Critical acclaim for Gloria Vitanza Basile's
GLOBAL 2000:
BOOK I

EYE OF THE EAGLE

"The most nerve-wracking, maddening, teasing hunt to come my way in years. What a story!"
—*Desert Sentinel*

"A plot that keep(s) the reader turning the novel's pages."
—*Publishers Weekly*

". . . A novelist with a remarkable talent."
—*Los Angeles Times*

"Devastating new thriller. Basile's pacing is tense and her research flawless."
—*West Coast Review of Books*

And now Book II of Gloria Vitanza Basile's explosive

GLOBAL 2000:
Book II

THE JACKAL HELIX

THE JACKAL HELIX

GLORIA VITANZA BASILE

PINNACLE BOOKS NEW YORK

This is a work of fiction. All the characters and events portrayed in this book are fictional, and any resemblance to real people or incidents is purely coincidental.

GLOBAL 2000: THE JACKAL HELIX

Copyright © 1984 by House of Lions, Inc.

An original Pinnacle Books edition, published for the first time anywhere.

First printing/April 1984

ISBN: 0-523-41961-9

Can. ISBN: 0-523-43082-5

Cover art by Paul Stinson

Printed in the United States of America

PINNACLE BOOKS, INC.
1430 Broadway
New York, New York 10018

9 8 7 6 5 4 3 2 1

Dedicated to
Melvin M. Belli, Esq.

BOOK ONE

AMADEO REDAK ZELLER
ZURICH, SWITZERLAND
1918

Prologue

COMPIEGNE, FRANCE
November 18, 1918

Even the wind stood still this day! The world, itself had stopped for a brief moment in time.

A train, anachronistic as a dinosaur, lumbered to a dead stop deep into the mist-shrouded forest of oaks and beeches. At precisely eleven o'clock A.M. *on this earth-shattering day several somber-faced, uniformed men climbed wearily and warily aboard the railroad car on a siding at the bend in the tracks. Marshal Ferdinand Foch, supreme commander of the Allied Forces, his aides with Herr Matthias Erzberger, spokesman for the German Military High Command signed the ceasefire to end the Great War.*

In Paris . . . twenty thousand sang the "Marseillaise" as people danced wildly in the streets to accompanying bottles of foaming champagne.

In the United States . . . people, people swarmed into the streets, singing, dancing, crying, laughing jubilantly, shouting "Praise God!" and hugging one another.

In London . . . pandemonium. Joyous, frenzied celebrants mounted demonstrations that often exceeded the bounds of human decency. There were drunkenness, brawling, even fornication in the streets. Tankards of beer, booze, opium—anything to dull the pain of war . . .

3

In Berlin . . . the shattering news marked the beginning of years of bitterness and hatred. The war, with its economic disasters, personal miseries, and starvation, already staggered the mind of an obscure little corporal lying on a hospital cot, blinded from exposure to gas at the Belgian front weeks before; he heard the news, and lurched, unseeing, back to his hospital bunk where he collapsed into apathy and disillusionment.

In Russia . . . Moscow to be exact, the news passed with barely a murmur, for the Red army, committed to Lenin and the Bolsheviks, was determined to decimate the White army in civil war!

In the Middle East . . . the last remnants of the Turkish Ottoman Empire lay in total collapse.

In Zurich . . . at the same hour, same day, Amadeo Zeller detrained at the cavernous Bahnhof and, moving with the pedestrian flow, proceeded along the Bahnhofstrasse to a sedate graystone building off the Parade-Platz to plant the seeds of World War II.

World War I was ending. World War II was about to begin.

Chapter One

ZURICH, SWITZERLAND
November 18, 1918

Amadeo Zeller emerged from the crowded Bahnhof depot and was overwhelmed by the celebrating hordes. It was the same everywhere; delirious celebrants braving the icy winds. He was surrounded by the din of discordant singing, yelling, screaming people, ecstatic with joy, almost suffocating him. From the opposite direction came an um-pah-pahing brass band playing the Swiss national anthem. Cymbals clashed, sending birds into flight, drums banged loudly, brass horns tooted discordantly. The escalating clamor turned to a howling reminiscent of a madhouse.

Uniforms of all colors passed Zeller as he strode the length of the Bahnhofstrasse. He elbowed his way through a colorful, disorganized panoply of flag-waving, beer-guzzling, amorous men and women who had lost control of their senses. Clusters of laughing men huddled for protection against the elements and a swirling humanity. It was enough to turn Zeller's stomach.

He swung a sharp left off the Bahnhofstrasse onto Parade-Platz hoping for reprieve; instead he encountered more confusion, an overly joyous mob bowling him over. Incredible, thought Zeller; in this icy chill the people were sweating.

Zeller pressed on, tugging on his collar, shoving furry ear-muffs into place, pausing momentarily to get his bearings. Craning his neck, he peered up, squinting at the pigeons in midair, momentarily robbed of their domain, the Platz itself. There . . . up ahead . . . the Suisse Banque Royale, his destination.

Swiftly he moved forward. Hoarse voices babbled. Christ! Would it never end? Several women clutched him passionately, kissing him, upsetting his composure. Annoyed at the uncontrollable propulsion engulfing him, Zeller pulled away, hugged the graystone banking houses, shielded his slim, wiry frame from the riotous mob.

At last! He stopped before the impressive graystone, peered up at the Great Seal of Zurich emblazoned in gilt over the entrance doors. He stared fascinated at the three headless saints depicted on the seal, carrying their heads jauntily under their arms. He thought about the legend. Three third-century saints—Felix, Regula, and Exupernatus—had been grimly tested for daring to convert ancient Zurich—Turicum—to Christianity. Decius, the town governor, had them scourged, boiled in oil, and forced to drink molten lead. But the final reward for their attempts to convert Zurich was a headsman's ax. Legend further claimed the intrepid saints had picked up their heads, walked to a nearby hilltop, and lay down to rest in graves they had dug themselves.

But that was then, and this was now. Today *Amadeo Zeller's* faith would be tested!

How would he fare in this twentieth-century equivalent of the scene of ancient legend? Would he convert Zurich to Zeller's laws or emerge from the arena carrying his own head jauntily about as did these depicted saints? Shuddering inwardly, he entered the building, relieved by the stark, austere silence of another world which the raucous outer din and clamor dared not penetrate.

The very building assimilated the character of its occupants, oozed a distinct odor of power. Recently in London he had detected the same unmistakable odor while conferring with men in prestigious banking houses. The scent peculiar to men of power was not easily forgotten.

Fishing for a card from the pocket of his chesterfield he walked briskly past a guard who barely noticed him. Zeller squinted at the logo on the card, moved to a wall directory, ran his gloved finger down the length of printed titles, pausing at Omicron Ltd . . . Suite 333. Good.

He boarded a caged lift, slammed the clanking gates shut, and was lifted slowly to the third floor. He exited and moved along the cold, dimly lit corridor, looking at the numbers over each door. A lone gaslight positioned midway on one wall produced flickering shadows on the walls, ceiling, and floors. For all his industrious scrutiny, Zeller was unable to locate Suite 333 and cursed aloud. Stymied, he moved back and forth, pausing before an unmarked door between Suites 332 and 334. His patience wearing thin, he muttered, "Damnation!" The unmarked door must be 333!

Why the charades? He rolled down the sable collar of his coat, reset his fur cap at an angle acceptable to the men on the other side of the door, and wiped his boots meticulously on the horsehair mat.

Zeller's eyes lit up in anticipation. Gripped by a feeling of circumspection, he faltered. The moment held great expectations for him. He *knew* once he stepped over the threshold of Suite 333 he could never go back, never! Inhaling deeply, he knocked on the door.

Thirteen months later on December 22, 1919, Zeller's indoctrination into Omicron Ltd. terminated. At age twenty-two, he was on his way to claim a great fortune. Emerging from the bank building on Parade-Platz he raced through the snowy Bahnhofstrasse to the Zurich Bahnhof terminal, rushing past people with travel itineraries in hand. Zeller ran swiftly, waving his ticket overhead, shouting to be heard over the raucous crowd.

The steam-spitting iron behemoth moved sluggishly forward on the tracks. Zeller frantically hastened his pace, crashed into— without apology—teary-eyed crowds waving farewells to a horde of army veterans.

The locomotive-lurched forward, evading him. He ran faster. He could not miss the train! He must not! Sprinting in swift pursuit, tossing valise and briefcase onto the rear platform, he grasped the outstretched arm of a one-armed veteran and jumped aboard.

Panting heavily, he mopped the sweat on his forehead, thanked the veteran, and, stuffing the ticket in the breast pocket of his fur-lined jacket, retrieved the valise and briefcase. He entered the overcrowded train unprepared for the boisterous din of voices upraised in song, catching a phrase or two of the German lyrics to "Mademoiselle from Armentiers, Parlez-Vous." He negotiated his way past the broken and maimed veterans on holiday leave from nearby military hospitals.

The veterans guzzled from hip-pocket flasks, momentarily relinquishing their personal traumas and dehumanizing infirmities to whiskey. For them, the ceasefire had long since ended, the war of living about to begin; each was concerned with how he'd handle his personal nightmare. Some were blind, a few armless, legless, most bearing hideous burn and surgical scars, and all unable to come to grips with their fate.

Zeller, sighting a lone seat at the end of the car headed for it. Reaching it, Zeller shoved his valise in the overhead rack. He wriggled into a window seat facing the war relics. On his left sat a woman suckling an infant. Tucking his briefcase protectively under his right arm, he turned his body slightly.

Cursing the inequities of brutish accommodations and held captive to the pungent stench of raw humanity, Zeller suppressed a rising nausea. Jarred by the shrill train whistle, the grating friction as the train switched laboriously to new sidings, his nerve ends sizzled. He could endure much, but each passenger with his or her distinctive odor, combined with stale foods, whiskey, beer, and cigar smoke had turned the car into a hell for him.

Zeller's ostentatious alpine garb, thick knickers, heavy ribbed stockings, durable walking boots, fur-lined jacket, and earmuffs drew sullen attention from the impoverished passengers. Veterans recoiled at his marked affluence, a decided contrast to their shabby garments. Zeller, unaffected by their innuendos, removed his hat, revealing stringy brown hair, a high prominent brow and an angular profile. Shoving earmuffs into place, he reset the hat. Good, he thought. Keep warm and minimize the din. Now if you can rid yourself of the god-awful stench . . .

The aura of icy imperturbability he exuded precluded any intrusion on his privacy. Zeller's eyes—you couldn't look at them without a second glance—were opaque, nearly colorless. A flaring temper, seldom expressed, sparked them with fiery hues. Zeller loathed his eyes for the unsolicited attention they aroused, a liability given the specialized nature of his work. Dark-lensed glasses, a recent fad at Lausanne University copied from the dashing French and German officers in the Great War, had swept the campus and everyone wore them. Soon, he would too.

Zeller was probably the only man aboard who was anxious to reach his destination. He had people to see, people to avoid, great distances to travel in treacherous winter snows, projects to carry out at great personal risks. His agenda was tight, his life in peril every moment; he dared the impossible. *He had plotted against Omicron.* Several plans for detours that he had crammed into his travel itinerary as protective devices left him little time to fritter away. Every moment counted. If Omicron *knew* what he was up to . . .

Zeller packed his Meerschaum, lit it, sucked vigorously until the bowl glowed brightly. A master at ferreting out enemies and sensing dangers, he scanned the passengers' faces. None indicated immediate threats to him. He relaxed, succumbing to the rhythmic swaying of the straining train on its uphill climb. An introvert, Zeller smiled a tight bitter smile, fixing indelibly in his mind the ploys Omicron had implemented to beguile, persuade, and manipulate him to their way of thinking.

His elitist mentors had disdained him. *Class-conscious prigs!* The invisible lines, drawn at once, separated them from Zeller. He had indulged this coterie of power brokers, and in this indulgence learned they avoided the public eye as they'd avoid a venereal disease. Invisibility was their strategy, a tactic devised to pursue specific goals. Once the goal was reached, they stood benignly to one side.

The invisible banking titans, undoubtedly the most frightening men in the world, who wielded a special brand of power, were the very men Zeller intended to defeat. Before *they* tasted the fruits of *his* victory, Zeller would crush their aspirations with his bare hands.

Zeller had yet to make his mark in the world, but who at age twenty-two had done so? Despite this, he'd had enough. Zeller, furious, had fulminated for almost a year. A year! At cross purposes with Omicron for a year. It had taken that long because of an operation called the Madrid Assignment.

The Madrid Assignment! His destination was Madrid. Yet on this day Zeller purposely headed thousands of miles in the opposite direction, to Admont, Austria. Plagued by burning questions Omicron had refused to answer, Zeller needed answers. Very well, forced to depend on himself—his life at stake, not theirs—Omicron had forced him into an adversary position. While feigning to comply with their directives, Zeller had devised a strategy to avoid what he viewed as total destruction.

Christ! Didn't they understand it was sheer suicide to engage in high-risk political gymnastics without protective umbrellas in an alien land? Suicide held no place in Zeller's plans; he had not yet begun to live! He barely knew his own potential. Anyone who met him and assessed his remote demeanor and unique intellectual capacities was either struck with a sense of foreboding or sought a way to exploit his talents in *their* dreams of empire. Clearly, Zeller had his own dreams of empire and entertained no intentions of being done in, yet.

How vigorously he'd protested against the constraints forced on him by the Zurich power consortium, who insisted on his visibility while demanding their total anonymity. Zeller, with excruciating patience, had masked his rising frustrations during the long hours spent deliberating, amending, modifying, and redefining his association with the invisible, austere figureheads. When he recognized the merits of the alliance, an agreement was struck that ultimately provided his entrée into a world he hadn't yet dreamed of.

Let these petulant princes have their way! Omicron was made up of second-circle men, buffers to the Zurich banking hierarchy; they stood this side of the veil to the invisible banking titans. Imagine. For a year he'd trained, lived, worked under the same roof, perhaps had seen them in passing, but never *knew* them, not by name, or physical description and barely by reputation. Omicron had personally trained Zeller, setting forth stringent, irrevocable guidelines in the Madrid Assignment.

What a surprise lay in store for them!

Deliberate attempts made by Omicron to minimize points Zeller believed crucial to the success of Madrid Assignment had forced him into defensive maneuvers. Disenchantment at their collaborative efforts escalated. Zeller had refused to imperil his life needlessly, and when he expressed discontent at this tactic or that and haggled over strategy he deemed dangerous to his well-being, their response enraged him. "Do not trespass in verboten corridors, Zeller."

"Never burden yourself with trivia. Take no detours. Never cloud an issue, confuse or permit yourself to be sidetracked. Once your goal is logically concluded, keep it in sight without deviation. *Verstehen*?"

And Zeller, a master at duplicity, had sagaciously amended his posturing, aware that his survival depended upon his own wits. He no longer demurred or posed problems. He *knew* what must be done. So he'd answered by rote, *"Jawohl, mein herrs, ich verstehe."* In the main, however excellent their advice seemed, the deeper he probed the situation the more he doubted their efficacy. Never, *never* would he trust the instincts of provocateurs posing unproven, unworkable theories against his own instincts.

Outside the train, the snow flurries thickened. Overcast skies darkened swiftly as the train scaled higher altitudes into the snowy Alps, moving closer into the eye of the storm. Temperatures dropped noticeably inside the car.

Zeller buttoned his jacket, turned up the fur collar, burrowed down into the muffler around his neck, and, clutching the briefcase at his side, thought about the situation. The aphorism that a man should know his enemy to overcome him was apparently not a part of Omicron's beliefs.

Contained in the precious briefcase was a highly classified dossier, intimate data on a prominent family of Spanish nobles residing in Seville, Spain. Considered a very important family in that nation, they possessed enormous wealth and power: landed estates, foreign holdings, gold and emerald mines in South America, and more. The patriarch of the family, Don Diego de la Varga, a decorated hero of two wars, was held in high esteem throughout influential banking circles of the world.

All this Zeller understood. After acquainting himself with all aspects of the family's long, glorious history, he believed in their social importance. What galled him were the irresponsible statements articulated by those at Omicron. "Your targets, the de la Varga family, will not be missed in the chaotic uncertainty of a nation in transition, one on the brink of civil war."

Not be missed! A family as important as the de la Vargas?

There had been moments in the past year when illogical, seemingly capricious statements had instilled in Zeller a sense of menace, but this statement, surpassing all others in its stupidity, had signaled real danger. *If* he embarked upon this mission unprepared, his annihilation was certain. Did these elitists think him to be utterly without wits? Did they consider his youth a measure of his naiveté?

According to these coup-planning sharks, no shades of gray existed in their strategy. How uncomplicated and theoretically faultless they appeared in the first few months. How flimsy and filled with holes was their final plotting!

Despite their differences, the men at Omicron had taught him plenty. Their paraded expertise and clever talents drew appropriate raves from Zeller, for he shrewdly reasoned, let them be the masters. Content yourself, Zeller, to be the uniquely gifted, fledgling assassin whose refined talents they think they can implement at their whim. These were cunning, ruthless men, who ordered death as you might a cup of chocolate. That he fell into the same category never entered his head; he considered himself a precision tool, an instrument to be used to pave the way for Amadeo Zeller's destiny.

By subordinating himself to their egocentricity, their loathing of Zeller became apparent. His low-keyed manner infuriated them because it concealed an essential evil quality to his nature, one he never revealed to them. They *knew* it lurked behind the bland facial mask, and *knew* also that nothing escaped him. That once a man had made an enemy of him, he possessed the facility to file away names, faces, and deeds for future retribution. It was true. Zeller never forgot slights or threats, and thus far in his young life anyone who had tried to harm him had been harmed.

No man had ever viewed Zeller's bedeviled, ravaged soul!

In the final ninety-day Omicron briefing, Zeller, precariously suspended between outrage and supplication, had played his role superbly.

They were wrong! God Almighty, those insufferable elitists were wrong!

And because they were wrong, whether by incautious evaluation or plain stupidity, Zeller was forced into an offensive role. He had figured the angles, measured personal risks and avoided in-fighting and confrontation with his mentors. Their rancor and displeasure came at too dear a price—death. *His!* But the men at Omicron must remain his special insurance against foul play until *after* Madrid.

Zeller felt the train slow down. He scanned faces with professional detachment, searching for the one face that could spell life or death. His skillfully honed instincts always working, he left nothing to chance.

He repacked the pipe, lit it, reflecting on his prudence. Any man in his profession who embarked upon such a mission ignorant of his target was an imbecile! It was like bicycling on a high wire over a pit of voracious crocodiles; one false step converted you into a gourmet dinner.

That was it, wasn't it? He was not to survive the Madrid Assignment! If he should conclude the task successfully—what then? Instant eternity by a hidden gun, an unseen blade, an accident perhaps?

Zeller hadn't seen it clearly until this moment! Distrust was inherent in him; he knew how swiftly cashiering took place once assets were converted to liabilities! *Bastards!* Accidents in high-stakes crap games occurred too frequently to be ignored!

In St. Gallens, the train took on new passengers. Zeller left the train, purchased a box lunch, and reboarded hugging his coat in the icy weather. He pulled the furry ear flaps down over his ears and quickly ate cheese, rolls, and pickles. He cursed his mentors, blaming them for the freezing temperatures, the discomfort of the straight-backed wooden seats on which he was forced to ride, and for his inability to obtain first-class accommodations. If those damned fools had answered the questions plaguing his orderly mind, he wouldn't be on this *verdamne schleppe* about to freeze *das hoden*!

Their stubborn refusal to explain *why* the de la Varga family was targeted for extinction had provoked his curiosity. *How had the Spanish nobles incurred Omicron's wrath? What desperate conspiracy drove Zurich to eradicate an entire family?* Nothing! They told him nothing.

Zeller's discontent had forced him into clandestine action. He had journeyed to Lausanne, Geneva, and Lucerne to research the subject, and had found skeletons lying dormant, amid freshly unearthed information, skeletons threatening to come alive. Forced to gamble, Zeller made the proper assessments.

What emerged as the result of his snooping was a five-century-old vendetta between a defunct terrorist brotherhood, Compagnia della Garduna—Society of Martens—and the de la Varga family of Seville.

Five centuries old! How credible could ancient history be in contemporary times?

Forced to question this extravagant possibility, Zeller reflected on the caveats stressed by Omicron. Counseled time and again not to deviate from his singular purpose, he had stubbornly rejected their warnings. Instead he had guardedly persevered, checked and rechecked facts. With clarification from trustworthy experts he abstained as best he could from flights of fancy.

Now he knew too much to quit! Desertion of the cause would easily convert him into a *corpus delicti*. His only option . . . forward and onward!

Six hours later Zeller detrained at Bregenz, Austria, used the comfort-station facilities, sped to another track, and boarded a better train. He lucked out. *A compartment!* Seven passengers grudgingly made room for him.

Zeller shoved his valise in an overhead rack, squeezed into the space made for him, and studied the passengers' faces and attitudes, his briefcase at his side.

Less than an hour out of Bregenz, he sensed danger. Outside, the texture of darkness changed, shifted in smears and patches. A slow-burning in his belly signaled the need for closer observation. He stared intently at the other passengers and then at the train compartment with an air of professional detachment, noting the exits, one outside the car, the other leading to a corridor, the wood-paneled walls, the red velvet window curtains. Nothing seemed amiss, yet he sensed danger.

Speculation is foolhardy, Zeller told himself as the iron colossus stopped at small towns with infuriating frequency. The engine's clamorous sounds as it pulled the train higher into snow-bound mountains along barely passable ridges in the provinces of Tiro, Voralsberg, and Salzburg, prevented conversations.

Someone was staring at him—a child. What was she—seven, eight years old at the most? She was smiling. Zeller stared at her, sternly and the smile dissolved. She hid her face in her mother's lap.

Ten minutes to Salzburg—only one passenger remained with Zeller. A stern ferret-faced, pear-shaped man, who masked his emotions behind brooding eyes shielded by gold-rimmed bifocals. The man's presence intimidated him. *What was it about him?* Studying the man under lidded eyes, Zeller pretended to sleep. The face alarmed him. *Damnation!* He knew the face! But from where?

Their eyes locked in recognition. In that brief second there flashed the unmistakable violence of a predator. The message clearly signaled danger. Zeller searched his brain, his heart pumping furiously.

The train slowed convulsively in its approach to Salzburg. Zeller moved. In seconds he retrieved his valise and briefcase, had one foot out the compartment door when it happened.

Too late! The burning sting of steel, a misplaced thrust aimed at his heart, caught Zeller in the left shoulder. His bags spilled onto the platform. He turned to his assailant and shoved hard against him, knocking the knife from his hand as he prepared to stab him again. The knife fell to the compartment floor. Zeller pounced on it, held it blade up as the other flew at him in a rage.

His expression was one of shock and astonishment as he fell, impaled on the knife.

Zeller, wanting to twist and shove it deeper, instead let go. He leaped from the train, backtracked, recovered valise and briefcase, and, snaking his way through a small crowd of late-night travelers, sighted a carriage at the end of the boarding platform. He ran for it, bleeding profusely, pain sizzling his upper arm.

Zeller thrust several German marks at the driver, entered the carriage on one side, left by the other, and ordered him to take off. Crouching low behind freight wagons, he circled behind the train, doubled back along an inner track, panting heavily. He reboarded the train and took refuge in a compartment occupied by a middle-aged woman.

Zeller eased toward the window. As the train lumbered forward he saw his assailant standing in an arc of gaslight, clutching his stomach wound, searching furtively about the platform. Zeller didn't breathe easily until the train was a quarter hour out of Salzburg. He needed to think. His eyes leapfrogged across the red velour and wood-finished compartment to the stiff-lipped woman, who overtly disdained his disheveled appearance. She spoke to him. Unable to hear over the train's din, he gestured his helplessness. Leaning across the aisle, she repeated loudly,

"You are bloomin' well bleeding to death!" she indicated to the blood pooling on his vest.

What a clever mouth, it speaks! "A jealous husband . . . ."

"Rather sticky, eh? Here give us a look," she insisted. "Don't do a shy bloke on me. I'm a nurse, recently deprived of portfolio." Her strong English accent made her words barely comprehensible to him. "Off with your jacket, luv, be quick. Blood supply runs out if the tap remains open—just like a barrel of wine." Accustomed to having her orders obeyed, the woman retired his disconcertedness with expertise. Zeller, unaccustomed to solicitous females, found himself curiously compliant to her orders.

His jacket was finally shed from one arm. She shoved a linen square between his teeth. "Bite hard. That's a luv." She grabbed a black satchel lying next to a lizard portmanteau and popped it open. Zeller scanned the contents. *The damned woman was a walking apothecary!*

"I'm Lady Margaret Ainesworth." Her tone implied he should recognize the name. He did not. "My late husband, Lord *Wellington* Ainesworth, was killed at Armentiers—a beastly place.

His aide de camp, his *own* man, for pity's sake, mistook him for a bloody Gerry one hour before news of the armistice reached the front. What rotten luck, eh? Bite hard, now! Do you have a pain powder on you—I'm fresh out.'' He shook his head. ''Prepare for the fiery bite of Lucifer,'' she muttered, applying antiseptic solution to the jagged cut. ''You'll be needing stitches if I'm any judge.'' Glancing at her diamond watch fob, she added, ''Vienna is next. Lord knows you'll find enough quacks there willing to sew you up. Do it or you'll be toting a mean scar—if not infection. Need I tell you how swiftly gangrene sets in? No matter, the bandages will do for the present.''

Zeller studied her as she deftly bound his shoulder. He decided she was eccentric to the teeth . . . dowdy, dressed less fashionably than her kind. *Remember, a war just ended, Zeller.*

''What exactly do I call you when you lack sense and the proper manners to introduce yourself, my good man?'' she scolded.

Zeller, barely audible, identified himself.

''What's that? Fabrizio Caragini? *Professor? A bloody Eyetalian!*'' She sighed tolerantly. ''Ah well, one must be charitable these days.'' She cleansed her hands with alcohol, opened her lavishly stocked food hamper, retrieved two silver cups and a flask bearing a British family crest, and poured cognac in each.

''*È veritá, professore, i gran dolori sono muti.* It's true, great sorrows are suffered in silence.'' She handed him a cup.

Zeller artfully waited until she sipped her drink before he tasted his. He observed her over the rim of his cup unable to ignore the covetous way she guarded her lizard portmanteau. She exemplified a neophyte courier, invisibly manacled to the case, bound by a sworn oath not to let it out of her sight. *Why?*

She guzzled cognac like a seasoned tippler, burped without apology, hardly aware of Zeller's scrutiny, and began babbling non-stop about her Middle East experiences a decade before the Great War began.

''You see, luv, certain men in government believe my knowledge of the region and its people qualifies me to embark on this mission for Sir Arthur Balfour. The recent British mandate to establish a homeland for Jews in Palestine brings focus to the area.'' She poured cognac generously.

Zeller politely refused. He desperately needed time to think. Her words made interesting copy, but not now, not while physical pain assaulted him and mental anguish wrecked his composure. ''May I suggest you stretch out and catnap?''

"I never sleep." She burped loudly, guzzled the cognac, poured herself a refill, and, pulling the lizard portmanteau closer, fixed her eyes stonily at a point above Zeller's head. Slowly lulled into slumber, the lidded eyes opened, closed, snapped open again before falling to half mast and finally closing tight.

Zeller painfully slipped his jacket over his shoulders. He spread his coat over him, praying she wouldn't disturb him. He needed to think.

Think, Zeller, think! Salzburg—the attempt on your life!

An instant replay of the near-fatal scenario flashed in his mind. His failure to trust his instincts and anticipate the attack ate away at him. Why? And who, for Christsakes, was the assailant? Who wanted Zeller dead? An inch or two to the left and the blade would have pierced his heart! The feeling he knew the man persisted. Think, man, think!

Zurich! . . . The Consortium! Omicron! It could be none other. Had he asked too many wrong questions? Had his subterranean moves been reported? Had he suddenly become a liability?

Sulking, mulling morosely over the facts, solved nothing. Everything irritated him—the train sounds, the monotonous rhythm, Lady Ainesworth's snoring, and his damnable burning wound. The continuous drop in temperatures iced his bones.

Zeller shifted focus again to the Britisher in critical assessment. She wore dated, tailored clothing, fashionable a decade ago. The fabric bespoke quality, the tailoring impeccable. An eight-strand pearl choker graced the long, aristocratic neck.

Authentic? Imitation? Which? The diamond and sapphire watch fob and diamond stick pin over her prim shirtwaist needed no lapidary's authentication. His eyes riveted irresistibly to the lizard portmanteau.

He stared fascinated at her face; the jaw dropped, the mouth loose, shapeless, the breathing rhythmic. Unable to ignore the inner urgings, Zeller made his move. Cautiously, silently, one eye on the woman, he removed from his briefcase a smaller black case containing several vials. The woman snorted. Zeller froze. Her eyes opened, she yawned and fell into deeper sleep, her hand tightening over the portmanteau.

Zeller marked time before stealthily retrieving the silver flask from her hamper. Uncapping it, eyes darting to the snoring woman, he emptied the contents of one vial into it. Quickly he recapped it, placed it back in the hamper, and, slipping the empty vial into his briefcase, settled back, a knowing look sparking his eyes. A tippler on awaking *usually* reached for the hair of the dog.

Now, to test the theory.

The sounds of a door opening alerted him. Instantly he feigned sleep. A conductor and his brass-buttoned assistant entered the compartment. The assistant removed the ticket from Zeller's pocket, canceled it, and stuffed the paper back.

"*Der Schlaffner?*" Lady Ainesworth's eyes widened brightly. "Don't overlook *mein fahrkarte*." She extended her travel docket for its perfunctory cancellation and, yawning, slipped it into the hamper as the two train employees exited, closing the compartment door behind them.

Zeller sat up, yawned, and, reaching for a blanket, solicitously offered to cover her. "Better to sleep while you can."

She declined politely. "Not since Armentiers have I slept a full hour in one night." She uncapped the flask and poured a cup of lethal cognac, observing Zeller wrap the blanket around himself.

Zeller feigned drowsiness. He watched as she guzzled the drink. She refilled it, gulped down the contents, and wiped her lips with a serviette. She tongued her lips, savoring every drop, and replaced the flask and cup neatly in the hamper.

"Bloody slow train, you see, lulls you. The monotony of it all is hard to combat." She yawned, stifled it as if to be caught in the act was tantamount to committing a mortal sin. Her hand clutched the lizard case.

The thought forming like a piece of sculpture between his closed eyes required time. *One hundred . . . ninety-nine . . . ninety-eight . . .*

The clever mouth yawned again. Good. Eighty-four . . . Eighty-three . . .

Busy scenes, countless voices inside his head readied him. He moved swiftly to the door, slid it open—nothing. He closed and locked it, pulled down the window shades on the door window and those at each side of the door. Then he lowered the gas jet and the compartment grew dim. He worked swiftly, yanked the woman's neck forward, removed the pearl choker, and removed the watch fob. He caught sight of the label inside her jacket—a British Redfern, no less, authentic upper-class tailoring. Pocketing the jewelry, he released her lobster-claw hold on the portmanteau, slipped the case between his valise and briefcase on the seat opposite her.

The train was slowing. He glanced at his watch. Five minutes to the next scheduled stop. He stared at the woman. Something between them remained unfinished. Sprinting to the door, he unlocked it, peered in either direction of the corridor, went back inside, relocking the door. At the woman's side, he felt the area of her midsection, and smiling, tugged at her shirtwaist and camisol. *Voilà!* A money belt!

He sprang open a pocket knife, sliced through the canvas, and yanking fiercely on it, removed the belt from around her waist. Shooting a cursory glance at its contents before dumping it into his briefcase, he experienced a trembling excitement course through every nerve in his body. With added zeal he worked swiftly to put the woman back in order. He managed to cover her with a blanket just as the train lurched to a stop. Good. She appeared to be in deep slumber. He took a last look about the compartment; his eyes fell to the diamond stick pin. Quickly he retrieved it, rolled up the window shades, unlocked the compartment door, and, bowing to the dead woman in mock salute, detrained with his newly acquired wealth.

LEIZEN
STYRIA PROVINCE, AUSTRIA

Zeller, alert to possible dangers moved cautiously through the icy predawn bleakness, waiting for the few travelers to board the Vienna-bound train before entering the deserted comfort station. Moving with deliberate, well-paced movements, he emerged a half hour later from the unendurable confines, completely transformed into the person of Professore Fabrizio Caragini.

All traces of Zeller lay hidden beneath a black mustache and goatee, the opaque eyes camouflaged by dark-lensed pince-nez glasses. His hair, darkened with oil to a slick, patent-leather gloss, was combed severely to one side and hidden under a rakishly perched brown beaver fedora, snap-brimmed from front to back. The suit he wore was black serge, frayed in places. His shirt was white with a detachable starched wing collar, the cravat bold and flowing. The coat, draped dramatically over his shoulders, exaggerated his flamboyance. An affected list to one side of his body produced a lilting flair to his gait. The disguise, planned in advance to conceal his identity in Admont, now served a dual purpose.

Skilled assassins in pursuit of Zeller would not recognize him!

Professore Caragini moved in that curious gait to the end of the deserted train depot and hailed a lonely driver seated atop an open sleigh. Settling back in the leather seat, he pulled the fur lap robe around his booted feet and legs.

"*Guten morgen, mein Herr,*" the warmly dressed driver said.

"*Guten morgen.* Admont, *bitte,*" he replied in an Italian-accented German.

The dawn of another day glowed against ice-topped mountains. Swirls of windswept snow, gusting along the village streets, spiraled a path to the east toward Admont, Zeller's destination. So far the hunt had been excellent. His body swayed lightly with the movement of the sleigh as dull sounds of horses' hooves pounded the snow trail. The passenger knew the pickings in Admont would surpass all else. His personal Rubicon lay momentarily to the east.

Chapter Two

Professor Caragini was ecstatic! *What a haul!* The fates had fed him a fortune. Contained in the lizard portmanteau was a fortune in precious jewels; diamonds, emeralds, rubies, a handful of sunburst black-star sapphires, unset, a few mounted in platinum. There was more. Gilt-edged securities, pay-to-bearer bonds, and the money belt? Several million British pounds, sterling. The unexpected bonanza had dimmed his anger over the attempt made on his life. By investing wisely a man could live like royalty.

But, not Amadeo Zeller. The fortuitous windfall wasn't enough to realize the visions he'd nurtured this past year. Visions of a financial empire so vast in scale, he dared not breathe the blueprint to any man lest they declare him insane.

Earlier at Leizen depot he'd dumped the cache into his valise and briefcase. He'd cut out the solid-gold crest, slashed the portmanteau to shreds, and concealed it in his overcoat pockets. Now, as the horse-driven sleigh journeyed him over precipitous slopes to his destination, he discarded the remains bit by bit over cliffs, committing them to an icy grave.

The majesty of the dawn illuminated the panorama with surreal lights. He'd seen Austria in the spring, and decided nothing he had viewed in life was as breathtaking as this.

He knew that hibernating under thickly layered, wind-whipped snow, awaiting rebirth, lay buds of vividly colored anemones, verdant forests, and purple tangles of brambles. But now, he stared in fascination at the scenery as the sleigh pulled over twisting snowy roads. Towering majestically in the distance, mantled regally in snow that resembled ermine, these Austrian mountains left him breathless. The grain of sky grew more distinct, the sun rising higher. Its brightness forced him to avert his eyes. But nothing quenched the slow-burning fires of expectation. Excited at what brought him to Admont, he estimated he'd finish in a day or two, then move on to Madrid to prepare for the deadly rendezvous. He daydreamed for the next two hours.

ADMONT, AUSTRIA

An ancient Alpine village. Rosy-cheeked peasants, busily at work were digging themselves out from under a record snowfall. A tinkling of sleighbells echoed through the near soundless streets. Festooned horses pranced dragging sleighs over trackless streets. Peasants glanced up with provincial curiosity; they knew a stranger on sight.

Professor Caragini booked lodgings at a hostelry, placed his depredatory wealth in the hotel safe, and following a spartan breakfast walked briskly in the cold bright morning.

Admont Library. Stunningly Churregeuresque. A lavishly ornamented Renaissance and Baroque building loomed in the near distance. Alcoves nestled decorously into its facade contained numerous statues on pedestal bases. Incredibly magnificent it rose against the brilliant sky, a wailing symphony of medieval splendor. Caragini paused in appreciation. Massive carved wooden and brass doors reflecting a glissade of glittering sunbursts gave off a hermetic appearance. The architecture was sheer artistry!

Caragini entered the cavernous building, quickly scanned the interior and, listing to one side, headed for the stately desk, signed the registry. He contributed a nominal sum to the poor box. He paused a moment to indulge in the library's opulence, his eyes adjusting to the dancing shadowy interior. He fixed on wall and vaulted ceiling frescoes by the Austrian artist, Bartolomeo Altomonte. Sheer artistry! he muttered in wordless awe. A profusion of decorative walls, gilded alcoves, floor-to-ceiling bookcases filled with hand-bound leather tomes. Rare first editions and priceless centuries-old manuscripts were kept under lock and key behind glass doors.

A spiral staircase stretched to open galleries on a second level, housing meditation chambers, additional alcoves, and thousands of books. He was at once curiously affected by the place, One day I shall own such a place! he told himself.

An hour later, his thoughts weren't as euphoric!

Frustrated, short of temper, growing angrier by the moment, Caragini cursed at the totally chaotic index and filing systems. Unwilling to bring undue attention to himself, he asked no assistance from the library staff.

Satan be damned! He had a timetable, a deadline to meet by July 1. At this rate he'd be here a year!

He felt compelled to wade through the inefficient filing system. He began at the beginning, meticulously examining each card, letting none escape his attention.

As the sweating Caragini pulled index cards, trying to make order from disorder, not far from him a tall, unsmiling man wearing a black cassock moved his six-foot frame through the sanctuary. Brother Heinrich Schuller, enveloped in brooding solitude, moved to the enormous picture window overlooking the snow-laden monastery grounds. An aura of elegance surrounded the man. Sandy brown hair fell in androgynous waves below his ears, framing an expressive, finely chiseled face. His midnight-blue eyes were shadowed by dark hollows. A hawkish, arrogant profile reflected discontent, a coiled intensity waiting to lash out against the slightest provocation. Always congenial, polite, considerate, deferential to a fault, he usually displayed a conciliatory, attentive nature. Today, his disconsolate mood was a warning to acolytes in the library; one look at Brother Schuller and they steered clear of him.

Numbed by his recent trips to Bavaria, his beloved homeland, Heinrich *knew* how fear contained within oneself becomes magnified. How deeply it festered in his soul, constructing impenetrable walls. The ultimate truth, the black lightning that splits and destroys, was surfacing, forcing him to examine it.

Earlier, when he began his stroll through the library, Brother Schuller had seen Caragini. He had a fleeting after-image of the visitor's obvious frustration, then weightier things pressed on the custodian's mind. He stretched his eyes beyond the snow-mantled trees to the majesty of snowcapped mountains towering in the distant landscape. Countless civilizations had come and gone, but the mountains endured forever. Why couldn't men endure forever?

Brother Heinrich felt a madness swirl inside him, ponderous darkness settling upon his spirit. The sight of his beloved Bavaria and Germany blighted by political turmoil and bloodshed had stripped him emotionally.

The horror of revolution in the streets had sickened him. World War I had ended. Germany was doomed to annihilation. Shame, degradation, starvation, and economic hardships weren't enough to punish the Germans. The victors of world war had redrawn the map of Germany, stripping it of everything including its national pride. Geographical resolutions to the Great War had embittered Europe and this was interpreted in Germany and Bavaria as blueprints for another war in the not too distant future.

Brother Schuller felt an anger deep in his soul.

And those Bolshevists! Those scheming Red cabalists had infiltrated Germany, overthrown Berlin, and captured Munich with their bloodletting coups. Schuller sighed. The Bavaria of his youth—gone! Swallowed by a republic! A Bavarian Socialist Republic proclaimed by Kurt Eisner! The irony of Eisner presiding over a predominantly Catholic government and conservative Bavaria was unpalatable to the cleric. The Wittlebachs had fled in terror. Now, a foreigner ruled. Bavaria, under siege of revolution, was anathema to him. He found unacceptable the idea of Stuttgart besieged by strikers, agitators, rabblerousers. It was all a shambles! The Daimler Motor Works under restraint; sailors engineering revolts at Frankfurt! At Kassel, the entire garrison had revolted, submitted without benefit of a bullet! In Cologne, forty-five thousand men had turned Red. Everywhere, the same madness. Dusseldorf, Leipzig, Magdeburg—did it matter? It was the end of an era! The end!

Lenin's success in Russia, his capricious butchers causing rivers of blood to flow, had instilled abnormal fear among the Germans. The overflow of Red fever beyond their borders, revolution turning the Rhine crimson, the increasing swell of bread lines, the incalculable losses as printing presses turned out paper marks at an astounding rate, angered the German people.

The war had boiled over into snowbound Munich, where the snow turned crimson with rampant bloodletting. Eisner, assassinated, was replaced by Ernst Toller. He and two Bolshevists,

Max Levien and Eugen Levine, insane fanatics, had ordered Munich Cathedral turned into a revolutionary temple! Heinrich Schuller had predicted the hell that followed. The extreme right battled with the extreme left and brought Munich to its knees.

Levine proclaimed himself president of the Bavarian Socialist Republic, waged merciless war against the bourgeoisie one disastrous winter. People were starving, freezing, becoming ill with numerous diseases, dying, as a continuous battle was waged in the nearby village of Dachau. It was horrifying to see the Reds defeat German troops in an unforgettable bloody coup.

Brother Schuller had fled Munich, sequestered himself at his estate at St. Bartolema in the vicinity of Berchtesgaden at the Austrian border. Many intellectual luminaries, seeking temporary refuge from the bloodletting, arrived daily at the hilltop sanctuary. Heinrich listened intently to scholars argue the dangers of a Bolshevik takeover. Their doomsday prognostications, antagonistic to his pacific nature, had caused him an unshakable melancholia.

His friend Oswald Spengler was provoking widespread controversy with his recently published book, *The Decline of the West*, advancing the belief that the culture of Europe was entering its final stage of existence, that following a period of technological and political expansion, the course of the world would change irrevocably! His friend Spengler further predicted that man would fly to the moon in the not too distant future! Imagine . . . a man of Spengler's intellect advancing ludicrous theories? Everyone quietly suggested he suffered from early senility.

To further compound Heinrich's growing dilemma and deep depression, two additional friends, both fanatical anti-Semitics, Alfred Rosenberg, an artist and architect, and Dietrich Eckhardt, a poet, journalist, translator, and alcoholic, who was also addicted to morphine, agreed with Spengler!

Heinrich's face changed at the thought. Not dramatically, but from within, revealing his contempt and disbelief.

Brother Schuller's introduction to a fourth man, Eckhardt's protégé, Adolf Hitler, a pale, haggard young man, offered the only stimulation, the only ray of hope. Released recently from a military hospital following recuperation from bullet wounds and gassing sustained in the final days of combat, Hitler, substituting for an infirm Eckhardt, spoke before hundreds of German nationalists in beer halls.

Brother Schuller was unable to ignore Hitler's words as the

man, full of animation, vividly described the intolerable depriva-
tions he had witnessed in Berlin. The images were burned into
the minds of his audience. He described the shame of surrender
shared by his comrades following the armistice, a distrust of the
homefront that was embracing Bolshevism. Hitler had wailed,
"The war was fought in vain! The sacrifices, privations, deaths,
injuries, were all in vain! The wounded, the maimed, the survivors and the dead Germans left on the battleground sacrificed in
vain!"

Bitter, vengeful over the terms dealt Germany at the recent
Paris Peace Conference, the obscure corporal's oratory held
audiences spellbound. He dared to speak about matters others
dared not even think.

"Everywhere Bolshevists are in power! All are abusing the
power. In Berlin, Budapest, and Moscow the beasts reign in
terror. A frightening people . . . in frightening times . . ."

Brother Schuller lighted an English Oval cigarette, recollected
words of his guests in his Bavarian mountaintop retreat. The
terror of Berlin under siege, immobile under the iron fist of
striking workers, came alive when graphically described by his
guests. Berlin without electricity and transportation! Grave food
shortages, bitter house-to-house fighting with cannon! Machine
guns! Strafing airplanes against rifles and deadly grenades! What
madness!

Heinrich shuddered. *Nightmares!* Too many had besieged him.
Day and night struggles in all the cities, people fighting for their
lives against the Bolshevists! Anarchy! Devastation! The war
was over but the revolution was tearing his beloved Germany
and Bavaria apart! Fanatics, keenly trained in the manipulation
of men's minds, presented untold dangers to the Germans.

Brother Schuller rocked gently on his feet. Turning, he swept
the library, his eyes holding briefly on the frustrated Caragini.
Puffing his cigarette, he turned back, focused upon those last
few days he spent in Munich.

The Freikorp, a resistance group of German soldiers led by
General Ritter Von Epp, had liberated the city. The Red leaders
were rounded up by the determined strike force and jailed, their
underground nests destroyed. The Red terror over, the White
terror was about to begin.

Brother Schuller, like the other thousands watching the victory
parade, experienced pride at the sight of the Ehrhardt Brigade
wearing swastika-decorated helmets, goose-stepping as they passed

the Felderrhalle along the Ludwigstrasse that day in April. But he fled in terror when Catholic worker hostages were executed in retaliation for the seventy Freikorp lives expended in the bloody coup!

Munich had escaped the iron heel of Bolshevism and its excesses, but at what cost? Would the bloodletting never end? When would man's inhumanity toward man end?

However impassioned his dedication and allegiance to his beloved Bavaria and Germany, the truth was, Brother Schuller was relieved to be back in Admont. If he could wave a magic wand, he'd leave war and politics to those militant bastards who profited from promoting those twin evils. What if the politicians and the industrialists who promoted wars got a taste of what they wholesaled to the lesser man—the sheep over whom they ruled?

The cleric turned from the window, cursing silently all who'd been a party to his ruined trip home. He had planned to hunt stag in the enchanting forests of Bavaria. He had planned so much.

Ah, well, the best-laid plans of mice and men. He moved past the filing alcove and caught sight of Caragini. He intensified his scrutiny of the man as unobtrusively as possible. Overwhelmed by familiar sensations, he padded quietly to the registry, opened the large book, studied the flowery script;

> *Fabrizio Caragini, Professore, Milano University. Scholar, Ancient Spanish History.*
> *Subject: Ancient Monastic Order of the Zaragoza-Vascongades.*

Heinrich Schuller's spirits soared. He glanced again at Caragini. *A scholar!* Scholars, a rarity in Admont since the war, were warmly received. Schuller, a lonely man, thirsted to communicate with his intellectual equal. Currents passed through his body like ripples through a snake. At last, a man he could assume would be disinterested in the military, to whom he could speak without faltering as he had before the Spengler fanatics! He observed Caragini, resisting an impulse to approach the Italian scholar. Contemplating him, noting again the subject of his inquiry, Brother Schuller frowned. He regarded the man's presence, the study of so ancient and remote a subject . . . suspiciously.

Was it possible? Was it possible he was a spy sent to catch him for a minor infraction? At once on guard, Heinrich Schuller backed away, eased himself into a shadowy alcove not far from Caragini, observing the man.

At eight the next morning, Caragini thundered into Admont Library determined to rectify the gross errors of the previous day. A hostile look contorted his features as he peered about, seeking someone in charge.

A colorless sun, seeping through the towering lead glass windows of the marble-columned temple, imbued his surroundings with supernatural luster. He ignored this previous enchanting effect and glowered.

"Guten morgen, Herr Professor. I am Brother Heinrich Schuller, Custodian of Admont Library." His German was fluent, a smile brightened his face. "You seem distressed. What may I do to alleviate it?"

Caragini's eyes reflected coldness. "Are you aware your category listings and cross filings defy classification? I've wasted an entire day trying to decipher the damned system!"

"When a mere question might have eased your pain?" The monk's infectious laughter rippled through the chambers. "I am, I confess, painfully aware of the system's inadequacies. It is totally archaic." He toned down the amusement. "The only reparation possible, dear *Professore,* is total annihilation of the existing systems and implementation of a new. At the speed with which our holy order moves, a millennium will pass before we catch up with the twentieth century."

Schuller's words and attitude dispelled some of Caragini's indignation. Schuller beckoned to him.

"Come, *Professore,* I see we share common interests—the Zaragozas. I am an authority on the subject. I am the researcher and historian of the holy order."

Falling into step alongside the solicitous cleric, Caragini estimated his age at approximately forty. Solid muscle strained under the cassock. He moved with the nonchalance of an aging athlete.

Brother Schuller led his guest through the cavernous cathedral to a spiral staircase leading to the galleria. Threading their way up the stairs, the cleric compulsively inspected the guard rail for dust. He spoke softly, his knowledgeable words caused an ebullience in Caragini.

"The Zaragozas . . . nomadic militants . . . a nefarious lot, the whole of them. In Christ's time they inhabited areas bounding the Red Sea. Following the crucifixion of Jesus of Nazareth, the Zaragozas began a peregrination over the face of the earth, ending up in Spain—Seville or thereabouts, taking refuge in the monastery. An alliance formed with a group of brigands attracted unwanted attention from the crown. Ferdinand and Isabella mobilized the combined forces and called them Compagnia della Garduna, Society of Martens. As an abettor of the crown's political aims, the brotherhood became a second tool of the Inquisition, to subjugate the Moors and expel the Jews from Spain.''

On the galleria level they proceeded to the last alcove. Brother Schuller lighted a gas jet on one wall, dug into his cassock pockets, produced a ring of keys attached to a geodesic emblem, a decahedron. Selecting one key, he walked the alcove's length, his left hand trailing along the locked glass cases. ''Ah, here we are. Actually the brotherhood adopted the combined names Garduna-Zaragozas.''

Bull's-eye! He was on the right track.

Unaware of Caragini's inner jubilation, Brother Schuller rolled a ladder in its track before the cases. He climbed it, unlocked the compartment, and delicately removed a large leather-bound tome. He descended the steps, toting it tenderly, and carried the precious item to a table at the end of the narrow confines.

Caragini spoke hesitantly. ''A family of Spanish nobles—'' ''—the de la Vargas,'' the cleric replied with instant recall. ''Ah . . . mortal enemies, if memory serves me correctly. Ah . . . yes, yes, indeed.'' He turned the pages slowly.

Several hours later, Brother Schuller, his memory inspired by his attentive listener, was relieved to find Caragini amply knowledgeable on the subject and dismissed his earlier concern at possible chicanery. Accepting the scholar as he was represented on the registry, he rhapsodized: ''How seldom I meet a peer with whom conversing does not become an exercise in futility,'' he said. ''Honor me, Professor, be my guest at dinner.''

Caragini's sharp assessment of the cleric signaled propositions he wished to avoid; he felt the naked appraisal, the kind a man gives a woman who interests him. But in that instant, he decided, why not? Time allotted him before the Madrid Assignment was precious. If it speeded his journey?

The secluded snow-covered, thatched-roof cottage was a monument to simplicity. Its cracked plaster and worm-ridden beams gave the appearance of dilapidation. It was situated in an isolated glade nestled among giant oaks, their overburdened branches heavy with snow.

Vesper bells sounded in the near distance. Monks, heads bowed, hidden under hoods, moved through snow-banked parterres and loggias to evening vespers, oblivious of the two men about to enter the cottage nearby.

Heinrich opened the door with a proprietary grin, permitting his guest to enter first. "My secret hideaway, Professor. Few are privy to it." He closed the door, the need to explain bursting from his lips. "I am not a man enslaved to worldly goods. My estate pays the holy order a stipend. Here, at Admont, I am the exception rather than the rule. I am a wealthy man, even *after* donating a substantial sum to the order."

Caragini shivered slightly. A raw sensation, a mystical vision shot through him. Schuller, mistaking the movement, moved briskly to the fireplace, placed a lighted taper to the prepared kindling on the hearth. "In summer, the shade trees cool the cottage magnificently. In winter—unfortunately—they make it colder. You'll warm up in a few minutes, you'll see."

The statement proved correct. A crackling bright fire fired the logs, casting a rosy warmth through the room.

A table set for one, appointed with bone china, solid silver flatware, Austrian crystal goblets, was swiftly rearranged and now accommodated two. The cleric wound a gramophone resting on a high counter nearby, placed a cylindrical tube in place, and set a lever in motion. Mozart filled the cottage. "I hope you enjoy Mozart. *The Abduction from the Seraglio*. I am hopelessly addicted to Mozart . . . Born in Salzburg, you know."

Schuller paused in his meanderings, caught by the curious look on his guest's face. "Hardly abstemious for a theologian is that what you're thinking?" He sighed. "I admit I strain at the bit," he said, pouring a light dry wine. "Liebfraumilch a Rheinhessen from the village of Oppenheim," Heinrich said, clinking glasses. "Twenty-five years in devoted service to the holy order is enough, *jawohl*?" Standing before the fire, he searched Caragini's opaque eyes in total fascination.

"Only a man steeped in luxury can make so succinct a statement."

"Steeped in luxury? I was born to it—far from poverty's door. May I call you Fabrizio? I find it easier to converse if we sweep aside formalities, *nein*?"

"Of course, Brother."

"Call me Heinrich."

"Heinrich, then." The room was charged with a sexual tension. Caragini, playing the game, intended to learn what he came for.

Heinrich, a gourmet cook prepared *Geschnetzeltes*, thin slivers of veal, braised in butter, caressed by a delicate herbal cream sauce; served with *Rösti*, mouth-watering pan-fried potatoes served in thin pancake style; baby artichokes, smothered in garlic and oregano complemented the entrée, and the wine was an Austrian white, a superb Neuchatel. Heinrich, expansive and loquacious, grew incautious; he spoke effusively of his youth at his estate on the Konigsee, at St. Bartolema, displaying photographs of the manor and his priceless collections of oils, wood carvings, sculpture and rare paintings. "Some consider these pornographic, but to me it is art in its purest form." He rambled on, speaking openly on subjects ranging from politics to love, death, and mankind.

Unaccustomed to such openness and boasting, Fabrizio listened raptly, his swiftly calculating mind seizing the pith of what he heard.

"Ah, Fabrizio, Fabrizio, what have they done to my beloved Germany? It is a ghost land. I saw it crumble before my eyes. This Versailles treaty is a pine box transporting Germany to a burial ground. What will I do? What *will* I do? I suffocate in a life no longer rewarding to me. War has changed everything." His tone grew dramatic. "I must leave the order—does that sound blasphemous—retire to my private lair in Bavaria. Once the prince-bishops resided there in summer, formed *glorious* hunting parties, rode *gloriously* to the hounds to find that one *glorious* stag as trophy in the most *glorious* country God created. A heaven on earth, where man can shut out the brutal, ugly world, live graciously, free of prying hypocrites. *And,* Fabrizio! What of this insanity of a workers' revolution spreading infectiously westward at an alarming pace?"

As Heinrich revealed his innermost thoughts and emotions several things occurred to Fabrizio. First, the cleric, raised in luxury, had abandoned it for a spartan life, one that fell short of his expectations. Second, his self-indulgent personality had rendered him incapable of abandoning earthly goods to live the life of a true ascetic. Third, this sybaritic martyr preferred the company of younger men in ways beyond the intellectual.

Heinrich pulled back a wall drape, revealing a large gilt-framed mirror that reflected both their images. "What a day of revelations, Fabrizio. Meeting you is the high point in my life. It draws me closer to a decision. If I remain in Admont, I shall atrophy in heart, spirit, body, and mind.''

Fabrizio sniffed the wine's bouquet, sipped it delicately with the air of a connoisseur, allowing it to caress his palate. Their eyes met, held in wordless communication. In evaluating the stakes earlier, Fabrizio had decided he would play his part because he needed information. Breaking eye contact, he raved over the superb cuisine.

''Your intelligence reflects a power I find irresistible and stimulating,'' Heinrich said. ''Dare I speak without being *misunderstood*?''

He opened another bottle of wine. ''I sense compassion in you, an understanding of the unrequited yearnings buried deep inside me. You put my spirit at ease, and that, my friend, is an art few men are capable of demonstrating.''

Fabrizio savored each morsel of the sumptuous dinner. Heinrich grew bolder.

''When society frowns on the expression of deep and profound feelings, what do you do? Do you yield to the sensations surging through the corridors of the soul or do you force yourself to dissolve them?''

''You do nothing, dear Heinrich. The feelings grow until no hope exists for either containment or dissolution until, one day, they demand release. And nothing, no power on earth can control those feelings.''

Their eyes met again. Heinrich, was besieged by powerful emotions, his eyes imploring to be understood. Caragini was impatient, ill at ease, and annoyed. Yet in that annoyance he retained a curiously detached attitude, giving the matter little importance.

''Your trouble, dear friend Heinrich,'' he began, ''stems from your being an elitist. Given everything in life, what need have you of ambition? You *want* nothing from life and complain because you *get* nothing. For such a man, there can be no exaltations, no victories, no thrill of risk taking. He is resigned for all time to wallow in self-pity and is of use to no one—not even to himself.'' Caragini wagged a sly finger at him. ''You are not elevated above the self, Heinrich. How have you concealed your deception from the hierarchy of this holy order?'' He chided gently, mischievously; his desire was not to offend—not yet.

"You see? I *was* right. I singled you out, placed you on a higher plane of thought than most who frequent my library. How perceptive. You saw through me." Heinrich was delighted. He poured more wine. Rising, he placed water to boil in an espresso machine on the wood-burning stove. "I will tell you more of my childhood. My domineering mother emasculated my father. He wallowed in self-pity. And I, simpatico to his misery, acquiesced to my mother's dictates until I no longer could endure watching my father's total disintegration. He took his frustrations out in alcohol and opium. And I—ran away! To Tibet . . . India . . . oh what does it matter, where? I meditated, studied philosophies advanced by men worthier than I, searching desperately for inner peace, ways of improving my lot in life. Alas, for a time I was hypnotized into believing that virtue—if it exists at all in men—consisted of championing the poor, underprivileged man. I believed the answer was to dedicate my life to the betterment of mankind. Ah, Fabrizio, I tried, how I tried to attain the selflessness of ego; instead I ended up a poor deluded fool. I admit to many things, but not to being a hypocrite. I am utterly devoid of piety and virtue. Shall I confess my loathing for the wretched masses of humanity I encountered? My contempt at their indolence, lack of ambition, refusal to elevate themselves above the circumstances of their birth? What a price I paid for my loathing! Beleaguered by intolerable guilt, the afflictions of Saint Anthony, the tortures of the damned rained down on me. I became celibate, abstained from spirits, tobacco, gluttony, drugs. I studied with the anchorites, failed miserably. Now I confess to failure after twenty years. A wasted life, Fabrizio, is all I can boast. *A wasted life!*"

Brother Heinrich sipped his wine, stared at the amber contents. "Whatever else I am, I remain honest. At least—that. I *am* worldly. I *am* a bon vivant. I *am* a libertine. Some men pretend to be what they are not; some try to cover up and drop hints that they are *not* what they are. I, unable to pretend to what I am not, refuse to cover what I am. I am determined to experience all this life has to offer, each day of my life, else I shall go mad. Today we met. Something whispered to me, 'Heinrich, you are at a pivotal point in your life. This man Fabrizio is here to create changes in your life. If you fail to grasp the moment, you will miss everything.' "

Precisely at this moment, the fraudulent Caragini formulated plans. He placed his knife across his plate.

"Heinrich, you're a gracious host. I can imagine nothing more rewarding than to know you better. First, we must talk. My time is limited. My journey saps my endurance. Perhaps if we complete my task expeditiously, there may be time to—"

"I understand. Please, be comfortable, warm yourself before the fire." With renewed hope, Heinrich retired to his bedroom.

In the sitting room, Fabrizio cooled his heels thumbing through the voluminous manuscript on the desk. In the bedroom, Heinrich undressed, refreshed himself with perfumed water, slipped into a quilted burgundy-velvet dressing gown and slippers. He returned to the living room, his mood expansive, his manner grandiose.

Caragini took in the changes, tightly.

"Very well, what is it you need know about the Zaragozas?" Heinrich asked.

"Everything."

"*Everything?*" The cleric rolled the word over in his mind. He closed his eyes, creating the setting in his mind. "Very well; it was the fifteenth century . . . the symbol of the age was the Dance of Death in which cavorting skeletons led men, women, and children step by merry step to hell. The world, viewed as evil, was drowning in waves of dissent; authority was challenged; social, religious orders were collapsing, all was chaos and madness. Criminals owned the streets. Commerce languished, hampered by economic disaster. Spain, the Iberian Peninsula, was a nation divided. . . ."

"We've come very little from those days, *ja,* Brother Heinrich?" He poured more coffee. Heinrich ignored the irony and shrugged indifferently. Locked into a different time warp, Heinrich sipped the coffee and continued.

"Isabella of Castile and Ferdinand of Aragon and Sicily, determined to change the course of history, married in 1469. The Inquisition became a tool to determine whether Spanish Jews sincerely converted to Christianity. . . . Into this hotbed of mayhem, corruptibility, and barbarity add a criminal brotherhood. The Compagnia della Garduna. These brigands, seduced by Isabella into serving the Crown, thrived. When the Inquisition ended . . ."

Once past the egocentric personality, Heinrich displayed formidable talent in research. His memory, sharp as a scalpel, enabled him to expound for hours. Fabrizio learned more than he knew, *far* more, but it was not enough. The Garduna helped to expel Jews and Moors, and this soothed the growing disquiet among the baronage and actually boosted Isabella and Ferdinand's dream of empire. Rewarded handsomely and permitted freedom to exist as they chose, the Garduna soon formed a vital alliance with the Zaragoza monks. How they tyrannized the people! Starting with sanctioned raids upon the Moors and Jews, they soon preyed upon the entire populace. They flourished, grew increasingly prosperous, and, in their bold metamorphosis from employees of the Crown, soon became despotic figureheads selling protection to members of the government. A refinement of their crimes elevated them above the label of brigands.

"How spectacular they were, Fabrizio! Reorganization into a disciplined, cohesive, criminal network permitted them full control in every nefarious activity imaginable with impunity. Protection rackets, kidnapping for ransom, forgery, larceny, sabotage, extortion, blackmail, even murder. They lived like pashas, very civilized, with dignity. What a time for lucrative dealings! Cohesion of the brotherhood, you see, was guaranteed by the tenets set forth in the Seven Garduna Parchments."

"Garduna Parchments?"

"Yes. Seven in all."

Caragini pounced on this point like a jackal contemplating a feast. "What exactly are these Seven Garduna Parchments?"

"Ah, my dear Fabrizio"—Heinrich kissed his fingertips in a gesture of delight—"the treasure men kill for."

"*Treasure?*" The blood-engorged veins at Caragini's temples throbbed.

"Blueprints . . . organizational laws and by-laws, statutes set forth in a step-by-step procedure, actually refined to a science by farsighted Zaragoza scribes. Fifty articles written in ancient, cryptic codes on seven separate parchments. One without the others is meaningless. The coded chronology for a grand design— the genesis of a criminal network, powerful as any government, meant to operate as a second government within the infrastructure of a governing nation."

Caragini sipped his wine, his eyes hooded, trying to remain calm.

"The intent was brilliant. Each parchment, placed in the separate custody of Garduna leaders in the seven branch offices of the brotherhood at Valencia, Cordoba, Barcelona, Zaragoza, Cadiz, Toledo, and its main headquarters in Seville, would only come together at a critical time, ordered by the grand marshal. However, a pressing problem tabled the relocation of each parchment." His voice fell to a hush. *"The irresistible force met an immovable object!"*

Caragini's eyes widened.

"Blinded with power, the Garduna-Zaragoza crime syndicate rode herd on Andalusia province, indiscriminately acquiring whatever suited their fancy without resistance from those they robbed. The Zaragozas coveted a lush hacienda, fantasic lands, vineyards, citrus, olive groves, grazing lands, a sprawling villa, and the ruins of a thirteenth-century Moorish castle. To the Zaragozas, the estate represented the *ne plus ultra,* the crowning achievement of their career, termination of nomadic life and a base to train future assassins. Unfortunately, impediments obstructed success."

"Don't tell me," Fabrizio interrupted. "The lands belonged to the Spanish nobles—the de la Varga family!"

Heinrich smiled approvingly, as a professor to his bright, attentive student. "A very *special* family, its patriarch an extraordinary conquistador, General Federico de la Varga. Recently he had laid at Isabella's feet lavish gold and silver treasures from the West Indies, Mexico, Central and South America. While the Zaragozas plotted to break the hacienda's security, kill off the peons, and slay the family, the general was in San Lucar de Barramedas, being knighted by the queen. Her appreciation of de la Varga's grand gesture resulted in declaring his properties free from taxes, in perpetuity. No succeeding Spanish monarch could revoke the decree or strip the family of their land under any circumstance, even during a state of war, *if* no ruling authority prevailed." Heinrich sipped his wine, observing Caragini's interest.

"Need I convey to you the result of this royal edict upon the Zaragozas? All other business was tabled as they fought against time to confiscate the coveted lands *before* the royal seal was affixed to Isabella's proclamation. Alas, their timing was off! And so began the worst bloodletting in history between a criminal band of thugs and Spain's most honored subject." Heinrich narrated from memory, as excited as his guest.

"Efforts to circumvent Isabella's edict frustrated, the Garduna combine grew more daring. Antonio Vasquez, grand marshal of the brotherhood, *dared* solicit protection money from de la Varga to insure him against vandals. Confrontation between the menacing crime overlord, Vasquez, and the dynamic, utterly fearless de la Varga, ended in verbal catastrophe. Sufficiently enraged de la Varga denigrated Vasquez, ridiculed him openly, had him thrown off the lands by a leviathan Moor, Jamal Montenegro, the general's confidant, a former Moorish warlord saved from death by de la Varga. Vasquez's fate was graphically described by the Moor, should the brigand chief dare trespass again. Humility, strength, and avid dedication to de la Varga sat strong in that bloodless face, and Vasquez, noting the threat retreated and retrenched.

"Open war followed. Brutal raids and marauding sprees ferociously hurled against de la Varga culminated in the wholesale slaughter of the innocent. The abduction, rape, and subsequent death of Don Federico's daughter triggered in him a barbarian's reaction. He dispatched a courier to Madrid to the queen.

"The courier, intercepted, was returned to the Spanish noble hacked to pieces; a note attached to the bloodied remains called it an object lesson, an indication of de la Varga's impotence against the terrorists. Oh, my dear Fabrizio, what courage it took to live in those days!

"And so, de la Varga hired his own army, taught them to shoot, and launched a personal crusade against the enemy, dedicating his existence to their extinction. The Guadalquivir River flowed crimson to the sea with the blood of de la Varga enemies! In time de la Varga, a military strategist, recognized the futility of defensive tactics against well-organized terrorists. Unable to implement offensive attacks, he would inevitably lose. Holed up behind the fortress, he could defend it for so long. Prevented from hurling one surprise blow, *un solo golpe terrifico*, what hope had he? It was time for desperate action.

"And so one night, Jamal, the Moor, slipped through enemy lines, reached Madrid, and returned a week later with an army supplied by Isabella. The next raid hurled against de la Varga was met with an unexpected counterattack by formidable, skilled warriors, who decimated the aggressors and sent what remained of them into hasty retreat.

"Did de la Varga end it right then and there? No! To crown his victory, he and a squad of men rode into Seville, raided the magnificent house of Antonio Vasquez, arrested the grand marshal and other members of the society's hierarchy, confiscated ledgers, books, and an innocuous-looking scroll that contained the Seven Garduna Parchments. Yes, there was a golden ring, the seal of the brotherhood, in the shape of a gold marten.

"The queen held court in the halls of the Alcazar, where she directed her wrath against these *master* criminals whom she had unwittingly endowed with unlimited powers during the Inquisition. They *dared* collect taxes, did they? Act as a *second* government? Infuriated at their usurpation of imperial powers, Isabella foolishly *leaked* her intentions to her advisers. The rumor mills spread fear among the offenders. Before sentence was pronounced, thousands upon thousands fled Spain in anticipation of Isabella's wrath. Until her advisers convinced Her Majesty to declare amnesty for the Garduna's crimes or suffer the severe deprivation of needed workers in Spain. Isabella acquiesced. Following her demise in 1504 A.D. the Garduna-Zaragozas kept low profiles, hired spies and scribes to scour the royal archives to locate and retrieve their precious ledgers and the irreplaceable Seven Garduna Parchments.

"The ledgers, delivered to them without the parchments, infuriated Vasquez and his brotherhood. Perusal of the ledgers proved them facsimiles—copies of the originals! Who, then, had the originals? Additional spies scoured the queen's former quarters and the Alcazar. Nothing! Meditation, logic, and reasoning turned up one possible suspect—Don Federico de la Varga! It could be none other—on this they agreed. Patience became their tool.

"Ten years passed. Targeted for their fury, de la Varga lands were infiltrated. Spies, disguised as day laborers, were caught, expelled, and often killed by the Moor and his men. These former criminal czars, unable to reenter the lucrative marketplaces where once their skills had greatly profited them, appeared at cross purposes with one another, and with drawn daggers, each blamed the other for their dismal insolvency. The Garduna chose to sever relations with the Zaragozas, determined to forage on their own. Soon they involved themselves in a variety of petty crimes, but never again operated on so grand a scale as they did before they clanked sabers with Don Federico de la Varga."

"What became of them?" Caragini asked quietly.

"They integrated with the population and went underground."

"No! I speak of the parchments."

Heinrich's cheshire-cat grin irked Fabrizio Caragini. "How judicious of you to ask." He tossed more logs on the fire, stoked them, replaced the poker, and stretched his athletic frame. He poured hot coffee, using cinnamon sticks soaked in brandy as swivel sticks. He gave one to his guest and stifled a yawn. "To reply to your question, I do not know. After five centuries . . . tracing their ultimate resting place—if indeed they still exist— would be a monumental task.'' Heinrich stretched out in his deeply cushioned leather chair. "What an ambition!" He shifted his focus sharply on his guest. "Is this *your* intent?"

Caragini yawned. A fiend at burning midnight oil, a nocturnal being, why should he feel such drowsiness? "What makes the parchments so priceless?" he asked, stifling another yawn.

"I never saw them. Few scholars claim that honor. Written as they are in ancient hieroglyphics, few attempted it. But wait . . ." Heinrich pondered a moment. "A very *special* scholar, Brother Xenofonte from Trento, Italy, claims the secrets contained in the Parchments rest solely in some unique manner of recruiting and training neophytes to the cause. Yes, yes, I remember. . . . Twelve steps must be followed in exact sequence— not one step eliminated in the training." Heinrich sipped the hot coffee, periodically peering at Caragini. "From what Xenofonte claims, personal choices and recommendations from the hierarchy meant nothing. Each recruit was judged on his own merits. Fear instilled in the neophytes' minds played a major role in keeping them virginal. The hierarchy of the combine, those who moved pawns about, remained anonymous. For example, Antonio Vasquez, the grand marshal, might have served in name only, while the actual plenipotentiary remained invisible.''

Caragini blinked awake. *The Invisible hierarchy of Zurich! The consortium!* The similarity jarred him. Fighting fatigue, he examined the similarity between Omicron and the Garduna. It sounded too close to be mere coincidence. He mopped the sweat on his brow. Heinrich was talking—what was he saying . . . ?

"My research ends in the seventeenth century, Fabrizio. The Garduna flourished sporadically as a gang of thugs who waged war against virtually anyone. The Order of Saint Pachomious at Trento picks up where my research leaves off." Heinrich, a twinkle of amusement flickering in his eyes, leaned forward in his chair. "Fabrizio . . . why do you wear a false beard?"

Vaguely Caragini's hand shot to his chin, smoothing the goatee into place. He offered an explanation. "To—uh—look older. Be taken seriously by my superiors. Youth pays a dear price." He climbed out of a ten-foot hole with a half inch of rope.

Something was terribly wrong! What in damnation?

His head whirled, his vision grew hazy, his movements slowed down. His reflexes refused to obey his commands. He stared into the fire, his host watching him like a spider about to pounce on a fly.

Chapter Three

A man has no better thing under the sun
Than to eat and to drink and to have lots of fun.

Ecclesiastes 8:15

The fraudulent Caragini tried desperately to form words, but the task was made impossible by loose, rubbery lips. Confused, he slumped in his chair, eyes flaring like splintered shafts of fire before sealing off all light. The coffee cup fell from his hand onto the floor, spilling over the floral-patterned carpeting. Heinrich moved swiftly, picking up cup and saucer, setting them on a table. Gathering his guest up in his muscled arms, he carried him into the bedroom, placed him lengthwise on the four-poster.

He had landed his prey!

Ebulliently he proceeded to the pleasurable task of disrobing his guest. First the boots, then trousers, jacket, vest, shirt, lastly the longjohns, by far the least attractive but necessary part of the man's apparel. Heinrich lighted two candles, placed glass chimneys over each, and set one on each of the two tables at bedside. The added illumination enabled him to appraise his prize. The body, young, sturdy—not athletic but well formed—certainly not the most beautiful male body he'd seen. Suddenly his eyes froze, riveted to the patch of dark crotch hair. Drawing one chimney lamp closer, the flickering flame illuminating the area of his focus, Heinrich experienced shock.

A Jew! God Almighty! Circumcision!

Heinrich sensed trouble, *serious* trouble. At times he won-

41

dered if he'd inherited a madness, for in his recent desolation of spirit, he had felt a slow inner deterioration, a sense of being sucked into quicksand. So much had happened . . . If he took another step over that rigidly imposed line . . . ?

Heinrich needed assurance. A spur of fear ran up his backbone, lodged itself in his parched, cracked throat. Wading through a welter of conflicting emotions, he rationalized. *Caragini!* Was it *just* possible? Could he? Sweet Jesus, *don't* let him be a spy sent by the Monastic Council of Internal Affairs to trap him in a compromising situation!

That's it! That excoriating letter waiting for him on his return from St. Bartolema! Nothing compassionate, nothing appreciative for his long years of service. The contents shaking him to the core, plunging him headlong into a sordid accounting designed to ruin him.

> *Three previous reprimands, Brother Schuller, for despicable sexual escapades reported to us . . . your salacious proclivities and degrading behavior unbecoming a cleric of your stature has shocked the council. You leave us no recourse but to issue an ultimatum. The lecherous debaucheries must cease! One more reprimand, the faintest tinge of scandal . . . and stipend or not, you shall be stripped of all credentials and discharged in disgrace.*

Those pathological ingrates! No thanks for the countless cases of rare brandies and wines sent to them in harrowing times! Affixed to the vile epistle was that condemning seal and twelve illegible signatures. *Damn them!* Heinrich had burned that indictment instantly, but the wretched, caustic words, etched indelibly in his brain, only deepened his depression and recent suicidal bent. Anger inevitably replaced the depression and he grimly determined to finish the hypocrisy. He'd do it! Perhaps the time was at hand?

Heinrich returned to the moment. He had work to do and it must be done immediately. He searched frantically through Caragini's clothing for a bursa containing identity cards and travel permits. Locating the items, he moved closer to the fireplace, utilizing the bright lights to scrutinize the papers. Shuffling through them, he heaved a sigh of relief and replaced them carefully. So much for that! His guest, according to the papers, was genuine—not a spy.

Damnable Monastic Council! The worst possible offenders *dared* threaten him? What was the harm in the games he played? Carnal interludes between consenting soulmates? Why spoil the night by dwelling on these outrageous, pontificating sinners who themselves formed a decaying society of misfits and took pleasure in the subjugation of the lesser man to please their own petty egos? Not after his elaborate preparations on this night!

Focusing on the pleasures at hand, he poured a glass of wine, approached the bed, prepared for the unveiling. He sipped the wine, placed it on the marble-topped table, and removed the goatee and mustache from Fabrizio's face. The man looked ten years younger! The result sparked desire in Heinrich.

But a Jew! Bedding down with a Jew? He'd heard fantastic stories—incredible tales concerning their voracious libidinal drive.

For as long as he remembered he preferred a man's company to any woman's. Most women were shallow, empty-headed, silly creatures whose every word and action was predictable. He understood very little of women. All sham and no substance, they pretended to live in a world only they perceived.

Stop it, Heinrich! Stop justifying that which needs no justification!

The monsigneur who had led him along the primrose path to his first homosexual experience had summed up the harsh realities of man's existence. "Since all morality is *man-made*, and therefore ephemeral, there exist no grounds for condemnation of personal taste and individual temperament." From that day forward Heinrich's life had exemplified this credo . . . and this Caragini undeniably sent blood coursing through him, electric shocks of excitement pounding at his temples. His cobalt eyes ravished the youth's body in repose; he exulted in his cunning in luring the unsuspecting victim to his bed. Caragini's was not the strapping, thickly muscled body he preferred, but it elicited a manly response from his organ.

His hand caressed his erection. He whispered, "The blood speaks, Fabrizio. Blood moves between us, pulsating, communicating desire. It transcends all religions," he added as if this absolved him of any sin. He reveled in the hardening of his erection. He was too far gone to permit differing religious persuasions to spoil pleasures of the flesh; whatever momentary guilt he had felt was now gone.

He bolted the front door, shoved a heavy chair against it, extinguished all candles in the sitting room, tossed logs on the fire, and returned to the bedroom with wine and glasses. He emptied the night bucket, poured fresh water into it and placed it under the bed. He closed shutters, pulled drapes closed, added more logs to the fire in this room. Warmed by the fire, he glanced at the myriad shadows flickering through the room. The gramophone played Mozart's *Marriage of Figaro*.

Heinrich, a romantic perfectionist, insisted that everything, including the setting, be conducive to his sexual pleasures. If one thing was awry, the slightest thing, it could ruin everything. Now, he caressed Fabrizio's genitals with perfumed water, rejoicing at the formidable mass of flesh growing in his hands. Finished, he placed the bowl on the nearby commode, and, padding to the opposite wall, tugged an oversized cheval glass on rollers from behind a drapery, positioning it next to the bed, angling the mirror precisely so his and Fabrizio's body were reflected perfectly. He stared at the large circumcized shaft nestled amid the dark curly pubic hairs. He listened. Fabrizio breathed steadily.

Anticipation seized him. Wetting his parched throat with wine, he considered his earlier action of slipping a sleeping potion in his guest's wine amply rewarded. His cunning was about to pay off.

He hardened again, delighted at the tingling inside him. The chastity imposed by that damnable council had left him numb. No more! Certainly at the very worst, the consequences, if any materialized, wouldn't affect him. The council had facilitated the plying of his craft. What was the difference? Awake or asleep?

Enjoy Heinrich! Enjoy your bounty, sate your thirst!

He commenced his sexual symphony. From the night-table drawer he removed the aphrodisiacs dispensed to him by a friendly Munich apothecary. He daubed a few drops from one vial on his swollen member, did the same to Fabrizio's. Waiting for them to take effect, he selected another vial, poured droplets into his wineglass, and gulped it greedily. Placing the empty glass on the night table, he proceeded to prepare his guest for the next ritual. He spread Fabrizio's legs apart, leaned over him, and applied his mouth to the large, pendulous testicles. His erotic manipulations, artistically precise, heightened his responses. He squirmed, wriggled, permitting sensation free expression. Myriad fantasies worked his brain. Periodically he glanced into the mirror, observing his sexual ministrations, growing hotter, highly impassioned. Nothing stirred his passions like reflected images.

He caressed Fabrizio's face, slapped it gently, whispered endearing words, and moving over him kissed him ardently, his long hard cock and hairy blond balls rubbing sensually against the other's. He fluttered a length of wispy silk veiling over Fabrizio's body, drawing added stimulation as involuntary shudders rippled through his guest's body.

Turning Fabrizio over onto his stomach, he placed a pillow under him, elevating the buttocks. He spread the slim, boyish moons apart, inserted a dropper containing muscle relaxer, and greased the anus to facilitate penetration. Heinrich's erection, unbearably hard, demanded release. Grasping Fabrizio's hips, he lifted them to him, and, once lubricated, moved past the sphincter and drove into him, barely completing penetration before the body under him began to writhe. Seized with violent spasms, Fabrizio grunted, groaned, and moaned pleasurably despite his drugged stupor.

Heinrich smiled. From the moment he set eyes on the professor he had sensed a complicity beneath the surface. *Why* had he played so hard to get? No one could fool Heinrich Schuller, *no one*. The writhing under him accelerated the brewing storm in his loins. Rhythmically, he thrusted in and out, in and out, prolonging the ecstasy. Catching their reflections in the mirror, he stepped up the momentum. Breathlessly, he paced himself, one eye on the mirror, storing mental images of the appealing erotica in his mind. He approached the plateau of ejaculation, his eyes like fire points. He stared down at his throbbing penis, pulling it out slowly and gliding it back a fraction at a time until the sensations chilled his spine like a thousand icicles. ''God—oh, God!'' he groaned, unable to prolong the ecstasy. A last violent thrust before the bursting semen held him suspended amid celestial configurations and the lower depths of debauchery. He fell heavily over Fabrizio, waiting for the cacophonous sound in his head to subside.

For a long while he lay there, pulling the down covers over them, until he felt his penis go soft; it plopped out of its own accord as Fabrizio's sphincter contracted involuntarily. Heinrich rolled over on his back, panting; he studied his quarry. No changes in breathing were evident, no fluttering eyelids, no mobility at all.

Well, Heinrich Schuller—why not?

Looming over Fabrizio, he indulged his tongue in caresses, alert to the slightest sign of consciousness. He tongued the

Italian's growing erection, marveling at the thick phallus. Turning slightly to catch their reflection in the mirror, his eyes widened in desire. Inside his hot mouth, the thick penis jerked spasmodically; he stretched his mouth to accommodate the huge member. Heinrich stopped, swore he heard a groan, but before he paused to observe Fabrizio's face, he felt two hands on his head directing the slow, sensuous movements, pressing him closer until he nearly gagged.

Easing himself from the strong grip, he glanced at the closed eyes. He might have stopped if the body under him hadn't undulated, responded sensually. Encouraged by this affirmative body language, Heinrich returned to his pleasure, thrilled by the reciprocity of his partner. How perfectly glorious, he thought. What utter perfection!

Fabrizio's body arched off the bed, pressing harder against Heinrich, his breathing more pronounced, eyeballs flickering under lids. The cleric sucked eagerly until the other drove so hard and deep that retreat was mandatory. Heinrich refused to end it. The gamble paid off. The cock exploded in his mouth, the body shuddered, and he screamed aloud.

Unbeknownst to Schuller, Caragini had awakened moments earlier, in a hangover haze, at first unaware of his seduction. Protests forming on his lips were quelled by the sensations of sexual ecstasy. A split second before orgasm, Fabrizio garnered his will as never before, forcing into mind the fantasy of a woman performing the act, replacing the image of Heinrich.

A hoarse, guttural, animal cry arose from his throat. The bed shook under them. Fabrizio bolted upright, eyes wide, nearly scaring the cleric into cardiac arrest.

Startled, apprehensive, the monk retreated, eyes fixed on those awesome colorless orbs reflecting red diamonds in the fire glow. He stopped breathing. The eyes registered no sign of menace—no danger.

The sharp planes of Fabrizio's face softened, relaxed, settled into a little-boy look.

Silence . . . interminable silence punctuated by the harsh, scratchy sounds of the gramophone. Heinrich arose, cranked it up and stood before the mirror.

Fabrizio lay against the pillows, in a half-reclining position. Between the drugs, wine, and muscle relaxant, he felt no rectal discomfort. A dull ache at the base of his skull, a slight inability to focus his eyes, a slight tremor, told him the story. He'd been drugged. But why? His focus cleared and centered on Heinrich. The cleric stood before the mirror, masturbating, his eyes fired once again with lust.

Fabrizio pulled himself up to a sitting position on the bed, his mood one of forced detachment, his expression seraphic.

"You were saying, Heinrich, your research ended in the seventeenth century. Tell me where to pick up the story."

Heinrich was startled. Stupefied by Fabrizio's total disregard for what happened earlier, he burst into paroxysms of laughter, doubled over in mirth. Was it possible? Was it just possible he and Fabrizio were fated to become soulmates?

The crackling, spitting sounds of burning logs on the hearth captured his attention; the fire had burned to embers. He placed more logs on the fire, resurrecting it, and replied mechanically to the question, his mind racing in another direction.

"Have you ever searched for God, Fabrizio?" the cleric asked quietly.

"I am not a godly man, Heinrich." Caragini frowned. He wanted answers to his questions.

"I just learned, neither am I. It is a revelation. It means I am finished with deception. You know how long I've searched for God? In all the countless library naves, in thousands upon thousands of books, I've searched every page trying to find the answer. I have nearly gone blind seeking Him, burning the midnight oil, but no more. Was it Maimonides who wrote: 'Words heard in a dream are divine when they are distinct and clear and the person uttering them cannot be seen.' Dreams belong to God, Fabrizio, and I have heard Him speak to me this night. Shall I tell you what he said?"

Chapter Four

The Zurich Christmas parade of marchers in nightshirts, clanging cowbells and tooting horns, had failed to exorcise the spirit of winter. The new decade was ushered in by a record snowstorm, which halted the wheels of commerce in this city of gold.

Rosy-cheeked work crews shouted, "*Neujarsabend*—Happy New Year!" They worked feverishly to clear the streets of snow. A colorless sun dimmed the formal bow of the new decade, but it didn't obliterate the enticing fragrance of fresh breads, strudels, and pastries that permeated the Alstad. On nearby Lake Zurich, boats, the only transportation during emergencies, carried the Swiss to their families to celebrate the holidays.

Standing at the window of Suite 333 at the Suisse Banque Royale, Kurt Von Kurt, an overfleshed, paunchy, bull-necked man in his forties, totally hairless, stared down at the work crews in the Parade-Platz. His bald head rose from thick shoulders; his face was a colorless fleshy mass with black, piglike eyes narrowed in apoplectic rage. This was not the usual posture for the senior man of Omicron. But nothing about his presence here today on a holiday was usual.

He jerked the burgundy velvet draperies on brass rings hurriedly together to shut out the offensive pigeon droppings smearing the windowpanes. The diffused light converted the wood-paneled conference room, the book-lined wall shelves, and the elegant furnishings to a lackluster drabness.

Von Kurt, a master at pleasing the hierarchy of invisibles occupying the top floors of the bank building, padded back to the polished mahogany table, sat down stiffly in a high-backed, leather wing chair at one end. Here they had sat, in Suite 333, at the same conference table frequented for a year by Amadeo Zeller, investing their time, training, confidence in a man for the clandestine Madrid Assignment.

Where had the trio gone wrong?

Von Kurt, with his companions, Karl Berne and Fritz Guggenheim were tough, shrewd manipulators of men, born predators, exponents of a highly refined Machiavellian philosophy. By making themselves indispensable to the Zurich consortium, they had themselves become an integral part of the power hierarchy. A peculiar breed unto themselves they had to be faultless or it was curtains for an entire operation and themselves. Stone-cold professionals selected from the ranks, they had long since paid their dues, and sat content at the foot of the power pinnacle awaiting their turn to play king of the hill. Because of these men, the ivory-towered moguls had tasted increased power, and in return their coffers were sweetly lined with riches and prestige. They marked time for the day they, too, would occupy the ivory towers upstairs.

Von Kurt finger polished his gold watch, his florid, heavily jowled face telling of his inner displeasure. On this day, this man of authority, feared and respected by his associates, fought for control. He sipped a glass of white wine, lifted his eyes over the rim, staring at, but not really seeing Karl Berne, the man seated at his right.

Berne, a slim, bony man, two years Von Kurt's junior, was cynical, domineering, and ruthless—a hard-nosed bird, opinionated, puffed with his own importance. Yet it was fascinating to observe his obsequious behavior before the two elder men. His sharp-beaked features and glaring hostile eyes made him resemble a hungry scavenging vulture. Berne removed a monocle from his left eye, blew on it, wiped it with a linen handkerchief, wondering where they had erred with Zeller. Berne replaced the monocle and lit a fresh cigarette. He bore the mark of a chain smoker, thumb and forefinger stained brown. He glanced impatiently at Fritz Guggenheim, seated at Von Kurt's left, waiting for him to read the report in his pudgy hands.

Fritz Guggenheim, the third man who was shaping Zeller's future, was short, rotund, with a high forehead and a rosy-cheeked cherubic face. He was fortyish, conservatively dressed, wearing gold-rimmed spectacles. A rich, red mustache, spread across his upper lip, widened out across his cheeks, ending in twisted, waxy ends at a point where his sideburns began. A thickly cropped shock of red hair falling from a neat center part was slicked into place at each temple. Brown eyes in their red-veined whites were riveted on the communiqué, reading each word, each line, as if it were a dagger aimed at him. Guggie, a deadly man with an uncanny aptitude for facts and figures, doubly blessed by inherited wealth, sat forward in his chair like a coiled python. He crumpled the communiqué in his hands, tossed it disgustedly on the table, glowering at it as if it had taken on a life of its own.

Each man alone was formidable enough; together they formed an intimidating defense against all offenders in their midst. Although not fully accepted into the oligarchy's inner circle, they were its eyes, ears, brains, arms, and its far-reaching tentacles. Lesser men shuddered at the power of Omicron. Few knew these men could move mountains.

Today, these mountain movers never before put to the test, felt impotent, fully shaken. Shaken by a piece of paper balled on the table! The damnable contents had ruined their holiday. A day dedicated to enjoying festivities with their respective families—disrupted by that damnable message. The offensive communiqué was a coded dispatch any moron could understand, from a trusted agent in the field, named Macbeth. Because it posed complexities beyond their wildest expectations, they were baffled by it, and until they understood its most profound meaning, they were relegated to remain in Suite 333. The conundrum must be unraveled! It must!

At issue was Macbeth's unblemished ten-year record with Omicron against the untested record of Amadeo Zeller. A year's investment of their time and brains in Zeller, if subverted, could capsize their individual dreams and destroy each man.

Too goddamned much depended on a man each loathed with passion!

Guggie read the message aloud, slowly, as if he hoped to unravel the mystery between each word. " 'Call—off—the—dog— Zeller. Am—seriously—wounded. Advise—or—expect—my—defec-

tion. Signed Macbeth.' So? What does it mean, this call off the dog, Zeller?''

"It means, Guggie, we are in trouble, *ja*?'' Von Kurt placed his gold watch on the table, folded pudgy hands, wringing them together. "First we locate the *dummkopf* Macbeth.''

Twenty-four grueling, frustrating hours later the trio stood at the shortwave unit in the next room observing a dispatcher decoding a message just received, not from Macbeth but from another agent, named Hamlet. It was brief, graphic, describing the altercation between Zeller and Macbeth at the Salzburg train depot. Hamlet claimed Macbeth had spotted Zeller on the train at St. Gallens. Fearing Omicron had ordered his demise, Macbeth had pulled a knife on Zeller and fell helplessly under Zeller's blade; he was now near death. Macbeth's identification was based on an undisputable fact: colorless eyes. How many men with colorless eyes wore ostentatious alpine garb and smoked Meerschaums? Hamlet's addendum to the message reinforced Macbeth's implied threat. *"Call off Zeller or Macbeth defects!"*

Following the cold recital of facts they retreated to the conference table to dissect, interpret, and deliberate upon the chaotic complications.

It was night again. Karl Berne pulled back the drapes, rang for a waiter to clear the remains of their dinner. An hour later, evidencing signs of strain, the trio approached a logical solution, jointly concluding that however serious were the obstacles clouding the Madrid Assignment, both Macbeth's Moscow job and Hamlet's Berlin assignment balanced out to zero compared to Madrid. Losses sustained by sudden shifts in strategy for Moscow and Berlin were absorbable; Madrid's loss was not. Capable agents in the field could be recalled, and reassigned to Moscow and Berlin. Madrid was very special.

Four hours later they made several decisions. Radio messages dispatched to Hamlet denied Omicron's culpability in a death plot against Macbeth. They insisted Macbeth's position with Omicron was unassailable. Hamlet was urged to convey their profound regrets to Macbeth and assure him that necessary funds would be dispatched at once to any conduit of his choice. He was further urged to impress upon Macbeth Omicron's gratitude for bringing Zeller's presence in Austria to their attention. A tag line followed the message. "Instruct Macbeth to look to other sources if his paranoia persists.''

The complex embroidery was not completed. Back in the

conference room, the men picked up their needlework and stitched together an intriguing design. They spoke German, as usual.

"We disregard nothing, *ja*?" Von Kurt drummed the table with his pudgy fingers. "Everything has its purpose, even that which remains hidden to the naked eye. Macbeth's paranoia concerning Omicron must be rooted in personal guilt. He has reason to believe we sent Zeller to kill him, ja? *Gut!* So! Macbeth and Hamlet are kaput. We prepare Malvolio for Moscow. Othello for Berlin. Shylock will handle the contract in Madrid— and Zeller."

Berne verbalized his thoughts. "Did Zeller act instinctively? Macbeth, after all, was the aggressor in the lethal contest."

A ray of hope sparked his associates' eyes, then dimmed quickly. "Karl, one blatant fact overshadows all else. What in damnation was Zeller doing in Austria? He should be in Spain!" exclaimed Guggie.

He was right; the disquieting fact drove them to find immediate answers. A renewed search through Zeller's past was required to abate their fears.

The men were forced to confront a situation they refused to accept at face value as they distributed among themselves the thick files compiled on Zeller.

"What did we overlook?" Berne lit a fresh cigarette with the butt before he snuffed it out. "Did we indiscriminately pass over data pertinent to the man's character?"

"Should our investment in Zeller prove a folly—" Von Kurt began, sorting out the papers before him. "I dare not conjecture."

"Let us not forget that the hierarchy demanded Zeller." Berne blew out smoke from his nostrils. "Do not forget *they* kept after us."

"A peremptory challenge from the august body and we complied?" Guggie, barely audible, seemed to lean on some invisible inner support.

"We glossed over nothing!" Von Kurt insisted. "*Nothing!* Not even to please the consortium. Our job was to unveil the Zeller profile, ferret out the ambiguities or distortions deliberately reported to create an improper one." He mopped the copious sweat from his hairless brow. "Zeller's vagrancy spells disaster for us. He knows too much. What quirk in Zeller provoked such inexcusable insubordination?" he asked, each word dripping icicles.

"Retaliation against Macbeth is understandable since the man came at him with a knife," Guggie mused aloud. "He protected himself. No importance can be attached to the act of self-defense except a superior skill." Guggie spoke above a whisper. "In felling Macbeth he felled the champion."

The others glanced at Guggie vacuously. Von Kurt shoved his gold-rimmed bifocals into place. "Before we leave these chambers, the truth will out."

A lengthy perusal of the files commenced, each man vividly reflecting how it was that Zeller, an unknown, had penetrated ivory-tower sanctuaries. As if they could forget! Their memories sparked alive.

In May, 1918 bloody battles still raged relentlessly in remote villages with curious names like Ypres, Flanders, Verdun. The Americans had entered the Great War in May 1917. They spread across Europe, infecting the people with their songs: "Tipperary," "Over There," "Mademoiselle From Armentiers, Parlez-Vous?" Heard daily on crystal sets, the songs had injected an air of buoyancy into the frightening darkness of panic, change, agonizing frustrations, and excruciating uncertainty. Globally, the era proved one of pure insanity; man's inhumanity toward man was never as devastating. The Great War viewed naively by the people as the war to end all wars fell short of the goal. That deadly plow of war, running out of control, began furrowing fecund fields, sowing seeds of future wars. Thirty-seven million men had lost their lives amid intolerable conditions created by a new military concept—trench warfare!

Nine months before the war machines gave up the ghost, special recruiting agents prowled through the universities of the world seeking raw material, new causes, for the power brokers of the world.

Reports sent directly to numerous power consortiums flourishing in Europe, examined critically, alerted them to the existence of an unusual young man at Lausanne University. These austere, astute power brokers, viewing the growing desperation besetting Germany and German-held territories, calculated to the day the Kaiser's defeat. They predicted the war's end to the day and set about skillfully plotting future wars, designing ingenious means to fill their coffers.

Against the background of personal misery, economic and political chaos, amid winds of uncertainty, poverty, and despair, the young man spotted by Omicron agents was placed under day and night surveillance. A closely knit ring of specialists compiled a diary of the young man's activities. The judiciously collated information, compiled by seasoned agents, took shape. Someone spectacular emerged . . . Amadeo Zeller!

Von Kurt read aloud from his file. '' 'Zeller, a talented, highly articulate Marxist-Socialist, possesses unique abilities. He employs the allure of ideology to harness the latent energies of discontented students swayed by his oratory. . . .' ''

Guggie read from his file. "It says here, 'Zeller demonstrates the power to whip an audience to a frenzy. A sedulous student of propaganda, he employs drama and excitement to its best advantage.' ''

''And,'' said Berne clearing his raspy throat. ''According to these reports Zeller is unlike anything the recruiters had encountered. 'His artful demagoguery, extraordinary intellect, and stamina are seldom seen in a man of his youth.' Bah! He is their personal messiah! Ridiculous garbage!''

Berne sipped the hot chocolate served earlier by their personal butler working in a nearby kitchen on the third floor. Clearing his nicotine-burned throat, he sorted through other reports.

'' 'Amadeo Zeller is perfect for Omicron!' '' Von Kurt sputtered. '' 'We submit he's too perfect to be real!' '' Von Kurt studied the signature of the agent submitting the report. ''Ironically Macbeth endorsed him.''

Each man took a turn at reading excerpts from the files.

'' 'Zeller's speeches on campus at Lausanne University electrify his audience.' ''

'' 'Conviction of his own self-worth oozes from him like sap from a maple tree.' ''

'' 'Beneath the facade he displays to the world lurks a mercurial personality. Zeller is not a man to be ignored, rather one to be artfully used by political giants as a device to move people, places and things—the world, if need be, into places to suit him.' ''

''Read that again, Guggie,'' Von Kurt ordered, caught by the words. Guggie obliged. They mulled over the statements in burning silence. ''Poring over this voluminous material, interjecting our thoughts, seems a bit ludicrous now, after the fact,'' Von Kurt stated flatly.

They persisted, determined to find something—anything to help them swim out of deep water and reduce the powerful undertow threatening them.

Zeller's progress reports were scrutinized, as were the weekly evaluations dispatched routinely by responsible recruiters. Each report, viewed in a new light, grew more provocative than the first—they couldn't learn enough about Zeller.

"We learned of Zeller—when?" Von Kurt asked, scowling darkly.

"After the recruiters notified the hierarchy. Did you forget, Kurt, how furious you were over the breach in protocol?" Guggie pressed.

"*Jawohl . . . ja, ja.*" He nodded, leaning back in his chair, reflecting.

For the past fifty years the hierarchy had nurtured a bold, ambitious plan. Selection of the *right* man was essential to the success of this highly covert assignment. Errors in judgment were unthinkable.

Years ago, before their time, recruiters, given a list of mandatory requirements, had searched in vain for an exceptional man qualified to promote the special project incubating in the minds of the ivory-tower moguls. In half a century no man had qualified. Only one attempt could be made in reaching for the coveted brass ring without lifting the lid of secrecy from it. The choice of necessity demanded perfection.

Profiles of Zeller arriving in dribs and drabs from several recruiters working independently of each other had bypassed the three men, reached the hierarchy's desks, and for a time became the best kept secret since publication of Ernest Renan's *Life of Jesus.* Eventually the three men were briefed on the framework of the Madrid project and the Zeller files turned over to them. Struck by Zeller's potential, they saw in him the embodiment of the fifty-year-old dream that would bring to fruition their own personal ambitions.

So, under third-level scrutiny, Zeller had passed through an invisible portal to a plateau of incomparable power, unaware of the *invisible* hands busy at work jockeying him into a future he hadn't yet dreamed for himself. Instantly the three men had launched into a meticulous in-depth evaluation of the man touted so lustily by their superiors. What they had learned at the outset had prompted comprehensive investigation of Zeller by discreet professionals, men better equipped to remain aloof from the mass hypnosis that eventually victimized most recruiters exposed to silver-tongued orators. The investigators worked in tandem, but apart from the Omicron recruiters. The professionals infiltrated student and faculty fringe areas at Lausanne University as disinterested parties, undetectable in crowds. All-seeing, all-knowing, all-hearing and -telling for a price, they sent volumes to the three men, including candid photographs of the subject in the company of highly controversial political figures of the day. It had taken them nearly a year of researching Zeller to convince themselves he was *right* for the Madrid Assignment.

And so, on this day, one of four dismal days spent on this can of worms wished on them by Macbeth, they searched to find where they had erred, if indeed they had erred at all.

Karl Berne, growing impatient, suggested they get to the meat of the matter. "Suppose, my friends, we commence from the beginning?"

He began to read:

AMADEO REDAK ZELLER: Born April 20, 1896, in Varesi, Italy, out of wedlock. Abandoned by his university professor father before birth, cast off at age five by his promiscuous mother. Responsibility for raising the precocious lad was relegated to what Zeller referred to as a covey of black witches masquerading as Sisters of Mercy at a Catholic orphanage. He was never permitted to forget the numerous deficiencies demonstrated by his mother. Further denigrated because his father was not Catholic, black thoughts hounded him. Destructive, antisocial forces coiled inside the lad, cleverly concealed under the facade of a seraphic countenance, unusual eyes, bearing the vaguest hue of blue. Constantly beleaguered by unbearable reminders of his illegitimacy, Zeller marked time until he escaped.

Zeller survived as a street urchin, living by his wits. He robbed, cheated, lied, stole to stay alive. At age twelve he was off the streets, sheltered by a kindly printer in Milano who offered him refuge from the abrasive world. He became a printer's apprentice and for the next several years his impressive mind, fed daily with subversive literature and propaganda printed in the shop, absorbed information about the rapidly proliferating cancers of discontent spreading throughout Europe. Rooted firmly in his mind were the words of Karl Marx, Schopenhauer, Giuseppe Mazzini, Garibaldi, David Lloyd George, Lenin, and a wave of Bolsheviks currently in vogue since that bloody Sunday when they carved names for themselves in that icy tomb called Russia.

Zeller paid the printer back for his kindness by robbing him of a precious sum of money. The loot took him to Lausanne, where he matriculated at the university with countless other fanatics of the era. He worked his way through the university by availing himself of the knowledge he'd gained as a printer's apprentice. He got a job in a printing shop. Enabled to read the material before publication, he used the information to impress his professors and fellow students, thereby implying a gift of prophecy.

Zeller learned the power of the printed word, the added magnetism of a modulated voice, proper placement of emotions, facial expressions and body movements.

The continued abrasive times, war at every border, on the sea, and in the air, provided a compatible climate for the absorption of Marxist-Socialist philosophies. In his third year at Lausanne, he displayed a fanatical desire to emulate Lenin. Zeller, bringing himself to the attention of campus radicals, was instantly embraced by activists and political malcontents who hung on to his every word. Their combined efforts provided this demogogue with suitable platforms to ventilate his Marxist venom.

On the fifth day the three men showed signs of strain and exhaustion. Much to their consternation and annoyance, the answers they sought, buried in an avalanche of manila folders, still evaded them. The time could have been spent more fruitfully.

Karl Berne, wearing one thick sweater over another and a woolen shawl over his shoulders, rubbed his face in a gesture of impatience and picked up the reports. "Shall I read to you from Otto Leger's report? He's a reliable man. Something contained in his report intrigues me. A key to Zeller's personality?"

"Otto Leger is a most perceptive man. *Ja, ja,* read," urged Von Kurt.

Berne, fatigued, shoved the burden to him. Von Kurt yawned, picked up the report, and, stretching his arms, rotating his shoulders, glanced at it.

. . . Zeller skillfully manipulates the students. Thoroughly proselytized by him, they venerate him with dedication.

Zeller is *power* without direction. He is a self-proclaimed emancipator of mankind, the voice of humanity thundering for emancipation after centuries of oppression.

I personally question if this human dynamo can be harnessed, reassembled, redirected in ways to suit Omicron. The question of his malleability is essential. Should he demonstrate a willingness to be reshaped, remolded, to conform to Zurich's requirements, speculation over Zeller's political potential staggers the mind.

Von Kurt slapped the report on the table, restraining a rising anger. "Of what purpose is this searching . . . searching . . . searching? The testimonials are the same—*ja*? A loner, no family, no love interests, no visible ties to subversives—perfect for Madrid!" He poured a large tumbler of cold German beer, retrieved from a windowsill. He sipped half, belched, grunted without apology, wagging a hand in the air. "I am finished."

"Perhaps we overlooked a word, a sentence, some clue—" Berne's mathematical mind worked like a computer.

"We analyzed everything and found nothing! How much longer do we perpetuate this farce?" stormed Von Kurt.

Guggie scanned the papers in his hand, eyes widening in interest. "I fail to recollect this report," he muttered aloud, drawing their attention. "Listen, Kurt . . . Karl . . ."

Zeller, denounced by an informer for distributing revolutionary pamphlets, robbed his *second* employer, escaping arrest by crossing the border into Germany. His money exhausted, he grew desperate for food and shelter. Reduced to the most wretched poverty and debilitation, Zeller was approached by the Okrana, the Russian secret police. The Okrana convinced him to become a Russian agent.

The moment he received his first paycheck, he informed on several acquaintances at Lausanne. The Okrana arranged for all charges against Zeller to be dropped. Back at school, totally exonerated of the charges previously leveled at him, he went from being a paid informer to the role of a Socialist agitator. When questioned by our recruiters concerning Okrana ties, Zeller treated the subject as incidental. Ties between them, he explained, had been severed by mutual agreement.

"Mutal agreement?" Guggie stared at his companions. "I admit I dislike Zeller, and I try not to let my personal reaction to this preening peacock interfere with rational judgment. But, I do question this alliance, *ja*?"

"*Nein*, Guggie. He was a free agent then. So, he paid off some debt, returned to school. He was young—when was it? Three—four years ago?"

"It doesn't explain the business with Okrana, Kurt." He shook his head, jowls quivering.

Berne, deeply engrossed in the papers he read, barely heard the others. "The day Zeller made *this* speech, our recruiters labeled him a hell hound of revolution. *This* speech was the turning point in Zeller's life. It brought him to the attention of the hierarchy."

Berne continued reading:

It must be clear even to the blind how necessary a determined fight is against every pope, whether he calls himself a rabbi, pastor, abbe, patriarch, mullah, or pontiff. No less avoidable at a given stage is his fight against God, whether he goes by the name of Jehovah, Buddha or Allah. Religion, my dear friends, is an opiate. Faith is serfdom. God and priests are necessary to workers as chains to slaves. It is insufficient to be merely a believer; every workman must become an agitator, a propagandist against ecclesiastical organization. Your mission is not to reform churches—but to destroy them. I repeat, d-e-s-t-r-o-y them.

Berne placed the speech before him on the desk, avoiding eye contact with his associates. Icy barriers threatened to melt under a rash of accumulated, unspoken reprimands. He personally had advised against Zeller's recruitment under any circumstances. The third man in command of the trio had had no clout. What good were his carefully compiled notes!

Von Kurt's gastrointestinal problems drove him from his seat. He pounded his stomach with a balled fist, as if this would help embattled digestive demons decide to ease up on him. Disgruntled, unable to disguise his abhorrence for Zeller, he paced around the room, burdened by dyspepsia. He unbuttoned his trousers, letting his bloated belly hang loose. Locating his voice amid a gurgling of intestines, he suggested a more matter-of-fact approach.

"It is impossible, I tell you, to fathom the complexities and mentalities of political zealots who are ready with fire, ax and halters. We worked a year with Zeller, *ja*? Do we—any of us—really *know* him? *Nein*. I confess to you, Von Kurt is no psychiatrist—but a good judge of men? *Jawohl*! Zeller to me is a stranger. Of him I know nothing more, nothing less, than what is spread out on the table before us. Reports! More reports! Some accurate, some overblown! But we had these reports a year ago. Upon these reports we predicated a judgment—*ja*? Now, *after* the facts we question reports. We knew then, know now, and know forever how facts can be doctored, changed. New files constructed—old files destroyed. We know this, yet we relied on these reports. So—we are immobilized for a time. We wait, mark time, and hope we have not erred.''

Guggie lit up a cigar. ''Zeller went to Salzburg, *ja*? Why? How do we determine why?''

Berne scratched his thick shock of brown hair nervously. ''If confronted, Zeller will lie or tell the truth. Which? How can we be sure? A schizophrenic is the most convincing liar.''

''Schizophrenic?''

''You think he is afflicted with schizophreeeenia?'' He drew the word out, absorbing it. ''You are speculating, Karl, *ja*? Something you know is not shared by Guggie and me?''

Berne shook his head, waved the cigarette smoke from his face distastefully, and took an opium pill. ''It's here, before us on the table. Each recruiter distinctly profiled separate sides of this man. Zeller is many personalities, each sharply defined.'' He slapped his hands on the table in a gesture of finality. ''You said it yourself. Who between us knows him? Can we claim intimate knowledge of Zeller? In one year he held himself aloof—''

''—as we held ourselves aloof from him?'' Guggie interjected.

They fell to a brooding introverted silence, each afflicted with unidentifiable emotions. The blatant truth upset their equilibrium. Their disdain for Zeller had dated from long before their initial encounter with him. In some oblique way, Zeller represented a silent threatening force to them. Had they instinctively sensed a sinister menace in the man?

Each one was forced to set aside personal rancor and prejudices, compelled to sustain an air of professionalism when dealing with Zeller. Their memories backtracked. They tried to recollect those slim, ephemeral moments when they had personally felt threatened. The resurrection of yesterdays was a distinctively odious task. Von Kurt spread before him a map of Austria, secured each end with a paperweight.

''First we deal in tangibles, *ja*? Take a look here. . . . Nothing! Nothing in Vorarlberg, Tirol, and Salzburg province is remotely connected to the Madrid Assignment! Perhaps he travels on personal business?''

"So, what personal business took Zeller to Austria?" Berne asked. "Did some dark hidden corner of his life elude us?"

"Does he traverse sinister corridors cleverly concealing quirks in his nature?" Guggie asked solemnly, scratching at his three-day beard. "Why should we care . . . unless he jeopardizes Madrid?"

Silent, noncommittal, each man slumped in his chair recalling moments when Zeller's downright obsequiousness, too compliant to suit them, had created doubts in their minds. Aware that Zeller was mercurial, inconstant as the shifting sands of time and without an ounce of loyal blood in his body, they made important decisions.

On January 5, 1920, in the dismal bleakness of night, as a storm approached Zurich province, resolutions were passed. The three men made two sound and solid decisions.

Von Kurt articulated the resolutions. "First, Macbeth's altercation with Zeller will not be discussed beyond the walls of Suite 333. The subsequent demise of Hamlet and Macbeth, if brought to the hierarchy's attention, will be written off as high-risk involvements. Second: Omicron's most trusted agent will be groomed and dispatched to Madrid covertly to observe Zeller's moves and report directly to us."

"Shylock!" Guggie hissed the name, appalled. Karl Berne glanced sharply at Von Kurt for affirmation.

"Shylock," he said succinctly.

They concurred. Despite Zeller's possible dissembling, he *was* perfect for Madrid. If they searched for a century . . .

Unfortunately they didn't have a century. What they had was Zeller, their personally trained specialist, an assassin comparable to none, who knew the assignment by rote. Later, *after* the mission was brought to fruition . . . if Zeller proved troublesome . . .

The austere Omicron hierarchy was gathered in the penthouse suite of *Suisse Banque Royale*, in the same graystone building housing the trio. Twelve men in all, their attention was riveted on a sudden shift of politics in Russia. The flux of enormous fortunes siphoned from Russia since 1917, pouring into Swiss bank accounts at an alarming, yet welcomed rate, was the subject of scrutiny. Trusted couriers, emissaries of the remaining Russian nobility, were arriving incognito carrying staggering sums in gold coins, fortunes in gem collections, priceless art, jeweled icons hidden from the Reds.

Russian nobles marked for extinction, wearing varying disguises, had escaped Bolshevik terror and fled to their villas and mountain retreats in Austria, Switzerland, Bavaria, and Italy, prepared to assume new identities and lives.

In Zurich secret lists were devised and fortunes assessed. The hierarchy determined that at the *right* time, names would be leaked to the *right* parties, with proper addresses. Then— extermination. Incalculable fortunes—without heirs to claim them— would be theirs. A few properly forged signatures, and *voilà*! At this moment in the diabolical plot, *Rahmen Ruski* was born in their minds.

The consortium scrupulously regarded the Bolshevik revolution while seated in luxury, eating Beluga caviar from golden plates, pouring French champagne from golden cups, smoking costly Dutch cigars. The Red uprising they had financed, aided, and abetted was winding down into an enormous sea of blood and tears, a vale of grief and hunger. How cleverly they had predicted Russia's emergence from the revolution as a vast cemetery, a howling desert of desolation. But enough now! The contagion of worker's revolutions was spreading westward, infecting Germany, Poland, Austria, and other nations. It must be stopped. It would be stopped!

The three men left Suite 333, descended the caged lift to the ground floor, walked outside in the crisp, cold night air, their breaths steamy as they expressed fatigued New Year's greetings to each other in parting. Each boarded his personal sleigh, was covered by furry lap robes, and left the dimly lit Parade-Platz, heading homeward at last. Sleigh bells jingled, horses snorted and neighed, their festooned heads bobbing up and down as their prancing hooves fell in dull thuds along the snowy roads. Kurt Von Kurt had promised his family he'd take them to Basel, to the Vogel Gryff festival, the Feast of the Griffin.

Von Kurt brooded. How could he think about griffins when the greedy jaws of the jackal, Zeller, gaped open, ready to devour and harness immutable power that had remained constant for centuries? Would the jackal, Zeller, if abandoned, turn against them? If their judgment proved wrong? How could it? When had they been wrong?

*   *   *

In the penthouse suite of the Suisse Banque Royale the power hierarchy took pause. Should trouble arise, *real* trouble, they'd be prepared. Amadeo Zeller's speech, that godless speech, had warmed the gold flowing through their veins.

They had found their godless man! A machine to suit their purpose. Retooled, redesigned, oiled sufficiently, he would perform like a robot.

The twelve men of the hierarchy left their golden towers in golden sleighs, driven by golden horses, and traveled their separate ways to personal dens of iniquity, free to succumb to jaded passions of the flesh, giving little thought to the oblique, serpentine monster they had venerated moments ago.

Amadeo Zeller was warming up in the bull pen.

Chapter Five

BUENOS AIRES, ARGENTINA
January 5, 1920

Victoria Valdez alighted from the cabriolet in a petulant rage. She stormed through a high-walled courtyard overwhelmed by a profusion of verdant fronds, past the iron-spiked gates of the Valdez mansion on the Plaza de Salinas Grande. She strode past the coterie of solicitous servants, who, catching a glimpse of their señorita, quickly retreated. *Ay de mi*! She was talking to herself—the worst of all times, *por Dios*!

Victoria, cursing aloud to the saints in heaven and demons in hell, *anyone* foolish enough to stand in her way, strode through the enormous wooden and iron gates into the villa proper, negotiating the graceful sweep of the spiral staircase with the finesse of a charging bull, the staccato sounds of her leather boots echoing like a swarm of click beetles. Spanning the stairs two at a time, she reached her boudoir, grasped the gilded winged horse handle, opened the door, and slammed it hard behind her, the sounds echoing through the villa.

She whipped off the flat-crowned sombrero, sailed it across the room, spilling a cascade of damp fiery red curls to her shoulders. She yanked at the leather bolero, unbuttoned the white silk shirt, flinging it to the floor. The calf-length black leather trousers fell from her waist to the floor in a heap. Off came the boots, gloves, and everything else until she stood naked. Her eyes, fire points of crushed emeralds reminiscent of the gemstones mined in the primitive Argentine reaches of Muzo and Chinquinquira near Tierra del Fuego, sparked dangerously. She was beginning to hate this room, this pastel elegance, the manor, the pampas, Buenos Aires, the gauchos! All of Argentina was becoming her enemy!

Her pale skin flushed deep crimson. Furious, filled with discord and a feeling of betrayal, she paced around the room, naked, unable to believe what happened. *Que atrocidad!*

She poured a hot bath, tossing in bath crystals, perfumes, anything in sight, thinking how she had fled the Vasquez hacienda in the middle of the night, traveling from the pampas to Buenos Aires, some four hundred kilometers over very rough terrain, leaving her family, her father, after the ultimatum handed her.

And on her eighteenth birthday! To be told she was bound in a contract of marriage to a man she hadn't seen, didn't know, purely in the interests of amalgamating two fortunes, was archaic! Barbarous in these modern times! The protests had weakened her, drained her of strength, but not the desire to flee. She needed to think . . . think!

Shoving her mass of red curls atop her head, spearing it through with a bone hairpin, Victoria stepped into the hot marbled tub. A hot bath . . . relaxing . . . invigorating, like a tranquilizer, enabled her to think clearly. She needed clear logical thought as never before to guide her through a bottomless pit of despair.

An hour later, with fresh perspective, she stepped from the tub wrapped in thick toweling, rubbing her body vigorously. She sprayed cologne over her body, worked creams into her tender skin. Her mind working overtime, she knew her next course of action.

The dreams have ended, Victoria. Reality flooded her senses. She reentered the boudoir, moved toward the escritoire. She poured herself a cup of steamy hot chocolate from the silver service tray placed on the shelf by a servant, popped a sweet confection into her mouth, and sipped the chocolate daintily, her mind racing with thoughts. *Go ahead, do it.*

Seated at the escritoire, she removed a sheet of scented stationery bearing the Valdez hacienda double inverted V for Verono Valdez, embossed in gold. Dipping a white and gold feathery quill into a white onyx inkwell, she began to write:

Don Francisco de la Varga
Calle Cervantes, Numero 33
Madrid, Spain

Mi querido señor de la Varga:

A week ago on the eighteenth anniversary of my birth, my father, Don Verono Valdez, announced that you and I are bound together by a contract of marriage, a marriage, señor, dutifully binding two strangers in an amalgamation of two fortunes. Argentinian and Spaniard are to be sacrificed to perpetuate a dynasty! A barbaric act I felt had long since been abandoned.

Of course I protested, to no avail. My protests were ignored. Further I ranted, raved, fought against such forceful coercion and underhanded collusion. My demands for autonomy, the right to choose my own mate, in marriage go unheeded. I threatened suicide, the worst possible embarrassment for the affluent, highly respected Valdez family. Alas—the only alternative offered me was life in a cloister!

A life of total abstinence and deprivation is so appalling and incompatible to my nature, I was forced to make a compromise. The drama between my resolute father and myself ended at his suggestion that I write to you, correspond for a year, to become better acquainted. To this I agreed—what choice had I?—and hope that if you also harbor disaffection for the marriage contract, at least it will not be said that we made no effort to rectify what must appear as arbitrary to you as it does to me.

Therefore I am initiating the first move. I herewith introduce myself to you properly, enclose several photographs taken of me recently. You know my background, I suppose, for my father and yours have been fast friends since they fought side by side in the Spanish American War.

It is only fair to advise you in advance that I am a wholesome but not beautiful woman. Truly, I am plain, on the stout side from eating too many sweets. I am dark of skin, black-haired, and not accomplished in the lesser arts. My humiliation is my inability to become the expert horsewoman my father desires—my girth encumbers me. The gauchos dare not refuse to ride with me but I see it in their faces. They loathe the task.

In cementing truth between us I admit to being ungifted in

the social graces; I lack coordination; I am forever stumbling or dropping things. My papa insists it is lack of concentration. *Ay de mi!* In addition I lack any culinary talent. I usually create disasters unfit for pigs.

De veras! I am also boring. My studies affected me only slightly. Daydreaming is my most proficient talent. It is best you know in advance the quality of goods for which you contract.

Es verdad! I am deficient in handling monetary matters. Budgets, household funds are complexities my poor mind cannot fathom. The more I have, the more I spend, and usually on frivolities. Let us not put the cart before the horse. To please two sentimental fools, I willingly commit myself to writing, however much of a bore it is.

Since I am unable to think of another thing to say I promptly end this letter awaiting your response. Respectfully, Victoria Valdez.

Victoria, you little devil—you did it!

ADMONT, AUSTRIA
January 5, 1920

Brother Heinrich carried a bottle of vintage burgundy and two crystal goblets into the bedroom of his cottage. Seated on the bed, nude, lotus fashion, Fabrizio Caragini watched as Heinrich poured the wine. A fraudulent mask of sexual contentment concealed whirlwind convolutions of his brain. Heinrich, also unclothed, handed him the filled goblet.

"How do I induce you to prolong your stay here?"

"I have overstayed my allotted time."

"It is not enough. Ah, Fabrizio, we must seize the opportunity to be together again." They clinked glasses. "Tell me, quickly— when do we meet again? I shall die until then."

"It depends on things in Trento. It was not figured into my itinerary. Heinrich, be a dear—fetch me some water. The bratwurst was salty, *ja*?" He placed his glass on the table. "I shall not sip my wine until you return."

Heinrich smiled flirtatiously. He left the room to get the water carafe. Fabrizio made his move. From his jacket pocket he removed a vial of liquid, emptied it into Heinrich's wineglass, and replaced the empty vial in his pocket.

Colchicum autumnale. The *perfect* aphrodisiac for Schuller! He got what he came for; it was time to move on, time to burn bridges behind him.

The cleric reentered the bedroom airily designing mental blue-prints for his next rendezvous with Fabrizio. "Your leaving twists a knife cruelly in my heart, my dear Fabrizio. For whatever it means, it wasn't only sex with you. Your mind seduced me."

They clinked glasses. Heinrich gulped his at once. Smacking his lips, he held his glass outstretched for more wine. Fabrizio obliged, his eyes equally flirtatious. Seated on the bed, his legs dangling over the side, he placed a robe about his shoulders, held the glass ready for a toast.

"To our last night together," began Heinrich, "until we meet in Bavaria, my love. May tonight surpass all other nights." Before he brought his glass to his lips, he groaned softly, doubled over, gripped by acute pain. It passed. He exhaled in relief, shook his head in wonder. "You may be right, Fabrizio. Perhaps I spiced the food more than usual." Sipping his wine, Heinrich took little notice of the color glints surfacing in the opaque eyes, the closed, hard look of hostility creeping over Fabrizio's face.

"Do you remember, Heinrich?" Fabrizio purred softly. "The first day we met, you said, was a turning point in your life. That my arrival would create changes in your life you might miss if you failed to grasp the moment? How prophetic. You see, Brother Heinrich, I intend to create a major change in your life, the most important of all."

Something was happening to Heinrich. His skin flushed deep purple as spasms of pain knifed through his chest, upper abdomen, shoulders, and neck. Attempts to signal his discomfort failed. He gasped, fell to his knees, the wineglass spilling on the carpet. His bulging eyes fixed on the rolling goblet, fascinated. He gasped again, the feeling of suffocation gripping his lungs. Cobalt eyes veined in red whites bulged progressively from their sockets in silent appeal for the other man's help.

Caragini, inscrutable as a Buddha, observed the other's prostration with detachment. The poison took its hideous, deadly course. "Shall I describe that change, Heinrich? Or have you already guessed? Ah, you know. Death . . . yes, death. Excruciating, painful death.'' His voice was soft, caressingly soft.

Heinrich was faring badly, in the grip of seizures, nausea, and retching. Pains, so acute they contorted his body, twisted his features hideously. Behind the immobilizing pain over each eyeball, Heinrich vaguely saw Fabrizio dressing calmly as if the spectacle on the floor were nonexistent. Sounds from Heinrich grew minimal as he gasped for breath. Catching the dying man's eye, Fabrizio bowed with dramatic panache and prepared for departure. He cleaned the room of any remnants of his presence, paying little mind to the wretched man converted into a purple-hued gargoyle. Fabrizio poured a glass of wine, placed it in Heinrich's stiffening, contorted fingers.

Caragini glanced casually at the cleric, placed his brown beaver fedora on his head, snap-brimming it lengthwise, and, picking up his briefcase, stepped over the dying man without a trace of emotion. In the sitting room, he paused briefly at the large desk, opened a drawer, and removed a metal box. He dumped the contents into his briefcase, picked up the priceless tome containing the Garduna-Zaragoza history, and placed it in the briefcase.

He glanced about the room and spat contemptuously at the man with whom he'd been forced to barter intimate physical services for precious information. Leaving the monastery grounds in the dark of night, he pulled up the sable collar of his coat and trudged through the snows until he reached his hotel.

The lengthy journey toward Madrid continued. He was on his way, wiser and wealthier. He carried, in addition to Lady Ainesworth's fortune, the deeds to Schuller's property in St. Bartolema, Bavaria, plus numbered bank accounts and the secret symbol for the dispersal of funds.

As his train wound eastward he thought, he too would one day gallop along those forest lanes Heinrich had described, with the hounds bellowing in the distance, and perhaps catch a glimpse or two of a stag bounding over fallen trees, just as the prince bishops had done long ago. The life of the gentry suited him as it had that pathetic old fool Schuller. That pitiable, ridiculous, grotesque man with a hatred for humanity and a neurotic fear of entering the living world of men and women in which he felt powerless to function, a world from which he had divorced himself, deserved the fate he had been dealt. Caragini justified his actions against the cleric with a feeling of inner satisfaction. Heinrich's problems no longer existed; hadn't he solved them for the poor fool?

Four days later, Zeller's train lumbered through the Brenner Pass between Austria and Italy in the historical region of Trentino Alto-Adige. Traces of its ancient conquerors—Romans, Ostrogoths, Franks, Lombards, and the prince bishops of the Hapsburg— were visible everywhere.

Affluent travelers, untouched by the war, gazed beyond the train windows, held captive by the awesome, ethereal sight of the stunning, snowcapped Alps majestically haloed by vaporous mists drifting low over jagged peaks. How they all rhapsodized— men and women alike—over Trento. Many argued over recent ceding of Trento to Italy by the Versailles treaty, after a century of Austrian rule. Their impassioned remarks, thought Zeller, exceeded the bounds of friendly discourse.

They felt that Trento, a medieval city of architectural gems— stunning cathedrals, ancient castles, arcades, fabulous museums, glittering palazzos—and graced by numerous piazzas, imposing statuary, masterful frescoes, tombs, painted facades and its famous Fountain of Neptune, belonged to the world and should not be used as a pawn between nations.

Amadeo Zeller, now using the cover of Konrad Gruber, Professor of Spanish History at the Bavarian Academy of Fine Arts at Munich, had not planned so tedious a detour to Trento. *Let it be the last stop before Madrid!* he told himself.

Chapter Six

Professor Konrad Gruber, sporting an extravagant Kaiser mustache, strutted pompously in his somber, brown suit, white starched wing collar, and thin black cravat. A Derby hat set squarely on his head, pince-nez glasses perched on his nose, he carried his briefcase in one hand, walking stick in the other. He booked lodgings at the Tyrolian-styled Trentino Alto Hostelry at the foot of the hill leading to Castello Buonconsiglio, an ancient castle located a short distance from his destination.

He stopped for a breakfast of *caffe e latte* and hot fresh rolls, paid his bill, and trekked up the mountainside in a stiff military strut, a gait far different than that of Caragini. The only trace of Zeller was in the eyes, his giveaway, opaque eyes. Pausing periodically en route, he pretended to the nonchalance of a botany professor on a field trip, pausing to sniff the early spring flowers, examine the budding shoots thrusting themselves through brown earth. The entire city and surrounding mountainous country-side were washed in a glaring brilliance of sun, which heightened the natural beauty of lush, verdant lawns, colorful flora, sweeping tree-lined paths.

At a fork in the road, Gruber turned left. He continued up the hill, past the enormous castle, his eyes widening appreciatively at its endless succession of indescribably beautiful courtyards, loggias, passageways, halls, footbridges, towers, graceful parterres, and breathtaking hanging gardens in which the Middle Ages and Renaissance were interwoven. Up ahead, the scene, a momentous one to Gruber, came alive. Trickles of sunlight burst obliquely through the treetops, creating a magical atmosphere of shadows pierced by shafts of light.

Compelled to pause by an inexplicable force, he felt instantly transported to a level of immense power. Energy coursed through him, and at that moment, he saw his destiny. Amadeo Redak Zeller would be a giant among giants in the world of man. In the past he'd speculated upon his future. Now, at this moment, and for all time, he knew, *actually* knew *who* he was and *what* he'd attain. He had been driven his entire life by something he never clearly understood. He was sixteen when he first imagined himself a powerful force. Today, he felt exalted, as if his spirit had expanded. His eyes, reflecting the sun's rays, filled with jagged streaks of light as if an inner conflagration illuminated his being.

"And I have only just begun," he spoke aloud, as if a continuum of what lay ahead paraded across his inner vision.

Retreating at once into the shell of Konrad Gruber, he moved forward, certain that destiny favored and guided him.

Hadn't everything fallen perfectly into place?

He stopped before enormous wooden gates between two high walls to read the bronze plaque affixed to the pillars.

MONASTIC HOLY ORDER OF SAINT PACHOMIOUS, he read aloud as he rang the bell.

Brother Cipriano, a jovial man in his fifties wearing his monk's habit, sandals, and a skullcap to cover the tonsure on his head, waddled like a penguin, maintaining a short distance between them. He spoke animatedly, lisping slightly, his eyes sweeping the hip-high field of flowers along the path.

"Yes, yes, I understand, Herr Professor," he replied to the barrage of questions fired at him by Gruber. "You *have* come to the right place. Who but Brother Xenofonte is better qualified? He confessed the last survivor of the order," he said with inborn pride. "You understand you will find a very old man. He has remarkably retained all his faculties. You will be patient, however, with him?"

Herr Gruber nodded.

Brother Xenofonte, an inscrutable octogenarian, remarkably well preserved, peered up at him with unwavering walnut-brown eyes from behind steel-rimmed spectacles, set awkwardly on his nose. His penetrating gaze was filled with dynamic intensity. Rising, he limped slightly. He pulled a chair forward for his guest, gestured to it, and returned to his seat behind the enormous, wormwood desk, an unpolished monstrosity occupying most of the room. Behind him, picturesque stained-glass windows overlooked bowers of hanging flowers on a brick portico. The windowsill was covered with riotous herb seedlings in ceramic pots. Nearby, on a wood-burning stove, a kettle of briskly boiling water hissed steam. The octogenarian patiently steeped a pot of tea as he listened to Gruber's introduction. "Ah . . . *Signore Professore*, where . . . how did you learn of my work?" He spoke in Italian.

"The Bavarian Academy. It is my intent to do a thesis on the Zaragozas." Gruber observed the older man pour tea into two cups.

"*Va bene*. You are a colleague then, of my old friend, Fritz Lehrman?" The cleric broke up brown sugar lumps in the steamy tea, then added thin lemon rinds. Avoiding Gruber's eyes, he spoke with disarming innocence. Tell me, *Professore*, is Fritz still manic over the Bavarian Illuminati?" He smiled enigmatically. "The last time we visited my ears refused to stand up straight for a week. His political zeal fatigues me, yet I would not miss a visit from Fritz for anything." Periodically Xenofonte shoved his bifocals up, peering through them.

"*Jawohl*, Fritz rambles. Happily I report he has recently abandoned Weishaupt and the Illuminati. Now he demonstrates surprising enthusiasm for Communism and that spawn of the devil, Lenin." Gruber's features jerked. "The war raging in Fritz Lehrman is between Communism and Socialism these days. Which to champion? He does not know. It's the Versailles treaty, my friend. Its damaging terms affect all Germany. Even here—Trento is now Italy—no longer Austria, *ja*? You see? We are, all of us, affected by the outcome of those infernal Paris Peace Conferences. Not you, *Framonaco* Xenofonte. What need have you to burden yourself politically?"

The monk shrugged, slurped his tea from a saucer noisily, with gusto, smacking his lips. He wiped his lips with his fingertips, muttering sotto voce, "Such a young professor. Why resurrect a monastic order of antiquity? Men of your age and caliber seldom find the past interesting. The future, *ja*, but seldom the past.

What is it you want from Xenofonte, Herr Gruber? Speak up . . . Speak up.''

Gruber without hesitation imparted what he'd learned from Schuller as if he had lived forever on an intimate basis with the Garduna-Zaragoza Brotherhood. "Now then, what can you add to validate these facts, Framonaco?"

"The deathbed confession of the last Zaragoza survivor."

"The last? Are there none others? None of the Garduna? No one left to perpetuate the vendetta against the de la Varga family?" He suppressed his zeal. "Do they live free from century-old threats, then?"

"Who lives free from threats in these times? Drink . . . drink your tea, *Professore*. It invigorates."

Gruber complied. "Are you up to answering a few questions?"

"Ask me what you will. I only request that you first read my manuscripts. Answers to most questions are contained in them. It is time for my nap. Read . . . read until I awaken." He yawned. "I promise to be more receptive." He placed two enormous manuscripts before Gruber on the desk. He finished his tea and, moving to a threadbare piece of furniture of unknown vintage, stretched out languidly on the sofa, his glasses shoved high on his head. In moments the old man was asleep,

Gruber frowned slightly. An amused tolerance and a scowling annoyance were apparent for a moment before he picked up the first manuscript. He read the title page and turned to the next.

PROPERTY OF
HOLY MONASTIC ORDER OF SAINT
PACHOMIOUS

Trento, Italy

HOLY ORDER

OF

ZARAGOZA VASCONGADES

HISTORY
1822–1900

Catalogued: Historian:

File, Spain Ancient Orders   Brother Xenofonte

AUTHOR PROFILE

Brother Xenofonte abandoned the priesthood at age twenty-five to pursue studies in religion, sciences, and human psychology. Due to his labors, the ancient Order of the Zaragoza has emerged, a triumphant record of scholarly labor.

Brother Xenofonte pursued his studies at the University, the School of Oriental Languages, and the College of France. In 1850, he was commissioned by the Ministry of Inscriptions and Belles-Lettres to investigate the libraries of Spain, Italy, and Austria's collections of Arabic and Syrian manuscripts. In 1852 he received an appointment as attaché to the Departments of Manuscripts in the Bibliothèque Nationale and began his writings for the *Revue of the World*. He took his degree and was elected to the council of the Société Asiatique. In 1860, he began a massive search for the lost Monastic Order of the Zaragoza, which dated back to the time of Christ.

Master of numerous languages, ancient and modern, erudite in the lore of ages and locales, expert in the technique of investigations and interpretations, imbued with the ideals and methods of modern sciences, he is master of many languages, histories, and traditions.

In 1880 Brother Xenofonte applied to Saint Pachomious for retreat from the world to complete his important works. A list of Brother Xenofonte's other publications appears in the last book of this study with the bibliographies of his research.

A Historical Note . . .

Spain, on the brink of disaster, approached the nineteenth century with a war of independence against Napoleon, insurrection against Joseph Bonaparte, civil wars, mutinies, pronunciamentos, the persecution of liberals by reactionaries, of reactionaries by liberals. The yoke of Spanish dominion abroad was about to be lifted by one Simon

Bolivar and a piece of paper known as the Monroe Doctrine. These consecutive disasters took their toll on Spain and her people; she would never be the same again.

Spain's backbone, the people, were in dire straits; starvation, unemployment, and inflation created internal cancers that could not be exorcized. The nation was treading a downward path to decline and total prostration. The Royalists, the nobility, were joining military juntas to preserve Spain from French and British domination.

Very few paid attention to the impressionable youths, those who would be leaders in the future. Many became victimized by shrewd dissemblers left behind in the cities— daring, cunning men, whose only concerns were selfish gains and self-serving political ends.

Thus, in 1822, the nation, in transition, tottered precariously between external forces, threatening to destroy the nation from within by an onslaught of criminal activities and civil corruption. The Compagnia Della Garduna, the Society of Martens, a criminal brotherhood, had merged with the Zaragoza-Vascongades in an organization known henceforth as the Garduna-Zaragoza combine, in Seville, and spread terror through Spain.

Elsewhere, previously documented, can be found the ancient origins of the Zaragoza Order. These writings deal with its history and the disappearance of the order today.

Brother Xenofonte

SEVILLE, SPAIN
October 31, 1822

On this day, in the year of our Lord, 1822 A.D., a violent storm struck the city before dawn. Dark skies hovered over this ancient city of caliphs and Moorish warlords. The pealing of the *giralda*, the bell high atop the Moorish minaret of Abou Yakob, summoning Sevillians to prayer, was periodically punctuated by wrathful thunder and jagged lightning bolts rupturing the heavens.

But the unusual horde, caught in the pelting deluge, poured through narrow, twisting, cobblestone streets not in the direction of the mosque or cathedrals across the plaza; instead, they streamed through the enormous bronze doors of the Byzantine courthouse.

For on this day, much was at stake.

Inside the crowded courtroom, Spaniard and Moor prayed together. "*Sancta Maria, Mater Dei, ora pronobis peccatorius nume et in hora mortis nostrae.*"

Catholic and Muslim negotiated ardently with their gods as each awaited sentences to be passed. The burning question: *Life or Death?* Which would prevail?

Lightning bolts sent splinters of colored light through the stained-glass rotunda overhead, splashing vivid kaleidoscopic colors around the room, drawing awesome stares from the people.

Don Francisco de la Varga, the Spaniard, a titled nobleman, a *hacendado* of vast wealth and influence, felt impotent in these moments. Abdul Montenegro, the Moor, a bull of a man with glittering ebony eyes, de la Varga's aide de camp, close adviser and blood brother, wondered if the forces of nature had ordained so wrathful a setting for the unfolding drama.

The chamber doors adjoining the courtroom opened. A flickering glow of candlelight obliquely picked out the foreboding scene: a tribunal of crimson-garbed judges entered the cavernous, vaulted room and took their places on the bench. Black hoods over their heads told the story: *death to all prisoners!*

Loud gasps of dismay rocked the courtroom.

Spaniard and Moor stared, dumbstruck. Their eyes traveled to the prisoner's dock, their attention riveted on the faces of their sons, Esteban de la Varga and Muhammed Haj Montenegro, respectively. Not twenty years of age, they sat chained in irons like savage beasts.

They lifted cold eyes to a cordoned-off section behind the prisoners' dock where thirteen Zaragoza monks sat. Throughout the long, arduous trial, their snide, aloof piety, seeping through masks of fraudulent benevolence, had plagued the Spanish grandee.

Guilt eroded Don Francisco's heart. What stroke of fortune had terminated their duties for the crown and returned them to Seville to find their sons arrested, falsely charged for murder and countless ambiguous felonies, forcing them through a farcical trial, a gross travesty of justice?

Maldito Dios! In their absence, the enemies of their ancestors had seduced their sons and ten other young nobles. The impetuous, misguided youths seated in the shadows of the gallows, a heartbeat away from death, had unwittingly usurped a brand of authority, unprepared for the consequences of their involvements.

Was this to be their finish—death?

Spaniard and Moor froze their attention on the Judas goats. Their perpetrated sham had undermined the entire court! Witness after witness had cleverly paraded past the court, each testifying to the guilt of the twelve young nobles. *Maldito Diablo!* The tribunal of judges, court officials, the crown's prosecutors—all of them were part of the corruption! *Murderous swine!*

The Garduna Parchments in exchange for their lives!

They had demanded the only thing Spaniard and Moor were unable to part with in exchange for the only thing in the world held dear to them.

Never! de la Varga vowed. *Never!* Spaniard and Moor had vowed the Parchments would never fall into the blackguard hands of those assassins. And *never* would they forfeit the lives of their sons!

How incredible were the complications *and* implications of their inherited legacy, thought Don Francisco as he observed the court. The location of the parchments, the most coveted secret since the days of Isabella and Ferdinand, had lured clever, enterprising spies in the guise of scholars to Seville, in search of the precious items. Too many had already deduced far more than was palatable to Don Francisco.

But there was more.

For years the Garduna-Zaragoza Brotherhood had conspired, murdered, and brazenly ordered the death and destruction of anyone who stood in their way, with full impunity. Proof of their satanic conspiracies, documented in what inept defense counselors had alluded to in the trial as a *mysterious* log book, was never located. Its contents, therefore, inadmissible as evidence, was labeled hearsay and capricious fancy. The ledger allegedly contained details of every nefarious crime committed by this criminal brotherhood, including the names of their victims, methods of persecution, and the fees charged for each service.

The appalling, unpalatable, devastating truth plunged both Spaniard and Moor headlong into depression.

There could be no last-minute strategy to exonerate their sons and their ten companions! No spectacular coup de théâtre! *No coup de tête!* No eleventh-hour miracle or the conjuring of a mysterious rogue, who on cue would dash into the courtroom at the last moment to astonish prosecutors, elate defense counsels, and confound those ignominious tribunal judges by producing the necessary testimony to clear the condemned scapegoats!

For, he, Don Francisco de la Varga, possessed the alleged ledgers! He held the key to the twelve lives in the prisoners' dock!

The Spanish noble was drowning in a sea of indecision. The choice was his: *Spain or the lives of a dozen impetuous fools.* That he was forced to choose infuriated him. Yet . . .

How many times had he weighed the consequences of the abominable legacy? He actually possessed the power to unmask the Garduna-Zaragoza assassins. But how, without forfeiture of the priceless parchments? *How?* The ledgers would identify these obnoxious and corrupt criminals, but their exposure presented a complexity of dangers, multiple dangers. If produced in court, the contents could destroy innocent men, devastate the Spanish government, its people and the church. Publicizing the ledgers' contents was analagous to committing high treason in Francisco's mind, and was, in addition, perilous. He'd be unable to cope with the guilt of causing the anarchy, civil war, and bloodshed that would surely follow. Even more risky, expulsion from the church of Rome would doom de la Varga. For the clergy, themselves listed in the ledgers as the Garduna's most frequent clients, had ordered innumerable deaths. Highly placed men in government had also ordered assassinations.

This fearless man cringed at church reaction. Rome permitted no man to threaten its longevity. At the papacy's disposal to protect itself were the implements of Satan: lies, savagery, tortures, death. Further, what assurance had he, if he produced the damaging ledgers so that the twelve nobles would be saved from the gallows, that lethal accidents wouldn't later befall them? *He had nothing!* No deals were possible. No bribe large enough to appease either the prosecution or the tribunal, for they too had used the Garduna assassins' service!

Neither Spaniard nor Moor tarried to hear the tribunal articulate what the black hoods conveyed earlier. Taking a last look at the issue of their loins, Spaniard and Moor strode from the courtroom. Behind them, deputies rapped for order. The long-drawn-out words of the chief magistrate echoed in their ears.

"It is the judgment of this imperial tribunal that the guilty be hanged by their necks. . . ."

Outside in the driven rain, the sight of carpenters working diligently in the prison courtyard, erecting scaffolds to accommodate the multiple hangings on the morrow, added fuel to the fires raging in the nobleman. De la Varga paused briefly, his smoldering cobalt eyes flaring angrily.

"God Almighty! Look at them, Abdul! Before the verdict was spoken, our sons were condemned!"

They boarded a waiting carriage, bearing the de la Varga crest and coat of arms, pulled by a team of six matched sable Andalusians. The driver sent a whip singing over their heads. Instantly the carriage lurched away from the curb; it charged furiously through the pouring rain, horses' hooves exploding on the cobbles like pistol shots.

Inside the carriage, Spaniard and Moor, suffused with rage and mortification, jostled unceremoniously about in their seats, buried their feelings in meditative silence. Don Francisco broke silence to articulate his thoughts. "This Mephistophelian brand of justice is finished. The blood of our blood shall not become sacrificial lambs for those butchering pagans on the morrow. Those evil plotters, working the diabolical embroidery of Satan while sipping the blood of Christ from silver chalices, will not live to view the fruits of their iniquitous labors. On this oath, I swear my life, Abdul. Arrangements will be made, not ordinary arrangements, but *special* arrangements, defying assassins to kill again with impunity!"

Ten minutes later the carriage pulled to a stop before a deserted, decrepit building along the Guadalquivir waterfront, between the bullring and the Tower of God. De la Varga handed the Moor a list of thirteen names—the Zaragoza Judas goats—before alighting from the carriage.

"Wait, *amigo*." Don Francisco held Abdul's robed arm a moment and peered into the Moor's onyx eyes. "Hear me well, Abdul, my brother. The madness exploding at trial's end will not end at dawn according to the scenario of the Garduna-Zaragoza Brotherhood. On this day the scenario will undergo a major rewrite according to the dictates of Don Francisco de la Varga and Abdul Montenegro." He put the dripping wet list in the Moor's hand. *"These false prophets are dead men!"*

Skirting mud puddles they disappeared inside the ancient building.

Inside the dismal, cold, leaky, bare-walled room, illuminated by three dripping candles on the table, they met with a covey of specialists whose talents equaled, if they did not surpass, those in the Garduna.

Assets were liquidated to negotiate a pocketful of miracles. One miracle would suffice; two would buy them immortality. Enormous sums changed hands. Arrangements were finalized between the principal parties, negotiations ended in two hours.

Now, for the miracles.

The sprawling Hacienda de la Varga, a short distance from Seville, encompassed thousands of lush acreage in the heart of Andalusian countryside. A thirteenth-century Moorish castle lay in ruins at the northern perimeter of the estate. Once the resplendent abode and manor of the Montenegro warlords, it stood as a silent reminder of a glorious, historical past, of a wealth of generations of Spaniards and Moors whose blood, shed in brutal warfare, fertilized the lands. Peaceful coexistence, bartered at a dear price, had ultimately rendered their relationship priceless.

Broken walls, battlements, embrasures, bastions projected from solid fortifications were in shambles. The bartizans, miraculously intact along the ramparts, resembled a citadel of antiquity. The villa proper had withstood the ravages of time.

By late afternoon, the rains stopped. The sun, in repose behind angry black clouds, penetrated long enough to dissolve them and remove the chill from the land. It was an omen, thought Abdul, as he made supplications to Allah.

Pray Allah, most merciful of Gods, let it be a good omen.

Midnight. Twelve prisoners, disguised, ironically, in monks' habits, left their cells to negotiate dark, smelly, underground passages and labyrinthine tunnels of the prison complex to the freedom oiled by their money, prestige, and social class. Willing surrogates, felons serving life sentences without hope of reprieve, had replaced them, their martyrdom providing financial security for their starving families.

Shortly before one A.M., a swiftly driven carriage bearing the de la Varga crest and coat of arms heaved lurchingly through the main hacienda gate and, turning right, headed toward the rear of the property, then, swinging a sharp left, pulled up at the edge of the castle ruins. Two elated, scruffy-looking passengers, their features wan and gaunt, jumped from the carriage and ran in the direction of the towering Moor, who signaled them forward with the lighted torch held aloft in his hand.

Abdul led his son and Esteban through darkened passageways, down two flights of stairs, and moving along the dark, musty smelling corridors, to a sequestered area away from curious eyes and loose-tongued servants. An ebullient Don Francisco stood at the door of the marbled room, greeting them with joyous tears. Nearby were two copper and wooden tubs filled with steamy water. Fresh clothing and a table laden with a banquet of food and wine awaited their pleasure. He indicated the tubs. "First a bath and then, my proud cocks, a serious discussion, the nature of your involvement with the enemies of our ancestors in whom you naively placed your trust. *Por Dios! Que atrocidad!*"

Both parents flushed with apprehension and relief as their sons lazed indolently in the hot wooden tubs. Their sons were home— nothing else mattered. Admonishments could wait—no?

Esteban de la Varga and Muhammed Montenegro were unable to control their curiosity at the surroundings, some thirty feet belowground in marble-walled rooms adorned with pillars and gilded latticework. They stared in silent wonder at the elaborate floor candelabra, adorned with mythological creatures carved in filigree silver and gold, illuminating the area with no less than fifty lighted candles. Faded, time-worn paintings dating from the thirteenth century adorned the walls, running the length of an indoor pool, exquisitely tiled in decorative mosaic. At either end of the pool stood two statue-decorated water fountains, tunneling steamy water through ancient underground conduits from a hot springs a short distance from the castle ruins. Don Francisco shrugged the questions forming on their lips.

"Where you are is not at issue, momentarily." The grandee shuddered inexplicably. He scrutinized the lads, noting their emaciation, prison pallor, the dark circles under their eyes. He pulled a chair closer to the tubs, addressing himself to the reprobates.

"Once an act of rebellion is begun there are no limits to which one will go until the rebellion is checked. Talk between us is essential. Dialogue must be understood. Stressing the urgency of our plight without previous briefing is difficult; therefore I implore you to listen. Trust in what I say to be the truth. You were betrayed, condemned to die by the eternal enemies of our ancestors, the Garduna-Zaragoza Brotherhood. Had we not intervened, they might have succeeded. Listen to me, both of you, and hear what I tell you. You must learn in life what you can lay open to scrutiny, what must be secreted, what must be shown in half lights, to whom and why. If these lessons go unlearned, you cannot survive. While you stewed in jail, contact was made by the enemy, dictating terms under which you would be exonerated of all charges against you.''

''What terms, Father?'' Esteban's curiosity was piqued.

''Your lives in exchange for priceless papers over which our combined families have exercised custodial powers for centuries.''

''And you hesitated? Are the papers more valuable than Muhammed's or my life?'' Bewildered, Esteban tensed, his eyes narrowing.

''Listen. I said *listen* to your father! You and Muhammed promiscuously wholesaled an inordinate amount of trust to these assassins and it backfired. Neither Abdul nor I intends to censure the imprudent insubordination you demonstrated in our absence, nor will we ask *why* you felt it incumbent to hone your manhood among such scum. Their seduction of you is equally unimportant, presently. First, without delay, the responsibility of your heritage must be stressed, clearly understood. Truly, our shame is in not confiding the legacy long ago.'' The hacendado lighted a *puro* for each of them to smoke. From a nearby sideboard, he poured thimble-sized glasses of Manzanilla from a decanter. Handing each a glass, he sipped his and continued the litany.

''Disobedience, resistance to parental authority, must cease. You must hear me, fully attuned to my words.'' The distinguished cavalier began his account with General Federico de la Varga and Jamal Montenegro, describing how their ancestors became custodians of a legacy that had blighted the two families with untold suffering, massacre, and bloodletting. He described the countless times when he and Abdul had wanted to destroy the legacy, ending the evil afflicting the families. ''Alas, we are descended from royalty, duty engrained in our mentalities. Descendants of the conquistadores do not shirk duties.''

Esteban and Muhammed, sobered by the don's words, emerged from their tubs, dried their lean, hard bodies with linen sheets.

''We are fighting time. Shortly after dawn twelve surrogates will die on the gallows in your stead. You must understand the ramifications involved, the extreme measures we were forced to employ to save you. Above all understand this, my sons, we took no pleasure in sending other men to their deaths in your place, but you could not be sacrificed.''

Esteban stropped a razor, prepared to shave off his beard. ''You have our ears, Father,'' he said, exchanging perplexed glances with Muhammed.

Don Francisco gestured for silence. The older men exchanged

glances of concern at the approaching sounds; loud chattering voices, leather bootheels striking against stone. Esteban grinned easily.

"It must be Antonio Vasquez and the others, Father. Don't concern yourself. Antonio suggested we all congregate here until *after* the hangings."

Before Spaniard and Moor voiced displeasure or questioned Vasquez's knowledge of this underground sanctuary, the doors burst open, admitting a force of exuberant, laughing men. Men who less than two hours ago sat in cells praying for their lives. Stunned at their presence, livid at their jocularity, Don Francisco de la Varga, moving to repulse the youths, was held back by Abdul's silent urging. Both men moved to the edge of the crowd, observed the vigorous backslappings and fraternal hugs with bitter reservations. The don seldom raised his voice; the strength of his personality was such that he projected his mental climate by the look in his eyes. At this moment, his wrath exploded in a subdued, controlled tone. "Do you hear their vainglorious boastings? *They* cheated death! *They* bested their enemies! Abdul, our sons are *muy loco*!"

Antonio Vasquez, gregarious, impeccably dressed, a youth with coal-black hair and eyes of ebony, in vocalizing their fortuitous flight from the prison to his companions, attempted to conceal his wide-eyed fascination at the subterranean rooms all Seville believed lay in ruins.

Neither Spaniard nor Moor noticed Vasquez's reaction, the wild agitation, the trembling uncertainty in his manner, for their thoughts were at cross-purposes with the impenitent scoundrels. Don Francisco de la Varga viewed their behavior as irresponsible, transcending the bounds of decency. Unable to chain his discontent or convey further solicitude and patience, he strode to his son's side and drew him away from the others, venting his anger.

"I find it inconceivable—in bad taste—for you and Muhammed to engage in this blatant revelry in utter disregard of the gravity of the situation. Have you no conscience? You, Esteban, of all people, condoning these brazen-faced baboons, *actually* encouraging a celebration! You treat this dirty business in Seville as remote, frivolous, and—"

"Father," Esteban protested, "I took no part in this. Antonio took charge. Admittedly his decision is clearly in our best interests. Where in Seville, on this of all nights, would we, any of us, be

safer than here at the villa. Especially in these, uh, chambers."
He paused. "Why have you never revealed these rooms to us?
Are there family skeletons buried here?" he asked.

Don Francisco took umbrage. He studied his son as he had
never studied his son before. "We must end the charades,
Esteban. If I minimize the dangers facing us I would be guilty of
a gross error in judgment. Reprieve from the gallows did not end
the matter; it merely compounded the dangers. By undermining
Seville's legal system, we have created a hornet's nest. Madrid
must be assured that justice has been served on the morrow.
Vigilance, circumspection, the devising of a calculated strategy
to determine your and Muhammed's future must take precedence
over premature celebration."

Before Esteban offered a defense he was whisked away by a
laughing Antonio Vasquez, luring him toward the other celebrants.
Glancing back at his father, imparting a gesture of helplessness,
Esteban fell into the gaiety of the moment.

Abdul, moving closer, placed a consoling hand on the grandee's
shoulder. "Why do I feel the fool who provides nuts to men with
no teeth?" Don Francisco asked, sighing. Then with renewed
vigor, he hissed through clenched teeth, "How dare they indulge
in frivolous behavior? Shortly twelve men will die due to gross
stupidity and miscalculation in judgment demonstrated by our
sons, and they have the unmitigated gall to celebrate? *Por Dios!*
The Dance of Death parades through the streets of Seville like a
black plague as cavorting skeletons lure men to their deaths. And
these insensitive baboons celebrate!"

Abdul pressed a glass of wine into the hacendado's hand, but
it failed to assuage his outrage. "The fools have learned nothing!
Thick-headed stallions! The lot of them! May God help us! We
have sired fatuous oafs."

"Be tolerant, *amigo*. Consider their protracted confinement in
a prison unfit even for infidel dogs." Abdul spoke soothingly.

Don Francisco de la Varga broodingly removed from his
pocket and slipped over his forefinger a gold ring shaped like a
marten, the symbol and seal of the Garduna Brotherhood. It had
been removed earlier from a secret vault, in the hope of adding
to his explanation of the legacy. He stared at it, his head bent
like that of a dying bull stopped by the muleta thrust. He
weighed the burdens the symbol implied, the veins at his temples
pulsating, his face flushing. "No one is safe, my friend, until
this dirty business in Seville is finished."

Glancing past Abdul toward the entrance doors, he froze at the sight of a trusted servant, Emiliano, beckoning to him. He *knew* what the man's presence signified. Cold, clammy sweat oozed from his body. Both Spaniard and Moor hastened toward him.

"A visitor on urgent business awaits you in the study, Excellency."

Taking a last look at the boisterous, fun-loving youths, eating, drinking, jesting as if nothing beyond these walls touched them, Spaniard and Moor departed, winding back along the wooded path to the villa, their steps quickening behind Emiliano's lighted torch.

Who, at this ungodly hour? Unless . . . ? Mopping the icy sweat from his brow, Don Diego strode back in silence, the sounds of his thick silver spurs clanking noisily along the path.

The ornate porcelain clock adorned with pink roses and cupids atop the fireplace mantel chimed three times. It was three A.M. Emotions antagonistic to de la Varga's usual uncompromising courage gripped him at the sight of his special courier, Armando. The ferret-faced peasant in the grandee's employ respectfully accepted the proffered glass of wine. The amenities over, Armando somberly related bad tidings—disaster! Disaster had struck. In dire jeopardy were the miracles negotiated earlier that day. "Four Zaragoza assassins are dead, nine escaped the trap set for them, bent on retaliation," Armando continued, breathlessly. "Be circumspect in all movements this night, Don Francisco. Among the twelve nobles is a traitor bought and paid for by Garduna-Zaragoza silver. Now here is our plan. At dawn when the hangman commences his ritual, our men will grab the traitor. Word reached us that he will not be among the dozen headed for the gallows." A tight smug smile twitched his lips.

De la Varga's noble head angled obliquely at the courier's words; his features jerked and paled. Glancing tremblingly at Abdul, he somberly imparted to the courier their distinct disadvantage. "It is finished, Armando. There no longer exists any opportunity to pare down the search for the traitor. The prisoners, released at midnight and replaced by surrogates, arrived earlier. Spread the word. Remind our friends that our enemies are demons from hell. *Cuidado me llamo!* Barricade themselves if needs be. *After* the hangings on the morrow we shall convene to construct the proper strategy to combat the assassins, and the traitor—whoever he is—shall be caught and punished, *una vez para siempre. Cuidado, amigo, vaya con Dios!*"

"*Gracias. A Dios, patron!*" The courier bowed respectfully and rode swiftly off the estate, prepared to spread the alarm.

Spaniard and Moor moved swiftly. Servants skilled in weaponry, awakened from slumber, were dispersed throughout the hacienda, ordered to defend strategic positions. If danger approached, they would signal by firing three successive shots.

Scrupulously examining all priorities, Spaniard and Moor walked back to the villa. Their primary concern: the traitor! An evildoer in their midst, having once betrayed their sons, was prepared to repeat the infamy. The question weighed carefully was this: could the Judas wait to be meted just punishment, *after* the charades at dawn? Protocol demanded the presence of bereaved family members at the gallows. Seville must be persuaded that justice decreed by the tribunal be carried out according to the court's dictates. The fathers of the condemned men would then convey personal grief to the proper officials. *And so it would be written!*

The traitor could wait.

Encumbered by the scope and magnitude of their pressing problems, Spaniard and Moor dutifully parted company to prepare themselves for the contrived drama set to unfold at the gallows, unaware that neither would rest eyes upon the other again.

At 3:45 A.M. a full moon rose in the heavens. Unruly winds tunneling off the Mount of Angels whipped balls of tumbleweed across the hacienda lands, rustled the silvery leaves of olives, saturated the night with aromatic scents of ripe orange, lemon, almond blossoms, and that nocturnal aphrodisiac, *dama de noche*.

Creeping surreptitiously forward, concealed in the myriad shadows of citrus groves, nine cloaked men moving swiftly with unfailing agility and adroit expertise, gained entrance to the hacienda de la Varga. The guards were abruptly overtaken and garroted. The nine assassins cautiously approached the villa.

An hour later, the assassins emerged from the villa, wiping blood from their knives. An assessment of their demonic handiwork brought smug, satisfied expressions to their glittering eyes. They returned to Seville, glutted with malicious satisfaction, prepared to gloat further at dawn.

For these men, ignorant of the drama played at midnight at the

Seville prison complex, would attend the hangings. The multiple deaths, symbolic of their ultimate triumph, was too exotic a victory to pass up. Then, according to plan, *after* the hangings, the world would be theirs.

Had they possessed an iota of knowledge about what was transpiring in the castle ruins, history might have been rewritten.

The frolicking over, Esteban and Muhammed Haj, singing to themselves, bade farewell to their companions. Observing the horse-driven carriages thunder off the estate, they wound their way toward the villa, warding off unabated winds. Both men felt a sudden chill. The singing stopped. The usual night sounds— chirping crickets, lowing animals, prowling cats and coyote howls—were absent.

They were not their fathers' sons for nothing. Animal instinct working at once, Esteban hissed, "Something is wrong—drastically wrong, *amigo. Vamos, pronto! Cuidado!* Not even the cocks crow!"

"I feel as if ghosts walk alongside us, ghosts with invisible faces," Muhammed Haj said softly, at once cautious. He fell into step with Esteban, moving lightly, stealthily, exercising caution, unprepared for the horror about to assault them and forever bury their youths.

Muhammed Haj saw it first. He froze. The macabre scene spread before them. Stunned disbelief flooded his handsome countenance. His nostrils dilated, his azure eyes turned cobalt. An inhuman wail of denial crashed through his throat.

Arrested by his savage outcry, Esteban stopped in his tracks, stared at the horror etched into Muhammed's stony profile. Following the Moor's line of vision, Esteban adjusted his focus until the grisly scene cleared. He staggered under the impact, and reeling, lurched toward a portico arch, doubled over, as-saulted by involuntary spasms. He vomited.

Four lances were driven into the ground at the perimeter of a mosaic-tiled water fountain, washed by the flickering shadows of two lighted torches. Death's-head emblems over crown and thorns shimmered in the wavering light. Impaled upon the signature lances were the decapitated heads of Abdul, his wife, and two daughters. Their mutilated bodies lay hacked to bits and pieces scattered on the ground.

Recoiling from the ghastly desecration, Muhammed Haj forced himself to examine each body. Blood-streaked, dust-caked heads, their expressions grotesque, a final glimpse of life before it was snuffed out. A rising madness turned him into a howling madman. The wailing lament, louder than the first, was more chilling than anything Esteban had ever experienced. Recrimination followed as Muhammed ranted, raved, cursed, tore at his clothing, lashing insanely at himself, as if in this self-ravagement, he would find solace. But his grief and despair refused to subside. He moved in crazy circles, making several revolutions around the fountain like a lost, forlorn animal. Images, dim and out of focus, communicated an unreality he refused to accept and in this unreality he was prepared to do himself bodily harm.

Esteban saw it coming. No match for the Moor's superhuman strength in this moment, he still dared leap out at him, hoping to restrain him. Infused with the strength of stampeding bulls, Muhammed picked up the Spaniard, flung him clear as if he were a straw puppet.

Esteban landed hard against a stone wall, shaken but intact. His approach grew cautious, tentative, his voice soft, compassionate. Nothing! No words or gestures penetrated the inner world in which the young Moor had locked himself.

Maldito Dios! To see a man go mad before your eyes . . .

Like an unchained beast, Muhammed lumbered about, eyes lighted to fiery points.

Esteban was so concerned about Muhammed's plight that he had unconsciously blocked his thoughts. Struck at once by electrifying images, he uttered hoarsely, "*Madre de Cristos!* What of my family?"

Esteban sprinted across the courtyard, disappeared inside the villa. He scaled the grand staircase and ran along the upper corridor to the master bedroom. Suddenly he stopped; he stood before the double doors, afraid to open them. Garnering his strength, he flung them open and froze, rooted to the spot, his senses paralyzed by the onslaught of violence and human degradation visited upon him. He whipped out a handkerchief, bowled over by an unbearable stench. Slowly his eyes swept the chaos before him. A configuration of unending crimson reached out at him. Blood splattered the walls, sheets, pillows, carpeting! Blood everywhere!

His mother and father, stripped naked, decapitated, lying in pools of blood oozing from the open stumps of their necks, drew his eyes magnetically. He fell weakly against the doorjamb, his ashen face contorted. Sweat poured copiously from him. He lurched dizzily forward, blindly striking out at tables, chairs, lamps, desperately trying to support the horror that pressed on him like a stone weight.

He steadied himself at the canopied four-poster, blinking at the ungodly desecration on the bed. Then he doubled over and fell to his knees.

When he could, he mustered strength, leaned back against a brocade wing-back chair near the hearth, gasping for breath, his nose still covered to shut out the ghastly stench. Esteban's eyes trailed unseeing to the fire on the hearth. He blinked, attempting to adjust his focus. He blinked again, his head turning sharply, unwilling to believe the apparition forming in his sight.

Mother of Christ! It was no apparition!

Two skulls, burning amid crackling flames and sparking embers, charred beyond recognition, stared at him, black holes where only hours ago familiar eyes were housed. The overpowering stench, he realized at last, was a mixture of cremated flesh, seared hair, burned bones, and blood. A concoction from Satan's apothecary was all that remained of his father and mother.

Esteban fled like a man trapped in purgatory. In moments he stood on a second threshold, screams lodged in his throat like lumps of hard coal. The sight of his three, sexually abused, virginal sisters, was more appalling. They floated in pools of blood, mutilated beyond identification.

Maldito Cristos! Who had done this to them?

Esteban, losing control, fled the horror. At the stairwell, he stopped, an after-image flashing across his brain; a glittering image amid a tidal wave of blood. He forced himself bit by bit to backtrack to the master bedroom. Swallowing hard, he moved toward the bed. He saw it; a gold ring in the shape of a marten reflected in the light. He stared at it, confused, disorganized thoughts running rampant in his head. Leaning over, he removed the ring from his father's swollen finger with difficulty, wiped it free of blood, and, without a trace of emotion, slipped it into his trouser pocket. He moved mechanically out the door to the landing.

A sudden dizziness came over him. He staggered, plummeted forward, sprawling like a bird with its wings clipped, and landed in a heap at the bottom of the stairs. He lost consciousness.

He came to, moments later, unable to think. Blinking hard, he forced his attention on the ceiling. Memory returned, and with it the nightmares. Feeling came in bits and pieces, in the struggle of picking himself off the floor, to his knees. He crawled the length of the foyer to the study door, and using what strength remained, laboriously pulled himself to his feet.

He closed his eyes and, leaning against the door, troubled, hot and cold chills alternating through him. It was worse with closed eyes; he snapped them open.

Steady Esteban. Keep your sanity. Pause. Regroup.

He could not. His weight, heavy against the door, flung it open; he fell into another nightmare. The room was a shambles! It seemed that a hundred stampeding elephants had thundered through the study. Heavy furniture was overthrown; wall cases containing priceless art objects were irreparably destroyed; bookcases were toppled, books strewn about in wild disarray; costly oils slashed from their frames; marble sculpture overturned, fragmented into a hundred pieces; it was all insanity! The oversized mahogany desk was violated, its drawers wrenched out, their contents hurled on Persian carpets. Who had done this? Why?

Robbers? Thieves in the night? Murderers? For what had they searched? Why the defilement—the wholesale slaughter?

Esteban de la Varga, at nineteen, felt himself sinking into madness. The penance of a thousand sins was hurled upon him.

A pale pink glow of moving shadows and tricky lights flooded the courtyard. Hints of the birth of a new day whispered behind the Mount of Angels. Muhammed Haj, calmer now, caught sight of Esteban emerging from the villa. The look in Esteban's dull eyes communicated at once that the diabolical fate meted to his family matched that meted to the de la Vargas.

He advanced slowly toward Esteban, a slip of paper in his outstretched hand, a list containing the thirteen names found on Abdul's remains.

Thirteen names! "Zaragozas who testified against us!" Four names were crossed out—nine remained. Other markings were jotted alongside, secret symbols of antiquity taught them both by Abdul in their formative years.

Following the four names was a symbol: an inverted double cross within a circle slashed by four vertical bars—it signified death.

Esteban glanced at his friend. "Muhammed, tell me what my mind swears cannot be."

"I am unable to do so, Esteban, for my mind, too, thinks as yours."

"The Garduna-Zaragozas did *this* to our families? Not content with setting an entire legal system against us, they did this too? From where comes their power? Surely not from Madrid! Pray tell me what manner of monsters these are?"

Muhammed Haj picked up a lance, and in a hard thrust, stabbed the earth with it, watching as it quivered. "Look here, on the lance. Their insignia: a death's-head over crown and thorns—a bold, audacious mark." His eyes trailed to the pile of corpses, the remains of his family lying neatly on the portico tiles, covered with sheets. He had thoroughly and neatly prepared them for a funeral pyre. "I call upon Malik, protector of hell, to dispose of these infidel dogs with a torture unmatched by any devised in his kingdom."

Alerted by an unusual noise, they glanced about the arena of death. Muhammed Haj sprang like a wildcat to a crouching position, knife in hand. Esteban froze. Muhammed hissed: "It's Armando!" He leaped forward. "He's wounded!"

Esteban rushed to the man's side. Reaching bloodied fingers out to both men, staggering, falling, his bloodied and battered body gashed in a hundred places, he was slowly losing life. Before he fell at Esteban's feet, he imparted valuable information, providing the youth with vital pieces to the massive puzzle forming in the minds of both Spaniard and Moor.

Esteban picked the dead man off the ground, carried him to the portico and laid the body next to the Moors. He closed the dead eyes and folded his hands over his heart. Drawing himself to his full six-foot height, Esteban cried out, his spirit in revolt against the deity who had cursed his and Muhammed Haj's family. "From this moment forward I shall become Satan's disciple! He is far more credible than you, who has never shown us your face! And I swear on this day to avenge our loved ones according to the tenets of Lucifer's handbook—not yours! Any fraudulent hope you instilled in the hearts and minds of our enemies shall evaporate, and death shall drain their blood without mercy!"

"Praise Allah! Blessings and peace be upon us!" Muhammed Haj joined in supplication.

Swifter than the eye could see, Esteban lunged for the knife in Muhammed's scabbard and stabbed his own arm. Blood spurted in a stream. He held Muhammed's arm as the Moor stabbed it, and placed the two wounds against the other. "Blood brothers forever. Two hearts, two minds, two souls united as one for all eternity."

Muhammed repeated the words.

Shortly after dawn, twelve surrogates kept their rendezvous with death. Their bodies, suspended by ropes from around their necks from overhead scaffolds in the Seville Prison courtyard, dangled and swayed in the rising breeze. Dark, ominous clouds clustering overhead kept the area as dismal and drab as the moods of the crowd. A black-garbed priest bleated a litany in Latin.

Less than fifteen feet away, the traitor, their paid informer, Antonio Vasquez, evaluated his precarious position. Death of the Zaragozas meant immunity for him. Who, if no witnesses existed, could pin the jacket of betrayal upon him? Having worked both ends against the middle, he intended to emerge from this fracas unscathed, untarnished, and wearing the laurel wreath of victory. Glancing furtively at the throng, his eyes picked out Esteban de la Varga, moving forward. Vasquez tentatively inched toward him, waiting for the proper moment to act.

Esteban inched through the crowds, a hooded falcon perched securely on his thickly padded left wrist. His hazel eyes searched each face. He stopped abruptly. *There!* He spotted the assassins. Behind him, Vasquez made his move. He moved to Esteban. Esteban glanced at Vasquez, nodded, and removing the leather hood from the predator's eyes, boosted the bird into the air. The golden falcon, a diversionary tactic, cleverly designed to create pandemonium, whirled arcs overhead, swooped down time and again on the screaming, panic-stricken humans desperately attempting to disperse and escape its talons.

Screams, shouts, cries of alarm and terror gripped the frenzied mob. Elsewhere among them, eye contacts were made, silent signals acknowledged, and instant bearings taken. The twelve nobles moved forward under cover of the commotion, prepared to converge on their quarry.

The falcon, whirling overhead, made a final dive, landing atop the hangman's scaffold.

The Zaragoza assassins, ignoring the commotion caused by the falcon, chose that moment to gaze again at the dozen dead men. Scowls creased their hard-lined faces. They tensed, their composure shattered. Disbelief fired the wrath on their blood-engorged faces. This couldn't happen! Not to them!

By the beard of Satan! They had been swindled! Beguiled! Tricked! And by that charlatan, Antonio Vasquez!

The impassioned assassins guardedly searched the immediate area for Vasquez, for the men who should be hanging from the gallows this day.

Too late! Esteban and his companions fell on their targets with drawn knives, sinking stilettos into the black-hearted Zaragozas again and again. Simultaneously a band of hard-riding horsemen, screaming, kicking up mud, fell on the crowds, dispersing the frantic hordes with swift saber swipes.

The courtyard, filled with screaming humans, braying horses, and shouting horsemen, became a blur of frightened humanity scattering toward escape routes. The horsemen, another diversionary tactic dreamed up by Esteban, had created their cover. The Zaragozas lay dead.

At nine A.M. churchbells tolled the hour.

A silent, sinister desolation drenched the muddied courtyard littered with dying Zaragoza assassins.

Somewhere a lonely trumpet sounded.

But wait . . . only eight bodies lay strewn about the muddied potholes. Where was the ninth? The young nobles, concealed in a nearby stable overlooking the arena of death, leaped to their saddles and rode fleetfooted horses back to de la Varga villa to ponder the maddening disappearance of the ninth Zaragoza.

Professor Konrad Gruber closed the manuscript and stared at its cover. *How could the history of century-old dead men benefit him?* What he needed desperately was an in-depth profile of the living—not the dead! He needed to know the present generation of de la Vargas, their habits, moods, social and political mores, their strengths, and beyond all else their weaknesses.

Silence . . . brooding silence, interrupted only by the snores escaping the sleeping Xenofonte's open mouth. A rash of questions seared Gruber's brain. Rising, he moved to the potbellied stove, poured hot water into a teapot. He filled his cup, added brown sugar lumps and lemon twists, and stretched his limbs. He lighted his precious Meerschaum pipe, drawing on it. He sipped his tea and finally sat again, manuscript in hand. He located his place, turned the page and read the heading.

CONFESSIONS OF FRA HUMBERTO

Last Survivor

Monastic Order of Zaragoza-Vascongades

1 November 1822

Upon regaining consciousness, I believed I had truly died and gone to hell. My body was wracked with excruciating pain. I heard the churchbell toll nine times. *Nine times for nine dead men?* No, it merely tolled the hour.

My vision cleared, and my first perception was of the twelve dead men on the gallows. Memory returned. We had fallen under the knife, my brothers and I. Lifting my head off the muddied ground, my focus clearing, I saw their dead bodies sprawled in muddy puddles and soggy earth, bleeding to death from the multiple lacerations inflicted on them.

I wondered if the dead could bear witness. Not those on the gallows, for their souls had long since begun their peregrination to hell. Had they paused en route to await the arrival of my dead brothers, hoping for escort to Satan's kingdom? Waiting for me? No! I vowed death would not sink her tenacious claws into my skin, for it was up to me to settle the score with both de la Varga and that black-hearted villain, Antonio Vasquez. My life, I believed, was spared to bear witness to the fraud perpetrated on the gallows, to reveal the surrogates who, for coins of silver, cheated the court system of Seville. Madrid would find this travesty interesting—no?

More dead than alive, I dragged myself from the courtyard moving painfully along back streets, hiding from inquisitive crowds in alleyways, behind trash and litter piled high in the streets until I reached the monastery. Instantly, upon my passage through the gates, the custodians of the order, fearing the worst, ordered the enormous bronze and wooden gates closed, forever banning the public from setting foot upon the grounds.

When I had healed, our neophytes were assimilated into the Seville order and I left Spain, to go in search of Antonio Vasquez. That viper must die for his treachery to our brotherhood. This I vowed as I had when I took my vows to be true to the Zaragoza Order.

*   *   *

Professor Gruber, startled by the noisy clearing of phlegm from the awakening Xenofonte, closed the manuscript, placed it on the desk, and relit his pipe.

"Ah . . . still at it I see, *Professore*." Xenofonte sniffed the air, enjoying the scent of fresh pipe tobacco. He stretched, yawned, and, pulling his ponderous weight off the sofa, padded across the room, peered under the tea cozy, nodding contentedly. He poured a cup and moved to his chair behind the desk.

"What happened to Antonio Vasquez?"

Xenofonte tossed him an enigmatic look. "You haven't finished?"

"Certainly you could save me precious time? About Vasquez?"

The scholar shrugged, replaced his glasses. "For a time he basked in the confidence of de la Varga and the Moor. When Esteban appointed a task force to uncover the traitor in their midst, Vasquez was placed in charge of the assignment."

"How nice for Vasquez."

"Precisely."

"Let me speculate. With Vasquez cleverly in control, the traitor would never surface."

"Excellent, *Professore*. You clearly perceive the rewards of so clever a move on his part to ingratiate himself to de la Varga. Fearing for the well-being of his friends, lest Madrid learn of the charades played with destiny on the gallows, and Esteban urged them all, six months later, to leave Spain and settle elsewhere. The ninth Zaragoza was still unaccounted for, and Esteban believed the last survivor would in some demoniacal way retaliate."

"What happened to the Garduna nucleus?"

"Ah, the Garduna. They too fled Spain, buried themselves in other countries under different identities, making new lives for themselves. They took up residence in Germany, France, Switzerland, Corsica, Sicily, and South America. Esteban and Muhammed Haj remained in Spain, for in that nation lay their destinies. However, contact was maintained by employing the emblem of the marten, the symbol borrowed from the defunct Garduna."

"Pray tell, *Framonaco*, what precisely is so valuable about the Seven Garduna Parchments?"

"Ah . . . the truth. Cabalistic tenets set forth by ancient scribes. Blueprints, *Professore*. Blueprints for the creation of a potent force. An organization capable of toppling governments."

Gruber sat forward in his chair, trying to quell the excitement tingling in his body. He sipped his tea to relieve a sudden dryness in his throat.

"The legacy weighed heavily on Spaniard and Moor. They evaluated their perilous positions. Muhammed Haj learned to decode the parchments. He found appalling truths. The identity of the first Garduna grand marshal was revealed as one Antonio Vasquez! *Coincidence*? Or was it possible the Antonio Vasquez of their time was a descendant of the Vasquez of the fifteenth century, just as he and Esteban had descended from the Montenegro and de la Varga clans? The information lay heavily on their minds.

"Esteban had immersed himself in the trial transcripts; he located the false testimonies and trumped-up charges against them. Appeals to the crown brought action, not swift action, for it took two years before the tribunal judges were taken to task for their part in the corruption. Instantly unseated and given severe reprimands, they were denied retirement stipends."

"When did Fra Humberto arrive at Saint Pachomious?" Gruber asked.

"Twenty years *after* his flight from Seville. He became a nomad in the years between, going from one pathetic little cell to the next in various monasteries throughout Europe. He began, almost at once upon his departure from Spain, to leak information to de la Varga in Seville, naming Vasquez as the traitor. Proof, ample proof, was provided to Esteban, always through an intermediary. And so it was that specialists, fueled by de la Varga money and revenge, were dispatched from Seville and poured over the face of Europe like bounty hunters, determined to track the traitor, return him to Spain, if possible, if not, kill him.

"Ah, *Herr* Gruber." The octogenarian sighed. "If Fra Humberto had come to Saint Pachomious sooner, those priceless parchments would be here, under lock and key, where they belong, with the remaining Garduna-Zaragoza relics. Alas, he was an anchorite of a monastic order apart from ours. Steeped in the ways of his order, Fra Humberto maintained his silence for two decades before articulating his provocative odyssey to me." He indicated the manuscripts on the desk. "The work of a lifetime, *Herr* Gruber. Reason for my existence on earth. Payment for the space I occupied among men. Does the information embellish your history of Spain?"

"Yes, yes, of course. But you have not fully explained Antonio Vasquez or the mystery of his disappearance."

"Ah. Something about this scoundrel appeals to you, no?"

"Judas, the betrayer of *your* Christ, I found as interesting as Jesus himself. Do you disagree?"

"To a historian, everything has validity. Death adds perfection to the most imperfect man and time frees him from defects."

Xenofonte fanned the hot tea with his hand, sipped it gingerly, noting Gruber's impatience. "You *are* persistent. Very well. By the time news of Fra Humberto's hatred reached him, Vasquez had left Spain for Austria. His position apparent by then, he lost all perspective when he learned de la Varga assassins were in hot pursuit. Fleeing the Austrian hamlet, taking sanctuary where he could, he fled village after village, in constant fear of his life.

"Didn't he stop at some point to reconnoiter?"

"Yes, he did. Curiously enough, his meanderings halted abruptly. Within a decade he emerged an affluent man. Divine providence, I suppose. He married, settled in the Bavarian Black Forest, and raised a family."

"My, my. Suddenly Bavaria takes on importance in my life too."

"What's that, *Professore*? Speak up."

"Nothing important. Then de la Varga's men failed to locate him?"

"Time and time again. Esteban finally deduced that Vasquez was protected, protected by one or more persons of power and influence. Else how would he escape his pursuers moments before their arrival? It was always the same. Vasquez, warned in advance, took flight."

"And what of Vasquez?" Gruber interrupted, unable to mask his rising fervor. He was getting close. He must know, he must!

"He died a raving maniac, spouting nonsense on his deathbed about the priceless Garduna Parchments. In an effort to exact a deathbed promise from his sons to take up the gauntlet against the de la Vargas, he suggested that the parchments, stolen from the house of his ancestors by the Spanish grandee, were in Seville on de la Varga property. If his sons fought for them, the legacy would be theirs, but he cautioned them to beware of others who had every intention of stealing them from the de la Varga family."

"Yes, yes, go on, *Framonaco*," urged Gruber.

"Alas, the sons regarded their father as a pathetically deluded fool. Reflecting bitterly on the long, unrewarding years of hardship when pressed into involuntary travel to strange alien lands, they labeled Antonio's words as the ravings of an old fossil whose moth-infested brains got eaten up at last. To show their contempt and utter disregard for him they assumed new names upon his death, denying both Vasquez and their Spanish heritage. Thus the Vasquez lineage was lost. I found no purpose in pursuing it.''

Gruber left the monastery mulling over the information. His time in Trento was nearly over. Madrid awaited him. What had he learned? Would any of this suit his purpose? He had yet to read the last half of the second manuscript, which contained the lineage of both the de la Varga and Montenegro families. He had to make his plans soon. How would the present-day families of Spaniard and Moor fit into his scheme of things? He hadn't found the keystone, the one vital piece upon which Zurich's strategy depended.

One fact was clear in his mind. The Madrid Assignment must succeed. He could not fail! If he did, he'd be killed. And if he succeeded? Would death be his reward? Unable to shake this possibility from mind, he returned to the hostelry, attacked his supper with avidity but drinking sparingly of wine. His head must be clear for the work on the morrow.

Early the next morning the red-clay-tiled roofs and church spires in Trento resembled glazed peppermint ribbon candy as the sun melted the snow. Gruber, en route to the monastery, stopped at the confectioners to purchase a box of Swiss chocolates for the scholar Xenofonte.

"Chocolates for me, *Herr* Gruber? I would have preferred my favorite brandy. Ah, well, we can't always realize our deepest desires, can we? Thoughtful of you." He tossed the box casually on the desk and set about preparing tea. He flourished a plate of creme-filled *pastachiotti*, Italian cookies, a rare delicacy. Gruber accepted the tea and passed on the cookies apologetically. They sat opposite each other. Xenofonte's eyes, deep in their fleshy pockets, peered intently at Gruber. "We are almost at an end here, *Herr* Gruber. Tell me, do I fall heir to Brother Schuller's fate?''

Stunned, Gruber feigned innocence. "I do not understand. Who is Brother Schuller? Did I meet him here?''

Xenofonte smiled. He sipped his tea, wiped his lips, sighing.

"You destroyed the illusion by denial. What is written on your face reveals the truth—not your words. I too was trained in dissimulation. The art of deception was once my forte. You forget I gave up the priesthood. Never mind. I am finished, I have justified my existence on earth. So how will it be? Surely, Gruber, you plan something more imaginative than chocolates laced with cyanide?" He grimaced. "You men from Zurich possess little imagination."

Gruber decided to drop all pretense. Actually he liked the old man, a rarity for him. His voice dropped to a soothing tone. "You know I must do it. My esteem for you is inestimable, but I have no recourse."

"Why—for the love of God?"

"If, following my departure, another comes making inquiries, he would torture you for information, be far less merciful than I. You would be forced to reveal the nature of my inquiries despite any disinclination on your part to betray me. They would show you no mercy—none at all."

"Since when have assassins become merciful? Their victims would not endorse so foolish a concept. Killing is final. Torture need not be part or parcel of the act." He sighed. "You are all the same," he insisted quietly. "You came only for the parchments. They are not here. On my honor. Search all you will."

"Others have come in search of them?"

"Why should I tell you? You intend to kill me."

"I promise to be merciful."

"As merciful as you were to Heinrich Schuller?"

"It was an object lesson he had to learn."

"What logic is that? Teach object lessons to the dead?" Xenofonte witnessed the frost forming in Gruber's unusual eyes. Lifting the hem of his cassock, he thrust forward a grotesquely twisted ankle. "The last man from Zurich too was merciful. This is a sample of his mercy."

"*Zurich!*" Gruber exploded. "You bray on and on about Zurich! Why do you assume he was—I am from Zurich?"

"I told you. You are all alike. The faces change, the clothing at times is unique, the disguises are humorous. But the souls, *Herr* Gruber, the souls cannot be disguised. Men like you reproduce themselves like cockroaches. In Italy today they wear brown shirts. In Germany, what moves them? A color? A design? A symbol? Yes, men like you are swayed by symbols and colorful panoply. In Russia it is the color red, as crimson as blood. Oh, what does it matter? Do what you must.''

"The parchments, you claim, are not on the premises. I didn't expect to find them here. Why did they—those who came before me—assume it?"

"What audacity, *Herr* Gruber? Mother of God, you scoundrels assume too much. Knowing my fate in advance, why would I further confide in you? Besides, I need bargaining power.''

"Sorry, my friend, no bargaining power for you. Personalities shape no decisions in these matters. Your fate was charted in advance."

"I think I should enjoy dissecting one of you. You challenge the cleverest minds."

"Describe these men from Zurich, Xenofonte."

"I thought I did." Xenofonte shrugged. "Very well, you insist on it. Ruthless, tyrannical, grasping, insane. It's in the eyes, Gruber," he said, touching the corners of his eyes. "The eyes of the dead or truly blind. You move through life burdened by the guilt of the deeds done your fellowman, yet, you are the first to scream foul."

They parried back and forth, using words for weapons, for the better part of the morning. Gruber, losing patience, loathed the clergy Xenofonte represented. "Abominations of mankind, your colleagues. They are, collectively, devils hiding their evil behind the shadow of a nonexistent Christ, brandishing crown and thorns before the hypnotized masses to keep them enslaved. Hypocrites all!"

"How did you do it to Schuller?" the scholar asked quietly.

"*Colchicum autumnale* in his precious vintage wines."

"Sweet Jesus! I drink no wine, thank you!" He shuddered.

"In your spring water, then, or tea. Make it easy on yourself."

"I've had my fill until tomorrow."

"For the love of your God, choose your own demise. You do eat lunch?" He glanced at the clock.

"Not if you intend to poison me. It's quite messy, Gruber."

"How did you learn of Schuller?"

"Homing pigeons travel faster than trains."

"You *knew* when I arrived? Still you confided in me?"

"Not at first. You gave yourself away. Dr. Fritz Lehrman from Munich is a figment of my imagination. In your verbose explanation you conveyed *who* and *what* you are."

"Ah, I shall stop myself from such lengthy explanations

henceforth. Feed my curiosity, Brother. Why did you indulge me when you knew who I was? *Why?*''

"What you learned here will create changes in your world. Lacking both the perceptions and sorcery of a Merlin, with no crystal balls to facilitate prognostications, I am forced to deal in facts. The facts substantiated for centuries a noble Spanish family who has risked life, limb, and property to prevent the alleged Garduna Parchments from surfacing and falling into the wrong hands. One must therefore logically assume the reasons to be compatible to the moral and ethical concepts of a forthright people—''

"—or a frightened, covetous feudal overlord unwilling to share his good fortune with others.''

"Hardly. What man inclines himself to suffer torture, brutality, unhuman debaucheries—even murder—for the base things in life? No man in his cups remains a bulwark against opposing forces at great personal sacrifices if the alternatives are less threatening. Such men are fearless. You are not motivated to be used as a tool of men superior to you to receive the baser things in life. Power and riches are your goals. Ambition oozes from you like the last stages of paresis.''

Gruber's eyes narrowed in annoyance. "One question and you may choose your own demise.''

"Back to that, again, eh? Decent of you. I want no undignified paroxysms when I voyage to meet my Lord. A weightlessness, a drifting sensation to facilitate my journey, will do.''

"Opium, then, it's settled. My question is two-fold.''

"We bargained for one! Ah, well, it is futile to go toe to toe with you on so picayune a matter. Speak up.''

"About Vasquez. You spoke of decoys, protection? You wager he sold information for protection?''

"How else did he outfox his pursuers? Fra Humberto believed this with conviction. Flight, decoys, cleverly manipulated escapes do not come cheaply. Remember he became affluent.''

"Vasquez on his deathbed contended the parchments were rightfully his. He believed them to be in the hands of the de la Varga family. Those who came before me—these men from Zurich—did they read the volumes you masterfully compiled?''

"Ah, then, you do appreciate my work." Xenofonte's eyes lighted.

"Brother Xenofonte, your impressive credentials bowl me over. One day in the future, knowledge stored in the brains of men of your ilk will be preserved, not decompose. A means to salvage, record for posterity, such talents will prevail.'' Gruber lighted his Meerschaum, aware of the peculiar apprehension forming in the octogenarian's face as he attempted to determine Gruber's state of mind.

''The answer is yes. They read the manuscripts.''

''How many? Do you remember how many came here? It's important.''

''Not to me. Too bad you intend to do me in. I could best Scheherazade's record and remain alive for more than a thousand nights. I have many stories to tell.''

''You try my patience. I do not have a thousand nights to waste.'' Gruber puffed the pipe, irritated at parrying. ''Not even a thousand minutes.''

''You only battle time because of your burning ambition. How masterfully *they* use your talents. They seduce only the most ambitious, for only among such men can they hatch their treacheries. You ambitious men—what a fiery lot—use hell and damnation to malign. You wield venom with expertise while your masters in their remote towers, far from the arena of battle, feign innocence, express outward shock at the dastardly deeds done by devoted servants. Once finished with your vile acts, you ambitious men are soon bridled, put down in secret plottings and covert maneuverings, broken and murdered because your knowledge threatens the well-being and impeccable social standings to which your ivory tower titans pretend. What then, *Herr* Gruber?'' he asked, stretching the words scathingly. ''The ambitious, clever human tool is dismantled, done away with, leaving no hint of impropriety to cast dark shadows on their flawless reputations.''

Gruber perceived at once both the wisdom in Xenofonte's words and the clever attempt to throw him off balance. His silence prompted the scholar to toss delicious bait at him. He bartered.

''The answer to two questions you aren't clever enough to ask me, in exchange for a bottle of my favorite brandy.''

''You said you *didn't* drink.''

''Wine, *Herr* Gruber. I detest wine.''

Gruber wagged a playful hand at him. ''How astute of you. To acquire the brandy means a trip downhill into Trento. On my return, *Framonaco*, a squad of carabinieri in ambush would seal my fate, no?'' He laughed like a parent chastising his son.

''What a fiendish mind! The brandy is sold here on the

premises. For three years I've been denied this luxury. Since this is to be my departure, may it not be euphoric? Ah, but never mind. I shall tell you just to prove your cleverness is lacking.'' He opened the box of chocolates. "You're certain they aren't tainted with cyanide?" Gruber shook his head. The scholar gobbled up a brandy-filled chocolate cream, chomped it noisily, and searched for another. "Not once did you question the subjective nature of my writing. How it was I knew intimately the workings of the de la Varga mentalities, *Professore*?''

Gruber's eyes narrowed to slits. *The man was a fox!* "*Molto bene, Framonaco.* You are the clever one. Had we met under different circumstances—''

"—you would do exactly as you will do. There is no salvation for your kind. Long before your time you will be a dead man. Everything you touch will die before its time. One day you will recall my words with clarity. By then it will be too late.''

Gruber's heart solidified against the old man. It was time to set aside foolish games and sentiment. His expression communicated his impatience.

"Yes, the Garduna Parchments do exist. In the wrong hands, irreparable damage will devastate any who oppose them.''

"And," Gruber added, "they are secreted someplace at the de la Varga hacienda in Seville, no?''

"For your edification, I sent Fra Humberto's confession to Esteban de la Varga. I am his first cousin. Second cousin to the man who you intend to set dogs against. General Diego de la Varga, Spain's most esteemed hero of both the Spanish American War and the recent Moroccan Campaign.''

Astonishment, skepticism, apprehension, combined with disbelief. "Why do you choose to tell me this?''

"Because you haven't one chance in a million of acquiring the parchments. Not for Zurich. Not for yourself.''

A few brain cells at the back of Gruber's brain exploded in that instant. He knew. He had guessed as much when Schuller mentioned the parchments. What were his words? Xenofonte's?

"The kind of treasure men die for! Blueprints for powerful organization that can topple governments!"

Zurich! The consortium! The ivory-tower titans! They were after the parchments!

Once he delivered the treasure to Zurich—what then? The demise of the ambitious servant? He smiled internally.

"You, *Framonaco*, are a true gentleman and scholar. Where do I procure your favorite brandy?"

"In the corner behind the door is a flag. Place it outside the door in the flagstaff holder. Someone will arrive shortly."

"This isn't a signal of sorts to summon a militia?"

"You called me a gentleman and scholar. I won't disappoint you."

Gruber complied with the instructions. He returned and went to work. He withdrew his vials from his briefcase, selected one, popped the cork, and carefully touched his tongue to it. Good, it was the proper vial. He picked up a water glass from a counter, emptied it, rinsed it with tea, and wiped it dry. He spilled a few drops of the drug into the glass, swirled it, coating the interior and rolled it between his palms to warm it. Lighting a candle on the desk he held the glass over the flame until the fluid evaporated.

Brother Xenofonte, perched in his chair like a caged eagle, glared stonily at the ease and expertise of his guest. A knock on the door brought Gruber forward. A young acolyte delivered the brandy. He wordlessly accepted the money. Xenofonte chuckled as he worked rosaries between arthritic-ridden fingers.

"Herr Gruber, we approach the moment of truth. Tell me who you are. You are *not* Gruber, *not* Caragini. Who then? When I meet your maker, I should like to assure him how infinitely clever is the centurion he placed on earth to do his bidding."

Pouring brandy into the glass, he bowed slightly. "Amadeo Redak Zeller, at your service."

Xenofonte nodded knowingly. "Amadeo, a derivative of Asmodeus," he mused. "You are of the hierarchy, after all." At Zeller's total confusion the monk added regretfully, "I am not faulted. You do belong to the men of Zurich."

Zeller's features hardened. "I belong to no man. One day, *they* shall belong to Zeller."

"You do not disappoint me." Xenofonte stared at the brandy in the outstretched hand. His cynical, contemptuous eyes lifted to meet the colorless eyes of his assassin.

"Take your time. Hold the glass in both hands, that's it, now roll it. The heat from your body creates a chemical reaction rendering the contents potent. Euphoria is a sip or two away."

The octogenarian did as Zeller instructed. "So, it's time. A serpent must eat another serpent before he becomes a dragon, eh? You are determined to snort fire. I drink to your professionalism. We are, all of us, mere specks on a horizon of swarming locusts.'' He downed the brandy in two gulps.

"Not I, *Framonaco*. If you envision Amadeo Zeller in that bleak picture, rest assured he will command that swarming ambitious horde.''

The dying man opened a desk drawer, removed an ornate, hand-carved rosary with a large wooden crucifix attached to it. He slipped it over his neck. "Beware, Zeller, of those who stack the cards and do not themselves play the game.'' The glass in Xenofonte's hand fell to the floor. He slumped in his chair. His features, devoid of sadness, fear, or regret, reflected a crafty smile as if in some way he had put one over on his assassin.

And he had. Xenofonte, dying from an incurable metabolic disturbance of unknown etiology, had begged for death in recent weeks. Zeller had just provided him with the means.

Observing him, Zeller frowned. The man was dead. Too soon for the poison to have run its course! With no burning itch to probe the reasons for this he swiftly picked up after his death tableau, rinsed the glasses, half filled one with brandy, and placed it in the dead man's hand. He slipped the precious manuscripts into his briefcase, extinguished the candles, exited the cottage, and, inhaling sweet scents of flowering jasmine, moved with agility off the grounds. Jasmine would forever remind him of Xenofonte. What a shame! What a phenomenal brain lost forever.

Madrid.

He must get to Madrid, swiftly, without delay. He'd made his decision, one so powerful it intoxicated his senses. His cover in Madrid would be Antonio Vasquez! Imagine the hornet's nest he'd stir in the proper circles?

Seated in the private compartment shielded from interlopers, Zeller familiarized himself with the de la Varga family lineage. Esteban had married an Italian contessa. Two sons died of mysterious maladies. A third son, Diego, born late in their lives, coveted and adored, had grown to manhood, became a man unlike any de la Varga in centuries. Courageous, born to command, he demonstrated a penchant for the military. He was educated at St. Cyr Military Academy in France.

Muhammed Haj, matrimonially inclined, journeyed to his ancestral home in the Sudan, returned to Seville with his stunning passion-flower bride who bore him twins, Oman and Raffi. Raised with Diego de la Varga, the trio was inseparable until

Oman, for some reason not explained, was denied admittance to St. Cyr. Nonetheless he joined Diego as his aide de camp in the Spanish American War.

On his deathbed, Esteban had summoned Diego and in the presence of the Moors discussed the complex burdens of the legacy. Strangely, his words, unlike his father's and his father's father, contained an ominous message. "Times are changing, my sons." He included Oman and Raffi in his circle of family. "Muhammed Haj and I have borne witness to incredible changes in our lifetimes. You will witness even more marvels in this twentieth century. My request, my dying request, is to persuade you all to familiarize yourselves with the Seven Garduna Parchments. Burn their contents into your brain. Be aware, if the need ever arises to form a consortium of power on a vast scale, the means to achieve these ends are spelled out clearly in the parchments. Such power is capable of toppling governments, able to bring other nations to their knees. In the wrong hands the parchments can devastate Spain *and* our families. You must swear blood oaths to hold sacrosanct and inviolate, in perpetuity, the inherited legacy. The building of a dynasty, a family dynasty, pyramiding wealth from foreign lands through mergers, marriage contracts, and sound business investments, will unify the family structure, forming an impregnable, cohesive bond of love, loyalty, and silence in all affairs. Let no stranger penetrate our strength or topple our dynasty."

Zeller dwelled on this section of the manuscript until he knew the contents by rote. The full import of Esteban's deathbed pronouncement was unclear in his mind.

Galvanically charged thoughts exploded his senses; it came together for him and he *knew*. He knew!

The Madrid Assignment was devised in order to acquire the Garduna Parchments! A power that could topple governments! Bring nations to their knees!

He was trembling. Anticipation of what lay ahead stimulated his ambition. He flipped through the pages of the manuscript, found his place. Only a few pages remained. He glanced out the train window. In the distance was the sweeping azure sea of the Italian and French Riviera. Soon the train would cross the border into Spain.

His first stop, Barcelona, was to establish contacts in that seaport city swarming with foreign agents and provocateurs. Then, when the time was right—Madrid!

Chapter Seven

None of the servants dared tell Victoria Valdez how foolish they regarded her recent behavior. Imagine locking herself up in her bedroom—in *darkness*—stubbornly protesting Don Verono's demands and the terms of what she called an archaic marriage contract! Two months! They refused to speculate on the outcome and closed their minds to this foolishness, hoping whatever it was between father and daughter would end. It was too much! *Dios!* What pandemonium she created in their lives, running them ragged at all hours of the day and night!

Francisco de la Varga hadn't shown the decency to respond to her letter. *Fool! You burned that bridge before you crossed it, didn't you?* Lying apathetically on the silken chaise lounge in her drape-drawn boudoir, she wallowed in the bitter fruits of her carefully laid plans, dissatisfied with the harvest of her meticulous sowing—total disdain and disregard from de la Varga, from her father.

Accustomed to having her orders obeyed by a vast retinue of servants at the snap of her aristocratic fingers, she found herself totally confused in dealing with people at long distance. With little concept of time and distance, what measure had she of the wide ocean between Argentina and Spain and the time it took

109

even the swiftest liner to cross the vast body of water to deliver the mail?

What really galled Victoria was her impotence, her inability to manipulate her father as she'd done in the past. What good was this dramatically staged scenario—created to dissolve her father's resolve—if he never visited her to repent his dictatorial demands? If she lost this cherished art what chance had she to manipulate the world to suit her whims and fanciful caprices? Too young to understand parental ultimatums and bargaining power, she had struck out against her father and found herself outwitted by a formidable opponent. The trouble was they were as alike as two peas in a pod. Victoria possessed her father's way of managing things to his own advantage, his calculated charm and underlying cynicism.

The impetuous darling of Argentine society, atrociously pampered, her slightest wish gratified on demand, had grown up headstrong, hedonistic, highly susceptible to the lure of danger. Astutely crafty in her ability to charm, her innate talent lay in the expeditious managing of things to her personal advantage. At least she had thought so all this time. Now she trembled inwardly, frightened by what she considered a lack of power. In eighteen years she had observed her father in numerous poses, as businessman, father, husband, financier. His lack of concern for anyone's point of view except his own in cementing business deals, the absence of illusion and a general cynicism in both business and personal relations, had subconsciously set a role model for her to follow.

Victoria picked up the letter on her table, stared at it, recollecting lessons taught her by her father years ago.

"You don't win a point by going toe to toe with a stronger opponent, you win by stalling for time, avoiding the in-fighting— and waiting. When you find the weak spot, you charge!"

Insensata! Fool! You pitted yourself against the master! Only fools give up one dream in quest of another before the first materializes!

Victoria flung off the satin coverlet and with it her imagined infirmity. She scurried across the room, flung open the French doors of the swan-breasted balcony, hurriedly tearing open the envelope, wincing at the acute glare of the sun, and paused to inhale the sweet cloying scents of roses, orange, and pomegranate blossoms. Inside, she drew the casements closed.

Victoria, hollow of cheek, a hint of shadow under her eyes,

padded back to the chaise on thick pastel carpeting, her eyes sprinting over the letter's contents. She glanced at the enclosed photographs, an ecstatic sigh escaping her lips. A sudden quelling sensation brought her hand fluttering to her breast. Her throaty giggle burst into amused laughter.

A montage of curious expressions flooded her face. *Is this to be believed?* Coming alive again, Victoria joyously reread the letter:

10 February, 1920

Mi querida, prometida:

Your letter arrived this morning, prompting my immediate reply. However sympathetic and in agreement I am with your expressed sentiments, we, you and I, cannot disregard tradition, long an established practice in both Valdez and de la Varga families. Marriages are more than emotional involvements. Responsibility facing us, as inheritors of affluence, cannot be disregarded. It is not my intent to limn our roles, only to offer you balm. One day we shall regard your premature fears and reaction to the nuptial agreement in good humor.

I confess my quandary, *mi querida*, at the photographs you sent me. My father, Don Diego, who prides himself as his memory, described you to me as a creature of slender grace, quick wit, and boundless energy. With hair the color of a fiery sunset, eyes like green gemstones, and boasting an expertise in horsemanship that has captured his fancy for nearly four years. When first he saw you, you rode with the gauchos on your hacienda near Santa Rosa, on a black stallion called Chaco. He described you as a mix of wind, fury, and unbridled passion. Why, señorita, would my father deceive me? Or is it possible that a strange metamorphosis has occurred in you, capable of changing your hair of fire into the black of coal? I doubt that your beauty has faded at so youthful an age and you have swollen to the proportions of a cow. Was the blithe spirit stripped from the enchantress recollected by Don Diego—or did he, in all candor, exaggerate to provoke my interest?

Alas, *querida*, the photographs were keenly disappointing. But since there can be no roses without thorns, I accept the good with the bad. Perhaps before our scheduled nuptials you will demonstrate courage and transform yourself back to the scintillating creature rhapsodized by my father.

Enclosed are two photographs of myself, if only to impress upon your fanciful imagination that Spaniards are not in possession of two heads, a tail, and do not snort fire. Now, so you may get to know me better, I shall tell you about myself.

I am studying law, political science, and international finance at the University of Madrid. Here in Spain, the future of the world seems grim. Due to Spain's neutrality in the Great War, we suffered no enormous death toll or abominable aftereffects. But . . . something is happening here. Curious and inexplicable circumstances threaten Spain's existence. An influx of strangers, rabble-rousers, and political agitators began arriving before the armistice to create a new climate of dissent. Workers' riots spring up everywhere, always led by strangers, unknown enemies infusing fear in the hearts of Spaniards. I tell you this, *querida*, so you will understand the nation in which you will one day live and raise our children.

Spain was not born in a vale of tears, her infancy was not fragile, nor was she cradled and breast-fed in the soft arms and bosom of history. She was not beguiled by the sweet-smelling scents and lusty promises of ambitious conquerors. Spain was raised sternly, the soul forged in iron, her perception of the world sharply defined. Created to the music of thunder, born on primitive sands and rocks, twisting through the wild tempo of time, Spain has breathed her breath of life into men like my ancestors and me. What a likely heritage for a de la Varga?

Why do I burden you with a past history you must know equally as well as I, for your father, Don Verono too, was descended from the *conquistadores*, no? Our lives are richly endowed with an undeniable heritage, *querida*, one we cannot take lightly.

Forgive me. My unbridled passion often sidetracks me. It was not my intent to overwhelm you at this, our first encounter.

Respectfully I must end this letter, for my presence is expected at the lecture hall, where a breed of men speaking with new voices and using alien words to Spaniards has captured the imagination of the university students. This night, I shall attend with my friend Esteban Escobar and hear for myself, what, if anything, these self-proclaimed messiahs can offer Spain.

Adios, querida. Pray your next letter to me shall be as amusing as your first, and less dramatic. With affection, I am yours, Francisco de la Varga.

Victoria, trapped by her childish attempt at dissembling, flushed crimson, yet secretly nurtured delight in her attempted fraud. She stared at the photos. Essentially they were identical; both, the image of Francisco de la Varga, tall, exceedingly handsome, standing with the panache of a strutting matador before a vaulted stained-glass window. A starburst of light behind him threw his face into soft focus. The sight of him, the power he oozed, raced her heart to an unbearable beat. The second photo, altered slightly in developing, included a second head alongside his, one with devil's horn, several puffs of smoke emanating from its nose, and a tail coming out from behind him.

Victoria's irresistible laughter echoed through the villa. Downstairs the servants took pause. The *Señorita* Victoria was laughing? *Por Dios! Es verdad?* A miracle? Could they breathe easier? What a devil she was when she didn't get her way! Now perhaps, they could perform their chores in peace.

Victoria lay on her bed, on her stomach, elbows propped up, face cupped in her hands, staring at the photographs, fantasizing over Francisco de la Varga. Why was her heart fluttering? Why did her knees feel weak, like water? What is this curious breathlessness, this elation pervading my senses? What leaves me parched and wanting? The questions assailed her, and Victoria *knew* the answers were somehow wrapped up in Francisco, her Prince Charming. When she considered her foolishness in sending him those silly photographs of Carmelita, she could die! And those countless candles she'd lit, knelt before, and prayed—and prayed, and prayed to all the saints in heaven and demons in hell—whoever had listened to her laments! Oh the shame of it all! She had made herself ill! Two whole months locked in her room, refusing to live, driving her family mad and the servants up the walls. And for what?

Well, the drought had ended, the foolishness drained from her. She summoned *Doña* Teresa, her *dueña,* and ordered her to summon up a *bruja,* the woman who prophesized the future. The fluttery woman, with dark flashing eyes, waddled away, wondering what her charge was up to, as if she didn't know. Trouble! It was always the same. But she looked alive! Hadn't she bloomed?

Color had returned to her face. Did *Doña* Teresa dare hope the wild tigress was tamed in some mysterious manner?

Victoria, ebullient, leaped from the bed, sweeping up letter and photographs, and flew across the room to her escritoire. She propped the photos against a vase of freshly cut blood-red roses. Feather quill in hand, pale-crested stationery on the desk before her, she took on a dreamy-eyed expression, and promptly responded.

30 June

Mi querido prometido:

Your letter arrived on this date. The flush of crimson lingers on my face. I beg your forgiveness at the childish deception I employed in my previous correspondence. You must think me a foolish untutored wretch of a girl.

You told me little about yourself. Truly, you spoke of Spain as if I were betrothed to her—not you. Is your preoccupation with your heritage, duties, and obligations of such magnitude that you intend to give our future an ancillary role? I am not criticizing, merely inquiring. Your photograph, while revealing your soul, does not describe you. What is the color of your hair? Eyes? What do you enjoy—music, books, operas? What?

Here in Buenos Aires we are not as touched by the war's aftermath as you on the Continent. At times I grow bored with the empty chatter of giggling females in whose company I am forced, more often than not, to learn the social graces of women in our class. Pouring tea, serving teacakes, and chocolate to bird-brained females who haven't a solid thought to contribute to the betterment of the world is anathema to me. Thoughts of running away to become a nurse or to serve some useful purpose entered my head while groping my way through a tortured adolescence. Had I made attempts toward those ends, my father would have confined me to a cloister.

It is reasonable to assume, since my mother was born in North America, that I inherited from her what my father refers to as my "damnable, stubborn wild, gringo streak." From him, a breeder of bulls, a hacendado of enormous stature here in Argentina, comes my romantic nature. I make no apology for either since I am a composite of both my parents.

Querido, Francisco, in all frankness you have captured my fancy. Your humor, charm, and sensitive words warm me, abate the wild rebellion that often possesses me and took hold of me last January when I wrote so horrid a letter to you. May I call you Paco, a more affectionate, shortened version of your name used by the gauchos on the pampas?

What is it I sense at your mention of so many foreign rogues infesting Spain? Do they pose a menace to you? To your family? I sincerely hope not. To contemplate a future in a land where the very earth trembles in fear and uncertainty is not my idea of a place to raise a family and build a dynasty. Forgive my bold, audacious manner. I was raised to be frank. It is part of my female nature to be filled with apprehension at your political doings in Madrid. Usually I admit to a bravery seldom found in women of my age.

Please extend my felicitations and those of my family to yours and especially to Don Diego, to whom I owe a debt of gratitude for generously recollecting a fourteen-year-old girl.

Enclosed are several photographs of me. One on my stallion, Chaco, taken at our hacienda in the pampas, is for your father. The others, taken on my eighteenth birthday, are for you. Affectionately, your *prometida*,

Victoria Valdez

So began the love affair between Victoria Valdez and Francisco de la Varga. For the next three months, Victoria lived only for the mail. She wrote Francisco a letter each day, often two, in case a ship sunk or the mails were lost. Victoria wanted Francisco to be reminded of her every moment of every day, just as she lived, breathed, and dreamed of him.

Gone were the demons tempting her rebellious nature. She embraced her family with dutiful devotion. One evening at dinner shortly before Don Verono left for Seville to bind the marriage contract with Francisco's father, Don Diego de la Varga, her father expressed his relief at her recent awakening. He upbraided her past disregard for her parents' feelings. "You wounded us deeply, Victoria. Remember this now and for all time. A wound either kills or is cured and forgotten. But a wound between blood will bleed forever because it pierces the heart. Never again alienate yourself from family because *you* cannot submit. Obedience forms the basis for knowledge and knowledge paves the way to a richer life."

"Father!" she remonstrated in wide-eyed innocence. "From

whence come those strange ideas? Haven't I always obeyed your word without question?"

Don Verono blinked astonished black eyes, choked on a morsel of spiced apple dessert, and swiftly reached for his wine to clear his throat. The distinguished man of noble grace, with a gray mane and muttonchop whiskers, caught his wife's bemused, knowing look.

"Please, Father, don't hold me in contempt." Victoria spoke in an alien, controlled voice. "It isn't easy for the young to understand the older generation's ways. So many complexities of tradition, never fully explained to me; how do I grasp them? Perhaps before you leave for Spain you will instruct *Doña* Teresa to teach me all I must know before I prepare for the nuptials. Now if you'll excuse me, I must keep an appointment with *Doña* Clemencia."

"The *bruja*? Are you mad? Why do you stoop to the superstititons of peasants?"

"Purely diversion, Father. Dissolve your displeasure. A lonely woman must do something for amusement when a vast ocean separates her from her fiancé." She excused herself, assured them her *dueña* would accompany her, kissed both parents, and departed in a flurry of excitement.

"If I live forever, *querida* Veronica, I shall never understand that girl," Don Verono said to his wife, a statuesque American beauty, the image of Victoria.

Veronica smiled patiently, sipped her Manzanilla delicately. "You are not so old, my dear, not to recognize love? Can you not see your daughter pines for her betrothed?"

The don's eyes widened in astonishment. "*Por cierto y por verdad*? Really and truly?" He felt his impatience subside.

Veronica Miles Carter Valdez, heiress to the Carter Meatpacking millions, lifted dancing emerald eyes flashing contentment. "*Despues de la lluvia sale el sol*. After the clouds the sun shines."

"*Por Dios*! At last!" he muttered, heaving a relieved sigh.

"Bear in mind, *querido mio*, there are no roses without thorns."

It was almost midnight. The fragrance of orange and lemon blossoms hung like a veil over the exclusive residential section of Buenos Aires. As the Valdez carriage and four horses moved out of the area, hardly a sound emanated from the grilled doors and courtyards of the great houses, for most were asleep. Along

darkened city streets the calls of a watchman echoed the hour.
The moon was riding high in the sky. Lamplighters had long
since gone home.

Victoria's senses pulsed deliriously like a pounding surf in her
ears. Soon she would *know* her and Francisco's future. Had her
father made the right decision in contracting their marriage? Not
that she harbored doubts now that she and Paco proved so *right*
for each other. But it wouldn't hurt to be certain—would it?
Besides, the *bruja* might give her a hint or two to help preserve
this love she felt for Paco. How could anything be wrong
between two people who fell into perfect harmony through written words?

The driver eased the carriage through twisting streets in the
shabby part of the city. Low ramshackle houses leaned on curves
and corners. Shuttered houses were refuges for strange, unfriendly neighbors, *Doña* Teresa told her, grimacing. There were
no lights at all. Here the moon formed grotesque shadows on
narrow spaces between hunched buildings.

"I tell you, let us return home. This is a place for dark
purposes, silent and mysterious goings-on," *Doña* Teresa
cautioned. "Why do I let you talk me into such things? Why?
The night breeds danger." She retreated in her seat.

"Stop it! Stop croaking like a frog. You're trying to frighten
me and it won't work," Victoria scolded harshly.

The carriage pulled to a stop before a wretched house. The
driver peered below him through a hole. "Is that it, *Doña*
Teresa?" The dueña peered out through the window, nodding.

They got out of the carriage, moved toward a dark alcove
draped with a shredded, filthy curtain through which the vaguest
hint of light was visible. A hoarse, grating voice seared by age
and brandy cried out, "What evil brings you here?"

Doña Teresa was all for leaving at once. "Stop this nonsense,"
Victoria remonstrated. She called out, "Is this—are you *Doña*
Clemencia?"

"*Pase adelanteo*! Enter!"

The women walked hesitantly through the opening, moved
along the dark, dank hallway overrun by rats, dogs, cats, spiders,
and other nocturnal creatures. They entered a shabby room,
where a hag sat rigidly before a broken table, her features
indistinct in the flickering candle glow. She was smoking mari-
juana or something equally foul-smelling. Victoria, on her signal,

sat in the small chair opposite her. *Doña* Teresa swiftly retreated to a corner, barely visible in the dark shadows.

The *bruja* lighted two small earthen pots filled with herbs. Instantly black smoke spiraled upward from them. The *bruja* searched her client's upturned palms, tracing lines, mumbling incoherent incantations. This strange creature, the subject of many awesome tales and superstitions, lit another candle, staring at Victoria's hands. Victoria leaned closer, wondering what it was the woman saw that disturbed her. Now she raised the candle, peered ominously at the young woman's aristocratic features, wide blue eyes, and hair of fire. Victoria was not prepared for what followed.

"You, woman, are the daughter of Satan. You are not a vestal virgin. Prepare yourself for a life of woe, for you are tempted to love a man who will abandon you to Lucifer himself."

Victoria, unprepared and unwilling to hear such words, drew herself up imperiously. Squinting her eyes in the dim glow, she searched the *bruja's* inscrutable features. It was an ugly face deeply lined like a contour map, deeply lined and abominable. Shivers played along her spine. *Go, Victoria! Go while you can!* Suddenly helpless, unable to move, something beyond her will kept her frozen to the rickety chair.

"Is it truth you seek or fairy tales?" rasped the hag.

Intimidated, Victoria whispered, "Truth, *por favor*."

The *bruja* snorted, then, with a dignity that sat strangely upon her withered walnut face, speckled with hairy moles, held up protesting hands before her. "Go! I can tell you no more. Go from my house, you are enveloped in maledictions!"

Victoria, by now perplexed, incensed, and curious, demanded answers. She reached into her reticule, placed a substantial amount of silver on the table. Instantly the coins were swept off the rickety counter top.

"Go, I tell you. You are surrounded by the fires of Satan."

Doña Teresa sprang to Victoria's side, pulling her to the door. She cursed the *bruja*, rued the day she agreed to participate in this loathsome business. They argued in a mixture of Portuguese, Spanish, and Indian dialect. *Doña* Teresa let loose a string of curses that could boil water. The *bruja* recoiled, poured out a stream of her own contempt, and demanded them to leave her house at once.

The last words Victoria caught as they fled back along the same dark corridor into the night air were, *"The spirit is in the bottle; if not controlled he grows and grows until he overwhelms the one who lets him out, but to the one who masters him, he brings great rewards.''*

Victoria understood none of this—nothing at all.

On the ride home, the *dueña* was strangely silent, mulling over the *bruja's* words. ''She was honest, at least. Deceit comes with difficulty to the *bruja.*''

By now the feisty daughter of Don Verono Valdez was furious. ''There is a great difference between honesty and those hallucinations she dreams up with the assistance of peyote!'' she snapped, taking personal umbrage that the *bruja* had dared speak to her in such a demeaning fashion.

Doña Teresa wisely held her own counsel. She had no intentions of imparting to Victoria the essence of the *bruja's* words. A prophecy of enormous malignity is what *Doña* Clemencia had read in Victoria's hands. *Heartbreak, sorrow, violence, and fires!* Fires meant the subject was surrounded by numerous deaths. That all who moved within her earthly sphere would be despoiled by powers greater than Satan's wrath. For certainly Victoria bore the mark of death. Three crescents in a row at the base of her thumb showed that she was born afflicted by the planet's influences. She was marked by destiny.

Doña Teresa shuddered, wondering if she should confide in the *Señora* Valdez. What was the good of it? What purpose could be served? She would merely shrug it off. The Norteamericanos did not believe in seers, *brujas.*

Por Dios! Better she keep an eye on her charge, no, better yet, both eyes would be needed for so exacting a chore.

BOOK TWO

THE END OF A DYNASTY

Chapter Eight

MADRID, SPAIN
October 30, 1920

The madness commenced at dawn. Intermittent rifle fire, exploding hand grenades, sporadic gunfire from handguns created a
drifting pall of smoke over the city. Zealots hurled bombs
indiscriminately, razing buildings to the ground, maiming and
wounding people. Terrorists banding together crept forward in a
phalanx of power bent upon total destruction.

By early morning the warren of twisting alleys fanning
out from the Puerta del Sol was packed with revolutionaries,
who had rendered the Calle del Alcala impassable. Bombs hurled
at the buildings embracing the deeper curve of the half-
moon-shaped plaza exploded, raining glass shards and crushed
concrete.

The federal buildings, clustered around a semicircle of graceful trees on an indolent parkway, trembled against the weight of
thousands of insurgents. Government officials, their faces glued
to the windows, mopped sweat from their brows. A Minister of
the Interior, recuperating from an assassination attempt, sniffed
the scent of death and destruction hovering over Madrid. He felt
powerless to circumvent the tidal wave of revolution. The Workers'
Union had won! The minister called his aides back to the conference table. "I called for an emergency session of the Grand
Council for this day at noon. Antonio Vasquez has won his

123

opportunity to sit at the drawing board and bargain with the council.''

Outside, violence and strikes were the order of the day. Placards, banners, signs, all protesting unfair labor practices, hung in doorways, windows, shop fronts, and draped decorously from the wrought-iron balconies of the Hotel Paris, facing the plaza. From these balconies, curious onlookers jammed tightly together; correspondents from London and Paris, eager for a story, enthusiastic tourists with box cameras, college students lured by the excitement spreading through Europe, self-styled soldiers of fortune, spies, counterspies—all had flocked to Madrid hoping for that ultimate thrill—a real battle. Less courageous souls huddled behind shuttered windows, terrified at what amounted to civil war. Thundering loudly below them, ceaseless chants promoted mass hysteria.

"Free the people! Free the people! Down with oppressors! Cut out their hearts as they have cut out our souls! There shall be no more rich—no more poor—no more masters! Only workers in a workers' state!"

At eight-thirty A.M. the *guardia de civil*, shocked by the assault upon Madrid, frantically deputized hundreds of men and called for help from neighboring cities. Within the hour the new recruits vanished. Cut telephone wires had isolated Madrid from the rest of Spain.

Lieutenant Lazaro Fuentes, moving back and forth between the men sandbagging the federal facilities, frowned, preoccupied with events of the past nine months. An unknown, nameless, faceless army of men became apparitions to the military police. How do you kill specters, the *guardia* officers wondered. Do you shoot a specter through the heart? Slash off its spectral head, take it by its spectral throat and cut off its spectral neck? No. You scoff and minimize each incident, precisely what the *guardia* had done publicly all this time.

Wires of confirmation did not arrive from Seville . . . Cordoba maintained a silence . . . Granada, Zaragoza, and Valencia offered no support. . . . Fuentes brooded. To further frustrate the *guardia's* efforts at tight containment, the Minister of the Interior chose to enforce his show of command by calling an emergency session of the Grand Council! He had dared summon to Madrid every remaining millionaire land baron, industrialist, and politician of the old social order—targets of assassination all!

The Workers' Union officials gave them until midnight on this All Saints' Eve to negotiate terms or a general strike would cripple every factory in Spain. Luring the land barons into a hotbed of revolution! What gross stupidity! Taking unnecessary chances with their lives doubled the *guardia's* workload. Why hadn't they had the sense to convene in secret away from Madrid?

Fools! Colossal imbeciles! They deserved the fate awaiting them.

Fuentes moved back and forth along the barricades, testing the sandbags, approving or disapproving the work as he saw fit. He would never understand Antonio Vasquez. Why the need to risk countless lives when the outcome of this day had been foreseen? Only one man knew the outcome of this risky business—Antonio Vasquez! And Vasquez had shrewdly connived to move all the queen's men into position.

The queen would be checked! Why jeopardize the lives of those who might prove useful to them in the new order of things?

Francisco de la Varga yawned, awakened moments ago by sounds of gunfire. Was he dreaming? He felt the quivering body of Victoria Valdez moving closer to him on the bed, her arms entwined about his neck and shoulders, her hair, the color of burnished fire, spilling across his bare chest. Pleasurable chills shuddered through him. Memory returned, bringing life to his flaccid groin. His hand groped under the sheet, caressing his erection. He loved the feeling of tumescence. It provided him with a sense of inner power and masculinity.

They were together in Victoria's suite at the Hotel Paris. Wasn't it marvelous how, *after* two solid weeks of resisting her, *she* had finally seduced him? He smiled inwardly. How admirably he had kept his passions in check like a pious prelate. Last night before the fireplace . . . Francisco sighed contentedly.

Outside death preened its feathers in preparation for the Dance of Death soon to parade through Madrid streets, yet they had wined, dined, exchanged smoldering looks, and made love as if nothing counted beyond the moment. The message in Victoria's eyes, explicit, his momentary shock melted into infinite amusement as she postured about as a worldly courtesan. Their love turned torrid vis-à-vis the mails, but how it bloomed the instant they met! Francisco smiled in recollection. And last night . . . This fireball of unbridled passion would settle for nothing short of flaming ardor and lust-filled nights. Last night he'd leveled his hazel eyes on her coolly, assessing her motives. Unable to conceal his amusement, he chidingly called her an Argentine *bruja*, a witch conjuring up a romantic brew. How could he know why her viridian eyes clouded over and became distant for a brief moment. He tried to make her smile.

"So you intend to seduce me, *querida*?" he had chided her.

"I left Argentina against parental orders to come to Madrid. Unless I know in advance that we are compatible, I refuse to marry you."

"And break the hearts of two old friends who planned this matrimonial coup?" he taunted. "Plenty of time for seduction *after* the nuptials, *mi amor*." He kissed her as a brother might kiss an impetuous sister. Victoria, seizing the opportunity, kissed him wantonly, leaving them both breathless. Eyeing her askance, as life stirred in his loins, he felt a trace of mild censure in his voice. "This is the innocent virgin I will marry? A quiet, sedate woman of refinement chosen to bear the de la Varga heirs?" His smile was indulgent.

Actually he was marvelously attracted to this contumacious wench—they were much alike—but his recent involvement with Antonio Vasquez had left him little time to court her properly. Victoria had arrived in Spain at an inopportune time, just as this business with Vasquez began perking to a boil.

Last night, Victoria refused to be mollified. "It's now, Paco, or I return to Buenos Aires at once. Wild horses will not transport me here again!" Storming about the sitting room, opening wardrobes, tugging at steamer trunks, flinging clothing about wildly she ranted, "I shall leave this world of supercilious jackasses! What appreciation do you have of a real woman? You wouldn't know what to do with one if your life depended on it!"

Victoria had stopped short, her face blushing a bright crimson. Francisco had no way of knowing these were not Victoria's words but the words of a stranger she'd met in Madrid, a man who had vilified Francisco to her.

Something disturbed Victoria. Francisco saw it in her expression as she lowered her eyes and turned from him, fussing with a flower in a vase. In moments she had nervously stripped the petals from a rose.

Francisco, a high-born gentleman, showed mild annoyance. Allowing his future wife to become a target of gossip was unthinkable. True, the supervision of *Doña* Teresa had afforded them little privacy. Their communication had been limited to fragments of speech, deep looks, smoldering moments of silence, and this had frustrated the young lovers. But at that precise moment, Francisco was angry.

"You go too far, *querida*. When you allude with vitriol to my masculinity, my desire to repudiate your attack grows as consuming as my desire for you." He had placed his champagne glass on the table, leveled hot eyes on her, and, moving slowly across the room to her side, drew her into his arms, kissed her, gently at first, then with increased fervor until their hearts beat deliriously. Several breathless moments later, he held her shoulders, lifted her flushed face to his, and peered into her eyes.

"I admire your confidence, *querida*," he said softly. "You know exactly what you want and have every intention of getting it. But the next time you make such bold statements, I promise I shall turn you over my lap and do what your father should have done long ago. Now if my part in the melodrama sketched clearly in your mind is to lie back and appreciate you, so be it."

An hour later miracles were in the works; forgotten was the pressing business, forgotten was Antonio Vasquez and *Los Desheredados*, the Brotherhood to whom he'd sworn a blood oath.

He began to mutter phrases that permeated the entire evening. "Incredible. Simply incredible."

Shy, awkward at the outset, Francisco was thrilled by her urgency and soon vented his hedonistic bent. *God Almighty, how he loved her*!

Together they had subordinated all thought, permitting only the mysterious secrets of sexuality to quiver through them. As they joined together, responding rhythmically to the other with natural simplicity, Victoria confessed to experiencing womanhood in a way she would cherish the rest of her life.

Francisco came alive for the first time in a year; he told her so. The revolution, the rigors of creating a new Spain, had left him little energy to appreciate the fire-haired vixen. But now he forgot politics in the warm willingness of her sweet-scented body; he had gained new life. Firm inviting breasts had excited him to new dimensions of pleasure. Her soft flesh and hair of dancing fire aglow in the candlelight gave rise to incredible excitement in him. Victoria was all eagerness, surging against him in erotic frenzy. They kissed deeply, her body jerking spasmodically when he touched her secret places. She was alive, burning with passión. Ecstatic sighs, deep, low in her throat, her perfumed scents, everything about her fired Francisco's passion. He seemed unable to get enough of her. When he entered her willing, well-primed body again, she gasped, shuddering against him, then in a powerful pelvic thrust locked her satiny legs around his waist. The explosions were galvanic. When he was brought to climax, they were fused together so fiercely that falling away from each other was impossible for several moments. Once they disengaged, they shuddered erotically and clung together, loath to part.

No matter how rigid Francisco's morals had been in the past, his resolve had disintegrated. This creature from Argentina, in demanding his physical love, had emerged victorious last night, but this morning he wore the laurel wreath of contentment.

Francisco was fully awake now. He shook Victoria gently. "Victoria, listen! Am I dreaming? Are those real guns? Mother of Christ! They *are* real," he shouted. "It's happening!" He sniffed the air. Who could mistake the smell of cordite wafting through the open French doors to the balcony?

A loud rap at the door brought reality into sharper focus. He cursed aloud. Damned champagne always left him fuzzy-headed. He cocked his head, listening intently. Two short raps were followed by a succession of short raps. *The signal!*

Bolting from the bed, he leaped to the door shouting hoarsely, "All right, *vengo, por Dios!*" and dashed for the balcony, one foot inside his trouser leg, tugging them on as he hopped, and stumbled.

He stood rooted to the spot on the iron balcony, peering down at the teeming crowd of revolutionaries in the streets. Secret thrills shot through him. What an extraordinary sight! *Vasquez had won! The power of one man had moved thousands into action!* Por Dios! *The man was incredible.*

The action in the streets stirred him into action. *Damn!* Victoria's seduction had kept him from being with Antonio when it started! He had to leave, to be a part of the new Spain, the culmination of months of hard work.

Back inside, Francisco grabbed the remains of his clothing; he finished dressing amid effusive apologies, thin protestations directed to the petulant Victoria. He promised to pick up where they left off.

"If you live long enough!" she retorted icily. Ignoring both the remark and the edge to her voice, he kissed her, slipped into his jacket, and heard her mutter something about *another* woman.

"What utter absurdity, *querida*. This is not the time to prove the extent of my love for you. We shall devote the rest of our lives to that. Be sweet. Be understanding in these, my final days of dedication to Spain. It is nearly ended."

Victoria watched him leave. Quickly she reached for her silk dressing gown, slipped into it, and dashed across the room to the balcony. She leaned over the balustrade, breathlessly waiting for her lover to appear through the entrance below. She hardly looked at the chaos in the streets. How could she, when her heart played havoc with her senses?

Stunned observers positioned in nearby balconies stared lecherously at Victoria. She picked out Francisco as he flew out the hotel doors and was swallowed up by the mass of humanity. Victoria shouted, waved frantically to no avail; the din of the horde drowned out her voice.

Damn the revolution! Damn the wrong timing! Damn it all!

Victoria flashed briefly on the turbulence below, unmoved by any of it. Mentally assessing the consequences of her rash exodus from Buenos Aires a week *after* her father's departure from Spain, she flushed with the guilt of her actions.

Ay de mi! If her father *knew* she was in Madrid . . . that she had seduced her betrothed before the nuptials? *Por Dios!* She dared not contemplate his fury. At this very moment Don Verono was in Seville finalizing the marriage contract and she had already consummated it!

Victoria's mother had left for Chicago to attend the bedside of her dying father, Miles Carter. Victoria had booked passage and with her *dueña* left for Madrid and Paco. She was worried to death over changes in his recent correspondence. Francisco's had extolled the virtues of a new revolutionary political climate in Spain. His fanaticism had created in her mind the image of an exciting, romantic swashbuckling conquistador. Each letter had swelled him to heroic proportions. He was El Cid, Don Juan, all heroes of history, a knight in shining armor on a dazzling legendary white charger. His letters had swept her off her feet. For weeks Victoria had conspired to reach Madrid and seduce her fiancé. No hideaways with mistresses for her husband's pleasure would mar the main *casa* on Victoria Valdez's hacienda! She told herself if she and Francisco proved uncongenial, what better place than romantic Spain to find the *right* lover?

Now she was here, terribly in love and frustrated! Something disturbed Victoria. A disquieting, intangible force destined to drive them apart had emerged. Oh, it was nothing you could point to and see with your eyes. A secret side to her beloved Paco, implied by his clandestine behavior, one he refused to discuss, had emerged almost at once. Victoria's fanciful, idealistic, romantic nature had turned it to a *casus belli*. She simply couldn't cope!

Oh, what jealousies she conjured up! Images of a bevy of concubines hidden in various hamlets in and about Madrid flashed in her mind. Francisco, *too* handsome, *too* affluent and passionate a man, must have amassed a stable of *putas* willing to spread their legs for him, devour his manhood at the flick of an eye.

Confronted boldly with Victoria's capricious hypothesis, Francisco had good-naturedly denied the allegations. She quickly countered, "Why then do you cut your visits with me short, denying me the love and attention I need?"

He had laughed and playfully admonished her. "What is this display of petulance, my Argentine beauty? I should be seducing you, not the other way around. Now, be sweet and patient."

Last night proved they were simply marvelous for one another, hadn't it? She grinned at the memory of the guileful seduction and, tossing her tousled fiery curls off her face, contemptuous of the disorder in the streets, Victoria, for the first time noticed the admiring bystanders gaping at her.

Her firm breasts with nipples ready to burst through the sheer bodice of her silk wrap, her swirling cascades of coiling copper curls falling in wild disarray, crowning her beauty and framing her pale skin, flawless as a Raphael painting, she was voluptuous womanhood at its most appealing. Whistles, catcalls, smacking kisses, loud as pistol shots, turned her cheeks crimson, firing her electric eyes.

Victoria bristled angrily. The audacity of a man dressed in alpine garb, actually staring at her through long glasses, incensed her. She stared back haughtily until the rogue had the decency to lower the glasses. Adding insult to injury, he bowed salaciously and tipped that silly alpine hat to her. Communicating her displeasure, she bridled, stalked inside, annoyed at the message in his eyes, and slammed the French doors with a loud bang.

Insufferable ass! Impudent cad! How dare he?

She paced the floor, furious at herself. *What do you expect when you comport yourself like a low-class whore lusting after Francisco?*

A litany of self-doubt exploded from her lips, followed by a string of blistering curses. She lit a cigarette—a recently acquired habit—paced the floor, puffing with marked agitation, her brain roiling with scorching thoughts. Nothing was going right. *Doña* Teresa was being difficult, insisting on returning to Buenos Aires. The temper of the times frightened her. She harked back to the *bruja's* prophecy. This craziness of revolution demanded too much of Francisco. She could compete against any woman, but how do you compete against the biggest of all whores—revolution? If she had any modicum of sense, she'd pack and leave before her father discovered her presence in Madrid. But when had *sense* entered in affairs of the heart? *Paco! Paco! If only I didn't love you so much!*

Victoria poured a hot bath. *That* man, the one with binoculars, incensed her. How dare he ogle her with obvious lust? Sprinkling bath crystals into the water, she paused, frowning in thought.

Something about him . . . From where did she recall him? His clothing stood out among other men in Madrid like a bull's penis in heat; you couldn't ignore it for long. *Ay de mi!* A pox on him! A pox on revolution! A pox on Spain!

She stepped into the tub, immersing herself, luxuriating, wondering if she had given *Doña* Teresa too many sleeping powders last night? She was still sound asleep. It was almost ten o'clock.

Sponging herself, Victoria gave a start. She *remembered* where and when she had encountered the alpine *burro!* She tensed, the scene vivid in mind.

Two weeks ago Victoria was quarreling with her *dueña*. That soothsayer and part-time psychic, a crochety woman in her fifties who loathed Spain and wanted to return to Argentina, had suddenly realized Victoria's intention to seduce Francisco. That solid proponent of Victorian morals had raved and ranted all morning. "Your flagrant behavior must cease! All Madrid speculates on your comportment, Victoria! Have you no self-respect? No pride."

Victoria countered hotly, "None at all, you old warthog! I told you my intentions, so stop snapping at me with false indignation."

"I only know that I left Buenos Aires with a pure and innocent virgin in my charge. God only knows what I shall deliver to

Don Francisco on his wedding day!'' the older woman had wailed.

Victoria needed no reminders; she knew her faults better than anyone; she needed time to work them out. She loathed defending her actions to anyone on the basis of morality. Furious, Victoria had stormed out of the hotel suite, descended the spiral staircase to the lobby with deliberate aplomb, inescapably drawing admiring eyes. She stood out like a precious jewel in her divine emerald-green velvet costume suit and hat. Men and women alike studied the cut of her clothing, her grace of movement, as she strolled so casually about the crowded lobby in these troubled times.

Aware of the admiring glances, she feigned indifference and, sauntering beyond the desk, peered through the large lead glass window at the snappily dressed *Guardia de Civil* in their incredibly bizarre *monteras*, black patent-leather caps designed like those worn by matadors in the bullring, milling in and about the swarming people.

Inclined to a shopping spree, Victoria strode boldly out the hotel doors into the dazzling sunlight, and, opening her parasol entered the pedestrian flow. What followed had made so curious an imprint on Victoria's mind she could not imagine how she had forgotten the episode and the man. Or had she blocked both from mind?

A fall sun fanned brightly overhead, sending shafts of light through verdant trees sprawled lazily around the Plaza of the Puerta del Sol. Animated people gathered in busy clusters, seemingly occupied in life-or-death issues. Victoria breezily snaked through swollen crowds, unalarmed at the skirmishes erupting in the square. Quick thinking *Guardia* soldiers containing most brawlers, infuriating many bystanders, gave rise to a savage outburst inches from where she walked. Instantly tussled, shoved, pushed by a crazed few and flung hard up against a building, Victoria, distraught at the sudden peril she faced, felt strong, steadying hands on her, one about her waist, the other guiding her by the arm to an alcove of safety.

She spent several harrowing moments fending off further pummeling, catching periodic glimpses of her benefactor. A young man with compelling colorless eyes, dressed in alpine clothing, stared boldly at her as if he couldn't get enough of her. Disquieted by the secret message contained in his glance, color rushed to her cheeks.

"Permit me, *señora*." He spoke a highly accented Spanish.

"*Señorita*," she corrected adamantly, accepting the outthrust reticule he retrieved from the sidewalk, where it had fallen from her hands. "*Señorita* Valdez, from Argentina. I'm in residence here at the Paris. Is it always so hectic in Madrid? The scent of revolution hangs heavy in the air." Unnerved by this man, Victoria purposely volunteered information to correct the misconception evident in his eyes. She was, after all, without chaperone. She barely heard him introduce himself.

"Antonio Vasquez, at your service. I know who you are." He bowed slightly with an insufferable self-assurance that irked her.

"It is only fitting I thank you for your chivalry, Señor Vasquez. My fiancé will reward your gallant behavior."

"Stay clear of the streets," he commanded authoritatively. "Your class of people—dressed the way you do—invite dangerous confrontations in these troubled times!"

Victoria, fascinated by the near-colorless eyes, stiffened. "How do you know me, *señor*? We have not met socially."

"That's true. I am a friend of Francisco de la Varga. I have seen you together. Your photographs grace all the newspapers. Your coming nuptials are the talk of Madrid."

What Victoria didn't know and had no way of exploring was the extent of his longing for her. From the moment Antonio Vasquez set eyes upon her he had lusted after her. In his mind, she formed a composite that epitomized woman. Dreams of possessing Victoria Valdez became so unbearable he had contrived ways of meeting her away from Francisco. Earlier he sighted her leaving the Paris. In moments he had incited a minor skirmish in order to display his gallantry. Now, her presence, her perfume, intoxicated him, stirred deeply rooted passion in him.

Victoria, without a glimmering of his intentions, held herself aloof. Vasquez's feelings, masked by a showy, superficial cleverness, came to light soon enough.

"Forgive the bold candor of a man who knows what he wants and will move the earth to get it. I love a spirited woman with determination and courage. You, *querida*, possess all the qualities I need, desire, and admire in a woman," he gushed.

"*Señor*! You are too presumptuous!" she snapped looking at those near-colorless eyes and trying not to stare.

"I make no apologies for my presumption. I had to make myself known to you if only to tell you you do not belong with

Francisco. He is not man enough for a woman of your spirit and ambition."

Victoria sputtered indignantly. "And you *are*, I suppose!"

"I intend to fight for you if it means stealing you from under de la Varga's nose."

"Y-you, y-you, brazen cad!" she sputtered in umbrage. "You call yourself Paco's friend?" She lifted a gloved hand to strike his face; it was caught in midair, held tightly, drawn slowly to his lips. Kissing it, his eyes conveyed disturbing messages. She strained against him, but the crowd pressing closer made it impossible for her to flee. Vasquez drew her closer, kissed her outraged lips. Aghast, she savagely pulled away from him, wiped the burning imprint of his lips from hers as if they were contaminated.

"I will not apologize for taking from you what will be mine."

Victoria turned in a huff, kicked a few shins, elbowed her way, and furiously snaked through the crowd with such haughty propulsion the crowds parted to make room for her. She ran through the lobby doors into the hotel, scurried up the spiral staircase, and took the caged lift to the third floor. She entered, slamming the doors hard, locking them, fully unnerved. She moved to the sideboard, poured herself a glass of sherry, gulped it down, forcing his taunting image and mocking laughter from mind.

Impudent bastard! How dare he take such liberties? If Francisco got hold of this odious jackal he'd whip the brute within an inch of his life!

Victoria stepped from her bath, dried herself off, spraying cologne and talcum all over her body. Feeling tarnished, violated by Vasquez's touch, her loathing for him, Spain, and the fermenting insanity of anarchy became intolerable. Why she had later failed to mention the cad to Paco puzzled and disturbed her. It was not her nature and inclination to conceal her wrath, yet something had prevented the unveiling of her emotions in any confrontation. Vasquez's audacious manner had aroused a maddening curiosity, which instinct forced her to conceal.

Vasquez's had been the face she'd seen several times in partial shadow when she and Paco had dined out, ambled about the plaza or cantered in the park. And recently at the bull fights. Always concealed behind a veil of mystery.

It was eleven A.M. when Victoria finished dressing. Outside,

Madrid was in revolution, inside her hotel suite madness was about to erupt. It began with a loud knock on the door. The double doors burst open with a loud crashing sound. Victoria glanced up as a procession of porters carried a profusion of magnificent flowers, gaily adorned baskets, elaborate porcelain vases containing white roses, and marked with enormous satin bows with notes and cards tucked into each arrangement.

Depositing the items in every nook and cranny, before the stupefied Victoria and her *dueña*, they filed out the door, leaving the occupants gazing about in wide-eyed wonder.

Victoria flitted from basket to vase, picking off the cards and notes. Reading them, she dismayed. They were from Antonio Vasquez! It was his doing. The notes alluded to his chivalrous nature.

"Forgive me, *querida*," Victoria read, "I apologize for not campaigning more vigorously for your affections. I must blame my pressing duties for depriving me of the precious time needed to pursue your love. Will you forgive the dilemma of a wildly beating heart that has fallen madly in love with you? Do not, I implore you, commit yourself to de la Varga. Delay your wedding plans until I, a *real* man, can lay the earth, moon, sun, and stars at your feet. My problems are only temporary. Shortly my affluence will increase beyond wildest dreams. *Querida, por favor*, support my requests until I can claim you as my beloved spouse?"

Victoria read all the notes; they said the same thing with slight alterations. She ripped them to shreds and tossed them into the fireplace. Before she embroiled herself in a network of lies and deceptions with Francisco, she quickly had the flowers sent to local hospitals. Summoning *Doña* Teresa from the adjoining suite, she sent orders to the concierge to refuse flowers from anyone except Don Francisco de la Varga.

Victoria threw herself on the sofa, her conscience tearing at her. Why suddenly did she feel disloyal to Francisco?

Outside on this All Saint's Day, revolution and demons were at work. Only the revolution was on Francisco's mind. But, this Vasquez had found the means to deliver a garden! Imagine.

Shortly before noon twenty imperturbable millionaires whose money controlled Spain rode in a cortege toward the Federal Building to keep their appointment with the Minister of the Interior.

The Calle de Alcala was jammed with British Daimlers, American Welch touring cars, German Benz, and a few horse-pulled carriages. Crack-shot bodyguards, well armed, tense, and riding shotgun for their *patrons*, controlled their itching, their eyes searching the hordes for the sight of any obstructor who dared interfere in their duties. These men would not hesitate to kill in the line of duty.

Don Verono Valdez, dressed elegantly in the style of an Argentine nobleman—black velvet suit, short jacket, white silk shirt, and flat-crowned sombrero *Cordobes*—spun the thickly rawled silver spurs over his hand-crafted leather boots, nervously avoiding Don Diego de la Varga's troubled countenance. The Argentine was wary, silent at the dissenters' strength, his outrage intensified at the conspicuous absence of federal troops. Taking umbrage at the insurrectionists and their damnable uprising at so inopportune a time, he cursed his own stupidity.

Only that morning before dawn, instinct had urged him to return to Argentina. Something he could neither identify nor isolate was terribly wrong. Furious at his future son-in-law, Francisco—the scoundrel had refused to confer with him in Seville—he'd been forced to make this trip against his better judgment. About to transfer to the young stallion his most treasured possession, his beloved Victoria, in addition to an enormous fortune, the fool had been hard put to find time for him! What manner of man was Francisco? Certainly he was not cut from the same fabric that distinguished Don Diego from his fellowman. *Damn the devil*!

Victoria needed a strong, steadying influence. Second thoughts solidified behind a bland mask. Was Francisco right for her? Don Verono needed reassurance of Francisco's inner strength, for soon the combined Valdez–de la Varga wealth would rest in his hands. Could he meet the test?

Don Diego, introverted, seated at the Argentine's right stared vigilantly at the compressed humanity at either side of the *avenida*, observing their loathing, staring eyes follow the motorcade to the Federal Building.

A loud rumble, followed by a barrage of gunshots, too close for comfort, startled the car's occupants. From the leering, twisted lips of the hordes came imprecations, seething shouts of hatred and jeering. Sticks and stones hummed overhead; bullets sang over their heads. The mob surged forward, rocked the automobiles precariously. The stench of cordite hung over the plaza.

Don Valdez exploded. "Sainted Christ! This is no place for Victoria!"

Don Diego, dressed less flamboyantly than his guest, wore his snow-white hair with leonine grandeur. He concealed his innermost fears discreetly but couldn't subdue them.

Faces, God those leering faces that once expressed serenity, simple, ingenuous happiness, affection and contentment! How easily human emotions convert benevolence into primordial visages. He saw in the crowded countenances the viciousness of mankind—hatred, treachery, degradation, ingratitude, and savagery; a spreading poison converted them into brute force. The venom, no overnight phenomenon, as the Minister of the Interior naively suggested, was the diligent application of subtle propaganda transmitted to their minds by agent provocateurs.

Don Diego experienced a momentary repulsion and wild denial that he belonged to this species of weak men who must be led, who could not think for themselves and were easily persuaded into ignoble schemes. Flushed with mortification as his temper flared, he brought it under control.

How dare he sit in judgment of weak men? Francisco, his own son, had fallen into disrepute with the very weaklings he condemned! Ghastly thoughts like lines of fire raced across his mind. *Francisco*! Where will I find him? Where do I begin to look? If he accomplished nothing else this day, his son must be found and told the truth! He'd put it off for too long. Far too long!

Don Diego had not, would not confide his son's perfidy to Don Verono—his abhorrent involvement with the terrorists, *Los Desheredados*. The repercussions might jeopardize all he had strenuously worked for: the marriage between two formidable families. He tried to calm himself, subdue his qualms by patience, detachment.

Mother of Christ! How do you detach yourself from the seething humanity engulfing Madrid? Never had the people paid Don Diego such dishonor. *Never*! General Diego de la Varga had, in the past, ridden these streets in glory, praise and, veneration due to the hero of two wars. Now this?

The automobile lurched, jolted to a sudden halt stalling the engine. The driver, Matteus Montenegro attempted to kick off the engine. His young face, belied by premature baldness was barely visible behind a multi-colored beard.

Frustrated, he half-turned in his seat, one eye on the gun in his brother Pablo's hand. "It's sheer insanity to proceed, Excellency. We had best retreat."

"My brother is right, General." Pablo spoke ominously, both eyes on the unruly horde. "Look, murder breeds in the hearts of these animals. They lust for blood. I tell you, Excellencies, the bloodletting will be Vasquez's glory."

Don Diego gave the Moors a sharp hard look. Then, for no reason except to feel the security of a concealed pistol he lurched forward. A swift, hot gust of wind whooshed past the hidalgo's ear, sending this old warrior to the floorboard of the car. He grabbed hold of his companion, urged him to the floor. "*Maldito Dios*! An assassin's bullet missed us by a hair!"

Pablo, instantly alerted, shouted, "It was too close to be a miss! Don't wait for another to finish what the first failed to do."

Don Diego opened the rear door, nudged the Argentine into the streets. "We'll be safer among the crowds, *amigo*." To the Moors he shouted, "Find shelter. Meet me at the office of the ministry!"

Instantly the two older men were swallowed by the crowds.

The Moors studied the line of fire, fixing on a sniper's nest atop a graystone building next to the Hotel Paris; their perception was distorted slightly by the thickening haze of black gunsmoke. Matteus held his brother's steady gaze. Words between them were superfluous. A mystic telepathy moved between the brothers; each knew instinctively the other's thoughts. Pablo, gun in hand, leaped from the automobile and, snaking through the crowd, trailed the two noblemen at a safe distance. Pablo's skill as a bodyguard was honed to perfection; he would countenance no accidents befalling his beloved Diego de la Varga. *Pray Allah, most merciful of Gods, hear my supplication.*

The sniper's nest. Antonio Vasquez stripped two slovenly gun-men of all vestiges of pride. "Fools! Idiots! No orders were given to kill those two! *Los Desheredados* cannot afford the consequences of your insubordination, even if you parade it as stupidity!" He had planned the coup meticulously, training his men, measuring angles of speed, fire, and distance of the moving vehicles; planning who would die first, when and at whose hands. Twenty swiftly executed assassinations had gone down in the past twenty-four hours according to his strategy;

more were planned. He needed no trigger-happy, braying *burros* to abort prematurely what must be done with scrupulous precision.

Under lidded eyes, the embarrassed gunmen flushed hotly at the severity of the reprimand. What did they know of the complications of insurrection? They glared sullenly, avoiding Vasquez's eyes. Vasquez and his poker-faced gun-toting sentinels disappeared down the iron stairwell into the building.

Tunneling through the congested hordes, rudely pushed, shoved, pulled apart by the embattled crowd along the Calle de Alcala, Don Diego shouted to the Argentine. "Confine yourself to the Hotel Paris, *amigo*. Once the Grand Council business ends I will meet you there. *Cuidado*! Go! Move!"

Propelled savagely into the swelling masses, Don Diego was shoved against a building, forced in that moment to witness the shocking spectacle of Matteus hurtling through the air to his right. Behind them the Welch automobile, rocked by the mob, was overturned, set ablaze. Fire exploded into giant flames, licking upward. Don Diego recoiled in horror, his protestations unheeded by the leering crowd. Angry, distraught, gravely concerned over Matteus, he could see nothing of the young Moor.

Matteus, several yards ahead of the don, unable to move against the pressing vise hold of an angry mob, was forced to move in their direction. Confusion, disorder, and mayhem occurred with frightening rapidity all around them: It was difficult to concentrate on any one act of terror. Don Diego watched as the mob fell away from the burning auto, the heat so intense, hands were held up protectively over their faces. The car, flame-streaked, began to billow black smoke. Upraised fists, clenched hard, shook at the burning machine as if it were responsible for the people's woes.

Don Diego stared at the scene swimming before him as if he were viewing an imaginary vision. But, this was no vision! Snarling sounds from swollen savage throats demanded the blood of their enemies. Hands stretched up to him, curved, clawlike, ready to seize and annihilate him and the class Diego represented. He broke their hold on him and ran forward into the melee.

Propelled by the mob—with no control over his personal destination—for the next half hour, Diego discerned the unmistakable precision of a well-orchestrated ballet of violence. The average man could easily overlook the mechanics of the riot, but to this former military strategist, the earmarks of astute planning and expert manipulation of the crowd's emotions distinguished this *coup de theatre* from a spontaneous uprising.

The pandemonium escalated into unsupervised chaos. Screaming, persistent wailing, shouts, ear-splitting gunfire at close range dazed and sent Don Diego reeling into the arms of uncontrolled beasts. Who had moved them to such frenzied pitch of revolution? Who indeed?

Antonio Vasquez! Valgame Dios!

Pummeled by the mob, unable to extricate himself, Don Diego felt a sudden surge of change. The rioters fell away, moved as if by unseen forces. He stumbled, fell, and, scrambling to his feet, bolted forward, heading across the plaza through a break in the horde, unaware that Pablo, wielding a gun like a club had crushed a few skulls to liberate his beloved *patron*.

A dog leaped at him, fangs barred, jaws snapping ferociously, and was stopped in midair by a bullet. Erratic bursts of gunfire, coming from behind stacked sandbags at street corners and on rooftops, strafed the crowd, sending them scattering in all directions. Feverish, impassioned men with maniacal eyes rushed at the grandee, crashing into him, their wounds spilling blood on his fastidious attire.

Don Diego cursed Vasquez. He cursed the unbridled mob, the insurgents, and most of all he cursed the *Guardia de Civil*. Where for the love of Christ were those ineffective, uniformed dandies? *Where*? By the burning balls of Lucifer! Probably in hiding!

Glancing furtively for an avenue of escape and finding none, Don Diego halted abruptly, immobilized by what he saw.

Francisco! His son stood less than twenty feet away, at the center of rabble rousers, passing out inflammatory propaganda designed to further incite the mob into vocalizing their discontent. A rifle was slung over one shoulder, criss-crossed bandoliers over the other. *Francisco! No! No! It can't be!* But it was his son, in the flesh.

It was true, then, all of it? The rumors, snide remarks, glaring hostile looks from his contemporaries had spelled the truth? Here now, in the open, the unpalatable truth stared back at him.

The Spanish nobleman felt a sinking sensation at the pit of his stomach.

Francisco, his son, a radical! Association with men spreading venom in Spain was no longer conjecture, but truth!

Shattered, the grandee leaned heavily against the water fountain, steadying himself, mopping sweat from his brow. All reserves of hope were destroyed. The complexities of Paco's involvement in the reign of terror rushed to him with alarming reality. He had judiciously hired specialists to investigate the extent of his son's radical activities and involvement with *Los Desheredados*, to assuage the pain in his heart and diffuse the cruel rumors. He needed reassurance that the rumors were unfounded. The investigators, explicitly instructed to proceed cautiously, had employed the utmost discretion in their inquiries.

But Francisco *had not* used discretion! Instead he had paraded his political fanaticism, openly flaunting radical rhetoric for all to hear. Disgrace, for the first time in centuries, threatened to crush the house of de la Varga, pulverizing all hopes and ambitions he entertained for his only son. Now all that remained was the bitter taste of ashes in his mouth.

Where had he gone wrong? His firstborn, his only son, heir apparent to the de la Varga millions, had demonstrated repeated unwillingness to come to terms with his destiny.

Francisco, an exceptionally bright, highly complex student at Madrid University, had surpassed his father's expectations. Despite this, a wedge of darkness drove father and son apart in spirit, mind, and deed. In recent months the rift grew deeper, the hurt acute.

From early childhood, Paco, a driven soul, battled unseen forces that wrought havoc in his personal life. An undeniable restlessness of spirit prevailed throughout puberty. He grew into a distracted, willful scoundrel, demanding full autonomy in his life. Unfortunately the demands paved the way for rebellion and acceptance among antisocial forces with whom he felt kinship. Remonstrations, severe punishments, threats, pleadings, even whippings meant little to him. Priests, beseeched to help bring about a transformation in the lad, ultimately admitted defeat. Military schools, after two weeks, tossed the scoundrel out on his hind quarters. The outcome inevitably ended in his full autonomy.

Then . . . a miracle!

The metamorphosis. Was it possible? Two years of calm sobriety following his matriculation in law school brought scholarly achievements to Francisco, a revelation to his parents. It was inconceivable that Paco would ever revert to his previous ways. He was a man at long last! Alas! The period of calm proved only a prelude, masking deeply rooted emotions that ignited into his recent anarchistic affiliations with the Disinherited, *Los Desheredados*.

It took Don Diego but a moment to flash on the past, his eyes fixed on his son. Incredible! That Francisco de la Varga was an enemy of the state denied every principle for which the revered noble family stood. The ugly rumors six months ago had embarked him on covert investigation. At that moment, and even now, Don Diego swore an oath. His only son would not die for so worthless a cause as the mad-dog politics of Antonio Vasquez!

He faced the issue of his loins, shuddering at Francisco's wide-eyed appearance. If Victoria Valdez, due to arrive in Spain in December, saw him in such disarray, she'd bolt!

Sharp repudiation fired his eyes. He felt sick at the ignominy of his plight. One thing was certain—he could not permit Don Verono to see Francisco in so deplorable a state.

Francisco, fighting the throng, did not see his father immediately.

Pressing forward with renewed vigor, the don shoved, clawed, elbowed his way forward toward the slim-hipped, tousle-haired younger man, reining his wrath. Obstructed by a new wave of rioters, he pulled out his pistol, fired into the air, twice. Nothing. No one heeded him or his gun. A cannon would not impact on this mob.

A sudden break in the horde. He came closer, closer, and grabbed hold of Francisco's elbow with an iron grip. He shouted to be heard.

"Francisco! Francisco!"

Francisco's head jerked about, electric green eyes searching the immediate area. He craned his neck above the crowds, still searching, and trying as he did so to knock off the restraining grip on his arm, unaware that the hand was his father's until Don Diego, in a sudden outburst, grabbed the offensive pamphlets from his son's hands and flung them angrily into the air. Ready to clout the offender, Francisco stopped short in recognition.

The awkward moment passed. Embarrassed, like a child caught trying to pull off a prank, the young radical frenetically ran his fingers through his curly hair, his eyes on the fluttering pamphlets in the air about them. Then, out of habit, he embraced his father as if this pardoned him from all wrongdoings, and, making feeble attempts to retrieve the pamphlets, shouted against the din of gunfire and frenzied cries. Scooping the pamphlets off the ground, he resumed his litany. *"Comrades!* Awaken to this infamy. *Vive la Revolución*!"

"Francisco! Stop this foolishness. We must talk!"

"Not now, Father. There is much to be done! Comrades, stand up and be counted. The time has come—"

"We talk now!" Don Diego's blue-veined hands grasped his son's wrist, fingers of ice and steel tightening their grip. Their eyes locked. Francisco patiently but firmly disengaged his father's hand. Don Diego, not to be put off, repeated his efforts, tightening his hold. "You must hear the truth, my son!"

"Go home, Father. Madrid is too dangerous for you today. You will never understand me, nor I you. So to what purpose would dialogue between us serve? Go home, I beg you, sir. Leave Madrid! I tell you, return to Seville! Politics aside, I love you and do not want you hurt." Francisco averted his head, then as quickly jerked his attention to his father. "Why in damnation are you here in the first place?"

Grabbing at any straw, the don shouted, "Victoria will arrive shortly. Do you want her to see you like this? Don Verono is here in Madrid with me. Your discourtesy to him is unforgivable."

His words fell on deaf ears.

Acts of violence at all sides of them frustrated his efforts. Deafening screams shattered his eardrums. A helpless brute, felled nearby by bullets, dropped to the ground, was trampled on by maniacs and left to die. He grew fatigued.

The scene, horrendously graphic, became for de la Varga an insane ballet; apart one minute, thrown together the next, he fought with Herculean strength to hang on to his son, while all around them, with equal fervor, the intent players in this drama struggled to keep them apart.

The crowd changed direction; once again father and son faced each other. Grabbing hold of his son, abetted by the miraculous appearance of Pablo who prodded the young rebel with his shotgun, the stars in this drama took refuge in a sanctuary between the trunks of an ancient flowering almond and a bronze statue of a Miura bull.

"Listen to your father," Pablo growled with menace, "or taste the sting of my gun. "Be a man, not a puppet, Francisco!"

Francisco's eyes, narrowing, bore into the Moor's resolute black-sapphire eyes. He had known Pablo long enough to know the Moor never made idle threats.

"This is neither the time or place to discuss vital matters," said Diego, mopping the dripping sweat from his brow. "You force my hand. I implore you, take every precaution. Protect yourself or drown in the treacheries and deceits initiated by those in whom you've placed too much trust. Oh, Paco, dangers not revealed to you will destroy you and our family. You must neutralize the brewing storm clouds, the hazards to which you've exposed yourself. Do you understand? You repeatedly ignore my urgings to come home. You must learn of the forces working against you, you must circumvent the impending tragedy." He grabbed his son's jacket lapels, as Paco moved to flee.

Pablo cocked his shotgun noisily, his energy and bold stance at once arresting the younger hidalgo. The Moor stared into Paco's eyes, noting the unusual dilation, fatigue lines, and shadows ringing his eyes. "You will listen, Paco, if shooting you is the only way to obtain your ear."

"I love you, Father, but you represent the enemy. The old social order must be destroyed. The new will liberate Spain from the shackles of feudal hyprocrisy. To this I have sworn a blood oath!"

"Oh my son, what have those demons done to you? Do you hear your words? You call *me* the enemy! You would destroy me—your family? All we represent? Can't you see? *Maldito Dios*! How do I make the blind see? The deaf hear? How? What do I do to make you understand? You have been hoodwinked! Yes, hoodwinked by the art known as camouflage. Of making white appear to be black by holding up to contempt and ridicule all honorable traditions. In a word, perversion. Yes, Francisco, *perversion* reduced to a deadly system by this foreigner Vasquez, who orchestrates revolution in Spain. When will you awaken to his treachery? To the truth?"

Francisco feigned indifference. He drew himself to his full six-foot height, eyes unyielding, not forgiving his father. Don Diego, aware of the formidable barrier between them, persisted. "The man you revere, to whom you've sworn allegiance, is a pretender. He is not who he claims to be, however successful his deception in Spain. He is the instrument of a nameless organization, an inner circle, men of power, who, finding Spain at her most vulnerable hour, intend to rapaciously devour her. He has duped our nation's most promising intellectuals, *you*, the university students! How well he must please the hidden hands behind the plot to seduce Spain. What's wrong, Francisco? You seem confused. Don't be. Antonio Vasquez, an enigma to most, is a beginner. He can be felled if we act now. Don't you understand: Behind him there exists a nameless circle of power, and behind this another still more secret circle, also nameless. Soon I will know them—all of them."

The conversation was too abstruse for Francisco. He gave his father a reproving glance, angled his head, searching his face in testy silence. He shifted the *cartuchera* over his shoulder, his eyes impatiently skirting the nearby crowd.

"I see. You do not believe me. Ask yourself, my son, why I would embroider such facts. To deceive you?" Don Diego snorted contemptuously. "Family does not deceive. Strangers with ulterior motives are the Machiavellians of the world. The man Vasquez is a born dissembler. His tracks are well covered." Pausing to clear his voice, he continued. "I don't know it all, but I will. I *will* know the man's entire story. And when I do, by God . . . when I do—"

"Are you finished? I must go, Father." Francisco's eyes, bloodshot from lack of sleep, took on the appearance of a drug addict's.

Despite Pablo's vigilance, the young fanatic broke free. The crowds thickened. Across the square a bomb exploded a carriage. Francisco shouted over his shoulder. "Go, Father! Get off the streets! I beg you, go! You too, Pablo. Go!"

An insurgent calling to Francisco removed a *cartuchera* of ammunition from his shoulders. Together they disappeared into the boiling horde. Pablo made an attempt to follow but was restrained by Don Diego's firm grip. "It's too late. Let him go. I've lost my son."

Observing the goings-on between father and son through high-powered binoculars, Antonio Vasquez stood on a balcony of the Paris Hotel wishing he knew what they were saying before Francisco de la Varga was gobbled up by the throbbing masses. Shifting his focus, he followed Don Diego making his way toward the Federal Building, the Moor running interference. He lowered his glasses. Everything was falling into place according to his strategy.

Enemies would be disposed of on this day by avid disciples. Time is what Antonio Vasquez needs. Time is my only ally!

A commotion in the congested street below drew his attention. Plate-glass windows in a storefront shattered, an outpouring of shards and spiky splinters rained down on the crowd. There was machine-gun fire from sniper's nests. Strikers' placards fell to the ground and were trampled over by the fleeing people caught in a cross-fire between anarchists and sparse squadrons of the *Guardia*. Across the Calle de Alcala beyond the immobilized street cars abandoned on the tracks, another building burst into flames. Sirens wailed in the distance. Rioters jerked their heads around, their attention riveted on a lorry train trundling closer into the mass confusion.

"*Muy bien, amigos*. It goes well, no?" Vasquez, pleased with the well-orchestrated mayhem, left the swan-breasted balcony with his entourage and disappeared inside.

Not far from the Federal Building a wave of men armed with sticks, stones—anything to use as bludgeoning instruments—poured off the lorries into the fan shaped plaza, daring any man, armed or not, to obstruct them. Maniacal desperadoes just released from jail moved in a phalanx of death across the square. Having bartered their freedom to fight against the government forces they meant to enjoy their roles.

Don Diego saw them coming and hurried forward. He understood their confusion, *knew* he meant nothing to them. To die for nothing at the hands of lunatics for being in the wrong place at at the wrong time was anathema to him.

The sudden clattering bursts of horses hooves striking cobblestoned streets, raucous bursts of cannon dispersing the crowds, made room for the *Guardia's* cavalry. The mounted soldiers charged, infiltrated the plaza scattering every man, woman and child in sight. In moments the madness abated.

Don Diego paused at the entrance of the Federal Building, stunned by the acute silence. "Pablo, see there." They both stared at the ghostlike plaza in disbelief, their eyes sighting at once the *Guardia* officer, Lieutenant Fuentes, a duplicitous, sticky-fingered vessel of corruption. Although Don Diego scowled at the man's presence he marveled at the clean sweep of insurgents orchestrated by his men.

"*Verdadermente, amigo*, if it takes Lucifer to crush the violence in the streets, Fuentes must be appreciated this day."

"*Quizas*, excellency. Men like Fuentes are a sickness." Pablo, his reaction minimal, followed his *patron* inside the government building to the office of the ministry.

Two hours later . . . the ministry office was in an uproar.

The Grand Council is incredible, thought Don Diego, viewing his contemporaries in a true light for the first time. God forbid!

Was he as antiquated, as out of touch with reality as were his peers? Jolted by the vast difference between his thinking and theirs, he listened as arguments exploded on all sides of him. Nothing made any sense.

Politics, world strife, injured pride, insufferable class prejudices, arrogance, everything the old social order promoted, plagued the meeting, obstructed progress, preventing rational solutions to Spain's afflictions. Blood was spilled in the streets; bodies were piled higher than sandbags; flesh-eating vultures, awaiting their cues in the wings, prepared to devour Spain, and these besotted numbskulls resolutely clung to their demands: increased profits, lower wages, tighter federal control to subjugate the masses in this crumbling society where the rich got richer and the poor grew destitute.

The Minister of the Interior, a portly man in his fifties, sporting bruises and weals, acquired two days ago in an assassination attempt on his life, chaired the meeting, offering appeasement, proffering solutions aimed at ending the workers' rebellion.

"Spain is up for grabs, about to be seduced by foreigners, an alien breed of political tigers with bared fangs, dripping greed and avarice. If the council fails to amend its time-worn, ineffective remedies, Spain is doomed. In this frustrating time of panic, change, and agony, Spain must be steadied, sustained, and supported, else this appalling history in the making will not be quashed."

"Spain needs no Workers' Union!" insisted one of the millionaire industrialists from Barcelona. "I say no negotiations. Weed out the scum! Destroy them! Deploy federal troops to decimate any man advocating unionization. Let the *Guardia* resolve the situation!"

The millionaire hard-liners clapped their hands, stomped their feet in agreement, glowering at the Minister of the Interior.

"Is it possible my words fall upon deaf ears?" The minister was exasperated. "Listen to me! Hear my words! Brute force, torture—not even death will quell the birth of new ideas infecting our people. To stop the insidious destruction in our land we must bargain with the opposition, listen patiently to the whirlwind voices. If we ignore them and attempt to suppress them by military force, they will call a general strike nation-wide and shut down all industry. It's that simple. And Spain cannot afford economic disaster!"

"No! No! No!" the voices arose in protest. "No talks!"

The minister insisted. "Antonio Vasquez, spokesman for the Workers' Union, awaits word to be summoned, to negotiate on their behalf. He promises to end all insurrection if we sit down and talk."

The Grand Council stiffened perceptibly at the mention of this man's name. Disturbed glances were exchanged.

Antonio Vasquez, eh? Empowered to speak for the dissidents? How did such a man garner unto himself these extraordinary powers? He performs miracles for the workers. Could he perform better miracles if he received monetary reward from the millionaires? Land? Riches? Yes, money! The greatest fertilizer could persuade the most scrupulous of men to violate the Commandments.

Don Diego observed his contemporaries through critical eyes. Clowns, blockheads the lot of them! For too long they had subscribed to a caste system that considered itself invincible by the power of their money. It was true. Irrevocable splits in the nation's politics had created turbulence in Spain. It was also true and more realistic to understand Spain's neutrality in the Great War. Men and women, expelled from their countries for a variety of treasonous acts, as suspect in their morals as they were in their politics, had descended upon Spain like swarms of drones around a queen bee eager to commence fertility rites. But these grand nobles had ignored the warnings, took no action to expel or deter the mutinous breed flooding the university corridors, backstreets, parks, plazas, wherever a crowd could be found to promote their soapbox oratory.

Don Diego snapped out of his reverie. Votes were cast. The majority—twenty against one—placed their faith in the military. Feudal minds, accustomed to letting the military do their dirty work, preferred hiding behind the booming protection of military weaponry, unconcerned that those *same* weapons might be used against them. They advocated *counterterrorism*!

Fatuous! Imperceptive! Imprudent architects of destruction!

Don Diego, the one dissenter was unable to check his wrath. "Fools! *Tontos*! No fool serves himself wisely. Are you ignorant of the perils of military juntas? If we relegate indiscriminate and unlimited powers to the *Guardia Civil* and militia, corruption will proliferate. We can say farewell to the Spain we know. What you carelessly toss aside by this hasty vote spells death for Spain—for us. What does it matter if we hand Spain over to the rebels or the military, eh? In either case we lose and relinquish all influence to guide Spain's destiny."

Before protests formed on the lips of those millionaires who resented the words of a general who no longer believed in war, a strafing of machine-gun fire whipped across the room, over sandbags, shattering windows, splintering tiled frescoes off the high, ornate moldings. Books flew off the shelves, ashtrays spiraled off the mahogany conference table, crashing to the tile flooring. Chairs toppled as the men dived to the floor amid falling debris. Plaster exploded into dust clouds.

Choking, sputtering, coughing, the frightened, shocked council members clutched the air. Jolted by the approaching sounds of rifle fire, they scurried about, yelling, creating vast confusion.

The doors burst open. The Moors, Pablo and Matteus, wielding shotguns, waded through the congestion searching for Don Diego. Matteus sprang to the window, leaning his body flat against one wall, peering cautiously into the courtyard below to assess the mob's action. The Grand Council members ran for their lives, the spur of fear at their tails, curses on their lips. Matteus signaled Pablo to extricate Don Diego from the wreckage. They all departed the room, fled into the upper corridor of the lee side of the building. Pablo pulled off Don Diego's coat, helped him into the shabby coat of a laborer. Behind them Molotov cocktails exploded the conference rooms, Matteus shouted in a loud booming voice, "*Vamos,* pronto!"

The trio descended the stairwell through a heap of dust, plaster, and wooden beams. They ran through the building foyer, out the iron-grilled glass doors.

Lieutenant Fuentes, that sleek black-eyed cat, and his death squad stood poised in a semicircle, fixed bayonets fanning at the mob, holding them at bay.

Don Diego's glance whipped past the soldiers and zeroed in on the guarded obscenity behind them. He grasped Pablo's arm for support. The Moors, transfixed, stared at the atrocity, their breathing labored, audible gasps escaping their lips.

Don Diego felt sick to his stomach. The atrocity—*Mother of Christ!*—was the remains of a man nailed to a wooden pillar, hands tied, in a pose of crucifixion, and elevated over the heads of the mob. A cavity, where once a face existed and was blown away, was grotesquely framed by matted, blood-soaked white hair coagulated with torn shreds of flesh and oozing brain matter. The crucified corpse hung limply, the body sagging, held up by a wooden cross-beam under its armpits, nailed to a wooden post. Its upper torso was bare; the ragged remains of black trousers ripped open in the groin area revealed a bloodied mass of flesh and blood where genitals once pulsed with life. Bloody boots dangled freely, half off, thickly rawled silver spurs on their heels.

Don Diego felt a hammering in his ears, blood-engorged veins at his temples about to burst, as the need to vomit out the creeping sickness inside him sought release. Images plagued him, forcing him to look back again at the revolting sight. What jarred him so? He'd seen death before in various guises. Then he saw it—recognition was absolute. *The silver spurs! Jesus! Mary! Joseph! It was Don Verono Valdez*!

"Don Verono!" The words, barely audible, brought the Moors' heads around. They stared thunderstruck from the corpse to their Don as the hidalgo, losing composure, fell against Matteus, the acute pain in his guts like knife thrusts over and again. General de la Varga had witnessed atrocities, thousands of barbaric rituals, but not here in civilized Spain!

The ravaged corpse, symbol of the mob's growing hatred for Spain's upper classes, was all that remained of the Argentine. A turbulent, acrimonious emotion coursed through him, maddened him. A few hours ago a live man with a beating, caring heart had occupied that multilated desecrated body. But there was more to sicken this man, far more. The body, riddled by gunfire, had been left with perforations like a sieve. Darts dipped into a poisonous brew and fired into the body had swelled it abnormally; it resembled a bloated porcupine, its quills prepared to discharge at an enemy.

Sweat poured off the Sevillian grandee. *Damn the devil! Damn God! Damn the universe and its people who hadn't risen above animal instincts*! A thousand questions ran rampant in his brain. *Why*? Why Don Verono? For what—his money? Had he unwittingly flashed it in the wrong circles: Fallen prey to murderous vandals in the streets? A foreigner, traveling under diplomatic immunity as Don Verono did, had always been afforded protection in the past.

But this isn't the past! This is now! And now madness prowls the streets of Madrid!

He lunged forward, only to be held in check by the Moors before anyone saw the violence in his eyes. "We must claim the body!" Don Diego hissed, struggling against their iron grasp.

Unable to extricate himself, he sternly ordered them to release him.

Pablo ignored the order. "Later," he hissed above a whisper. "Friends, whose only interest in this sickness plaguing Spain is to bury the dead, will claim the body for us. The body will be tended, Excellency, returned to Argentina with a proper complement of bodyguards and letters of sympathy to family members. To intervene at this moment can prove fatal to you—to us."

Sighing heavily, the don acknowledged Pablo's sagacious remarks. "You are right, of course," he told the devoted Moors whom he loved as sons. Skirting the crowds, avoiding the incendiary areas, he was led carefully from the riot area.

Later, and before Spaniard and Moors left Madrid that day, Don Diego resurrected old and solid friendships. Within the next few weeks they traveled to Toledo, Barcelona, Granada, and back to Seville to confer with more *special* friends. All agreed that those men in the shadows, eager to wield power in Spain's new regime, those who had conspired with Antonio Vasquez to suck the life blood from Spain, would pay. *By God, they would pay!*

Two weeks later Don Diego assembled the Moors before him in his study at the de la Varga villa in Seville. "Find Francisco! Return him to Seville, by force, if necessary! The dangers to him as a de la Varga threaten his life every moment the truth is withheld from him. He *must* be told why the hidden forces leveled against him will not let up until he is dead and our families are dead! Even a fool deserves to be forewarned if the dangers bind him inextricably in a web of intrigue from which there is no escape!"

By November 20, the intense search for Francisco had produced few if any results. Then came the shocker. A letter arrived from Francisco. Don Diego tore it open and read:

My dearest father:

I am writing to you to confirm the date of the wedding. January 31, 1921, is the date Victoria and I have agreed upon. May I rely on you and my family to make the necessary arrangements? In conforming to tradition, the nuptials shall take place at the hacienda. Victoria shall arrive one week before to tend to womanly things. Trusting this meets with your approval, I am, your loving son, Francisco.

Elated, Don Diego scurried about to confer with his wife and family over the coming nuptials. There were things to be done, people to be reached, plans to make this wedding the festive occasion they all so sorely needed.

Chapter Nine

While the women of the de la Varga household prepared for the nuptials, Don Diego and the Moors frequented the underground vault of the castle ruins, perusing the log and record books of the ancient Garduna-Zaragoza combine. Matteus, excellent at decoding, sat back, sweating profusely in a cold, damp room. He had placed his work papers before his brother on the wooden plank table. A satisfied look was on his face.

Pablo, scanning them swiftly, shook his head. "Impossible, you have erred in decoding."

"Why will you not believe I am as capable as you?" a frustrated Matteus retorted. "I tell you, I worked with painstaking effort. My work is accurate."

"Then consider it pure coincidence—nothing else."

"Not conspiracy?"

"Certainly *not* conspiracy." Pablo retrieved the code book from this brother's hand and with an exasperated air reworked the transcribed material diligently.

"What is it?" Don Diego buttoned his sheepskin jacket to ward off the underground chill. He moved closer to the brothers, a benevolent smile on his lips. The rivalry between them bordered on farce, for between them was a deep devotion. "What stokes your wrath, Matteus?"

Matteus scratched his beard sullenly, waiting for Pablo to confirm his findings. His confirmation came like thunder clap.

"By the Holy Scriptures of Fatima! It *is* the truth!" Pablo exploded. "You are more expert than I, for I failed to detect what you perceived in a twinkling. The name passed by me, meaninglessly." Matteus grinned. Pablo thrust the translations of the Garduna ledgers at the Spanish noble.

"*Por favor, señor*, examine these translations. May Allah forgive my blunder, my wise, astute brother. You are undeserving of my wrath. See, here, Don Diego, the name *Antonio Vasquez* appears in detailed documentation of treacherous acts perpetrated against the de la Varga family, both in 1501 and in 1822. You must decide, is it truth, coincidence, or a plot? Is it possible the traitor who betrayed our ancestors left a legacy of vengeance to *his* heirs as *ours* left one of custody and safekeeping to us? Would a Vasquez *dare* return to Spain to attempt another betrayal?"

Don Diego, confused, stared from one to the other, unable to grasp the full import of the controversy until he perused the translations. Instantly he fought the images rising in mind, reserving his comment until he pulled from the vault the writings of his father, Esteban. These he pored over exhaustively under candlelight for nearly two hours. Finished he wearily placed the precious papers before him on the desk, his expression unreadable. He glanced at the Moors over the rim of his bifocals, the truth confirmed in his eyes. He nodded slowly.

"The name *Antonio Vasquez*, clear as crystal, is thusly written."

Pablo's unyielding inquisitive mind demanded, "What does it mean? What is the significance of Vasquez's presence in Spain?"

"It means serious business. We must dissect the intrigue and come to logical conclusions." Don Diego shoved his glasses onto his head, massaged his throbbing temples, and reset the bifocals over troubled eyes. He accepted the hot chocolate Matteus made over a brazier, pondering the significance of the discovery.

"The man, Antonio Vasquez, presently collecting bits and pieces of Spain like a thief in the night, is either the descendant of the traitor who betrayed our ancestors or he is too well informed on matters held sacred to us. *Which*?"

"Is it then, coincidence," Matteus persisted, "or some diabolical plot?"

"A plot!" Pablo was adamant. "I tell you, a plot! The emergence of Antonio Vasquez in Spain, a man who in several months makes himself so prominent, reflects a skillfully executed design. I admit . . . I admit parts of the puzzle are lacking, but observe his moves. You must admit the plot thickens, no? Truth runs deeper than what meets the eye."

"Only a Cagliostro can solve the unsolvable," Matteus lamented.

"There is a way to find the answers, my sons." Don Diego began doling each a section of the Garduna ledger for their perusal.

For the next two hours there was silence; you could almost hear the wheels whirring in their minds, the occasional pauses, to clarify a point or two; they never admitted defeat, yet their expressions reflected the enigma.

Don Diego's ambivalence grew disconcerting. "It cannot be coincidence. Yet what else but coincidence can it be? Too many heterogenous twists and turns in these addenda pose a curious dilemma."

"Why would any sane man assume such a name in a country where doing so might prove lethal to him?" Pablo insisted. His brother shook his head.

"You know how many men in Spain have the name Vasquez?"

"Vasquez with an S, *sí*. But with a Z?"

"Spelled with an S or a Z matters not," Don Diego insisted. "Of concern to us is the Machiavellian Antonio Vasquez who is presently running herd on Spain with incalculable power and unlimited funds. He is protected, financed; and it falls to us to unravel the mystery. Conjecture is as ridiculous as spitting into the wind. Only a personal confrontation with Vasquez can provide us the answers. Do we wish to learn the truth? Are we prepared for it? If, Pablo, as you suggest, some diabolical intrigue hatched outside of Spain necessitates the use of a decoy, use of the Vasquez name, it is a possible clue to the mystery and will shed light on the viper's intent in Spain. Give the devil his due. We shall retire and sleep on these thoughts."

When they convened in the vault the next afternoon, working feverishly against time, the underground chamber exploded with Pablo's electric voice. "*Señor*! Why was it not clear to us at once? I have solved the enigma! *The Seven Garduna Parchments!* Yes, don't you see? It is to confiscate the parchments that this Antonio Vasquez thunders about Spain with so much importance!" Pablo explained the totality of the plot. "Is it not true, the hacienda has been plundered every thirteen years since 1822? Eritonces, how many provocateurs came to us in the guise of servants to snoop about in the in-between years? Only Allah knows.''

The way Pablo saw it, the Vasquez who fled Spain in 1822 had bartered for protection. ''It is thusly described, Excellency, in your father's writings. Don Esteban's relentless pursuit of Antonio Vasquez brought to light the existence of a nefarious, subterranean body of assassins who converged once every thirteen years upon the island of Malta to compare strategies with their counterparts from various nations of the world—''

''And you believe them to be former Garduna members? Yes, yes, I remember.''

''Those same men converged to plot in secret the death of kings, princes, even presidents—any and all who oppose their precepts. They dared plot the future, the religious and political fates of all nations. Don Esteban recorded that these men were former Garduna members who had fled Spain and dispersed to other nations following the slaughter of the Zaragozas in Seville in 1822. The Zaragozas were dead, long live the Garduna. Bear in mind, Antonio Vasquez was Garduna, not Zaragoza. The unassailable fact is that they too thirsted for the seven parchments.''

''Will it never end?'' Don Diego muttered.

''Not until they clutch the parchments in their greedy fists.''

''What you set forth in this chain of logic is that Vasquez, in 1822, left Spain on the run and bartered for protection.''

''*Si*, Don Diego. He bartered protection for disclosing the whereabouts of the Garduna Parchments.''

''Protection by whom?'' asked Matteus.

''That, dear brother, is the important question.''

Don Diego, sipping sherry. lifted his eyes, focusing on some remote inner vision. ''They are closer than even I imagined,'' he said in a quiet, disturbing voice. ''I smell them as I smelled the enemy in war.''

The Moors gazed at him, unwilling to confide their personal hunches of the inexplicable, unseen forces at work. Each, in the grips of premonition, had not slept a full night in many moons. Before locking the underground vaults that day, decisions were made. Despite the depressing prognosis for the future, they renewed their pact to guard the precious Garduna Parchments as had their ancestors.

Pablo, on orders from Don Diego, left Spain in three days for Italy, embarked upon two specific missions. The first, to seek the counsel of artists skilled in the production of counterfeit paintings and sacred writings, men who received incredible sums for their talents. The second, to travel northward into the Dolomite Alps to Trento, to investigate the writings of Brother Xenofonte, second cousin to Don Diego de la Varga.

The day after Pablo's departure Don Diego received a large parcel delivered by special courier. He watched the courier drive off in a war-salvaged lorry, reentered the villa heading for his study, staring apprehensively at the parcel. He recognized the markings of the sender, an investigative firm from Trieste.

Don Diego sat behind the hand-carved desk of Abdul Montenegro, grandfather to Pablo and Matteus. He dreaded viewing the contents, he was concerned that his deepest suspicions would prove true. He poured a thimble-sized glass of Manzanilla, a potent cherry made from grapes grown in San Lucar de Barramedas. He sipped it, feeling a glow course through him at once. Unable to put aside the dreaded chore, he opened the packet with a pen knife and was overwhelmed at the massive contents. *Por Dios!* It would take forever to sift through so much.

He summoned Matteus at once. Together they set about the task, placing all the data in sequential order, integrating as they did all previously compiled data on the subject. They worked diligently, night and day, a wild-eyed urgency spurring them feverishly as if the forces they waged war against were time and life itself. Within five days there emerged a sharp, clearly defined profile of Antonio Vasquez. They uncovered the inner workings of a man's evil genius—not Antonio Vasquez, but Amadeo Zeller! The growing dread ignited within Don Diego's mind. "*Maldito Dios!* Matteus, what chance did Francisco and the other university students have under the man's Rasputin-like power? My first suspicions merely scraped the surface!"

Matteus said nothing. He drank in Don Diego's most confidential remarks concerning Vasquez/Zeller. For days they pored over the collected data, sifting facts from rumor, placing it in perspective. Murky confusion, swimming about in their minds, was encumbered by the many holes in Vasquez/Zeller's past. Distortions confounded by time and distance masked the true purpose of his presence in Spain. Nothing overt tied him to the Seven Garduna Parchments; still, Don Diego worked on.

Walking the distance between castle ruins and the villa proper, both Spaniard and Moor tugged up the collars of their sheepskin jackets to ward off the gusty cold wind rolling off the Mount of Angels.

"*Why* the conspiracy was engineered against the de la Varga family grows clearer. *Who* engineered the conspiracy to steal the parchments eludes me." Don Diego tapped his head. "The answer is here."

The Moor arched an eyebrow. "Do not be disconcerted at what appears to be passivity in my silence. My brain throbs, Excellency, with thoughts of a conspiracy of great magnitude advanced by this fraudulent Vasquez. Why am I confident that it takes more money to finance than this man Zeller could amass in his young life? Does it not seem so to you?"

"Oh yes, Matteus. Yes, yes. I grow more convinced of this each moment. The enemy has been a blight in the lives of all de la Vargas. Due to their invisibility and because they multiply in numbers, our task seems endless. We await one word, something, *anything* we can use to cut into their network—whoever they are. But, Matteus, if we cannot . . . you must listen carefully to what I tell you; be prepared to follow my instructions to the letter, *entiendes*? To be forewarned is forearmed."

Pablo returned to Seville before Christmas to reveal his secret weapon before the thunderstruck noble and his brother.

"It's a miracle!" Matteus exclaimed, marveling at the magic his brother performed before their very eyes.

Don Diego fell into instant delight. "It is perfect, Pablo. Dissolve the contents of the parchments! Should they fall into wrong hands, of what use are they? Once in the safety of the rightful protectors, the writings can be made to reappear!"

The miracle: *invisible ink*.

The elation of Spaniard and Moors was immeasurable.

From the moment Don Diego conveyed to his family the fact that Francisco had decided to marry Victoria Valdez on January 31, 1921, the women of the household were ecstatic. Inborn curiosity propelled an avalanche of questions. How large a wedding will it be? *I don't know*. Would their three daughters suffice as bridesmaids? *I don't know*. What will they wear? What style, color, and motif did the bride prefer? *I don't know. I don't know. I don't know*. Should they cater the wedding in Seville or handle it all at the villa? *I don't know*. What of foods—drinks? Champagne, wine, or both. *I DON'T KNOW*! Tossing up his hands in frustration, Don Diego pled *non compos mentis*, and, turning over Francisco's letter, insisted they interpret it as best they saw fit. He quickly sought refuge in his study. Fathoming the labyrinthine corners of a man's mind was less intimidating than the unfathomable complexities of a woman's world.

Moments later it dawned on him that Pablo had made no mention of his trip to Trento. Summoning the Moor, he put the question to him. Pablo, unused to dissembling, shuffled about on his feet, his dark eyes the color of Moroccan figs, stared past the hacendado. Unable to suppress the facts or mask his own alarm at what he'd learned, he paced the floor, venting his spleen until the story was told.

"How many men have the colorless eyes of that devil Vasquez?"

Don Diego listened, his features blackening. The bludgeoning truth, worse than he imagined, tied into the Trieste reports with alarming coherence. "Go, Pablo, summon your brother. We must recapitulate our findings." In his momentary solitude Don Diego experienced a sense of futility. On the battlefield, in command of thousands of lives, his leadership had ultimately led to triumph—not defeat. Apprehension gripped him. How, he wondered, could he structure victory into his plans when his mule-headed camel's ass of a son refused to implement the needed strategy to save his life? *How*?

The Moors entered the study. "The date is January 5, 1922. Tomorrow you both go to Madrid to find my son. Abduct him if need be, but do not return *without* him!"

For the next several days, Diego became the victim of a form of psychosis, an obsessive dread of isolation and loneliness. He fought against it with every weapon at his disposal. He sat at luncheon, listening to the chattering of his three effervescent daughters, who were intoxicated with their brother's forthcoming nuptials. He regarded them solemnly. Soon he must select proper suitors for them as carefully as he had brought together Francisco and Victoria Valdez. He listened with concerted effort to their ceaseless babbling. A half hour later, if his life depended upon it, he was unable to recollect a word they had uttered.

Pablo returned within a week, dejected, emotionally outraged at both the aborted mission and at Francisco himself. Nothing! He had heard and seen nothing, not even a whisper to project hope into his beloved Diego's heart. For the next several days they both brooded, reviewing all possible options.

There were none.

Matteus, determined to find the scoundrel, arrived at the hacienda five days later, *without* Francisco, but with plenty to report. He found Don Diego, alone in his study, the drapes drawn, obscuring the dull rays of a colorless sun. A sense of foreboding clung oppressively in the air. For several moments he did not acknowledge Matteus.

The Moor came around the desk, placed a sheaf of newspaper clippings before his former general. Diego glanced at them apathetically. His depression was such that nothing short of his son's presence would lift it.

Matteus turned up the wick of the sputtering oil lamp. Impatient with its lack of illumination, he pulled back the drapes, flooding the room with sunlight. He turned back to the grandee.

Diego's eyes were glued to the photographs in the news clippings. Matteus began. "That girl. Francisco's bethrothed has been in residence at the Paris Hotel for three months. *Three months*! All this time . . . *Señor*, with respect, I say to you, if he were here, I would gladly wring that *gallo*'s neck. Your son is in Barcelona. He returns to Madrid in one week. The *Señorita* Valdez confirmed her arrival here in Seville one week before the nuptials."

"One week is better than we dared hope. And my son?"

"In Barcelona, wallowing in the excrement of subversives! Agitators, agent provocateurs! Sewer rats!" Matteus spat. "Oh, Don Diego." The Moor shook his head ruefully.

"Go, Matteus, rest. You are exhausted. Your brother is concerned over your delay. Put his mind to rest."

Alone, Diego admitted to a slight mood elevation. Victoria's arrival meant the wedding plans were intact. Good. A blessing to be counted. Had she melted Paco's resolve? Convinced him of the *real* priorities in life? What was there beyond love, respect, consideration for family and the perpetuation of a new generation? God Almighty! He wanted to believe that simplistic solutions eradicated nightmares! Could Victoria be the answer?

Earlier that day a steady rain had fallen. By late afternoon the sun had cleared angry black clouds and illuminated the heavenly valley. Now, in the darkness, he felt the need for a brisk walk. He sought solace among the stars.

Dressed in the traditional attire of a hacendado, tightly fitted trousers flaring over his leather boots, he smoked a *puro* as he moved along the ramparts, his thick spurs clanking noisily against the tiles. He inhaled deeply; nothing smelled better than fresh earth following the rain. It cleared the sky, polished the stars to a jeweled luster, and gave man the feeling he was a part of the great universe.

On the high walls a change of guard was in progress. He nodded to them, moved on, and, pausing at the outer perimeter of the courtyard, pondered the heavens. The face and deeds of the imposter Amadeo Zeller intruded on his thoughts. Why had he tarried? He'd known from the beginning it could be no other way, yet he'd failed to take deliberate action. The procrastination had ended. In a week he would consummate the work of many months. The decision made, he returned to his study, stretched out on the sofa and in moments fell into deep slumber.

SUNDAY, January 25
SIX DAYS TO THE WEDDING.

Pablo rushed into the study, a sealed envelope in his hands. "For you, *señor*, an urgent message—the courier insisted."

Don Diego broke open the seal on the parchment, his eyes swiftly going over the contents. Pablo saw his *patron* shake, his face flushed. The don rose to his feet, frenzied eyes searching . . . searching the corners, walls, seeing nothing.

He flung open the study doors, stepped outside. Pablo followed the don's slow movements under portico arches, searched the wan, deeply lined face reflecting a tortured soul. Don Diego paused, looked beyond them, eyes brilliantly lighted. He reached to touch his forehead, found it dripping wet.

"You see, Pablo? Sweat! When ice flows through my arteries, the sweat of guilt saturates my conscience."

"Guilt, *señor*? Why do you punish yourself?"

"Guilt and fear," Don Diego insisted. "I've seen all forms of fear. I am not a cowardly man, but I recognize the fear icing my blood, chilling my responses until even the Andalusian landscape shudders, writhes, and cowers in a storm of unshakable panic, reflecting my fear. It crushes, distorts my perception."

"*Señor*, I tell you, you have done more than any father can do."

"Have I? Had I spoken to my son at the proper time, no

stranger offering Francisco immortality could have seduced him.
My grandfather, *por Dios*, failed to instruct my father, Esteban,
and saw the dastardly results! My father taught me my heritage
at the right time, avoided any possible repetition of so macabre
an act, and I, Don Diego de la Varga, properly oriented to our
legacy, failed my own son. How do I reach him? How do I tell
him of the responsibilities he is charged with beyond any he
might imagine?'' Fear huddled over his brain, atrophying what
thin sparks of courage remained. The bravado he mustered to
keep from falling into madness was fractured by the message
contained in his hands. He thrust it from him to the hands of the
Moor.

"Death closes in on all sides of us. I feel it. The message you
read confirms it. My best friend—victims of assassination—are
dead. You see, Pablo,'' he continued as Pablo's eyes skimmed
the contents. "Twenty-four in all, slain. Spain's most honored
men, bred from generations of fearless men, descendants of the
glorious *conquistadores*, who endowed Spain with wealth, fame,
glory, and a memorable history of power, are gone! Yes, Spanish giants slain! Men deserving of a better fate, slaughtered by an
invidious enemy; their haciendas, industries destroyed. Do you
see it, Pablo? The pattern is clear. I am to be the last sacrificial
lamb!''

"No! No, *señor*! Do not utter such words! *Los Desheredados*,
those nameless dogs of revolution, dared assail authority? Lift
bloodied hands against the established order—against so enormous a force arrayed against them? It makes no sense, Don
Diego—no sense at all. The *people* provided life for *Los
Desheredados*. They were the support system behind all this
mad fanaticism—''

"How well Antonio Vasquez primed the blood brothers, eh?''

"Then explain to me, *señor*, why the signals echo from
hacienda to hacienda, from peon to noble: "*Morte a Los
Desheredados! Vive España! Vive Guardia Civil*! Is it not possible
the tables are turning?''

"Oh, Pablo, Pablito, if you listen and observe long enough,
the fine line of truth emerges. Don't you see? The truth, visible
from the beginning, takes shape. "Once Vasquez and the unsuspecting *Desheredados* attain their goal, annihilation for the blood
brothers will come at the hands of the Guardia de Civil, who thirst
for a military *junta*. Then Vasquez, prince consort of the military.,

will be crowned their king. Don't you see? It was clear at the outset.''

The dull thudding sounds of fleet-footed horses and carriage wheels interrupted them. Matteus entered the study, ran to open doors to the portico. "She is here, Excellency. *Señorita* Valdez has arrived.''

They reentered the study. Matteus went directly to the wall safe, opened it, and withdrew a large black velvet case. He placed it on the hidalgo's desk, an expectant look in his eyes. Don Diego opened the case, revealing jewels dating back to Isabella of Castile. They stared in wide-eyed appreciation at the tiara, four tiers of multifaceted diamond-studded rosettes set on platinum stems. Don Diego held it up to the light, the stones shimmering like prisms. It was a work of art, exquisitely crafted. He placed it back in the case alongside a four-strand diamond necklace and earring pendants.

"I shall go to greet the carriage, Don Diego," Pablo said, leaving the study.

Don Diego picked up a stunning solid platinum cross, three inches in length, two in diameter, one inch thick. Its smooth lines, plain symmetry unadorned save for a diamond-crusted family crest at its center, made it an Isabella heirloom of enormous value. Don Diego lifted it from its niche, pressed a barely detectable spring. *Voilà!* It opened in half, forming two diamond-crusted crosses, each stone no less than a full carat. He snapped the platinum sides back to back transforming it into a solid diamond cross totaling one hundred twenty carats. Three blood-red diamonds at its center formed minuscule roses with emerald gems in the shape of leaves. "The cross once hung around Isabella's neck. It was given to Don Federico de la Varga by Her Majesty in gratitude for the riches of the West Indies, Mexico and South America," he told Matteus. "Keep these with the rest of the jewels, until the wedding day. Matteus, you do understand all we've discussed these many weeks? No doubts exist concerning my instructions?"

"Only one, Excellency. Why me? Why not Pablo? I am not as forgiving a man as my brother.''

"Especially because you are *not* as forgiving as Pablo, you will endure. You are not a worldly man, but you know the world, Matteus. You possess a commitment, dedication, and depth of knowledge beyond your years. You, my son, were born old. You are fair, a man of taste and dignity, a gentle man whose morality does not preclude killing an enemy. You are a just man.''

"You know all this, Excellency? Better than Matteus knows himself?''

"Search deeply within yourself. Is it not a fact that you have heard inner whisperings?''

"Yes, yes a fact, *por cierto y por verdad.* I dared not confront it.''

"The need to marshal your inner strength may be at hand,'' Don Diego said, staring off at some remote vision. "Come, let us not keep our honored guest waiting.''

As Don Diego left the study to greet Victoria Valdez, Matteus carried the velvet cases to the vault. *One of us is crazy! Don Diego must be growing senile! Why do I not see the man reflected in his eyes?*

Matteus scratched at his bushy, black, brown and red beard. To offset his prognathic hirsutism, a premature baldness had stripped his young temples bald as a knee and, this impediment was covered by a cap which he yanked off, and slammed on the desk in vexation.

Am I such a man as the one painted in Don Diego's head?

Chapter Ten

HACIENDA DE LA VARGA
January 30, 1921

One by one the six cloaked riders spurred their horses, struggled up the rocky incline, crushing pebbles, snapping twigs underfoot, bridle paraphernalia and saddle leather straining noisily with each movement. Moving nimbly at the top of the ridge, they wheeled the sweaty beasts about, facing the darkening vistas from the Mount of Angels. The hacienda de la Varga sprawled below them, held fast in their sights.

Winds tunneling in gusts over the rounded hills whipped at the riders mercilessly. Each man, intimidated by his unholy mission, cast wary eyes at the barreling black clouds in the southern sky. Guardedly they crossed themselves and glanced furtively at their leader, seated on a coal-black Andalusian stallion a few feet ahead of them. What was it about him? Something perverse and exquisitely evil about Antonio Vasquez had committed them to his cause. *What*? Whatever—it was indefinable.

Antonio Vasquez, shifting in the saddle of his dancing horse, concentrated on his objective through binoculars. He was waiting for something—a signal of sorts. Everything had to be perfect; there was no margin for error.

He had done it! In less than a year he had crushed and nearly crippled Spain! Before midnight it would be finished!

Blood brothers of *Los Desheredados*, terrorists conceived,

165

organized, controlled by Vasquez, committed to die willingly for causes they dared not abandon, suffered momentary conflict. Francisco de la Varga's demonstrated guts in betraying his family had shaken them to the core. How would they fare?

Vasquez, riveted to the scene below, pursed his lips tightly under the thick black brush mustache. His eyes were as rigid as his posture in the saddle.

One man knew the desperate game he played. Shortly it would make no difference. Don Diego de la Varga would be dead. Vasquez smiled, the end was in sight. He had passed himself off as a native, charming all, the aristocracy, bourgeoisie, and proletariat alike, and seduced Madrid as she had never been seduced in her life.

Vasquez turned from the scene. He leaned toward the rider next to him, nodding approvingly. "It goes well, *amigo*." He flung to one side the bulky rain poncho he wore, fixed the time at five-thirty P.M. His eyes lingered on the miniature portrait of a red-haired, green-eyed vixen framed in the watch.

Prepare for me, Victoria Valdez. It shall be mine—all of it—as you shall be mine, because I will it so.

"Mi vida, mi alma, amada mía," he cooed. "It is impossible to stay away from you. After tonight, I shall devote every hour of the day to you." He rained kisses on her soft, silky skin, whispering between each, "The sooner I depart, the sooner I shall return."

"How can I believe you? You left me in Madrid, night after lonely night."

"This is the last of it, I promise. I too tire of this intrigue. I shall convey my apologies to my father and family upon my return. Tell them I love them desperately."

"I beg you stay. If not for your sake or mine, then for our unborn child."

His lips fell upon hers, silencing her, passion springing in him. *"Especially* for our unborn child," he whispered huskily. "At midnight, I shall return. Say nothing of my visit here. To no one, understand? Especially not to my father."

She shrugged, sighed, muttered weak protestations of apology and assurance, and sank against his strong, vigorous body. She was both woman and child in need of love and reassurance. Before permitting him to leave, she moved under the spill of gaslight. He must see the pain and grief etched into her porcelain features, her red-rimmed, swollen eyes.

Noticing her black garb, his eyes sweeping her from head to toe in puzzlement, he sobered. "What's wrong, Victoria?"

"My father is dead." Her voice faltered. "Murdered—no, slaughtered on All Saints' Eve by—by those scum you call blood brothers. They impaled him—crucified him, in public. It was terrible!"

His eyes turned hard. "Lies! Lies, Victoria. Where did you hear such lies?"

"Your father and the Moors attended him, shipped the body back to Argentina—what remained of him. While I, Paco, was spending time with you in Madrid, conceiving a new life. My father was on the high seas, dead, and I was with you." Tears spilled down her cheeks.

He held her tightly, comforting her, petting her. With his final kiss on her lips he made promises.

"I promise as God is my witness, nothing short of death will prevent my return tonight. After the wedding I shall make a full inquiry into Don Verono's death. I swear the guilty shall be punished."

She melted into her lover's arms, accepting his ardent and profuse kisses. Breaking the embrace, he left her reluctantly but with firm resolve.

Victoria observed her lover exit through the French doors onto the balcony, swinging his agile body over the balustrade and descending the rose trellis to the courtyard below. Clouds moving northward darkened the land in hues of blacks and grays. Victoria clutched at the life growing in her belly—no larger than a cherry pit—and went inside to ward off sudden chills and rising nausea. Off came the black frock she loathed for what it represented—death. She had shed tears for a week, torn apart by guilt, although the comforting support from Francisco's family was profuse. The extent of the mutilation done her father was never graphically described, Don Diego recounted the ghoulish event as an unfortunate episode, converting her father into a statistic of revolution. Grateful for his discretion, she pressed no further. The Madrid newspapers had luridly reported the crucifixion of an unidentified foreigner in the courtyard of the Federal Building. When she read of the ghastly crime, Victoria made no connection between the deplorable incident and her father. After the aching revelation she refused to believe the truth. Hysterical denial followed.

Victoria preferred half truths to nightmares, for she and death were not on friendly terms. Often she eyed that invisible shrouded figure of uncertain dimensions with the same awe in which she viewed the Deity, for both possessed the awesome powers to give life and expunge it without contest.

Seated before a low dressing table of inlaid mirror and mother of pearl, she brushed out her bright coppery hair, viewing her reflection in the ormolu mirror, thinking that life, at best unpredictable, had become meaningless for her until she took it in hand. Victory had come when she finally tasted Francisco's love.

That night Francisco had placed a twelve-carat diamond ring on her finger, a brilliant stone of exquisite fire. Victoria had squealed happily. Officially betrothed, each wanted the other more than life itself. The diamond merely brought reality into sharper focus.

After All Saints' Day, they spent many nights together, but it was always the same. Before their delight was consummated, there came a knock at the door. Victoria neither saw the intruder nor heard the spoken words, but the pattern took shape and form. The inevitable knock on the door meant Francisco's subsequent departure. Furious with him, a growing wedge of anger and resentment blocked their relationship. Finally, in desperation, she had cleverly charmed a few of Francisco's friends to learn more about her fiancé, but few would talk.

The night before she departed for Seville, the knock at the door came as usual before the consummation of their burning ardor. Instantly Francisco broke away. Victoria's frustration fed her brooding disquiet. She was too much a woman to share her man with anyone else, even with an idea, if it meant he would abandon her to pursue that idea.

"I must leave, *querida*," he told her, dressing swiftly. "I must go."

"To that *man* again?"

"What man?"

"Don't be coy. I know where you go—what you do. Esteban Garcia told me what takes you from me and to whom you show your loyalty. You always jump when *he* summons you!" Her petulance obvious, her mimicry of a poodle on its haunches, begging, infuriated him.

"Esteban conjures up curious fantasies. His world is unreliable, *querida*." He slipped into his shirt, tucked the tails into his pants.

"I loathe him. He frightens me," she insisted.

"Don't be foolish. He is a great man. You don't know him."

"I tell you I loathe him."

"Why?"

"Why not? He always manages to take you from me."

Francisco laughed tolerantly. "Just like a woman," he said, shrugging into his jacket.

"I can imagine the conspiracies you stitch together, the intrigue." She began her litany. "Very well, if you choose to change your mind, I will not hold you to the marriage contract. Break from me now, Paco, or else consider me part of your life, with every right to know what is going on."

"I find your sass intolerable, Victoria. Don't issue ultimatums to me!" Francisco's voice for the first time grew frosted.

Right then, at that moment, she should have informed him of Vasquez's loquacious promises to steal her away from Paco, describe the flowers and notes. She had every intention and the opportunity to confront him with the viper. Instinctively Victoria held back, aware of the peril in combatting Francisco's fierce loyalty to the man, the jeopardy of placing her love in the balance against their friendship. That night she wavered. She had destroyed all proof—the notes had fallen prey to the fire on the hearth—and without proof her words would appear the rantings of a woman scorned. "I loathe him. I don't trust him!"

"Who?" Francisco had asked cagily.

"Who? The man who manages to time his intrusions perfectly and summons you only when we share intimate moments together!" She rushed to his side. "Please, Paco, let's go to Seville together, marry and take the first liner back to Buenos Aires! Here, the world has gone mad! International intrigue threatens Spain's lifeline. Terror in the streets! Uprisings! Revolution, murder, assassination! Why do you lust for any of this? You are not of these people. These men are aliens who infect minds. Why must you give birth to their insanity?"

He listened, curiously puzzled at her outburst. She had not spoken of politics since her arrival. He gathered her into his arms, misunderstanding. "Poor Victoria, *mi amor*. This is frightening you. No wonder. You are too confined here. I should send you to the villa in Seville for rest and relaxation. I too desire peace, *querida*. It will come. But only because I, a Spaniard, a proud noble, am honor bound to ensure Spain's future." He stroked her fiery hair, endlessly fascinated by its luminosity.

"Oh, Paco, you are *first* a man. Second a noble Spaniard." She slammed the door behind him angrily. With his departure that night came a growing disaffection for Spain, its politics, and Francisco's friends.

Now as she bathed and readied herself for dinner, she reflected, pouring scented crystals in the steamy bath. Unable to isolate or quench the flame burning in Francisco, she blamed herself thinking she had pressured him. Pressed for an ultimatum—Spain or her—would he have abandoned Spain and opted for her? Might she have induced Francisco to renounce his involvements with Vasquez?

She slid into the hot tub, rubbing perfumed oils into her skin. Victoria chose to believe the all-consuming pull from the opposite direction was strong enough to defeat her personal ambitions with Francisco, that the masterminding behind his political seduction, more powerful than her sexual seduction and love, was too formidable a force to parry. Hadn't she sampled Vasquez's bold determination?

An hour later she stood before a gilt-edged cheval glass fully dressed, reflecting a vision in misty amber silk. Her breasts were filling out, conforming to the miracle of growth in her body. The ashen, wan appearance of the past week was absent. She loathed black, refused to wear it on this the eve of her wedding. And on this *special* night, the groom was absent. *Mas vale tarde que nunca*. Better late than never, Victoria.

Victoria considered the estrangements between Francisco and his family; their uneasiness, constant regrets at his absence had long since passed the apology stage. Francisco, each parent had confessed, remained the enigma he'd always been.

Victoria moved back to the dressing table, perfumed her wrists, temples, earlobes, and pressure points, her eyes trailing to the notepad where earlier, while daydreaming, she had artistically penned a heart with her and Francisco's name on it.

"So, *Señor* Vasquez, de la Varga is not man enough for me," she muttered aloud, scornfully. "You can believe one thing, he, not you, will be present at my wedding tomorrow."

She took a last approving glance in the cheval glass and left the room in a rustle and swish of silk and lace.

*   *   *

Antonio Vasquez's binoculars held on Francisco de la Varga
until he got behind the wheel of the waiting Daimler and drove
off the Seville estate. Glowering, he lowered the glasses, brooding,
mystified at the Spaniard's untimely presence.

*Maldito Dios! Francisco de la Varga! What in damnation was
he doing in Seville when he was scheduled to be in Cordoba?*
Fanning the hatred curling his lips into a twisted leer, he regarded
the hidalgo. Deviations from planned strategies spelled trouble.
Was it some trick? A plot? Where was he headed now?

He considered de la Varga, born to riches, power, and privilege while he, with nothing, no doting parent to guide him,
forced all his life to scratch like an animal for survival, had
accomplished miracles in Spain these past months. Vasquez,
forced to check his inner hatred for Francisco, permitted no man
to read on his face what was imprinted upon his brain.

Omicron had taught him a bag of tricks.

Admont and Trento taught him expediency.

*Madrid had taught him how vendettas perpetuate themselves
for centuries.*

Forced to amend his strategies *after* he arrived in Madrid, his
decision to use the name Vasquez as a cover had failed to elicit
the expected response. Penetration of the de la Varga inner circle
was nearly impossible, their resistance to outsiders was inbred.
Cracking that *invisible* chain of command that held the de la
Vargas of Spain aloof to outsiders, and worse, getting past the
Moors protecting them—a formidable feat in itself—Vasquez
had tabled the task.

The warnings, profuse and intimidating, seemed to say, "*You
do not mess with the Moors*! Their protective powers are legend.
Men passing themselves off as something they are not, instantly
spotted, are dealt with in the mysterious ways of their ancestors."
Those in the know shuddered and swiftly changed the subject.

Vasquez had located the weak link—the Achilles' heel—in the
three months. *Three months*! Don Diego de la Varga's own son
was the weakest link in the Spanish lion's chain of command.
How easily the fatuous oaf had been seduced! His heart quelled
at the easy task.

Vasquez clicked open the solid gold watch he carried. *Ten more
minutes*. His dream was about to burst into reality. He studied
the portrait of Victoria Valdez, assessing the diamond necklace

and earrings she wore in the tintype. The Argentine heiress was his!

Vasquez bit his underlip in vexation. Last October 31, he had waylaid a pretentious hacendado, relieving him of identification, moneybelt, jewelry, and personal effects—including the gold watch—before turning him over to the impassioned mob. Vasquez had no idea that his victim was Victoria's father until after he had perused the documents, and when he did, he felt queasy, uncertain, but it was too late to rescue the man. To do so would have imperiled his life. By then he'd worked the mob to hysteria. So, the millionaire *happened* to be in the wrong place at the wrong time for his personal good. For Vasquez, the timing couldn't have been more fortuitous. Fate, his adoring fairy godmother, had provided her adopted son another bonanza—a moneybelt containing a fortune in convertible legal documents! Any qualms felt at the revelation of the Argentine's identity dissolved when he calculated the extent of legal claims possible against the Valdez estate by cleverly manipulating these documents. He remembered the searing lessons learned under Kurt Von Kurt's tutelage.

Strike when the iron's hot, for opportunity is ephemeral at best!

Because he believed anything was possible to men who practice the art of dreaming, he dared dream with dedicated ferocity the dreams few men dared dream. What began in Admont, proved fruitful in Trento, was about to multiply in Madrid. Monetary acquisitions would render him independent of Omicron. Power fueled by money would equalize his standing with those financiers. Why shouldn't he sit in lofty places, calling the shots? He deserved more. Craftier, more talented, extremely ambitious, he could outwit them any day.

Hadn't he uncovered *Shylock*? Their special assassin sent to spy on him and ultimately waste him? Somewhere between Madrid and Seville on a broiling desert wasteland, the careless executioner had fallen prey to coyotes; his bones stripped of flesh lay bleaching in the sun.

At six P.M. Don Diego addressed the Moor. "Matteus, tell me you understand the responsibility I put upon you, the dire consequences if you underestimate a man's character."

"Excellency," Pablo pressed, "there is little time."

"Yes, yes, I understand," insisted Matteus, fumbling with the cap in his hand, anxious to depart before the storm worsened.

"You will follow my instructions to the letter, Matteus. If what I suspect comes to pass—"

"If I fail to intercept Francisco, Excellency?"

"Value your life—and ours. Do not fail."

"But if we do *not* connect?"

"*Ay de mi*! Return here with God's speed and we shall retrench."

Matteus checked the chambers of his handgun and shoved it into his waist. "What of the *Señorita* Valdez?"

"After the wedding tomorrow, you will leave for Buenos Aires, to remain there until this whirlwind in Spain is reckoned with."

Don Diego embraced Matteus as a son and watched the brother leave the study. "*Cuidado, amigo. Vaya con Dios.*" He watched them brave the pouring rain en route to the stables.

"My brother," Pablo began quietly, as rain whipped down on them in a fury, "we have never spoken in ultimatums. Should Kismet choose to alter the course of our lives, you will protect Francisco with your life, no matter the peril to yours. Should distance and time separate us, communicate to the address I gave you in the Sudan, in the utmost secrecy. Pray Allah shall grant us peace and time to live together again, side by side as brothers." They embraced, tears flooding their eyes.

Matteus quickly sprang to his saddled horse, rain cape in place, and, braving the heavy downpour, headed off the estate toward Villefrance de los Barros, where he hoped to intercept Francisco de la Varga, according to the itinerary sent to Don Diego. The Moor had no inkling that Villefrance had no place in the bridegroom's itinerary, that on this day he had covertly visited the villa and then approached Cordoba, some fifty kilometers distant. His presence at the hacienda might have helped to avert the bloodshed and slaughter brewing in the soul of that odious provocateur Antonio Vasquez, upon whom the fates were smiling of late.

Don Diego stood under the portico archway peering at the fading horse and rider. *Buena suerte, amigo. Vaya con Dios.* His lips moved in silence, his troubled eyes on the storm. The wind grew shriller, gustier. Tumbleweed balled through the courtyard. How incredibly still it was in the villa. He sighed. *Irony of ironies*! It was the eve of his only son's wedding and the groom was missing.

Don Diego believed in tomorrow, that man must always be on the move, for inaction meant death. Man could not prevent the world from revolving about the sun; likewise he could not stay motionless gazing at the moon. He must move else his heart and blood must halt. For the dead there are no tomorrows. For every living man there will always be a tomorrow. The key was to remain alive. He prayed aloud.

"You hear, my son? Wherever you are, stay alive!"

He went inside, shuddering in the chill, poured brandy from a crystal decanter, sipped it sparingly, and, pausing briefly before a portrait of his son at age sixteen seated astride a spendid Andalusian stallion, experienced another chill. The consequences, should Francisco fail to return to the villa this night, took a lethal grip on his heart. Yesterday, when covert information reached him, describing in detail Francisco's intentions on this night, he planned strategy for Matteus.

He shuddered again, seemingly unable to shake the inner qualms. He placed his empty glass on the silver tray. This night, by God, would mark the beginning of the end for that vile cobra, Vasquez.

Don Diego left the study, padded through the grand walkway of highly polished wooden floors, his eyes wandering over the enormous beams of wood—wood so heavy, it sinks when tossed into the sea, so hard, it blunts the edge and shatters the handle of any ax used against it—over the hand-carved furniture with gilt and deeply colored rich leather to the cool tiles of hand-set mosaic flooring in several *salas* he passed. Enormous cloisonné vases filled with giant garden blooms placed throughout the grand villa emanated sweet, heady floral scents. Silk tapestries and priceless Goyas and Botticellis graced the walls. Pastel Persian carpets were scattered over highly polished flooring and in between long tables in the smaller salons lavish wedding gifts were displayed. There was Spode china, Austrian and Venetian crystal, silver services crafted by Spanish silversmiths.

Don Diego, nodded in passing to a scattering of industrious servants but failed to note the few servants in attendance preparing for the wedding festivities or that many more were absent.

Victoria sat at an ornate escritoire in a smaller salon, neatly listing wedding gifts and their donors in a notebook, unaware that Don Diego stood under a domed archway studying her in silence, trying to find a way to gracefully discuss his son's political transgressions with her. Sensing his unwavering gaze, she raised her eyes in greeting, then quickly lowered them lest he discern the duplicity behind them.

Damned Francisco and his revolting chicanery! In agreeing to become party to his deception, she forgot her inability to keep secrets from those she loved.

"I regard my son's sanity in leaving your side this night as terribly lacking, Victoria. Who in his right mind would abandon so stunning a creature on this, a night to be cherished forever? Is it possible he failed to inherit the de la Varga genes and hot-blooded passion?" Profuse apologies for his son's absence became a bit of a bore, so he added, "Pressing business I suppose. You must insist, *after* the nuptials, that Francisco perform his uxorial duties diligently." He kissed her outstretched, perfumed hand.

"How does one tell the son of Don Diego de la Varga what he must or must not do?" She replaced the white-plumed pen in its holder, closed the book, and, standing, took his arm.

They walked leisurely through the villa to the larger salon. Patting her hand affectionately, he sighed, stripped of his usual verve and panache. Pretense evaporated under the strain of many months.

"How strong and beautifully spirited you are. I like that, Victoria." He reached into his dinner-jacket pocket and removed a black velvet case. He walked her to the large gold-framed mirror over a credenza, stood her before it, and placed the Isabella diamond necklace around her neck. Victoria sighed, ogled, and shrieked in delight. As she inserted the earrings in each pierced lobe, he suggested she was as strong-willed as the queen who had gifted his ancestors with the exquisite jewels. Then he spoke conspiratorially. "Before the others come down to dinner, we must talk, you and I. You are my last hope, child."

In speaking his heart, confiding his deepest concerns and mystification at Francisco's attitude toward family and country, Don Diego displayed the anxiety of a parent who loved his son without qualification and seemed bewildered by his son's failure to reciprocate in kind.

"Perhaps, Excellency, if you were candid with him?"

"Yes. Yes, precisely. Unfortunately the information needed to lay my case properly before my son arrived only a few days ago." He sighed. She poured two glasses of sherry from the crystal-and-silver decanter on the low table before them. She handed him a drink. They clinked glasses. "To you and Francisco, *querida* Victoria." They sipped the sherry. "Tonight it shall be finished. Matteus has left for Villefrance to intercept Paco and escort him home."

Victoria froze. *Què atrocidad! How could she tell him*?

"My desire is for you to keep Francisco in Buenos Aires—"

"Your son, Don Diego, cannot be persuaded to do what he does not fancy himself doing."

"Find a way. *Por amor de Dios*! Find a way? Surely, Victoria, you are woman enough to keep him at your side until the madness and dangers here subside?"

"What dangers, *señor*?" A sinking sensation extended to her toes. I should have known his commitment to *Los Desheredados* was such—" She stopped, the faux pas blatant.

He angled his head obliquely, disenchantment etched in his tortured eyes. His words were an indictment. "You know? You know of his abominable activities? You sanction his opprobrium?"

"Oh, no! Lay no such heavy burden upon my soul, Don Diego. I sanction nothing. I confided nothing because I know nothing. Perhaps Paco's friends will tell—"

"They too are mixed up in this dirty business?"

"Yes, I suppose so. They are alike." Victoria on her feet paced alongside him, her silken gown rustling diamonds, shimmering brilliantly in the candleglow. "I saw the gradual changes in him, impassioned zeal. I tell you Paco is possessed with foreign conspiracies against which he measures Spain's political climate. Infernal intrigue consumes him. Mysterious comings and goings at all hours of the night. When questioned, he hides behind masks of secrecy. I prevailed upon him to desist in this covert madness. Shall I tell you what I received in return? Censure! Caustic condemnation! Ultimatums. Never speak thusly to me again, he spoke with bold temerity. Tell me what to do. I love him desperately."

Outside, the ill-tempered winds howled fiercely. The storm moved full-force against the villa bending trees, banging shutters, shattering glass. Raindrops splattered through the chimney flue onto hot fires on the hearth, hissing loudly.

Don Diego stoked the burning logs. Victoria stared into the

roaring flames. "If you had only confided in me sooner . . ." He paused. "We must try to resurrect the future of hope from the ashes of the past's discontent. Will you at least promise to keep him away from Spain?"

"I will try, *señor*. Overprotection has never been a wise remedy when dealing with a rebellious child." She spoke from knowledge.

"Our mistakes as parents are plentiful. My generation, in refusing to cede the reins of power to our sons, have robbed them of manhood. We failed to recognize in them the same stuff that made us conquerors of destiny early in life. To salvage what we can is the only option open to us if we wish to keep Francisco alive."

His intent was not to alarm the girl, merely to spur her to awareness of the hazards involved. Victoria sipped the remains of her sherry. She felt a traitor. Her inclination was to make a clean breast of things. She blanched. "Excellency, Francisco *will not* be home for dinner. He was here earlier today." Her voice quivered. "He promised to return at midnight," she hastened to add, at the sudden paleness of his features. "He swore me to secrecy. Now I am overwhelmed by an all-pervasive fear." The *bruja*'s flaming words seared her heart and soul.

"W-what a-are y-you s-saying? Francisco h-here? Today? Without seeing m-me?" Feeling compromised, he fell against the chair, the life drained from him. "Truly, Matteus will not find him. Surely he will return empty-handed. Pray, child, you made no bargain with the devil this day or you have sealed Francisco's fate."

"You know, then, where he is? Where he may be found. Send someone after him, I implore you."

How could he tell this innocent-eyed bride that he, Diego de la Varga, had no weapons of negotiation left to barter with the gods for Francisco's destiny? Muttering vague excuses about unfinished business, he left the salon, and in his wake, Victoria, clutching the life in her belly, clung to what remained of her sanity.

Matteus whipped his horse furiously, spurring the fleet-footed animal beyond physical endurance. He left Villefrance in a rage. *Por Dios! Burro insensato*!

Paid informants revealed that Francisco de la Varga had been in the village over a week ago. *A week ago!* Cursing aloud he paused to water his horse, then swung to the saddle, spurred the frothy-mouthed animal into a wild gallop, and headed back to Seville. His thoughts stormier than the black night, he vowed it was neither appropriate nor his duty to take the hidalgo to task. But, if Paco were within his grasp . . .

Allah had endowed him with a brain, one that Don Diego had crammed full of knowledge. For what purpose, if not to think? And Matteus was thinking . . . thinking . . . that rooster's cockscomb needed trimming. While he was at it, why not wring Paco's neck?

Barely able to distinguish the black outline of the ancient Moorish castle in his approach to the hacienda, he cursed again. "By the hairy black balls of Moloch, if that pain in the *culo* isn't home when I arrive . . . *Para todo hay tiempo y modo*. For everything there is a time and a way, he told himself.

The six cloaked riders, less than half a kilometer from their target, slowly walked their horses, concealing themselves, taking cover in the shadowy pockets forming in the diminishing light. Sweat poured from their stony faces; the scent of the kill turned their dark eyes to fire points. They strained against the blustery wind, yet retained their unhurried pace. Somewhere a coyote howled. A snorting bull raced up a hill, commandeering a few stray cows into cover. The bells riding herd on the wind grew closer . . . closer . . . more melodic.

Chapter Eleven

Cloying floral scents saturated Victoria's senses, giving rise to nausea she fought to control. She stared at the sterling silver candelabrum, one of four spanning the length of the table, each heavily encrusted by winged horses and mythological creatures.

Four solemn people sat at the dinner trying to elevate their spirits. Don Diego, at the head of the table, toasted his wife at the other end. *Doña* Florenzia, a gentle, snowy-haired stately woman with patrician features, smiled, speaking in asides to *Doña* Teresa, Victoria's *dueña*, whose present mood was blacker than her ebony hair. Victoria, seated quietly at Don Diego's left, listened to Francisco's three younger sisters chattering like mad hens, their conversation alternating between tomorrow's nuptials and disappointment over the inconvenient storm.

Don Diego, directing his conversation to Victoria, hoped to lift the pall of gloom created by his son's absence. "We Andalusians, with our abounding love for life, display a morbid preoccupation with death. Did you know there is inbred in us a taste for the tragic, evidenced by our passion with bullfights, our gruesome statues of Christ and the martyrs?" He paused to sip his wine. "Yet, truly, love dominates our life. It's not for nothing this is the home of the infamous Don Juan. His real name was Miguel de Manara. A curious thing. He was a wealthy, licentious man, whose total disregard for life and money became inextricably bound up in his final journey through life. Legend claims, Victoria, he departed the scene of a drunken orgy one evening, encountered a funeral procession, and through some mysterious powers discerned the partially decomposed corpse as his own. Accepting the apparition as a sign from God, he renounced all worldly goods, joined a monastic brotherhood, and for his remaining days on earth collected the bodies of executed men for burial.''

Victoria shuddered. Why wasn't she able to shake the *bruja*'s prophecy that death would surround her? Why?

"My dearest husband," interrupted the gentle, eternally romantic *Doña* Florenzia. "On so propitious an occasion, would it not be more fitting and proper to speak of beauty? Especially the eternal beauty of Seville?" Turning her attention to Victoria, she rhapsodized. "Every crossroads is a garden. Flowers burst through stone walls, festoon the trees, invade the streets. My dear Victoria, before returning to Argentina, Seville is a must for honeymooners. The Maria Luisa Park, scented with tangarine trees, is so perfect a setting for love and romance. The intoxicating scents of heavenly orange and lemon blossoms transport the soul to paradise." She clutched her ample bosom. "And its winding, narrow little streets are a perfectly conceived setting for a Verdi opera. Old houses mingle with secondhand shoe stalls and antique shops. Whitewashed gardens with wrought-iron lanterns overflow with a profusion of vines. Every window hides demurely behind iron grills bristling with spikes. Ah, what *amor* goes on in that inspired setting . . .''

Victoria, playacting her way through dinner, barely listened. The *gazpacho*, barely touched, the rack of lamb, embellished with fragrant garlic and mint sauce, nauseated her in her delicate condition. She feigned hunger, but each bite was minute, and she delicately sipped wine between each mouthful, raving over the marvelous cuisine. Quick to observe the vacuous expression creeping into Don Diego's features, the absent twirling of his wineglass, Victoria, despite the warmth of crackling fires on the hearth, experienced sudden chills.

Soft, throbbing flamenco guitars in concert with the rich, impassioned gypsy voices sent a shudder of melancholia through her. Externally she reflected the joyous bliss of a blushing bride. Nothing was further from the truth. She felt guilt-ridden, useless, her pride rapidly disintegrating. Here she was on the eve of her wedding, forced into social strangleholds without benefit of the groom. She felt worse than the inclement weather and equally as unwanted. *Damn*, Francisco, anyway!

Three orange marmalade cats pranced regally into the dining room, one after another, imperiously disdaining the diners, moving about exploring new scents and sounds. Victoria observed them momentarily, an increasing homesickness gripping her. *What the devil was she doing here*? Her mother had buried her father, Miles Carter, in Chicago and returned to Buenos Aires to be greeted by her husband's dead body. Finding Victoria gone, she returned to Chicago, where the newlyweds on their honeymoon, intended to rendezvous with her, then return to Argentina.

But that was *tomorrow*, and this was *now*. And right now, Victoria was lost. God only knew how lost she was! Never mind what the Argentine *bruja* had prophesied! Victoria was tired of inventing fictions, pretending one emotion, feeling another. Confusion had set in. In the polyphonic clamor of her thoughts, one fiction did not exclude another.

She was at once a star in four separate dramas running concurrently on four stages under the proscenium arch of her consciousness. She was the romantic, idealistic Juliet, ready to die for Romeo; a stalwart Portia fighting injustice for her lover against the forces of Shylock; the rhapsodic Dulcinea to Don Quixote, the brave knight errant bent on wiping evil from Spain's borders; the immortal Mimi of *La Boheme* transformed discreetly into innocence, sweetness and vulnerability. She was everyone and no one. Bent totally to Francisco's will, assailed by second thoughts and the burning memory of an ugly, wicked *bruja*'s words, she wondered, did love make her heiress to misery?

Spooning the *membrillo*, an acrid sweet, orange-flavored aspic made of quince, she grimaced at its tartness and delicately laid a bit of *machego* cheese on her tongue to soothe the palate. The silent, sudden absence of sound caused her to glance up expectantly.

Don Diego's pale preoccupied blue eyes glanced up, the silence breaking his concentration. A long, measureless pause followed. Tilting his head obliquely, he strained to hear through the storm's sounds. His posture brought the room into abrupt silence.

The stark absence of flamenco music and singing voices startled him. He held a hand in midair, cautioning the diners against making undue sounds. His eyes cut sharply across the room. *Por Dios!* Pablo! Don Diego froze. A string of curses spilled from his lips. *"Maldito Dios! Vive Dios! Voto a los ajenos de Dios!"*

All the curses under God couldn't avert what was written long ago and was coming to pass. Heads turned toward Pablo.

The Moor, valiantly supporting himself between pillars of the dining room archway was deteriorating rapidly from the butchery done him moments before, his attempts to warn his beloved don failing. Blood-veined eyes popped their sockets, excruciating pain shuddering through him sapped his strength alarmingly as he tried desperately to hold the gaping folds of flesh together across the bloodied knife wounds. The butchery done him was incomprehensible.

The diners, immobilized by paralytic shock, their throats frozen in terror could not breathe, cry out or whisper. Then, suddenly the nightmare continued.

Lightning bursts of fire split the night. A staccato of bullet fire exploded glass windows, raining glass shards like stilettos on stupified diners. Terrorized into action the women scrambled to their feet like awkward birds in disorganized flight. Behind them, Pablo sank slowly to his knees, his face contorted in pain, bloodied hands leaving ghastly scarlet streaks on the pillars before falling in a heap like a ravaged animal. Ricocheting bullets, their wailing sounds panicking the women, bounced off the walls. The women hesitated, their focus shifted across the room.

Five menacing figures stealthily approached from all points, smoking guns in hand. Instantly, the women, cut down by high powered guns, became a potpourri of flesh, skulls, intestines erupting in a swirling mass of humanity. *Doña* Teresa, muttering madly, blamed a *bruja's* prophecy for this satanic nightmare before she fell over onto the rack of lamb, her pendulous breasts marinating in meat juices, eyes twisted grotesquely upward. Behind her, bodies heaped onto bodies in final embrace.

Don Diego, immobilized by bullets lodged into his lower back, unable to circumvent the evil orbiting toward his family these many months, called out to Victoria in desperation. "Go, my child, save yourself!" Spewing bullets ripped him apart. He seemed to rise off the floor, his cheeks filled with displaced air as he fell back, fingers clutching the tablecloth, pulling it after him, spilling dishes, stemware, candelabra, everything. He landed on the floor, on his side, his eyes darting past the five killers to the sixth man, standing well to the rear of the gunmen. Their eyes locked.

"*Asesino, muerte sangrienta!*" He rasped before the *coup de grace*, fired by one of the killers silenced him forever.

Reality, colored by imagination lurched crazily in the nodules of Victoria's brain. Visual distortions, false perceptions vigorously antagonizing what her brain recorded, left her dazed, frightened, uncertain. She noticed a bloodied striation rippling across her breasts, dripping onto her gown, yet she felt nothing. *Nothing!* She lifted emerald eyes from one murderous devil to the next, cursing them. Pain assaulted her and she clutched at the table. Her blurred eyes sharpened focus in time to see Antonio Vasquez spring catlike behind the five assassins. White smoke and fire burst from the muzzles of two guns held in his hands.

She actually saw Vasquez shoot the killers!

Sounds diffused, everything blurred, she sank to the floor as a dead weight shoved her into a tunnel of darkness.

Vaguely she heard a voice, Vasquez's voice. "You cannot die!"

Wafting in and out of consciousness she managed a few words. "Y-you w-were a f-friend, a-after all!" Her head fell heavily, sagging to one side. Blackness engulfed her.

Vasquez, on his knees, listened to her heartbeat. He caught sight of the Isabella diamonds at her neck and ears in the dazzling play of candlelight. Excitement coursed through him. Studying her with peculiar detachment as he deliberately removed the blood-stained jewels from her body, he dipped the diamonds into a wineglass, washing away the blood, and wiped them on a serviette. He slipped them into his jacket pocket.

The de la Varga villa was deserted. Servants participating in the betrayal, paid off by unknown couriers had fled and were killed for their efforts. The terrorists who had done the mule work lay dead at Vasquez's feet. He moved about the room kicking at dead bodies with his booted foot; he could leave no one alive to identify him. What a masterful, incomparable *coup de de main*! He worked swiftly, borrowed a Daimler from the stables, and sped to the infirmary of the Virgins Macarena Cloister. He pressed currency into the Mother Superior's hands, begged her to save the patient, promising a nominal bonus if she worked miracles for Victoria. "Just keep her alive! Understand? Do not let her die!"

Vasquez left before questions were asked for which he had no answers. Pushing the Daimler to excessive speeds in the storm, he raced against time. He must get to Cordoba before eight P.M. In this the final chapter in the life of Antonio Vasquez, he must disappear. Amadeo Zeller anxiously awaited in the wings, eager to begin the legal manipulations for the conversion of de la Varga assets. One last scene remained in this high drama before the curtain rang down on a successful run-of-the-play. And then—opulence, wealth and power.

Consciousness returned to Pablo in spurts. A moment passed before the ghastly array of bodies, heaped grotesquely about the blood and flesh splattered walls and floor, imprinted vaguely in his mind. Pain spasms assaulted him, shattering his senses, Commanding Herculean strength, Pablito grasped a nearby chair, clung to it, pulling himself up tottering under the jarring tonnage pressing down on him—pain! Pain as he'd never experienced it, and no wonder! His entrails spilled from the gaping wounds in his stomach. How he managed was a miracle. He pushed the pale intestine back inside of him, folded the flesh overlapping it. He peered about the room, wild-eyed, searching . . . searching. Ah! A pillow. He shoved it hard against his belly, the pain growing more tolerable, eased by the pressure. Inching along one wall, he yanked at a drapery cord, bound the pillow to him and, heaving laboriously accomplished the incredible feat, miraculously transcending the pain threshold until he felt numb.

A singular thought drove him—*Matteus! He must find his brother!* Matteus! Matteus, my brother, where are you?

Matteus, the unseen, unknown witness to the slaughter had seen it all, down to the last bloodied *infamita!* Shaken, helpless to circumvent the tableau of horrors he fled the scene prepared to fulfill his promise to his beloved Don Diego. To have imposed himself in the mad dog slaughter would have meant his own demise. He could not permit it. Not that he feared death—he didn't—but that vow to Don Diego became his *raison d'être!* Extricating himself from the proscenium of massacre he headed for the castle ruins. He had things to do! Things that must not go awry!

Pablo crept toward the castle ruins, each step taken reducing his chances for survival. The miracle? He was still alive! A blood-soaked pistol, grasped tightly in trembling hands, he shakily descended the stone steps to the lower vaults of the castle. His massive bulk flat against the walls for support, each step sheer agony, he inched forward. Blinking hard, unable to focus definitively in the near darkness, he stopped suddenly.

There . . . he saw it! A flickering candle casting vague moving shadows. Sweat poured off him, mingling with the rapid loss of blood. *Think,* Pablo! *Think! Someone is violating the sanctum sanctorum! Allah, praise Allah, spare me a few moments longer!*

His sight dimmed, perceptions turned hazy, less definitive. The gun in his hand shook uncontrollably. He could take no chances. He cocked the gun's hammer, and with super-human strength pulled the trigger.

Amplified sounds echoing through the cavernous vault alerted the trespasser. As quick as his assailant, he turned, crouched low and fired, spewing a rapid barrage of white fire and thunder.

"Matteus! Don't shoot! It's me, Pablo!" The words lay unspoken, frozen on Pablo's lips. It was too late, the bullets had ripped out his eyes.

Matteus approached hesitantly. Then, recognizing his brother, sank at once to his knees, wailing anguished, tormented sobs as he observed Pablo in the final throes of a hideous, painful death. Matteus prepared a supplication to Allah.

He bowed his head, trying to block out all vestiges of the recently witnessed *danse macabre* that had plucked from him all he'd held dear in his life. As bloodied images and the revolting nightmare of white fire and fiery bullets were forcibly relegated to the dark side of his brain, he spoke to his God Allah.

"Many times in the past we have spoken, oh merciful, most compassionate of Gods. I have sought you but you avoided me. I called to you, but you listened not. Now I implore you to send your messenger of Death to embrace the soul of my beloved brother and your son. Place your strong fingers upon his trembling lips, enfold his soul tenderly beneath your shrouded wings and keep him in your presence for all eternity, oh most merciful Allah."

Matteus, finished stared at the eyeballs of his brother lying on the earthen floor nearby, convulsed with loathing.

"You shall be avenged, beloved brother. All who died on this black night of infamy shall be avenged. He, who is responsible shall never sleep a full night without the nightmares of Moloch to destroy his soul."

Quickly, Matteus, on his feet, moved to a marbled wall. He

pressed a hidden panel; an opening appeared, as heavy walls gave way to an inner crypt. Matteus picked up Pablo's body, carried him into the icy unlit chamber, laid him on a marble slab, crossed his hands, shut the empty eye sockets and placed a robe over him. He backed out, lit a torch, returned and holding the flame to the wall, slowly turned in a three-hundred-sixty-degree circle. The flickering oil torch illuminated the crypts of all the de la Vargas and Montenegro families since the days of Isabella.

"Allah forgive me for not placing into your hands the bodies of my beloved Don Diego and his cherished family. But I must do the bidding of my master, for he has prepared to sacrifice his holy temple so that his useless son may live."

The Moor exited, shoved the enormous marble wall back into place. He studied the bloody pools leading to the blank wall, a slow, ineffable smile flickering briefly on his face.

Let the beast wonder. Let them all rot in the arms of Moloch!

Chapter Twelve

"La ilyaha, ilya Allah . . . There is no God but one God, Allah the merciful, most compassionate God . . . Blessings and peace be upon thee . . ."

The first chantings of the muezzin from the minaret high above the city called the faithful in the streets to prayer; his throaty modulations, bouncing on the winds, echoed through the city. A flaming western sky, slowly obscured by darkening storm clouds, formed a stunning backdrop for the Mezquita de Cordoba, the eighth-century mosque, a proud citadel, an eternal glory of caliphs and Moorish warlords.

Amid swiftly dispersing crowds and tourists scurrying to their destinations, Francisco de la Varga paused briefly, listened to the muezzin's chant, and shifted his focus to the rapid changes overhead. Black clouds abruptly terminated daylight. Paco hurried along, for his was a pressing appointment—*he had a rendezvous with death*.

He had a haggard, strained look, the eyes of a fanatic, as he sped hastily through the narrow, twisting, aromatic Street of Flowers, heading for the rising passage of steps joining the rear of white stucco buildings with red tile roofs. He was almost there.

A huge gust of wind, rolling in behind him, propelled him forward, and he landed at the threshold of the enormous ornate doors of the mosque. He entered and was immediately struck by the pervasive scents of paraffin, Oriental incense, and the stench of antiquity. Moving forward on the balls of his feet, he traversed the narrow walkways at one side of the spectacular interior.

Raindrops struck the overhead rotunda and jarred him. His eyes lifted upward, trailing along the delicately carved cedar ceiling past the double domed capitals atop sleek pillars—remnants of the ancient Visigoth church razed to make place for this mosque centuries ago. He cautiously searched overhead catwalks leading to numerous lofts, shifting his scrutiny back over shadowy walkways, pausing at the slightest noise to listen.

Francisco eased forward, opened a door leading to a *maksoureh*, one of the many meditation chambers opening off the length and breadth of the mosque. Closing the door behind him, he slipped a bolt into place, locking it. He breathed easier, removed his rain cape, and spread it over a chair. His familiarity with the room implied his presence there many times before. He knelt before a small altar, crossed himself, stared into a sputtering candle wick in its red glass container, his lips moving in silent prayer.

"Sancta Maria, Mater Dei, ora pronobis peccatoribus nunc et en hora mortis nostrae . . ."

Finished, he whipped out two concealed weapons, both 9mm Campo Giro automatic pistols, and deftly sprung the magazine from the grip, checked the ammunition, and shoved it back into the chamber with a loud metallic click. He placed the guns on the altar shelf carefully. He inspected and replaced two ingeniously hidden blades tucked into his boots.

Muy bien. All was in readiness.

A curious, unexpected sound brought up his head, he cocked it, listening with cat ears.

Steady now . . . calm yourself. The first time is always the worst. What worries have you? Arrangements were made.

He had never killed before. Yet tonight, in less than an hour, three despicable men, Workers' Union officials who were destroying Spain from within, would die at his hand. Yet . . . struck suddenly with a prick of conscience, he asked himself one question.

What was he doing here on the eve of his wedding?

A sane man would be home at his bride's side. Was that it? Was he insane? Was madness infecting his brain, eating away at it until he could think no longer? These thoughts assaulted him nearly melting his resolve. He lit a *puro*, took two puffs, and flung it savagely to the floor, grinding it out with booted heel.

If he did not believe that Spain faced an enemy more lethal than any encountered on a battlefield, he would not be here, risking his life. The enemy *must* be destroyed! The stodgy, opinionated, antiquated relics of the older order must be uprooted, else Spain would die.

Francisco, neither large nor imposing at nineteen, measured an inch under six feet. His was the classic beauty of a poet and deep thinker, but a shock of brown curly hair and an impish smile marked him as a roguish scoundrel. The eyes, a greenish hazel, masked volumes of stored-up emotions. Imperious, self-indulgent, he had flung off the confining strictures of upper-class morality nearly a year ago when he joined his fellow students in rebelling against the establishment to follow the precepts and policies of a very special man.

Antonio Vasquez. The man had illuminated Paco's mind. Until this genius had enabled the university students to clearly see their views, Francisco and the others had possessed no vision at all. Vasquez preached death to the timeworn precepts by which Spain had lived in past glory. He insisted that Spain was dying for clinging to ancient tenets. The Vasquez credo was: assassinate the important men of Spain and we shall begin anew with fresh ideals, revitalized by the young blood of our grand, glorious nation.

Francisco glanced impatiently at his watch. Victoria's image stared up at him, nearly melting his resolve. *Damnation*! Why on this of all nights? Couldn't it have waited? No! Antonio had insisted upon this night. "One night each month the union officials meet in Cordoba. The assassination must occur *away* from Madrid or Seville."

Francisco had agreed—why delay for another thirty days? Why indeed? Mother of Christ! He was tired . . . tired!

The assassination had caused rivers of blood to inundate the nation but had been unsuccessful in bringing Spain an inch closer to the anticipated victory. The ends certainly had not justified the means. Was it all for the glory of Spain? Broken promises to his father—to Victoria? How could he justify the unhappiness and hardships imposed upon them. False messages had been sent to his father from Madrid, charting a fraudulent itinerary for this day while he was immersed in the plotting of three assassinations in Cordoba! What deception! What duplicity and cunning! What sort of a man had he turned into in less than a year? He hardly knew himself.

Only this morning he had prayed, rising in the darkness to travel across town to his own private place of worship, the Plaza Delores behind San Miguel Church. In this secret spot where walls and flowers gleam in violet shadows, he had found no solace. Images of his bride had intruded upon his prayers. The anguished face of his father receded into the background, an expression of stern disapproval etched into his distinguished features. Disquieted by the unrelenting images and turbulent feelings these images unleashed, Francisco decided to leave the Plaza Delores with dispatch. Driving the British motor car at excessive speeds, he arrived in Seville for his tête-à-tête with Victoria.

En route to Cordoba after his disquieting moments with Victoria, a jumble of disconnected thoughts had assailed him. The revelation of her father's brutal murder had devastated him. His knowledge of the incident was limited and vague. He'd been occupied with other matters. Fortifying himself with brandy and reminders of Vasquez's words, he had floored the accelerator over precarious twists and turns in the roads, the voice of his mentor clear.

"My brothers, consider, if you will, violence, murder, and assassination as purely rational acts deliberately devised to further the political aspirations of those who perpetrate them. Since we, the minority, are too few and too weak to withstand open warfare with government forces, we must resort to covert action. We must weaken both the hold and will of the possessors of political power to win our civil rights, long denied us. We must establish and foster a new order if Spain is to survive. . . ."

Francisco, a devoted disciple, had immersed himself in brotherhood activities until Victoria arrived in Madrid. He shifted about, agitated. *What is it, Paco? Pangs of conscience? Now?*

Yes, yes! He was glad it was over. All hot-headed radical involvements with Vasquez would end this night! Jesus! How he vacillated. Would it really end for him on this night? The sudden duality of his nature frightened and appalled him. How could he define the intoxication charging through him at the night's expectations. Torn apart between his father's admonitions and Vasquez's constant encouragement, why did the word of his father reach out to take a stranglehold on him tonight of all nights. "A de la Varga can best serve Spain from the podium of government, not by insurgency!

Would he be the same man *after* he killed three men. Did he have the right to judge, condemn, and sentence with three swift bullets? The self-interrogation ceased abruptly. He tensed, cocked an ear, listening. *Something . . . what?*

He heard it again, clearly. He sprang to the door, forced his body flat against the wall. He did not breathe. He did not move. He listened, senses heightened. A moment passed. Nothing. Beads of sweat popped out on his brow. Stepping back, he took a gun from the altar shelf, gripped it firmly, and with his free hand turned the key in the lock soundlessly. He slid back the bolt, cracked open the door, and peered about the shadowy marble hall.

In five nights no intruders. Why fancy one on this night? What compelled his rising paranoia? Ruses, evasions, deceptions. Entrapments by the enemy! Damn it! He was not a felon, yet in less than a hour he would become the vilest of men—a murderer!

"You are not criminals, my brother. Rather agents of Spain, sworn to crush enemies. You shall be exalted for the deeds you perform for Spain, rendered homage, and granted immunity in a future life!"

Vasquez's revolutionary rhetoric had convoluted what the university students had believed as gospel all their lives. Now, as trigger words buzzed in Paco's head, sweat poured off him, his stomach churned as if acid were searing his innards. He needed sleep. The confining room allowed him no real rest, no daydreams. It brought reality into sharper focus.

The sounds again, more definitive, horses' hooves, carriage wheels assaulting the cobblestones, horses whinnying, straining against their bridles; fierce winds; loud, heavy rainfall whipping tree branches, buildings; and the noisy banging of shutters somewhere—all of them jarred his frayed nerves. In the confusion of sounds one was unmistakable. An automobile came to a noisy stop in a street.

Lines furrowed his brow. Ten minutes had passed, twenty to go. He clutched at his gurgling stomach—he was hungry. Damn! Empty stomachs heightened anxiety. He should have eaten!

Francisco gave a start, sprinted to the door, placed his ear against it, listened. Hesitant footsteps approached. *Damn the devil!* Contributions to the poor box of five hundred pesetas had brought him needed privacy this night. Signs posted at the entrance—he'd seen them—declared the mosque closed to the sightseers.

Footsteps! Louder, closer, like clicking castanets echoing through the cavernous chamber, each step clearly discernible. Francisco listened with cat ears pressed against the door. The footsteps were those of a man who knew exactly where he was headed.

Finger tightened on the Campo Giro trigger, Paco carefully unlocked the door, opened it a slit, peered through the slim spear of light. A moving caped form swaggered toward the meditation chamber—his! The gun slipped in his sweaty palm. Quickly shifting it to his left hand, he dried the clammy hand on his trouser leg, then regrasped the firearm firmly, prepared to decimate the interloper.

He squeezed the trigger . . . froze! He gasped aloud, recognition burning his brain like white fire. "*Por Dios!* I could have killed you!" he shouted hoarsely. "*Maldito diablo!* I nearly shot you, Antonio. The shadows, dim lights . . . near darkness and the wind sounds . . . I couldn't make you out. Why are you here? What's wrong? Is something wrong?" He paused, inhaled deeply, leaned against the wall, deflated like a jellyfish hiding from its enemies. "When I think I could have killed—"

"You didn't. Perish the thought. Look! I am hale and hearty." Vasquez's soothing, placating voice allayed the Spaniard's fears. He forced a silver brandy flask on him. Francisco gulped greedily and returned it. Vasquez peered about the darkness of the *maksoureh*. He tugged at one of the straight-backed wooden chairs. "Sit, *amigo*. You appear distraught. There is little time; we must speak in truths, Francisco. This is our concern—the truth, *verdad*?" Pulling at a second chair, he sat opposite the Spaniard, his expression somber. "Tonight, you will abandon all plans to slay the union officials." He raised a hand to ward off Paco's shocked retort. "Rumors of betrayal reached me."

"Betrayal? What betrayal? I don't understand. Tonight everything computes with precision. I am ready tonight. Another time I may not be here. Who speaks of betrayal?"

"Fuentes—straight from the horse's mouth. He is our ally."

"*Lieutenant Fuentes*? That butcher? The man who executes on the spot—without trial? Since when has he become *our* ally, Antonio?" He shook his head. "No. No! I say it is foolish to delay. It must go down this night. This night must mark the end of our enemies!"

"When Fuentes indicated possible treachery, I deliberated,

sent him to Cordoba to prepare for you in the event of foul play. I too grew disturbed. So, with five of your blood brothers of *Los Desheredados* I rode to Seville, hoping to intercept you before you left for Cordoba.''

''Why? You *knew* I was in Cordoba!'' Paco stiffened imperceptibly.

Vasquez inclined his head sheepishly. ''I confess to putting a man on your tail—a backup should things go awry. Paco, in contradiction to *our* strategy, I learned you arbitrarily left Cordoba for Seville earlier this day. When my courier wired me in Madrid, I pondered your moves. It struck me you may have learned of the betrayal, so we boarded the express to Seville to measure my information against yours.'' He mopped nonexistent sweat from his brow, ''Your strategy confused me, *amigo*.''

''What are you trying to say? There's little time—''

''What I am trying to tell you and faring badly at it is—we—uh—all of us—witnessed an unfortunate tragedy.'' He made a gesture of futility. ''How do I tell you, Paco, when I do not believe what these eyes witnessed? Oh, my dear *amigo*, how do I soften the blow?''

''Mother of Christ! Get on with it! I don't know you. You've never been reluctant to make a point.''

''They were killed. All of them! Your family—victims of bloody massacre. Do you understand? All—including your fiancée!'' His voice dropped to a dramatic hush.

Involuntary shudders gripped Francisco. He gasped, disbelief in his eyes. The word reverberated in his brain. He stared at Vasquez obliquely, eyes distended. ''Is this some attempt at humor—''

''Humor! *Humor*! *Por Dios*! You think I would jest about butchery?'' He affected mortification. ''I *saw* it happen! *We* saw it! Your blood brothers and I stood like impotent bulls. Outnumbered ten, perhaps fifteen to one—who took time to count—we were impotent I tell you! And the weapons! The caliber of their weapons made ours look like toys.''

Vasquez, the consummate actor choked up, convulsed with sobs, mopped real tears from his eyes, fooling Paco completely. He pressed more brandy on the woebegone lad.

Francisco, stupefied and vacant-eyed, fell back into the chair, shoved the outstretched hand and brandy flask from him as if it were contaminated. ''No! No! No!'' he cried in wild repudiation. ''You are mistaken. Yes, that's it, you are mistaken. No one dares harm a de la Varga! What you say is unacceptable! Not until I see it with my eyes!''

Hysteria twisted Francisco's mind, bending it to his will. The sight of Vasquez brought things into perspective. ''W-who d-did t-this? W-who was responsible? You saw it, Antonio! Tell me!''

Vasquez averted his dupliatous eyes sadly.

''I asked, who? Tell me. I see it in your eyes.

''You—see—it—in—my—eyes.'' He dragged out the words. ''What you see in my eyes is a vision of their butchery burning in them. *Who*? Who. You ask who? Who else—the Workers' Union! *Que atrocidad*!''

Vasquez broke away, stutted about the small confines, arms waving dramatically. ''I heard them! I saw them! Voices carried in the night. Much was vague. They spoke of labor grievances. We were unable to get too close—understand.''

However shattering and incomprehensible was the blow dealt him, Francisco weighed words against instinct, sensing something far more ominous.

''There is more, *amigo*.'' False tears escaped Vasquez's eyes. ''The massacre of your family failed to appease them. The bastards burned the villa! Yes, Paco, arson! The vipers added arson to their heinous deeds. Come with me.''

''Where?''

''To evaluate our position, replot their demise with the same cruel dispatch meted your loved ones on this infamous night.''

''They did this? Workers' Union officials? The very men—''

''—you intended to kill on this night.''

''Those animals *murdered* my family!''

''They beat us to the game!''

''*A game*! You call it a game?''

''A game. Played according to the rules. A cold hard fact. War is impartial.''

Francisco, wild eyed, stared into those colorless eyes. A thunderous pounding at his temples distended his eyes. He seemed unaware that his hands had grasped Vasquez's throat, and were tightening . . . tightening.

Without alarming him, Vasquez deftly grasped Francisco's hands, slowly releasing the lethal hold on his neck, easing free. He cleared his throat several times until his voice returned, his concerned eyes fixed intently on the Spaniard.

''Christ! What have I done? What am I doing? Twice in one

night I have nearly killed you. What's happening to me? Am I losing my mind? Tell me, Antonio—what's happening?''

Vasquez pressed more brandy on him. "Sit down. Listen to me, my brother. When I heard of impending betrayal, my only thought was to reach you and abort the mission. I vowed, yes, I did, if I failed—if something unforseen happened to you—I would pick up the gauntlet to fight your cause. Now, I, your blood brother, Antonio Vasquez, swears an oath. I shall devise their deaths in kind, until their followers cow in submission. We shall show no mercy! No compromise is possible with *Los Deseredados!*'' Vasquez paced the confines, using a collapsible fox-headed cane to dramatically punctuate his words.

Silence—strained silence between them—punctuated by the storm's ravages, echoed in the mosque's rafters.

"No. No, Antonio.'' The Spaniard spoke above a whisper. "No one, only I shall taste the blood of vengeance. Not you, not anyone else, shall take on *my* responsibilities. It is *my* affair. I shall conclude this nightmare in *my* own way. On this their night of triumph and gloating they'll not expect counterattack. So my act shall prove an expedient.'' Pacing furiously, Paco forced Vasquez into a chair. Vasquez, shoved hard against one wall, sat frozen for moments, feigning awe of the Spaniard.

Vasquez, a master at projecting a Damon-and-Pythias-like intimacy, his acting flawless, counted on Francisco's fierce pride to cloud the issue. He knew precisely how to incite the younger man. It was not for nothing that this dissembler approached the zenith of his dreams.

"You are certain, Antonio, it was *not* Lieutenant Fuentes and his butchers who killed my family? He is no friend of the de la Varga family. My father opposed military juntas—what Fuentes advocates. No. It cannot be Fuentes. Only you and I knew the machinations of this night's involvements. Just you, Antonio and me. I told no one.''

"I dispatched Fuentes at Cordoba *after* betrayal warnings arrived. Surely, Paco, you don't think that I—''

"What happened at my villa? It *actually* happened as you described it? No chance of error?'' Francisco pressed fervently.

"You imply I have cause to deceive you?'' Vasquez affected dismay. "*Ay, mi querido amigo!* If you believe me capable of deception—that *I* would falsely dissemble to a blood brother—that *I* could trick and delude the sagacious Francisco de la Varga, gives me more credit than I deserve.'' He picked up a handgun, thrust it at Paco. "Go ahead, shoot me! Be done with it! I'd as soon be dead as denigrated by you. You, whom I've loved as a brother, think me a dissembler, a fabricator!"

Francisco waded through the melodramatic outpourings and flagrant flattery in discomfort. He thrust aside the gun, stared dully at Vasquez, his guts churning. Something about all this rang false, but it swam about hazily and disconnected in his head, just as the drugged brandy swam through his bloodstream. Something was forming in his mind. Thoughts collided with other thoughts, veiled by the brandy. Nothing made sense. He felt sick. He trusted Vasquez with his life. Unfortunately Francisco was too young, too inexperienced to discern the totality of the seduction.

Vasquez packed his Meerschaum, aware of the Spaniard's intense scrutiny. His brows arched delicately. "Forgive me, Paco, you were about to say something?"

Paco repeated himself. "They, uh—killed—uh—my entire f-family." He paced the words. "W-when they l-learn I am alive, they will kill me. Someone wanted my family dead. Who, Antonio? You must know! Very few plots are undertaken without your knowledge." He grew guarded, his words measured. "They killed my bethrothed, you said? Who slaughtered her father, crucified him before the Federal Building on All Saints' Eve day?"

Vasquez was perfect. His wide-eyed reaction, designed to convey shock and disbelief, brought an end to the business with the pipe. He shoved it into his pocket. "Incredible! Are you certain? But why wasn't I told? A conspiracy, eh? You think it to be a conspiracy? To what ends? Why? For what purpose?"

"I do not know. *I do not know!*" Francisco wailed in anguish.

"For now, erase it from your mind. Blood brothers, dispatched to Madrid, will uncover a conspiracy if one exists."

"*If* a conspiracy exists! Of course it does. Someone *permitted* the atrocity! The villa was secure; armed soldiers walked the ramparts. The military! Where were the military to stop the union slayers?"

"*Ay!* Francisco, in these troubled times you ask for miracles? Wide chasms split the nation's politics! The Workers' Union succeeded in keeping the matter covert. No leaks. No hint of their intentions fell to wrong ears. Had I not traveled to Seville to find you, had I not witnessed the atrocity, God knows how long the matter would be hidden from Madrid. What's the purpose in this? You shall be avenged, my brother. *Los Desheredados* take care of their own."

"No survivors, Antonio? Not the Moors? The servants? No one?" He reholstered the Campo Giro under his cloak, swaying slightly at the double vision afflicting him.

"None. In that fire—"

"Fire? Yes, yes, you mentioned fire." He paled.

"A shambles remains, *amigo*. Give it up for tonight. You need rest."

"No! I said no! It is my final word, Antonio!"

"Maldito demonio! Then, be finished with it! When you finish, meet me at the old fort, La Calahorra. Together we shall return to the smoldering ashes of your hacienda."

Departing the mosque in the downpour, Francisco drew his cloak about him protectively. He observed Antonio sprint across the plaza to the waiting auto and disappear inside. Turning, he sprinted through the murky, deserted streets, lashed with stinging rain, toward his destination, vaguely aware of haunting flamenco music floating out from the houses.

One thing struck him—the absence of Vasquez's usual, *"Bueno suerte, amigo."*

Aware of Francisco's fate on this night, Vasquez had no intention of keeping the rendezvous at La Calahorra, this night or any other. He sped back to Seville to begin the immediate conversion of de la Varga wealth into assets for Amadeo Redak Zeller. Having ensured against any possible escape for the Spanish noble, his thoughts turned to Victoria Valdez and the Seven Garduna Parchments.

He'd done it! By God, he'd done it!

So far, Vasquez thought, nothing—in accordance with his original plan—could have been easier. He found it mystifying that Francisco de la Varga had even begun, as it was said in secret, to challenge the authority of Antonio Vasquez.

Chapter Thirteen

Three hours ago he was a prince!

Now Francisco was a fugitive!

A fugitive, running from the law, hunted like a savage beast. *Santos de cielo!* How had things progressed to such insanity?

Incredible! Francisco de la Varga, a noble born to the best of two worlds, cowered like a whipped puppy in the dark corner of the ancient fort. His resolute, desperate attempts to piece together the chaotic chain of events since he departed the mosque failed.

Three hours ago . . .

He arrived at the appointed rendezvous. He saw them; his enemies sat at a wooden table piled high with printed matter. Three union officials, his intended victims, huddled together, in the shadowy, smoke-filled room, lit dimly by a solitary light bulb hanging by a cord. Cracked walls, peeling plaster camouflaged by torn, yellowing posters of the greatest of all matadors, Joselito, bespoke an era long gone. Cockroaches, spiders, lizards scurried about randomly. Odd he should remember these and very little else after. He remembered kicking in the door, standing crouched in the doorframe as the shocked, older men glanced up at him.

Francisco's guns went off in rapid-firing order!

Por Dios! How the blood splattered as whirling bodies lifted into the air, twisted by the bullets' impact. Stunned by the electrifying explosions, the men screamed, lashed their arms about the air like rag dolls, as bullets hit them time and again. One man who had nothing to lose shouted hoarsely, cursing Francisco. *"Señor, Señor* de la Varga! Fool! *Tonto!* How easy you play the idiot to the dictates of a master criminal! *Pobre desgraciado!* What deception he spins on you!"

A fusillade of bullets terminated the man's tenure with the Workers' Union. Moving through the makeshift office, he had examined each body, dazed by his own brutality and the rapidity of events. Certain each was dead, he had crossed himself, reholstered his guns, flung his cape over his shoulder, prepared to leave. *Bravo!* So far it fell according to plan.

Nada de eso! Not quite.

The minor commotion that followed the slayings should have afforded him cover; instead he found himself staring into the hollow muzzles of six military-issue rifles, fixed bayonets aimed at his heart. Sober-faced men in Guardia uniforms moved in on him. At that moment, the scent of betrayal wafted past him. Antonio was right! It was unclear *who* might have issued the orders, but the Guardia had executed them and the stench of their perfidy hung heavily in the air.

Lieutenant Lazaro Fuentes, that pantherlike soldier of the Guardia de Civil, advanced stealthily. Moving about the room, he examined with maddening detachment each of the bodies, kicking them over with a booted foot, loath to touch them. He purposely avoided eye contact with Francisco, and the Spaniard understood that the officer could not permit his men to witness the slightest hint of possible collusion. He snapped orders to the men in his Andalusian-accented Spanish. *"Vamos, pronto!"*

Francisco peered at the officer. *Fuentes!* Why Vasquez trusted him baffled him. Francisco made rapid assessments. Fuentes, out of his jurisdiction, would be loath to try any dirty business in the presence of the Cordoban Guardia Civil! In Madrid Fuentes was on probation for several major infractions of the Civil Code. Precisely what they were, he couldn't recall.

During the next several moments, as chaotic as they were, Francisco kept his wits about him, surprisingly containing his temper. Unable to ignore the exegesis of dangers immediate to his person, he reviewed the blueprints etched vividly in mind. By now nothing was going according to plan.

Flanked at all sides by six-guns, Francisco was marched out of the death chamber along dark, dank corridors, shoved out the building entrance into the driven rain. Drenched to the skin, shivering in the cold wind, he observed the Guardia officers signaling to someone further back along the street in the pitch darkness.

Standing there, Paco's mind raced back over the dying union official's last words. He recalled something—what? Yes, yes, he had called him a fool. An idiot! *"You were deceived, señor! How easily you play the idiot!"* In that instant, as the words roiled over in his brain, just how much the amateur he was shone vividly.

Francisco de la Varga . . . you are a marked man!

He'd seen it in Fuentes's bloodless eyes!

Right then, in that moment, he made an extraordinary decision. *No one, not Fuentes or his butchers, would kill the last de la Varga!*

Standing in the downpour, his head and face drenched, he furtively evaluated all possible options of escape. *None!* There were none at all! Not with all this armor aimed at his heart!

What next? Like a fool bearing witness to his own foolishness, he blamed another for his own gross miscalculations in judgment.

Vasquez! Why hadn't the son of a bitch restrained him?

He had lost his senses, else what gave him the unmitigated gall to assume that he alone could withstand the plots and betrayals aimed against his family? Most men, in the wake of his family's mass murder, would have collapsed, incapable of rational thinking.

Damn the devil! Vasquez should have restrained him!

The cold, biting rain had sobered him. Decisions must be made. The military police, mumbling incoherently, peering askance at him, signaled something was drastically wrong.

A lorry driving rakishly along the slippery street pulled up abreast of the Guardia. Francisco flung back his rain cape, revealing his holstered guns. "Do your duty, *caballeros,* you failed to disarm me. Far be it from Francisco de la Varga to obstruct justice."

On the whole it seemed stupid for a criminal to reveal both his identity and his weapons. But Francisco, a student of the law, had just invalidated Fuentes's orders to *"shoot the assassin at the slightest provocation."* The surrender of his weapons placed a veil of immunity around him. Shooting an escapee was one thing; it was another to murder in cold blood an unarmed man, especially when that man was the son of Don Diego de la Varga of Seville. One guard, acting alone, might have disposed of the impudent grandee easily. However, four soldiers who might render different versions of the story? Assassin or not, he was the son of Spain's most venerated war hero. The questionable death of a man of de la Varga's prominence could wreak havoc upon them; repercussions could prove fatal. Fools they were not.

Disgruntled, drenched, and short of patience, the Guardia slapped handcuffs on their prisoner and shoved him into the rear seat of the lorry. Two officers climbed in and sat at either side of him. Two climbed into the front seat alongside the driver. The remaining two officers scurried back into the building.

The lorry was old, its brakes faulty, and its clutch, sturdy enough for back roads or in city travel, was a definite liability on a long haul of some fifty kilometers . . . in a storm.

After several false starts the driver got the engine going again; it moved cautiously along the deserted dark streets and twisted alleys until Cordoba lay behind them. The driver followed the curve along the Rio Guadalquivir, striking ruts in the road, jostling the passengers unmercifully. Visibility was poor. Headlights bounced rakishly over the muddy roads, minimizing visibility further, creating havoc for the driver. The soldiers furtively eyed the road's edge, fully aware of what lay beyond the shadowy mass—deep crevasses. One inch over the boundary . . .

The rough ride joggled Francisco's brain, confirming the precariousness of his circumstances. Sharply defined in his mind, the intrinsic dangers became his only reality in the ensuing moments. Death surrounded him. He smelled it. He had left Cordoba alive. He would not reach Seville in the same state of health, unless . . . *Think, Francisco, think!* The rain was trying to tell him something. What?

Rain . . . Rain . . . something about the rain . . . What?

The Guardia, unusually silent, added to his disquiet. One man could be bribed—perhaps two—but five? Not all were sympathetic to nobles.

An obstruction in the road brought the lorry to a halt. They were two miles from Cordoba at a bend in the road, at river's edge, just before it turned sharply inland toward Seville.

The bad-tempered duo in the front seat, forced to brave the torrential rain and clear the path of brambles and uprooted trees, felt the brunt of the innuendos of the two soldiers guarding

Francisco. Their disparaging remarks momentarily took their attention from the prisoner.

It was now or never!

Up went his manacled hands, high over his head, his fists, balled hard, came crashing down on the skull of one man, stunning him. Before the second soldier reacted, fists pounded his face, drawing blood; handcuffs tore through an eyelid. The first man, recovering from the blow, lunged confusedly for the prisoner. Twisting his body, Francisco held the other in a hammerlock. He struggled to reach the blade in his boot, grasped it, and shoved it into the man's groin.

Wrestling free, he pummeled the second guard with hard sure blows, closing the other eye. Before the driver could move free of the steering wheel to assist his hapless companions, Paco leaped clear of the lorry's rear door, and in two loping strides reached the edge of the road. He sprang over the edge, fell, rolling down into the gulley, relaxing his body in the soggy, bramble-filled underbrush.

Bullets fell dangerously close on all sides of him in the murky blackness, missing him. His battered body rolled to a stop, caught in a heap of sharp, jagged rocks and spiny brambles. He barely made out the Guardia at the very top of the rocky palisade, floating in misty pockets of ebony fog. The rising vapors became his allies. The aimless gunfire, impotent in the thickening haze, was expended in desultory fashion at the fleeing felon.

Paco moved swiftly under cover of the storm, the instinct of survival strong within him. Lacking direction, visibility, he ran blindly in any direction, escape uppermost in his mind. He stopped suddenly, remembering. He had promised to meet Antonio Vasquez at La Calahorra.

La Calahorra. Where in damnation was it? He thought a moment, picturing in his mind how far the Guardia had traveled. Backtracking, getting his bearings, he rubbed his icy hands to stimulate circulation.

Goddamned handcuffs! How to get them off? *How?* He pulled, tugged, drawing blood where they cut into his flesh. Wincing at the searing pain, he cursed the loss of his guns. If only he had kept one—at least. Trudging over rocks and brambles, soaked to the skin, he tracked back and forth in the black bowl of night, searching for the old fort. A jagged bolt of lightning sizzled across the sky. A miracle! For a split second he saw the outline of his destination near the old Arab mills along the waterfront.

La Calahorra! The fort dated back to the time when the Moors occupied Spain. *Gracias a Dios!* The perfect place to rest, get his bearings, and find answers to the questions in his head.

He entered the dismal structure stealthily, wading through the hay and dung strewn about the earthen floor, his eyes furtively searching everywhere. No Antonio Vasquez! He moved through the lower level, his eyes adjusting to the dark. Ample time had elapsed since he departed the mosque. Had Vasquez been here and left? He struck a match, held it over his watch. The hour was late. He could not blame Vasquez. Tossing off the soggy cape, he contemplated the wisdom of taking refuge here, waiting until dawn before he got under way. He stretched his icy fingers, rubbed his aching wrists, and then he saw it.

A ladder. It hugged the wall to the upper level; above that another reached clear to the tower. He scaled it easily. Three quarters of the way up, he leaped to a catwalk. Climbing to the lofty reaches, he swung to the second ladder, pulled himself to the highest point, and peered through broken embrasures to the ground below. The northern, eastern, and southern approaches to the ancient fortress were visible to him. No covert access was possible; he would spot the interloper first. Sighing in relief, he descended one tier, located the dryest corner, and huddled against a wall, conjuring up the comforting benefits of a hot fire and a bumper or two of brandy. He shivered. His teeth chattered. Gripped by a relentless chill yet strangely feverish, Francisco arose from his sanctuary, warming his hands before he swung with agility up the ladder again.

His vision was dull. Straining to peer through the drizzle proved fruitless. Wearily he returned to his corner, huddled, his fatigued, lidded eyes descending to half mast. He blinked, fighting off the debilitation and despondency. He reached for, took hold of, and clung desperately to fleeting images of his beloved Victoria, forcing her beauty to hold fast in his mind. Hair of fire, drenched with sunbursts . . . glittering eyes; defiant, yes, arch at times, but consumed with love . . . the lilt, flow, the swing of her hips as she walked, talked and made love . . . her innocent candor . . . By God, it took his breath away. Pleasurable shudders inflamed his body; memories of their shared intimacies restored life to his flaccid groin.

Sweet, sweet Virgin! What manner of beast am I? Immersed in sensual pleasures when . . . oh Sweet merciful God! Victoria is dead! My family is dead!

His heart did battle with his mind; his heart refusing to accept the truth. Her husky voice whispered to him, endearingly, "You have let me experience womanhood in a manner I shall cherish for as long as I live."

For as long as she lived!

Demons wrought havoc on him. Victoria was dead! His unborn child was dead. His family—all of them were dead! It was finished. All that remained were the blinding memories.

Midnight! No sign of Vasquez. Scanning the lower reaches of the tower, Francisco caught sight of the connecting ladders. Inexplicably he kicked them away from the catwalks. He heard them crashing to the ground, suddenly wondering what had forced him to cut off his only egress. *Oh Christ! What was happening?*

Something was wrong. His skin crawled; hot and cold flashes alternated with such rapidity they left him shaken. He swung to the upper catwalk, peered through the embrasures and froze.

The Guardia de Civil—everywhere! In all directions! Enough to pursue an army. *Bastards!*

Flushed with anger, he leaned back away from the tower walls, flattening his body against the curved inner walls. Then, springing lightly on the balls of his feet, he covered all sides of the tower.

It was the same—on all sides!

Uniforms holding lanterns approached. He was surrounded! Had he remained on the ground level. . . . A sinking sensation gripped him. *Betrayal!* Only he and Vasquez knew of this rendezvous! Had Vasquez been caught? Arrested? Forced to talk? No! *Never!* Antonio would never betray him. His only recourse was to move.

He leaped through openings, scurried cautiously in the rain over the clay-tiled roofings, slipping, nearly falling several times. His manacled, cut, and bruised hands bled profusely. Falling debris and loose tiles fell with loud crashing sounds to the courtyard below, drawing unwanted attention to his flight. Oh Christ! He was done for.

"Quick! The roof! The assassin is fleeing!" Words punctuated by volleys of fire at his heels split the tiles, cracking them underfoot, spewing up clouds of pulverized clay.

Francisco zigzagged, crawled, swerved, and, ducking live fire, dropped level by level along the fortification wall leading to the water. He leaped to the soggy earth this side of the Guadalquivir River, picked himself up, and sprinted forward into the black-shrouded night, escaping his pursuers by seconds.

Suddenly struck by a bullet, he spun around. He lurched, stumbled, but would not stop. Even when the pain spread fiery tentacles in his lower arm and upper shoulder, he would not be deterred. By now, the raging fever in him forced him ahead. He was bent on preventing those mysterious forces that annihilated his family from killing off the last of the de la Vargas. He headed in the general direction of Seville, which seemed light-years away, bullets wailing all around him.

The chase was on!

How long had he been running? Hours? Days. Weeks? He stopped again, terror shuddering through him, listening. Bloodhounds! *Bloodhounds! Por Dios!* They howled war cries as bullets sprayed overhead. How much longer could he last? He floundered. The pain intensified. Rain, like spiny cactus thistles, lashed at his face. And the pounding! The pounding in his chest, so unbearable he felt his lungs would burst.

His dull, thudding footsteps, making fresh tracks in the muddy ground, frightened him. Amplified in his mind, they sounded like a hundred footsteps in pursuit. He was losing blood rapidly. What drove him forward was the desire to avenge his family's deaths.

Gunshots! Louder! Ahead of him, behind him, at all sides! God Almighty, help me!

The barking dogs drew closer, sounded fiercer, more predatory. Francisco drove himself like a demon without direction. Abruptly he pulled up short. He heard it; he swore he did! The river was close, very close! Sounds of turbulence, of rushing water came at him. It was no illusion! *God Almighty!* A few more running steps . . . Gun bursts hammered in his ears! He hesitated a moment too long. Another bullet shattered the shoulder of his wounded arm. The impact sent him headlong into the swollen river rapids. The frantic hubbub subsided; he faced the cobra of fear as he never faced it before.

He felt himself drifting, flung every which way in the turbulence; even as he clung to the floating debris, he felt himself powerless. Hours later—he had lost all sense of time—he disentangled himself from the floating mass, struggled to his feet, and found himself standing hip deep in the water. Overhead was a dense black foggy mist. He trudged, slipping, falling, and crawling finally to the riverbed. He fell, unable to move, until his racing heartbeats subsided.

Victoria . . . I promised I'd be home at midnight—instead we shall rendezvous in eternity.

Consciousness came and left him. Blood! He was losing too much blood. Somehow he managed with his teeth to rip apart a sleeve from his shirt. An eternity later he had finished, and with a twig made a crude tourniquet. On his feet again, with no recourse but to keep moving, he plunged forward blindly. All at once, he pulled back. Too late! Razor-sharp brambles cut his face, a spiky thorn nearly tearing an eye from its socket. Too late to avert the natural gladiators of the earth from ravaging him, he fell, twisting over on his back, clutching at his torn face, fearing he'd been blinded. Every bone, nerve, and muscle in his shattered body refused to function. He lay there, immobile.

Something was trying to form in his mind. Fragmented words, sentences, images, the series of events leading to this betrayal. Nothing. He could make nothing out of nothing.

But something had been made of something! What? What had heaped destruction upon him? His father had tried! *God Almighty!* he had tried to tell him something. That day in Madrid! With Paco wielding the gun against him! He had tried to tell him—tell him—something about Antonio Vasquez. *What?* So many things had been said. The crowd, the noise, the gunfire and insurrection— who could hear clearly?

"Vasquez is not who you think he is. He is someone else. An instrument acting for a nameless organization . . . Behind him a nameless organization and behind this, still another. Soon I shall know them all!"

A pall of black mist pulled him toward infinity.

He awakened, certain he was dead and gone to hell. An eye cracked open, then the other. A black presence hovered over him. A beast! He recoiled in terror. His eyes sharpened their focus. Vision cleared. Turning its enormous head from side to side, glazed black eyes gazing askance, the beast converted into a black stallion nudging him with its powerful snout. Francisco blinked hard.

He wasn't dead! He was alive! The horse would provide sorely needed transportation. He cast a speculative eye at the sky, searching for a break in the storm. He expected no miracles, for winter rains in Andalusia can be formidable enemies. Marshaling what remained of his will to live, he managed somehow to mount the beast. Delirious with fever, drifting in and out of consciousness, he headed to the only refuge he knew—the Hacienda de la Varga.

How long had he been here—an hour? Two? Slumped over his horse, his face buried in its thick mane, Francisco found himself on a high ridge on the Mount of Angels overlooking the villa. At the same spot from which Antonio Vasquez had stood not long ago, planning to acquire the coveted de la Varga lands.

Burning with fever, ridden with unquenchable thirst, Paco lifted his bleary eyes, trying desperately to put the scene in focus. Vasquez's words echoed in his muddled brain.

"Arson! Fires destroyed the villa! Everything reduced to rubble."

Why had he come here? What desire had he to view what had become a crematorium for his family? A hundred reasons to flee the place nagged at him. A thousand more kept him here. *Duty!* Duty to his family, to himself, reared its demanding head, duty commanding bravery, courage, and determination to avenge the wrongs done them.

Slits of light seeped through his bleeding eyes under their swollen lids. The moon appeared from behind the last wisps of storm clouds. He blinked, steadied himself against the stallion, and with superhuman determination lifted his head, staring down at the scene below under a spill of moonlight. Slowly focus cleared, bit by bit, so imperceptibly he failed to grasp the importance of what communicated itself to his brain.

Lighted torches burned in the courtyard. Horses, automobiles, and men, uniformed men, clustered about in small groups. The Guardia! They had come for him! Where would he go? What would he do? He could not return to Madrid. Never to Cordoba! Remain in Seville? Not now. He was a wanted criminal. A blood brother of *Los Desheredados*. The Disinherited possessed the means to effectively destroy any defector or betrayer, even a de la Varga! God help me!

But wait . . .

Holding the weight of his head with his manacled, bleeding hands, he cursed at the tricks his eyes played on him. It was impossible! He was going mad! Vasquez had told him the villa had been destroyed by fire, that he'd witnessed it with his own eyes.

What was happening? Francisco rubbed his eyes, increasing the burning, distorting the image, yet between the pulsating burning he saw it! He saw it as certain as he stood here this moment.

Mother of Christ! The hacienda, intact, sprawled across the land precisely as he had left it. He saw no signs of arson, fires, destruction!

He was going mad! Mad! Agonized cries escaped his lips. He dug his heels into the animal's flanks and galloped wildly off the Mount of Angels back toward the sanctuary of the Guadalquivir and his destiny.

You've lost all control! You're seeing things you wish to see, not reality, he told himself, spurring the animal into a frenzied gallop.

A sudden perception of his folly tore at him. Inner revulsion, bitter hatred, and a deep-seated violence raged at the unknown forces that had spawned the recent vicissitudes in his life. How could he have known that the black-hearted devil who had initiated the evil upon the de la Varga family had already prepared his vice-regency over all their wealth and affluence.

He rode furiously, his fever raging without mercy. Wherever he took pause to search for possible obstructors, an eruption of gunfire would blast his eardrums. *Mother of Christ! The Guardia was everywhere! How had they picked up his scent?*

He spurred the exhausted horse, demanding more of the beast than could be delivered. Somewhere between Seville and San Lucar he paused. Streaks of white-hot fire whizzed overhead, a bullet catching the side of his temple, stunning him. His body spun in recoil, fell off the horse, landing in the riverbed of mud. Gunfire resounded like cannon fire, splitting his eardrums. The sight of blood seeping through dirty, mud-caked fingers both enraged and weakened him.

Bastards! Stinking, foul scum sacks! When would they cease?

Against the tricky predawn lights, Francisco's vision cleared. He spotted several uniformed soldiers on the river bank a hundred feet away from him, poking at the tall reeds with their bayonets.

Blackness mercifully devoured Francisco. The strength sapped from him, he no longer cared, not for anything, including life.

He awakened late that afternoon. Vague thoughts and fragmented memories came at him, nothing making sense. A powerful flood of pain at the base of his skull immobilized him. With painstaking effort, he moved his hands to one side of his neck.

Hot sticky blood confirmed his suspicion. Earlier, when he fell off the horse, his head had struck a rock. His lower back and legs were without feeling, incapable of motion.

The night had ended. Terror immobilized his senses. How long had he lain here? How many days? How many nights? Was it only hours ago that he had lain next to Victoria, reassuring her, placating her, promising to return, never again to part? He did not know. He could not think. The young Spaniard was a short distance from Death's portals. Not long ago he had been the hunter. Now he was the hunted. Would God be merciful? Debilitated by pain and loss of blood, he felt himself precariously perched at the edge of madness.

Holes in his memory left gaps in time. Memories came and left him; irrational images, sketches of people—faceless, nameless men without shape or form. Everything was without definition. Conscious briefly, then unconscious as nightmares danced diabolically in his mind, he made nothing of the illusory images.

A moment's clarity came. He asked himself what did it matter if he lived or died? He would welcome death, if it came; it was the only remedy to a luckless situation.

A rash of images. Hair of fire, eyes of emerald jewels. Who was it beckoning to him from the distance? She was crumbling away, like an enormous icon, melting in a fire of hell. Deep within him he felt a presence. Of what? A deep basso-profundo voice echoed over and over inside his head.

You are not dead, Francisco de la Varga. Preserve your sanity. Think! You must not die. You promised . . . You promised Victoria. . . . Oh, God! She's dead! They're all dead!

A rustling of leaves, dull thudding sounds of running footsteps against the soggy earth, awakened him. An enormous figure hovered over him. He tried to refine his focus under swollen lids. Everything was a blur. A thrashing tangle of arms and legs silhouetted against the foggy mist formed ambiguous images in his mind, none recognizable. A stone weight pressed against his chest, crushing him. A face, a great face of frightening dimensions, leered at him. He fell into a whirlpool of blinding lights.

Chapter Fourteen

Powerful tides ripped across the Mediterranean. Herculean winds swept back and forth over its brooding surface and crashed ferociously against the hull of a tuna scow, plunging it headlong into the storm. The vessel heaved, pitched dangerously, fishtailing rakishly like a whale in death throes. The helpless man below deck, strapped to a bunk, groaned and moaned with seasickness. A swaying lantern hanging from the bulkhead in the crude, makeshift cabin created eerie lights and shadows on the bruises of the body lying on the bunk bed. Covered with a mass of welts and abrasions, the young man shuddered, strained against his bindings, his face swollen beyond recognition. He forced hard against the puffy slitted eyelids to focus on his surroundings.

Nightmares returned. Visions that were not visions but reality came to him. Unable to control the rapid rise and fall of his body temperature, he sweated bullets of fire and ice, each change forcing him nearer the consciousness he prayed would never return.

But it did return. God wasn't listening. A dim haze over each eyeball, fanning into light, activated his vision. He blinked, forcing more light in. Feeling, beginning at his toes, traveled slowly upward like a current of weak electricity until his brain snapped awake. Awareness brought on uncontrollable nausea.

He wanted to vomit, tried to, came up empty, only to start the process over again. His stomach backed up, delivering bitter bile to lodge in his throat where it burned like acid. His body was aflame. Water. He needed water.

He strained to move, unable to budge an inch. Vague, ambiguous shadows shifted through the haze. His senses sharpened. The stench of stale fish assailed him. The pungent smell of rotting wood increased his nausea.

He tried jogging his memory. Nothing. His panic increased. He kicked his feet furiously, strained against the ties, but the pain, too intense, halted further attempts. To breathe was an arduous feat. His eyes darted to the door. He saw the bolt slide open. He recoiled, retreating into the shell of his body, alert yet helpless at the pain biting into him. He endured agonizing hell, uncertain of his fate, as a dark, shapeless hulk, standing in the open doorway, entered, closing the door behind him. Its dark visage remained indistinct to Francisco de la Varga. He lay back fearing the worst.

''*Señor*?''

The voice! Where had he heard it before? Recognition took place. A bull of a man stood over him, shedding foul-weather gear. His upper torso, disproportionately larger than the rest of the body, grew more familiar. A shock of black hair like porcupine quills around a receding hairline seemed to grow like nails. The dark glistening eyes instantly became those of a solicitous bloodhound. In the lantern glow the multicolored beard shone fiery—friendly.

Matteus, the Moor, prepared an injection of morphine, observing the patient. The opiate was transferred from needle to bloodstream.

''In time the pain will pass.'' The Goliath rubbed Francisco's arm until the burning ceased.

Memory returned in bursts of shock and confusion and with it the countless demons pursuing him. ''Matteus!'' His senses were jolted by the rush of morphine. ''God help us. From where did you come?'' Tears spilled from the Spaniard's eyes.

The Moor loosened the bindings, elevated the patient's head and shoulders, tucking a rolled blanket under him. Francisco gazed numbly at the deep abrasions and pus-infected burns ringing each wrist. His left arm was bound in a sling.

''Two bullet holes. You have lived at the center of hell, *mi amigo*. Rest for now. We talk later,'' the Moor instructed quietly.

"Matteus—is it true?" The words, just above a whisper. "M-my f-family—d-did t-they—were they k-killed?"

The Moor stiffened, asking frigidly, "Do you want truth, Paco? Or lies like those fed you so many months."

Francisco shot him a reproving look.

"It's true." The Moor sighed. His words stumbled from him. "No thanks to you, they are all dead. The *Señorita* Valdez, my beloved brother Pablo, were also killed. Slaughtered by the men you trusted with your life. *Your* blood brothers. For too long you have remained blind to the death surrounding you. Now see what blindness and deafness to your father's words have reaped."

The Moor's words faded as the opiate coursed hotly through his body, relaxing every ache and spasm. In the widening arc of light spilling from the lantern as the boat pitched, heaved and rolled giddily over an angry sea, Francisco focused on the Moor's grim features. He felt strange; a hot rush of euphoria pervaded mind and body. His highborn arrogance, about to erupt in an avalanche of condemnation, reprimanding the Moor's tone of voice, dissipated. Morphine. The god morphine took reign, turning him lethargic, uncaring, weightless, without concern for anything, himself included.

Earlier, for a fleeting second, he wanted to kill, maim, massacre all those who had slaughtered his loved ones. As quickly as the hideous nightmare became reality, it faded. Now, what did anything matter?

Matteus attempted to spoon-feed him soup. Francisco, unable to ignore the Moor's estrangement, shook his head vigorously, held his lips together, stubbornly refusing nourishment. Finally he shoved the spoon away. "First, *muchacho*, you eat it," he whispered hoarsely, the paranoia behind his words unmistakable. He trusted no one.

Matteus smiled wanly. "It might have served you better if your suspicions were aroused many moons ago, *amigo mío*."

Shame-filled eyes averted the Moor's. Francisco's lips parted submissively. In went the soup, five spoonfuls. Unable to take more, he shook his head, lifted himself on one elbow, wincing at the pain. He was more lucid now. He silently questioned his bandaged arm.

"Bullets, two, upper arm and shoulder. I removed the shells. Is your memory impaired? You recall nothing before I found you?"

"Bullets?" He blinked. "Why would anyone shoot at me?"

"You play the assassin, you reap the rewards," the Moor quipped dryly. "You were hunted, shot at by the Guardia and those stragglers of *Los Desheredados*, your blood brothers. *Bribón!*"

"You lie! Why do you spin lies now?"

"Why would I lie to you, Francisco? For three days and four nights you escaped your pursuers, hiding from them, playing them for fools." Navigating his towering bulk over the plank floors to the cabin door, he bolted it. The vessel had outridden the storm at last.

He turned to the Spaniard. "Listen to me. Hear my words well. Your blood brothers did the job on you." He placed a vial on the table. Francisco's eyes fell upon it. He gasped aloud, sucked in his breath, recoiling in horror. "Why do you turn away? Do you not recognize the eyes of a friend? The eyes of Pablo, my brother. Shot from his head with *my* guns. *Mine!* I picked them off the ground, placed them in this vial in alcohol to preserve them and remind me every day of my life that the man responsible for the atrocity lives. He lives until I shall mete out to him the justice he meted out to your family and mine. My bullets did not kill Pablo. He was nearly dead. With his last breath he made certain I would abide by the trust and faith placed in me by your father Don Diego." He crossed himself religiously. "Your blood brother, Antonio Vasquez, killed your family and Pablo. Antonio Vasquez!"

Francisco turned from the revolting sight, sickened. A delayed reaction to the Moor's final condemnation echoed in his brain. "Antonio Vasquez? No! No! It cannot be him! No, I tell you!"

"Your mind refuses to accept the truth. *Muy bien.* Shall I put it to you succinctly? Yesterday, a mere five or six days ago, you were unquestionably the wealthiest man in Spain. You held within your grasp the scepter of power, the world at your feet. Today you are someone else. Never to be the man you were— not for a long time—a glorious future ends in disgrace. Why? Your false perceptions, perverse, intractable stupidity, brought calamity to your family, destruction upon you."

The Moor towered over Francisco, observing the bruised, bullet-shattered body he had resurrected from death's doors, wondering at his blind loyalty and obedience, trying to assure himself he had made the proper choice in saving this *burro*. "You were the subject of a long search by the authorities. Hunted like an animal, shot at with less consideration than is shown to an infidel dog.'' He removed his jacket and began to shed his woolen shirt.

The Moor had saved his life. Francisco owed him that, but to attack him personally while he lay inches from death, in so infuriating a manner, was something the hidalgo's ego refused to accept without stern rebuttal. Silence! How dare you speak to me in so demeaning a manner!''

''I say to you, listen. And listen you shall in whatever manner I choose!'' the Moor retorted. ''The heinous crimes committed against the House of de la Varga have brought about a few positive results, *amigo*. Your penance is to be *me*! I shall remain at your side for the rest of your days as a constant reminder of your blackhearted perfidy. You, Francisco de la Varga, are as guilty of the deaths of your family, your beloved fiancée, and my brother Pablo as if you had killed them yourself!''

''Stop it! You are killing me! I am still at death's door,'' came the anguished cry. ''Do you wish to push me into the void of eternal damnation? Leave me in peace! *Dejenos en paz!*''

''If it were my choice? Yes, by Allah! Yes. For the willful denial of your birthright, your insufferable conceit, inflated self-importance! But mostly for consorting with duplicitous men who seduced you without cost to them! *Maldito Dios!* A lowly street whore would have demanded payment, but you? Oh, no! You merely lay back and permitted the unholy rape. Why in the name of God did you permit yourself? What weakness lurks deep inside you? What madness permitted the betrayal of family? You cut off communication, brought dishonor and death to your family. You permitted this devil's disciple to become your God, your mentor, and finally your downfall. Strange, Paco, how the stench of his abomination failed to overpower you. Even a jackass will not step into the manure of another.''

Francisco shook his head in silent, stubborn denial of the truth. He blocked out the painful words, concentrating instead on the swaying lantern, listening to the sea slap against the creaking hull. ''If you loathe me why save my life?'' he asked *sotto voce*.

''Don Diego's sentimentality in saving his son's worthless hide escapes me. His last request binds me to you for life. So, get used to it.''

Stinging tears spilled onto his discolored, battered face. He swallowed humiliating remorse when the Moor's words fell upon him, lashing him with brutal candor. How could he logically explain Antonio's seduction of him? He barely understood it himself. Perhaps he was mad. Deranged!

Stripped to the waist except for a thin leather pouch strapped to his upper torso and another at the waist, Matteus placed various objects on the table. Turning up a mattress corner of the bunk, he pulled out a large flat parcel and tossed it across Francisco's legs. "When you can you will dress in this clothing. Meanwhile my duty is to prepare you for the lengthy voyage ahead of us." He sorted out the documents and, shuffling them about on the table, placed them in an order conforming to a peculiar inner mental design.

"By what authority do you dare speak to me thusly?"

Matteus, although servile at times, was not a humble man. "By the authority vested in me by my beloved lord and protector, Don Diego de la Varga, who bound me to you the day you haplessly became one of the Disinherited."

"He knew? My father knew of my affiliation with *Los Desheredados*? With Antonio Vasquez?" His eyes grew wild.

Matteus gave him a cold assessing stare. *The opiate! It must be the drug. It did strange things to a man's mind. One minute you make sense, the next—did he remember nothing?*

"The closeness between us evaporated once you became a radical politico." The Moor's eyes followed the other's line of vision. He was staring at the sharp knife on the table. Matteus picked it up, tossed it into the air, snatched it quickly as it fell, balancing it on the palm of his hand and smirking contemptuously. "You still feel loyalty to those butchers? By the beard of the Prophet, what a job they did on you, *amigo*! God willing, I shall endeavor to undo their evil and rewash your brain, *Signore Bonifacio*. In approximately five hours this poor excuse of a fishing boat will arrive in Ajaccio, Corsica—"

"*Signore Bonifacio? . . . Ajaccio?*" He shot inquisitive, hostile eyes at the Moor.

Matteus hurled the knife into the table; it quivered for several seconds before stopping. He pounded the table, indicating the papers spread out before him. "It is all here, the instructions clearly written, *Signore* Bonifacio."

"Stop it! You know who I am. Don't do this to me! *Mother of Christ!* You are driving me insane!"

"Who you *were, Signore* Bonifacio. Who you were and no longer can remain if you wish to live. Perhaps it is just as well if

you die.'' He spat. ''You never honored your name in the past,
but by God you shall honor this one, if I have my way.''

''This is preposterous! You are preposterous!''

''And your father—is he too preposterous?''

Cowed, Francisco stared at the articles on the table. Passports,
visas, letters of credit, property deeds, banknotes, Swiss and
French currency. What else?

''Legal documents bearing the name Vivaldi Fornari Bonifacio,''
the Moor began. ''I submit each to you as your father requested.
Listen. It is important for you to know and understand—no
matter how it shocks you—the evil machinations of the man who
calls himself Antonio Vasquez.'' He began to read the information submitted by a Trieste investigation firm, records lifted from
Omicron's files. He read for nearly an hour.

'' 'The man, Amadeo Zeller, a known assassin in very elite
circles, was once affiliated with Organization C, better known as
a society of assassins. This man, *Señor* de la Varga, is a man to
be watched warily, he is a cagliosto of the blackest sort. He deals
only in results, feels no curiosity for the agony of his victims.
We know he went to Zurich in November 1918, remained there a
year, and later emerged in Spain, using the cover Antonio
Vasquez. Our investigators reported Zeller's presence in London
a few months ago, where he consorted with men involved in a
notorious conspiracy. A mysterious fourth party involved in the
conspiracy to assassinate targeted members of British Parliament
departed; we believe the man was Zeller. Facts substantiate his
presence there at the time.' '' Matteus sipped water from a
goatskin to wet his lips.

''Vasquez is too young to have acquired the despicable reputation profiled in these reports,'' Paco muttered quietly.

The Moor ticked his beard thoughtfully. ''Satan was recognized at birth for the evil of his soul.'' He continued reading.
'' 'Firmly entrenched in Spain, Vasquez fans the fires of insurrection while covertly presenting himself to the authorities as an
ally. Actually he works hand in hand with the Guardia Civil, who
conspire to solve civil disobedience in ways that make the
Inquisition pale. Vasquez allied himself with dissidents, the
Workers' Union, with whom he cemented strong ties in Barcelona long before his arrival in Madrid. The university radicals,
taken with his fire-and-brimstone manner, allowed the seeds of
rebellion to be sown in their minds.

'' 'Who are the *Hidden Hands* from whom he takes orders? It is the next logical question, *Señor* de la Varga, one to which we presently plead failure. The information has eluded us for decades. The facts are as follows: the organization—fronted by banking institutions—originates in Zurich. Among the invisible giants are reputed to be several of the world's most powerful and affluent men. We do not deal in rumors; therefore we feel it unfair to start one. The moment we obtain dependable facts we shall forward same to you. A fact, *señor*, as painful for us to report as it will be for you to hear: In Madrid, Vasquez organized a terrorist brotherhood, *Los Desheredados*. Among those duped into joining him are sons of Spain's most devoted royalists. Your own son—' "

"Stop it! I've heard enough!" Francisco cried hoarsely. Unwilling to believe in his own victimization, he pressed, "Anyone could have written those lies. A man as important as Vasquez must have thousands of enemies!"

The Moor lifted black glittering eyes, focusing on the Spaniard. "You still persist in placing Vasquez on a pedestal? What is this mulishness? Paco, it is too late to play games with your head. What will it take before you sew together the pieces of the conspiracy that decimated your family? Can you not see the duplicity in the beast?" Matteus led Francisco over the roughshod road again, as Don Diego had commanded. He explained the legacy of the Seven Garduna Parchments, pointing out the appearance of the name Antonio Vasquez in the de la Vargas' past history. He touched briefly on the real Antonio Vasquez, how he had affected the lives of both Spaniards and Moors.

Paco's thinking capacity diminished by the euphoric state induced by the opiate, he waved the Moor off. So much crammed into his brain at one time overwhelmed and confused him. And all this talk about secret brotherhoods! He tried to sit up, couldn't. He fell back against the bunk bed. He insisted, "I need to walk, Matteus. I need air! If I don't move, my legs will atrophy!"

"Better your legs than your head." The Moor seemed relentless.

He helped Paco to his feet, walked him about the cabin, a step at a time, three, four minutes at the most before Paco collapsed, totally exhausted. He lay against the bunk as Matteus, back to the business at hand, held up a letter. "From your father. Shall I read it?"

"No. Let me." Paco held the letter in trembling hands as the Moor busied himself opening the parcel of clothing. He laid out various articles on a chair and the bunk bed. He shifted the lantern to a wall peg above the bunk bed so the spill of light better illuminated the letter. Francisco stared at the contents, a hard lump arising deep in his throat. He began to read:

My beloved son: Delivery of this letter to you by Matteus means I am dead at the hands of Antonio Vasquez. . . .

Francisco stopped, wild denial in his eyes. "It says here . . . my father claims . . . Matteus? How could he know in advance the identity of his assassin? I do not understand. Why didn't he take measures to circumvent the deaths . . ."

"What must I do to convince you of what I myself bore witness to?" The Moor placed a rolled blanket behind Paco's head. "It is the truth! I swear it upon the soul of my departed brother Pablo. By Allah! I saw the massacre! I saw them die! And after they killed your family, Vasquez turned the guns on his own men. Your father *knew* in advance what Vasquez really wanted—the Garduna Parchments! The truth, no matter how painful, must be understood. This man—whoever he is, Vasquez, Zeller—came to usurp the de la Varga wealth. With your help he attained his goal!"

Francisco winced under the undeniable truth. He accepted the hot Turkish coffee, which Matteus had boiled in a pot in the makeshift galley in a corner of the cabin, and turned in defeated silence back to the letter:

How I tried to dissuade you from consorting with that devil . . . A year following the armistice, discreet inquiries, made abroad concerning de la Varga holdings by unidentified parties, came to my attention. The inquiries, coincidental to the civil unrest in our nation, caused several world financiers to believe our business advisers were involved in secret negotiations geared to upset the sensitive economic balance in our nation and theirs. In alerting me to the imminent dangers, their assumption was clarified. Considerable sums of money were changing hands. Mergers with foreign interests were being effected in curious, covert ways, unveiling very clever manipulations of the stock market in London and Wall Street.

In the misery that followed the armistice, I was warned that a force would soon disrupt Spain's politics. That this force would erupt at Madrid University; further, it was clearly pointed out that civil unrest precipitated in Spain would tear the nation in two.

Needless to say, it came to pass. Shortly after Antonio Vasquez appeared, it became clear that he was the force described by our friends abroad. When I learned, my son, that you, of all men, supported Vasquez, advocated his philosophies, emulated his politics, and persuaded *our* friends to provide the platform he needed to promote his politics, I tried desperately to reach you, to make contact with you and discuss the matter. All appointments I set up, you arbitrarily broke. You became unavailable to me.

Ill-boding rumors came to my ears and I feared for your safety. You forced me to procure all available information on the man. Secret records reveal his true loyalties. Let it be known they bear no resemblance to any you might bear for Spain.

Spain was not the target of Vasquez's treachery; it was a means to an end. The end? A carefully executed plot, the implementation of a clever strategy aimed at controlling the de la Varga wealth and what lies behind that wealth, an inherited legacy. Matteus will explain it in detail.

Recently I learned that the *plot extends beyond the annihilation of our family*, into other dimensions, possibly to Argentina and beyond that, Chicago, in the United States!

I had worked swiftly to bind the marriage contract between you and Victoria, hoping to remove you from Spain. That day in Madrid you pushed me from you. Oh, my son, we had so much to discuss. That same day Don Verono was slaughtered by Antonio Vasquez. His money, valuable papers, and vital legal documents were removed from his person. In the wrong hands they can move mountains of wealth.

Then, following the butchery on All Saints' Eve day, the systematic assassination of the nobles began, close friends disposed of one at a time. It was all subterfuge, my son. Subterfuge to get at me, at what I hold inviolate. All was done to impress and dazzle you. He kept the de la Varga family for the very end, *after* he had duped you. Do you see it now? I took what precautions I could, but since you are reading this letter, my precautions were obviously ineffective.

Know, Francisco, know it well! Our family fell prey to the evil menace and adroit manipulations of Antonio Vasquez, who is not Vasquez at all, but another man, far more evil, more menacing than the face he presents to you. I shall not belabor the irrevocable past. You must listen to my words, hear them from across the grave to which Vasquez committed me. Listen as you have never listened in your life. Burn them into your soul, heart and mind! Matteus is to be trusted. Accept his guidance, for in your absence, I transmitted my knowledge to him. From birth he has understood his binding commitment, an obligatory part in this legacy, which at times has been a curse.

The Seven Garduna Parchments must never fall into enemy hands!

Matteus will inform you of their value. Carry the legacy forward into the minds and souls of your sons. Together, you will generate the power, will, and strength to enable you to return to Spain and reclaim your birthright. Take warning! Unless you marshal forces superior to those demonstrated by this man Amadeo Zeller, you are to avoid him at all costs. *Do not tangle with him!* You will lose all, including your life. Only when the power is yours can you combat this lethal foe. *The time must be right.*

Matteus will deliver into your hands the gold ring of the Marten. It will open doors, introduce you to *friends* throughout the world who can be depended upon for assistance.

Money, funneled over the years into foreign channels, is available and at the disposal of Vivaldi Fornari Bonifacio. This identity, and your destination, will keep you alive. Properties, bought and paid for in other nations, cannot be traced to de la Varga sources. Monies from the liquidation of certain assets in South America, deposited to numbered accounts in Zurich and Geneva, identifiable by the symbols to be found elsewhere among these documents, will enable you to draw on the funds without danger of exposing your true identity.

Plan astutely. Take time to adjust to your new identity. Wear it cautiously. Trust *no* man, save Matteus. Follow these instructions judiciously. Burn the name Amadeo Redak Zeller into your memory. He is a master at disguises. He will employ a long list of cover names in his lifetime, but the name Zeller is the one he will use at the top.

Find him, Francisco. Swear on the blood and souls of your family to avenge the wrong done us. Death as punishment is too sweet for such a man. Once Matteus reveals to you the extent of this man's evil I trust you will devise a scheme to exact just penance.

Know that our family has been bound to the family of Moors for five centuries. The documents will explain. The father of Pablo and Matteus was my right arm. Matteus shall be yours.

You cannot, must not, remain in Spain! Else you shall be killed as they killed me. You cannot stand alone against Zeller. Understand this. Your life must not be wasted.

Perhaps I will never know if you are still alive, and if the Seven Garduna Parchments escaped Zeller. From wherever my spirit alights I shall endeavor to watch over you. May the blessings of God be upon you, watch over you, and instill in you the needed courage to perform a just execution of your duties as son to Diego de la Varga.

The letter, signed, sealed in wax with the family crest, fluttered from Paco's hand, falling to the floor. The irrevocable hand of God had sealed his fate. *Sweet, blessed Jesus! What have I done?*

The truth pierced him like double-edged daggers through his heart. He could trust no man in Spain. What diabolical planning!

Convulsed with sobs, he turned, facing the wall. He grew quiet, the tears stopped. Francisco observed the playback of events with the detached fascination of a person watching a three-reeler.

It was true. He could not deny his total seduction by the clever Machiavellian Vasquez. As pictures played in his mind, he recollected how he and countless Madrid students had succumbed to the dissembler's rhetoric. When suddenly Francisco was singled out, flattered by the attention of a man who openly scorned the fawning adulation of hundreds of students, why wouldn't he experience inner exaltation? What nineteen-year-old would shun the enviable position of standing at the center of attention, the envy of his classmates?

Francisco pondered . . . one night—when was it, how in Christ had he overlooked it?—Vasquez had boldly spelled it out for him, like graffiti on a wall.

At the Café Madrid, over dinner, shortly after they had met, Francisco spoke out. "You are a Bolshevik, no, Antonio?" he had asked.

Vasquez's amused laughter filled the room. He shook his

head. "I assure you you're mistaken. Bolsheviks neither like me nor loathe me. For now, they merely ignore me. The worst degradation, Paco, is for a man to be ignored. Be hated! Be adored! But never, *never* be ignored." He sipped his wine in genuine mirth.

"We met two months ago, Antonio. At times I feel I've known you always. Other times, you are a stranger, a man of mystery."

"No, no, no, *amigo,* not a stranger. What I am is a man of destiny. That's why you feel you know me. An immortality exists in me, one that connects to you university students. But enough of such talk. Let us drink a toast, Paco. To the man I was, to the man I am, and to the man I shall become." They clinked glasses. "I admire you, Paco. You are a man with an aim in life. I too have an aim—to get all I want from life."

"And that is?"

"To be like *you.* Possess what *you* possess. Control all *you* control." He'd lifted his wineglass as if he were studying the wine's clarity and smiled sheepishly. "The de la Varga fortune." Vasquez's laughter had resounded through the café, making light of his declaration. "Oh, yes, and of course, very shortly, the Valdez affluence. How clever of you to consolidate fortunes with the Argentine."

Francisco had joined in the laughter. "That's some ambition, Antonio. Until recently you knew nothing of my existence, now you covet both my inheritance and my future bride's."

"That's true. You were born to riches. I was not so fortunate. I was forced to dream, Paco. Dream, scheme, plan, plot, work hard to acquire what is necessary for my future. The demand exceeds the supply, you see, so I must work industriously to make up the shortage."

"Too bad, Antonio. Your dreams, schemes, plots, and whatever must exclude de la Varga holdings. I personally control nothing."

"Your father is not immortal, *amigo.* One day the burden shall rest upon *your* ability, *your* integrity, *your* cleverness to make it work. Pray, do be prepared for so tremendous an undertaking. Nothing, Paco, is as loathsome to me as a man unprepared to handle riches."

"That, Antonio, is a burden I neither anticipate nor desire for many years. I know not the taste of greed or avarice or of ambition."

"Because you were born to riches," Vasquez had said quietly.
To be like you! Possess all you possess. Control all you control! The de la Varga fortune.

And he, Francisco de la Varga, the camel's ass of the century, had laughed with Vasquez!

"I swear to you *Signore* Bonifacio . . ." Matteus's voice came to him through a dark tunnel. He had missed the prologue. Something concerning the massacre of his family.

"The deed took no more than a half hour. A half hour? Six family members, twelve servants, and Allah knows how many more." He poured more coffee for the Spaniard. "He came to Spain spreading his gospel while in the pay of the Guardia. No one saw through his disguise. He collected the terrorists, tore Spain in two, then, hired by the Guardia, betrayed his blood brothers. He wiped out all traces of his guilt. He remains a friend of the Guardia Civil, protected at all costs, immunity ensured for all his crimes by the forfeiture of the pawns he collected, a long list of the Guardia's enemies."

"What are you saying?"

"What am I saying? I am telling you *Los Desheredados* no longer exist. The Guardia rounded them all up and executed every last one. Oh, yes, Paco, they were betrayed by their mentor—Antonio Vasquez! The five assassins who emptied their guns on your family and mine were slain on the spot with Vasquez's guns! *Dale al diablo lo que es suyo!* Give the devil his due and you will see him clearly for what he is."

Matteus guzzled the remains of his wine. Paco, beginning to feel the pain returning, winced, not at the physical pain but at what the Moor conveyed.

"You are saying that Vasquez now has the power of the military behind him? That he stands all-powerful? More powerful than the nation itself with the de la Varga fortune supporting him?"

The Moor leaned forward on the table, his bearded face cupped between two powerful hands, nodding ruefully, hoping the Spaniard understood the full significance of his words. "He stands all-powerful but only for a time. Only until you absorb the contents and power of the Seven Garduna Parchments. And then . . ."

"And then?"

The Moor stood up straight. "Before we come to that point

we must first approach Vivaldi Fornari Bonifacio. A noble Genoan family related on your mother's side of the family. Pay attention, *signore*. The real Vivaldi died of consumption in youth. A trust established for him at his birth and invested wisely has accumulated substantially. The assets of the trust, purchased by your father years ago and reinvested after the Bonifacio family was murdered by political dissidents, have multiplied considerably.''

"You are a fount of knowledge," the Spaniard said tightly.

"Pay attention, *Signore* Bonifacio, I must cram into your head much information before questions are asked of you for which you have no answers." He prepared another injection of morphine at the sight of pain contorting the other's face. As he worked he continued the briefing.

"We shall reside in Corsica, by design rather than by choice. The Fornari Bonifacio family, absentee landlords for many years, own vast lands in Corsica, including quartz and marble quarries, forests, fruit orchards, farming and grazing land. You will have little difficulty being accepted, if it suits their fancy. But take heed of my words. The Corsicans are a curious lot. They trust no one and despise strangers. Common ground must be found upon which to meet in understanding and respect. The Corsicans will observe you silently with an inborn caution.

"I speak their dialect; you fortunately speak Italian, their native tongue. They speak French rarely and only when Frenchmen invade their lands. The time we spend in Corsica cannot be calculated, so prepare yourself for an extensive stay. Men in Spain, fully trustworthy, will inform me in time about what is happening at the hacienda. They will observe that viper—"

"Not now, Matteus. *Por favor*. Until after I have mourned my family and my beloved Victoria, my mind is not attuned to anything but the moment."

The Moor nodded in understanding. He collected the morphine kit, placed the vial of eyeballs into his shirt pocket, and, slipping into the foul-weather gear, left the cabin, permitting the Spaniard to rest.

Francisco stared solemnly at the rotting, wood-beamed ceiling, at the swaying shadows created by the lantern. Thoughts and images flooding his mind, replayed without form, out of synch. The words of his father echoed from a grave.

The plot extends beyond the annihilation of the de la Varga family. To Argentina—perhaps Chicago!

Victoria belonged in some way to both places. Could this be merely coincidence?

He shut his eyes briefly, then lit a cigarette, puffed on it for a time, sickened by the fatuous blindness that had permitted him to subordinate himself and everything that had meant anything in his life to this man Zeller. His besotted witlessness, if measured, would crown him king of jackasses. Would he ever understand the flames of hell enough to circumvent them in his life? The inconsistency of his behavior boggled his mind. Repudiating the wise dictates of the man all Spain revered, his father, he had permitted a man like Vasquez to feed him with slick oratory and to destroy him.

Deception, for God's sake! It had all been deception!

Where was his sense of balance—his intelligence? All his life he'd engaged in mortal combat with himself, demanding autonomy. His father had told him in desperation, "You see and hear only that which is compatible to the wild beatings of your savage heart, instilled by barbaric passions and a thirst for life. Once, Paco, it was acceptable behavior—when Spain was young," his father had said. "Modern-day thinking and its restrictions merely confuse you."

It was true—he had fought for and won autonomy. God Almighty! What a price he'd paid!

Everything had been taken from him by a man who used his cleverness to steal the de la Varga properties and create his own world of power!

Francisco felt wretched, alone, frightened, his self-esteem at the lowest ebb in his life. Wealth and riches, the social standing to which he was born and had taken for granted, no longer existed. The name de la Varga stood for something special in Spain. He had reduced it to nothing. He was a stranger to himself. For the rest of his days he would remain a stranger in a land of strangers. Of what use was it to continue?

Morphine flowed through him . . . morphine. It dulled his senses, dimmed perception; it elevated him to a sea of weightlessness, a plateau that diminished pain and thinking. He felt a warm rush flood his senses; an undulating heat permeated his body, propelling him into a warm tunnel where he saw, actually *saw* himself swimming about, floating, soaring above the surface and diving into a sea of tranquillity before plummeting downward into a dark abyss of forgetfulness.

*   *   *

Long before dawn of the next day he stood on deck dressed in the elegant attire of an affluent Italian. The newly born Vivaldi Fornari Bonifacio moved with a limp, his weight supported by a gilded lion's head cane. He would arrive in Corsica, a near-dead man, but in style. The bruises on his face and body, the healing bullet wounds, were all reminders of the living hell from which he'd emerged.

The fresh scent of sea air, the fine salt spray, felt invigorating; still he wrestled with conscience. A collision course between thoughts and emotions imprisoned his mind. He felt like two different people with separate personalities trapped in one body; one grateful to have escaped, and the other critically observing him. His hold on reality was so fragile he conceived abysmal pitfalls and failure ahead.

Observing him from a short distance, Matteus glanced out at the turbulent seas. For a time, he too fell victim to shapeless images, bloodied recollections that stretched achingly across his mind. He recollected how he had hidden among the ranks of military police during the manhunt Vasquez and the Guardia Civil had initiated to find Francisco. He had skulked about for days following their forays in and about Seville. While the fastidiously dressed Guardia diligently patrolled the Las Marismas marshlands, Matteus had roamed in closer to the bird-and-animal sanctuary where by chance he stumbled across Francisco. The man Vasquez had set his butchers to find was lost to them.

Taking every precaution, the Moor had floated the body through tall reeds of the tributary leading to the main river, out of the soldier's range. Next, the expropriation of a river boat. A long trek downriver at night had taken them to San Lucar de Barramedas, where among waterfront hovels he had booked lodgings and sneaked the dying man inside, past the *concierge*.

A grouchy, uncooperative physician was roused from slumber to examine the near-dead Spaniard; he had vehemently protested the expending of further energies to save a man who was a hair from death's door. He argued that loss of blood, lack of nourishment, protracted periods of unconsciousness, and God knew what else caused him to make such a dim prognosis. The Moor's persistence, however, in addition to a large sum of money, had intimidated the physician into performing miracles.

A week of uncertainty passed. Francisco's return to consciousness had kindled hope in both physician and Moor. The frequent administration of heavy doses of morphine were gradually reduced, yet were still needed. The physician had explained it carefully.

"To preserve the patient's life, the priorities lie in the reduction of pain. Excessive pain is the *killer*! The inability of the heart to absorb, withstand, and combat protracted assaults of severe pain does the body in. With morphine the future looks less dim."

As Francisco mended, Matteus, busily at work, negotiated passage to Corsica with the skipper of a fishing scow in Cadiz. A few nights later, a long boat ferried them from San Lucar to Cadiz. They had barely boarded the trawler, set to sea, when the Moor, glancing back toward shore, had sighted squads of mounted Guardia troops converging on the port authorities. But he and Paco had escaped, alive!

The trawler pitched prodigiously, upsetting Vivaldi, lurching him from his reverie to reality. On this day, February 25, 1921, the Spaniard, Francisco de la Varga, was buried at sea with all the personal effects that could betray him. His personal Rubicon lay ahead, enshrouded in mystery and intrigue. Sighing deeply he spoke out.

"Tell me, Matteus, are you to be my conscience?"

"No, *Signore* Bonifacio, merely your steering wheel."

Both Spaniard and Moor turned their eyes on the giant shadow looming in the near distance.

"*Poco a poco*, step by step, one goes a long way." The Moor spoke Spanish softly amid the crashing sounds of the sea against the hull. Then he spoke in the tongue they would speak in the future, Italian. "*Allora*, circumspection, *signore*. Understand?"

Vivaldi Bonifacio understood perfectly. Before they came above deck, Matteus explained the dangers. "It is imperative you know and understand what can happen. Captain Zacharias, the trawler's skipper appears to be a benign man. I caution you in advance. The look of peace scrawled on his cunning face and on those of his men masks the souls of assassins. Captain Zacharias's approach is conspiratorial, Vivaldi. His seamen's shabby attire is designed to project an aura of paupery. But it is all a masquerade, a tool used for extorting higher fees for the unique services he performs."

"*Unique* services?" Vivaldi got the picture. "He promotes the escape of men fleeing one country for another for whatever the reason, *sí*? Then what's the problem, Matteus?"

"The problem is he often earns a second fee for betraying those to whom he offered protection. Anything you do to displease him will mean imminent betrayal. Should a client suggest an additional sum, a bonus, outside the price fixed for his services, Captain Zacharias will light up like a brilliant sunburst blessing you, *una vez, dos veces, tres veces, cien*—"

"Speak Italian, *per favore*. Did you offer him a bonus for our safe arrival?"

The Moor, listening for usual sounds, had signaled a negative answer with his eyes. "And be marked as fools? No. Zacharias's duplicitous ways are known to *friends*. His reputation is widespread. The wise avoid him."

"And we, the desperate are forced into league with the devil. Is that it?" The Moor had nodded, and leaped to the door, listening with cat ears.

"Foul play usually occurs as his passengers sight their destination. At the moment their spirits soar and their guard is down, he moves in. Unexpected foul play takes place, a knifing or garroting followed by a watery grave *after* the captain robs the carcasses. Failing in this, he reports the escapees to port authorities, pleading his innocence in the transportation of vicious criminals who invariably "forced" him at gun point to enter into a criminal conspiracy."

Vivaldi sighed despairingly. "Is our life to be a series of brutal confrontations? Never-ending bloodshed?"

"Let us concern ourselves with immediate dangers—none in the future." The Moor had loaded a revolver and tucked it securely into the scarf sling in which Vivaldi's injured left arm was sheathed. "If needs be you will shoot to kill. We are five against two."

"Five against one and one half," Vivaldi muttered bitterly.

"Pray Allah you are strong enough at the proper moment."

"What does that mean?" Vivaldi snapped.

Now here they were before dawn, expecting the worst. Vivaldi stood on deck. It was his first visit topside since boarding the trawler at Cadiz. The Moor hovered at a slight distance, standing at a point closer to the bow for a better vantage point. Tense, yet giving every indication of outward calm, his dark eyes scanned the crew, wary of any false move. There . . . almost on cue, the man appeared.

Captain Zacharias stepped from the engine room, weaving his

way forward unsteadily, combating the pitching and yawing of the sea. "There, straight ahead, she stands, *signori*."

A special look, a current of understanding and complicity, passed between Spaniard and Moor. Captain Zacharias narrated with brio. "Corsica . . . a spectral, indifferent giant perched on the gray horizon. A gargantuan shadow of mystery, an island, an enormous rock jutting from the cobalt sea and thunderous splashing white surf. Separated above water from the larger island to the south: Sardinia. Did you know these islands are connected underwater like Siamese twins?" He struck a friendly, disarming pose, affecting to be a knowledgeable seaman.

Vivaldi glanced at him and turned, feigning interest in the panorama. Matteus moved in, positioning himself as a bulwark against foul play, at the eye signal passed from Zacharias to two of the men. They came, first one seaman, then the other, armed with knives and garrotes. Matteus sidestepped the first, sent him plunging into the frothy pitching sea. The second came at Vivaldi, knife outthrust. An iron grip on his wrists caught him by surprise and Matteus twisted the blade inward and, with a swift leg movement, caused the assassin to lose his footing on the slippery deck. He fell on the knife.

"Now, *signore*, shoot!" Matteus said. Vivaldi reached for the gun with his right hand, winged Zacharias, and shot at the remaining two assassins.

Matteus picked them up bodily, heaved them overboard, leaving Zacharias, stunned, backed up against the engine room, his feet entangled in the netting, bewildered at the sudden turn of events. He pulled from under his filthy sweater a knife and a handgun, dropped them to the deck.

The Moor leaped forward. "You will pilot the ship into the harbor, Zacharias, and leave immediately for another port. Do you understand me? And if you ever so much as recall a hair on our heads or make reference to either of your passengers on this trip, you will spend sleepless nights, haunted to eternity, for it is well known that Moors have an endless bag of tricks, which they use without hesitation." He shoved Zacharias into the engine room, ordered him to set out for the port of Ajaccio, standing over him, gun in hand.

On deck Vivaldi gazed at the alien, foreboding-looking island looming ahead as an enemy to be conquered. What would the future hold for Vivaldi Bonifacio? His eyes fell to the golden ring of the Marten on his left forefinger. His curiosity had been aroused when Matteus insisted he wear it; he wondered how the ring would fit into his future when in the recent past it had sealed the fate of his family and Victoria.

Vivaldi Fornari Bonifacio. Would he ever come to terms with this new identity? Become more Italian than Spanish? Why in God's name had his father chosen Corsica? What was the logic behind Don Diego's thinking? Why not Sardinia, where Spain strongly influenced the language and culture?

Why Corsica?

In the faint pink glow of a newly born sun about to burst on the horizon, Vivaldi regarded Corsica. Its early history, veiled in mystery, and its modern-day customs were never clearly fixed in his mind. An enigma to the outside world, one fact was indisputable, Corsica's history had played a determining role in keeping strangers from her shores.

Matteus, handcuffing Zacharias to the helm, joined Vivaldi on deck.

"Is it safe to leave him to his own resources?" Vivaldi asked.

"If it were not, be sure I would not have left him alone."

"I have as much to learn about you as I do about Corsica." Vivaldi turned back to the island panorama. "What will we find here, Matteus?" It was a rhetorical question. "Seneca, exiled here once, wrote a consolatory letter to his mother defining Corsicans as savages, barbarous men and women. What he said was, 'The Corsicans' first law is vengeance; the second, to live by robbery; the third, to lie; the fourth, to deny the gods.' " He sighed heavily. "To such a place we are exiled. Is Corsica the price I pay for my folly?"

"Better Corsica than death."

"Seneca's words are immortal, but, *mi amigo,* pray Corsica has lost all traces of barbarism."

Lost in the silence, against ocean swells and an able engine putt-putt-putting toward the harbor of Ajaccio, the Moor adjusted his eyes to the horizon, a throbbing crimson and white-gold sheet of pulsating lights that blinded the eyes, illuminating the harbor scene. They were approaching the Sanguinaries.

"We are fortunate to be alive, *signore.* The small fortune paid to this scum, Zacharias, provided us no insurance against our safe arrival. You saw how easily we could have been killed. Do not exclude possible treachery from mind—we have yet to set foot on Corsican soil, eh? Stay alert."

Stunned by lack of sleep, exhausted from the long vigil over his charge, Matteus still could not permit fear to cause errors of judgment. About to begin life anew in alien lands and prepare for a future of blood revenge, he began to put his mind in order. *As smooth water reflects the image of all objects within its range, so must the mind be kept clear to reflect its opponents' moves and prepare the way for immediate, appropriate, accurate responses. If the surface of the water is disturbed, its images will be distorted. If the mind is occupied with disturbing, improper thoughts, it will not comprehend an opponent's intention.* Lesson one in the training of Vivaldi Bonifacio—to enable him one day to recoup the great losses of recent weeks—was about to begin.

Vivaldi was struck by pangs of conscience. The Moor had risked his life to save him, not once, but many times. Both were suffering the nightmares of Seville, yet he had offered the Moor no balm, consolation, or sympathy. *Damnation!* Where was his compassion? He owned no exclusive franchise on sorrow or heartaches!

Vivaldi glanced at the manacled Zacharias, then shifted attention to the scenic panorama. They were not tourists; they had no desire to partake of gaiety, old churches, museums, or breathtaking landscapes, yet both men focused intently on Corsica.

An ancient lighthouse rose from a craggy rock and extended from the island itself. The Isle of Sanguinary—the Island of Blood. Vivaldi shuddered. Intermittent whistles from fishing boats setting out to sea collided with the incessant screeching of gulls. Above the piers and quays of the harbor stretched the city of Ajaccio, a mass of whitewashed houses, hexagonal red-clay tiles, glowing with a high gloss in the sunlight. Splashes of bright Corsican reds, Mediterranean blues, golden-rod yellow, and Irish green materialized into swaying palm trees, Genoese watchtowers, canopied sidewalk cafés, and an exotic array of impressive yachts.

They had arrived. There could be no turning back.

Both men stood on a quay observing Captain Zacharias leave the harbor for some other port.

"Why do I feel it is not the last time we hear of Zacharias?" Vivaldi said quietly.

"What does it matter? We shall do what we will when that

time comes. Now remember, *Signore* Bonifacio, do not pronounce the word Ajaccio as the Spanish, *Eye-ee-ah-they-o,* but as do the Italians, *Eye-ee-ah-chee-o.* Remember this at all times, you are an Italian who speaks French, Spanish, German, whatever. . . ."

Chapter Fifteen

"You are *Signore* Bonifacio? *Signore Vivaldi Fornari Bonifacio?*"
The shock on the bank manager's face was total.

Don Carlos Mazzeppi, a dirty, used-up man with evil eyes and
a weak mouth, wearing a worn, black serge suit, stared at
Vivaldi, then shifted his focus to the Moor. Stringy, yellow-
white hair fell around a wizened face framing dark, owl eyes that
had seen all there was to see in his fifty-eight years.

In the background, a gramophone played Puccini. "Corsicans
cannot be all that barbaric," Vivaldi said to Matteus in Italian.
"Imagine. *Tosca.*"

They sat opposite each other in *La Banque Nationale Francaise,*
sizing each other up. Mazzeppi smiled, showing his yellow,
shark teeth as he studied the welts and discolorations on Vivaldi
critically. He gestured with a bony, tobacco-stained hand. "How
did this happen to you, *signore*?" He opened a pill box and
popped an opium pill.

"A minor accident, a regrettable fall from a horse. A sprained
arm as incapacitating as a broken one." A look of long suffering
appeared on Vivaldi's face. His glance fell to the pill box.

Spreading out the identification and letters of credit on the
desk before him, Mazzeppi mopped his sweaty brow. "*Piacere,*

signore. It is a pleasure to serve you. It has been too long since a Bonifacio has come back to Corsica.''

''Ah, then, you know my family?''

''But of course, *signore*. We Corsicans believed for many moons that a Bonifacio would return to help restore our lands to their former glory. To our displeasure we became a department of France, instead of Genoa. But you are not in Ajaccio to vacation, judging from these documents. What is your pleasure?''

''To assume full tenancy of my lands.''

''Fully tenancy?'' For a moment Mazzeppi's face reddened. ''Ah, yes, full tenancy. For a long time, *signore*, you have been an absentee landlord,'' he temporized.

Spaniard and Moor exchanged glances. ''What exactly does that mean, Don Mazzeppi?''

''It means, *signore*, the ways of our people may not conform to your expectations. Your lands are leased. To terminate a lease becomes difficult at times.''

''I may not be so inclined. An examination of the books of account—if profits are indicated—might prove it advantageous to keep the leases intact.''

''Examination? Books of account? *Profits? Signore*! There are no profits! But of course you jest. You must know all this from the reports sent to your bank, no?''

''No.''

''But, *signore*, the tenants do *not* work the lands!''

''Suppose you tell me exactly what it is they *do* on my lands?''

''Tenants? Tenants are—tenants! They live on the land. Eat off the land. What else?'' The banker threw his hands into the air in a gesture of futility. ''But this is not my concern. I make no inquiry into the books.'' He snapped his fingers several times.

From across the room, a mousy-looking man, a bookkeeper programmed to respond to finger snapping, glanced up from his desk, sprang from his chair as if by electric impulse. He sprinted across the room, his waspish face screwed up inquisitively. His name was Victor Barbone, a small man, weightless as a bird in appearance. He wore a striped shirt with a white starched collar, red satin garters on his sleeves. His stoop-shouldered appearance, a by-product of his profession, hardly matched his youthful looks and the hint of bulging muscle under his shirt.

''Barbone, bring me the estate ledgers of Vivaldi Fornari Bonifacio,'' Don Mazzeppi snapped, emphasizing the name.

Barbone hesitated, cowed by the silent command in Mazzeppi's coal-black eyes, then disappeared into an adjoining room; he returned blowing a thick dust layer from the ledger cover and with defiant aplomb placed it on the desk before his boss.

Mazzeppi imperiously opened the ledger. He licked the fingers of his right hand, thumbed page after page, frustration and annoyance seeping through his artful serenity. "*Signore,* you own so much property. Which do you desire to examine first?"

"Suppose I review the ledgers at my leisure and make the determination at the proper time." Vivaldi made this a statement.

"You wish to sit here, at the bank, to read the books?"

"No. My hotel. Perhaps, Don Mazzeppi, you can recommend a suitable restaurant in Ajaccio?"

"But of course, *signore.*" He scribbled an address on a card. "The very best in the city. Mamma e Carlu. Excellent food, I assure you. Carlu is my cousin. *Adieu* to you."

As Vivaldi and Matteus left the bank, stepped into bright Corsican sunlight, Don Mazzeppi snapped his fingers again. Barbone scurried to his desk. "Listen to me good, Vittorio. You go to my cousin, Carlu. Tell him to observe these two *birbante,* eh? Set on them an accomplished spy who will not be detected. Then, alert your brother Chamois, eh? We must know *everything* they do, to whom they speak, where they go, and how they are treated here in Ajaccio. If they are friends to anyone, I must learn to whom, understand? They must learn *nothing* of our involvements. Should they approach the French authorities, demand an inquiry into the business and legal affairs of Vivaldi Fornari Bonifacio, it means, for us—the end! *Madonna de Dio,* we shall be forced into the *maquis!*"

Vittorio Barbone understood too well. He locked his desk, pocketed the key, slipped into his black serge suit jacket, picked up a leather satchel, and, lifting a bowler from a wall peg, peered inside the compact crown fitted with a small handgun. He placed the hat on his head, walked through the doors into the street.

Don Mazzeppi waddled from his desk into a caged alcove. He stepped into a walk-in safe, raised the gas jet on the wall for better illumination. He sorted through several ledgers, shoved his glasses from his forehead down on his nose and reexamined the pages. A frown creased his face. He popped another opium pill to dull the excruciating pain of duodenal ulcers.

Seated at the small wooden makeshift desk, he traced entries on the pages with short stubby fingers. He paused periodically to mop the sweat pouring off his brow. He'd seen enough. He closed the ledger, replaced it in its compartment, locked the drawer, turned down the gaslight and shuffled heavily along the worn carpet to his desk. He placed a sheet of paper before him, dipped a plumed pen into an inkwell, and scribbled: *"A rapid, smooth liquidation is necessary. Contact Chamois Barbone to do the job on Bonifacio and the Moor."* He signed it "Mazzeppi."

Ajaccio, a city of contrasts, of squalid suburbs and palatial mansions, Byzantine cathedrals and spartan *chiesas* abounded with marble statues and a profusion of monuments dedicated to Corsica's most famous son, Napoleon Bonaparte I. The military fort with fancy uniformed soldiers on watch seemed antiquated. Its streets, overrun with humanity, were maddening to traverse. Foreigners instantly spotted as an oddity were stared at, jeered, and ridiculed, especially by the street urchins.

Vivaldi and the Moor walked to the café through quaint streets lending a far different atmosphere than any in Spain. Intrigued, they passed garbage piled high in the peopled streets, past mounds of pulped lemons equally as high.

"Why do Corsicans use so many lemons? Surely they don't eat them as Spaniards eat oranges?" the Moor muttered.

They moved on through the shouting confusion, past dirty, scrubby houses next door to palaces. Lines of glaring white washing stretched across narrow streets like signals of surrender. Young lads hawked contrabrand wares; horse-drawn carriages clattered noisily past them on the cobbled streets; dung permeated the air. No sweet essence could disguise the pungent odor.

Ajaccio was madness! Music hammered away, blasting their eardrums; accordions, guitars, hurdygurdies, at every street corner competed for attention. From the houses stacked together like rectangular blocks, the music of Puccini, Verdi, Ruggerio, even Wagner played on gramophones, all at once, turned the day into a cacophonic nightmare. The shops in a tangled maze of streets were like smelly corridors with their own splendid confusion; strings of lemon, colorfully arrayed vegetables, purple and green figs bursting in ripeness, chestnuts, olives, sausages, cheese and anchovies, and stalls where fresh fish of indescribable ugliness lay on slabs: squid, octopus, eels, mussels, oysters and only God could count the numerous variety of shellfish!

"Ah!" Matteus exclaimed in a sudden burst of enlightenment. The lemons are used on the fish."

Vivaldi's nostrils were assailed by the sweet pungent aromas of seed spurting melons. And there, in the middle of this gastrointestinal nightmare, stood Mamma e Carlu's café.

Mamma e Carlu's, a piece of Corsican Victoriana, was half mansion, half hovel. An atmosphere of restraint prevailed despite the lush marble cupids, tarnished gilt mirrors, and cracked whitewashing. The newcomers to Corsica took an outside table under a colorful canopy, ordered a breakfast of hot breads and coffee.

People bargained for foodstuffs with mule drivers, and men strolled arm in arm, in groups of two, four, even six. They paused to argue, make points, oblivious to any save themselves. The music of *La Bohème* suddenly rose above the cacophony of operas and Caruso's rich tenor voice permeated the narrow streets, bouncing off the whitewashed government building at the far end of the piazza, past the fort, into the cul-de-sac where the café catered to a motley assortment of patrons.

Corsica was a distinct cultural shock for Vivaldi. Matteus accepted it in stride.

"Obviously, the café is a combination meeting place, message and package depot, general store, and place to exchange gossip," Vivaldi remarked to the Moor, his eyes trying to take in everything at once.

"It is also a place where hidden eyes observe us from secluded alcoves," Matteus added, watching the café's patrons through discerning eyes.

"Then it isn't my imagination? You too sense it?"

"It is controlled, the low-toned conversation, bordering on hostility. I fear in some cases it goes deeper. These are men who never see more than they intend to see, but who know everything that goes on."

Constrained politeness from the waiters, their constant fussing, brushing imaginary crumbs from the table, rearranging glasses, silver and table linens from one spot to another, grew annoying, prevented any discussion between Vivaldi and Matteus. More disconcerting were the purposely casual eyes, indifferent stares from men partially hidden behind newspapers. Mamma e Carlu's was obviously a favorite spot of men of questionable character who earned questionable livelihoods for even more questionable purposes.

Neither Matteus nor Vivaldi felt comfortable. Something in Vivaldi's brain waited. He sipped his coffee from a saucer, continental style, his eyes arrested at a point beyond the Moor, narrowed in thought.

"That man, behind you in the shade, along the flower box, dark suit, gray fedora. I think I know him."

The Moor did not move. "Impossible. We know no one here."

"I tell you I know him."

"Who, then?"

"My memory is hazy. Madrid. I associate him with Madrid and Vasquez."

The Moor was very still. "Has he seen you?"

"Yes. He too is attempting to put it together."

"You bear no resemblance to who you were. The bruises, swellings—all excellent camouflage. Do not concern yourself or worry." Matteus glanced up casually, attempting to summon a waiter. In that second he got a clear view of the man in question.

"He is an agent provocateur," Vivaldi insisted.

"Better you remove from mind the possibility you will be recognized. I shall pay the bill. Wait here for me. I will hire a carriage to take us to the Fornari Bonifacio estate, *va bene*?"

Vivaldi nodded, glanced blandly at the familiar face, then took the Moor's advice. He flipped randomly through the pages of the ledger. Here and there he caught sight of blatant inconsistencies. Curious debits and credits he was unable to make out. He turned page after page, his finger moving from left to right. Outrageous! The books bore traces of falsification. He closed the ledger, sipped his coffee, glancing up and down the street. If a superficial perusal produced flagrantly fraudulent entries, what would an in-depth audit produce, besides Don Mazzeppi's apoplexy?

Matteus had prudently suggested they move slowly, take things a step at a time until they stood on solid ground and knew the Corsicans better. Vivaldi concurred. Once they settled on the Bonifacio estate . . .

Vivaldi lighted a thin cigar, acutely aware of eyes boring into him. Vasquez, the master, had taught him to detect unusual movements in a crowded room. Had he learned his lessons well? He glanced casually about, spotted the first incongruity. A motionless figure of a man in a darkened doorway close by. Heavy, well paunched, in his thirties, dark lizard eyes hanging low in their pouches under thick, fleshy lids. A bulge under his jacket on the left side—he was armed.

Vivaldi felt sick. It was too soon, way too soon. Dizziness, nausea, a parade of painful images cut through him like an electric current. He sipped water, fixing in mind the geography of the place. Where in hell was Matteus? What was taking him so long? Vivaldi, having experienced an obsessive dread of weakness and isolation in the past few weeks, was filled with dread. He was coming to depend on the Moor too heavily. He must relinquish this destructive fear gripping him. He lit a cigarette, blew out the match, when he spotted a second alien presence zeroing in on him.

A slouched figure at the edge of the sidewalk, his boyish frame against a building wall, one knee raised, foot flat against the wall. A cap pulled low over shaggy brows formed a shadow over his fleshy beaked nose, and a cigarette dangled from the corner of thick, twisted lips.

Amateurs! Rank amateurs! He had learned his lessons well! Neither man demonstrated the requisite detachment needed to excel in surveillance work. The air of menace both meant to exude was laughable.

Matteus beckoned to him. Collecting the ledger and leather case, Vivaldi paid the bill. Matteus moved swiftly across the congested street and helped Vivaldi to a waiting carriage. Every eye in the café, it seemed, stared after the strangers. Demonstrating a cavalier grace, Vivaldi paused before boarding the carriage. "And who are you, my good man?" he asked the driver.

"I am called Andrea Doria. Descendant of the great Genoan general, *signore*. Ah—do not appear disbelieving. What remained of General Doria's courage dissolved long before a speck of his blood mingled with mine. The four-centuries-old battles he fought are dim in my memory. You see, *signore*, here in Corsica, we are all descendants of royalty. Kings, even emperors. Today I drive a fiacre for hire, content to earn enough to feed my family. However, I much prefer to gamble. A Corsican needs little else."

Vivaldi, glowering darkly, was sorry he asked. Seated next to Matteus, he muttered, "Remind me never to ask that question again. Will every Corsican we meet deliver a history lesson?"

Matteus suppressed a smile. The driver, instructed earlier by the Moor as to their destination, cooed to his horses. The carriage rumbled through streets alive with people and activities.

Vivaldi glanced at charts and maps of the Fornari Bonifacio properties. The estate, as he saw it, was several kilometers north of Ajaccio, along the west coast. Land encompassing several thousand acres should be profitable.

The perky carriage, drawn by festooned, red-tasseled horses, trotted past vast market gardens, picturesque farm buildings, verdant pasturelands and a coastline that was unequaled for elemental beauty anywhere on earth. Vivaldi and Matteus focused intently on the extreme changes once they negotiated the coastal route, past a disorderly tangle of peasant carts and stubborn mules that impeded their progress out of Ajaccio.

Vivaldi dwelled on something Don Mazzeppi had said to them. "Do not tamper with the *maquis* and avoid traversing the easement running through Bonifacio properties whenever possible." Vivaldi repeated the caveat to Matteus, adding, "Tell me why the Corsican bank president referred to the area so ominously."

"Political prisoners, fugitives from the law, take refuge in the *maquis,*" Matteus explained. "It is an area even the police do not traverse, for all those who commit blood vengeance take to the *maquis* because no laws exist to protect such men. As I understood the land titles, the French government set aside a portion of Bonifacio lands. The right of egress and ingress, and sections of the *maquis* itself, are held sacrosanct for these criminals."

Vivaldi listened for as long as he could. Under the narcotic's languorous effects, he dozed for a time, was awakened momentarily by changes in the terrain and sudden shifts in temperature. The ride grew exceedingly rough on their bodies; every lurch, jolt, bump over every rut in the dry, dusty road, was imprinted on their backsides. Their discomfort was forgotten in moments as the splendor of Corsica's interior greeted them. Nature exploded on all sides of them. Ancient olive trees, bent and deformed over centuries into curious shapes and grotesque formations, stunned them. Steep granite walls along narrow, corkscrewing roads were barely able to accommodate the carriage. They passed jagged promontories, precipitous valleys, mountains with razor-back humps, descended into broad fields. Then, suddenly, the air filled with an exhilarating sweetness they had not experienced before. Ahead of them, a mist arose from the earth in what appeared to be an ethereal, mythological land, far removed from any earthly thing they'd seen.

"The *maquis*, *Signore* Bonifacio," the driver, Andrea Doria, proudly announced.

Inhaling the splendid profusion of floral and herbal scents, Vivaldi and Matteus were treated to exotic botanical splendors. An alien world to them. Trees, their branches spreading every which way in a tangle of branches with other trees, formed lacy patterns of indescribable design. Steam appeared to escape the earth in misty vapors, and rising in drifts moved through the *maquis* like specters of startling shapes and forms, protecting the men who took refuge in it.

Vivaldi, suddenly arrested by the Moor's rigid posture, noted his upraised hand in a gesture of silence, his eyes fixed on the driver. Turning slightly to Vivaldi, his eyes signaled to a position on the mountainside beyond red granite monoliths.

Vivaldi spotted a black and white ballet of sheep woven through the mountain flanks, lost in a mangling perspective; they appeared oddly crabbed between centuries old trees strewn about, shaped and petrified by the elements into a strangely Brueghelesque scene, more a canvas than reality.

"Do you sense their presence? See them?"

"Sense who? See who?" Vivaldi saw nothing beyond the panorama.

"A hundred eyes peering down on us."

Vivaldi, shot with fear, shuddered. Or was it getting colder at this altitude? He tugged up the collar of his coat, unable to still the shivering disquiet. Observing the Moor feel for the security of his gun failed to bolster his waning courage. Each became more aware of their surroundings. They were traversing the *maquis*. Now in. Now out, but closer to primitive landscapes.

The carriage, creakier, more uncomfortable, jogged over bumps and craters. They climbed higher, to somewhere near the sea. Vivaldi, increasingly aware that this land was saturated by strange, mesmeric forces, was awed at the sight of hallucinatory lights, lacing in and out of towering trees forming delicate swifts in the sky.

"Stop the carriage!" Matteus thumped the driver's shoulders, shouting, "I said stop!"

The nervous driver, pulling hard on the reins, braked the wheels to a screeching, sliding halt, causing gales of dust in the road to arise behind them. Before his passengers collected themselves, Andrea Doria retrieved the sawed-off shotgun from under his seat, leaped from the carriage, and was halfway down the hill before the congested air cleared. "*Por Dios, señor*, fly from this place! *Cuidado! Ay de me!*"

Forgetting for the moment the necessity of speaking no Spanish, Matteus propelled Vivaldi into action. They jumped clear of the fiacre and sprinted forward, swiftly clearing the carriage some fifty feet before the booming sounds of gunfire exploded the bomb-rigged carriage. They dived into the bushes, flattened their bodies against the ground. Under them the very earth shuddered.

Glancing behind them, they blanched at the incredible devastation. Horses, thrown into the air, came down stiff-legged, their bellies ripped open, entrails pouring from them. The carriage, totally demolished, rained to earth in splintered pieces amid broken rocks, pebbles, and geysers of dust. Screaming animals lay bloodied in the open craters and potholes, nearby.

Vivaldi, appalled at the sight, doubled over at the pain of fear knotting his stomach. He shook uncontrollably and, wiping the dusty sweat from his skin, cried aloud. "Sweet, sweet Holy Mother! Not again! Not here! We left it all behind us, didn't we?"

Matteus, gun in hand, hunkered forward between a broken spiked-iron fence and stone pillar. A timeworn, faded sign, hanging lopsided, bore the barely detectable printing: TERRA FORNARI BONIFACIO. He turned to Vivaldi, glanced past him at the scene of the explosion, commanding, "Stay here."

Sidling cautiously, skirting the perimeter of the wreckage, trying hard not to suck cordite smoke and chalk dust into his lungs, he waved the thickly congested air before him, peering in all directions, walking in dislocated circles through the wreckage. He took pity on the dying, disemboweled horses and delivered a bullet to the head of each until their suffering ceased. His instinct worked triple time. His eyes trailed casually from the slashed granite towers jutting up from the road to the mountain. Matteus tensed, alerted to danger. What could he do?

Enemies without faces, shapes, or form surrounded him. Matteus smelled them as a beast sniffs a scent in the winds. In a cautious tigerlike movement he moved behind a spinning carriage wheel, grabbed it, ending its revolutions.

Vivaldi, disregarding the Moor's order, had crept in behind him and, sorting out the wreckage, made his observations. "The bomb had little power. Not everything was chewed up and spit out in pieces." He lifted the charred remains of the ledger book, blackened at the edges but intact. "How was it you sensed the danger?" He blew the ashy dust from the smoky remains.

The Moor, intent on the enemies stalking them, barely heard Vivaldi. "Come, we approach the land of your adopted ancestors to learn what other maledictions Moloch devises on this unholy day."

Vivaldi persisted. "How did you know? The bomb? The driver?"

"He addressed you as *Signore* Bonifacio. I never told him your name. What's wrong? Are you feeling badly?"

"The pain. Always the pain. It's past time for the morphine."

"Will it not wait?" Matteus inserted fresh cartridges in the Campo Giro's chambers. A quick wrist snap forced the cylinder shut.

As he and Matteus threaded their way through overgrown brush leading to the iron-spiked gate, Vivaldi glanced over his shoulder. "Who in Corsica wants us dead? *Why?* We might as well have stayed in Spain. Nothing's changed. *Nothing!*"

"Do not hold a mirror to your fears, Vivaldi. When among dogs, you must play the lion. Display bravado when your bones rattle in fear. We shall learn who and why in good time. We have outfoxed them. Soon, if we continue to prowl like lions, their curiosity will force them to show themselves."

Before Vivaldi reacted, he felt the Moor's strong, steadying grip on his arm, guiding him forward. Vivaldi persisted, "Who? Who are they?"

"Whoever wishes us dead." It was a simple, forthright reply. Moving in, climbing over the broken, rusty gate, Matteus cautioned, "Remember, play the lion even if your heart is that of a dove. *Avante!*" The sudden pull on his arm sparked impatience.

"Well, which is it? Go or stay?"

"Look there, up ahead. The house."

Vivaldi's face flooded with contradictory emotions. Shock, disappointment, astonishment, curiosity raced helter skelter through him. He could not believe his eyes. "God Almighty! What is it?" He moved forward, his pains forgotten, assessing the incredible architectural jumble. It resembled an ancient citadel, yet a more honest appraisal would describe it as a mad combination of citadel, cloister, palazzo, and fortress, a potpourri of several structures fused together to form some monstrous design from the mind of a demented architect. Off-shaped windows and doors, some round, some rectangular, defied classification. Ten doors fronted the property; they would later learn eight were camouflage, two functional. The carriage courtyard, overrun with weeds and neglected for centuries, had been abandoned.

"Who was it said, 'There is nothing new under the sun'? The theory is disproved, Matteus. This monstrosity will take a lifetime to restore."

"First, we must live long enough to contemplate such an undertaking."

Matteus guided him to the left of the enormous complex, through archway ruins, past pine and cypress trees, grape arbors, around broken, neglected statues and dried-up water fountains, over stone footpaths overrun with dry, brown weeds.

Vivaldi stopped, reacting to the same stimulus Matteus sensed earlier. He felt alien eyes trained menacingly on them. The hairs on his neck stood on end. Guns out there, somewhere, were preparing to kill them. He hissed aloud.

"Mazzeppi! Son of a bitch! Who else wants us dead, here in Corsica?" He tapped the charred ledger against a hitching post. "It's Mazzeppi, I tell you! The books were doctored. Crude tampering and a messy cleanup. The rogue oozes dishonesty. To cover his greed he wants us dead!"

Was it relief he saw spreading over the Moor's features? It was! Matteus lifted the Campo Giro from his waist, reholstered it securely. "So! Mazzeppi falsified the books. To him we are better dead than alive. Good. Very good. Now we know how to handle ourselves. I estimate at least a dozen men out there waiting to liquidate us."

"I need morphine," Vivaldi pressed.

Matteus scowled, peered about. "There, ahead of us in the grape arbor, a more sheltered area. It is unwise to allow our enemies to think you are ill or believe you unable to cope with realities."

Vivaldi moved as languidly as a feudal landlord inspecting his properties. Once under the thick foliage of the grape arbor, they worked swiftly. It took a moment: a sharp jab in the vein . . . the needle replaced . . . it was finished. A warm glow flushed through Vivaldi's body. Matteus draped the jacket around Vivaldi's shoulders, whose left arm was still in a sling. Vivaldi swayed unsteadily. He held onto an arbor post, waiting for the light-headedness to clear.

Matteus slipped the morphine case into his jacket pocket and moved into the clearing, his eyes sighting possible defenses in the terrain. He pondered a solution to the present dilemma. *How?* Corsica was rougher country than Don Diego's appraisal of it. How easy a task it would be to kill them off, dispose of their bodies, and no one the wiser. No one! Vivaldi was too vulnerable for confrontations with mountain savages; survival for both rested in the Moor's hands.

Merciful Allah, if ever I needed you, now is the time to demonstrate your presence.

Matteus returned to Vivaldi's side and took his arm. "Come, we move about as landowners. If you recall anything of Antonio Vasquez—" Vivaldi cut him a sharp reproving look. "The manner in which he commanded, spoke, and moved about, strike that attitude, understand? Keep in mind, a spider from birth is a weaver. So like the spider we shall weave words, deeds, and actions. Take your strength from mine. Do only as I command, understand?"

Moving through the tall grass, halting suddenly, their eyes swept past the estate's perimeters down toward the vast sapphire sea, a sheer drop of several hundred yards. To their left, inside ferocious walls the sight of incandescent orchards captured their sights. Blissfully trickling waters from mountain streams, the sight of Dantesque gorges of clear crystal water splashing audibly as it tracked out to sea arrested them. In all Spain no such exotic paradise could be found; it was a scene to inspire poets, thought Vivaldi observing the great trees of Corsica, tragic duels of rock and pine, tormented branches stretching horizontally over the sea, deformed in a single direction by phantasmagorical winds. Overwhelmed by the panorama he attempted to share the moment with the Moor.

Catching him in profile, Vivaldi, shaken back to the moment, began to duel the fear twisting his guts. For Matteus, frozen into a pose of alert caution, resembled a gargoyle. Heightening the supernatural effect was the sharp landscape, vertically jutting palisades of muted umber and phosphorescent granite, towering into icicle peaks. The snowcapped heights of Mount Cinto in the far distance, visible through branches of pine of exaggerated heights, soared beyond the rings of diaphanous white mists.

Then he heard it. Just as Matteus heard it.

The sounds echoed past their ears . . . the cocking of gun hammers . . . mountain boots crushing pebbles underfoot . . . dry twigs snapping, cracking. Expecting the worst, Spaniard and

Moor pivoted slowly, searching every inch of the landscape. Menace and death were riding herd on the wind, and the wind turned icy as the sun moved behind vaporous clouds of mist.

Vivaldi saw them, his eyes locking on an awesome sight less than thirty feet away. Conversely, Matteus relaxed, now the enemy was visible. Later he would explain how fear of the unknown often produced a paralysis worse than death; it presented a greater threat than hordes of a visible army armed with every warring device known to God and man.

Seven craggy-faced Corsicans with beady eyes advanced stealthily through the archway ruins, luparas in hand, closing in from all points. More were standing on the slopes. Shepherds appeared from nowhere to observe with provincial curiosity the scene enacted below them.

The Corsicans became the landlords, catching trespassers red-handed!

Vivaldi became a lion. *"Buon giorno! Buon giorno, signori.* I bid you welcome to Terra Bonifacio. I, Vivaldi Fornari Bonifacio, am landlord of these vast lands. And this is *Signore* Montenegro. Ah, you must be neighbors come to pay your respects? Welcome. Welcome."* He bowed with the gallantry of a cavalier.

The flinty-eyed Corsicans, unable to conceal their contempt for this dandy's affectations, exchanged glances, their guns relaxing. This clown was like no other they had encountered. They studied the Moor, knew him instantly. Here was the force they expected, not the milk-fed, besotted caricature attempting to manipulate them like some puppeteer!

Vivaldi persisted. "Are you neighbors or caretakers?"

The Corsicans smirked. One man prodded them toward the house with his gun. Spaniard and Moor fell into step between them. Vivaldi muttered between motionless lips, "Who are these men?"

"Our *executioners,* they think."

Several moments later, inside the great house, descending a stone stairwell, Vivaldi viewed the architectural jumble of the house-museum with a curator's curiosity. Prodded unceremoniously through enormous bronze and wooden doors into a cavernous room below the first floor, Vivaldi's curiosity heightened. *What's this? What's this?* Eight door exits? Eight stunningly crafted ecclesiastical throne chairs, in sad need of renovation stood in a circle under a massive iron chandelier containing eight tiered niches for candle tapers under massive layered cobwebs and dust? What in *damnation*?

A vendetta room! The house was built around a vendetta room. The ritual eight of everything, *especially* doors, to facilitate escape—a medieval curiosity!

"Sit!" came the terse order.

Six men took their places, leaving two chairs for the newcomers. The seventh man stood guard at the door, the eighth started a fire on the hearth. A long-limbed Corsican wolfhound lumbered inside and curled up at his master's feet.

A black-jawed, fierce-eyed Corsican with a scrubby beard and short black hair was paring a chestnut with a small razor-sharp stiletto. The room filled with silence. Only the snap-crackle-popping sounds of a beginning fire were heard. The obvious leader spoke up. The voice was thin, high, raspy.

"For twelve years this has been our home. What will you do, landlord? Throw us off the property?"

It was Matteus who picked up the gauntlet before Vivaldi blinked an eye. He spoke a Corsican dialect, in a voice oozing with authority. The two men fell into a heated debate; Matteus, respectful at times, alternated between contempt and ridicule. "We are newcomers to your land. Is this your brand of hospitality? My shock is such that I dare not convey such lack of respect to my chief. When your people sought asylum in our lands, it was given, no questions asked." The Moor reproached the Corsican but not without rebuttal.

"You come to *our* land, to Corsica without our knowledge and with no warning, demand the books of account? After a thirty-year absence you expect a warm welcome?" the Corsican demanded harshly. "You expect us to turn over the lands we have cared for—"

"*Cared for?* You call this mass of garbage—these broken ruins cared for?" Matteus spat into the dirt.

The Corsican sat forward in his chair, his flinty eyes like daggers. He would not permit this man's contempt to mar his image among his fellow Corsicans. He tossed the chestnut angrily aside, spoke brashly in the falsetto voice of a dwarf, using the stiletto to punctuate his words. "Who are you that we Corsicans must honor your imperious insults?" Chamois Barbone demanded.

"Men sworn to blood oaths as you. We honor sacred ties and

do not molest our brothers in foreign lands unless they endanger our existence."

"Bah! You complicate matters."

"You would execute *us* for Mazzeppi's bungling? For the fraud done upon Bonifacio estates?" Matteus's disdainful laughter echoed through the room. "You honor a petty embezzler who pockets fisfuls of money and lacks the finesse to cover his tracks? Mazzeppi is a bungler! We view with contempt such unprofessional work; it provokes disrespect. Only artists can perform the bookkeeping miracles needed to fool the experts!" Matteus, rising from his throne chair, swaggered toward the stupefied Vivaldi, winked slyly at him, and, taking the ledger from him, tossed it at the Corsican's feet. "The work of a buffoon. Believe me, a suckling child could do better."

The ballet of hand movements, facial expressions, and outbursts of temper between Corsican and Moor needed no interpretation. Bright flames on the hearth removed the chill from the room. Vivaldi felt its warmth and that generated from the Corsicans close scrutiny of him. They stared at him as if he were of a different species of man, studying with provincial curiosity the elegant cut of his boots, breeches, and the fine tailoring of his coat. They noted his lidded eyes, slowed-down movements as he smoked his cigar. They assessed the bruises and weals on his face, the arm in a sling, but fixed interminably on the gold signet ring on the forefinger of his right hand, the ring of the Marten.

Chamois Barbone prodded the Moor. Matteus retorted blandly, "Ask him yourself. You speak Italian."

The Corsican opened one of the eight doors, whistled sharply. Instantly the Corsican wolfhound leaped to his feet, pranced outside friskily. Barbone closed the door, lifted a calfskin bag off a wall peg, complete with pelt, legs, and tail. Holding it dramatically above his head, he forced a thin stream of water into his mouth until his thirst was quenched. Replacing it on the wall peg, he wiped his mouth with the back of his hand and sauntered cockily back into the circle.

Standing before Vivaldi, staring at the dandy for what seemed an eternity, he was observed by his men stonily, the butts of their cigarettes dangling loosely from their lips. A steely-eyed impatience settled onto their features. Chamois sucked at his gold tooth, jerked his head at Vivaldi, indicating the bruises on his arm. "An accident, *signore*?" He clucked his tongue regretfully.

Vivaldi merely nodded.

"I am called Chamois Barbone. Perhaps if you ignore the ill wind we transported to your house earlier, we can mend the broken bridges between us, eh? It is better to understand one another, no? The world grows smaller. Friends in other nations can become assets. Listen, it's best we make adjustments for this misunderstanding, *d'accord*?" He spoke in French, alternating to Italian, often sneaking in dialect.

In an unexpected move, Barbone leaned over, kissed the ring on Vivaldi's finger. Over his head, Spaniard and Moor's eyes locked, a silent warning communicated between them. With the panache of a street-wise hood, Barbone arrogantly staked out his territorial jurisdiction. "Here in the *maquis* between Ajaccio and Calvi to the north, from Calvi to Porte Vecchio in the southeast, I am in command. Hundreds of men take orders from me," he remarked, scratching his crotch. "Is the *Signore* Bonifacio amenable to a discussion that will clear the air? Your man indicates an injustice was done you by Don Mazzeppi, the bank director. My brother, boss of all bosses in Marseilles, will study the matter and pass judgment. You say the ledgers are falsified? Very well, what is the sum involved?" He glanced at the charred remains. "Well, *signore*—how much?"

Vivaldi shrugged. "Without the original ledgers it is foolish to hazard a guess."

"Take a chance. A mere approximation will do. Several thousand francs, perhaps?"

"More," came the soft reply.

"Many more thousand?"

"Without the books—"

"I heard you the first time. It is not necessary to chew your words twice in my presence," he squeaked in his dwarflike voice. "You refuse to hazard a guess? It matters not. Adjustments shall be made. So, take a chance—a mere approximation. Come, come, you have some idea."

"Very well, Corsican—a guess. *Millions of francs!*"

Chamois's expression benign, he shrugged. "In thirty years?"

"Millions of francs *monthly* for thirty years."

Smoke exploded from Barbone's lips. He lunged into coughing spasms, gasping for breath. He spun around, faced Vivaldi, doing rapid calculations in his head, his mouth agape. Chamois paced the dirty tiles, scuffing up debris with his boots. Unable to mouth the proper words, he savagely bit down on the soggy cigar clamped between his teeth, severing it and finally flinging it from him. "Higher in the mountains near Niolo is a house, too cold for us to occupy in snow country in the winter. We stay here at our convenience, *d'accord*? Later, at our convenience we move."

Vivaldi hard-lined it. "Don't confide your business to me. I insist you inflict no more charades on us. Two fine horses and a carriage blown up needlessly!"

"And you shall pay reparations to the driver," Chamois retorted.

"*I pay!*" Vivaldi, outraged, his face turning a mottled purple, exploded. "You design the evil plot, then expect them to pay for the damage you caused? My dear Chamois Barbone—you are not dealing with an Englishman!"

Barbone gave him a look that defied classification and laughed outrageously. Wily eyes carefully searched the handsome features, looking to spot vanity and weakness, a clue to enable him to mount an attack on this strange citadel of contradictions. Vivaldi, mistaking the look for total acquiescence, asked Chamois to suggest the names of competent workmen to clear and tend the estate. All the Corsicans laughed uproariously.

Chamois laughed the heartiest. In his squeaky voice, between peals of laughter, he lowered the parameters of defense. "Ah, *signore*, you are a jester. It is good that you laugh, it cures many maladies. You have been away too long, landlord. You have much to learn about Corsicans. You don't *know*. Here we are all sons of kings and emperors."

The Corsicans laughed in a body. Chamois sobered. Instantly the laughter ended. Chamois ambled to one of the escape doors, flung it open, held his hand to his lips. Gone was the dwarfish voice; it changed into a melancholy wail, the lament peculiar to those of shepherds calling to their flocks.

"The *irrenzina*," Chamois explained. The squeaky voice had returned. "The shepherd's call lets all concerned know you are under the protection of Chamois Barbone. So that you understand and bear him no malice, my brother Vittorio Barbone, bookkeeper at the bank, took orders from Don Mazzeppi. The situation bears remedy, *d'accord*? Understand that I remain in the *maquis* because like most Corsicans of honor, I am a fugitive. One night, perhaps, your African shall prepare dinner and we shall speak of future alliances—"

"The Moor is not my servant," Vivaldi snapped. "He is my brother in blood. An associate. A partner in my business." Unaware of the clever baiting, he caught Matteus's disapproving look too late.

Chamois stood in a languid pose, leaning against the chair he had vacated earlier, one foot crossed lazily over the other. "Ah, business associate. Blood brother? What has the Moor done to earn so lofty a position?" He grinned, showing short, tobacco-stained teeth. "Where are the bodies buried, *signore?*"

"What business is it of yours where they are buried, Corsican? Do I ask you similar statistics?"

"Here everything is the business of Chamois Barbone. To challenge me for such an honor you must first go to Marseilles to make yourself known to my brother, the number-one boss."

"Of what, Corsican?"

Chamois laughed uproariously. "You Italians! Jesters. Not even the Sicilians display the courage of the *Unione Corse.* In these troubled times in Italy, they cower in fear. Listen, you know who comes in and out of the port of Marseilles without interference? Eh, Bonifacio?" He tapped his chest proudly. "You will learn. You will learn."

"We crave no demonstrations of courage, Corsican. For now our only concerns are the Bonifacio properties."

"Ah, *molto bene.* It is understood then, no investigations? We are in accord?" Chamois nodded to his men. The men moved in a body out of one of the exit doors. One of the fugitives paused to relieve himself in the room. Matteus politely suggested the weeds needed more watering than the house. The Corsican hitched up his trousers and left.

"From Ajaccio shall come a driver and carriage to transport you back to your hotel," Chamois announced in passing. The Corsicans disappeared as quickly as they had appeared. Spaniard and Moor moved in behind them to observe the various paths taken by the Corsicans in their approach to the *maquis* below the property.

The circumstances of Matteus's conversation with Chamois aroused Vivaldi's curiosity. "Explain, Matteus. I hardly anticipate the company of such men running loose in our household."

"Simply, they came to kill us. We escaped the bombing earlier. A swift bullet through our heads would have ended it, our bodies dumped into an *arca* for decomposition, before running our remains to sea."

"You managed to liberate us. *How?*"

"I assured them you possessed no interest in prosecuting a Corsican for *any* wrongdoing. I suggested you sat at a higher level in an organization like the *Unione Corse*. I also suggested if harm should befall us, they'd taste the wrath of our brothers from around the globe. And because it is unwise to tell *any* Corsican you are without kith or kin, I merely let it drop that at least ten men as highly placed as you knew of our presence in Corsica."

Vivaldi was aghast. "You dare classify us as like them? You have done us both a disservice!"

The Moor's gaze fixed on the Spaniard. "Explain, please, the difference between the Corsicans and *Los Desheredados?*"

Momentarily, Vivaldi turned from him, unable to contest the blatant truth. He stood before the fire, snapped open the lid of his watch, studied the time, lingering on the tintype of Victoria Valdez.

"We are alive," the Moor insisted. "Nothing else matters. It is true, when you lie down with dogs you catch their infirmities. If we must, we will, to survive and restore order out of the chaos in our lives."

"That man, Mazzeppi," interjected Vivaldi somberly, "took opium pills. I find pills more acceptable than the needle. Please order some morphine pills for the apothecary."

Matteus hesitated. "They are less effective. Your need will grow, not abate."

"I prefer them." Vivaldi peered around the vendetta room. "Shall we look upstairs in this monstrosity? Take inventory? By God, I dread taking the first step."

Matteus lighted two candle tapers and joined Vivaldi. Together they explored a limited area of the dark, dank interior. High stone walls stretched three floors to a vaulted ceiling. Stone steps hugging the walls were overrun by spiders, nesting scorpions and rats scurrying for cover. At each floor level open gallerias overlooked enormous rooms below. Each level was graced with fireplaces of the same gray stones overgrown with a sickening, greenish moss and more cobwebs. Vivaldi ran ahead and, after counting twenty rooms, he stopped, bewildered. A short peek into each of the rooms branching off the dismal corridors, darkened by windows overgrown with leafy foliage and rambling ivy, further dismayed Vivaldi. The furniture—the paltry existing pieces, warped by time, inclement weather and lack of care disintegrated upon touch. Worse, how in God's name would they ever rid the stench-filled house reeking of antiquity and raw animal scents of the putrefaction that violated the senses?

Two hours later, they left Terra Bonifacio in dismal silence. The driver promised them by Chamois Barbone had not materialized. So, they began the descent of the narrow, craggy steep incline, shuddering as they passed the earlier wreckage and near fatality, to the valley below, elated at the sight of a makeshift train stop.

Later, aboard the rickety train transporting them to Ajaccio, Vivaldi regarded that monstrosity of a house. He vented his thoughts. "Inventory on this day borders the disastrous, Matteus,"

"Count your blessings. We are alive and together," boasted the lord high chancellor of optimism.

"Why do you place such faith in me? I am not equal to the dreams my father entertained for our future in a land ruled by barbarians."

"I am painfully aware of your shortcomings. My purpose is to amend those deficiencies and convert liabilities into assets."

Vivaldi's glowering scowl mellowed. Suffused with despair and mortification he wondered how they'd fare in this alien land, relegated to living without the luxuries and fine amenities of the life to which he was born. A sudden unleashing of the pent-up jackals of fear petrified his emotions.

Time . . . Time was needed. Wasn't it the healer of all wounds?

Chapter Sixteen

On a sweltering night late in July, 1921, in the infamous North side of Chicago, a mean little gangster with a tigerish temper named Hymie Weiss, one of Dion O'Banion's general staff of hitmen, invented what would become one of gangland's favorite murder methods, *taking him for a ride,* and proceeded to execute his first victim. As one life was snuffed out, another struggled fiercely to life through the birth canal in a breech birth.

Victoria Valdez, hemorrhaging severely in the final stages of parturition, was admitted to St. John's Hospital shortly before midnight. A desperate battle was waged against death to save both mother and child. Heavily sedated, her pale, wan face, as colorless as the white sheets on which she lay, Victoria remained lifeless in appearance.

The birth occurred shortly after midnight the morning of July 31. There existed no correlation between the two incidents except for the violence involved in the death of one, the birth of the other.

Veronica Carter Valdez rocked silently in the chair alongside Victoria's hospital bed, pondering the *bruja's* prognostication as Victoria had related it to her on her arrival from Spain. She rocked in the chair next to the bed in the flower-filled, dimly lighted room, her shadowed eyes never leaving her daughter's face. Victoria, admitted to the hospital under an alias, was presently guarded by Pinkerton men, stationed outside in the sterile hospital corridor, and with good reason. Veronica vividly recalled the horror story Victoria had narrated from the moment she had met Francisco in Madrid up to and including the murder of the de la Varga family. Driven to within an inch of sanity, Victoria, having experienced hell and come back, had not fully recovered. For months she had relived that night of horrifying drama, unable to erase from mind the wholesale slaughter committed before her very eyes.

What Veronica Valdez had been unable to discuss with her daughter was the real evil behind the infamous massacre of the de la Varga family—Antonio Vasquez. For in Victoria's skillfully programmed mind Vasquez was a saviour who had slain the assassins. The appalling scene was etched vividly in Victoria's mind; the images imprinted deeper and deeper until she believed with conviction what her eyes had witnessed. Antonio Vasquez, so thoroughly despised and misjudged, had been absolved of any wrongdoing or possible guilt in the killings. Hadn't he saved her life? Bravely transported her to the Seville infirmary where two bullets were removed from her body?

Victoria had awakened an hour before midnight, her wounds less critical than originally surmised. A fierce compulsion drove her to leave the hospital bed—Francisco's promise to return to the hacienda at midnight! Wrapped in a rebozo, she escaped through a terrace window and stood weakly against the balustrade, the cool wind and rain clearing her mind. She knew what she had to do, where she had to go.

To the outskirts of Seville. To the hacienda de la Varga.

She found a horse tethered to a hitching post, borrowed it, and rode along the muddy roads and soggy ditches for nearly an hour. The villa gates loomed into sight, as the moon drifted out from behind ebony clouds. She rode swiftly to the main villa.

It was dark, deserted, locked, bearing no signs of life. She spurred the animal to the rear of the villa, dismounted, and crept cautiously through the shattered glass doors of the dining *sala*. Her head throbbed as she crossed the slaughter grounds, her hands shook, and moving forward, she lighted a taper from a flickering candle burning in a red glass before a religious icon in a wall niche.

What she saw as the flame flared reinforced the earlier trauma. Forced into confrontation with the grisly scene of mass murder, slaughtered bodies, blood-splattered walls, overturned furniture, Victoria had fled the room. Nausea surfaced and she tottered dizzily.

What followed was vague. She had scaled the steps to her boudoir, dressed, taking money, travel permits, passports, her jewelry case, and descended the steps quietly, pausing momentarily before the smaller salon for a last look at the undisturbed wedding gifts. The clock in the foyer struck midnight. *No Francisco!* Victoria fled. She ran to the stable, saddled and mounted a fresh steed, and rode off the hacienda grounds, driving the lathered animal to his limit.

In Las Marismas she hired a driver to transport her to San Lucar Barramedas and from there boarded a stage to Lisbon. She booked passage on the first liner to Buenos Aires, and for three weeks fell heir to mal de mer and morning sickness. Confined to her cabin, under a doctor's care, Victoria grew more distraught and anguished, in her nightly battle with demons.

Victoria arrived home in March. Her mother, in double mourning for her father and husband, listened carefully to her daughter's tragic tale. She had described her original assessment of Antonio Vasquez, his attempts to seduce her. "To think, Mother, the very man I loathed actually turned up that night, but a moment too late. I vindicated him at once when I witnessed him slay the five murderers who destroyed Don Diego's family and me. God forgive me for hating him!"

Veronica had heard the lament time and again, as Victoria mercilessly crucified herself for misjudging Vasquez. Fearing her daughter's condition might worsen, she said nothing about the letters she'd received from Don Diego before his demise, naming Vasquez as Don Verono's murderer. If later Victoria thought her mother's repetitive questioning concerning Vasquez as impertinent or excessive, she didn't complain, for in a sense repeating her answers cleansed her of the terrible guilt she bore in not confiding in Don Diego. The remorse for having discredited Vasquez abated after a while. "If only I had cultivated Vasquez. I might have helped to avert the tragedy," she moaned to her mother.

On the bed, Victoria's eyes fluttered open. Veronica, at once on her feet, daubed the perspiration from her daughter's forehead. "Darling . . . are you awake? It's over, everything is just fine."

Victoria's heavily lidded eyes fluttered open. "Darling, do you hear me? It's a girl. A beautiful baby girl. How do you feel?"

Victoria's eyes widening, her weak voice was just above a whisper. "How do I feel? As if a main artery in my body is plugged into hell . . . A girl?" Her dismay was apparent. "Oh, Mother, did you say a girl. I wanted a boy, I prayed for a boy."

Veronica applied a cool compress to Victoria's burning forehead. "What will you call her?"

"Valentina, Miles Carter Varga," she replied without faltering. "She'll never know her father and I were cheated out of marriage. You can arrange for a proper birth certificate, can't you, mother? List her father as Francisco Varga."

Three months later, Victoria stumbled across Don Diego's letter to Veronica while rummaging through her desk. Her shock was total. Her first reaction, disbelief, was converted to belief as intelligence set in and logic compelled her to face the facts. When her daughter's health had improved beyond any danger point, Veronica was encouraged to impart the truth. Veronica's story took on a hint of the bizarre. They sat in the solarium of the great Carter mansion along Lake Michigan at tea.

"In July, before Valentina was born, I was advised that a certain Amadeo Zeller of Spain made legal claims against the Valdez estate in Argentina. Six million dollars to be exact. An aggregate sum, claimed Zeller's barristers, that your father borrowed over the years. Demand payment was never enforced, because Don Verono, I was politely told, promptly paid interest charges, reducing the principle only slightly. Of course, dear, I refuted the entire claim. Unless your father was a demon incarnate and lived a double life, which he wasn't and didn't, he couldn't have incurred debts of such magnitude without my knowledge. You see, Victoria, as an independently wealthy woman with shrewd business sense I personally had underwritten all your father's business loans. So, how do I believe this fraudulent in-depth audit of the books which indicate liabilities in excess of six million?"

"You don't, mother! You will fight this man Zeller! I mean fight him to the end!" Victoria was outraged.

"Complications are endless. Zeller, it appears is affiliated with the Bank of Argentina in some covert way. The issue, it appears, is more political than financial. What makes it sticky is the bank possesses intimate knowledge of your father's involvements in several confidential dealings."

"I don't understand, Mother. Who is this man Zeller? What

has he to do with anything?'' A new, hard edge to her voice lanced at her mother, demanding answers.

Veronica obliged and brought her daughter up to date. ''I hired the special services of a reliable, reputable investigative firm in London, shortly after the claims against the Vasquez estate were filed. Submitting the name Amadeo Zeller to Sir Arthur Duns Scotis in London apparently set off several alarms. Sir Arthur's instant feedback came from three firms on the Continent that fed information to the Queen's Investigative Agency on a reciprocal basis. From the firm Bello, Bellomo and Mario Romaeo in Trieste came information, the *identical* information supplied to Don Diego in Seville.''

''Don Diego hired the services of an investigative firm? Why?'' The nurse brought the baby Valentina to her mother for suckling. As Victoria accommodated herself to the greedy infant, she pressed her mother for more information.

''It seems, Victoria, the man you knew as Antonio Vasquez is actually Amadeo Zeller. Don Diego, before his death, had advanced the name Vasquez to Trieste. They, in turn supplied Sir Arthur with their findings on Zeller. London perused the man's dossiers and background. Well, my dear, the most amazing information sprang out of a virtual Pandora's box! Duns Scotis was not surprised. The disposition of the de la Varga wealth in Seville, Madrid, and in other European cities was suddenly being handled by Zeller. What intrigued Sir Arthur was the *modus operandi* Zeller employed. A definitive pattern in the confiscation of the de la Varga wealth materialized. Observing it, something took shape and form in Duns Scotis' mind. This man Zeller, a newcomer to financial centers had emerged seemingly from nowhere with enormous wealth. Recently Sir Arthur dispatched data to me on the suddenly reclusive Zeller including a newspaper article from Trieste. Bello, Bellomo, and Mario Romaeo fell victims to a clever bombing incident. Naturally the Zeller-Vasquez files were destroyed. Perhaps stolen? Two additional information conduits, one in Paris, the other in Brussels were meted similar fates—bombed. Suddenly, my dear, it's as if this man Zeller never existed—not Vasquez or any other alias he had assumed to mantle his activities.

Victoria pulled away from the greedy, suckling infant, examining the situation judiciously. ''But he does exist! *If* as you say, Zeller and Vasquez are one and the same I can prove he exists! Mother! We must not permit him to escape criminal prosecution!''

"I assure you, Sir Arthur has no such intention. Zeller is the sort of criminal he enjoys setting elaborate traps for, baiting him with innocuous lures, sparring with him until he is trapped in the very web he spins."

Sir Arthur Duns Scotis, Veronica went on to tell her daughter, had not been chief inspector of Scotland Yard for thirty years by playing innocent games of cops and robbers. His real talent lay in the psychological understanding of master criminals. Following the bombing incidents, Sir Arthur, concerned with the preservation of his evidence, had walked into Scotland Yard one day and gotten a stenographer to retype the reports on Zeller. He placed the originals in a safety-deposit vault in the Bank of England. The copy and work papers were locked in his safe. A week later the office was burglarized, the safe cracked, and the Zeller files had vanished.

Duns Scotis, wisely, after conferring with the new chief at Scotland Yard took the man's suggestion and moved the Queen's Investigative Firm to new covert offices behind a dummy organization. "Hire a new breed of sleuths to track Zeller," The S.C. Chief urged. "All you men look alike. I suggest you hire some of those men from the Colonies—Pinkerton men—I hear they assume a variety of disguises."

Duns Scotis moved swiftly. Where once the Zeller files occupied prominent places in the wooden file cases, dummy files were set into place containing memos: CASE CLOSED. SUBJECT DECEASED. The investigation, however, continued full speed ahead.

"Sir Arthur lost no time in contacting me. His professional recommendation was that I change my name, leave Buenos Aires, place the Valdez estate business in the ablest legal hands and continue litigation in a highly covert manner hiding behind the veils of a dozen dummy corporations, you know, dear, as a smoke screen. So, I followed his advice, collected you and moved back to Chicago, here in the Lake Michigan mansion in which I grew up. Communication with our lawyers in Argentina is handled through the law firm that handled the Miles Carter holdings. I quickly enjoined them to place pre-dated liens on the Valdez estates in an effort to outmaneuver Zeller. Pray we can outfox him."

Recently, Victoria, shown photographs of Zeller found it difficult to reconcile the black-haired, mustached Vasquez with the light-haired, clean-shaven Zeller. "I find no resemblance in the two men, Mother. Perhaps in the eyes? Yes, only in the eyes do they share a similarity."

"Only the eyes cannot be disguised, Victoria," her mother had counseled.

Now that Victoria knew the full story, she despaired.

Veronica soothed her daughter's ruffled composure by appealing softly not to jeopardize her life by burying herself in the past.

"Pray, Mother, Valentina grows up looking exactly like me."

"But, darling, she does. She is the image of you."

"Good! I shall make her into my own very secret weapon. You'll see!" Her eyes sparked. "Has any word come from Francisco? Can he be alive or dead, Mother?"

"Sir Arthur is attempting to learn what may have happened. The mails take time. One day, perhaps, planes will fly the Atlantic just to deliver the mails. Until then, we must make do with ships, however slowly they travel."

"Oh sure, and one day soon we'll fly to the moon!"

Veronica knew that in that moment of decision to move from Argentina to America, she had altered the course of her daughter's destiny. Pray God it was for the best.

Victoria picked up the newspaper, read the headline:

AL CAPONE FLASHES DEPUTY SHERIFF BADGE IN FRACAS. The article said that Capone was booked on four charges: driving while intoxicated, assault with an auto, carrying a concealed weapon, impersonating an officer. . . .

She set aside the paper, concerned with the violent wave of crime and bloodshed erupting in Chicago. "Mother, I begin to think we'll need an Al Capone to decimate that devil, Zeller."

Chapter Seventeen

While Victoria battled personal demons in Chicago, in Corsica, Vivaldi, at war with the Corsicans, stood transfixed at a mountain ridge at the northern perimeter of his property, helpless to stop the appalling fires ravaging a forest of stately pines. His shock was impossible to conceal. The rage in him swelled; his body trembled in anger. He called to Matteus. Before his disbelieving eyes, the trees metamorphosed into charred monoliths, stripped of their greenery.

It was ghastly, he felt ill. Black smoke burned his eyes, lungs, parching his throat. Through the thickening haze he spotted Matteus dragging two Corsican peasants up the mountain by the scruffs of their necks.

The Moor disgustedly hurled the culprits with terrific force at Vivaldi's feet. The rage in his eyes competed with the blazing hot fires on all sides of them. He spat derisively, "Here are the arsonists. I caught them red-handed!"

Vivaldi stood before them, scanning their faces. "Is it true? You are the guilty torches?"

"But of course." The cocksure man called Carlos scrambled to his feet, assisting his companion. Dusting their trousers, eyes defiant, scornful, contempt oozing from both, they locked eyes with Vivaldi.

"You confess you started the fire? You destroy my property and dare admit to the act?" Vivaldi turned red.

"Why not, *signore*? You dare import labor from Sardinia and Elba! Corsicans do not submit to the trickery and treachery of a stranger!"

"Bastards! You refuse to work and deny that right to other men?" Vivaldi raged, fumed, cursed, and damned them.

"Why should we work and be less than emperors?"

"I shall continue to import labor, damn your hides!" he stormed.

"And we shall continue to burn your lands!"

"All the others—the chestnut, citrus groves—"

"—was our doing. *Sì, signore,* it was us." Carlos beamed.

"Damn you, is there no remorse in your souls for the damage you've done? For whom do you work?"

"No one. We do this on our own, as good Corsicans."

"Who is boss of the *maquis*?"

"But, *signore,* everyone knows. Everyone who is Corsican."

"Refresh my memory," Bonifacio commanded.

The Corsicans turned mute. Matteus signaled Vivaldi not to press. "Let it go. We shall take up the matter with the right person."

"Let it go?" Vivaldi bridled furiously. "Let it go, you say? I'll show you, let it go!" Like an enraged bull tearing up sods of earth before charging, he paced before them and swung with fury, knocking their heads together, cursing, kicking at them.

Behind them the fires had spread beyond control. No fire brigades, no neighbors, would come to their aid.

"To make friends with you Corsicans is an effort in futility. To recruit your labor is madness. Here, all you *emperors* prefer a life of crime to an honest day's work."

"But of course, *signore*. Were we meant to be less than Napoleon?" They smirked—broad, infuriating grins.

Vivaldi, at his wits end, stalked off the only plot of ground untouched by fire. He swung to his saddle, rode the Andalusian stallion off the estate, his heart beating furiously. *It was the last straw!* He loathed the Corsicans, detested everything about their baffling demeanor. He must leave this damnable island of pompous Corsican *emperors* or go mad!

Riding swiftly through black smoke, he reached the military compound to the north of Porto. Until recently German prisoners of war had occupied the premises. Now mainland convicts were housed there and used to build roads and repair bridges.

Sweating, out of breath, Vivaldi stood before the pear-shaped, fiftyish prison governor. He pleaded, cajoled, begged, even tried bribing the man for assistance. But the governor, a fawning political appointee, without backbone, sucked noisily on a prickly pear, indolently picking seeds from between his teeth. "The prisoners are here to build Corsican roads, mend bridges, and repair underwater conduits. They work, *signore*, for the Department of France—not landed estates. First, before work permits are possible, you must talk with the authorities in Marseilles."

"But I see them working for the landed estates at Porto and Calvi. Why not for me?"

"Eh?" He spread his hands in a helpless gesture.

"Where do I procure workers for my lands? Those miserable beggars burned my forests, the groves! *Burned them!* They feel no remorse—none at all!" Not since his arrival in Corsica had his anger been fanned to so feverish a pitch.

"Listen, *signore*." The governor spoke in conspiratorial tones. "Listen to me. Say nothing to another soul that the governor gives you such ideas, eh? Go to Sardinia, Sicily. Even Greece will recruit labor if you vouch for their safety. *D'accord?* You arm them, see?"

"*Arm them?* Are you some crazy man? You are spouting anarchy! Blood will flow!"

The governor raised a pudgy hand to his lips, gesturing caution. "But of course." The Corsican's sly grin turned obscene. "Kill them all off, start anew with the children. It's the only way to rid them of the emperor complex."

"Mother of Christ! You are mad. You are all mad on this god-forsaken island! Lands must be worked, crops harvested, and you let it rot on the trees!"

"Not me, *signore*. Like all good Corsicans I take only what I need to fill my belly when I go hungry. What more do we need than food and a roof over our heads to protect us from the elements?"

He accompanied Vivaldi out the door of the ancient concrete citadel, bumbled along the neglected portico, kicking up pockets of dust. The cocking of a gun hammer brought Vivaldi's head up. Two gun blasts startled him. He whirled about, facing the man. The governor was blowing the tip of his smoking gun like a movie gangster. Across the courtyard two attempted escapees, trying to climb a barbed-wire fence, lay dead. "You see how a Corsican solves a problem?"

Vivaldi stared from the shapeless oaf in uniform, glistening with rows of sharpshooter medals on his chest, to the dead men, his anger replaced with incredulity. He strode out of the prison complex, swung to his saddle, and galloped furiously to Terra Bonifacio.

Vivaldi felt total defeat. He loathed Corsica. And the Corsicans viewing him obliquely, reciprocated. They sensed his rejection. The Moor, conversely, was held in high esteem. United in mind, body, and spirit, Matteus, possessed the strength to enforce his point. Of him it was said, he is a Moor who makes a fine Corsican. Of Vivaldi, little was said, for he posed a puzzle to Corsicans. Aware of their censure, Vivaldi's remoteness increased. *What did they know of him?* Of the insomnia that drove him closer to madness?

Vivaldi asked himself if he'd been born under a jinxed star. Everything in his life was wrong, turned sour. The cards were stacked against him. He felt persecuted by the gods in heaven, condemned by the devils in hell. He felt singled out, taken advantage of, mistreated, plotted against, robbed of earthly and spiritual goods.

Week after week, month after month, he tried to understand his dilemma. One year was stretching into two. With pain and anguish his constant companions, he pushed himself beyond endurance, renovating the great house, growing more dependent on morphine. Attempts to do without it resulted in sleepless, sweat-drenched nights for weeks on end. The only remedy was found in exhaustive physical work until he fell in total fatigue each night. He was firmly entrenched on an endless merry-go-round, spinning aimlessly toward a mental and physical breakdown, and morphine was the panacea.

The vendetta room became his special passion. He set to work, scrubbing, cleaning, restoring, renovating, peeling off layers of cosmetics applied by the previous tenants until one day something spectacular emerged. From under the grime came stunning hand-set mosaic tiles. Natural woods came alive. The room changed into an opulent oddity. Eight reupholstered throne chairs, in burgundy velvet, their natural rosewood polished to a satiny gloss, proved to be valuable, costly antiques. A wild shopping spree in Marseilles produced wrought-iron chandeliers, standing candelabra, and hundreds and hundreds of sorely missed books to fill the wall cases Matteus had lovingly built. A large desk and matching throne chair near the hearth overlooked the circle of eight chairs under the chandelier. Finished, this became Vivaldi's sanctuary.

No matter how often surgery was performed on the great house, nothing suited Vivaldi. The massive house, rebuilt countless times in its history, began a monstrosity and remained one. Attempts to bring portions of its facade into a semblance of harmony failed. Large sections of the house were closed down, including the squat, brutal towers topped by metal spires, which served no function except to provide sanctuary for thousands of cuckoos, owls, occasional hawks, and peregrine falcons. Beyond the rear courtyard was a greenhouse, butchering shed, and game house.

Despite Chamois Barbone's assured promise of protection, Matteus amassed a formidable gun collection. He refined animal instincts to an art. Vivaldi needed time to come to grips with the traditional differences between himself and Corsicans. Matteus, determined to minimize the risks for human emotions and loyalties, no more or less capricious than Corsican winds, bore watching. The arsenal grew from day to day, week to week.

For added security, they mended broken stone and brick walls about the estate, rebuilt property gates, sealing all possible means of ingress and egress. Guard dogs joined the ménage—Dobermans, German shepherds, Corsican wolfhounds. Their ferocious growls, snarling fangs, snapping bites discouraged the bravest of trespassers.

Shortly after their arrival, on a daily trek through the estate, Spaniard and Moor came upon an ancient military citadel with towers, battlements, embrasures, ramparts, and dressage rings for horses. Empty rooms, overrun with weeds, once the living quarters for men in suits of armor and capable of housing over a hundred men, sprawled the length of the battlement wall. The citadel, a veritable fortress, undetectable to the naked eye, was located some three kilometers from the great house west of the main gates close to the sea wall, yet camouflaged by a thick belt of tortured, wind-shaped trees.

They climbed the ramparts and gazed beyond the gnarled trunks and branches to the coastline and the absolute serenity of the wooded knolls. Matteus studied the perspective with a keen, discerning eye. Delight provoked an unguarded thought.

"Perfect. It is absolutely perfect! The day we begin to recruit and organize the power of the Garduna, it shall be here, within these ancient battlement walls.'' Below, striding boldly amid overgrown weeds like a grand landlord estimating the property's worth, Matteus measured distances and in the manner of a warring general picked out defenses and possible weaknesses in the fortification. He was unaware of the sudden paling of Vivaldi's features.

Staring at him in silence, observing his elated antics, his own expression ashen, Vivaldi panicked. How clever he'd been when Matteus broached the subject of Don Diego's plans concerning the Garduna Parchments. How quickly he switched the subject. This day was no different than the others, thought Matteus scowling inwardly. Both men returned to the house, estranged. Don Diego's carefully constructed blueprints were collapsing in the decay of silence, collecting dust, and dying of atrophy. Matteus lacked the strength to breathe life into their skeletal remains.

For the next month, Vivaldi buried himself in the vendetta room, refusing to leave. Paranoia, the jaguar of fear assailed him. Erratic hot and cold seizures sapped his strength. Attempts to honor his blood oath culminated in repetitious journeys into drugged oblivion. Only then could he escape the shackles and burdens imposed upon him.

''I am not a maker of miracles, Matteus! Do you understand? I am not your Allah, not even Moloch, who can conjure up miracles to suit your purpose!'' He ranted at the Moor. ''I know! I know amends must be made. I tell myself this a hundred times a day. But, how? In God's name how? From where will come the strength needed to negotiate the superhuman task waiting to be born in those Parchments? I am plagued by conditions beyond my control. Singled out in Spain by a total stranger, destroyed for things that occurred centuries before my time on earth? What chance have I? I tell you destiny has dumped on me. Dumped! Dumped! *Dumped!*'' For Vivaldi no end was in sight. His only reality was morphine; he lived for it. At times he felt he'd kill for it.

An increasingly puzzled Matteus, unable to mend the broken fences of estrangement between them, grew aware that the Garduna Parchments were the thorn in Vivaldi's side. Yes, it was true. Each time he reminded Vivaldi of their goals, he was severely and caustically reprimanded, the objectives torn asunder as foolhardy, unworkable, without merit. What was this malady Moloch had caused to descend upon Vivaldi? The physical pain was long gone. What then was this growing dependency on the drug?

Plotting strenuously against the insidious enemy obstructing their progress, Matteus, one night, collected every needle and morphine vial in the house and destroyed them. It failed to produce miracles. Vivaldi always bought more.

Vivaldi's features grew cadaverous, his eyes glazed over, his expression, haunted. On the few good days, he took jaunts about the property with an eye to multiplying his possessions, with rhapsodic dreams of increasing this crop, reducing another. What a marvelous performance! The air of a Spanish grandee, who at the snap of his fingers commanded hundred of peons to do his bidding, was deflated in moments of clarity, shattered by the blatant truth: no peons existed in Corsica—only emperors and kings! *And in Corsica Vivaldi was not a grandee!*

And so it went, up one day, down the other.

Betrayed by time itself, Vivaldi walked endless stretches of spectacular beaches and coves against a crashing surf, through the fragrant *maquis* and wooded lanes.

Each morning the sun seemed to keep pace with Vivaldi's revolution of thought. It would appear with a silent burst of light in the same place on the horizon; at noon it poured concentrated rays of fire on his dark, gloomy thoughts, then sank mysteriously into the sea each night, giving life to his depression and inner hell. The monotony of sameness gripped him, keeping him in constant agitation. Such were the days, hot and heavy, melting one after the other into the past.

The night descended upon him like a benediction, and for an hour or two after shooting morphine he enjoyed oblivion. Still the nightmares persisted. From midnight to dawn the images of the past tortured him. Poisoned by self-hatred, he became like stone. Detachment had not come easily. The stiff penalty he had paid for it was addiction. In that marvelous stillness pervading the earth between midnight and dawn, deception became the fiercest for Vivaldi, for this was when his inner world waged merciless battles against him. For Vivaldi there would be no rest, no peace, no eternal paradise.

How guileful he became when the Moor's attempts to assuage the anguish repeatedly failed. Reassurance, compassion, the pledge of eternal support if he would but forfeit the morphine were met with vacant eyes, then sudden explosive ebullient promises. "Next time decrease the dosage, and it will end the addiction."

When Matteus complied, there followed tirades of condemnation. "You are killing me! That's it, you want me dead! You force me to excruciating pain! You and your Allah would make me suffer the cataclysmic nightmares of Zeller, my family, of my beloved Victoria and my unborn child! I tell you the demons will not disappear without morphine!"

"In two years morphine dissolved nothing!" the Moor fired back one evening.

And so in January, as Corsican church bells tolled in the New Year, Matteus, totally alienated, unable to endure Vivaldi's deterioration, issued an ultimatum. "In the past year you've developed no insight into Corsica and its people. You've no concept of the high personal cost to us both brought about by your perpetual self-indulgence on this carousel of dementia."

Seated on a throne chair in the vendetta room, reigning over an imaginary kingdom, Vivaldi stared with the dull-eyed vacancy of an opium smoker. All that mattered to this disinherited noble was anticipation of his next fix. The daily resolutions to reject morphine evolved into empty oaths when another personality arose from the ashes of the man buried deeply in the loins of his mind.

"Procrastination is your existence—your god!" The Moor hurled imprecations of disgust and disappointment. "Nothing has improved. Daily resolve is consistently broken. If I forcibly withhold the morphine, you prowl about the house, a demon incarnate, an outraged beast stalking a lethal enemy, devising clever ruses to outfox me! Well, I am finished. *Finished, do you hear?* And *that* portrait!" Matteus strode about the room. "That portrait you commissioned of the *Señorita* Valdez! You hang it like a shrine in this room, in a *vendetta* room! You praise it as you would a religious icon! Worship it! Drink yourself into a stupor! Drug yourself and then you converse with her from the bowels of the dead! *Por amor de Dios!* You make future plans with her as if she were still alive—not dead! At times I listen to your insane soliloquy, wondering if it is not I who am deranged. *Por Dios!* I believe you even ejaculate before her image! She is dead! Dead! *Dead!* Do you hear me? She belongs to the dead past—not the world of Bonifacio!"

"You think I don't know it? You think I *really* don't know she is dead?"

"Then act it! Be a man!"

"I've tried," lamented Vivaldi, suddenly sagging from the unexpected verbal onslaught. "I've tried to bury my guilt in the whores of Bastia, Calvi, Ajaccio—even in Marseilles. Nothing works. My heart stops at the sight of hair the color of exploding suns. If the wench looks upon me with eyes the color of crushed jade, the ache in my soul renders me impotent. She was carrying my child, Matteus! *My child!*''

"It's always the same, some excuse or another. Something new to frustrate our purpose in life. Truth is no longer discernible in you."

"I'll try! I swear to you, I'll try. I'll end it now." He picked up his tray of needles and drugs, hurled them against the stone fireplace. "I am finished with it. You'll see. Beginning tomorrow, you'll see the man my father envisioned. I am young. Pray for me, Matteus."

The Moor's shoulders sagged. The scene had played too many matinees; the spontaneity of the star had staled. It was always the same, tomorrow . . . tomorrow.

If he had not promised Don Diego . . .

Two weeks later decisions were made. Matteus had had enough. Don Diego's disappointment, from wherever he viewed the shambles of his son's life, must be equal to his own. The life-style to which Vivaldi had fallen prey was incompatible with the Moor's. Allah alone knew the private corridors of hell Vivaldi traversed. Rendered impotent against the insidious drug enslaving Vivaldi, of what good was he to the Spaniard? Why remain at Terra Bonifacio?

He packed a valise and, descending the steps to the vendetta room, found Vivaldi, in the early stages of drugged stupor, barely able to look up at him. "I am here to bid you farewell. It is finished between us. So flounder in the sea of wretchedness Moloch prepares for you. You have sold out to him, and against Moloch, that devil incarnate, I have few persuasive powers."

Within the hour the Moor was gone.

Stunned, unable to articulate his thoughts and lacking the strength to combat the morphine, Vivaldi slipped deeper into the seductive embraces of drugs and alcohol. How long he remained in a stupor, he did not know or care. Periodically he'd catch his reflection in the mirrors hung between the eight doors of the vendetta room and trace the hollows under his eyes. He had metamorphosed into a wandering cadaver, roaming the fields of purgatory, searching for but finding no escape.

On March 15, a miracle!

Matteus returned, crammed with vital information designed to light vendetta fires under Vivaldi. This time, the plans of Don Diego would not be aborted. He was prepared to set fires to the prickly balls of Moloch, send him scurrying back to hell where he belonged, *outside* Vivaldi's body.

Vivaldi, engaged in soliloquy, sat in a throne chair before the portrait of Victoria propped before him on another chair. He glanced up, saw Matteus.

Drugged? Drunk? What did it matter, thought Matteus, it was as if he'd not been gone these past few weeks.

"Ah, Matteus." Vivaldi's voice turned conspiratorial. "Did you know we've been bewitched? Yes, yes, it's true. Corsica has bewitched us. This island of fascination and beauty, surrounded on all sides by sapphire seas, has captivated our souls. But you and I know, don't we, its Garden of Eden mantle is purely camouflage." He crooked a finger, beckoning the despairing Moor, his voice a ferment of ugliness. "You and I *know*, don't we? Its beauty is a coverup for a dark, sinister world of petty intrigues, death, a devilishly hostile people. We know." Vivaldi, on his feet, poured wine into a gold chalice on a nearby table.

"For all its indescribable beauty—" He waved his arms about like a high priest commanding the populace as he strode the ornate medieval chambers. "For all its beauty, poets and writers believe the island was designed by Mephistopheles to disguise its mysteries, hide from the world its vicious blood feuds, murders, and centuries-old vendettas. The flowers, none more beautiful the world over, have fed off the blood of man. How cleverly disguised. The world's most exquisite coral beds abound in Corsican waters. Do you know what transforms them into crimson magnificence?" Spurts of laughter escaped his lips. "The blood of millions fed the waters for centuries." Vivaldi moved to one of the floor-length mirrors between the eight exits.

"Take me, for instance. Am I not a handsome young devil? He studied his cadaverous expression in the glass, examining the harsh gaunt lines, sunken pallor, death's-head reflection. "Ah, well, perhaps not now, but once I was a handsome scamp. Come, Matteus, look deeply into my eyes. Tell me you see the soul of a depraved specter unworthy of trespass in Dante's Inferno."

Wearing an open-necked silk shirt and velvet trousers, Spanish style, tight to the knee, flared over his boots, a gun tucked into his waist, Vivaldi refilled his wine chalice, guzzled the contents, spilling crimson streams down his shirtfront. "Oops," he grinned.

The Moor edged in closer, gently removed the cup from Vivaldi's hand, led him back to the throne chair, then attacked him mercilessly. "Enough! The idiocy must cease! I refute this self-indulgent fantasizing! Agreed . . . Corsicans are a perplexing people. But let us be honest. Disaster fell like a plague upon you in Spain, where you were a prince and acted like a peon. In Corsica, no longer a prince, you court disaster by acting like one! Fifty whispering angels cannot steer your course unless you will it. Vindicate the guilt in your mind—burst the chains holding you. Cease suffering! You forced a habit upon yourself, without pause for self-inventory. Don Diego sent you to Corsica. Why? You asked the question in the beginning. Ask it again. And again! Why? Why? *Why?* Until you learn the answer you will remain half dead, chained in a purgatory of your own satanic creation. You moan, bewail, construct elaborate plots about the injustice done you by this exile, and all the while your eyes turn inward on past scenes. You court disaster in the present, denying your future, and have learned nothing of Corsica—nothing at all!" Matteus paused a moment. "If you choose a coward's life, blindness over sight, deafness over hearing, death over life, so be it. But I tell you, until the riddle of your presence in Corsica illuminates your mind, you will remain of no use to any man, least of all yourself." Matteus quenched his thirst from a calfskin *botta* of water.

"In the *maquis* are hidden bandits, brigands, criminals, exiles, thieves, murderers. The forsaken take to the fragrant thicket belting the island because law to them is meaningless, human life worth less than a sneeze. Centuries of oppression have made them what they are. Come to terms with these men. They are the means of generating a power to avenge the injustices done the Houses of de la Varga and Montenegro. For too long I was moved to disgust. I no longer pity you. Your display of cowardice is appalling. Yes, cowardice! When a man can no longer be the man he was, he loses his reason to live. If you think I take pleasure in holding a mirror to your soul, I assure you I do not. Your steadfast refusal to become the man you are, the man you are destined to become, is beyond my comprehension. Surely there remains enough de la Varga blood to build your strength? If your will is to destroy yourself, better I put a gun to your head than let this demon devour you bit by bit. The demon is you, Vivaldi, a monster created by drugs. You totter on the brink of disaster."

Pacing furiously as he spoke, pausing briefly before the ornate chest in which Vivaldi's stored cache of drugs lay in meticulous array in an open drawer, Matteus, in a siege of fury lifted the drawer from its niche and flung its contents into the open fireplace, where every vial and syringe shattered into pieces.

Vivaldi leaped from the chair, arms outflung. For a second it appeared as if he would pounce on the Moor, tear him apart with his bare hands.

Vivaldi whipped the gun from his waist, tossed it to the Moor. "Go ahead, *amigo*, do it! Do it and be done with it! It's the only way. I am everything, anything you say I am. I want to die. Don't you understand? I *want* to die! Do it!"

Matteus's features set grimly. "You are a sick man. It was a mistake to return. *Adieu*. I leave you to your personal hell."

"No! *Goddamn* you, no! You will stay! Hear me out! I have done it *your* way! I have tried to honor my father's wishes. You, Matteus, better than any *know* I am no Corsican. I understand none of their barbaric ways. I own land abounding with thick, rich forests, perfect for lumber. I negotiated for their sale. To attain my goal, I posted signs prohibiting grazing and hunting on Bonifacio lands. *Signore* Bonifacio is perfectly within his rights, yes? *No!* Can *Signore* Bonifacio recruit outside labor? *No! Signore* must throw open his lands to hunting and grazing before labor is made available to him. Shall I continue? Charred ashes, black stumps designate the graveyard of former lush lands once worth millions of francs. Does that end *Signore* Bonifacio's humiliation? *No!* Poachers audaciously appear to use Bonifacio lands for personal purposes without fear of landlord reprisal. *Signore* Bonifacio recruited labor from Sardinia. Suddenly Corsicans congregate, shotguns at the ready, to scare off alien labor. Well, *Signore* Bonifacio is finished! I am finished! I refuse to live among brutes. The Corsicans are an inbred race of men, comprised of all who have ruled the island in its past. They have assimilated the faults of past rulers but few of their virtues. I, for one, refuse to coddle these Corsican *emperors* who refuse to work. I cannot, will not, cope with their level of mentality. And the women! Bah! Scowling, unfriendly, suspicious—they treat me as a stranger!"

Matteus, posed under the archway leading to the stairs, tilted his head. "*No es verdad, señor?*" He spoke in Spanish. "You are a *stranger*. You remain a *stranger*, the absentee landlord in a land that despises *strangers*. The island shall remain your purgatory until you face the men of the *maquis* to test your manliness. You have permitted them to see your weakness. It was a bad move—a naked man poses no threat. When the weakness dissolves and you are looked upon as a man of strength, you will regain their respect. *Verdad*, they pause, drink your wine, but you will not coax work from them. Before your weapons of negotiation evaporate, come to terms with them and with yourself.''

"What do you suggest I do?"

"Suggest?" The Moor shook his head. "I grow weary of wiping your ass. *You* defecate—*you* wipe. Become a man. Do the manly thing.''

Vivaldi mopped the sweat from his brow; he breathed deeply, his eyes scanning the debris of opiates. His need was great. He gestured to the shattered paraphernalia. "Will you see me through this—I am uncertain I can live without it.''

"There is only one way.''

"I know. I know! How do I know if I can do it?''

"There is no other way. All else is deception.''

"I want to, *goddammit*! I want to give it up! Do you know the tortures of being haunted by hair the color of flaming fire? Eyes of verdant gems?'' His bloodshot eyes trailed to the painting propped on the chair. He paced, wrung his hands, and pounded his fist through the back of a throne chair, splintering his knuckles, drawing blood.

"Face reality. Make peace with Corsica—its people. Forget the past. Honor your sworn blood oath. Shall I speak to you of the daily conquests made by Zeller. The malefactor who destroyed your life brings victory, glory, political prominence throughout Italy.''

Vivaldi's lidded eyes fixed dully upon the Moor.

"It is true. I was in Italy to witness for myself Zeller's triumph over you. While you sit here rotting away, inch by inch, bit by bit, drop by drop with that daily dose of poison to dull your wit, erode your mind, lull you into false security, your mortal enemy reaps rewards and riches beyond credibility.''

"W-hat are y-you s-saying?''

"Shall I cite your enemy's accomplishments? Very well. Zeller is the second most important man in Italy. Adviser to Il Duce, liaison minister of finance. It is true. Shall I tell you how this was possible? The falsification of Don Diego de la Varga's last will and testament. Assets from de la Varga were transferred to Amadeo Zeller—not Antonio Vasquez—he was too clever for that—to *Amadeo Zeller*! Zeller, you see was financial consultant to Diego de la Varga—''

"That is a lie!"

"Of course. Who will contest it? Zeller possesses full autonomy. Don Diego's consultant—given power of attorney; another falsification—controls the entire estate. *Ay de mi!* You seem surprised. Surely you recognized this dissembler's talents when you were blood brothers? Brace yourself, there is more. Zeller converted much to cash. He lives in a grand palazzo in Rome, married to royalty. Ah, yes. A claim Zeller made against the Valdez estate in Argentina, naming himself a sizable debtor of Don Verono Valdez and contested by the widow Valdez, was recently settled. The *Señora* Valdez met with an unfortunate accident while traveling in Europe recently, I was told. I have sent for the facts. Perhaps a trip to London will be necessary."

Vivaldi was stunned, confused; he sorted through the cob-webbed maze in his brain. It did no good. He was too far gone. His eyes trailed to the portrait of Victoria. Words from across the grave reached out to him. *The plot extends beyond the annihilation of the de la Varga family, possibly Argentina, the United States. Study the Parchments . . . carry the legacy forward to your sons . . . do not tangle with Zeller until you have the power . . . the power . . . The ring of the Marten will open doors. . . .*

His head reeled. He felt sick. Never so sick in his life.

Matteus's voice was low and husky. "It was, from the first, a plot. Acquisition of the de la Varga lands, the wealth for conversion to Zeller's use."

Each word, gesture, intonation, was skillfully designed to incite Vivaldi. Facts supported by demonstrable evidence were offered—newspaper clippings, photos, headlines, letters. The Moor observed Vivaldi carefully as he rose to his feet. Standing before the likeness of Victoria, his words were directed to the Moor.

"You might have to wipe my ass for a week or two or however long it takes, for I will be incapable of doing it myself. At the end of two weeks, we shall determine if a real man lies beneath the facade of a worthless fool. Will you gamble with me, Matteus? Am I worth the effort? Will you, can you, help me exorcise the predatory Morpheus from my body and mind?"

Matteus observed him solemnly, weighing his own capabilities. "I will pray, make stronger supplications to Allah, to dissolve the power of Moloch, who presides over the tortures of the damned.

Someone has performed a bad *baraka* on you and the spell must be broken. We must catch Moloch in a weak moment when he, who never sleeps, is not looking.''

Matteus boarded up the wine cellar, hiding keys and tools in places Vivaldi would not find them. He led Vivaldi to his room, undressed him, placed him in bed, secured him with straps, covered him with down comforters. Locking the bedroom door, he barricaded the entrance with furniture and left the house. He saddled up the stallion and rode to Ajaccio to seek out apothecary Angelo de Rocca.

De Rocca, the rotund, pink-cheeked cheerful apothecary, wearing a white jacket over his shirt and trousers, stood at a counter in the back room of his shop, working a mortar and pestle near wall cases filled with apothecary jars: arsenic, belladona, curare, cyanide, strychnine, *colchicum autumnale*—the list was endless. He listened to Matteus's story and, pausing, wrote a list of instructions as he carefully prepared several calmative and pain powders. He judiciously resisted probing into the identity of this mysterious war-veteran friend, who the Moor had described as having sustained injuries during the war that had caused the addiction. "My friend desires to be done with the addiction. I cannot refuse him assistance."

De Rocca, shaking his head, waddled to the large window overlooking the Ajaccio waterfront, offered a dim prognosis. "A man must have supernatural strength to resist the seduction of morphine. Let us hope for the best, *Signore* Matteus. But you must heed my instructions, pay careful attention to my words. You will become a Cassandra to him, a sentinel exercising prudence every step of the way—understand? *Bene*. The patient begins withdrawing. The severity of his symptoms is dependent upon his tolerance—the quantity of poison previously consumed, the length of intervals between injections.''

De Rocca lumbered back to the lab counter, lighted a Bunsen burner, and heated a flask with black Turkish coffee. "So," he began.

"The symptoms begin with yawning, sweating, sneezing, and loss of appetite. Increased desire for the morphine sets in. Restlessness, depression, feelings of impending doom, magnified a thousand times . . . Irritability, muscular weakness, will precipitate an accelerated respiration rate. Anxieties will pervade his spirit, the symptoms I mentioned earlier, will exacerbate his condition in a day or two. Now comes the time to demonstrate Herculean strength. Chills commence, vasomotor disturbances, flushing, sweating, vomiting, diarrhea, abdominal cramps, pains in the lower back, severe headaches, marked tremors . . . *Signore,* he will exhaust you.''

"He will exhaust *himself, Signore* de Rocca,'' Matteus said softly.

"At this point he could die.'' The apothecary removed the briskly boiling coffee from the burning jet, held the flask gingerly with a towel, and poured a cup for each. "You wish me to continue, *signore?* We have only begun to scratch the surface.''

Matteus nodded, accepted the coffee graciously. "I must proceed. It is a life-or-death situation.''

"Truer words have not been spoken,'' continued de Rocca, sipping his coffee. "The battle rages between the forces of life and death. The patient refuses water at this point, *and* food. The body dehydrates. A marked loss of weight ensues. Now comes evidence of delirium, hallucinations, manic activity. *Si, signore,* even heart failure and death can occur. You must utilize all your wits at this juncture. The temptations of Christ will appear benign by comparison to the temptations facing you. To weaken, to end his stress, the severity of withdrawals afflicting him, will seem the only humane thing to do, and you can cease his suffering abruptly by injecting morphine into his system. Physiological equanimity is restored in five to thirty minutes. Should you give in to the temptation, the patient's addiction becomes aggravated and the devil's own watchdog, Cerebus, will not grant you a second chance. Should you demonstrate the consolidated forces needed to slay the morphine dragon, the symptoms will have peaked by ninety-two hours. The fifth day brings about their decline. The eighth day should end it. The patient should be amenable to water and food. Be forewarned, *Signore* Matteus, following the cessation of withdrawal, tolerance disappears. Should he take a dose equal to the amount used before withdrawal, death can result.'' De Rocca sipped his coffee. "I do not envy you this task. Your God, Allah, and his convoy led by a legion of angels must guide you on this journey through hell. Who is it you plan to rescue from hell's damnation?'' he asked subtly.

"A foreigner living in Mount Cumeta. Who he is is of little importance.''

"A man's life to you is of little importance?'' The hostility creeping into the Moor's eyes silenced him momentarily. "Once

Satan is shaken from his bones, take him to *Guagno les Baines*, a hot springs some eleven kilometers from Vico. The waters, one for drinking, the other for bathing, are miraculous, curative. They promote relaxation." He handed the Moor the parcels, placed them carefully in his basket. "God be with you, *signore*, and with your friend. He is a most fortunate man to have you."

De Rocca stood in the open doorway observing the Moor swing to the saddle of his black Andalusian stallion and ride away. Usually physicians were summoned in such matters, or the patient taken to the special villas along the Riviera for such treatment. In the past he had supplied vast sums of opium and morphine to the Moor. Certainly the Moor himself was not addicted. De Rocca knew an addict on sight. Countless French war veterans spent summers in Corsica, their use of morphine alarmingly vast. In Ajaccio itself, morphine powder was dispensed as a cure-all for everything from a bee sting to a headache. Only recently he had read medical journals from Vienna, describing the drug as most insidious.

Snapped from his reverie by his wife's voice, he turned to her. The small-framed bright-eyed woman rushed to him ebulliently. "She's coming home, Angelo. Our daughter is returning to us. Dariana will be home for Easter!" She hugged him joyously.

At Terra Bonifacio, the hell had ceased. Every tool devised by the devil Moloch, hurled against Vivaldi for the next several weeks, became ineffective. Matteus, his keeper and warrior, had waged war with death and won. They had defeated the enemy! How sweet was the taste of victory!

On this day, Vivaldi seemed to lose his cadaverous expression. He stood before the oil portrait of Victoria Valdez in the vendetta room in a calm, deliberate pose.

"Forgive me, beloved, for what I am about to do." He removed the painting from the wall, carried it upstairs to the main house, climbed the stone staircase to the third floor, hugging the wall.

In a storage room he wrapped it in a clean white sheet, then again in wrapping paper, tying it with a cord. He placed it among other relics of the past, staring at it for a time.

"I will never forget you, beloved. If somewhere you are miraculously alive and it is meant to be, we shall meet again. But for now, I must return to reality or be consumed by the ravaging fires of hell. You are my immortal beloved. No one shall occupy your place in my heart. Understand, my wandering into the unexplored dimensions of eternity must cease. The cave of my mind no longer returns the echo of your voice, but within my heart burns the eternal flame of your love. In me is a sorrow deeper than love, loftier than knowledge, stronger than desire. It is mute, its eyes glitter brighter than the stars, and its name is vengeance. It commands me, drives me to seek out the reason I no longer hear the echo of your sweet, sweet voice, beloved Victoria. And until I find him, mete out to him what was meted out to me, my family, to you, our unborn child, I shall submit to its dictates."

Twenty minutes later Vivaldi stood on the terrace facing the sea. Behind him the mountains rose, range above range, shaded from a delicate azure to a misty violet. Blue pine forests filled the air with a strong, pungent scent. Vivaldi inhaled deeply, filling his lungs with fresh, pure air, ready to face the future with resolute calm and a sense of rebirth.

Chapter Eighteen

Dariana de Rocca stood on the ship transporting her home to Ajaccio. Sardinia, off the port bow, was shrouded in a pale blue mist. Up ahead were the Straits of Bonifacio, known as the Corsican Gibraltar. Corsica loomed off the starboard bow, presently not visible to her. Bundled in a white great coat, her short bobbed hair concealed under a turban, with dark glasses wrapped around her eyes, she inhaled the first perfume of Corsica and at once felt at home.

The thin, raspy voice of a tour guide wailing through a bullhorn shouted to be heard in the approaching strong headwinds and wild, uncontrolled lashing of the sea. Frothy cobalt waters slapped against the ship's hull.

"Signori, attention please. Corsica, off the starboard bow . . . Off the portside, its sister island, Sardinia."

The tour guide waved his ecstatic passengers forward. They ran, box cameras in hand, springing from deck chairs, emerging from cabins, swarming around the elevated ramp where the comely young man and his bullhorn described and gestured to the approaching panoramic splendors.

"The four winds of heaven gather at this historic spot, the Straits of Bonifacio, in baleful lament as if in protest that these sisters were severed from each other after the great glacier

279

descended. *See, here, as we steam through the straits, beneath the water the islands are connected like Siamese twins.''* The ship negotiated the aperture dividing the sister islands.

Dariana had heard the legend, seen the chalky white cliffs of Bonifacio, its ancient Genoese watchtowers, the enormous pounding of galelike surf. She had felt the fury of four winds and never ceased to peer below at the coral reefs forming a curious spinal column joining the islands. Today, Dariana, preoccupied, merely stood at the ship's rail, inhaling cool, crisp breezes, unaware of the close scrutiny measuring her every move.

Not far from her, another passenger, paying no mind to the raucous bullhorn and the *ooohing, aaahhing* passengers, was riveted to Dariana. He was tall, broad-shouldered, dapperly dressed, wearing an expensive camel-hair coat. A snappy beige fedora sat jauntily on his head and dark glasses concealed his eyes; he resembled one of those cinema stars traveling the Continent incognito. Briefly his eyes fell from Dariana to the passenger list in his hand; the name, *Dariana de Rocca* was underlined in ink. Back to Dariana. He dropped the dark glasses slightly, peering above them, drinking in all of her from head to toe. At first glance, he appeared bland, a man able to blend into a crowd if he removed the dark glasses. But if one lingered a bit longer, one would notice there was something *special* about him, even the way he looked, with a studied eye, without expression, unreadable. The man was a professional.

He glanced at the address listed next to Dariana's name: Palazzo de Fiore Ciliegia—Cherry Blossom Palace. *Perfect! What luck! What a worthy courier she'd be. Above suspicion.* The girl was tailor-made for him. She was a resident—an official resident—at the palazzo of the liaison minister of finance in Rome! An unexpected bonanza! The camel coat made his plans.

Dariana relaxed, unaware that fate had just singled her out for a radical change in her life. She listened to the dry parched voice of the tour guide. She could, if called upon, give the passengers far better information about the *real* Corsica. She knew the land of her birth intimately. She smoked a cigarette, a shocking act to most, enjoying it fully. Dariana, her own woman, cared little for the opinions of others—either in politics, religion, or morals.

Not considered stunningly beautiful, Dariana was nevertheless enticing and eye-catching. Her expressive face, superior bone structure, the unwavering disquiet in the depths of her hypnotic eyes, the full red lips . . . drew fascinated stares wherever she went. The classic features, studied manner of concealing her true emotions, failed to indicate the presence of inner turmoil.

Dariana, disturbed by the strain of her employment as social secretary to the Contessa Marie Clotilde de Bernadorf Zeller, had made the decision to return to Corsica for the Easter holidays. She needed the island to cradle her in its arms until the chaos in her mind abated. She needed new perspectives, a return to reality from the insanity of the fascism infecting Italy.

Once through the Bonifacio Straits, a few more hours on this turtle-paced ferry and home—Ajaccio, she thought, and peace. Peace away from the contessa and her libidinous husband would restore balance to Dariana's disorganized life. She tugged the collar of her coat up. The strident voice of the tour guide cut into her thoughts.

"Corsica, the scented isle, is a land of history looming off the starboard bow. In Ajaccio, the birthplace of the great Emperor Napoleon Bonaparte, you will visit his tomb. The very place his mother birthed the remarkable son. . . . Meanwhile, fasten your sights on a curiously formed rock resembling a crowned lion—il leone coronato. Next to the Tower of Roccapina."

Dariana, inhaling the fragrances of this India of the Mediterranean, permitted a host of pleasant images to parade past her mind—childhood images stirring a deeply rooted nostalgia in her.

Corsica. Home. Is this where she belonged? Or was it in that swiftly paced marketplace of Rome where values and morals changed at a reckless pace? Where yesterday's devout friend became today's enemy and tomorrow's hangman? She shuddered at the thought of the fascisti *squadristi,* the terrorists who accompanied Il Duce and the new order, and what happened to all who disagreed with his politics.

The ash of her cigarette blew away into the sea. She returned to her deck chair, bundled up, and lying back, fished into her handbag for another cigarette. She placed it between her lips. Before she could light it, a hand extended from the deck chair next to hers, held her wrist, and, with his free hand, struck a match with his thumbnail, cupped it with both hands, and held it under her cigarette. Dariana accepted the light. Eyes behind dark-lensed glasses stared into her eyes. She thanked the camel coat, lay back, retreating into her thoughts. Then she was moved to glance at the gallant man, slouched in his chair, the brim of the fedora pulled over dark glasses.

Something about him? Familiar? She shrugged back in repose. Possibly a cinema star? . . . He dressed flamboyantly, well cut, costly tailoring, hand-made leather shoes.

So? Of what concern is it to you? She turned her thoughts to Rome. The land of romance, indolence, art treasures, luxury for the monied classes, had recently become mecca for frenzied revolutionaries, men who used words for bullets until Mussolini's audacious March on Rome early in 1922. How quickly the tenets reversed to bullets instead of words. What a strange lot, the fascisti. Pompous, strutting peacocks, always on stage, loquacious to a fault, unrealistic since the Great War's end, and yet so ambitious they had electrified the world! Suddenly fascism was looked upon globally as the cure-all for the strife of mankind, something extra special upon which were focused the eyes of the world.

Damn! Damn! Damn! Dariana, agitated by the recollections, rose from her deck chair and positioned herself at the ship's rail, unable to suppress her resentment. Her increasingly untenable position in Rome provoked unquenchable anxieties. She whipped off her turban, spilling her short flaxen hair free in a mass of curls, letting the cool ocean breezes caress her. She must cleanse mind of the contessa's problems, of the detestable Minister Zeller and Rome. She refused to taint her holiday with thoughts of them.

"Corsica, a lava of legends, land of brigands, bandits, resistance heroes, romantic outcasts, heroes of impossible valor, remains as backward as the Middle Ages. . . ."

Corsica. Dariana both loved and detested the island. Corsica's stunning landscape stood as a reminder that nothing ever changes there. Once she had believed in Corsica's future, but the antiquated ways of her people, the gross neglect and rape done her by France had soured her. The governers of the island cared only for their personal aggrandizement. Nothing was done for Corsica itself, *nothing*!

Dariana bargained for more from life than that meted out to the Corsican woman. God, she wanted more! She'd gone to Rome, even Naples, and now she was going home. Sighing, she flipped her cigarette into the sea.

Suddenly she spun around, head tilted, listening. She heard something, something that didn't belong in this environment. *There! A gunshot!* Dariana's eyes trailed about the deck, searching alcoves, doorways, stairwells. Nothing! She looked behind her and saw the Camel Coat. Her focus sharpened. He staggered toward her, eyes furtively searching passageways and lifeboats.

Then she saw the red splotch oozing from his coat near his breast, spreading. Her gloved hand darted to her lips to muffle the cry crashing through her throat. His hand, outstretched, holding a small packet wrapped in brown paper, was pressed into her hands.

"Take it for the love of God," he said in Italian. "Deliver it to the Moor in Ajaccio! Now, move! Do not let the slightest suspicion fall upon you. Look for the sign of the Marten. My trust in you is implicit."

Dariana, reacting instinctively, shoved the parcel into her handbag and reached out to him. He appeared to be crumbling, falling.

"Move!" he shouted hoarsely. "Fascist eyes are everywhere. I beg you, do as I ask."

"You need help."

"I said, go!" He coughed blood. "There is little you can do to save me."

It wouldn't be until later that she questioned her sanity. But for now Dariana moved as if with the wings of Pegasus. She joined the tourists listening to the guide's canned speech. She wanted to scream, *Help! Someone help this dying man!* How could she scream with no voice? Her throat was constricted by a fear she'd never experienced.

Tourists to the right. Tourists to the left, forward and aft, wedged her in tightly. She feigned interest in the guide's dissertation. Her mouth felt dry; her heartbeats accelerated unbearably. She heard pounding in her ears as loud as the surf on the shore. Surely she could turn now to look behind her? Was the Camel Coat bleeding to death on deck? She turned casually. Nothing at all. The deck was empty. *What the devil? What in damnation happened?*

She sucked in her breath, fell away from the crowds. Had hers been the only ears to hear, the only eyes to see what took place? Had she only dreamed it? She felt her handbag; the parcel was intact. It was no dream. She trembled, angry with herself. Fear was not one of her characteristics. She forced it to withdraw. Shoving her hands into her coat pockets, the handle of her handbag secure at her wrist, she fell back amidships. No one, nothing unusual, lurked about the deck. Tourists asked questions of the tour guide: prices, accommodations, dysentery, suitable cafés, the usual queries. Her thoughts turned inward. *Why had he picked her? Not because she was Corsican? How would he know this?*

Dariana, born and raised in Corsica until her fourteenth birthday, had spent her childhood and adolescence strolling the waist-high *maquis*. No one spends time negotiating this beard of the earth without acquiring a certain grace of movement and an ability to remain blind, deaf, and dumb when adversity strikes. The years spent away from Corsica hadn't dulled her wits. Thank God!

Who was this man who marked her as his special courier? What made him certain she wouldn't turn the parcel over to the authorities? Who was the Moor in Ajaccio? A Moor in Ajaccio! Look for the sign of the Marten. What Marten? What intrigue had she fallen into?

A man's momentary madness had infected her. Why had she permitted this? Questions assailed her. Had he vanished into thin air? It struck her at once. Overboard! Had he jumped overboard? Was it possible? She moved to the rail, her eyes sweeping back over the waters. Fool! What could she see now, five or six minutes later? He could have drowned by now! Dariana tensed. She could very well be under surveillance. *Do nothing to give yourself away, Dariana.* She gazed about. Incredible! Had no one witnessed anything?

Dariana scanned the passengers' faces superficially; her eyes trailed casually past their heads. She tensed, Two hulking figures walked forward from the aft deck. She knew them! *Sainted Mother, from where? Where in her past did they fit?* She searched her memory.

Fascisti! From the palazzo of the minister. Secret police!

Their arrogant, parade swaggering attempts at disguise and their hooded eyes gave them away; they were men of the new order. Dariana took hold of herself. Weighing heavily was this role pressed on her by a stranger, using cryptic, meaningless words. Startled by her thoughts, she both rebelled inwardly and grew paranoid. *A man was killed moments ago. No one minded, no one cared. Now the secret police of Il Duce! They must have seen it all.*

She resisted the impulse to fling the offensive parcel into the sea. What omen was making her a player in these cloak-and-dagger theatrics? What powers had lured her to the center of intrigue with such men? What would she do? What could she do? Worse, what evil visitation was she bringing home to roost on the doorstep of her parents. Her father, mother, and sister? She thought of her father, Angelo de Rocca.

Seven years ago he had taken a good look at his precocious, full-bloomed daughter swinging her long slender limbs in a sensuous gait, exciting the men in Ajaccio, and packed her off to clerical school at age fourteen. The apothecary, a pacifist, wanted no rutting young males to disenfranchise the girl so early in life, robbing her of her virginity, thereby forcing him into exacting vengeance—blood vengeance. He had no sons to pick up the gauntlet when he died. The proper safeguards rested behind the walls of a convent. Four years later when Dariana graduated with honors de Rocca beamed with pride. By then Dariana had formed solid opinions on life, love, and politics.

The absence of love, the kind she read about and dreamed about, a profound mystery to her, had caused her to overcompensate in other areas of her life. She became a skilled armchair politician who hadn't the sense to keep her thoughts to herself. At times, acerbic, often downright caustic in her assessment of the current fascisti regime, she had come under the contessa's sharp reprimand. Attempting to espouse her husband's contempt for women who interfered in a man's world, she'd end up saying, "Who really cares, Dariana? The world goes on as men will have it anyway."

Dariana's thoughts, spliced by the loud spurts of gunfire, magnified her angst. Apprehension curdled her spine. This time, the sounds were definitive, as unmistakable to her as to the panicked passengers. Oblivious to the earlier melodrama, they screamed, scurried for cover like animals seeking escape. Furtive, uncertain eyes darted in all directions unable to locate the source of their fright.

A series of loud crashes brought her head up; a door to a cabin on the foredeck was forced open. Two men—not the same she'd seen earlier—were chasing a frightened, bug-eyed steward, firing guns at him. The petrified man, forced to his knees, pleaded to deaf ears. One man held a gun to his head threateningly; his words were muffled in the wind. The tour guide swung in closer to Dariana.

"Secret police. Il Duce's men," he whispered, drawing an imaginary line across his neck with a thumb.

Dariana got the picture. She looked away, loathing the sight of the wretched man pleading for his life. Her lips were pulled together over her teeth, her dark stormy eyes seething angrily.

Grimly she recollected the parcel she toted, a legacy forced on her by a total stranger, some dying man who had disappeared as mysteriously as he had appeared. At once concerned by potential problems, she grew troubled. Quickly, as the two men she spotted earlier reappeared at the side of the cabin and wound their way through the frightened, scurrying passengers at the starboard bow, Dariana feigned disinterest, listening as their animated discussion reached her. Something about the stranger's disappearance?

"I tell you he was shot. I swear! When has my gun ever missed? Why search? He's gone. He was no illusion, I tell you." The sober-faced, hawk-nosed brute patted his piece, holstered under his jacket.

His compaion jerked his head in the direction of the sea. "He must have jumped. We searched all over; his body is no place to be found. Do not concern yourself, *Capitano*. It shall so be recorded in my report." The words provoked a vicious reply. The hapless steward was kicked savagely in the groin.

Dariana moved in closer, observing in stony-faced silence as the secret police slapped the steward, pistol-whipped him, knocking him into a semiconscious stupor. Bloodied, battered, and nearly comatose, the fool made what looked to be an impulsive move toward his inner jacket; he did not live to explain his action. Wood and glass exploded behind him as a cabin door crashed open on its hinges, shattering into fragments. The steward, thrown on his sides, rolled over several times. If he had concealed a weapon, he never reached it. The fascisti opened fired. The blasts were deafening. The steward gasped, blood pouring from between his teeth; he twisted, jack-knifed, gyrated in a series of writhing spasms before going taut, his staring eyes sightless.

The ship became a swelling boil of indignation. Three stewards stepped forward with the ship's captain, herding the passengers away from the scene of the violence. The second pair of fascisti guns demanded to inspect the papers of each passenger. The captain, a distinguished, white-haired, hard-bitten seaman, displaying a more determined strut than that of the fascisti, growled at them.

"I am in command of this ship. You Italians are in Corsican waters without jurisdiction. I will not permit an illegal search and seizure. If you wish, you may bloody well put me on report. But I warn you, all inquiries and searches without approval of the

French port authority in Ajaccio are out of the question, subject to severe reprimand by the government of France.''

Well versed in maritime law, cognizant of his rights, Captain Flaubere insisted that no fascisti butcher could step into his jurisdiction and make mockery of it. For a time they huddled, Italians and French, arguing in a mixture of languages.

Dariana felt sick. Why such vicious brutality? A parcel given her by a dying man? Gravely concerned that a search would reveal the contraband parcel, she considered the likelihood of returning to Corsica in a pine box. This would be no holiday, she thought, no holiday at all!

Three planned vacations in the past four years had soured. Each time something unforeseen had happened to prevent her from traveling home. And now? Why now were the forces arrayed against her?

Upon graduation from the convent school, Dariana had applied for and received the position as tutor to Contessa Marie Clotilde de Bernadorf of Austria, a noblewoman secretly shuttled out of that nation due to the instability of the government and its politics. She and the contessa, two years Dariana's senior, became fast friends; a schoolgirl's affection sprang up between them.

Spring of 1921, a harbinger of bad tidings from Austria, had brought news of a marriage contract binding Marie Clotilde to a prominent fascist lawyer, a formidable politician cleverly allied with a self-proclaimed man of destiny, Mussolini. It made Amadeo Zeller the most eligible catch in Rome society. It was whispered that Zeller, wealthier than Victor Emanuele, was second to Il Duce in power.

Dariana's plans to return to Corsica were foiled by the contessa's growing neurotic dependence on her. The Austrian was alone in Rome without kith or kin. The war had solved nothing. Intrigue, counterintrigue, flourishing secret societies forming strange alliances, and the growing threat of Bolshevism erupting in Germany had instilled terror in the hearts of Austrians. No one knew friends from enemies, and it grew worse.

The war had ended, but the frightening years of slaughter, destruction, and racial propaganda had left open wounds. Austria and Hungary had become two separate states. Germany, stripped of its industrial wealth and forbidden union with Austria, paved the way for the financial destruction of the contessa's family. The de Bernadorfs were forbidden to leave Austria. Her father, arrested for consorting with former German friends for needed business loans, was later killed, but not before he arranged a marriage for his daughter and provided a substantial trust fund for her in Swiss banks.

It was little wonder that Marie Clotilde, finding herself alone in Rome, clung to Dariana, pleading not to be abandoned. Dariana had promised to remain in her employ for a month following the nuptials. Reluctantly the contessa had agreed to the arrangement. It was only fair that Dariana take a needed vacation, wasn't it?

Not quite. Dariana's plans were scuttled when they moved into the ostentatious Cherry Blossom Palazzo. An overwhelming set of unexpected problems took precedence. The minister's social, political, and personal obligations had proven too much for the young, naive, distraught contessa. Helpless without Dariana, she had wailed, "You can't leave me in a time of crisis!"

And Dariana didn't. Such lamentations coming from any woman, noble or not, would have rolled off Dariana's shoulder like water off a duck's back, but Marie Clotilde's unique situation demanded *special* concern.

The contessa was plagued by a curious affliction, a psychosomatic condition, labeled aposiopesis, which created several problems. Her inability to express a clear thought, breaking off in the middle of a sentence as if she were either unwilling or unable to complete it, was as infuriating and embarrassing to Marie Clotilde as it was to those forced to suffer in her company. The results were disastrous. Things constantly went wrong where they should have sailed smoothly. It fell incumbent upon Dariana to solve household problems, hire and fire servants, instruct them in personal and social functions.

Of late, the contessa's condition had worsened. Before her marriage to Zeller the impediment had occurred periodically and only under stressful conditions. Under Dariana's patient care, she had improved considerably. Following her marriage, the impediment became more pronounced and she had begun to stutter. Zeller's cruel indifference, his brutal censure before guests, and worse, before servants, had exacerbated the condition. How Dariana loathed Zeller for displaying Marie Clotilde as a cumbersome burden he was forced to endure. In time, she found reason to suspect Zeller's overbearing, paternal attitude toward the contessa.

Dariana's ability to translate the contessa's convoluted phraseology had transformed her into an indispensable ally. The growing dependency of the Austrian on the Corsican woman had made separation increasingly difficult. There was so much more . . . more than Dariana had time to dwell upon at this moment.

She eased forward on deck, moving through the terrified passengers. The ship moved on, hugging the scenic coastline, The spell had been broken; death, terror, and fear formed an invisible barrier between tourists and their holidays. Stewards passed reassuringly among them, extending apologies. The Italian officers, explained the stewards, were attempting to do their duty in subduing a criminal. "No real dangers exist for the passengers. The matter is under control," they said.

Brutal deaths! Murder? Possible espionage—no real dangers?

Dariana shuddered, her thoughts spinning forward. Once she stepped off the ship and the parcel was discovered in customs? Fool! Endanger the lives of your family and your own! What would she do with the parcel? In God's name what had she become party to? She dreamed up a thousand consequences.

The ship lurched. *How agonizingly slow!*

"Your first trip to Corsica, *signorina*?" Dariana spun around sharply, fixing on the eyes of the hawk-nosed fascist agent as he politely flashed his badge. She took her time, composed herself.

"Is yours an official inquiry or a social one?" She smiled.

"Perhaps both."

"I am Corsican. Born in Ajaccio."

"And your business in Rome?"

"Officially?"

"Officially."

"I work there."

"So. Your papers, *per piacere*."

She laughed lightly. "After so many years I failed to bring them with me."

"I must ask you to come with me," he commanded brusquely.

"I doubt," began Dariana austerely, "you would desire to tangle with me unless of course you are prepared to make supplication to Minister Zeller and plead imbecility for your actions."

Hawknose turned beet red. He gave her a long searching look. "What have you to do with the minister?"

"I am social secretary to the Contessa de Bernadorf, the minister's wife."

It wasn't enough. His sharp, probing eyes searched hers. "Your visa, with permission."

Dariana complied, searching her handbag without peering inside it for the leather folder. She handed it to him, her heart racing furiously. Hawknose reluctantly disengaged his predatory eyes from her imperious expression, scanned the document, searching for something other than the information written on it.

Locating it, he slapped it closed, tipped his hat, clicked his heels together, and begged her to accept his regrets for having disturbed her. His profuse apologies and obsequious behavior alerted her.

She accepted the papers, shoved them into her bag and promised to commend him to the minister. After all he was only doing his duty. He would be remiss if he had not approached her, she assured him. In a voice loaded with idle curiosity she inquired about the hapless steward. Hawknose leaned in conspiratorially.

"A political wretch attempted the assassination of Minister Zeller early this morning on his arrival at the ministry. We trailed him to Osta Antica, aboard this very ship. Be careful, *signorina*. Take care of yourself in Ajaccio. It is, doubtlessly, the hand of the *Unione Corse*."

"Not the Sicilian Mafia?" Dariana, unable to resist the rub, added, "Certainly, *Capitano*, with pressures on the—" She stopped abruptly, aware she'd shown no concern for Minister Zeller's state of health. "Pray, is he well? The minister?"

Nodding, the Italian handed her his card. "It ensures your passing through Customs expeditiously." Dariana's mild protest that she needed no special favors and would take her time in line with the others fell to deaf ears, just as she wished it would.

"Anyone, *signorina*, in the employ of Minister Zeller is entitled to special courtesies. The stamp on your visa automatically accords you privileges, since it indicates special security clearance. You are, in effect, something of a diplomat with a diplomat's protection when you travel abroad."

Dariana blinked at the meaning behind his words. She thanked him, moved back amidships, lighted another cigarette, annoyed to find her fingers trembling. Buzz words flew about inside her head.

Automatically accorded privileges . . . security clearance . . . So, Minister Zeller had taken precautions to clear his employees with the Italian secret service, eh? Why was it necessary?

The frozen features of the dead steward flashed in her mind.

The wretched little man had been a decoy, dead now, but merely a decoy! The killer . . . Santa Maria! The killer was the man in the camel coat! The assassin! The *real* assassin? *Think, Dariana, think!* Dark glasses, camouflaging distinguished features? Fine-tailored clothing to be noticed, rather than promote obscurity? It made no sense—no sense at all. He had disappeared? *Where? How?* With so much blood oozing through the camel-hair coat, how long could he last? Were the police correct? Had he jumped overboard?

Overriding all her queries, the most important question boggled her mind. Why had he singled her out to be his emissary? *Why?*

Dariana had no answers, only questions. Then the questions stopped. Thoughts of Minister Zeller's close brush with death brought a rush of excitement, color to her cheeks. She pictured Zeller riding in his chauffeur-driven limousine, stopping before the office of the ministry in the Palazzo Venezia. Somewhere, somehow, an assassin lay waiting for just the right moment to pull the trigger!

Damn it to hell! Too bad he'd missed!

No one was as driven or dedicated to Zeller's destruction as Dariana de Rocca. He was the bane of her existence. It was not only his despicable treatment of the contessa. Dariana detested even more his galling assurance that she, like any other woman, was unable to resist his sexual overtures.

On March 15, a few weeks earlier, the murder of two Italian communist leaders of Comintern sent shock waves clear to Moscow to Stalin's ears. Il Duce's newly formed paramilitary corps, the MVSB, Voluntary Militia of National Security, prowled the streets in Rome sending the Reds into hiding, their leaders into exile.

At the Cherry Blossom Palazzo celebration was in order. There were clandestine comings and goings, covert powwows, future plotting, strategy aired, tactics turned over and over, and secret jubilation. Servants had worked late into the night, serving food and drinks to the silent army of men in Zeller's employ, and when the business ended, each ambled wearily to his quarters and fell exhausted on his bed.

Dariana, no exception, fell prey to sheer exhaustion. Supervising the impromptu gala had drained all her energies. In moments, she had fallen sound asleep. Habitually a light sleeper, Dariana, with a cat's agility to spring at any threatening interloper, had felt a weight on her chest, pressing on her lungs, cutting off her air supply. Gasping, she had awakened, immobilized by a man's body pressed to hers. His guttural, foulmouthed language flooded her cheeks with crimson. Panting, grunting, groaning over her as sharp pain stabbed parts of her unexplored body. What Dariana felt between her slender limbs was alien, revolting, abrasive, a hot trail of searing fire ripping through her. A rush of hot blood panicked her. She was suddenly aware of what was happening and violently angry. If the knife she had carried in Corsica during her youth had been in place, the rapist would have been slashed in two.

His hand clamped hard over her mouth, cutting off her air. Dariana's face had turned a mottled purple, her struggle against him was life or death—hers! The gyrations, erratic animallike thrusts inside her, had kept her pinned to the bed. His frenzied pumping brought release. His drunken ejaculation at that critical moment had saved Dariana from death. His hand relaxed, slipped from her mouth. She had sucked in air, gulping prodigiously, with loud grating sounds.

Then, quickly, her wits about her, she had jack-knifed her legs,.propelled his body off hers with tremendous force, and sent him tumbling to the floor. Scrambling off the bed, she frantically struck a match, lighting a wall jet, turning the control until the room was washed in dim flickering light.

She stood transfixed, shocked at her rapist's identity. She stared warily at the leering, idiot face, preparing possible defenses as an overpowering loathing came upon her. Standing over him, she eyed him with so power-saturated a look, one so controlled, it sobered Amadeo Zeller. Her mortification was communicated to his drunken stupor.

Dariana neither screamed nor cursed. She neither cried nor indicated her true feelings. In her exhaustion she leveled on him the Corsican eye, the studied look cast upon blood enemies, pregnant with promise of future retribution. Suddenly, unpredictably, she leaped at him. Confused, mistaking the move for amorous acceptance, Zeller opened his arms to receive her. Dariana had nuzzled against his neck, his ear. . . .

The scream, an animal shriek of a wounded tiger, crashed through his throat. He flung her savagely from him. She landed against the wall in the corner, where she sat dumbly as he clutched the side of his head, the hot gush of blood oozing from between his fingers like a geyser. Dariana, blood dripping from her lips, spat out half his earlobe, and wiped her mouth as if she'd been contaminated.

Zeller, cursing her drunkenly, yet sober enough to assail her in a voice just above a whisper lest he awaken the entire palazzo, sprang to his feet, growling, yanking at his trousers, his face blackened in fury. He was speechless, aware he could bring little attention to his defeat. But Dariana read the message in his colorless eyes: he would destroy her when the time was right.

She had dashed for the door behind him, turning the key in the lock, savagely upbraiding herself for her carelessness in not securing it earlier. Shoving a heavy chair under the handle, she collapsed on the bed, pounding the mattress with the fury of a tigress, thrashing her legs wildly in repudiation of the vile deflowering. Despite her vengeance, the sight of blood on the sheets appalled her. She cursed, raged at the bastard, bemoaning the loss of her virginity to so worthless a beast! What she had saved, hoping to bequeath it to the man she loved on her marriage bed as a symbol of her purity, had been stripped from her by a despoiler, a man she would hate for all eternity.

Daily she vowed to expose him to the contessa. How could she unveil Zeller's monstrous nature to the naive girl? Marie Clotilde, however, came to her own conclusions about what ailed Dariana. The sight of her pale, strained face, hollow circles under her eyes, immediate withdrawal from Zeller's company, avoiding him at every turn, signaled serious problems.

The contessa, a young woman of gentle breeding, immersed in the wretchedness of a loveless marriage, had taken in her stride the crushing blow of Amadeo's infidelities; they were the talk of Rome. A week after the incident Marie Clotilde called Dariana into the vine-filled solarium.

"Some men, unable to restrain themselves in matters of the flesh, Dariana, need constant gratification." She elaborated on Amadeo's accomplishments, his powerful influence with Il Duce, his recent appointment as liaison minister of finance. Fascism, the hope of the world, was doing marvelous things for Italy, wasn't it? Great men were permitted special privileges. Forced to remain away from home for extended periods, sent on missions for Il Duce, they must be forgiven for their indiscretions. "Our sacrifice is small compared to his," she had sadly insisted to the young woman recently brutalized and raped by her husband.

Listening to the habitual smokescreen of lame words and pitiful excuses, Dariana made an instant decision and put it to the contessa.

"It's time I return to Corsica, set eyes upon the graceful *moufflon* grazing on snowcapped mountains, inhale the perfume of wildflowers, listen to the soulful *irrenzina* of shepherds calling their flocks, and hear the mating cries of cuckoos."

Enough! She had had enough! Enough of Rome. Enough of the contessa! Enough of that fornicating, rutting Zeller! For days the sight of his bandaged ear had sent shivers of delight through Dariana. One of the servants had confided that the minister, on a recent fox hunt, had caught the animal. "The little beast had leaped savagely upon him, chewing off half his ear. Dariana's astonishment was such she had burst into outrageous laughter. "No doubt it was a vixen, *Sì?*" Plucking a ripe strawberry from a large bowl on the table she had winked at the cook.

There . . . up ahead, Ajaccio. The passengers rushed forward to the rail. Dariana was home now. She planned to enjoy Corsica and her family. But how was this possible, in view of the event aboard ship? Unwittingly made a party to another's intrigue, what awaited her in Corsica? *What?*

It was Easter Sunday. Mass was not on Vivaldi's list of priorities, but he dressed meticulously, selecting a fawn-gray suit, white silk shirt, vest, slim trousers, elegant gray suede boots, and a snappy walking cane purchased recently in Marseilles.

Matteus, shocked at this business of going to mass, made no comment. They rode to Ajaccio in a fine fiacre, cautious as usual, heading for the cathedral.

Ajaccio on Sundays—a walking promenade of flower vendors, women sellling glazed fruits and nuts, perambulating crowds. But Easter Sunday was madness! Crowds grew denser; tourists with box cameras obstructed traffic. Automobiles, appearing on the island, blasted horns, spooked horses, caused major traffic snarls. Curiously fascinated, the people clustered about the horseless carriage, making the streets impassable. In addition, long lines of people four and five abreast flocked to the cinema houses. Silent pictures from France, Germany, and America had arrived in Ajaccio. *The Birth of a Nation,* the current shocker, was the latest subject on Corsican tongues. *What to make of this land America?* Civil War scenes frightened them, but Lillian Gish became at once their *femme plus adorable actrice*.

Vivaldi and Matteus rode through the glitter of Corsican sunlight, listening to the sounds of bright young voices lifted in song. Wild excitement permeated every street. Smiling celebrants jammed the floral-filled streets, but it was the young children, decorated in greenery and exotic flowers, armed with collection boxes, singing with maddening persistence that elevated Vivaldi's spirits. He listened as Matteus left him before the cathedral: *"Frère Jacques, Frère Jacques, Dormez-vous? Dormez-vous? Sonnez les matines! Jésus mort, vit encore, Tra-la-la-la-Jésus!"*

Vivaldi entered the cathedral buoyantly, with a newborn feeling he was unable to explain. Something about this day told him it would be *special*. Was it because he needed desperately to feel a part of something? Someone? For too long he'd forgotten he was a man, with a man's needs and desires. Today marked a milestone; he was about to join the brotherhood of man once again.

When it did happen to Vivaldi, he denied it. Once before, during his romance with Victoria, he had experienced the magical shape love takes between man and woman. He believed that magic could occur more than once in a man's heart, and when it did, it brought a song to his heart and a ringing in his ears that accelerated the blood pounding in your veins. Vivaldi felt all these things and more. He was delirious. He desperately wanted to belong to another human.

He had come alive at long last! All because of a face, a shock of flaxen hair, dark telling eyes in which he'd seen life. *Life!*

He saw her emerge from church. A glimpse of silk stocking, high-heeled shoes—shocking by Corsican standards—and short hair! Jolted, he felt the fresh bloom of spring within himself. Floral scents sweetened the air and filled him with longing.

The crowds swallowed her up.

None of the gay street scenes affected Vivaldi. Struck by the images playing havoc in his mind, he searched frantically among the throng for another glimpse of this apparition that breathed life into him. In desperate pursuit he hunted up one street, down another, around the plazas, past the military fort, along the *Place des Palmiers*, the *Rue Fesch,* and *Cours Napoleon*.

Nothing! Was she an apparition? Had she not existed? Save for the brief flash registered indelibly in his mind, he had nothing. Suddenly a ferret on a wild-goose chase, he persisted, searching every face along the waterfront. He felt like a dying man marooned on a desert, afflicted with unquenchable thirst. Vivaldi, bewildered, failed to understand compulsive behavior. He understood less the curious sensation of longing deep inside him. Longing for a stranger? But was she a stranger? Hadn't he seen her somewhere in a dream? He continued to move along the waterfront, unable to deny the images or part with them. All he knew was he must learn her identity. He must.

There . . . suddenly on the esplanade, walking with a younger woman and an older couple. Vivaldi recognized the apothecary, Angelo de Rocca. It was enough. Tomorrow he would visit the shop to make proper and polite inquiries. He went in search of Matteus.

They stopped at a café for a *pastis* before driving back to Terra Bonifacio. Observing the celebrants, Vivaldi reminisced for the first time since their arrival in Corsica. In Spain Holy Week culminated in Easter Sunday, which meant celebration, fiestas, confections, cakes, cookies, songs, gaiety and family life. At Terra Bonifacio, life was synonymous with existence in a mausoleum cut off from the world, Vivaldi refrained from airing his thoughts with Matteus. Things must change, he vowed internally. His mortal enemy, Zeller, hadn't abdicated from life, had he?

The conversation at the next table piqued Vivaldi's interest. Obviously husband and wife, the middle class couple of modest means proceeded to enlighten him on mundane, picayune matters.

"My dear, how shocking! Short hair, short dress, high heels!"

"It's the latest fashion in Rome and Paris, no?"

"This, my dear spouse, is neither Rome nor Paris, It is Ajaccio. When in Rome do as—"

"Dariana de Rocca has always done as she pleases. She's a rebel with a mind of her own."

Vivaldi's mind stopped at the name: *Dariana de Rocca!* His heart sank. *The Apothecary's daughter?* He put to Matteus the burning question sticking in his throat. "Matteus, did de Rocca know of my morphine addiction?"

"From my lips he heard nothing. He is no fool, Vivaldi. He needs only to sum up the purchases we made in the past." The Moor puzzled a moment. "Why? Is it important?"

Vivaldi's face drained of its earlier exuberance. He rose stiffly to his feet. "*Andiamo.* I wish to return to Terra Bonifacio."

They left the festivities of Ajaccio. Vivaldi, silent, brooding, uncommunicative on the way home, buried the fire of hope he'd felt all day. How in God's name could he hope to be socially acceptable to the de Rocca family in view of his recent illness?

The moment they arrived, Vivaldi changed into casual country-squire clothing, and following a light repast took the Dobermans,

Madame and *Monsieur*, for a long walk through the *maquis;* unable to get the image of Dariana out of his mind. Vivaldi hadn't the slightest notion that when he first set eyes upon this woman, he'd been the subject of a stimulating conversation between Dariana and her younger sister Angelica.

At age seventeen Angelica de Rocca was a stunner. Her heart-shaped face and large brown doe eyes, dimpled chin, pouting lips, and a lush, ripe figure were enough to drive the young men of Ajaccio crazy. Drooling young, lusty men who overtly signaled their prurient longings were not for Angelica. Only one man, *Honoré*, captured her fancy. She was desperately in love and wanted to marry him. Unfortunately, until Dariana, the eldest, married, Angelica, captive to Corsican traditions must remain a spinster.

Angelica had conspired with her suitor a month before Dariana's arrival, begging him to conjure up a miracle. The miracles commenced the moment Dariana arrived. She was bombarded with prospective suitors, at the contrivance of the desperate couple, until she'd had enough. "Enough!" Dariana pleaded in desperation. "I refuse to take tea with anyone else, so you can stop parading the Corsican cock o' the walks to our house. I've had no time to enjoy myself, my family, Corsica, or you Angelica."

Angelica, in an overwhelming outpouring of pent-up emotions, burst into tears. She accused Dariana of selfishness, totally unconcerned with her sister's happiness.

"You entertain the wrong perception of me, Angelica. If you wish to marry your young man, if he is suitable, I shall speak to father at dinner. I shall insist that he desist in this archaic custom. I've no intentions of remaining an old maid; neither shall I marry just any man to avoid that eventuality."

Dariana brooded on Angelica's words during Easter Mass. She wasn't callous or unconcerned at her sister's dilemma or angry with her countless matchmaking attempts; it was simply that her mind was organized for a faster-paced life. Dariana realized how drastically she'd changed in her absence from Corsica. God! She repudiated the customs. She'd grown worldly. She had already discovered there was more to life than the confining strictures of Corsican life.

What a stifling lot, her former friends! In her absence from the island, Dariana had learned to handle consequential matters with little or no confusion. She loathed needless ceremony; she was frank, spoke her mind perhaps a bit too directly but she detested and lacked patience for beguilements and feline entrapments.

Mass had ended. They were walking out the cathedral doors when suddenly Angelica tugged hard on her arm." There he is! The one I've talked about. *Signore* Bonifacio is most eligible, Dariana."

Dariana, charming as always on this holiday but irked at her sister's matchmaking attempts, had snapped sharply, "Why tell me? I have no interest in gentlemen shepherds."

"Shepherd? Are you some crazy woman? He is a Fornari Bonifacio. Don't you remember the landed estates . . . vineyards . . . The Genoan family? For goodness sakes, have you forgotten Corsican history? You are some strange woman, Dariana. I think you've become a jaded Roman. *Signore* Bonifacio, for your information, is a well-educated man. A bit on the mysterious side, I hear, and young. Perhaps too educated. I think he is snobbish, too. He hasn't been to church until today."

"What's this *too* educated business? No man can be *too* learned," Dariana had snapped at her sister, then glanced casually over her shoulders at the tall, elegantly dressed young gentleman. For an instant their eyes met. She flushed clear to her toes. Then the crowds moved in and he was lost from her sights.

"A man so well educated does not bury himself in a land like Corsica without reason, Dariana," Angelica said ominously. "Usually he lives elsewhere, comes here periodically on holiday. Bonifacio is a hermit. He lives with a Moor—"

Dariana's head swiveled about. "What did you say? *A Moor?*"

"Yes, like a eunuch guarding over him."

Dariana tried to locate him in the crowds milling about the *Cours Napoleon*, but he was lost to her. Was it possible? Was it just possible the Moor of Ajaccio had something to do with this Bonifacio? Noncommittal through the Easter promenade along the esplanade at the shore, Dariana anxiously returned home with her parents. She helped serve Easter dinner with dispatch. Her father complained, "Why do you rush me? Today is *Pasqua*, a day of rest, relaxation, and family doings," he reprimanded. sternly.

"I am anxious to go riding through the *maquis*, Father. I feel stifled here in Ajaccio. I ache to breathe in the beauty of the island. And when I return, we must sit and talk seriously about Angelica and this suitor of hers."

"I had to ask," Her father muttered resignedly, picking up the newspaper over cognac and black coffee.

Matteus, mulling over the numerous mood changes occurring in Vivaldi on this occasion, puttered about the greenhouse, tenderly transplanting seedlings. Something had punctured Vivaldi's spirit between the time they rode to Ajaccio and the return trip. *What?* Why would he concern himself if the apothecary knew of his morphine habit? The addiction had passed. He was a different man from the one he was on their arrival, wasn't he? Glowering, he set about the task at hand. Perhaps in five years he might perfect the proper hybrid grape to grow on this impossible brackish land. Why hadn't Allah endowed him with his beloved brother Pablo's green thumb?

Overwhelmed, and enchanted with Dariana de Rocca, Vivaldi strolled the northern perimeters of his land, frowning in thought. Something spectacular had happened to him that morning. He actually *smelled* the flowers on the island. He paused to marvel over those spectacular *roses de noel,* roses of emerald-green velvet, indigenous only to Corsica. His senses sprang alive; he was perceiving life as he hadn't perceived it in years, not even in Spain. Nature in all its glory came into sharper focus all because of beautiful dark eyes and a name inspired by goddesses!

Vivaldi eased himself off the corniche, heading toward the *maquis* below. Behind him goat bells tinkled; stiff-legged sheep climbing to greener pastures were egged on by determined sheepdogs as steely-eyed shepherds on the slopes kept open eyes for poachers and wolves. Vivaldi sensed their presence but his thoughts turned inward as he designed the means to a proper social meeting with Angelo de Rocca. He must meet Dariana, he must. He quickened his pace, determined not to traverse the corridors of his private hell.

For the past six months, peace had still evaded Vivaldi. He slept minimally. His natural melancholy turned to brooding, and his bitter hatred for Amadeo Zeller became a disease. Succumbing to a partial paralysis of spirit and mind, he felt devoid of feeling, assaulted by nameless yearnings. He felt, at times, as if he'd become a madman, rioting in an empty house from which all other madmen had fled. His detestation of Corsica had not abated. Of late he silently cursed his dead father for condemning him to this giant rock, this millstone around his neck, this stone weight whose chief national product was death.

Vivaldi glanced at his watch. This morning, for nearly three hours now, the past had miraculously dissolved from mind. Something—someone inspiring—had freed his soul! The exhilarating experience had pumped hope through his veins. He could, by imagining this woman, Dariana de Rocca, stop black thoughts from violating his mind! *Was she some miracle? Was she?*

Vivaldi sighed deeply, inhaling large gusts of fragrant air, and with his walking stick flushed the tall weeds in his path, scattering those small wood animals at whose presence the Dobermans fussed. He paused on a ridge overlooking the *maquis,* just below the goat track. He stood very still, inhaling the fresh sea air, feeling energy permeating his being. God! How good it felt to be alive! He gazed up at the clouds, haloed with wreaths of pink fire in the vast azure sky—and beneath it all . . .

Vivaldi gave a start. *Was it possible?* Beneath it all was the enchanting shock of flaxen hair, flying in the wind, sparking dark eyes. . . .

Vivaldi, immobilized, shaded his eyes from the sun's bright glare. He blinked hard, unwilling to trust his senses. *Sweet, sweet angel* of god! . . . It was Dariana de Rocca, springing free as a gazelle through the *maquis!*

Silence shut out all sounds except for the wild, frenzied beating of his heart. He gazed with passionate yearning at the lithe moving figure breezing past the upper branches of heather and myrtle. Soft, warm wind, rustling through the reeds below, tunneled up at him on the bluff. The sable-coated Dobermans panted rapidly, their pointed ears standing like teepees, alert, listening to nearby woodpeckers chipping away at the tree bark.

Vivaldi lifted binoculars to his eyes, fanned them across the path, picking her out at once, holding her in his sights. He barely heard the chirping of birds, goat bells tinkling from a herd above him on the stately mountain, raucous braying asses higher up.

Earlier, when their eyes had locked before the cathedral, a flame had run over his body, invading his blood, consuming his bones. His heart had beat so violently he felt certain its pulsing was visible in his throat, at his temples. Now he felt the same all-consuming flame; the weight of his old agony lifted, fled into soundless space. God! He felt free, wild, weightless, and seized by sensations of joy and rapture. A thousand dormant emotions sprang to life. His spirit swerved like a beacon, directing him, pulling him inexorably toward the girl with irresistible force.

Vivaldi was unable to circumvent the mysterious forces of so awesome a hand moving things into place. It struck him—he needed love as he'd never needed it before; a wild, driving passion possessed him. Victoria Valdez was suddenly relegated to another era, another dimension in time, the dead, empty past.

A stirring in the brush alerted the dogs. Rising on all four legs, they turned to the south. Quickly Vivaldi whipped his binoculars about, searching. There! *What in damnation?* Two thugs, stalking the girl, moved surreptitiously toward her, darting here and there behind bushes, tree trunks, boulders. Was he imagining things? No.

When she paused, they paused, obscuring themselves as best they could. When the girl turned periodically to scan the area, her pursuers concealed themselves. *What the devil was this game?*

The plot was there, shimmering in Vivaldi's sights. At once the juices flowed.

He lowered his glasses, unslung his *lupara*, and, grasping it firmly, hand-signaled the dogs to silence. He moved forward cautiously, crouching low, out of sight, negotiating his way down the slope, staying close to the goat track to observe the scene below without being observed himself. *Move. Come on, move faster.*

Dariana's lingering was due to her sudden awareness of cat eyes staring at her. She had discerned soft footfalls behind her moments ago. Her instinct worked every second; she hadn't been born to the *maquis* for nothing. Here she had no fears, none at all. Her purpose was to find the Moor of Ajaccio. From the moment she arrived at the quay, Dariana had expected to be intercepted, relieved of the parcel pressed upon her by Camel Coat. She had exchanged warm, effusive greetings with her family when all at once, the man in the camel coat appeared from out of the blue. He wasn't dead after all! He was hell-bent on escape, for split seconds later the Italian secret service was in pursuit, followed by Corsican gendarmes on their heels. In that instant Camel Coat spotted Dariana and a conspiratorial look passed between them, a silent warning. That look had not escaped her father.

"Are you at the center of some devilish nonsense?" Angelo had asked his daughter. And Dariana, playing innocent, made vague reference to the incident on shipboard, matters, she insisted, she knew little of. A day or so later, her rash of curious questions concerning Moors and martens had incurred her father's anger. Angelo had pressed, sternly citing a father's right to know what this sudden interest in Moors and martens had to do with the man pursued by the police. Thinking quickly, summoning her wits, she nonchalantly laughed the matter off. "Some fortune teller in Rome told me my life was bound up with a *gallantuomo*—royalty, no less, whose coat of arms bore a marten in its shield. Somehow a Moor figures into it." Dariana's laughter had set the apothecary to brooding. He knew his daughter and recognized a fairy tale when he heard it.

Tell a lie, Dariana. Then tell ten more to cover the first!

"The only Moor I know," replied de Rocca, "lives on the Fornari Bonifacio estate." This statement burned in Dariana's memory when Angelica pointed to Vivaldi Bonifacio that morning.

Now, moving through the *maquis,* she regarded Vivaldi Bonifacio. She recalled how their eyes had locked. Had his interest in her centered on the mysterious parcel? If only to rid herself of that abominable parcel and bring no calamities to the house of her father, Dariana had decided to visit the Bonifacio lands to conclude the matter. She was sweating now.

Angling to her left, Dariana paused, leaned under a chestnut tree, and climbed the slope to a large flat rock, Virgin's Point, where the sweeping bayline of Porto was visible. *Porto?* Had she walked this far? She tethered her horse near Piano, the red mountains of Les Calanches in her sights, and set out on foot through the *maquis,* forgetting how warm it could be.

She stopped abruptly, inhaled intoxicating floral scents, her expression one of exquisite rapture. In Dariana's childlike fantasies, despite her education and knowledge of the harsh realities of life, lay a vague wild-eyed desire for Corsican brigands, pirates, and above all the exciting legendary Sampier, the great Corsican liberator whose legacy to Corsica was centuries of blood vengeance. Traversing the *maquis* this day, overwhelmed by childhood memories, she was filled with joy. She adored Corsica with profound reverence. She fanned herself. The heat was intense. Stepping off the flat rock, swirled by time into a curious, indefinable shape with jagged edges, she peered below at the sheer drop to the sea. Close by streams and flumes splashed over tiered, perpendicular mountains, and shade trees. She quickly looked around at all sides of her. Good! She was alone. Who would know, anyway? She felt mischievous, yet as she eyed the refreshing cool water and felt the sweat pouring off her, she didn't hesitate a moment.

She pulled off her boots and socks, unbuttoned her riding breeches, flung off her shirt and bra, and with a cry of wild abandon dived into the pool, swimming, splashing about like a nymph, rolling over and over like a beaver. She was singing a Corsican ditty when a few minutes later she stepped from the pool to dry herself off with large green fronds. Dariana pulled on her breeches, bra and, shirt, slipped her belt and knife sheath into place, buckling it firmly. She donned her socks, one boot, the other in her hand, when she sensed the presence of intruders. She stiffened, peered about, eyes darting in every direction. She was tugging on her other boot when the two stalking Corsicans moved in stealthily toward her. Cocksure, arrogant, taunting, they moved in closer.

It happened so swiftly it was difficult later to patch together the chronology of events. From nowhere came the tall menacing figure of Vivaldi and the Dobermans. Perceiving the two brutes to be up to no good, he rushed to the scene, enraged, lifting one man off the ground, hurling him several feet away into the sharp brambles. Turning, he connected a hard fist to the jaw of the second man, sent him reeling into a ditch. Stunned, the first man picked himself up, glowering, rubbing his backside and legs, and backed away. The second man, rubbing his jaw gingerly, bounced backward on his bottom as the Dobermans snarled and moved to attack. Picking himself off the ground, he ran in full retreat after the first hoodlum, and both young men, regarding him with astonishment, flew as fast as their legs could carry them into the lush *maquis*.

Vivaldi whistled, summoning the dogs to his side. Dusting off his hands, running his fingers through his tousled curly hair, he turned to the girl, expecting a measure of appreciation. Instead his eyes widened in surprise at the expertly wielded steel blade flashing menacingly at him. A look of majestic anger and cold sternness fell upon him.

"Fool!" she spat. "I could have handled them. Instead you've needlessly made two enemies." Cautious eyes whipped past him, searching the terrain furtively.

"From where I observed your predicament, you did not seem in control of the situation, *signorina*," he began reservedly at her censure. "As for enemies, I have little concern for them."

Vivaldi drank in her short hair, falling in strands across her face, the knife held expertly without trepidation, the sparking, militant eyes, flushed with excitement: It was an intoxicating composite that played havoc with his senses.

It was the way she wielded the knife, her lack of condescension, the slpendor and grace of an untamed animal that rendered Vivaldi inexplicably and irrevocably in love with Dariana de Rocca. In her hazel eyes, not as dark as he had first perceived them, he saw Corsica. Rebellious, unyielding, filled with an unmatched sensuous beauty that staggered the imagination. How to approach her? Would she bolt like a frightened thoroughbred, take off like a flash of lightning if he prematurely bared his feelings?

Dariana's breath came unevenly. She recognized him. "Oh, it's you. We saw each other at church this morning, no?" She gathered her wits as she resheathed her knife. "Forgive my rudeness, *signore*. I was momentarily shaken. You came to my defense like a true chevalier."

"A woman wandering alone in the *maquis* places her life in peril. It is the sanctuary for bandits, men with prices on their heads. They roam freely here. It is a haven for them."

"They would not harm me. I am one of them."

"A brigand? A bandit? Is there a price on your head?"

"No, no, no, no! I am Corsican. But what of you? Are you not in similar jeopardy?" She began walking back along the route she traveled earlier, unable to suppress her laughter at his suggestion.

Vivaldi fell into step alongside her as if they had known each other a lifetime. "I can handle myself. Permit me, I am Vivaldi Bonifacio. These are my lands, above the *maquis*." He gestured in a wide, sweeping arc. "Forgive my brazen approach. Corsican customs, I know, do not permit strangers to approach their women. Pray it does not affect our friendship, *Signorina* de Rocca."

"You know me?" She shot him a sharp glance. Ah. It followed he would ask her about the parcel. She geared herself. "You are no Corsican. From where do you come? For seven years I have lived in Rome where the violation of a custom rarely means a life-or-death crisis."

"I too am Corsican," he lied. "Born here, I lived most of my life in Genoa." *Another lie? How many more would spill from his lips?* He looked past her at sapphire seas, wondering at the sudden prick of conscience he felt at the deception. Honesty was suddenly imperative to Vivaldi, but he resisted. *Trust no one. Tell her nothing. Who can tell from where an enemy strikes?*

"May I escort you to my house to take tea? It would please me to escort you to Ajaccio in my carriage. The route you took is a long one. You must be exhausted?"

She nodded, wondering why she hadn't contested his claim to being Corsican. Why would he lie to her? Vivaldi helped her up the steep incline through the *maquis*. The profusion of scents, sights, and sounds stimulating her senses, Dariana's childhood flashed before her. "Please, let me pause a moment," she said in a voice above a whisper. "Just look at the sight!"

A brilliant filigree of orchards lay directly to the north, trees laden with fruits soon to be harvested. A black-jawed peasant emerged on a terrace. Sprawled along the rugged mountain, ancient shepherds wearing skins called to their sheep in that unique, forlorn melancholy way. Dariana listened intently, turning, peering, eyes transfixed at once to a point on a mountain slope at a grazing goatherd. "Look! There! How skillfully he works. You'd never know his presence."

It took Vivaldi several moments to locate the splendid *moufflon*, king of Corsica's wildlife. Its golden spiraling horns and sable ur glistened in the sun.

"See how well camouflaged he is? Look, his sentinels nearby are guarding him, alert to all dangers. Protection in its purest form, no?" Dariana spoke huskily in a low voice, hoping not to frighten off the *moufflon*.

Vivaldi, listening, no longer looked at the *moufflon*. His attention was riveted on Dariana. She dazzled his senses, occupied his desires. Something beyond pure lust drove him. In her eyes he'd seen radiance, tenderness, understanding, and a mysterious magnetism drawing him closer, closer, closer than he'd been to any living human. Where Victoria was the moon, sailing in a pale silver light over dark, precipitous cliffs, Dariana was sunshine, the life force that galvanized his senses and restored meaning to his life. In his mind, the two never approached. They were distinct creatures, one of heaven, the other of earth. "You appreciate the *moufflon*?" he asked softly, but his voice made love to her.

"The *moufflon* is Corsica. How early they learn the ways of man, the power of the gun. See? How wisely they keep their distance."

"Those men in the *maquis*—why did they accost you?" he asked once they continued back to Terra Bonifacio. In true Corsican fashion she shrugged and became mute.

"Who knows? The rutting season is in full sway. Perhaps the wind blew goat scents their way." She laughed softly.

Vivaldi found no humor in her words. "It would please me if you chose not to walk alone in this curious wild place. Since the war the men have become more desperate. I implore you, take care."

Corsica, never as appealing as it was as he walked alongside this scintillating woman, came alive for him. Dariana was engulfed in waves of alien emotion. Failing to understand why she resisted the impulse of remaining in his company, she suddenly concerned herself with propriety. She didn't want him to think her brazen and outspoken. She was quick to notice the brooding lights in his eyes when she expressed her views on the fascisti in Italy. How could she guess his sensitivity on the subject? No matter, she reined all inclination to speak on subjects usually reserved for men and felt disturbingly at cross-purposes with herself for concealing her true nature. Just for today she'd play the game, she told herself. *Just for today*.

A half hour later, as Dariana strolled about the stunning vendetta room, marveling at the masterpiece of subdued elegance and the impeccable restoration, flares of light sparked her eyes. She lauded his efforts, remarked at the enticing scents of pine cones heaped on the fire. She sauntered over to an étagère, admiring its contents, a collection of precious and semiprecious stones encircling a black velvet display mound topped by a gold ring in the shape of an animal. A fox, perhaps? She moved on, her fingers trailing over the texture of fabrics and woods, her curious and appreciative eyes sweeping the walls of books, bric-a-brac, and art objects. The heels of her boots clicked noisily as she moved over the tiles, circling back to the fireplace, where for a moment she warmed her hands in the cool room.

"Imagine, moments ago I was so warm, I went for a swim. Now, here, inside this curious room, I am cool enough to be warmed by a fire."

Vivaldi handed her a drink of *pastis*. "It is several degrees cooler inside. This will warm you." They clinked glasses in silent toast. Dariana sipped hers, trying to subdue her excitement.

Her eyes swept up the massive rock fireplace, stopped abruptly at the coat of arms fixed to its highest reaches. In the lower left-hand square of the gilded shield was a furry animal with dark piercing eyes, bushy tail, its open mouth baring sharp, pointed teeth. A muskrat? A fox? Marten? *A marten!*

The sign of the Marten!

Her mind and body tensed. She spun about, eyes darting across the room to the étagère. The gold ring! It wasn't a fox! It was a *marten*! As it fell together in her mind, she moved quietly back to the étagère, her focus riveted to the gold ring. Instantly images floated past—Camel Coat . . . the parcel!

Dariana wasn't certain what she felt at that moment. She was excited, flushed, at the threshold of discovery, uncertain if she wanted to take that last step, afraid it might infringe upon a relationship of which she suddenly found herself protective. At this moment, she knew she wanted to know Vivaldi Bonifacio better. The thought of defeat caused a sinking sensation to flush through her. Before she was forced to make any decision, the sound of descending footsteps on the stone steps leading to the vendetta room brought up her head. She gasped, stared into the onyx eyes of a Moor. As Matteus nodded politely to her, Dariana barely heard the introductions. Her mind, racing on another tack, heard the Camel Coat's ominous voice.

The Moor of Ajaccio! Look for the sign of the Marten!

Sweet, sweet Jesus! She had found him! How calmly she reacted to the cordial introductions. She was the epitome of charm and social grace to both Vivaldi and the Moor. How delicately she sipped her drink before the fire while her heart pounded in unbearable frenzy.

Matteus, stiff, formal, uninvolved in the obvious enchantment growing between Vivaldi and this woman, became acutely aware of Dariana's burning scrutiny. Her open curiosity created discomfort in him. He sensed a hundred questions forming in her mind, and disconcerted by the studied expression in her eyes, he finished his drink, prepared to excuse himself. He clearly saw how smitten Vivaldi was with her. Worse, what he saw in Vivaldi's eyes posed a threat, continued detours and delays, if not abandonment of their goal.

Vivaldi squirmed uneasily. Would the Moor's presence forever serve as a reminder of the bloody past? Burn daily like an eternal flame to remind him of his sworn duty, even if he felt repelled by it?

"Are you the man referred to as the Moor of Ajaccio?" Dariana asked Matteus with provincial candor.

Vivaldi failed to hear the question. He was actually contemplating marriage to this Corsican. Appalled at his own boldness, he chastised himself. How dare he contemplate a union? Who would marry him, aware that his existence was dedicated to blood revenge? He sensed in advance the questions forming in Dariana's mind. her reaction to the strange, compelling relationship between a fraudulent Corsican and a Moor had signaled warnings. Glancing at Matteus, he blinked, alerted by the expression on his face. In this moment, Dariana repeated her query.

"*Signore,* are you the Moor of Ajaccio?"

Now both Spaniard and Moor tensed, astonishment on their faces. Their eyes collided. Each sat forward in their throne chairs. Matteus took the initiative. "What a strange question, *Signorina* de Rocca."

"I do not mean my inquiry to be impertinent," she began, placing her drink on the table at her side. "But, *Signore* Matteus, *if* you are the Moor from Ajaccio, I have been commissioned in a most importune manner to deliver into your hands a parcel. Commissioned, I might add, at considerable risk to myself and family."

Artfully concealing his astonishment at the effrontery of so direct an inquiry, he admitted, "Yes, I am that person. Pray tell me how and why you came by this inquiry?"

Dariana glanced at Vivaldi tentatively, displaying momentary confusion. She awaited Vivaldi's permission to speak candidly. The expression in Vivaldi's face troubled her.

Vivaldi's thoughts at the moment thundered across his skull like rampaging buffalo; he dwelled on the foolishness of his impetuosity. *Marriage?* Was he mad? He hardly knew the woman. A few emotional tugs on his heart after a long dry spell and he was ready to draw a stranger to his bosom? *A Corsican?* He *was* mad!

The torment, floods of doubt, gushed forth. Was she *really* the apothecary's daughter? Had she been sent by enemies to worm her way into his affection on false pretenses, to hasten his demise. Plagued by these thoughts, he was unaware she awaited his permission to speak. When it dawned on him, Vivaldi nodded his permission halfheartedly.

And so, Dariana told of the shipboard incident from beginning to end, describing the Camel Coat, his approach, the pursuit by the Italian officers, reiterating what the secret police conveyed to her concerning the attempted assassination of the liaison minister of finance to Il Duce just before the ship departed from Ostia Antica. Because Dariana was no professional courier or agent provocateur, she failed to mention details that might prove vital to either the Moor or Vivaldi. She grew acutely aware of the sharp glances exchanged between these unlikely conspirators. Dariana failed to mention she was in the employ of Minister Zeller—not to deceive but to forget the man's existence. Questions asked of her by both men were answered promptly, without guile. But the name Zeller was not mentioned by her hosts or herself.

Expressing an urgency about retrieving the parcel, the Moor politely asked if Dariana would forgo the planned excursion through the Bonifacio property for another time. Dariana, delighted to rid herself of the weighty burden, suggested they return to Ajaccio at once.

The ride to Ajaccio was strained and quiet, Vivaldi settled into uncommunicable gloom. Dariana, who normally voiced her annoyance at silence she neither understood or deserved, was quiet. Sensing this to be a fragile period in their relationship, she dared not press. Suddenly desirous of knowing Vivaldi better, she sensed disaster, an alienation she seemed unable to circumvent.

The carriage lumbered to a halt before the de Rocca house. Dariana graciously invited them both inside. Vivaldi declined, lamely muttering something about the lateness of the hour. Perhaps another time? Did she have a choice? Dariana quickly entered her house, retrieved that troublesome parcel that suddenly changed her life around, and, running outside, handed it to the Moor. Vivaldi tipped his hat, thanked her with reserved politeness, and drove off.

The electricity between them fizzled.

Dariana stared long after the carriage left her sight. She was not fickle or impressionable. But she *knew* something extraordinary had happened between them earlier. She'd read volumes on magical communications of love, its inexplicable feelings, but hadn't dreamed it possible for her, until today. *Love had happened to her and was finished in less than a day!* She ran inside her house, up the stairs, into her bedroom, slamming the door behind her. She was furious, her anger thundering like kettle drums, yet she would not cry. She refused to shed a tear over something over which she had no control. She ranted, raved at the Camel Coat for making her party to his conspiracy. She furiously assailed Vivaldi for fostering duplicity. Who or what she appeared in Bonifacio's eyes mattered not an iota to her. But at least she spoke in truths! Her clear-sighted perception had detected deception in Vivaldi. Confined to her bedroom, Dariana paced the floor, angrily refusing dinner. She lit a cigarette and collapsed on the bed, staring at the smoky spirals reaching the ceiling. Her body, mind, and spirit fell into a state of confusion, a bewilderment she didn't understand.

An hour later, still fulminating at the odious and unfair cards dealt her by fate, Dariana jumped up at the soft knock at her door. Her father entered, a curious, ashen expression on his face. Wordlessly he handed her an envelope. Dariana accepted it, acutely concerned at her father's paleness. She studied the envelope. It bore the Bonifacio crest. Her heart quickened uncontrollably. Her nude body, under her silk wrap, trembled.

She opened it, her eyes radiant at the contents. She read:

"*Mia carissima, Signorina* de Rocca: This Easter Sunday when our eyes met, I knew instantly destiny had intervened in my life, directing me to your path. Later when you strolled the *maquis* that knowledge was reinforced. If I demonstrated an overwhelming urge to protect you against those hoodlums, if I overstepped Corsican customs or violated social mores, I beg your forgiveness. You dazzled my senses, stilled an articulate tongue by your presence. My heart sings so loudly I find it difficult to write. I respectfully ask you for the opportunity to become better acquainted. If we find ourselves in accord, if our souls vibrate compatibly? It is not my desire to overwhelm you, *cara mia*, but be advised I have every intention to ask for your hand in marriage.

Dariana whirled about the room, trembling inwardly with a joy and ebullience be had never experienced before. She was all woman, a *real* woman possessed of strength and frailties. She grinned at her father like a mad cuckoo bird. "He wants to marry me, Father!" She wagged the letter playfully under Angelo de Rocca's nose. "Here, see for yourself."

"What need have I to read when these eyes have seen your feelings clearly written in your eyes. You wear your heart openly on your face, Dariana. You must learn to be circumspect."

*   *   *

Within a week, Vivaldi and Angelo de Rocca sat together in the Corsican custom, drinking *pastis* while the bid for Dariana's hand in marriage was made. Two weeks later, amid high expectations and overt demonstrations of his love, Vivaldi sat with Dariana listening as the banns of marriage were announced in church. The date of the wedding was two weeks hence, on June 5. Angelica was elated; her engagement to *Honoré* was announced; she was married two weeks later.

Dariana, floating in the upper reaches of the stratosphere frequented only by lovers, was delirious. It was the happiest time of her existence. She felt as if she'd come into her own at last, into the full heritage that was woman.

In this state of rapture she wrote to the contessa in Rome, terminating her employment, asking her to share in her happiness by sending her blessings. Thoughts of the contessa revived the trauma of Amadeo Zeller and all its hideous complications.

Mary, Mother of God! How would she explain her loss of virginity to Vivaldi? Impaled on the horns of dilemmas, she struggled, thrashed about, devising ways to soften the blow, ease the pain to his manly ego. How would she lessen the pain of revelation? How? And what a revelation it would be! Would Vivaldi accept the truth without demanding to *know* who had deflowered her?

Two days before the wedding, heavily laden with the burden, Dariana spoke to her father in his lab. A potpourri of medicinal herbs and exotic poisons filled the workshop. Angelo glanced up, a ready smile on his face until he noted the worry in her eyes. "In three days you shall become a Bŏnifacio; why the sadness?"

"I wonder, Father, is love highly perishable? Do men's affections change quickly, for no reason at all?"

"Yes . . . Yes . . ."

"What is this ready yes, yes, you hand me?"

"Answers to both questions. Yes, a man's affection can change, often for no reason. The mind of man is a labyrinth of endless complexities and preoccupations. Its true functions and importance are not fully fathomed by your humble father. And, yes, love is highly perishable. Love must be worked on, handled with care, nurtured and respected before it truly blooms. It can produce beauty like nothing else in God's earth."

"Why do you dislike Vivaldi?" she asked quietly.

Angelo peered up at his daughter over the rims of his gold

spectacles. "If I disliked him, would I present him with the love of my life in marriage?"

"Then what is it you feel? You study him as you study those potions in the bottles lining your shelves, as you stare at the specimens on slides placed under your microscope."

Angelo shrugged, reaching for the jar of belladonna, measuring it carefully into his mortar. "I wonder, have I done the right thing? He is a complex young man. What do we know of him save he is a descendant of Fornari Bonifacio? The name is prestigious. You take a step up in the social ladder, but is he *right* for you?" The remark, absent of malice, oozed with concern for a loved one. "Illness has plagued him for the past year, Dariana. Recently a remarkable change has altered his disposition. Since Easter he appears well, exuberant, and in fine mental state. Your influence on him has produced miracles." He wisely refrained from describing the extent of Vivaldi's recent drug addiction, fearing she would instinctively defend him and cause a rent in the love between father and daughter. "Bear in mind, Dariana, passion can be destroyed with facility, but never created."

Dariana passed over the remark briefly, concerned with Vivaldi's health. "How ill was he? Physically? Mentally?"

"A little of each. Problems within weeks of his arrival. You know, typical Corsican resistance to *strangers*. How easy is it for an absentee landlord to communicate with Corsicans?"

"The perennial sickness still afflicts workers?" She nodded in full accord. "The Moor, father? Who is he? What is he to Vivaldi? How long have they known one another? They appear devoted."

"That, my child, only your future spouse can answer, I know only that they arrived in Corsica together. The Moor is highly protective of Bonifacio. He is also highly respected among Corsicans."

"And Vivaldi, is he too respected?"

Angelo de Rocca busied himself with the prescription tacked to his wall, purposely avoiding the question. Dariana pressed. The apothecary shook his head. "You ask questions of a man whose head is buried in mortars, pestles, Bunsen burners, and microscopes, my child. Personally, I know very little. It is a father's prerogative to speak sagaciously to a daughter about to marry. Know beforehand that no man is perfect and proceed on that assumption to build a secure nest, a strong foundation for marriage. 'Tis a far saner approach than to believe you start with perfection, only to discover countless imperfections. You risk less discouragement and fewer disappointments.''

Dariana turned from him, opened a few jars containing dried rose leaves and floral scents, sniffing each one. Sighing, she admitted, ''True, no man is perfect. Father, not even women can claim perfection.''

''Explain, please.''

''I too am imperfect.''

Angelo laughed. ''What woman isn't? I've never met any perfect—''

''I'm serious, Father. Really! To be imperfect when a husband expects perfection presents serious problems to any nuptial bed.''

Angelo glanced up, searching her unwavering eyes. ''If there is the slightest validity to what I am hearing, I swear the Creator is as cruel as he is heartless.'' Sighing heavily, he returned to his work. Her expression bespoke the truth. ''Does he know?''

''No. Despite my inclination to brutal candor I am reluctant to tell him the diamond dazzling his senses is flawed.''

''Would it make a difference between you?''

''What a question, Father. I dare not speculate.''

Angelo shoved his spectacles to his forehead and, pouring them each a cup of coffee from the flask over the burner, shook his head. ''It is said that men seem wiser than they are, that women are far wiser than they seem. This case calls for the ultimate display of wisdom.'' He scribbled on a sheet of paper. ''I desist in asking for the lurid details, Dariana, aware you would spare none. I am too old for the truth. So I shall counsel you, not as a father but as a professional. This time, be wise, learn the virtue of keeping silent.''

''The fact will become evident on a night when things between man and wife should be perfect.'' She sighed, listening to the music coming from the house. Closing the door, she shook her head tolerantly. ''Angelica is in seventh heaven. Listen to that soulful lament. It was not my doing, Father. I had no choice, despite my Corsican resourcefulness.'' She smiled wickedly. ''I managed to exact my pound of flesh for the unprovoked, rapacious attack on my person, yet it doesn't assuage my guilt, or my terror in facing my husband on our wedding night.''

''They all say, do not beat your breast when it is over. The world, my child, is a stage and in her time a woman plays many parts.'' He glanced up sharply, his robust face paling. ''*A pound of flesh? Unprovoked rapacious attack?* My God! What happened?'' he asked with parental urgency.

Dariana took the paper from her father's hand, read every word he'd written twice over, devouring the instructions in detail. She lifted her eyes to meet his. ''Will it work, Father?''

''In thirty years practice I've not had one failure. Here in Ajaccio, numerous children bear my surname, not due to my promiscuity, God forbid, but from the gratitude of their mothers!''

Dariana hugged and kissed him profusedly. ''You old scoundrel! You're a romantic, after all!'' She ran from the room.

''Dariana! Explain the pound of flesh—the rapacious attack!''

''Very well. I bit off half his ear!'' She felt the apothecary retreating into a cocoon of bewilderment, a half smile on his lips. ''Half an ear? . . . Imagine.''

In the weeks before the wedding, Vivaldi and Matteus examined the contents of the mysterious parcel Dariana delivered to the Moor. Chemicals applied to them revealed writings in invisible ink: comprehensive reports about Amadeo Zeller and his activities in the Fascist party, his appointment to the Quadrumviri, Il Duce's advisers, his marriage to a member of Australian royalty, plus sheafs of reports on illicit assignations, numerous concubines with their names and addresses. Sexual proclivities were graphically documented. A schedule of his comings and goings between the Quirinale and these numerous love nests followed a curious pattern. Was the man a satyr? Far more interesting to Vivaldi and Matteus were Zeller's political involvements.

An in-depth perusal of these documents hinted at the provisions of gold war chests supplied by foreign interests to encourage Il Duce's aims at colonialism. Reports of Zeller's personal assets were vague and ambiguous; tag lines attached by investigators read: *It becomes increasingly difficult to determine exact assets, due to numerous devices employed to veil ownership of various properties.*

Listed were former de la Varga properties in Spain and South America. Former Valdez properties in Buenos Aires. Several in joint tenancy with names unfamiliar to both Spaniard and Moor. Property in Bavaria, Switzerland, England and the Middle East. ''I want title searches on all these properties,'' Vivaldi told the Moor, secreting the documents in a special vault constructed in the vendetta room.

The days flew by swiftly and they all revolved around Dariana.

Was he doing the right thing by marrying her? Dariana was his conduit to life, love, and sanity. How would it fare between them? He was, after all, a man living a dual life. Francisco de la Varga was living in the fantasy world of Vivaldi Bonifacio; could the one be kept separate from the other? Dariana, a compelling woman of iron, one year his junior, possessed the maturity of a woman twice her age. The incident aboard ship had required courage, poise, and cleverness. She had braved numerous dangers to herself and family to deliver a parcel thrust on her by a stranger who might have rewarded her with death. Still? How was it Dariana, out of a shipload of strangers, had been selected to act as courier? The question plagued both Spaniard and Moor.

"Such men," Matteus insisted, "are not without wits. They pick a mark, knowing full well what they are about. They trust no one. What qualities were discerned in the Corsican woman to inspire such trust? Unless . . . perhaps they were acquainted before the ship left Ostia Antica?"

Vivaldi brooded. "The man she calls the Camel Coat is still alive. Aided by friends in Porto, I learned only recently, he has returned to Sicily. I shall make contact immediately to learn the reason she was considered a safe, dependable courier, to ease both our minds."

Vivaldi was soon to learn the delights of Dariana. Like a Beethoven symphony or a Botticelli canvas, they would increase with intimate acquaintance.

On his wedding night Vivaldi left his suite of rooms at Terra Bonifacio and headed for the bedchamber Dariana had decorated recently. For an instant he paused, his hand on the gilded cupid door handle, images of Victoria flashing before him. Swiftly he erased them, determined not to permit her memory to spring like a wedge of darkness and alienate Dariana. He must give this relationship every chance of survival; to this he swore an oath.

Hearing his footsteps, Dariana, inside, having prepared the large four-poster bed with fine hand-stitched linens and lace coverlets embroidered with her initials, quickly stepped down and crossed to the window, standing in the fiery pink glow of a lighted brazier burning perfumed scents.

Vivaldi entered. Dariana turned slightly, unfastened the shimmering white silk robe, letting it drop around her shoulders and slither to the floor. She stood naked, arms outstretched to him, a smile of ineffable beauty playing on her soft red lips. Vivaldi gasped, stood a moment in silent rapture, feasting on the vision before him; full, ample breasts, small waist, smooth, velvety hips and thighs glowing like transparent alabaster. She looked up into his awesome green eyes, the shivering of her heart accelerating.

Vivaldi opened his arms, and with a cry of mingled lust, love, and exaltation, he fastened his lips on hers. Fusing together like sculpted statues, he carried her to the bed, never permitting an inch of air between them until dawn. Dariana was everything he'd dreamed of and more. She responded to his loving overtures and embraces with tantilizing, honeyed expressions of a love so deeply rooted in her he felt overwhelmed, intoxicated by it. The double delight of finding her a virgin infused him with pride and devotion that made his heart race.

Vivaldi's gentleness following the first piercing thrust of his throbbing manhood into her pulsating body unleashed urgent passions in her. She became at once insatiable. Oh, how she loved this man of mystery who knew exactly how to please and fulfill her deeply seated desires.

That night Vivaldi ached to end the deception with Dariana. He needed to reveal his real identity to her, unloose all the pent-up emotions struggling to escape. God, how he needed the warmth, love, security, and confidence of a real woman! Fear kept the secret clamped tight in his soul. Emotions would never, *never* cloud his judgment again. The words of his father still reached across the grave to remind him, *"Trust no one!"*

As desperately as Vivaldi, Dariana felt the urge to strip her soul bare of all subterfuge. How she loathed perpetrating a fraud on him! Her father's wise counseling had offered her one of two choices. Tell Vivaldi the truth, risk losing him, or keep her mouth shut, build a solid relationship based on love and trust as if neither he nor she had existed before the moment they met.

What purpose would be served by confessing the manner in which her deflowerment came about? Would he believe her? Would *any* man believe such a story? Seven years in Rome, alone. Could she admit to being raped by her employer's husband? Would he believe how she had struggled against him? Marked him for life to forever remind him of the hellion he'd conquered against her will? No! His first question would be, "Why did you remain after the rape, for so long?" Her attachment to the contessa seemed a flimsy excuse when viewed by Corsican mentality.

So Dariana accepted her father's counseling, did what countless women had done for centuries when confronted with the nagging problem. By treating her vagina with alum for several days prior to the sex act, the interior labia had constricted, the lips had tightened. A small sack of chicken blood spilled at the proper moment on the bed sheets at the height of her husband's passion, when he momentarily lost touch with reality . . . and *voilà!* The miracle was performed.

What mattered was Vivaldi's happiness, and it had worked. A month after the nuptial night, she exacted a promise from him. "Please, Vivaldi, know one thing, and know it well. If you choose to stray from the bosom of our house, it is finished between us. No marriage vows in the world will keep us together in mind, body, and spirit unless we work at our marriage. I shall bring no children into the world if they are to be forced to hear disparaging remarks about either parent."

Vivaldi's heart melted, his unbridled love for her swelled each day. He felt his heart burst with happiness. He adored her, respected her intelligence, independent streak, her strength, her fearless and straightforward manner. God Almightly! She was refreshing, stimulating, and if he did nothing else in life, he would love her for all eternity.

When Vivaldi told her of his feelings, he had every intention of keeping his word.

And when Dariana listened, she believed Vivaldi loved her in a way she could never hope to understand, with a depth of emotion beyond any she dared hope to inspire. Her love for this marvelous dream-come-true prince, who fed her love beyond her capacity to endure, was beyond any dream she had envisioned for herself.

He assured Dariana she could have anything her heart desired but one—he wanted no nosy servants underfoot to pry into their affairs. Could she handle the household and wifely duties? Matteus, he promised, would assist her in every way possible, but the presence of strangers in his domicile, prowling into every nook and cranny, was anathema to him.

And Dariana, with stars in her eyes, couldn't have been more pleased, for she recalled the busybody servants and their myriad petty, unending complaints in Rome. She concurred ecstatically.

Terra Bonifacio became her paradise, Vivaldi, her eternal lover. She was Eve, he Adam, and God smiled down on this Eden, sparing them the serpent's presence.

Chapter Nineteen

But had God spared them the serpent's presence—or was evil waiting in the wings in this Corsican tableau of perfection?

Dariana floated about in delirious rapture for the next two months. Marriage to Vivaldi was her wildest fantasy come true. Nothing save Vivaldi's love held importance for her. She reveled in his love and attention; she worshiped him and he in turn melted in her sensual arms each night. The past never became a wedge of darkness between them; they never spoke of it. The future was too nebulous. Both contented themselves by living in the moment.

Vivaldi had yet to learn why fate had delivered Dariana into his life, to become part of his world, his existence.

On this bright August day, as they rode horseback through the lush, Corsican countryside headed for a weekend sojourn at the hot springs at *Guagno les Baines*, Vivaldi had no idea that before the day ended his life would take on a different meaning.

"Find us a suitable place for a picnic." he called to Matteus. The Moor, following at a respectable distance, waved his cap and sprinted forward at a swift gallop on his white Arabian stallion.

Vivaldi and Dariana slowed their horses to a canter as they traversed narrow paths through the incredibly dangerous red

granite peaks of Les Calanches. Dariana, shielded from the brash
sun by a flat-crowned straw hat, called to her husband.

"The day—when was it—I stumbled upon you and Matteus,
what were you speaking of?"

Vivaldi, turning in his saddle, remonstrated patiently. "*Cara
mia*, Dariana, Matteus and I speak of a number of things. Unless
you refresh my memory . . ."

"You were ranting on about some miracle—some miraculous
happening—"

"Then it had to be you we spoke of. I know of no other
miracle in my life." He grinned easily at her with adoring eyes.

"Truly you are cavalier. So many compliments bring crimson
to my cheeks," she retorted coyly. "Unfortunately the com-
ments had little to do with me. You spoke of the citadel as being
the perfect place. You were certain Matteus's earlier assessment
ideally suited some future plans. Are you planning to restore the
citadel?"

"What else did you hear?" His stern expression changed to
reproval.

"Vivaldi! I *wasn't* eavesdropping!" Dariana maneuvered her
mare past the last corkscrew turn, eased to the incline at her right
in a steep descent over pebbled terrain to the lower reaches of an
open meadow, wondering at the tinge of resentment in his voice.
By the time he caught up with her, Vivaldi had removed all
remnants of her inquiry from mind. Dariana didn't press. Why
ruin the weekend?

Moments later she spread a tablecloth under a spreading,
golden-leafed chestnut tree in the glorious shade, bringing respite
from the broiling intensity of the sun. Matteus kept his distance
and intermittently rewound the portable victrola. *Madame Butterfly*
waxed and waned valiantly.

"I am the most fortunate man in the world." Vivaldi spoke
expansively.

"Would you make that remark if I were not laying before you
a banquet fit for the gods? Cold *becasse*, French wines, cheeses,
fruits and sweets?" she taunted. "Please ask Matteus to join us.
Lunch is ready."

Vivaldi's eyes darkened briefly. He glanced in the direction of
his ever-present sentinel. "I wanted you to myself this weekend."

"You ask the impossible. Matteus is not a specter."

"I know. I *know*!" Reluctantly he beckoned to the Moor.

Matteus shook his head regretfully. "Newlyweds need time to

themselves." He took his plate of food and wine, positioned himself nearby but not actually in conclave.

"The past two months with you, Dariana," Vivaldi extolled, "were beyond my wildest expectations. Amazingly, not one incident has been directed against Bonifacio lands. No fires, no rents in the fences, none deliberately damaged. Not one shepherd has violated our grazing lands. I'd call that a miracle, no?"

"Who would dare now that a Corsican lives on the land? Attribute the peace to your wife's presence," Matteus responded.

Dariana smiled. *Ah! Vivaldi was no Corsican! You knew it!*

"Matteus understands your people better than I. My perception of them is not as favorable. God knows I've tried, Dariana. I daresay my experiences with them do not add up favorably for the Corsicans. They are a barbarous lot."

Dariana, on the defensive, insisted her people were like those of any nation, a reflection of their land, victims of history and their rulers. "What happened with Mazzeppi was merely a sampling of Corsican justice. He stole from the Corsicans, and they eliminated him. If you bear in mind that Corsica, for centuries, became a refuge for foreign exiles engaged in vendettas, you will understand the Corsican mentality." Dariana, busily slicing cheese, failed to note the lights flaring in the eyes of both Spaniard and Moor.

Vivaldi, chewing on the cold partridge was exasperated. "The Corsican mentality defies classification."

"So you consider it fair for the avengers of blood to wander homeless in the *maquis* while political fugitives from foreign lands live in comfortable homes in the towns?" Before either could answer, Dariana launched into a dissertaion on Corsica and Corsicans.

"Take the Corsican bandit. No one despises him; he is neither thief, highwayman nor killer, rather a combatant, an avenger as free as the mountain eagle. His fierce nature, untamable by any culture, seeks continuous ventilation for the internal fires raging in him. How little Corsicans know of the world beyond their shores, yet they thirst after exploits. It's true we Corsicans are by temperament jealous, warlike, ambitious, revengeful, eager for fame and in every sense, native-born warriors." Dariana paused to sip her wine, inhale the profuse herbal scents riding wild on the wind.

Vivaldi kissed her hand impulsively, delighted with her profound knowledge, equestrian prowess, and indefatigable spirit.

Matteus, feeling like the fifth leg of a camel, wanted to leave, but the subject held immense fascination for him. He nibbled at the cheese, posing his questions.

"I admit to boundless ignorance over these curious creatures whose god is Napoleon Bonaparte. What a fickle, insufferable lot!"

Dariana's amused laughter waned. "True, we are a complex people. How else do you explain our history. Strangers chronicle Corsican evolution as a life of national apathy with crime it's national product."

"I, *carissima*," interjected Vivaldi, "could not have put it as succinctly."

"Be generous, my husband, more forgiving. These malcontents, contaminated by the emperor complex, have permitted Corsica to go to seed. We are a poverty-stricken nation. But how do you condemn Corsicans when land-rich foreigners, absentee land-lords flocked here, bought the land outright for a pittance, forcing Corsicans, the natural inheritors of the land, to steal to feed themselves, then to flee into the *maquis* as outlaws and fugitives, forced to exist by their wits. With no recourse open to them, they earned reputations as cold-blooded killers, forced to become avengers. Corsicans live in a natural state of war; if not against a conquering army, they battle the forces of nature on the island. They are notoriously poor mountaineers, yet they inhabit the highest reaches, in areas unsuitable for cultivation. They are obstinately addicted to barbarous customs and change for no one, not even to better themselves."

"I envisage Chamois Barbone and his mountain brutes fitting the pattern you describe, Dariana, and find it difficult to believe they engage in open, honorable struggle."

"I was hoping for a more compassionate vision," she replied.

Matteus was reserved. "Conquerors must appear bold, but audacity has always paved the way for ruin. Barbone's audacity, laced with histrionics, grates the nerves."

Dariana split a ripe fig and gave half to each of the men. "People who have never stumbled or fallen can never hope to understand a downtrodden people." How could Dariana hope to fathom the cryptic looks exchanged by Spaniard and Moor? How could she know she was getting closer and closer to solving a major problem in her husband's mind? Excluded from the rapport between Vivaldi and Matteus, how could she know the depth of the commitment which bound the Moor to Vivaldi for all eternity. She trod on into deeper waters.

"Life can only become precious when one has suffered. When mistakes are made and later remedied, you develop compassion and in this compassion comes understanding." While she spoke, both men suddenly became still. Matteus observed the rapt interest Vivaldi displayed. And Dariana, the center of attention, recipient of their profound respect, was reaching into the very depths of her storehouse of knowledge. She continued.

"In Corsica the family is a kingdom in itself, its members, a cohesive lot stick together through thick and thin. An injustice to one is an injustice to all. You see, the family exercises justice through itself; the form is vengeance. Blood revenge, although considered a barbarism in most nations, springs from sense of justice and from the natural love of relations; its source is the noble, human heart. Don't you see?" She glanced from Vivaldi to the Moor with astute perception of their bafflement. "It's simple, *caro mio*. The vendetta is barbarian justice—Corsican justice." Her hazel eyes caught the sunlight angling through the spreading chestnut branches. "Family relations are held sacrosanct, the purest form of love demonstrated is that between brother and sister. It denotes the purest happiness the heart is capable of containing. It is not unusual in the highest expression of love for a wife to call her husband brother."

"Yes, my beloved sister," Vivaldi teased, kissing her hand.

"If you are not interested in learning about Corsicans, say so," she quipped sharply, the tutor in her reprimanding the pupil.

"Of course, sister." Vivaldi erased the smile tugging at the corner of his lips. "Please continue, I shall stop this boorishness."

Matteus, busily whittling a twisted twig of white heather into the shape of a pipe, did not break his concentration.

"I merely wished to impart, *beloved husband*, that love between brothers and sisters is considered the most durable relationship because it is free of passion. Corsicans believe the history of human woe began with Cain, the fratricide. Woe to him who has killed a brother or blood relative of a Corsican! The deed, done, the murderer must flee from double jeopardy: the fear of justice which punishes the murderer and the relatives of the slain, who avenge the crime."

Silence fell upon the trio . . . one in which the only sound was the howling wind. Falcons circled overhead and, sensing an upswelling current of warm air, turned imperceptibly, circling higher and higher on the updraft. Dariana, fearing she had inadvertently spouted words offensive to both men, collected the remaining food. Matteus rose to his feet and began to repack the picnic hamper. He moved away and collected the horses.

Vivaldi, moving closer to his wife, held her hands, forcing her to look into his eyes. "What do *you* think of vendetta, Dariana? In *your* mind can it be justified?"

"As a participant or observer?"

He did not reply. He was, absorbed, sorting out the facts she'd thrust upon him.

"Vendetta here, as in Sicily, is a reality, no matter how much a fairy tale it appears to foreigners. Corsicans are different. We were born different. Who can explain the undefined sensations that shake our souls? This response to the Napoleon complex, the ancient citadels as intact as our conquerors built them centuries ago, the barbaric rites of blood vengeance, the display of virgin's blood, and the forbidden *maquis* where homeless men in rags conspire ruthlessly?"

Vivaldi listened, thoughts rushing at him from every avenue of consciousness; something urgent was trying to take shape and form, something curdling the very bowels of his stomach.

The sun beat down on them as they rode off toward their destination. Dariana, at a wild gallop, needed to feel the wind whipping at her. How could she know the thundering thoughts riding herd on their minds. That the day had been a revelation to Vivaldi? Dark corners in his mind were suddenly illuminated; reasons for his exile to Corsica exploded like tiny bolts of lightning. What was it Dariana had said? *"Corsicans are avengers, free as mountain eagles seeking to vent the internal fires raging inside them! Corsicans, native-born warriors, live in a natural state of war!"*

At *Guagno les Baines,* Dariana, ushered to separate women's quarters, indulged in an invigorating bath, relaxing all her sore muscles after the long, hard ride. Vivaldi and Matteus, quartered in an area reserved for men, luxuriated in hot, steamy waters, relaxing in silence, but the wheels of thought revolved in their heads.

"You must think me a dunderhead! It's taken too long to germinate in my mind!" Vivaldi tapped his forehead in vexation. "Where else but in Corsica can forces be marshaled to implement the power of the Garduna? Corsicans, having inherited their natures from ancestral warriors, have refined criminal talents to an art!''

"Praise Allah! It took the words of a woman to clear the fog in your mind, Vivaldi. My sudden perception of your wife has transformed her in my mind to an angel sent in answer to my thousand supplications.''

They both thought of Chamois Barbone, his legendary brother, head of the *Unione Corse* in Marseilles. And that sleazy Don Mazzeppi, who, after the *accidental* death of the previous bank manager, had assumed managerial duties until Vivaldi arrived on the island to expose his fraud. The covert investigation Chamois had promised Vivaldi that first fateful day of their meeting had earned Don Mazzeppi his predecessor's fate—*accidental* death. "No question," Vivaldi confided to the Moor, "their criminal skills, however primitive, are diamonds in the rough.''

"It takes one man, with knowledge of special power to guide them," the Moor interjected, smoking a cigar expansively for the first time since their arrival to Corsica.

Spaniard and Moor quietly exchanged thoughts. Vivaldi spoke of the men he'd met in Chamois's company, recollecting their stoic silence, obedience without contest, disciplined skill in weaponry. They were a silent army of men, aware of all goings-on, confiding in no one. Power—they represented power. Collectively or individually they represented a nucleus of power. Begin with the nucleus, adding one element at a time, intensifying the power, swelling it to a higher pitch—the sky was the limit.

Vivaldi, ebullient as they dressed, asked Matteus to remain in the background for the rest of the evening. On this night, under the spell of a full orange moon rising to illuminate all of Corsica, he wanted time to be alone with the woman he loved.

A half hour later he walked with Dariana under the stars. He poured his heart out to her, declaring the depth of his love and affection. Between lingering kisses, he told her of his desire to raise a family in her image. There, under a chestnut tree whose serene vibrations seemed a hundred golden wings tinged orange by the moon, he made love to his wife. Each time was as exciting as the first; their union was fresh, sensuous, soul-shattering, rendering them both breathless and unquenchable.

Nine months later, Dariana gave birth to a son, Daniel. Their second son, Robert, would be born eleven months later. Dariana, the light of Vivaldi's life, gave him reason to live and prepare a future for them. That their marriage was heaven-sent was, in Vivaldi's mind, a foregone conclusion.

He could trust Dariana with the truth, now, couldn't he?

Seated at the edge of the great four-poster, observing Dariana suckle their son, he smoothed back damp strands of flaxen hair spilling around her shoulders; she had grown it long to please him. Vivaldi reached in, kissed her lightly, watching the stirring scene; the greedy, suckling sounds brought smiles to their faces. Vivaldi caressed Dariana, lightly touching her cheek.

Dariana, the strong, courageous, the brave, and the bold! What a marvelous influence! She radiated joy and happiness. She smiled and laughed. Nothing disturbed her unless it affected her family; then she'd be transformed to a whirlwind of protective motherhood. Her nesting instinct intimidated the staunchest foe. She backed her husband's word to the end unless she believed him wrong on an issue. Then, in opposition, she'd stick to her guns, until Vivaldi admitted defeat. When all else failed she produced her trump card: tears.

"Dariana. I have something to tell you. It's best you know . . ." he began, and in a torrent of words spoke for three hours about his real life. "You see, I am not the Genoan landowner you thought, but an Andalusian noble, well educated, a student of the law." An apologetic smile forming on his lips froze at her expression.

Dariana's astonishment was absolute. She listened, perched precariously between Vivaldi's anguish and the relief of his soulful unburdening. He described his agony over Victoria Valdez, their unborn child, something he never believed himself capable of discussing with another mortal.

The peace descending on Vivaldi was indescribable; the weight of his past trauma was dissolving. Was sanity within his grasp? Could he ignore the burning madness scorching his soul since the nightmares of Seville, Madrid, and Cordoba?

Silence fell between them. He awaited word from Dariana, a sign, a reprimand, indignation, *something* to indicate her feelings about the deception foisted upon her. Nothing! *Nothing!*

"Dariana?"

"Yes, beloved."

"Have you nothing to say to me?"

"I am collecting my thoughts."

"And?"

"I know nothing of the man de la Varga, the Spaniard you

claim to be. I met and fell in love with Vivaldi Bonifacio, father to our son. The man you are is the love of my life, my joy, my reason for existence. The past matters not to me as long as it does not cloud our future. Can you assure me of this?''

''I have sworn to avenge the death of my family, to kill the animal who desecrated all I held dear.''

''Does such an act loom in our immediate future—or the present?''

He shook his head. ''I know only his present whereabouts. Periodically a courier supplies me with information. For example the parcel to which you fell heir on board ship.''

''The Camel Coat? The assassin?''

He nodded. ''Presently the time is not right for vendetta. I will bide my time if it takes all my life.''

Dariana reached up, stroked Vivaldi's face tenderly, looking upon him with loving eyes. ''The hatred, the violence you carry inside you, can turn upon itself, become self-destructive.''

''You *know* this too, *cara mia?*'' Drawing her fingers to his lips, he kissed them, nibbled on them playfully. ''In the recent past it nearly consumed me. Since you've entered my heart, the hatred abated, retreated into my soul, surfacing less and less.''

''Pray it dissolves altogether, beloved.'' She finished suckling the infant, placed him in his cradle next to the bed. Observing her as he poured coffee for them in the sitting room adjacent to the bedchamber, Vivaldi thought that nothing equaled Dariana's spiritual beauty. Even her hands, strong, firm, powerful, yet slender, graceful, expressive, were an artist's rendition.

''How else can I show you my love,'' he murmured rhetorically.

Dariana jerked to an upright position over the crib, turned, alerted, eyes searching the candlelit room, somewhat startled. ''What did you say, Vivaldi?'' Eyes uneasy, she fluttered her hands before her face, walked to the French doors, swinging them open. She repeated her question.

''I said nothing,'' he told her, handing her cup and saucer. ''What's wrong? Tell me. Your face has drained of color.''

Dariana, still imbued with the unnatural sensation experienced moments ago, shivered in the balmy night air. ''For a moment I saw the countess standing here in this room. The image was clear, Vivaldi. I'd swear she stood at my side, reached out and touched me. Pray it is no omen.'' The cup in her trembling hands rattled noisily. ''Blessed Virgin, pray all is well with her. If only hers was the good fortune I received in marrying a loving

man like you, Vivaldi. Her husband is vile. A contemptuous
womanizer, a hateful man, who I fear has diabolic plans in store
for her. His soul is evil. He poses a constant threat to her. Poor,
poor Marie Clotilde suffers a form of . . ." Dariana compassion-
ately described the contessa's affliction, its aggravation by her
spouse's demeaning criticism.

"If your concern is such, if you fear for her life, feel free to
invite your contessa to Terra Bonifacio, beloved."

"Oh, thank you, Vivaldi. How fortunate I am to have married
you. I shall ponder the matter in short order."

What was this inescapable spell Dariana had fallen under?
Delicious, delirious happiness, overwhelming love, a joyousness
in merely observing her husband at breakfast. She counted her
blessings and compared them with Marie Clotilde's lot in life.
Fortunately Dariana's disturbing perceptions of the contessa's
personal problems were swallowed up in myriad household duties.
How swiftly the days flew by. Days melted into months and
months heaped up behind the adoring pair like precious pearls of
remembrance. Their first wedding anniversary was at hand.

It was summer. A resplendent summer! Terra Bonifacio, under Dariana's green-thumbed wizardry, abounded with fragrant
blooms and acres of scintillating herbal aromas. From the rear
terrace as far as the eyes could see, almond trees flowered with
heavily laden branches of cascading white blooms. Pray she
never awakened to find it all gone like some fantasy.

Matteus's true worth to Dariana and the Bonifacio family was
never fully realized until he departed on a trip to North Africa
and Sicily. In his absence Dariana was lady of the manor, the
chatelaine of Terra Bonifacio, tending to Vivaldi's and Daniel's
needs, the great house itself, without troubling Vivaldi in the
slightest. At first, she even found ample time to spend in the
greenhouse, where she grew hybrid flowers. She hadn't realized
her increasing dependence on Matteus. After two weeks she
marked days on the calendar, waiting for his return.

Meanwhile a monastic stillness reigned at Terra Bonifacio; the
blinds were drawn to keep out heat and insects. Everything was
spotless. The only intrusion on the stillness was occasioned when
Daniel's temperament needed venting or when the victrola played
Madame Butterfly, La Bohème, or Vivaldi's favorite, *Tosca.*

The music, a signal of sorts, intensified the lovers' intense
sexual needs. From wherever Vivaldi sat, in the great house or

outside within hearing distance, he would at the first refrain drop what he was doing and seek her out in moments. Arms around her, he'd swing her up the steps to their bedchamber, hot lips pressed on hotter lips, their hearts fluttering. Between kisses, stroking and nibbling at her swollen breasts, and caressing her round pregnant belly—he'd lay her sweet scented body on the fine linens and enter her honey-lubricated, hot, yielding body. Dariana, melting under his tender caresses, in the dimly shuttered room returned his love totally. Vivaldi, built like a stallion, took tender care in entering Dariana in her pregnancy, but once the juices flowed, they'd spend the entire siesta clinging together in erotic ecstasy.

Vivaldi loved the feel of total nudity, hot flesh against hot flesh. Dariana became his wife, mistress, concubine, his Delilah, Sheba, and Cleopatra. And like Dariana, he brooded sometimes wondering how much longer the gods would favor them in this love. Each was growing too dependent upon the other for love. The question creeping into his mind, too often of late, terrified him. What would he do if this paradise evaporated? If Dariana suddenly disappeared, for whatever reason?

One afternoon, in Matteus's absence, after erotic overplay, Vivaldi pulled himself up regally on the bed. "We cannot go on like this, Dariana, or we shall consume one another." He spoke quietly, his voice loaded with resolve.

"Then let there be spaces between our togetherness and let the winds of heaven dance between us. Love me and I will love you, but not make a bond of it; let it be a moving sea between the shores of our souls." Dariana smiled.

Vivaldi sighed wistfully. Even when she poured a bath for him, scented the tub, and rubbed his skin with oils, she moved in a regal fashion. He relaxed in splendor, but his thoughts were clouded by alien visions.

Dariana carried her second child with considerable discomfort. She didn't, wouldn't, complain, not while in the midst of counting blessings. The old wives' tales claiming the *second* child is less difficult than the first was erroneous. *Each pregnancy, a unique gift from God, is different and that ends it!* Dariana found herself endlessly fascinated by the birth process and begged Vivaldi to bring medical books back from his trips to France. In her spare moments, she'd pore over them, marveling at the human body, a temple of incredible fascination and unexplored vistas. She kept Vivaldi alive with endless questions and often ended in heated conversation over the destiny of her sons. How many had she wanted? Six?

Today as she moved sluggishly up the stone steps hugging the wall of the great salon past the first landing, she narrowed the number to no more than three. Exhausted, she gripped the polished oak banister, paused to inhale a deep breath, staring at the symbol of the marten on the step before her.

The sound of horses' hooves striking the cobblestones in the main courtyard brought a radiant smile to her lips. Swiftly, she descended the steps to the foyer, threw open the double doors to see Matteus on his Arabian stallion whip past her, kicking up misty brown veils of dust.

Dariana ran to the rear terrace, calling, "Vivaldi! Vivaldi! Matteus has returned!" She waved to her husband.

Vivaldi, approaching from the crest of the slope, smiled warmly. "Will you miss me as you missed Matteus when I depart for Marseilles?"

"Again, Vivaldi?" She gazed into his eyes. "Why? When?"

"Why? To purchase a lorry, a machine to expedite travel, and a few needed supplies." He grabbed hold of her playfully. "Pray explain the excitement you display at the Moor's homecoming."

"My dear husband, in Matteus's absence I came to realize he is my third, fourth, and fifth arms. I am at wits' end without him. You are always out on the land, or in your study poring over those mysterious manuscripts, my scholarly husband."

With an expression of exaggerated outrage, Vivaldi caught Dariana, spinning her around so hard he staggered but, gripping her tighter, planted a lusty kiss on her lips. "And where am I when Madame Butterfly sings her lament? Or when Mimi sings the love duet, hmm? All you need do is touch me to trigger the passion in my loins. When will we be done with this enchantment?" he chastised playfully. Her arm slid up around his neck, his across her back held her tightly; groping for her mouth, he kissed her until she melted against him. The enchantment ceased the moment Matteus entered. They broke apart to greet him.

Something very strange was happening. Matteus was noticeably aloof after Vivaldi left for Marseilles. He answered Dariana's questions with a terse yes or no, never dallying, and when Dariana wasn't aware of his scrutiny, he warily eyed her every movement. Dariana, sensing his ineptly masked alienation, made no inquiries; she too kept her distance and moved about the house in her usual duties.

Inside the steamy greenhouse, she set about repotting saplings. Outside, the wild cuckoos were chattering. Dariana glanced up at approaching sounds. Matteus, returning from a hunting sojourn, had to pass her en route to the game house to hang up and bleed his catch.

Awkward, ill at ease, he continued past her with a polite nod. Dariana, barely acknowledging him, continued packing the crockery pots. Matteus entered the game house, hung up the string of partridges and pheasants, and closed the door behind him. He sidled back through the wooden tables.

Dariana, unwilling and unable to remain a party to the silence any longer, spoke up. "Tell me what causes the estrangement between us. What's wrong? What causes you to study me like a specimen through a long glass?"

Matteus laid the shotgun on the table next to her, slipped off his hunting jacket, and prepared to strip the weapon.

"You, *signora*, are blessed with countless womanly skills and cleverness. Your most precious, I admit, is third sight. I, lacking duplicity and the social graces of the Romans, am unable to slip behind masks of benevolence. So, *signora*, I ask with directness and desire that you answer truthfully. How long have you been in the employ of Minister Zeller in Rome?"

Her lips formed several shapes, but her expressions were shock, curiosity, bewilderment, and anger. *"Minister Zeller!"* The outburst was unexpected. Momentarily, Matteus wavered.

Controlling herself, yet sensing something terribly amiss, she spoke economically. "For your edification, I was never in the employ of Minister Zeller. I was social secretary to his wife before they married. After the nuptials I went along as part of her entourage." Sputtering in outrage, she turned her back on him and continued repotting. "How is it you dare ask me so personal a question?"

Matteus took hope, for in her mention of the name Zeller, he noted her venom. In the interminable silence, he continued to clean his shotgun.

"I know you well enough to *know*, Matteus, you do not play the role of inquisitor for nothing." Dariana tossed him an opening.

The Moor took it. "In Sicily I encountered a mutual friend.

Don Marcobello sends you his felicitations and a message that he is indebted to you.''

A sapling fell to the earthen floor. Matteus retrieved it, placed it back on the table. Dariana was noticeably fatigued. She waved her hand listlessly. ''I know no such person.''

''The *Camel Coat*. The foiled assassin?''

Briefly her eyes lighted in recollection. ''He's alive? He escaped the Italian secret police? Il Duce's men? Well, if I had a moment with that reprobate, I'd give him a tongue lashing he'd never forget! Did you ask him why he singled me out of all the others to be his special courier?'' Dariana potted vigorously, taking her frustration out on the earth and plants.

''I did ask.''

''What?'' Dariana glanced up at the ominous words

''Why he singled you out among all the others.''

''And?'' She pushed back a wispy strand of hair falling over her eyes, ''Because you worked for Minister Zeller you'd be less suspect. He had every intention of contacting you in Ajaccio, but he was badly shot up.''

Dariana eyed him. ''The arrow moves one way, the mind another. Even though the mind moves cautiously and circles about, it still moves toward its goal. Be quick, Montenegro, ask me straight as an arrow.''

''Are you a spy sent by Zeller to infiltrate the Bonifacio domain?''

''Infiltrate—'' Several pots fell crashing to the floor. She was furious. ''A spy? You must be mad!'' She stopped abruptly, clasping her breasts with sooty hands, as if in so doing she could still the mad beating of her heart. ''Tell me, Matteus, very carefully, so I do not, cannot, mistake your words or intent. What has Amadeo Zeller to do with Vivaldi Bonifacio? *Tell me!* What does Zeller *know* of Vivaldi? I don't understand any of this.'' Her husband's strange odyssey—Seville, Madrid, Cordoba—swirled dizzily about her head.

''What happened aboard ship, then, was pure coincidence?''

Dariana's eyes flared; she sucked in her breath. ''*You* know, *I* know—nothing in life is coincidence,'' she began, dusting the fresh earth from her fingers. ''You told me I was selected out of all the others for reasons only the Camel Coat knew. Very well, the moving finger writes . . . pawns move into place to fit some scheme. And I ask you, I beseech you once again, tell me what in the name of your Allah and my God is this all about?''

Matteus, at once humble, salammed to her, begging forgiveness.
"Pray forgive a fool. It is imperative that your husband never
learn of these words between us." Matteus expressed profound
regret for upsetting her, but Dariana was not merciful.

She stared at him. "Charades are as incomprehensible as they
are distasteful. No secrets stand as barriers between my husband
and me. Now, Matteus, once again, before I go mad. What has
Zeller to do with my husband?"

"It is enough I am satisfied you were not sent as a spy,
signora. Nothing else matters."

"*Nothing else matters?* You say, nothing else matters? *It
matters to me!* By the burning balls of your Moloch, whom you
disparage often enough, I know what happens to Zeller's enemies!"
Dariana quickly desisted. What more could she say without
referring to the night of her deflowerment? A hatred as visible as
hers would not go unnoticed. She'd open the path for too many
questions.

In the days she awaited Vivaldi's return, time stopped for Dariana.
Her heart felt crushed, stomped on. It was her turn to avoid
Matteus. She'd cast oblique glances at him when he wasn't
looking. She experienced no sense of treachery from him, only
his undying devotion to Vivaldi, for which she could not fault
him. He was more than Vivaldi's factotum, more than a bodyguard.
He was more a paladin. No, not that, much more. He was too
much a part of Vivaldi's life; he was a vital link to the past. If
one depended on the other for life itself, the weight was on
Matteus's shoulder.

Dariana, a courageous soul, fearless and clear-sighted, pondered the relationship. How did Zeller tie into Vivaldi's past?
Was it Zeller against whom her husband plotted vengeance? Had
some diabolical plot of Zeller's caused Vivaldi's exile? She
regarded their life. Remote, isolated, away from the city, with
no friends to speak of. Matteus seldom left the estate. *And that
weapons arsenal?* She reflected on her father's words and found
herself entangled in a web of intrigue. If she tried to disentangle
herself, she found new snarls awaiting her.

Dariana's breasts were swollen with milk. She always knew
when it was time to suckle Daniel. She washed her hands,
entered the butter rooms, kneading the risen chestnut bread
dough, then patting it back into the large copper bowl and
covering it with warm towels. After washing her hands again,

she picked up the hungry, demanding Daniel. Seated in her rocker, she cradled the infant. In her mind she planned a special menu for Vivaldi's return from the mainland.

It must be select. Partridge smothered in ardent sauces, with fresh, garden-picked vegetables sautéed with scented cheeses and mushrooms. Of course her freshly baked chestnut bread. But first, to whet his appetite and put him in the proper mood, his favorite, Porto Vecchio coquilles, giant mussels and clams wrestled from seabeds, sautéed in spicy wine sauce, and a very delicate but heady wine.

And then, after dinner, she had much to discuss in their bedchamber. Having developed some insight into Vivaldi's flight from Spain, she now connected it to Amadeo Zeller. Her father's words echoed in her mind.

"Love that which happens to you and is woven into the threads of your destiny, what more is suited to your needs and desires than that which keeps you alive and happy?"

Dariana *had* happened to Vivaldi. Her life *was* woven into the threads of his destiny. She suited his needs, desires, and had kept him alive and happy. Now she deserved to be told the brutal truth. What she could expect? Because she *knew* Zeller. Because she *knew* him well, her fears were compounded and her personal assessment exceeded the wildest imaginings of a demented soul.

As she prepared dinner, an apparition came alive. Would it never stop? Marie Clotilde's presence, a clear mental image of the contessa seemed to materialize, arms outstretched, beckoning to her.

Dariana, Corsican enough to accept this as an omen paused to whisper a prayer. "Pray God protect her. Let no harm befall her."

Chapter Twenty

The Day Contessa Marie Clotilde received Dariana's letter announcing her forthcoming marriage to a Corsican, shock waves spiraled through her body, mind, and soul. She paced the thickly carpeted pastel boudoir at the Zeller palazzo, frantic, frightened, frustrated, bewildered at Dariana's abandonment of her.

Her pale porcelain features were without hue, her gray eyes, panic-stricken. She screamed internally, *What will I do?* Forced to watch her every move, measure each word—her husband's spies everywhere, watching, waiting, eager to report her slightest error—Clotilde viewed her life as a nightmare of horrors without Dariana's protection.

She flung open the French doors, gazed, with a slight chill coursing through her, at the Roman rooftops and city streets, seeing nothing, until the sun emerged in full glory, its invigorating rays giving her a charge of life. She regarded her childhood, a tapestry of fading dreams woven by a deluded father who had denied her nothing. God, if only he'd directed her to face life vigorously, with the determination Dariana exuded.

One man's influence! *One man* born a century before her time had doomed Marie Clotilde's life. Her great-great-grandfather, an illegitimate issue of Napoleon Bonaparte's loins, had caused his genes to flow in her blood. Everyone expected to find his genius in her!

334

She'd grown up thinking she'd let her parents down, first by being a girl, second by not being a Napoleonic prodigy more spectacular than the original. It had not happened; it was unlikely to happen; still the Bonaparte descendants prayed for that miracle.

She flung Dariana's letter from her in vexation. *Why am I doing this to myself?* This is ridiculous! Dariana has every right to love, marry, settle down, raise a family—she deserves happiness. *And I too deserve happiness!* She daubed at the hot tears stinging her eyes. Didn't she deserve a man who loved her and a family? *Damnation on you, God! Why do you permit such rewards to elude me? What have I done to incur your wrath?*

The contessa's marriage to Zeller was fraught with disenchantment, destroying her, bit by bit, day by day. She asked herself why she hadn't realized he was incapable of the love she longed for, needed passionately. Actually she'd known, deep in her heart, but had avoided facing the truth. Zeller, *overly* discreet, *overly* polite, *overly* protective of her, subdued and contained to a fault, was the quintessential blackguard, who seldom paraded his black temper before her. Insulting? Yes, he was that. Browbeating, fault-finding, derisive . . . all these too. His ingratiating manner before others suggested the noblest of intentions. To any onlookers he conveyed the concern of a doting spouse.

He was the curse of her life: she hated him. Daily she refired this hatred, for all the good it did her.

Marie Clotilde had roamed the palazzo for weeks after Dariana's departure in a daze. At galas, Amadeo continued to politely humiliate her before guests; no one noticed. Wasn't she the luckiest woman in the fascist social circle to have so devoted a spouse? Oh, God, if only they knew the truth? Only Dariana *knew* the tortures she suffered.

She went back inside, flung herself on the pale mauve satin chaise lounge, recalling how many times her rage held her mute while his friends and cohorts regarded her as inordinately stupid. The mystery was *why* she incurred such shabby treatment from Zeller. She'd brought no shame upon him. Her dowry was more than substantial; her breeding and social graces were impeccable. Why then? How had he managed to subjugate her, force her to submit, surrender to his whims, gratify his wishes? Was it because she didn't possess his ruthlessness?

Their sexual coupling had long since evolved into a sterile, dispassionate act; Her only role in this loveless marriage was to act as the potting soil for the propagation of Zeller's seeds. Luckily, in this unacceptable situation, she had circumvented conception by every device at her disposal. She would not carry his child! *Never!*

In Dariana's absence, she needed courage. This nervous affliction impaired her speech flow, but it didn't reduce her intelligence. Zeller's attacks on her character, morals, and behavior were increasing. Searching out Zeller's faults, she realized she could virtually paper the palazzo walls with his perfidies! She considered lies, hypocrisy and envy to be the tripod of villainy and at its center stood Zeller.

Days, months dragged by. Time in which Marie Clotilde resolved to take a firmer grip on herself. Was the power role Zeller played in the creation of a new Italy aphrodisiac to her senses? Was that it? Was that why she refused to look at the sham of their marriage? The nuptials, performed by Cardinal Bertelli at the Vatican Chapel was an example of just how far Zeller would go to achieve his ambitious aims.

Zeller, atheist by intellectual conviction, viciously anticlerical, had adopted strict Jewish traditions! And he wasn't a Jew! She didn't understand why he wasn't one thing or another and admit to what he really embraced. But to use religion as a bludgeoning weapon to force opponents into acquiescing to his politics . . . Something diabolical was infecting that twisted brain of his. *What*? That he secretly practiced Zionism didn't disturb her, she understood the wisdom in not openly flaunting his politico-religious persuasions since the Jews were once again in disfavor following the Great War. But that he flagrantly misused this persuasion, hid behind it conveniently, as it suited his purpose stoked her curiosity. He was deceiving Il Duce. The act was tantamount to treason!

It made no sense, none at all. Viewing him in the proper perspective she concluded, *Amadeo Zeller is the most dangerous man alive!* Yes, he was! Deceptive, lacking honor or principles Zeller was something other than what he represented to the world, someone base who employed numerous facades to keep at a distance anyone attempting to learn more about him.

Aware that her marriage, just short of being disastrous, needed repair or its death was imminent, Clotilde had taken to daily explorations of her body, wondering if something about her was totally repellent to her husband. Standing naked before a mirror, she had inspected every inch of her lush, ripe, womanly body.

With no barometer to measure its worth, she assumed that what she saw was a splendid morsel of femininity. Constant appraisals had brought about the inevitable—autoeroticism. It was either that, or without an outlet to fan the fires of passion searing her body—insanity.

She was young, teeming with life, in need of normal sexual expression. The mere touching of various erogenous zones had sent shudders of excitement through her, arousing dormant sensations her maturing body needed express. This fantasy world, preferred to the reality, enabled her to conjure up images of romantic young men making love to her. None bore the slightest resemblance to Amadeo Zeller.

Sauntering to the balcony, the contessa slammed the doors shut. She was young, in desperate need of normal, sexual expression and fulfillment. Enough! She'd had enough of self-pity, feelings of inadequacy! It was no way for a woman with the genes of a Bonaparte to behave!

A half hour later, dressed elegantly, she sat in the rear seat of her touring car en route to the heart of old Rome, embarked upon another senseless shopping spree. How many more shops would she haunt, buying articles she neither needed or wanted? How much longer would Zeller drain her life's blood?

Today, the shopping spree would *not* be senseless. The least she could do was purchase a wedding gift for Dariana and her Corsican peasant!

Once Rome was a flea market of ancient Gods, conquered peoples, a bargain basement, a tasteless heap of gold and marble, and more people crammed into the passages of the Colosseum than there have been ever since. Today, Rome, the gayest capital on the Continent, dressed in bridal finery, basked in the seduction of fascism. Mussolini, the man of the hour, was hailed by many Italians as a god, the spirit, essence, the force that would save the world. Look! Hadn't that flamboyant choreographer in his black shirt, knee britches, and patent-leather boots performed miracles for his people? Hadn't he stabilized the economy? Improved workers' conditions? Inaugurated ambitious public-works programs? And what of the Pontine Marshes? Il Duce, the worker of miracles, had succeeded. Fifty thousand acres of land reclaimed and under cultivation! The deed spoke for itself, didn't it? And what of the dreaded malaria? Hadn't Il Duce defeated that insidious, lingering inescapable malaise that had infected Italy for so long?

People marveled at this new phenomenon, Il Duce. The honeymoon days of his reign waxed grandly. People with smiling faces paraded along streets lined with mammoth posters of Il Duce's image towering over them, reminding them daily of their good fortune to be guided by this man of destiny. Passionate outbursts of song filled the air randomly. *"Giovanetti . . . Giovanetti . . ."* Magnificent shade trees lined the streets. It was a spectacular summer in Italy. A cloudless sky with the sun at its center illuminated Rome with dazzling brilliance.

Love and romance permeated the very air of Rome.

Marie Clotilde inhaled its essence as the splendid Burgatti-Bertelli open touring car wheeled along the Piazza Venezia. Glancing up at an enormous facade, a larger-than-life facsimile of Il Duce reminded her of another time. When was it—1922? Il Duce's bold March on Rome echoed throughout the world. That October day in Rome a panoply of tricolors waved atop towers in the piazza. Thousands of brass bands played inspiring march tempos. Rome had regaled itself in awesome pageantry to celebrate the birth of a *cause célèbre*—Benito Mussolìni.

That black-shirted, strutting major domo and his iron-jawed pretentiousness became an overnight sensation. A new age in history had dawned. Italy trembled in hope. The whole world placed fascism on glass slides and studied it with microscopic intensity.

And Marie Clotilde had been in at the beginning.

She inspected her makeup in a compact mirror. Reflected in it was another towering poster of Il Duce. Turning slightly in her seat, glancing up at the dramatic scowl on the giant's face, a smile played at her lips. A mesmerizing oratory had turned him into a national hero. Today, two years later, Il Duce was growing in power.

The chauffeur downshifted in the congested Rome traffic. Clotilde reflected. To think, she had fancied herself in love with Il Duce, such was his brand of magnetism. His sexual dynamism had captured the fancy of women, worldwide. She and Dariana had witnessed the birth of fascism. In October 1922 they had attended the rally in Naples where thousands upon thousands of black-shirted fascisti had marched thunderously into the *Piazza del Plebiscito* to listen to their leader's immortal words:

"Either the government of Italy is given to us or we shall seize it by marching on Rome!"

Marie Clotilde and Dariana had observed the phenomenon from the balcony of their hotel suite. The energy generated by this man had ignited the masses; their ceaseless chant echoed through the city for hours. *"Roma! Roma! Roma!"*

What a spectacle of power! The hysteria was infectious. To be in the presence of a world leader, upon whom the eyes and ears of the world was focused, was an incredible experience for the contessa. Her new husband, at Mussolini's side, dressed as splendidly as their leader, had induced a fierce pride in the recent bride. The novelty of her marriage and her infatuation with Mussolini had blinded her.

Following his public address, Mussolini had disappeared for several hours. Everyone, fearing the worst, searched everywhere; he was no place to be found. Party leaders feared kidnapping or assassination. The women of the fascist VIPs were ordered to remain in their hotel suites, under guard. Marie Clotilde's room, adjacent to the large salon where a consortium of fascisti convened to discuss the serious development, provided a marvelous opportunity for her to learn the truth behind Mussolini's disappearance. The walls were paper thin. The voices, angry, indignant, and laced with envy, painted a vivid picture of a sexual interlude with three prostitutes who had captured Mussolini's fancy.

"Imagine . . . it takes four or more women to satisfy him!" Clotilde had giggled in childish simplicity.

"It does not enhance your image, Contessa, to dignify such rumors," Dariana had scolded. She observed Clotilde drag two chairs to the door, prop them under the open transom.

"Stop being so—so—Corsican! Prim and proper! Proper and prim!" she whispered. "It takes a spark of truth to ignite rumors. Imagine, three times a day with each woman? How much is truth? How much fiction?" Before Dariana responded, the sound of Zeller's irate voice brought up their heads. Both scrambled atop the chairs to peek through the open transom.

"Mussolini's hesitancy, his capricious character, are totally unsuited to organization. My friends, I fear his leadership qualities are sadly lacking. His presence poses a serious threat to the party. He vacillates. . . ."

Dariana and the countess exchanged wild-eyed glances, neither daring to express what sounded like treason. Another voice made it clear that Amadeo Zeller received a severe reprimand. "Who is he?" Clotilde asked. "Italo Balbo," Dariana hissed back. "Be still, we are watching history in the making. Balbo is head of the *Squadristi!*" Clotilde made it clear she didn't care who Balbo was, only that he was a beautiful man. She listened as he talked.

"It falls upon you, *Signore* Zeller, to impress upon that brown-shirted Bolshevik that the fascisti will march on Rome *with or without* him." The conversation became then at once subdued; the gathering grew silent and stood at attention. Both women, standing on chairs sneaking peeks over the transom, noted at once the reason for the abrupt silence.

Mussolini. He strutted into the room, stepped up to the dais. Applause from well-wishers and foes alike drowned out the earlier discontent.

"Something about him . . . a *je-ne-sais-quoi,*" rhapsodized Clotilde. "What magnetism! The moment he enters the room—" She stopped, assessing the glowing after effects of sexual gratification unmistakably etched into his relaxed features. Both young woman knew that look.

That day, her idolatry for Mussolini declined. Her idol had shown feet of clay, reducing himself to the ranks of a mere mortal. The bloom of innocence gone, Clotilde flung off her naiveté and addressed herself to the autumn of her discontent. She came to view Il Duce in the same light she viewed her husband—with one difference. In Il Duce, she had found a true friend, his easygoing character putty in her hands. She entertained no such thoughts of camaraderie with Zeller.

The chauffeur made a right on Via Battisti to Via Novembra. At the Piazza Manapoli, he cut a sharp left traversing Via XXIV, then, another right, proceeding uphill toward the Piazza del Quirinale, the palazzo of King Umberto in their sights. They passed San Carlino Church. Clotilde frowned. The site of her wedding reminded her again of Amadeo.

Martino, the chauffeur, slowed down in his approach to the Trevi Fountain. Clotilde removed a white, silver-embossed card from her reticule. She read: *Argentio Silversmiths, en famiglia.* Good. Her destination was close by. Perhaps a stunning silver service . . . It was the least she could do for Dariana's coming nuptials. Imagine . . . a Corsican peasant for Dariana . . .

*   *   *

Miguel Bertelli, scion of the millionaire Bertelli automobile fortune, sat sipping absinthe with an entourage of hangers-on at Giorgio's sidewalk café in view of the famed Trevi Fountain. On all sides of him was a potpourri of café society continentals who hopscotched to Paris, London, Madrid, Berlin, the Costa del Sol, the Riviera when Bertelli moneybelts provided their fare.

Michael-Miguel to his friends—Bertelli was suntanned, too handsome for his own good. He possessed the irresistible combination of a Roman gladiator's physique, the smoldering looks of a Romantic poet, a passionate heart, and an unlimited fortune.

He wore the finest, Italian tailored suits, handcrafted shoes, frequented the best cafés, piloted a yacht with expertise, and recently began taking lessons in those flying contraptions popularized in the recent war. With medium brown curly hair, worn tousled, longer than fashion dictated, he was more a likeness of Fairbanks than Valentino, with the swashbuckling ways of the former, not the latter. His eyes were actually two shades of blue; lapis lazuli centers, ringed with cobalt, flecked with golden glints in the sunlight.

Michael had never been in love in his entire thirty years. Tired of the playboy image, yet aware of how attractive he was to women, he was, at times, not the most pleasant man amid company. What Michael wanted was the true love of a woman. He was eager to settle down with the light of his life and create a rash of bambinos in his owm image.

Christ, how the right woman eluded him!

At this moment, with a dozen or more, made-up faces, marcelled hair, and Paris fashions seated around him, Michael was desperately lonely and bored. Glancing impatiently at his gold watch, he smiled vaguely at the others. His eyes roved at the horde of sightseers. Suddenly his heart stopped.

He spotted her stepping off the running board of the Burgatti-Bertelli car a short distance from the crowded promenade. A vision in pale mauve silk, a thin moiré frock, and matching cloche wrapped about her head, partially covering a shock of golden hair, she moved through the open throngs, gracefully poised, without restraint, the stride of a sleek lioness about her. The face, indefinable from where Michael sat, remained in the profile until she turned. When she did, he was stunned by her indescribably translucent beauty. The manner in which she pursed those full, cherry-pink petulant lips jogged his memory. He *knew* her! From where? What could she be—in her early twenties? No more than twenty-five! Whatever she did cosmetically produced an irresistible woman. Look at the undisguised admiration she drew from passersby.

The sun, flaring over the ancient city, glistened on the marble statues with unbearable intensity. In this brilliance, he felt as if a magnet drew him to her. Bertelli rose to his feet, peeled off a handful of lire, tossed them on the table, and excused himself. "*Ciao, amigi*. See you back at the hotel."

When he looked up, she was gone, the automobile no longer in view. He craned his neck, searched the crowds frantically, wondering at the panic he felt. *Miguel!* You are some crazy *chou-chou*! Despite his own inner chastisement, he sprinted forward into the moving throng for a glimpse of his fairy-tale phantom in flight. Neck craned, eyes peering here, there, everywhere, he stopped abruptly before the massive Trevi Fountain where spectacular sculptures of lusty tritons hauled a winged chariot ridden by Neptune. Rippling water cascaded as cooing lovers tossed coins into the pooling waters, but his vision was lost to him.

Michael shoved his dark-lensed glasses to his forehead, stepped on a pedestal base, shading his eyes with his hand, searching all faces scrupulously, searching for a heavenly vision in mauve silk.

There! Off the *Via del Stampera* near the *Via del Tritone* where a hundred little shops could gobble her up in a twinkling and leave no trace of her. Michael stepped down, ran after her, stopping short a few feet from her, panting breathlessly. She was exquisite, more stunning from a closer perspective than he'd imagined. He observed her enter Argento's silversmith shop. He put himself in order, tugging down on the jacket of his white suit, ran excited fingers through his unruly hair, inhaled deeply, and languidly entered the sedate shop, giving no hint of his wildly beating heart.

The shop was modest, filled with elaborate, costly silver works of art. Argento, a snowy-haired, bent-over old man, stood in a respectful pose, pointing out the fine, exquisite detail on a costly silver service.

"I will take it," Clotilde said quietly, without negotiating a fairer price. She handed him her personal card, wrote down Dariana's married name and address. "Pack it carefully. Pray ensure its prompt delivery to Corsica." Increasingly aware of the man who entered the shop moments ago, she barely saw Argento nod. Nervous under his audacious staring eyes, she fought for control, measuring her words economically so as not to garble her thoughts. "The bill—send—it—to—this—address." *So far so good*.

"Corsica?" Bertelli picked up the card, scanned it, and replaced it. "*Signore* Argento, are you *ensuring* the *signorina's* purchase?"

Argento's bushy brows shot up imperiously. Clotilde turned to the stranger, captured by the most exciting eyes she'd ever seen. Her brain registered an instant image: handsome, self-assured, smartly tailored, and he smelled divinely. Here was the prince of her fantasies! She flushed, erotically aroused. Sniffing a whiff of his essence, Clotilde felt a warm, orgasmic rush in her vagina. Turning away lest she give herself away, she paid little attention to the tongue-lashing the silversmith unleashed upon this disbeliever.

"You dare suggest to the contessa that Argento's word is without substance? That he encourages sales which cannot be delivered?" the older man sputtered in outrage.

Michael's astonishment came from the referral to her as royalty. A contessa, yet! He projected as casual a tone as possible. "It would not be the first time goods failed to arrive in Corsica," he said pleasantly. "I cast no aspersions on the name Argento, *signore*. Yours is an establishment of high repute. My concern is with the waterfront thieves both in Ostia and Ajaccio, ports of exit and entry—"

"Your point is well taken, *signore*—uh—"

"Bertelli. Miguel Bertelli." He whipped out a business card with aplomb. "If you will pack and secure the items purchased by the contessa, send them to my freight offices—Bertelli Shipping—and instruct *signore* Destro that I will personally ensure the delivery to Ajaccio." He smiled, bowed graciously. "Now, *Signore* Argento, *per piacere*, honor me by extending your gracious manners. An introduction to your enchanting client. I do not wish to be misunderstood."

That's how it began. Actually they got off to a bad start.

"Contessa de Bernadorf-Zeller?" he repeated in a tone that made her want to instantly deny it. "Are you the minister's daughter?" Now he remembered. He'd seen her in the company of Minister Zeller at the Quirinale at a party Victor Emanuele had hosted in Il Duce's honor.

"No. I am his wife. Good day to you. *Mille grazie* for your able assistance." Instantly barriers were erected between them. She spun on her heels and left the shop. Outside she stepped briskly along the streets, angry at the hot tears brimming her eyes. His strong voice calling to her, hastened her step.

"Contessa! *Signora* Zeller!" He caught up with her, took her elbow, and steered her away from the moving crowd. "Please. I mean no discourtesy to you. By way of apology, take tea with me." Her heart, mind, and legs stopped functioning. She was trembling.

Eyes gazed into eyes, both smoldering. Everything in life, Clotilde believed, was timing. The time for her was ripe. Today, this moment, she was ready, ripe as a peach at harvest, ready to be plucked and devoured. He searched her eyes ardently, his heart racing at the secret messages he discerned. He read the message in her eyes clearly. She was begging for seduction.

Over tea, it was *small* talk and *big* talk. Two opposing forces reared, splitting Michael's feelings: a naive enchantment for Marie Clotilde and a vile loathing of everything for which Zeller stood. He avoided politics at first and told her about himself. He explained his life as an automotive designer, industrialist, and playboy. He had served in the army for less than a year, learned to loathe war and the military. Ever since, he had worked hard and played even harder. "The war dictated our position for a time. Conversion of Bertelli factories, retooling to make munitions and war materials seemed worthwhile. We are presently restrained from producing more automobiles. We are commanded—mind you, in *peacetime*!—to produce war matériel in full-scale production. *Carissima contessa*, whether or not you already know the design in advance, or refuse to clutter your pretty little head with such banalities, the fascisti have long since prepared the blueprints for World War II. Amadeo Zeller's edicts force Il Duce into demanding more and more war supplies. He lights the pyres of empire under the fascist throne. He is a greedy-jawed jackal, your husband."

Michael sipped his champagne. "*Per piacere*, forgive me. You probably haven't the faintest idea of your husband's politics. I am certain of this, else you wouldn't be his wife. Did I mention I appreciate your taste in automobiles?"

"The auto is my husband's taste." Clotilde deliberately slowed down her speech, affording her more than usual control. Michael picked up on what seemed marked hesitation.

"You are too young for the minister," he said.

"He is five years my senior."

"Do you always speak as if you are frightened?"

"Only when I'm flustered." She turned beet red, averted her eyes.

"And *I* fluster *you*?" He took her hand in his, studied the wide gold-and-diamond wedding band. "Good. *You* fluster *me*. And for Michael Bertelli, contessa, it is a first. I am unperturbable."

Marie Clotilde's heart stood still. Her pulse quickened. What was happening to her? She slipped her hand from his, cast furtive eyes about her. Why must this Miguel Bertelli bear so strong a resemblance to the prince of her fantasies?

Michael followed her gaze. "Do I offend you?"

"People staring at us might draw the wrong conclusions."

"Would it matter if I say I don't give a damn. Ah. Your husband's spies. Has he reasons to set them upon you?"

"You are as insulting as you are candid. I think I had better leave."

"Please. Do not go. I am suddenly without senses, saying, doing the wrong things. Rudeness is neither my style nor my intent. How can I make you understand? You entered my life as if fate willed it, as if I already knew you'd be here waiting for me. Yet now that I've found you, you belong to another. I am angry. Yes, yes, I seethe with wrath at the irony of learning you belong to a man I revile." Michael poured more champagne.

"I find it contemptible of you to demean the minister when he is not present to defend himself," she began, not believing a word she uttered. *Damnation! Why must I defend Amadeo?*

Michael saw through her.

"If thy associate is insane, *carissima contessa*, be thou sensible."

"I neither wish to parade the minister's virtues before you, nor his faults. If my relationship to Amadeo Zeller makes you uncomfortable, it is best I take my departure. You seem unable to cope."

"Contessa, you speak in truths. Shall we make a pact? I promise"—he crossed his heart—"not to refer to him unless you do. Have dinner with me at my villa." he pressed with renewed vigor. "Your husband is away. You needn't make excuses for your absence at the palazzo."

Go, Marie Clotilde! Run. Leave while you have a chance or else? That instant, if she had any sense, she would have fled.

But she didn't. Stiffening imperceptibly, she asked, "How do you know he is away?"

"We made a pact, remember?" he chided. "Shall we extend it to exclude all *fascisti*?"

Clotilde's eyes darted back to him. "Such talk is dangerous. You never know who is listening." Something nagged at her. She probed her memory. *Burgatti-Bertelli! The company had endorsed fascism; so why was he so bitter?* She asked him point-blank. "Why are you so antagonistic? You supported Il Duce, no?"

"Il Duce, *sì*. He is vital, fully committed to Italy at this stage in the dictatorship. He knows he must depend upon industry, so he does not intimidate us. But who can know so soon the outcome of a man's history. Il Duce's wisdom lies in the awareness that he cannot convert all of Italy. So he makes no attempt to convert the devil as long as the devil performs admirably, eh? But what of those who stand in his shadow? The riders of wild stallions are reputedly fiercer than the stallions themselves."

"We agreed, no politics, no *fascisti*," she whispered.

Michael Bertelli laughed good-naturedly. "For the pleasure of your company I shall serve the moon to you on a silver platter. Come, *contessa mia*. Somewhere a clock is timing us. Let us make haste, decide what to do with the rest of our lives."

With his hand in hers, he strutted like a vain peacock, fully aware that every head turned to admire the stunning couple who ambled along the *strada* to where Michael's custom-made sports car, a bright red Bertelli sat at the curb. All the way to the pinnacle of one of the Seven Hills overlooking Rome, Michael tried to fathom the numerous shifts in her speech patterns.

The thought was fleeting, quickly replaced by thoughts of adventure and great personal risk. Here, at his side, was the wife of a vile man, who had recently ordered the death of his innocent cousin, a man accused of espionage. He was shot to death while defending his villa, *Campo Stella* near Turin.

Trembling, he wondered how the Contessa Zeller could be used as a weapon against Zeller. He hadn't expected such a bonanza dumped into his lap—not today. Time would tell; meanwhile the clock continued to tick.

If Michael entertained thoughts of using Clotilde against Zeller in any future encounter, the scheme was swiftly discarded.

How do you contest the divine will of God? Neither Michael nor Clotilde knew the answer. Nor could they pinpoint the moment when their love became all-consuming. Michael actually believed they were made for one another, that they had existed in a previous life and found their way through reincarnation to the present to be together for all eternity. Clotilde, unable to describe or understand this rhapsodic existence in which she indulged every whim, every fantasy, believed she existed in a dreamworld where all wishes came true. She thought about Michael constantly. Every waking moment was spent contriving ways to spend time together.

She canceled appointments, refused to entertain, counted hours, minutes, seconds between each separation as though this would hasten the process of transporting her into Michael's arms. From the moment it began at Michael's villa, there was no turning back. Every moment spent away from him was agony.

The villa. Quiet elegance, furnished exquisitely, was secluded behind a high stone wall. This love nest became Clotilde's real home, for here amid the things Michael loved and surrounded himself with, she matured, mellowed, grew astonishingly beautiful. Michael's love nurtured and expanded her spirit to heights she never knew existed. Under his tender caresses, she quivered like shimmering silver olive leaves.

Time finally stopped for them. Clotilde, at last a whole woman, was fulfilled. She was like a running brook that sang its melody to the night. She ached for him, desperately needed his love to make her whole. The rapture of their first union melted into all others as if there'd been no beginning, no ending in sight.

Hours before they were scheduled to meet—it wasn't easy leading a double life—thoughts of Michael brought on orgasmic tremors, vaginal contractions, lubricating her far in advance of their union. For Marie Clotilde, this was a miracle. Thoughts of Michael brought on orgasm. Amadeo, when they coupled, was cold, bestial; in essence performing brutal rape, an act from which she derived no pleasure and came to abominate. Clotilde's absolution came in Amadeo's long absences from home, and in Michael's loving embraces. Dear God! How beautifully she wore Michael's love. Truly Clotilde believed she had never existed before Michael Bertelli brought her to full flower. Daily she gave thanks for God's generosity, for permitting her to taste true love and passion. At the root of her soul was a growing fear that others who saw her would also note how beautifully Michael's love became her.

Days, swallowed by months, gobbled up by a year, had passed too swiftly. Secret rendezvous away from prying eyes and blabbing tongues served to intensify the fires of unquenchable love. In the confines of Michael's villa, perched high atop Rome's ancient ruins, their love rivaled that of legendary gods and goddesses.

Periodically the ugly face of reality jarred them awake, forcing them to confront the myriad complexities of life.

Nothing was more jarring to Clotilde than those unbearable days Zeller returned from his political forays, to reconnoiter in mysterious comings and goings at the palazzo, surrounded with an entourage of black-shirted henchmen. The sight of Zeller's features, the sound of outbursts heard clear to the third floor of the palazzo, iced Clotilde's veins. And those colorless eyes! As Zeller regarded her, they resembled crystal balls she believed capable of searching into the depths of her soul. The controlled studied look of him at dinner reviled her. *Dear, dear God! To what monster did my father marry me?* What an actress she must be, to veil her thoughts so cleverly from him.

Clotilde trained herself to sleepwalk through their encounters, avoid Zeller like the plague, feign headaches, complain of protracted menstrual disorders, barring him from her bed, deterring his slightest attempt at performing husbandly duties.

God! What a deadly game she played!

Constantly on guard, certain to never, *never* let the Bertelli name pass her lips, she refused to ride in or speak of the customized Bertelli autos Amadeo favored, for fear Zeller's X-ray eyes would detect her infidelity. He would kill her! She knew it, saw it in his eyes. At times, across the dining table, they'd lock eyes in accusing silence, saying nothing—*nothing*! It drove her mad, but she rallied.

Aware that she strolled through precarious corridors, Clotilde's only defense was to avoid him at every opportunity. Nightly she prayed to Santa Teresa, imploring her to coerce Zeller into continued travel for Il Duce. *Please, please, devise a way to keep him away longer.* She would promise to light ten candles, twenty nightly if necessary.

And then . . . the miracle. Zeller announced he was leaving at the end of May for an extended trip abroad. The night before his departure they dined alone in the magnificently appointed dining salon.

"You look rather special tonight," he began. "I've really neglected you, haven't I?" Clotilde, sipping wine, shook her head. "Do I detect an improvement in your speech? But then, how could I? You've barely spoken lately. Why do you never wear the diamond earrings I brought from Africa? Yes, yes, I suppose we haven't complied with social obligations. In my absence, you could seek an escort, my dear. Il Duce keeps a staff of men for neglected wives. Very proper, indeed. I believe they are all eunuchs. He would not desire a scandal to brew among fascisti wives, you understand."

Clotilde, continuing to restrict her replies to yes or no or raising an inquiring brow now and again, barely listened. In her mind, Zeller no longer existed; he'd fallen away from her life like an old barnacle from an overhauled yacht. *Italian law be damned!* Clotilde cursed under her breath. She was his wife, and there was no way out. Wishing him out of her life was a luxury she could not afford.

"I've been informed you've been remiss in your social obligations, contessa," he said, sipping his cognac after dinner.

She shrugged. "It's true. A malaise of sorts, I suspect."

"Not malingering, Clotilde? Perhaps you should go to the mountains, the sea? Il Duce inquires about your health. He nags me about starting a family. Whether or not we desire offspring is not the matter at stake. A good fascist procreates. Suppose we give it concentrated effort when I return from Argentina?"

"Argentina? Why there?" she asked innocently.

"Actually I will travel to the new land, America. I'm fascinated with a place called Wall Street. It's rapidly becoming the financial center of the globe. But why do I tell you?" He sighed. "I wonder what goes on in that space between two ears. Do you have the faintest notion what Wall Street is?" It wasn't a question; it was scathing condemnation for what he perceived to be stupidity. "Contessa?"

Clotilde, studying the ten-carat diamond on her finger, snapped out of her reverie. "Forgive me. You asked something?"

"I asked if you cared to travel with me this time. I could use help with social commitments." He poured two brandies in crystal snifters and moved toward her.

God, no! Not tonight. The thought of his hands on me!

"You forget it was Dariana's social talents, not mine, that

kept the Zeller books in proper order.'' Clotilde's syrupy-sweet voice arrested him. At once his face turned cold, closed, affronted by the innuendo in her words. His hand darted to his mangled ear.

"You, madam, are mistress of the palazzo, not Dariana or any other scullery maid. And you best damned well see things run smoothly. The reports bode ill. To much time to squander with nothing to do. Suppose we convene in your chamber, madam. Il Duce is right. It's time we began a family."

"Next time. Plan accordingly. I am ill disposed. According to the church's edicts—"

"The church be damned! The papacy be damned!" snarled Zeller. A footman knocked, entered carrying a note on a silver tray. Zeller's anger quickly dissolved.

Clotilde, recognizing the pale blue stationery, grew brave. "Madame Scarletta, it seems, awaits your pleasure. My dear, it's best not to keep her waiting," she added snidely. "What an infuriating habit, Amadeo. Displease her and your statement at Fabergé will swell enough to provoke a coronary." She sipped her brandy, leveling cool blue eyes at him over the rim of her glass. "Her jewelry is exquisite."

Zeller, ignoring the acerbic comment, held the note, unopened, something in his brain clicking. "What's this? What's this, my Austrian contessa? What is this change I see in you? What boldness! What audacity! What happened to the innocuous limpet, the clinging, helpless, nonassertive child I married? A metamorphosis before my eyes? What a shame I am unable to sample this new, tempting dish." He scanned the contents of the note, without expression. Collecting himself, he sipped his brandy, stood up, pulled his uniform into place. With a proprietary air, he bowed, stiffly. "Madame Zeller, a genuine disaffection with social and political situations in our nation causes unrest. Momentarily I am committed to Il Duce, and our great cause, fascism. If, as a result of my devotion to duty, our marriage suffers, it is unfortunate. On my return, I shall properly mend the fences in our union."

Clotilde bit back her tongue, choking on an unuttered comment. Silent storm warnings flashed around her; she audited the peril and quickly fell to her usual role as mistress of the palazzo. Rising to her feet, she accompanied Zeller into the foyer. His bags lay in careful order. His manservant slipped the black leather knee coat over the ornate uniform, handed him fresh white gloves and a visored cap adorned with passementerie. Zeller clicked his heels together under the giant crystal chandelier in the entryway, kissed Clotilde's outstretched hand, and bid her *adieu*. Four burly uniformed guards fell into step, flanking him as they disappeared through the giant entry doors.

The Golden Medusa, Michael Bertelli's luxury yacht, sliced through sparkling lapis lazuli waters, southward bound from Ostia Antica along a stunning sweep of coastline. It was the last week of May. Orange domed Rome blazed fiery in the sun.

"Just think, my beloved, a whole month! At *least* three weeks." Clotilde dared not reflect the inner disquiet and trepidation churning through her. A premonition of doom hung heavy over her. Michael masked his disappointment. *Three weeks?* He had planned for three months—years—decades!

God! He loved Clotilde more than life itself. He rhapsodized over Positano. "It is sheer paradise, beloved, a village not far from Capri, an undiscovered world of primitive beauty. You will adore the villa," he promised, refilling her champagne glass.

On this day, the whole of nature conspired to provide a spectacular backdrop for the lovers, an indescribable dress parade as earth, sky, and water exploded in color profusions no artist had ever captured on canvas.

Once past the sweeping Bay of Naples, *The Golden Medusa* held to port between Sorrento and Capri, then, swinging past the Isle of Capri, navigated into Salerno Bay to drop anchor. Standing amidships, Clotilde and Michael soaked up the beguiling sights of the village seemingly carved from the precipitously sloping mountain jutting up from the water.

"Oh, Michael, if this is paradise, dish up a lifetime supply for us," she whispered ecstatically, her eyes drinking in everything at once as if she'd never be finished with it.

Vividly gleaming waters, dancing in the bay, reflected a misty purple with viridian overlays, lacy gray spectral pools.

"The ethereal effects transcend reality, Michael. I feel transported to another time, another life."

"Look—there." He pointed out a motor launch slicing the waters, headed toward them. "They'll pick us up and take us to—there." He brought her attention to an enormous rock jutting from the water at the southernmost point of the bay. Bitten into its side, carved steps spiraled up from the water's edge some fifty feet to the villa. Clotilde's eyes crept up the steps, stopping

at the massive cascade of brightly colored bougainvillaea showering down on bright red clay tiles of the villa roof, continuing
down to the retaining walls at water's edge. She shuddered
involuntarily, inhaling deeply.

"It is paradise. As close as I'll ever come to it, outside of
your arms." She was shivering. Michael removed his white
knitted sweater, hugged it about her shoulders, reassuring her.

"The hot sun does this—sends chills up and down your spine,
beloved."

"No, it's not the sun. It's you, your love, and because our
arms are empty of each other." How could Clotilde tell him
what it really was she felt? It wasn't the *right* moment. Would it
ever be the *right* moment to tell him? She'd never seen him as
relaxed, as content, as totally hers.

"Am I mad, darling? Totally without wits?" Clotilde moved
about the villa, staring awestruck at the exact replica of the villa
in Rome. She turned to him, questioning. "Right down to the art
objects?"

Michael laughed, a sheepish grin on his face. "It's a quirk.
Wherever I go, part of my life goes with me. I need to feel a
kinship with my world at all times. I delight in the new, Clotilde,
don't misunderstand me, but without the old, the new is
meaningless."

"What a marvelous thought." She tilted her head obliquely,
considering it. If she had kept part of Vienna in her world, she
might not have been so easily intimidated by Zeller, so alienated
in his world.

Dinner was served overlooking blue waters reflecting a stunning sunset poets would rip apart their souls to describe. Softly
in the background, a victrola played her favorite aria from
Madame Butterfly. "You remember everything." She sighed
ecstatically. "Cho Cho San's passionate lament."

Their favorite foods and wines were barely touched. An overwhelming sea of emotions gripped them. It was perfect, *too*
perfect, thought Clotilde, trying again to shake off the ominous
presence she sensed.

A flood of loving comfort spilled from Michael's lips. "Leave
him, Clotilde. Marry me. My uncle, Cardinal Bertelli, will help
us receive papal dispensation. He is aware of Zeller's anticlerical
thunderings. Zeller is not held in high esteem. Believe me, it is
not impossible to dissolve the sham of your marriage."

How close she came to capitulating. *How very close!*

"What exists between you and Zeller is not marriage. Why prolong the farce? Until we met I was a frustrated bachelor, playing at *la dolce vita.* I disavowed marital ties as archaic. Now, see me! Willing to sacrifice all for the woman I love!"

Clotilde, wearing a diaphanous beige silk peignoir, trimmed in ecru alençon lace, left the table, past the cascading floral bowers to the edge of the terrace as if she belonged in no other place in the world. She inhaled the perfumed night air, feeling Michael's warm breath behind her. She leaned against him, sighing huskily. "Michael, I love you with every breath I take. When we are apart, I can't breathe, I want only to wither and die." He moaned softly, buried his face in her scented hair. She turned, receiving his soulful kiss. The need to couple grew unbearable. Clotilde smiled secretly and Michael knew.

Moments later they lay naked on the enormous bed on a raised dais constructed to overlook the bay. In the soft candle glow, her eyes traced every inch of his body, her fingertips caressing his as he caressed hers, each committing the other to memory. Clotilde lay against his flushed, pulsating body, her head against his throbbing heart. "Yours is an uncanny gift, Michael, of making me feel the way a woman was born to feel. Your touch ignites every spark of life within me. You alone have the key to my secret world." She shuddered against him, trying to blot out that dark cloud hovering over her since they left Ostia Antica.

Michael, insistent, announced in no uncertain terms, "It's settled. You must leave Zeller. Look at you, Clotilde; when have you looked more beautiful? I am perfect for you."

She reached to him, pulled his face over hers, brought his lips to hers greedily. She directed his hands over her breasts, shivering at the sensation coursing through her. He manipulated her nipples with his lips in feathery strokes until they stood as erect as his love shaft. "Each day and night, every hour, every minute, I am reminded of you. You gave me life. You made bells ring in my heart, soul, mind. My senses, conditioned to you for all eternity, will die of slow starvation. I cannot marry you, beloved. I am carrying our child."

Shocked, bewildered, he jackknifed to a sitting position. *"You cannot marry me because you are carrying our child?* What logic!" He grinned, laughed in a spurt of good humor, a radiant grin animating him. "Oh, beloved! All the more reason to end this sham. We *shall* marry! You hear, we shall marry!" His body, a swift messenger of delight, grew hard against her. His charm ignited her. "What more can I say? What else can I do, beloved contessa, to convince you our love is ordained. Not you, not Zeller, no one can part us."

He rolled her over gently on her back, his strong fingers lightly caressing the slight rounding of her belly, his devouring eyes drinking in the swelling of her breasts. He marveled how nature hinted at the life growing inside her.

Melting into each other, rising to a plateau of oneness, they gave in to maddening passion, the escalating throbbing drive transporting them to a summit of starburst radiations, shimmering lights until the brilliance faded.

Later, smoking a cigarette on the bed, watching the smoke spiral upward, Michael insisted, "You must prepare for instant flight from Zeller! The Bertelli family maintains business contacts globally. Take your pick of countries—"

"No! We can't! We must not! He would kill us both."

"He wouldn't dare!"

"The laws of adultery favor him. beloved, we are star-crossed lovers—don't you see? My intuition tells me he *already* knows about us. Oh, it's nothing he's said or done; he's too clever for that. But, Michael, those eyes! Those all-knowing eyes. The way he looked at me this last time . . ." She shuddered. "As if he saw me for the first time in a new light . . . I watched myself saying, doing nothing to shed light on our love. I swear he could see the fullness of your kisses on my lips, your love indelibly etched on my heart. Oh, beloved, I would die before bringing harm to you or our unborn child. This must be our last time together. *It must!*"

It was the last thing he expected to spill from her lips here in this setting of tranquility and love. "Are you mad? I love you. Love . . . love . . . *love* you! Doesn't our love mean anything to you? I waited a lifetime to find you. You cannot desert me now, Clotilde." He was uncontainable, moving closer, embracing her, arms tightening their grip.

"I am not deserting you. I am saving—God willing—your life, my life, that of our unborn child. Zeller will not permit himself to be viewed in disfavor by his peers. He would kill you, be applauded. Then find a way to kill me. I know him. He's inhuman."

"Knowing this, you remain with him?" He clutched his head as if to stop the insanity of convoluted thought. "You admit he's monstrous, and abet this monstrosity by remaining with him! *Why?*'' He paced about the shadowy room in unabashed nudity. She loved him like this, natural, normal, human, compassionate, endearing. ''Listen to me, Clotilde. This is *your* life, *our* life, here and now. How we choose to live it is *our* business; not the state, the church, or God has the *right* to tell us what to choose for ourselves! We'll leave Italy, hear? You and I and our child are all that matters.''

For a few rapturous moments she almost believed him. A glimmer of hope sprang within her. He had sculpted her from virgin soil, shaped her, and now that she was his he couldn't bear to let her go. She was that missing rib, from which God created woman. ''D-do y-you—d-do you really think—''

Oh how they plotted, schemed, dreamed of an unrealistic future in the next few days. Strolling hand in hand about the estate, their souls wrestling for survival, they lived in a fantasy world. Neither would relinquish the hold on the other; they belonged together.

On the evening of the sixth day, a shadowy twilight descended. In the bedroom, Michael's body grew to fit hers over and again, and together they mentally sketched an image of their child, a boy. It had to be a son, created in Michael's image. How wondrous were the ephemeral dreams constructed on gossamer wings. How idyllic were their designs for a future.

Suspending thought, he sucked swollen kisses from her brimming mouth, as honey flowed between her legs. Their love was urgent, poignant, and Michael wanted to plunder her body, soul, and mind. He murmured sweet endearments, ''*Cara mia*, you are my everything.''

He purred, stroked their unborn child endearingly. No erotic fantasy had ever entered their love scenario. Curiously this made Clotilde very *special* to him. In Michael's past, any woman, after a week of coupling, grew stale, necessitating other avenues of stimulation to keep him interested. With Clotilde, the stimulus between them was so intense, they lingered at the pinnacle, never fully descending to earth. The need to protect so special a love intensified.

It was nearing midnight. In the silence, rapturous sighs gurgled low in their throats. Sexual release approaching, the power of Michael's loins rising to unbearable crescendo, they moved in unbroken rhythm. He held back the passionate thrusts, moved agonizingly slowly, retarding the sensuous, exquisite feelings until Clotilde gasped aloud. Passion turned her into a tigress. The momentum increased. They opened their eyes, drowned in their love as millions of starbursts exploded and fell softly to earth.

Michael's body convulsed. The expression on his face was different from any she'd ever seen. Clotilde gave a start. Different explosions popped in the vague distance.

"Get down!" Michael shouted roughly, pain and anger etched into his face.

Streaks of white molten fire strafed the room. Bullets burst their eardrums. Michael pulled Clotilde off the bed, forced her flat to the floor. Reaching for a buzzer near the night table, he pressed, summoning his men. "Stay down, Clotilde. Do not move!" he commanded in an alien voice. He crawled on his hands and knees over the floor to a wall cabinet, flung open a door, removed a handgun. Checking the ammo clip, he crawled to the far wall, rose to his feet, and, hugging the wall to the open terrace, peered cautiously in the darkness.

In the soft glow of moonlight, Clotilde discerned dark, bloodied streaks splattered on his forehead and shoulders. She cried aloud. "God! You've been shot!" Her hand covered her mouth to muffle her screams.

She slithered along the floor to his side. "Michael! What's happening? Tell me. In God's name, tell me!"

"Be silent!" he commanded. "I told you, don't move!"

Loud, angry voices split the silence. Sounds of running footsteps approached. The bedroom door, kicked open, was flung hard against the wall with a loud crashing sound. Shadows sprinted past the naked couple. Michael shouted directions. "The terrace! Shots fired from the terrace!" He grabbed his robe and followed them out the door.

Bullets, fired into the night in rapid succession, panicked Clotilde. She reached for her peignoir, slipped into it, and dashed onto the terrace. Michael was hurt, and like some crazy man he was running after the assassins! Bullets spewing like spurts of lightning, sounds of gunfire amplified in the night, drew her attention to the water's edge.

Below, in the inky darkness, a glittering of running lights from ships and boats at anchor lighted Salerno Bay. Clotilde heard loud, thudding sounds, shouts, obscenities, the sounds of engines struggling to come alive. She scanned the landing. A motorboat groaned to life. One of Michael's men shot a flare gun. The sky overhead burst into an umbrella of bright yellow fire; his men fired rifles at the moving speedboat. Instantly it seemed to propel itself into the air, exploded, splintered to pieces, and came crashing down, the boat and occupants fragmented into a watery grave.

Michael found her shivering on the terrace, eyes transfixed to the burning remnants on the water. "I told you to stay inside," he scolded gently, placing his arm around her protectively, leading her back inside. "Thank God, you're safe." He brushed her forehead with his lips. "You're shivering." He yanked at a coverlet from the chaise, wrapped her in it. "It's ended, Clotilde. Whoever it was can do nothing else."

He picked up a towel, wiped the blood from his face, pressed it to a shoulder wound, wincing slightly. He stepped out onto the terrace. His men returned. Michael conversed with them briefly, in hushed tones. Finished, he returned to Clotilde, casually poured her a brandy from a cut crystal decanter. "Drink this, *carissima*. Try not to be frightened. I'll return in moments. My men insist on checking the exits above the property to the Amalfi Drive."

She nodded mutely, teeth chattering, forcing the brandy to warm her intestines. Moments after Michael left, she heard running footsteps along the tiled portico at the rear of the villa. Loud, angry voices . . . more gunfire! Clotilde poured another brandy, gulped it down. Why didn't the trembling cease? She tried to put the earlier events in sequential order. She paced the floor, reached for a cigarette, lit it, inhaled, sputtered and choked on it, and, realizing she didn't smoke, flung it into the fireplace.

Love had made her incautious; fear was rendering her insensible. In the backstage of her mind, a cast of unwanted players had warned her, hadn't they? Something would happen to destroy her and Michael's happiness. For a year she had lived in dread, never knowing when the magic bubble would burst. Now it had happened. No one had to spell it out for her. She knew, really knew what would happen. For too long she had ignored the thoughts at the threshold of her consciousness.

Who, better than Clotilde, knew the madness lurking in Amadeo Zeller's mind? Born in the shadow of madness he was bound to take her with him. She was falling victim to vicious circumstance, victim of an appalling, fiendish burlesque.

Clotilde slipped into a pair of white flannel slacks and a short-sleeved sweater. Brushing her hair severely off her face, knotting it in a coil at the nape of her neck, she fenced mentally. Where had she erred? How exacting a role she had played with Amadeo before his departure! Clotilde's efforts had been so intense she failed to recognize the knowledge in Zeller's eyes. He'd made little mention of the changes in her but he'd noted them. She knew. And Clotilde dared believe herself victorious in her charade. One fox might outfox another, but Clotilde, ignorant in the ways of a vixen, would not permit herself to be crucified for the love in her heart.

By the time Michael returned, her bags were packed. He observed her in silence, amazed at her frenzied pace. "Are you going someplace?" he asked *sotto voce*.

"You think I would remain, now?"

"Yes. Now more than ever."

The sight of his bandaged shoulder and wounded forehead panicked her. "No! I'm leaving before I heap death upon you. Oh, Michael, it's the only way! God! I don't know what I'm saying or doing. I'm frantic, can't you see?"

He pulled her gently to a chair, poured more brandy. "Drink it," he commanded. "You cannot return home at all."

"Why not?" *As if she didn't know or guess!*

"Four of Zeller's butchers tried to kill us. One got away."

The glass slipped from her hand, fell crashing against the fireplace tiles. "Kill *us*? Not just *you*? He wants us both dead?"

"Let me put it more succinctly. A successful assassination is like a perfectly executed play in which each actor with the exception of the star knows their roles by rote. In this case the players were rank amateurs; the stars, you and I, behaved in an exemplary fashion—we are alive."

"He knows about us." Clotilde's voice was empty, flat.

"Yes, beloved, you can wager all you have that Zeller knows. Whether he issued orders to kill us is debatable since three men are dead. I must learn the fourth man's identity. Meanwhile, under no circumstances do you return to Rome. Zeller is a madman."

"No, Michael." She persisted. "My absence would be an admission of my guilt. My presence at the villa will create doubt in his mind. He hasn't the courage to ask me straight out—"

"*Courage!* The man is a bloodthirsty, man-eating jackal! He'll devour you alive!"

"He wouldn't kill me—not yet. He still needs me," Clotilde began, coolly, duplicity sparking her courage. "You see, my trust fund is due on my twenty-fifth birthday. If I had died tonight, the money would revert to another trust—it would never be his. If I disappeared, he'd merely produce fraudulent papers to twist the law to suit his purpose. I refuse to accommodate him in either design."

He stared at her, aghast. "All Rome believes the minister to be a millionaire. Why would he *need* your trust fund?"

"The difference between need and greed is hairline thin when fifty million in Swiss francs is involved, dearest Michael. Married to Zeller, I've perceived a few of his hidden talents—not all, but enough to understand what he wants and intends to get. Plots are carefully laid. The man never trusts to luck or fate; he creates his own circumstances and seizes the moment most men toss aside."

The Bertelli scion listened, staring at a stranger, his heart thundering with new, peculiar sensations.

"I refuse to let anything happen to you or our *love* child." Tears sprang to her eyes. "I will devote my life to preserve both our lives. I shall return to Rome. Zeller will receive his reports. Doubt will flounder in his mind. And you, my beloved Michael, must play a stellar role in the upcoming drama. You must report the incident to the local *polizia* and to the newspapers, describing graphically how you and a certain *unnamed* paramour were nearly gunned to death by unknown assailants trespassing your property. Quickly, you must find a trustworthy woman of my size and description who, for a sum of money, will agree to play the role. A foreigner, Michael, not necessarily Italian, *capisce*? Foreigners are inclined to promiscuous behavior, no? Persuade them—the *polizia*—of a likely motive. Robbery, perhaps? Meanwhile my very calm presence at the palazzo will make Zeller uncertain. He would expect precisely what you suggested, that I would never return for fear of my life. Doubt will assail him, hold him frozen for a time, forcing him to rethink his strategy. There is an axiom, beloved, that man must never cease watching other men, that the clever man watches without giving evidence of his watching. And I shall be watching Zeller's every move."

Michael Bertelli gnawed at his underlip in helpless frustration. Didn't she *really* know Zeller?

"A friend, a trusted friend in Corsica, will substantiate my presence there for these past few weeks. My reasons for traveling to Corsica? Health reasons. My pregnancy—"

"You're insane! Quite mad, you know. If you think for one minute you can deceive Zeller—"

"A pregnancy Amadeo will believe he caused. I shall make him believe it. What a story I shall embroider. The child will be stillborn. But he won't, Michael. Our *love* child shall live despite Zeller!"

"My God, Clotilde! You out-Herod Herod! You are Messalina come to life!" His eyes sparked fire. "I don't believe my ears! My eyes!"

"Believe both your ears and eyes, beloved. A new Clotilde stands before you, one molded by your love, one into whom you breathed life!"

"Don't speak of what you believe to be conspiracy. This posturing about in so deadly a situation tears at my guts. The jaws of the jackal will crush you."

Clotilde moved about the room, deaf to Michael's pleading. "I need a highly respected, quite brave lawyer, not necessarily a fascist. I have business interests I wish to protect so that Zeller cannot touch them." Clotilde stopped. "No. It shall not be necessary. I already have a quasi-benefactor—Il Duce. I shall ask him to recommend a lawyer to me. A highly respected *avvocato*—uh—what is his name?"

"Donato Donatelli," muttered Michael dispassionately.

"Yes, yes, Donatelli is perfect!"

"Il Duce's personal *avvocato*! He will report everything to Il Duce."

"Precisely." And when he shook his head, totally bewildered by her reasoning, she explained, "Donatelli shall transfer into any account I desire the bulk of my trust fund, with, of course, a respectable donation to Il Duce's favorite charity. I will subtly suggest I do not wish to burden my spouse with petty details, since he is dedicated to Il Duce's business. *You know what that means?*"

"Only too well, contessa. A wife stepping beyond the boundaries of the lord and master of a domicile. . . ."

She smiled maliciously. "If a wife cannot trust her husband?"

"The implications are clear, Clotilde. But I doubt *you* comprehend the complexities," he cried softly. "Besides, you are dooming our love, forever!"

"If you had been killed tonight, protecting me, where would I be? Forever shamed by the guilt of infidelity and adultery hang-

ing over my head? He cannot destroy us now. Don't you see?
Aren't we both alive? We foiled his plans!''

What extraordinary logic, spoken in a firm, resolute voice,
without arrogance, thought Michael, sensing their love slip slowly
from his grasp. Slowly his eyes lifted to hers in a passionate
silence and he knew, really knew in his heart that Clotilde would
have it no other way. A lethal hatred for Zeller burned deep
inside her, a thirst for vengeance, blinding her to all else. It was
as if she had died and risen again from the ashes of her discontented past, soared into the heavens, and returned to earth on the
wings of Pegasus, a reincarnated goddess of war. No good
would come of this; he sensed it.

Clotilde said in a soft, plaintive voice. ''He would hunt us to
the ends of the earth, knowing he's been made a cuckold.
Please, how do I make you see what registers so clearly in my
head, Do what I ask. Find that surrogate. Pay her well. Hospital-
ize her for shock, whatever you can. Be attentive to her. Shower
her with flowers, confections, perfumes; indicate your concern,
before witnesses.'' *Oh, how she conspired!* ''Your actions, reported to Zeller, will frustrate him. You say one of the assassins
is still alive? Even he can be fooled if you provide a surrogate to
fit the scenario at once. Delay the story for a day or two. Pretend
to suppress the facts, but when the story breaks, make it the talk
of Rome! A scandal, if needs be, within proper limitations, of
course. Who will dare contend your story? Authentication of the
minister's suspicions will be impossible. Men hired to observe
me will grow bored with my saintly comportment. Until a safe
means of communication is possible, we shall remain apart.''
She laughed conspiratorially. ''I daresay when he learns about my
trust fund he will become apoplectic.''

''Or declare you insane? Cause you to accidentally disappear off
the face of the earth!'' Michael snapped, outraged at her myopic
view of the situation. ''Are you insane to dare match wits with
Zeller? I shall make it a point to unearth all I can about
Zeller, and you, Clotilde, must promise, if I prove to you how
dangerous a man he really is, that you will leave him! Yes, yes,
I resist your plan, out of fear of sending you into this flesh-
eater's lair.''

''Once I plant a seed of doubt in Il Duce's mind, Amadeo
wouldn't dare harm me. There'd be the devil to pay.''

''Dear, dear Clotilde. What a child you are. How willing you are to tangle with hungry tigers. You will be consumed. And I will not permit it. When is our child due?''

''October.''

''I won't let you return to Zeller.''

They argued. In the next few hours he learned the extent of her stubborn determination. ''I can handle him now, thanks to your influence, Michael. I needed to believe in my worth; you gave me that strength and belief. I am no longer the shy, retiring, overburdened, emotional wretch I was a year ago.'' She pursed her lips, connecting something of the past and present. ''He cannot shame me; he has lost control over me.''

Michael was horrified. ''Our love must stand for something, Clotilde. We cannot be ships that pass in the night. I refuse to accept this fate. How would I know if something ever happened to you? In that maniac's hands you will never be safe. We cannot let it end this way.''

Her slender hands shot out, over his lips, silencing him. Her voice was soft, loving, consoling. ''This is madness. I must return to end the insanity. My love for you is more precious than life itself. I want you alive. *Alive!* Who can foretell the future? Amadeo travels a great deal . . . he has many enemies . . . perhaps an accident, or a well-placed knife? Oh, God, listen to me plot a man's death!'' She moved away from him, collecting her cosmetics, tossing them into her packing case.

Michael hurried to her side. ''Tell me what to do. And since you display Herculean strength, devise a kit to mend my broken heart.''

A moan escaped her lips; she fell against him. It had been a mad, mad, mad dream after all, a dream they had both clung to until the last possible moment. ''If there's a way for us, I shall find it. I promise,'' she whispered huskily. Clotilde, better than Michael, faced the reality of their predicament. Michael's enlightenment would come the hard way.

''If ever you need me, go to Cardinal Bertelli,'' he instructed.

''I won't knowingly endanger anyone's life.''

''Very well, then, unknowingly.'' Moving to an alcove adjacent to the bedroom, he removed a Botticelli from the wall, exposing a wall safe. He tumbled the dial, opened the safe, and returned with a black velvet sack. Placing it on the table, he unveiled the contents.

Clotilde gasped. She gazed admiringly at the hand-carved ruby sword and its diamond-studded hilt, an emerald at the hilt's center. "What has this to do with us?"

"The sword of Damocles—the replica of the original was fashioned after the sword used by Dionysus, the Elder, to teach Damocles how grave were the dangers surrounding those in life who appeared the most fortunate of all."

"I still fail to comprehend—"

"Collectors the world over have lusted after this priceless relic. Daily I refuse offers to display it in a museum or gallery. I will personally place the Damoclean sword in the hands of the curator at the museum in Rome, under the tightest of security precautions. Whenever you need me, you will contact him, authorizing him to display the jewel. Once I see it displayed, we shall somehow make contact and it shall be removed from display."

"If it should fall into the hands of thieves I should never forgive myself." Clotilde, aghast at the gesture, declined.

"Thieves do not concern me, Clotilde. If it should fall into the hands of some ambitious fascist, who covets it for the party—"

She stared at him, puzzled. "You don't mean to imply that the minister would stoop to so shabby a device?"

"It wouldn't be the first time. But that is another matter."

"Then, I shall not permit it. Find another way."

"There is none without the complicity of a third party. It's this or I shall shackle you here in Positano. We'll face it together."

"No. Michael, no!"

"Very well; now think of a code word to be used for the curator's convenience."

"Dariana," she said, as if the name sat at the edge of her memory waiting to be used.

"Dariana? Dariana it is."

Then anxieties, uncertainties, life-threatening situations swallowed up in passion, eternal declarations of love, they moved on the bed like playful seals frisking in balmy seas. From midnight till dawn they spent the time in wistful remembrance, ecstatic sexual release, catnapping in a tangle of arms and legs.

Chapter Twenty-one

"Dariana! Dariana!" Vivaldi called to her through the open terrace doors. Carrying Daniel in her arms, her belly swollen with child, she broke into a radiant smile at the sight of an enormous bouquet of her favorite roses. Vivaldi kissed her, lifted the infant from her arms; kissing his son lovingly, he stepped into the house. Dariana followed, selecting a vase. "Here, in my pocket," Vivaldi indicated. "A letter from Rome, for you." He did a shuffling sidestep to her amusement, offering his hip pocket to her.

Dariana removed the envelope. Recognizing the pale mauve stationery embossed with a gold de Bernadorf crest, she frowned, then hurriedly scanned the contents, her eyes widening in astonishment. "The contessa is coming to visit us!" She gasped, glancing at the wall calendar. "Good heavens! She's due any day!"

"Well," Vivaldi said, tossing the child into the air, coaxing smiles from him. "We can certainly accommodate your duchess."

"Contessa, Vivaldi—not duchess. She's due any day by ship. And due any day to deliver a child! My, my, what an incongruity. She wants the child to be born in Corsica!" Dariana sat heavily in a kitchen chair, staring at some inner image, a shudder running through her. She paid no attention to Vivaldi making those silly noises grownups make over infants.

"See! Daniel knows his father, don't you, *bellissimo*?"

Dariana failed to be amused. Her troubled mind focused on a premonition. She speculated: *If Vivaldi were to learn the contessa was married to Amadeo Zeller* . . . Her face became a mask. She slipped the letter into her apron pocket, busied her trembling hands arranging the roses, praying Vivaldi would fail to notice her sudden pallor. Seized with a sudden, vague fear, Dariana resolved firmly that Vivaldi must never know Clotilde was married to Zeller—*never*!

NOTES FROM DARIANA'S DIARY

August 15, 1923 . . . At eleven o'clock A.M. approximately one hundred and fifty-four years after the birth of Napoleon Bonaparte, a son was born prematurely to Contessa Marie Clotilde de Bernadorf and Miguel Bertelli. The coincidence of the infant's birth on the same day and hour, not far from the house of his famous ancestor, has brought attention to the child.

The child, named Darius Bonifacio, will be raised as our son, Vivaldi's and mine. His birth certificate, to be kept under lock and key, will read: Darius Miguel Bertelli.

Knowing of Marie Clotilde's desperation, I could not refuse her. I promised to do all in my power to comply with her request and, in return, she must do all she can to prevent Vivaldi from learning she is married to Zeller.

August 30, 1923. It was with great reluctance I bid the contessa farewell. Both she and Miguel returned to Rome. The baby, Darius, is gorgeous! The image of his parents!

Dariana was nursing Darius when Vivaldi and Matteus returned from taking the contessa and Michael Bertelli to the quay to board *The Golden Medusa* back to Rome. She failed to hear Vivaldi enter. For several moments Vivaldi stood at the threshold of the sitting room observing the suckling ritual. He glowed warmly, a strange tenderness flooding his senses. He listened, mesmerized by her honeyed tones as she fawned over Darius, inflamed with the aching desire to go to bed with her.

"You sweet, sweet thing. Yes, baby, you're safe, little Darius," she cooed. "Safe from that beast Zeller. He'll never taint your soul. No black shadows will torment you or harm a hair of your head if he knows nothing of your existence.'' She hummed a Corsican ditty, unaware of the shock registered on her husband's face.

Vivaldi faltered, replayed her words in his brain, his senses shaking him. He moved in closer to her, circling around behind the sofa until he faced her. She glanced up, startled at first, then her features relaxed into a rhapsodic smile.

''Dariana! Repeat what you just said!'' he commanded, his eyes fixing on the infant.

''What I said? I don't remember. What did I say? I was talking baby talk to Darius, I suppose.''

''About Zeller! *Amadeo Zeller!* What is he to Darius? What's this all about?''

Her deception of Vivaldi loomed ugly in her mind. She took hold of herself, unable to cling to her composure enough to maintain the lie. ''Darius is the issue of Miguel Bertelli's loins, not the contessa's husband. She is married to Minister Zeller of Rome,'' she added, keeping the information minimal, hoping to evoke some response from Vivaldi concerning Zeller. He gave her nothing, but required answers to his questions.

Vivaldi's queries bore an uncanny resemblance to the explicit barbs Matteus had prodded and probed her with on his return from Sicily. Dariana wisely held to the truth. ''Zeller is a horrible man. Their marriage, doomed at the outset, was a sham. Oh Vivaldi, he deliberately exacerbated her nervous affliction. Truly, he was driving the contessa mad, to render her incapable of managing the vast wealth of her trust fund. Strange how her affair with Bertelli ended the affliction,'' Dariana continued, explaining the love odyssey as Marie Clotilde had imparted it to her. ''She brought Darius to us because she fears for his life.''

Vivaldi, stunned at the revelation, studied his wife in silent admonishment as she recounted the love affair between Darius's parents. He wondered at Dariana's rancor when she spoke the name Zeller, at the vitriol dripping from her words. Dariana, having promised Matteus not to mention their conversation concerning Zeller, expected Vivaldi at some point to explain what Zeller meant to him. What was the interest he demonstrated in the man?

Vivaldi, dazed, inordinately tense, and deliberately obscure in his account of the enmity between himself and his arch enemy, avoided direct questions concerning Zeller. Here, he thought, was the pure essence of betrayal, the grand deception.

Perceiving Vivaldi's dark thoughts Dariana forced herself to be discreet. She dared not permit him to suspect how long she had harbored the suspicion that Zeller was the target of Vivaldi's wrath and vengeance. The blood was thumping behind her eyes and at her temples. If Zeller's name had produced vitriol in Dariana's words, images of the man exploded like guns across Vivaldi's brain. The idea of creating unbearable complications in his life with Dariana forced him to control himself. He could not, *would* not permit malevolence to turn him into a vile base thing again! His marriage to Dariana had helped him schedule this hatred, enabled him to examine and measure suitable responses with detachment. If he permitted hatred to consume him as it had in the past, he wouldn't live to reap his planned revenge.

How curiously moved the hands of fate! And now, God help him, the infant Darius would serve as a daily reminder of his sworn enemy! Was there to be no peace for him?

"I'm going for a walk," he told Dariana, distrusting his own susceptibility to her when she suckled a child. He averted his head and left the room, acknowledging her wisdom and astuteness, yet unnerved that never once in their relationship, had the name Zeller defiled their hearth.

He moved restlessly past the terraces toward the flatland. In retrospect, Vivaldi realized the name Amadeo Zeller had never spilled from Bertelli's lips. Not once! Was he a victim of a conspiracy of silence? Vivaldi found Miguel sincere, well educated, a politically astute man whose grasp on the pulse of international finance proved stimulating to him. He had spoken of impending war. He predicted drastic changes in the future. He spoke of passenger airplanes with capabilities of transporting hundreds of people around the globe at impossible speeds, Forced by so stimulating an encounter to dust the cobwebs from his brain, Vivaldi realized how remote a life he lived in Corsica.

Following the decision to keep Darius as if he were his and Dariana's own flesh and blood, Vivaldi had chided Bertelli. "Must I concern myself with the prospect of some *umbriago* appearing on my doorstep one day, guns blazing, shooting first, asking questions later, wanting to pluck the lad from my arms?" Miguel, at once defensive, blurted in agonized frenzy. "The child is mine, not her husband's! Your kindness and Dariana's devotion to Clotilde deserve the truth. The contessa is married to a

scoundrel! A heinous womanizer. A vainglorious politician en-
meshed in the upper echelons of the fascist government, with a
power equal to if not exceeding Il Duce's''

A power equal to if not exceeding Il Duce's. Imbecile!

The statement should have aroused apprehension in him. It
had not. That day, Bertelli had paused to view the stunning
gorges of crystal-clear water as he and Vivaldi ambled about the
estate. Wiping tears from his eyes, he dwelled on the circumstances of Darius's birth, his descent from Bonaparte bloodlines,
his birth on Corsica, and the stamp of illegitimacy he must bear.
''Branded for life, because a tenacious church system forces
humans into bondage, married to people with whom they have
nothing in common. I am a wealthy man, Vivaldi. The means to
raise Darius properly are not beyond my grasp. In Italy, the
stigma attached to bastardy is most unpleasant for any child born
to it.'' He related Clotilde's fears, the incident at Postiano, and
how Clotilde's cool thinking had miraculously dispelled her
husband's suspicions. ''The man is no fool, Vivaldi. Clotilde
fears he will one day explore the hoax, learn of Darius's existence,
and order his death. Should that happen, her fate is sealed. She'd
take her own life.''

That day, Vivaldi had commiserated with the auto tycoon,
admitted he too was not a poor man. ''Darius is in excellent
hands. Dariana's devotion to the contessa is boundless. No harm
shall come to your son.'' Bertelli had pressed a large sum of
money into Vivaldi's hands. Vivaldi refused it. Bertelli's inner
turmoil betrayed itself in the bitter green sparkle of his eyes, the
flush of his face. ''You must take it. I want Darius to lack for
nothing, to be well educated.''

Vivaldi's steadfast refusal to accept money resulted in a cryptic
compromise of sorts. It was simply a means to cement future plans.
''Your friendship, Miguel, means everything. One day I might
need a *special* favor. You, in Rome, might assist me. May I
count on you?''

For an interminable time, the two men had gazed at each
other. Vivaldi read volumes of unspoken questions in the Italian's
eyes. ''For the devotion you show my beloved and our son, ask
anything of me. It is yours.''

''Your words shall be cherished. Pray you never forget them.''

They had returned to the house to await the delivery of the
infant boy. The next morning at eleven at the birth of Darius,
Vivaldi, Miguel and Matteus drank a toast. Bertelli had reached

into his satchel, removed an object encased in black velvet. He placed it on Vivaldi's desk in the vendetta room, unsheathed the priceless art object.

"The contessa has provided a handsome trust fund for our son. I match the gesture with something a hundred times more in value."

The Moor gasped aloud. "The sword of Damocles!"

Bertelli, stunned, glanced apprehensively at the Moor. "You *know* the legend? The object itself?"

"It was a fable I learned as a child. Descended from the Almohad Dynasty, my people claim the myth equally as did the Greeks in Sicily. We believe its origin was with the Moors." Matteus moved in closer, placed silver candelabra closer to the ruby jewel, staring in awed fascination.

Once Bertelli explained his wishes, he had left to remain at the contessa's side until their departure that afternoon. In two weeks' time, the name Zeller had not spilled from any lips.

Vivaldi stood on the large white rock, at Virgin's Point, listening to surf below crash against the shore. The robust harvest moon turned the sea to a mirror of crushed orange jewels. It seemed to Vivaldi that everything in nature glowed with an icy-orange incandescence. Dariana's earlier words were crashing through his mind like live thunderbolts. Suddenly it struck him.

Destiny had dumped a windfall into his lap! A full-blooded future emperor was a powerful weapon indeed!

Most merciful Mother of Christ! The way was clear! The wife of his mortal enemy had placed into his hands the most powerful weapon devised by man. Her illegitimate son! God! What avenues of revenge were open to him!

Time, patience, care, proper training, and a resolute purpose would mold Darius into a perfect tool to effect Vivaldi's blood revenge on Zeller. A gun in hand, at the *right* time, at the *right* place, would provide Zeller with instant eternity.

Vivaldi left Virgin's Point, headed back to Terra Bonifacio along an upper goat track. Vivaldi paused, peered up through the tall branches of the pines, thinking, *Am I crazy?*

A single bullet for Zeller would be too simple, too kind. Vivaldi's scheme for Zeller encompassed plots in which death alone did not prevail. Long before the final stage of death unfolded, long before, Zeller would beg for death to relieve him of the torture and anguish drowning him. Oh, would he pay for the horrors inflicted on the de la Varga and Valdez families!

Expectation of his demise would filter into his consciousness, slowly. Warnings would reach him. Insidious gossip would thwart him. Rumors of his gross perfidies toward others would be leaked among the circles in which Zeller moved at the most inopportune times. His credibility would slowly rupture and disintegrate, bit by bit. And when Zeller's present provided him no further refuge from his iniquitous past, he would be sustained with fraudulent hope.

This was Vivaldi's plan, his goal. Upon these ends, he set his sights. Vivaldi no longer believed in a morphic God. But on this night, how he coveted the wicked, mysterious powers attributed to God. Would that he were God, only for the time needed to implement and bring his plans to fruition.

Vivaldi quickened his steps toward the house. It was time to seriously review the Seven Garduna Parchments! If the hour weren't so late, he would awaken the Moor to begin again the indoctrination, interrupted and tabled when he married Dariana.

Oh, God! He felt the power surge through him! Was the time ripe?

The Golden Medusa was fifteen minutes out of Ajaccio before they spoke. "What a gorgeous child, our son." Michael sighed wistfully.

"How unfair to deny him his heritage," Clotilde said, drained of emotion.

"What of us? Isn't it unfair to us—to me? Why am I unable to convince you? Argentina is not far. We can reclaim our son—"

"Why won't you believe me? Amadeo would hunt us down like dogs! Kill the three of us. I am the sinner, the adultress in the eyes of the church!"

"Damn the church! I won't be enslaved by archaic traditions! I won't live in bondage, Clotilde!"

"Say what you will. I am convinced God is punishing me, forcing me to part with our child. Oh, Michael, these many months away from you were torture. If I return to you, you will die and so will I!"

"Damn it, Clotilde! We are all destined for death. The only uncertainty lies in not knowing the exact moment death schedules our earthly departure. Why not take our pleasures? Enjoy our love in the precious time allotted us on earth? Why must existence be a damnation?"

Clotilde quietly described the format of her future. "I shall remain with Zeller, be a dutiful wife, bear him children and make do with a *damned* destiny as hostage in a loveless marriage if it saves your life and Darius's.''

"If you do not believe we control our own destinies, Clotilde, all hope for us is gone.'' Tears welled in his eyes.

Pressing her hands to her breast, she said softly, "We must be brave. Dry those tears of love, beloved.''

Michael locked eyes with her. "My tears don't love you! They blight, curse, and *damn* you for lacking courage to stay with me!''

"Don't! Don't break my heart!'' she pleaded despairingly.

"Oh, Clotilde . . . I could never break your heart. You are breaking both our hearts. Oh, my beloved, my sweet sweet love, how you loved me! What right have you to throw away our love, our child? I beg you to reconsider what you are doing to us.''

"Michael . . . Michael, Michael, beloved Michael, you would have me believe in fairy tales? That there is a future for us?''

"I will die without you.''

"You will die *with* me. I refuse to spend the rest of my life looking over my shoulder in the expectation that what began at Positano will culminate in sudden violent death.'' She lifted her beautiful face, and like the dawn a light broke over the darkness and she fixed on him. "Why do you fail to perceive the extent of my love for you? My sacrifice is to keep you alive. Alive there is hope for us, for Darius. Dead, there is nothing.'' Her fixed gaze caused tears to mist her azure eyes.

"And I thought you lacked strength, Clotilde,'' he said quietly.

"I am a survivor. You too are a survivor. I sense this in you. Whoever said it is impossible to love and be wise may have said it of the common man. You and I are not common; we are indeed rare. Between us we have begotten a rarer specimen in Darius. More than our love child—he is a child of destiny! Let us not destroy him! Darius is our hope for the future!''

"You realize, Clotilde, we have placed our son into the hands of total strangers? Yes, that precious child for whom you sacrifice our love, our life, will be raised by strangers!''

Suddenly bent like a helpless tree in a gale, Clotilde paled.

"Explain very carefully, so that I comprehend what you say, because Dariana is no stranger to me, but more a sister. A bond exists between us, a bond joins us, one stronger than God Himself. Be careful what you say, for a wound inflicted by speech can be more damaging than a wound inflicted by a sword.''

Michael gazed from her pale face out at the vast expanse of water. How would he phrase the restlessness of an overburdened heart, the draining fatigue he felt. The thoughts besieging him. Straightforward and to the point; it was the only way. ''I get the strangest feeling that Vivaldi Bonifacio is not who he claims to be. My very dear, sweet Clotilde, the man is no Corsican peasant! And the Moor? What a strange combination. Did Dariana explain his presence? How he fits into the family setting?''

''It was not my privilege to pry.'' A chill shuddered through her. ''Michael, you sense a deception? If you *know* something, I beg you, tell me!''

''No, no, no! It's nothing like that!'' He embraced her. She trembled against him, fear visible in her voice and body. It's nothing tangible,'' he admitted. ''It's just that—well, the Moor knew the legend of the sword of Damocles.''

''The sword of Damocles? What has it to do with anything?''

''I left it with Vivaldi for Darius's legacy.''

''You gave it to *our* son? To Darius?'' She *knew* what the priceless treasure meant to him. The magnanimous gesture left her breathless.

''Pray, Clotilde, our trust in Dariana was not misplaced.'' He reflected on Vivaldi's words. *One day a favor will be exacted from you.* How Faustian of Vivaldi. Michael knew precisely the pact he'd made with Bonifacio. The purpose behind the pact was what evaded him.

At dinner aboard *The Golden Medusa,* everything crashed down around Michael. In an angry outburst at so cruel a situation, he flung his champagne glass at the wall opposite him. ''What will I do without you?'' he shouted, unprepared for Clotilde's reply.

''Live . . . marry . . . have children.''

Michael felt ice splash against his emotions, numbing him.

Clotilde persisted. ''Divert attention from us. Never hint you even know me. If we meet socially, appear to despise me. Hold me in contempt, if you can. If Zeller has the slightest inkling, he will kill you, ruin Burgatti-Bertelli, and destroy me however it suits his fancy.'' Her words, flowing like a volcanic eruption, would alter their lives, drastically change the course of Darius's life as well as the lives of several unborns.

Michael's feverish lips silenced her with wine-honeyed kisses.

"Beloved, before time and distance widen the breach beyond our reach and sight, let us feast on the banquet of our love, so we may remember its heady bouquet for all eternity. My kisses will burn your flesh; our love shall be cherished for all time."

Together they surrendered to love for the last time.

It would be two decades before they met again.

BOOK THREE

DARIUS BONIFACIO

Born a bastard, adopted by a madman,
he was programmed to kill . . . kill . . .
kill . . .

Intermezzo

In the decade of Darius's birth global events were gearing up aimed at the destruction of Western Europe.

In Berlin . . . legendary, vice ridden, symbol of the violence and insecurity of an era coiled behind the sequined facade of the Jazz Age sat poised like a serpent waiting to espumate the terror of the days to come.

In Italy . . . fascism continued to thrive in its halcyon days.

In Russia . . . Lenin's death paved way for the bloody leadership of a narrow-minded, crude, bitterly jealous man, Joseph Stalin, a many-faceted mad genius who would reshape Russian bureacracy into a gargantuan monolith. Commintern was transferred from the vanguard of world revolution into the frontier guard of Russia.

In China . . . waiting in the wings of a bloody war theater, preparing to bask in a spotlight of butchery and massacre, Mao Tse-tung engaged in brutal warfare against Chiang Kai-shek and the Kuomintang in which millions upon millions of lives would be slaughtered.

In America . . . a nation escaping the drama and misery of the postwar era embarked on wild spending sprees in a Golden Age where it was rumored that the streets of New York were paved in gold. The bubble burst on Black Thursday. The Great Crash led to the Great Depression bringing misery and ruin to millions globally, escalating instability in Europe and hastening the decline of great imperialistic powers.

In Germany . . . a nation was struggling to be reborn out of the ashes and rubble of the war dead. In the wake of the Versailles Treaty came strange whisperings that Europe was being reshaped in the mind of Adolf Hitler, fueled by British and Russian moneybelts.

In Corsica . . . an astutely implemented strategy commenced shaping Darius Bonifacio's malleable mind.

Chapter Twenty-two

It was a moment of revelation and controlled jubilation. Vivaldi paced the vendetta room, moving as if, periodically, charged with electrical currents. "Now I understand the delays . . . the obstacles. Don't you see? Destiny delivered Darius into our hands. God agrees with our vengeance against Zeller, else why would the child come as he did, like a miracle?"

"What hatches in your mind, Vivaldi?" the Moor asked, stacking firewood in the corner of the fireplace wall. "You seem driven by the need to justify his presence—"

"A miracle, Matteus!" Vivaldi interrupted. "A miracle! The answer to our dilemma. What we've searched for since our exodus from Spain." Pivoting on one foot, he turned to the Moor. "Face the truth. I am not the *right* man to knit together the powers described in the Garduna Parchments. God, that I were such a man! The power needed to undertake a project so vast in scope must be implanted in the consciousness from childhood."

Vivaldi's eyes sparked green fire. "Oh, my dear, faithful, trusted Matteus, I see my deficiencies in your knowing eyes. The truth . . . I suppose I've known it forever." He moved before the fireplace, scrutinizing the coat of arms overhead, staring at each finely tooled design, reciting by rote the words of his father that came to life on that fishing barque—how long ago? "Carry the seeds of vengeance forward into the loins of your sons. *Sons!* Well, Darius *is* my son. Agreed he's not the seed of my loins, but he is the conduit to Zeller. Darius will be the power—not Daniel, not any of my unborn sons, but Darius!"

Matteus let the scheme dovetail in his mind. When it did, a precise configuration jackhammered over the horizon of his brain. As the images perfected themselves, he sparked alive, listened acutely as the Spaniard ranted.

"Never, *never* did I possess the credentials to negotiate so powerful a future, but Darius will! By God, the Garduna Parchments will guide his destiny. He will organize the power! Daily, the tenets will become part of his mind, body, and soul until he is aflame with the injustices done to the de la Varga family. Until the fires of vendetta are etched eternally in his brain!"

How perfectly things fell into place on the drawing board of Vivaldi's mind. Matteus, considering the Spaniard's impassioned words, held his judgment in abeyance. Praise Allah! Darius was still in swaddling clothes!

Vivaldi, cradling Darius in his arms, took daily treks about the estate, programming the lad through suggestion, bringing the vendetta against Zeller into sharper focus. He spoke firmly to the infant Darius, accentuating the imperatives of family cohesion, repeating trigger words: *vengeance* and *vendetta*. He exalted blood revenge, stressed the necessity of inner strength, emphasizing discretion and secrecy in family matters.

"Whether or not the genes of Napoleon course through Darius's veins," he suggested to Matteus, "is another matter. What counts is the constant repetition of facts into the lad's consciousness. Think, Matteus, think! The effectiveness of such indoctrination over the years?" He shifted focus to the child. "Some men, Darius, live for country, some for family, others for God. You, my son, Matteus and I, live for the total annihilation of a man who skillfully seduced me, slaughtered my family, robbed me of wordly goods . . . And for this he must pay! Our existence, yours and mine, is valuable only as it relates to a vendetta waged against our eternal enemy, Amadeo Zeller!"

The words . . . unwaveringly repeated, day in and day out, continued in ominous ritual, until months melted into years.

Observing these goings-on, permitted no entrance into the circle of conspiracy brewing in her home, Dariana was climbing the walls, fighting demons, unable to exorcise them. Vivaldi's preoccupation with Darius to the exclusion of his own sons, Daniel and Robert, was manifesting itself in sibling rivalry. When her apprehension escalated beyond her ability to cope, her Corsican instinct forced a study of the situation.

Something very strange was happening in her household!

Be circumspect, she told herself. Wait . . . watch . . . worry— but when had worrying ever helped a situation? Never had she forgotten how Matteus had questioned her employment with Zeller. That Amadeo Zeller was covertly interlocked with Vivaldi in some hideous conspiracy ate at her and cut away at the foundation of her marriage. Could she approach Vivaldi without unearthing a pit of venomous vipers prepared to poison her marriage? She could not. The stiff price she paid: silence.

Robert had arrived six months after Darius. Eleven months later a daughter, Sophia, brought joy and laughter to an otherwise glum household. Sophia's birth provided Dariana with needed respite. Her large doe eyes and ebony curls evoked ineffable delight in Vivaldi. The sight of him hugging, smothering the cherubic baby with fervor, had redeemed him in Dariana's eyes. Then the fascination wore off, and the sickness commenced again.

Vivaldi's incurable excitement at Darius's slightest accomplishments to the exclusion of those of his sons mushroomed the sibling rivalry.

Dariana, in silence, paid scrupulous attention to the keg of dynamite threatening to explode the Bonifacio domicile. How could she openly challenge Vivaldi's doting on Darius? She couldn't, and instead muffled her anger, bridled her maternal fervor, forced to bide her time. The sensitive situation demanded tact, logic, diplomacy and intelligent handling. It was her own fault— all of it—her own doing. She had encouraged Marie Clotilde to leave Darius with her—hadn't she?

Dariana! The safe port in a love tempest!

On the day she realized Vivaldi's inextricable estrangement from her, Dariana pondered the perplexing problem objectively. When and how had the marital estrangement escalated? Why Vivaldi's intensified involvement with Darius had turned manic no longer mattered. Vivaldi's constant doting was influencing Darius's behavior, negatively.

The detente between husband and wife honed Dariana's clear-sighted focus. She got the impression that her husband had some hideous investment in the lad. *What?* She didn't know. The complexities of Vivaldi's behavior, juxtaposed to Darius's erratic moods, confused and frightened her. She became jealous of the indefinable element disrupting her family, and determined to ferret it out.

Vivaldi, she noted, pushed Darius harder than he did Daniel or Robert. Unwilling and unable to close her eyes to the surreptitious goings-on and the secret conclaves held in the vendetta room, Dariana was driven to get at the truth as if she were under mysterious orders. Driven, clinging tenaciously to her dedicated mission, Dariana bird-dogged the daily ritual. She gave no hints of her clandestine meanderings, darting in and about trees, ducking behind bushes, stone walls, to conceal herself.

But she was unable to come within hearing distance of Vivaldi's exhortations.

Dariana, gifted with the ability of winnowing the false from the true, seldom spoke unless her words were strikingly accurate. Because her love for Darius was equal to the love she felt for her own flesh and blood, she sharpened her focus and persevered in her study of her husband and Darius with the intensity of a gem cutter.

Darius, at age two, was given to periodic fits of temperament and a moodiness Dariana attributed to the upheavals Clotilde had suffered during pregnancy and premature delivery. Beauty had settled into his burnished features, bronzed by the Corsican sun. Large eyes of azure, fired by secret thoughts clicking on and off, followed every movement and living thing with insatiable curiosity.

Glimpses of his dual personality appeared in spurts before he was three. In the absence of Vivaldi's watchful eyes Darius commanded an articulate tongue. He laughed spontaneously, without inhibition. Vivaldi's presence converted him instantly into a reserved, attentive child, somber of face, cynical of pose. However turbulently those green eyes sparked, his defiance failed to manifest itself physically. Dariana, brooding over his bridled anger, wondered if it was fear or respect that kept this emotion dormant, building to an inevitable day of explosive tantrums.

At age four, Darius's mind worked out his questions by ceaselessly asking Dariana or Matteus, seldom Vivaldi, for it seemed he expected the child to *know* the answers. Darius did not quarrel easily with his brothers, but the rivalry between them precluded peaceful coexistence. As Vivaldi gave willingly of his time to Darius, limiting that spent with Daniel and Robert, the two sons skulked and brooded, nursing worse jealousies. Upbraided by either lad, Darius would withdraw behind an unpenetrable fortress as if he'd been dealt an undeserved blow.

And all this was driving Dariana mad!

At age five, Darius demonstrated a penchant for the military. In Ajaccio, he ran after the soldiers at the fort, imitating them, using sticks for guns, stones for bullets. He would doggedly soldier the plaza, marching . . . one, two, marching . . . one, two. One day Matteus returned from Ajaccio with a toy brass cannon. Delighted with the gift, Darius thundered about the great house, feigning the destruction of imaginary enemies in each room. From morning to night, his voice echoed through the house, "Boooooom! Boooooom! *Boooooom!*"

Darius's games of war, his unique strategy in imaginary ambuscades, captivated Matteus's attention. Utterly fascinated by the lad's activity, he directed Vivaldi's attention to the childish, but well-constructed fort of stones, sticks, and pebbles lined up all abreast, representative of a massive army. Listening to "General" Darius's verbal commands hurled at imaginary stone officers and pebbled army, both men agreed Darius's clumsy attempts at defense could put several military strategists to shame. In a burst of enthusiasm, Vivaldi proudly decreed, "He takes after my *conquistadore* ancestors. What warring men they were, eh?"

Matteus' tolerant chuckle failed to amuse the scowling Vivaldi, struck suddenly with the maddening truth: *not a drop of de la Varga blood flowed through Darius's veins*!"

On Darius's sixth birthday, Dariana had had enough. A truce was imperative—not capitulation, but a truce. Combining sensibilities, Corsican shrewdness and zeal, she added to the mental cauldron zest of cleverness and inescapable charm. She confronted Vivaldi. "Daily, my husband," she began in soft, alluring tones, "you remind Darius what a *special* child he is, no? Does it surprise you that I agree with your assessment that a *special* child needs *special* schooling?" Her guileful presentation couched with innuendo proved an unwanted entrapment. Fantasizing over the day he'd confront Zeller with Darius, his secret weapon, Vivaldi was caught unaware in this mental jousting with his wife. He retreated into a glowering silence.

In the next few weeks, Dariana's calm determination that everything must be sacrificed to bring her goal to fruition proved to Vivaldi that he'd married a woman of iron determination. She persisted, prodded him constantly, repeated his words of the recent past. When Vivaldi had his fill of her cleverness, and victory spilled into her corner of the invisible fight arena staked out in the privacy of their boudoir, his acquiescence contained one *proviso*. "Darius will attend the school of your choosing providing he is not a permanent boarder. I expect him home on weekends, holidays, and during the summer."

"Why not a military school?" Matteus's sternly voiced disapproval of the Jesuit School at Bastia was ignored. "Because my wife selected the Jesuits!" Vivaldi deferred with a tinge of rancor. It was helpless capitulation, thought the Moor, displeased at the arrangement.

Departure time . . . early before sunrise, packed, ready to leave. Darius hugged little Sophia. He shook hands with a sullen Daniel, and Robert, grumbling, wiped sleep balls from his eyes, crabby at the early hour. Darius's departure solved nothing. A new set of jealousies chewed at the lads. *Why Darius and not them? Why did he get to go away to school?*

Their mother's strategy escaped them. "In Darius's absence you'll both grow closer to your father," she insisted. God! How she prayed for this miracle! She lavished hugs and kisses on the young man standing before her dressed in his knickers and jacket with a tag on his lapel citing his name, address, and destination.

Darius donned his peaked cap, crushing his curly hair and promising exemplary behavior. He boarded the waiting lorry, fired by a rush of excitement. Tears welled in his eyes, his lower lip trembled and as the lorry wound its way down the steep hill and Terra Bonifacio evaporated behind him, he turned in his seat, brushed away the tears, unable to control the rising expectation of adventure churning in his guts.

With profuse farewells to Vivaldi and the Moor, Darius boarded the iron colossus belching steam from its underbelly. The engine lurched forward. Darius peered back through the grimy windows until the somber-faced men were reduced to specks in the dim distance. Traversing the length and breadth of this island en route to a new life with the Jesuits, he viewed the panorama, aware for the first time in his life how insignificant he was to the whole of Corsica. Cowed by the world of man, he briefly examined his *droit de seigneur*. Away from Vivaldi, out from under the smothering protection given a feudal land-baron's son, Darius shuddered deeply, freely, a weight lifted from his young shoulders.

*   *   *

Two secretly elated youths waited until Darius disappeared from their sights before scuffing back along the circular courtyard, kicking up clouds of dust, each secreting his innermost thoughts. Daniel, an impatient lad, fired by Spanish and Corsican temperament, detested idle talk and the shadow of obscurity to which his father's doting of Darius had relegated him. Noticeably indolent, disinclined to action, he lacked Darius's patient and bottomless curiosity. He loathed books and tutors. When Vivaldi had asked him to consider studying law when he grew to manhood, he countered with a simple, why? "Here in Corsica, who obeys the law?" He made heroes of bandits and hillsmen, intrigued by the primitive shepherds in the *maquis*. He filled his idle hours with speculation and fantasy. He disdained study sessions, content to ride horseback through the mysterious *maquis*.

Robert possessed Dariana's beauty. He was soft in voice and features, compelling of eye; the bitter winds and harsh sun of Corsica's interior couldn't darken his fair skin. Hazel eyes smoldered in passion, yet bore no ferocity. None of Daniel's wild, untamed anger diseased him. He entertained little interest in hunting, fishing, or guns, preferring instead to bury his head in the clouds and his books of sonnets. One never saw Robert after his fourth birthday without a book clutched in his hands. His enchanting grin, wide-eyed speculation, and look of a devoted hound-dog puppy always managed to coax and wheedle extra cookies or sweets from Dariana.

Neither lad spoke as they ambled to the rear gate, yet each uncharacteristically heaved sighs of relief. *At last, kings of their domain!* But their inability to articulate their detestation for Darius gave them pause. The futility of expending energy to loathe Darius hit them smack between the eyes. Truly they secretly admired him.

"Darius has neither lied to us, cheated, nor has he been cruel. He always keeps his promises," Robert began the brotherly discourse.

Daniel reluctantly agreed, but figured the scales didn't balance out. "Something about Darius is different from you or me, Robert. His temperament isn't like ours." Robert shrugged. The whole thing was getting too much for him. Two days later both lads confronted Dariana, asking her to explain the differences between them.

Dariana was dressing Sophia in a pale maize cotton batiste shift embroidered with pastel flowers, tying up her lustrous curls in ribbons. She listened to their persistent inquiries and with placating diplomacy she described each child as distinctly unique, separate and apart from the other, all gifts from God to their parents. "Rejoice in the differences, dwell upon them, and be led to your chosen destinies by the innermost whisperings of each individual soul."

The lads listened, Robert with ears attuned to his heart. But not Daniel. He retained a secret cynicism, masking a heated anger that would color his temperament and his life.

Before the week ended, each missed Darius as if a part of their body, dismembered, had withered and died.

Chapter Twenty-three

Father Amalfi Franchetti sat in the library in the subdued light of great bronze-footed candelabra. There were smoldering red logs on the mosaic-tiled hearth. The walls were alternately lined with books, assiduously collected for years, portraits of the Jesuit's predecessors, leading to the papal portrait in full regalia, ending with Jesus Christ Himself. Indifferent to the books, the Jesuit tugged at garnet velvet draperies drawn across the window, creating a tenseness in the atmosphere that Darius Bonifacio discerned at once.

Father Franchetti sat in his gilt throne chair near the fireplace, distinguished as usual in this distinguished hall, slowly sipping from a golden goblet of wine. Beckoning Darius closer, he laid the goblet on a long vast table of carved oak and, wiping the corners of his lips delicately with his fingertips, glanced at the young man with affectionate reservations. "Well, my son, how many times has your presence graced these walls?"

"Ten, sir."

"Ah, yes. Ten times. Ten years. A decade. You are a man, no? Nearly sixteen years, *si*? Please, please sit down. I take it you are well. Ten times, eh? Each time we have carefully reviewed your curriculum. Now, soon, you will leave for summer vacation, once again." At the smile rippling across Darius's face, the Jesuit nodded.

"In this decade you've been nourished by alluring images of new worlds, old and new philosophies and, I admit, you are well disciplined in philosophy, the sciences, art, and literature. Where did we fail you, Darius?"

"I beg your pardon, Father?"

The Jesuit repeated the question. "Why, out of all we've fed your brain, do none feed your psyche as your military studies?"

Darius's address was gentle, his manner frank and simple, his smile open, without duplicity. "If I learned anything, Father, from my enlightened tutors, it was not to deny the real self. I come alive when I study history. It is a beguiling study—"

"Which you retain with lightning accuracy. I swear, your tutors come to me with wild tales. Do you know what they tell me? They swear you had intimately lived, through previous incarnations, every era of history you studied. That's how in tune you are with your studies." The Jesuit sipped his wine. "And this absorption with Napoleon! How do you explain your feelings about Napoleon? It poses an unsolvable puzzle to the Jesuit fathers!"

Darius sat stiffly in the chair opposite the Jesuit, uncertain where this was leading. "I'm not certain I can explain, Father. I know only that the moment the subject was introduced, lights clicked on in my mind and everything concerning the emperor— the Napoleonic Wars, his brilliant warring strategies and the tactics he deployed has held me captive. Perhaps in these aspects are mirrored my hopes, dreams, ambitions, and fears."

Franchetti turned the stem of his goblet in his slender fingers, his lips set in a secret, implacable curve. "You are indeed a phenomenon, Darius. Actually you astound me with that stellar intelligence and that uncanny photographic memory—if that's what it is giving you incredible insight to history—as well as the flawless articulation of political rhetoric. I confess at times you confound me."

"It is not my intent to confound you, Father. I merely search for answers," he retorted, always acutely aware of the thoughts passing in the minds of others with near-clairvoyant powers.

"Nevertheless I regard you with both marvel and constant irritation."

Darius remained silent. Each moment made him less secure in his position. Left-handed compliments followed by right-handed rebukes baffled him. Why didn't the father speak what was really on his mind?

"For the past decade I have recorded your geniuslike progress with dedicated fervor, praying for signs that labeled you, uh, *normal*. Normal, Darius, I could deal with, but not a genius. Not a *genius* who corrects me in the Scriptures and philosophy, a subject upon which I pride myself. I daresay you are *not* the most welcome student in my midst." His tone was facetious, but a sternness underlay it. "Remember, Darius, military men are usually evil men. Inexorable fate usually overtakes them. This is the evidence of history. Unfortunately, before their punishment is meted out, the innocent are lost. I had truly hoped you would become a man of peace. A great man of peace! Alas." He held up an envelope in his hand. "It has taken me a decade, ten long years before I could actually bring myself to write the contents of this envelope."

Darius sat forward, expectantly, unsure what that white envelope contained. The Jesuit sipped the remains of his wine.

"This then is my recommendation." He opened the letter addressed to *Signore* Vivaldi Bonifacio and read the contents. Darius listened without reaction, waiting as the Jesuit summed up his observations. "And so, after considerable deliberation and soul searching assessment, the Jesuit Fathers recommend that Darius be transferred to St. Cyr Military Academy the next semester. Darius has been gifted; he sees everything in the perspective of military strategies perceiving all solutions in terms of defensive and offensive actions. Astounding! Regretfully, at times despairingly I've wished and articulated that desire, hoping Darius would focus his genius on other than military matters. Dear God! All that interests your son is war! Warfare, generals and armies!"

Father Franchetti was wrong. A matter that most excited Darius contained no military shadings at all. *Summer vacation!* Time to spend with his little sister Sophia whom he adored. Images of Sophia, with the wind blowing that riotous mass of ebony curls framing her seraphic face, were what sustained him year in, year out, all these years. With her small hand clasped in his, those adoring doe eyes uplifted to his in hero worship, they had strolled about the Bonifacio lands through feathery green ferns and exquisite summer blooms engaged in the art of serendipity. How simple and uncomplicated a blithe spirit was Sophia. She loved Darius with innocent purity, trusting him implicitly. Ineffably delighted with her curiosity and wealth of questions, Darius had pointed out the land's beauty and its

inherent dangers, and upon occasion, encroaching on the bewitching *maquis,* he had picked massive bouquets of wildflowers
at the ancient citadel, seated on the ramparts of the broken stone
wall overrun with cascading bowers of fragrant myrtle, pink and
white heather. Oh, what stunning air castles they built! Enticing
princedoms in marvelous, faraway castles in which they reigned
as king and queen came brilliantly alive for them. They dreamed
of a magic carpet able to transport them at the blink of an eye to
the moon and the stars.

Oh, how Darius loved and cherished every moment spent with
Sophia. In her company he could be the child he was never
allowed to be during his formative years. Her adoring, uncondi-
tional love, demanding nothing in return, overwhelmed him.

Now, as school semester was coming to a close, Darius would
face a Sophia growing into womanhood.

At Terra Bonifacio, Spaniard and Moor, ensconced in the vendetta room, meticulously planned the annihilation of Amadeo
Zeller.

It was summer. Darius was expected in less than two weeks.
The Garduna Parchments were fully decoded, their organizational procedures scrupulously studied. Both men marveled at
the cleverly designed statues Darius had assimilated over the
years and memorized on the previous summers spent in dedicated seclusion.

Vivaldi was pleased. The Moor raved ecstatically over Darius's
unique talents. Truly, he thought, Allah had sent them the
warrior of all warriors to champion their cause. He ran his
tawny-skinned fingers through his black hair, streaked with shimmering gray. His beard, shaven clean for many years, was
growing back, a brighter shade than in his youth.

Soon, now, very soon . . .

The Spanish Civil War was two years old when Darius, approaching his sixteenth birthday, arrived at Terra Bonifacio for summer
vacation. That night, after dinner, Daniel and Robert drove to
Ajaccio. Darius remained behind, involved in a heated debate
with Vivaldi and Matteus over Franco's decision to seek aid
from the Axis nations.

"France will regret not coming to Spain's aid. You'll see,
Father," Darius insisted. "Her importance in world affairs is
declining. France, like other nations, permits Hitler liberties

because she is running scared. She helped create the monster, turned him loose, and hasn't the sense to see Hitler is stalking her, waiting for the proper time to pounce on her. Has anyone condemned Italy's bold and audacious colonialization attempts in Africa?" He snorted. "What is it France calls it? Appeasement. Even the British call the policy '*Appeasement.*' The calculated policy of surrendering to Hitler's and Mussolini's demands is called appeasement? *Mon Dieu, Papa!* It's a fiasco. Are the British lion and French leopard blind to the dangers if Germany and Italy intervene in Spain?" Darius mosied over to a large bas relief map on the wall in Vivaldi's study, thumped the area of Spain with the panache of an irritated history professor trying to make a point with dunderheaded students. "An imbecile can see the folly. Once Spain is tucked into their hip pockets, Il Duce and Hitler will swallow France, target their aggressions westward through Poland, and move down the Middle East to control the Mediterranean and the oil fields Russia has coveted for so long. In no time, all Europe will fall under the shadow of the Axis nations. Surely you see through their clever offensive? France must assert herself, reinforce her position, and form alliances with Great Britain and Poland. Unless they unite and move with grim determination to squash the German dictator, it will be finis for La Belle France, for Great Britain too. To delay is suicide."

Vivaldi and Matteus beamed at the lad's clear-sighted perception. Dariana had entered the room moments before and stood mesmerized by Darius's comportment, his clear, incisive grasp of the situation. But neither of the three were prepared for the next pronouncement.

"I want your permission to attend St. Cyr's Military Academy, Father," Darius began calmly. "We shall be at war shortly. It is foolish and incautious to remain unprepared in the face of the staggering statistics heralding war. Daniel and Robert should also go to St. Cyr, be prepared to serve France."

"No." Vivaldi's terse refusal demanded justification. "You are only fifteen years old."

"By St. Cyr's standards that's considered old. Besides, the Jesuit fathers tell me I speak with the maturity of a man twice my age. My logic is beyond my chronological age. I will be sixteen in August."

"I don't give a fig for the Jesuits' opinions. I am your father and you'll do as I say."

Darius staggered momentarily under the sharp rebuttal, then

regained his composure and spoke with clinical detachment. "When war comes and we display unpreparedness, let it be on your conscience if your sons are struck down for lack of tactical weaponry knowledge. A hunter with a wolf gun is no measure against a well-trained soldier."

"Darius! I have neither the patience nor the inclination to discuss a nonexistent war. Why do we speak in hypothesis?"

"Why? Because you must assume that Italy wants Corsica, Tunisia, and other French African colonies. Il Duce grows powerful. His war chests overflow with gold. He is colonizing everything in sight and no one checks him. Listen, Father, fascism is a tempting system. Il Duce maintains formidable military strategists to plot his conquests. Have you taken time to study his Fascist Youth Movement? He begins with the child in premilitary training. One day he will have a ready army of inspired soldiers. Even Germany has followed Italy's lead. Read *The Fascist Documents*, they chronicle the future. War is inevitable! There is a world beyond your *vendetta* room, Father, and it is stirring up powerful forces."

Spaniard and Moor grew introverted, each nurturing thoughts that suddenly threatened their world. Dariana linked her arm through Darius's and drew him from the upstairs study through the sitting room toward the butter room, reminding him of his promise to take Sophia into Ajaccio to visit her grandparents.

"Why doesn't Father listen to me? Don't they know what is happening? Don't they care?"

"Because, my son, it doesn't touch us yet. The moment it does, you'll see a swift response." Dariana kissed and hugged him. "How good to see you," she said, beaming. "I can't believe how you've grown. I hardly know you anymore."

"Locking the barn doors after the rape of mares is foolhardy."

"Darius! What words to speak in a house where females abide!" For a moment their eyes locked, then laughter pealed through the great house. "Be patient," she cooed, still smiling.

June flew swiftly. July evaporated. It was mid-August. Darius was crushed. Vivaldi gave him no opening to discuss St. Cyr. Attempts at conviviality with his brothers reinforced the rivalry between them. Nothing was going well until Matteus saved the summer by suggesting they celebrate Darius's sixteenth birthday by hunting the elusive *moufflon*. "What an impressive trophy those golden horns make over any hunter's mantelpiece," the Moor suggested provocatively.

And so it was that the experienced hunters gathered at the base of Mount Cinto two nights before Darius's birthday. Matteus called the lads around the fire to issue a list of imperatives. "Stay close to the seasoned hunters," he cautioned. "Don't venture alone onto the icy tors without a guide. As you climb higher into the cold each new step brings unexpected obstacles and enormous dangers."

For two days and nights, hunters traversed the mountains, returned each night, exhausted, hungry, frustrated at not sighting the *moufflon,* yet willing to commence afresh the next day. Darius's impatience with the old hunters drew a rebuke from the Moor.

"They content themselves to sit about campfires, smoking red clay pipes, tossing off bumpers of wine, and spinning tall yarns rather than tracking game," he protested.

"It's all part of the ritual, Darius. Be patient. Perhaps their courage needs reinforcing. Telling tales is as important to the hunt as the stalking and final kill."

Darius, despite Matteus's earlier warnings, persisted in taking detours on his own to pursue the *moufflon.* On his return, the Moor, in a rare display of temper, castigated him. He took the lad aside and spoke out of the hearing of the hunting party.

"Hear me, and hear me well, Darius. I am not inclined to chew my words twice. The *moufflon* is very clever, wise in the ways of man. He is cautious, tricky, infinitely better acquainted with the terrain than any human. Scores of hunters arrive in Corsica with dreams of hunting *moufflon* and never, *never* catch a glimpse of him. So clever is his imperial highness, he posts wary-eyed sentinels everywhere to protect him from hostile, gun-carrying intruders with murder in their hearts."

Matteus's words, meant to hold Darius in check, merely increased the lad's desires to confront the enigmatic beast. He slept fretfully that night, near the fires, chilled yet excited by his secret thoughts. He arose before dawn, scurried quietly about the campfires searching for extra food rations—brook trout and bread. He wrapped the fish in green chestnut leaves, shoved chestnuts in his pockets, strapped on his knapsack, and slung a *lupara* over one shoulder, the pellets in his pocket. He stole out of camp long before sunup, following the trail taken the previous day along a worn goat track, up the slopes of snowcapped Mount Cinto.

Darius had hiked past three climate zones without any sense of time. He traversed rambling countryside, rising hills, villages with slender church spires. He had waved to shepherds grazing their sheep, pausing to listen to their chant, a familiar sound of his childhood. The panorama changed dramatically from babbling brooks to swift torrents, high granite gorges, thundering waterfalls. Darius, enormously excited, paused to drink from the waterfall. These were the same harsh granite walls and snowcapped peaks he'd seen all his life from Terra Bonifacio and on train rides to and from school. What a revelation to see them close up!

He must have walked for three hours when he noticed a pink blush of dawn in the eastern sky. Fields of snow extended from a clear lake to the highest reaches of the summit, covered by blinding white ice deceptively camouflaging a perilous area unknown to Darius. The summit appeared speciously near, yet in his three-mile ascent the perspective had varied only slightly. Darius paused on the ridge, breathing heavily, his arms and shoulders aching from the tension. Time to eat, a snack, rest and continue the trek. He retrieved the trout from the knapsack, unwrapped the large leaves, bit into the food, stopped, hand poised in midair, arrested by the sight.

Moufflon! The Corsican monarch! Less than fifty feet away!

Darius would remember this moment forever. They eyed one another from a distance, the eager-eyed young hunter with knapsack and gun, and the *moufflon*, with glazed black eyes peering in profile at his mortal enemy—man.

Darius held out the food. The animal, arching his imperious head, fixed his incandescent eyes suspiciously on the young hunter. He sniffed the air, bridling slightly. Slowly, he backed off, wise in the ways of man. Darius spotted the sentinels moving to protect their leader as he inched off the snow-covered peaks to greener meadows below. They pawed the earth, prepared to charge and destroy the enemy. What impressive teamwork, thought Darius, observing the forward sentinels fall into place before their king. Just like a perfect military offensive! He followed the herd, losing all sense of time, direction and distance.

The most difficult part of the ascent over the snow track was gaining a foothold. He improvised by digging steps with the end of his *lupara*, and cautiously placed one booted foot after the other into each track. Suddenly an icy obelisk loomed before him, towering some thirty feet into the air, narrowing to a sharp peak. To climb further meant dangling in midair some nine thousand feet above the sea.

Darius felt incredible awe. Breathing heavily in the thinning air he turned in utter stupefaction, caught up by the breathtaking beauty of the panorama beyond the glaring white, shimmering mass. He stretched his vision across dazzling waters to the Tuscan Islands, to Italy where the snowy peaks of the Maritime Alps and the whole sweep of coastline from Nice to Rome was visible. To the south, Sardinia. To the west, the Spanish Costa del Sol.

Darius stood above the clouds, experiencing the heady intoxication of the view. A feeling of tremendous power galvanized him. He experienced sensations that would form the foundation of strength from which he would draw needed powers in the future.

The thinning air slowed him down, his breathing grew increasingly labored. Briefly, the sun surrendered to fleecy white clouds, and he felt chilled to the bone. Thank God Matteus had forced him to wear gloves and a cap. He'd never climbed this high before, hadn't known what to expect. The climatic changes were severe, unexpected.

Darius moved over a snowbank, stopped abruptly. There, several yards away on a snowy outcrop stood the majestic *moufflon* in his domain. Darius squatted, eased himself in closer, cursing his lack of foresight in neglecting to bring a camera. He didn't question his penchant for *moufflon*. He only knew some mysterious force drove him toward the beast inexplicably. He felt a curious kinship. He inched closer.

The ballet began. For nearly an hour his approach to the beast was resisted. The closer Darius got to him, the further the animal retreated.

Now . . . they stood twenty feet apart. Darius dusted the snow from an area of flat rock, placed morsels of food on it, and stepped back a few feet, coming dangerously close to the precipice.

He turned suddenly, feeling queasy. Without warning the earth trembled under him, the flimsy snow on which he perched disintegrated. He recognized the pitch of his own fear as he fell through air and snow. He reached frantically for something to grasp, anything to break his fall. Miraculously his fingers clung to an icy ledge; below him was a sheer drop of five thousand feet. He panicked. Sweat poured off his face in the icy temperature.

How long would he last before fear paralyzed him? Killed him before the actual death plunge?

In these moments Darius cried out for help. His voice ricocheted off snowy peaks, echoing feebly through canyons below. Warned never to look down when scaling precipices of treacherous heights, he committed the unpardonable sin and fell prey to a more sinister menace—vertigo! Held in its lethal grips, everything below him swam dizzily. The futility of his plight registered in his brain, unleashed uncontrollable nausea. Darius fought it strenuously. One twitch, the slightest move, his hands weakening an iota . . .

His eyes filled with unwanted images; twisting roads resembled strings, arched causeways bridging ravines. He hung by his hands like a circus aerialist, body suspended in midair. Darius focused overhead.

A shadow was transformed into the giant head and horns of a *moufflon*. Its eyes peered over the precipice ridge, its head tilted obliquely, the horns not far from Darius's hands. Relief surged through him. He hadn't fallen the distance he had earlier surmised. His hands cramped, growing weaker. How much longer would he last? Could he—if he lunged quickly—reach for the horn? What if the animal bolted, shook him free, hurled him into space like a rag doll?

Before this conjecture ran its course, the *moufflon* disappeared. Darius, still sweating, could bear little more physical punishment. His arms felt as if they'd pop their sockets. The backpack weighted him down and the *lupara* felt like a ton. *Think, Darius, think! Perhaps you can maneuver them off your back . . .*

In the name of the Father, Son, and the Holy Ghost . . .

This wasn't happening to him. He'd made no bargain with death—not before his sixteenth birthday! He forced his eyes downward, inch by inch on the wall before him. Was it possible? Were his eyes playing tricks? A few yards below, a parapet jutted out from a wall, like a ledge! He had no time for measuring his weight against the durability of the ledge. His hands were frozen to the ice he clung to for dear life. Propelling his body forward, he gathered momentum, swaying. The moment his body swung flush to the icy revetment, Darius let go!

Merciful Jesus! He made it!

Solid ice held his weight. Snow fell like silent thunder, showering him with clumps of powder. Winds howled through holes in the mountain. The pall of fear clung to him, chilling him. Frozen into immobility, he could not think.

Why hadn't he listened to the Moor?

Perched like a broken-winged bird over a swarm of salivating cats, he dared not move. Thousands of feet above and at either side of him, an incredibly blue sky stretched to infinity. Never in a million years could Darius have contemplated what followed.

He was freezing. His backpack contained a heavy sweater, sun goggles, and brandy for medicinal purposes. Could he, if he dared, turn his body about? He faced the mountain wall, not daring to move. The backpack extended at least a foot from his body, perhaps more. If he could slip off the pack one arm at a time . . .

First, the *lupara*. Easy now . . . Good! He lay the weapon at his feet without bending his knees. Now slip the strap from one arm . . . that's it, easy now . . . now the other . . . slip it off nice and easy. He was nearly home free. A gust of wind tunneled at him. He leaned in closer to the wall. *Voilà!* Off came the pack. He grasped the strap—it was slipping, slipping! He lost! He turned slightly in time to see it go sailing into space. The move broke off a piece of the icy shelf. Shuddering, Darius flattened his body against the wall, his shivering lips turning blue.

Thundering sounds, rumbles he was unable to distinguish, came at him; he swore he felt the very mountain itself tremble. But how could that be? Mountains don't move . . . unless? Impossible, there've been no earthquakes in Corsica! His lips moved in prayer.

Merciful Christ! Even Matteus's Allah, hear my supplication! If you see my plight, come help me!

Snow to the left, snow to the right, snow above and death below, he dared not move! Still the rumbling sounds came closer. To his left, he discerned a curious disturbance in the structure of the snow wall. *What is it? Am I going snow blind as well as mad?*

Everything was gone, snow goggles, backpack, food. He had no hammer, chisel, or grappling hooks to assist in his plight. It was only a question of time before he succumbed to the elements and died.

Poor Sophia. She'd miss him dreadfully. He hadn't spent nearly enough time with her this summer. She'd grown up, all right. . . . Thoughts of Sophia fired his anger at his predicament.

Damn the devil! Somewhere in his mind a solution existed. He had to think. He made a dozen attempts to ferret out avenues of escape concluding, a half hour later, that none existed. *If* Matteus and the hunters had tracked him to the promontory above, his tracks indicated he'd fallen. The hunters would retreat, send out search parties below to recover his remains.

Merde! Think, Darius! You can't just stand here!

He studied the wall before him, scraped at it with his gloved hand, reached at his waist for a knife, shaved away the snow bit by bit until he struck stone. The rumbling sounds stopped periodically, then recommenced, growing more audible. Darius continued to cut away the snow until he stood on an additional foot of icy ledging.

An enormous gust of wind tunneled at him and Darius thought it would blow him off the niche. Then he heard a loud savage animal cry. To his immediate left a portion of the snowy wall crumbled and fell away. The savage cry shook him, and turning from the wall, he stared into the glaring eye of an enormous predator. A fierce-eyed golden eagle hovered less than ten feet away from him. Darius did not move. He did not breathe. He held his knife-wielding hand outthrust. The winged predator turned, sensing an upwelling current of warm air. It circled, rising higher, higher on the updraft, and hung suspended at ten thousand feet. Suddenly folding its wings, the eagle hurtled toward earth in a compelling stoop maneuver after prey.

Darius sighed in relief. Dull thumping sounds caught his attention. Real or illusory? Iced to the bone, teeth chattering as the sun moved past its apex into western skies, he inched back against the snow wall as another portion of the ledge gave way. He dropped his body, squatted, arms wrapped about his knees to keep warm.

There! Again! Thumping sounds, louder than ever! He wasn't hallucinating! To his right were blinding crystalline snowy walls, to his left, blocks of ice, resembling marble. He *knew* what lay below, refused to look. His eyes fixed on the wall to his immediate left.

It shifted in contour! Jesus! It was crumbling! Breaking away, falling into space below him! A snow slide? Avalanche? *What in God's name? He'd be buried alive!* Crouched to one side of a snow-spouting geyser, he stared at the apparition in uncertain awe. The wall was breaking up! He saw a gaping hole widen. Summoning his courage, he forced himself to look upon the miracle. When he clearly discerned the strange sight, he stared, stupefied, unable to believe his eyes.

The moufflon! The golden horns of the moufflon!

The animal had burrowed through a honeycombed cave to save him. Man and beast eyed one another. Darius, motionless, dared not speak or flick an eye. The *moufflon,* withdrawing briefly, returned. He gazed imperiously at Darius, raising, lowering its head, retreating once again. Darius swore the animal attempted some form of communication. Numbed by the ordeal, Darius shifted focus to the obstacle preventing him from jumping—a four-foot open space leading to instant eternity below. One miscalculation, a fraction of an inch off in timing or propulsion and it was *finis* for Darius. Did he have a choice? No! If he wanted to survive this ordeal, it was onward and forward.

Darius inhaled, exhaled repeatedly until he got the circulation going in his body. He rubbed his fingers together, blew hot breath on them until they tingled. He slipped on his gloves, then, suddenly inspired, picked up the *lupara,* aimed, tossed it into the cave, observing the path it took as it curved in an arc, landing inside the opening. How could his body accomplish the feat? He measured angles, distance, and momentum. There wasn't the slightest chance he could gather the needed momentum to catapult his body into the cave. Dear God! It was suicidal to remain on the parapet and suicidal to leap. *No time for speculation, Darius, move!* He told himself if he survived he need never combat fear again.

He was stalling and knew it. A large hunk of snow gave way under his right foot. Darius crouched and sprang, arms outthrust, head pulled in, landing half inside, half out, his lower limbs dangling in midair. His icy fingers were digging, hand over hand deeper into the snow. He began to slip. He was falling . . . there was no way . . . oh God . . .

Coming at him at a brisk trot, from the dark cave, was the *moufflon.* He poked out his head, angled it, laid his horn close to Darius's hand. Instinctively, Darius did what was necessary. He swallowed hard and in a quick movement released one hand, grabbed hold of his lifeline to safety, then releasing the other, clutched the horn tightly. He felt himself lifted and dragged inside the cave, then hurled several feet into the air, landing a few feet within the secure darkness. Forcing his body into a lateral roll, he propelled himself closer to a shaft of dim light coming from the opposite end of the honeycomb. *Lupara* in hand, he moved painfully forward until the dim light grew brighter.

Vaguely he saw movement. The *moufflon*, backing up through the tunnel, emerged into daylight. Darius's heart pounded furiously. He was numb. Pausing now and again, moving when he could, he reached the tunnel to the entrance.

He made it! The *moufflon* had saved his life!

Emerging into the daylight, Darius's hands flew to the burning pain that seared his eyes. Shapes, forms, images, everything blurred at once. Shielding his burning, snowblind eyes with his hands, he stumbled forward, falling prostrate at the pinnacle base where earlier he'd placed food. His eyeballs felt as if hot coals were flung upon them. He fell to his knees, scooping up snow, packing his eyes until relief came.

Dropping his hands from his eyes, he peered about, barely able to make out the kingly *moufflon*, the wary-eyed sentinels at the perimeters of a circle ringing him like a king at court. Darius staggered to his feet slowly. A baby *moufflon* sprinted stiff-legged, stopped short like a child at play.

Darius saw it first. The sentinels, suddenly alert, sniffed the air, peering about the flatland. The hero who saved his life stood his ground less than five feet away. Darius purred softly, wanting to pet the sable-coated beast out of sheer gratitude. The *moufflon's* glazed eyes sparkled, shifted focus, his nostrils flaring. The sentinels pawed the earth.

Thunderous blasts of guns from behind deafened him. Darius froze at the shock and betrayal registered in the *moufflon's* eyes as it sank to its knees, blood spurting from a gaping hole between its eyes. Sickened at the sight, he whirled around to see the hunters shooting wildly. Two sentinels were instantly felled; their bleating sounds pierced Darius's heart. Blood the color of claret wine oozed from their heaving bodies, streaming in spurts onto the white snow. The spectacle of death felt like a dozen knives twisting savagely in Darius's heart. They struggled, tried to rise to their feet, but weakened limbs, in combat with death, succumbed.

As long as he lived Darius would never forget the grisly nightmare that followed. He spun around, his vision still impaired, but not so he was unable to detect the smiles of triumph on ugly, bearded faces. Without thought, without first weighing the consequences of his actions, Darius, *lupara* in hand, fired at the gloating men.

Vaguely he heard his name called before he blacked out.

* * *

Six hours later he awakened in his room at Terra Bonifacio. Three shadows hovering nearby were transformed into a solemn-faced, troubled Matteus, seated at the foot of the bed and Vivaldi standing at the window with a stormy countenance. A stranger sat in a rocking chair. He was Don Lupo Feruggio, a house guest, from Palermo, Sicily.

Memory returned to Darius with a jolt. He was back at the meadow atop Mount Cinto with the *moufflon*. He cried out in vexation. "They killed him! They *killed* him! Vile contemptible cowards! He saved my life—don't you understand? What right had they to kill so brave a beast?" he cried over and over in feverish despair.

It took Vivaldi an hour to string together the facts of Darius's incredible tale. Vivaldi, at last, huddled with Matteus and the Sicilian don. At least Darius had explained his rash behavior in the killing of two Corsican hillsmen, but it did not vindicate the act.

The Sicilian don, his hawk face without expression, snapped dryly, "*Va bene,* the Corsicans are dead. Your son's marksmanship is superb. *Allora, Signore* Vivaldi, there is hell to pay. Prepare yourself for the consequences."

Dariana moved closer from the shadows, gently chastising Darius. "Didn't Matteus warn you not to go tracking by yourself? You could have been killed!"

"He was beautiful, Mother. Imagine, he dug a hole through a honeycombed cave to rescue me." He recanted his story to a bewildered but attentive woman.

When he finished she turned to her husband. "And those butchers shot the *moufflon*?"

Vivaldi lumbered to the bed, sat down next to Darius, his expression somber. "You realize, my son, you have killed two human beings? Two Corsicans."

"They were despicable and deserved their fate!"

"Darius! You shot two human beings because they shot an animal or two? Do you not see the inhumanity of your act? Your lack of logic?"

Darius's passion, burning at furnace intensity, provided no room for logic or reasoning. Dariana's anxiety heightened. "Surely, my husband, they do not demand blood vengeance?"

"*Your* Corsican heritage can better answer what *they* will or will not demand." Vivaldi gave his wife a strange, compelling look. "Watch over the children. I shall set out the hounds. Be circumspect in our absence. We must find Chamois Barbone to rectify the day's wrongdoings."

The older man left the house.

It was impossible for Dariana to have any other thoughts than Darius's well-being. Darius's eyes were closed, feigning sleep. It's just as well, she thought, why instill the lad with my own paranoia until we know for certain.

Pulling the covers around him, she turned off the light and left, closing the door behind her. In the kitchen she set a large pot of coffee to brew. Darius's ornately iced birthday cake sat on a shelf in the butter room awaiting a ceremonial lighting of candles. She puttered about, busying herself, unaware this would be the longest night in her life.

The moment Dariana left his room, Darius sprang from the bed, took a moment to gather his strength before he dressed, and crept cautiously out of the room. He carried his boots down the stone staircase, easing along in the shadowed hall past the sitting room where his brothers and Sophia were playing the card game *rouge et noir*. He opened the front door, slipped outside, and sprinted to the stables. Donning his boots, he saddled up a gelding. He cantered quietly beyond the rear gate, then broke into a wild gallop in an effort to catch up with Vivaldi's lorry. They headed toward Mt. Rotunda.

Twilight descended. Darius, keeping the lorry in his sights, trailed at a respectable distance. He had no idea of their destination. He knew only that he needed to be a part of whatever it was he had caused to happen.

An hour later—or was it more—darkness enveloped the land, the only illumination a giant harvest moon. Darius trailed the steep incline toward the flatland where he saw Vivaldi park the lorry. It was at the end of a seemingly vanished winding path where lighted torches were posted outside a straw hut. Ancient bergers in sheepskin, with fierce penetrating eyes, carried *luparas* and stood guard at the entrance.

Darius slid from his saddle, tethered the gelding to a tree trunk, estimating they were somewhere high in the mountains of Niolo, the heart of bandit country. Creeping up the steep incline, he eluded the guards, circled around, and scaled the height between intermittent rocks, crouching behind them to conceal his body. Grabbing shrubs and rock projections, in a hand-over-hand movement, he pulled himself upward, coming closer and closer to the sounds of human voices engaged in heated diatribe.

He made it. Positioning himself at one of the windowlike openings, Darius squinted, trying to make out the faces in the shabby, lantern-lit interior. Hostility and hatred thickened the air. Darius, adjusting his focus made out Vivaldi, Matteus and Don Feruggio standing before a crude table before an imperious Chamois Barbone. Gathered behind them, in a semicircle, he counted twelve bearded and fierce-eyed barbarous men carrying menacing guns.

Vivaldi, dressed nattily in the attire of a country squire, stroked his recently acquired mustache, and in a sudden movement placed a white linen square before Barbone, on the table. The *maquis* leader scratched his beard, observing the wealthy landowner with inimical hegemny. He scrutinized the gold ring of the Marten on Vivaldi's left forefinger, sucking loudly on his gold tooth. His look was sardonic, his voice biting. "I am curious to see how you intend to explain away two deaths."

"I came to correct the wrongful deaths of your cousins," began Vivaldi. "Accidental deaths are puzzling—"

"*Accidental deaths!*" the Corsican bleated angrily, jumping to his feet, kicking back the box he sat on. "Your son *murdered* my cousins in broad daylight in the presence of witnesses, and you dare call it *accidental*?" He looked at the others. "But this is the final insult, Bonifacio. This is too much!"

"Yes. *Accidental!* Understand me, Barbone, I do not engage in capricious conversation." Vivaldi stared at the man's flat skull, his iron features, as he slipped the knot on his money pouch. He tossed the sack on the table. "I came prepared to pay reparations to the dead men's family."

"I spit on your gold, Bonifacio!" Chamois exploded. His spittle landed inches from the pouch. "What is money to us, eh? If you heaped it to the clouds, we would remain here, where we live, not like you in that costly house, the majority of which remains closed, unoccupied. Too splendid for the likes of Corsicans, no? You think money erases the murder done by your son?" He let flow the sickening bile of jealousy. The twelve Corsican men muttered approval, spurring Chamois on. "Here, our *honor* is at stake. Your gold insults us. That you came, daring to buy our honor as you'd buy a dozen eggs, will not be forgotten!"

"If I believed you," countered Vivaldi, "*and I don't*, I would have paid my respects to your brother in Marseilles, not you. Oh, perhaps you aren't aware we've become business acquaintances in the past few years?''

Chamois, disconcerted by the words, scanned the faces of the twelve Corsicans in scowling silence. Observing the interplay between them, the Moor tensed. *These crazy men preferred a gunfight to the end.* Arbitration to them was anathema.

Chamois, contemplating Vivaldi's words, opened the money sack, dramatically spilling the coins to the table from shoulder height, his astonishment evident at the sum. Vivaldi conciliated.

''More than enough to support the men's families, no?''

The Corsican reset the box in its upright position. He sat down, sucked on his tooth. ''In the unwritten laws of vendetta, the demands are blood revenge. This son of yours is *un augellone*, an evil bird. When the dead men were laid at the feet of their widows, my cousins, they wept with grief. They demand revenge. They made their vows at that moment. The women will cut not one strand of hair from their heads until it is washed in the blood of your son. The sons and daughters of my dead cousins will not rest until the skull of the young *augellone* lies bleaching in the sun, like this one.'' He kicked at the remains of a bleached sheep skull on the earthen floor.

''My son is a boy of fifteen.'' Vivaldi's voice grew deadly. ''What knowledge has he of vendetta?''

''The dead men's sons are under that age and know first hand its meanings. The blood of their dead ancestors demands retribution.''

''My son is incapable of deceptions. He studies with the Jesuits at Bastia and—''

''Priests? *Jesuits*?'' Loud guffaws exploded from the Corsican's thick lips. He spat onto the earthen floor. ''Then truly he is *un augellone!*''

''My son's life is meaningful. One day he will sit at the head of the Corsican brotherhood. Only he has the power to unify Corsicans!''

Darius, listening, gave a start. *What did his father mean—the brotherhood?*

''If you need exact your pound of flesh for the dead men, take my life. Spare the lad. I tell you, Barbone, only he has the power!''

''You're some crazy man, Bonifacio. I knew it long ago, but today the truth rings as clear as the tower bells. The deaths must be avenged! Corsican laws were born out of centuries of bloodshed and will extend beyond my time on earth.''

They parried back and forth, Vivaldi's mood growing blacker. ''Why will you not believe, Corsican, it was an accident? Unintentional? Kill my son Darius and you annihilate Corsica. He is truly the son of Corsica as only one man before him was.'' Vivaldi handed Chamois an ominous-looking papyrus, which he unfurled with a dramatic flair.

As they pored over its contents, Darius thought: *Son of Corsica? Me?* What the devil was his father manufacturing to free him of the vendetta?

Darius felt a snarling tug at his ankle. The Doberman, *Monsieur*, barked loudly, leaping at him in recognition, waiting to be petted. The commotion brought the Corsican hillsmen out of the hut, guns at ready. They shoved Darius roughly inside the shack to confront the hostile group—and the infuriated Vivaldi and Matteus. Staggered by the raw, primitive odors, Darius studied the Corsican, Chamois Barbone, his eyes fixed on the unusual tattoo on his muscled left arm: an eagle carrying a woman in its beak—*the sign of the emperor pimp*. Darius had heard of such men who do no worthwhile labor and live instead off the labor of women. Such men, the shame of Corsica, brought disdain to Darius's features.

''*Augellone!*'' Chamois spat the word at him.

Darius's contempt was readable. Vivaldi, moving to reprimand him, was held back by Don Feruggio's firm hand on his arm, a silent warning in his black ferret eyes.

Darius, swiftly calculating the sum of gold coins, sternly repudiated his father. ''You pay far too much, Father. Ten thousand in gold in exchange for my life? Understand, I feel no remorse. What I did, I would do again and again.''

''Darius!'' Vivaldi's voice rose in outrage.

''The *moufflon* saved my life. He did those butchers no harm! Those castrated killers of rabbits lacked the valor of the hunt.'' Hurling scorching contempt at the Corsicans, he demanded, ''Which of you warriors would kill a standing target, hang horns over your mantel, and run shouting to your neighbors, 'See my bravery this day. I caught *moufflon*!' '' Darius's hot condemning eyes swept the hillsmen's faces, then turned away. ''Collect your money, Father. Let them shoot me. Grant them the blood revenge they thirst after. These are mere women who sing songs of vendetta; they eat elephants and choke on flies.''

"Darius!" Vivaldi's stern reprimand shook the rafters.

The Moor addressed Chamois, his jacket open, fists on his hips, displaying in full sight of the others his unusual belt, containing myriad amulets and curious lethal weapons with no names. "Barbone," he said quietly. "Before you touch Darius Bonifacio, you will first contend with me."

Chamois squirmed uneasily, shifty eyes coveting the gold. Awkwardly he sat back in his seat, casually trailing his eyes from the gold to Matteus's belt, to Vivaldi's implacable features, to the Sicilian don, whom he respected, then lingering on Darius calculatingly before swinging back to the Moor. "I intend you no harm, Matteus, but it appears we must contend with an unsolvable problem."

"Matteus!" Darius intervened. "I fight my own battles! I believe in real justice, not convoluted Corsican justice that enslaves its people like animals in chains." He hurled imprecations at them.

Vivaldi's attempts to halt Darius's rash diatribe were halted by the stunning impact of seeing Darius as his own person. He stared at the young man, fascinated, bearing witness to the fruits of his labor.

"You have robbed us of honor!" Chamois snapped at Darius.

"You have robbed Corsica of nobility!" Darius countered hotly.

"You go too far for a stranger of Corsica!" Chamois's eyes narrowed hostilely. "You had best learn more about Corsicans before you grapple with our customs." His voice took on added harshness. "Corsican men sing no songs of vendetta! We are too busy dancing the *Moresca*, the weapon dance of war. The tears of our women lying prostrate over the dead bodies of their loved ones stimulate the men to vendetta. In the *maquis*, *Darius Bonifacio*, thorns grow sharp and profuse. Shall I tell you why? Because they are watered by the tears of our women, whose loved ones were slain there." Chamois turned from Darius, his defiant eyes lingering on the three elders representing him. "You are too late. The women of the dead men have already sewn pieces of their bloodstained garments into the clothing of their oldest sons as reminders of their duty in vendetta."

"Tell them to unsew the pieces," the Moor commanded.

"It cannot be done." Chamois sucked his gold tooth.

"It *will* be done. Resolve it." Vivaldi's voice grew deadly.

"I tell you, no. It cannot be done! Families are involved, relatives. From village to village, district to district, valley to valley, war will be waged. Blood will be shed. I suggest you return to Terra Bonifacio and make a fortress of it.''

"And I," Vivaldi spoke deliberately, drawing himself up to his full six feet, "suggest to you, dissolve this vendetta against my son or you shall regret any action brought against the House of Bonifacio."

"*You, signore,* are the *visitor* to Corsica, not I.''

Vivaldi spoke quietly. "If this island of Corsica would vomit forth all the blood poured out on it in past vendettas, it would overwhelm the cities and villages, drown its people, turn the sea crimson to North Africa."

Chamois sucked his teeth and shrugged. "It is our destiny, *signore*. What can we do?"

"The destiny of my son is not to die worthlessly in a matter of unjust blood revenge." Vivaldi caught the peculiar look in Darius's eyes. Matteus averted his eyes. Vivaldi continued. "Before you make decisions, you had best discuss the matter with your brother, the big gun in Marseilles."

"Ajaccio is *my* jurisdiction," the Corsican muttered sullenly.

"Times in Marseilles are critical," Vivaldi began, lighting up a cigar. "Recently your brother outsmarted both the African and Neapolitan syndicates. Mercurio expected and received my cooperation. He desires the brotherhood to become the most powerful fraternity in France—the world perhaps."

Chamois cut him a sharp, probing look. So! Bonifacio and his brother were amicable, eh? Bonifacio spoke the truth. Recently all brothels in Marseilles were forced to shut down during a power struggle. Mercurio was cleverly hidden away while the other contenders killed themselves off. The African syndicate had wrapped their enemies in concrete caftans and plunged them into the Bay of Marseilles. The Neapolitans, wielding Thompson machine guns, had shot down their enemies in broad daylight. When it appeared the Italians would emerge victorious, Mercurio revealed the strongholds to the authorities. The following day, Mercurio Barbone, more solid than before, was back in business. Chamois's personal ambition included a move to Bastia to control the remaining families on the island, then—Paris! The *ne plus ultra* of his career was to pimp in style. How Bonifacio fitted into the scheme of things was not revealed. Chamois scowled. The crime syndicate powered by the Barbone family was based on prostitution, gambling, and protection rackets. Recently he had smuggled a thousand Bedouin and North African slave girls into Marseilles and sold them for such high prices that Mercurio contemplated broader plans to include Chamois. That plans of such magnitude were not revealed to him was as annoying as it was demeaning. The highly sensitive matter could bring dishonor, even death if not handled properly. That Bonifacio knew of such plans and he himself did not, made him cautious.

"Find an alternative," Vivaldi demanded.

Barbone wiped his sweaty brow, took his time lighting a cigar. On his feet, leaning over the crude table, he contemplated the coins. Observing him, the Sicilian Don Feruggio, silent throughout the heated contest, was keenly aware of Chamois's pride. He interrupted the Corsican's silent war. "Perhaps, *Signore* Barbone, you might consider the services of a *parolanti*?"

Twelve strong Corsican voices arose in protest. They argued, grumbled fiercely, in firm opposition to the Sicilian's suggestion. *The services of a mediator?* Bah! Too often they ended up with less than direct settlement with the accused. The presence of the Sicilian don who knew intimately the rules of vendetta provoked their anger. The Sicilian, suddenly the focus of their wrath, stood his ground with the inscrutability of a Buddha. One power-saturated glance from Don Feruggio changed Chamois's belligerence to deference. The others, on a given signal, clammed up.

"The mediator, naturally, will be my brother, Dominic," Chamois snapped.

"*Naturally,*" the Sicilian replied silkily.

"As mediator he shall receive from the hostile parties oaths of reconciliation. I assure you, *Signore* Bonifacio, such oaths are sacred. The violator is despised by God and Corsica as destitute of honor and conscience. Rarely it happens, but upon occasion the oath is broken, for the demon makes his nest in the human heart as we all know. Pray let this not happen in your son's case."

"So be it."

"Vengeance, goddess of destiny for Corsicans, controls the history of our lives. Through a single passion man becomes a demon more unsparing than the avenging angel. Never satisfied with the firstborn—he would have them all."

The underlying threat, unmistakable, Vivaldi caught the look Chamois gave Darius. He paced before the Corsican, "Where there are mortal enemies, my Corsican friend, there can also be friends for life and death. Where vengeance rends the heart with ferocity, human love excites it to the noblest resolve. There can be heroic forgetfulness in the name of unity, a divine forgiveness among men, for nowhere can the Christian injunction to *love thy neighbor as thyself* be realized more than in the land of blood vengeance.'' His loquacity and phrase turning caught the men's attention.

Chamois blinked hard, tilted his head obliquely. ''What matters are not *your* fancy words, but our ways. So. You will hear from the *parolanti*, soon.'' Chamois hitched the money pouch to his belt. ''Pray your words take effect on him, not me, Bonifacio.'' His attention shifted to Darius. ''What will you do if you are permitted to live? What will you be?''

''Not that it is of your concern, *signore*. I shall be *moufflon*, king of all Corsica,'' he said.

''*King of all goats?* What a noble pursuit.'' Chamois laughed uproariously. The twelve Corsican hillsmen chimed in with explosive bursts of ridicule. ''This is the son who holds so glorious a future? He talks like a man, but where it counts he is a mere boy. Imagine, king of goats.'' Their laughter and guffaws echoed after them as they left the ramshackle hut. Outside the ridicule ceased. They regarded Darius morosely. Each had witnessed an extraordinary power in the lad, indefinable but nevertheless something unique. The mountain men harked back to ancient legends of Corsicans who once brought fame to their island. They had much to discuss on this night.

The hour of madness ended. The lorry carrying Darius trundled downhill to where he'd earlier tethered the gelding. Once secured to the vehicle, they moved on slowly over tortuous roads. Silence afflicted the passengers.

At Don Feruggio's insistence Vivaldi drove him to Porto to his friend's house. Alighting from the lorry, the don thanked his host, assuring him he had no real worries concerning Darius and the dead Corsicans.

''Assuredly the correct action will commence. I shall remain in Porto to supervise the *parolanti's* role.'' In a confidential note, he added, ''You could have saved your gold, *signore*. The Corsican is a nothing, a bag of wind. Vendetta originated with the Corsicans, but it took Sicilians to perfect the art. We shall meet in a week as previously discussed.'' He tipped his gray fedora, nodded respectfully to the Moor. Pausing, critical eyes on Darius, he tapped him lightly on the head.

''And you, young cock o' the walk, once you decide to become a hammer, strike as hard as you can, then make certain never to fall under the anvil of your enemy. You must learn honor, never display contempt for the ways of another man. And never open your head to let another see inside it, understand?'' Lighting a cigar, holding the match close to Darius's face, he studied the lad's expression critically. His smile faded, ''We may never see one another again, young hammer. I am destined for a natural death, but you had best be looking to your flanks all your days.'' He turned, waved, and strutted along the narrow alley.

''Who is this man, Father?'' Darius stared after the Sicilian.

Vivaldi gunned the motor and wheeled the lorry along the dark cobblestone streets, taking the coastal road back to Terra Bonifacio. ''You've heard me speak of friends. Don Feruggio is a *friend of friends*,'' Vivaldi said. ''He is an important man.''

''To whom?''

''To many people. Associates, businessmen, politicians, men high in government, his countrymen.''

''You said he is in exile, here. *To whom is he important?*''

''Darius, we shall speak of this at home. The roads are treacherous. They require my attention.''

They were almost home when Darius, unable to contain his silence, spoke up again. ''Why did you permit the man called Chamois to believe you are ignorant in the ways of vendetta? Why was it necessary to denigrate their fanaticism over blood revenge? You spoke of brotherly love in a way that contradicts what you've taught me all my life. Do your words change from day to day? Are they as changeable as the shifting sands?''

''Is it not written, 'There is a time and place for all under the sun' in the Bible taught you by the Jesuits?'' Vivaldo asked.

''I see. Adapt yourself to changing situations.''

''Exactly.''

''Then explain how *your* words are to be regarded. How do you trust others, expect them to be men of their words, if you are capricious?''

''Good, you ask the proper questions. We shall discuss this after supper, after we calm your mother, who must be frantic at our long absence. We shall talk, you, Matteus, and I.''

''And Daniel and Robert too?''

''No.''

''Why not? Are they not your sons also?''

''Yes. With you it's different.''

''Why?''

"Why? Because I have trained you, instilled in you the vision and power of your destiny."

"Why not to Daniel or Robert? They loathe me, Father. Is it too late to change their concept of me? Why did you permit the rivalry between us to exceed the bounds of decency?"

"You imagine things that do not exist."

"The hatred they feel for me is not imagined. It exists. Your words to the Corsican were, *'Where there are mortal enemies, there can be friends for life or death. A heroic forgetfulness in the name of unity, a divine forgiveness among men.'* You have not instilled this philosophy into my brothers and myself. Will you explain why you permit the hatred to grow between my brothers and me?"

Vivaldi missed a sharp turn in the road. "*For the love of God!* Not while I'm driving, Darius! These roads are treacherous enough—" He broke off, he wiped the windshield, hoping it would help sharpen his focus. "Matteus, what do you make of that—up ahead?"

The Moor leaned forward in his seat, cat eyes sweeping along the dirt road. Darius saw them first. He recognized the red sweater.

"Father! *It's Daniel and Robert!* Someone is trying to harm them!"

Vivaldi's foot hit the brakes. Matteus, gun in hand, leaped from the machine, followed by Vivaldi and Darius, their *luparas* in hand. The trio hid behind a boulder, grateful for the full moon illuminating the area. Two Corsican brigands were in the act of abducting Daniel and Robert.

Their positions were fixed approximately one kilometer from Terra Bonifacio, on a remote, seldom-used road that led to the ancient citadel on the property, then branched off into the *maquis*.

"We have to work swiftly," Matteus said in a strangely hushed voice. "Once the lorry takes off with the lads, they will be swallowed up in the treacherous paths of the *maquis*."

Vivaldi agreed. A thousand trails led nowhere and everywhere in that thickly forested area.

"Heed my words, Darius. Once we succeed in surprising the Corsicans, you grab your brothers and run back to the lorry. If things work against us, drive them home, barricade yourselves, and take up arms. There is no way of telling the treachery underfoot at this point."

"Chamois Barbone?" Darius hissed. Moor and Spaniard gave

him a sharp look. They did not confirm or deny the possibility. Darius understood what was expected from him.

"I shall go around to obstruct their path at the other side of the flat rock in case they outrun us," Matteus said, and vanished quickly in the shadows.

Vivaldi and Darius moved forward, in spurts, leaping from boulder to boulder. Vivaldi was unable to discern the identities of the Corsicans. He stepped into the full spill of moonlight ten feet from the action. "Stop!" he shouted, hurling rocks in the direction opposite to his voice. *"Firma!"*

The startled foursome glanced in the direction Vivaldi had hoped they would. One Corsican whipped out his gun and shot blindly in the night. Vivaldi took the opening, ran forward into the melee, catching them off guard. "Make one move and I'll put a bullet through your brains!"

Darius made his move. He yanked his brothers from the lorry, shouting, "Run swiftly, the lorry is behind the boulder. Stay inside."

Daniel and Robert sprinted ahead several yards only to stop at the blasts of rifle at their feet. The boys dove for cover. A loud booming voice in the night struck terror in their hearts.

"You two, come back here. Get into the lorry," said a third man on an elevated boulder, peering down at the arena of action. "Drop your guns, Bonifacio. You think we're foolish? That we Corsicans have not refined our talents to cover our action?"

The *lupara* spilled from Vivaldi's hands.

"You too, boy," he commanded Darius. "Drop the gun!" The voice, emanating from a shadow in profile, signaled his men to pick up the *lupara*. He slid off the boulder. Daniel and Robert were prodded back into the lorry. "Take the third," ordered their leader. "Three hostages will fatten our purses—" His voice was snuffed out, he gagged.

Matteus, springing from the shadows, had grabbed the menacing leader in a hammerlock from behind, disarming him. With the Corsican frozen before him like a shield, he ordered the other two brigands to cease and desist. "One move and your boss is finished!"

The Corsicans, losing their advantage, relinquished their guns to Vivaldi and Darius, who moved in swiftly to disarm them. "Go, Daniel, Robert! Fetch the lorry!" Vivaldi commanded. The boys left with dispatch.

"Matteus!" Darius shouted a warning to the Moor. The Corsican broke his hold. They scuffled. The brigand, whipping out a concealed gun was obstructed by the Moor who displayed quick fancy footwork. Moving behind, twisting the Corsican's upper torso he connected with a swift kick to his groin. Matteus snapped off an amulet from his belt. In a fast move he slashed at the brigand's face twice. "You're dead." he told the man flatly.

Nursing his groin, the Corsican bared his teeth and in a crouch position ready to spring at the Moor, snarled, "You black-skinned son of a whore's whore! Cut me will you?" The brigand leader, named Moto tried to lunge at Matteus. Instead he recoiled in horror, hands darting to his face. The feel of hot, sticky blood incensed him. He was powerless to move!

Darius observed the act in stupefaction as the victim fell back, gasping for breath. Violent screams about to crash through his throat froze, gagged him. His body writhed in agony; his black eyes bulged grotesquely.

Daniel, gunning the lorry's engine, came at the scene at break-neck speed, then slamming the brakes hard, fishtailed danger-ously to a standstill. Headlights fanned illumination on the eerie scene.

Darius, curiously engrossed in the drama of the dying man observed as Matteus stood over the victim, hand outstretched holding a death's-head amulet the size of a partridge egg. The Corsican, turning a mottled purple had chewed his swollen tongue to shreds. Massive spurts of blood spewed from be-tween his lips; he resembled a beast espumating ribbons of blood.

Turning from the dying man Matteus focused on the brigand trio. Panic striken, eyes on the amulet in the Moor's hand they recoiled, terrified. *Once the Moors ruled Corsica. To this day they were feared and revered for such mystic, ceremonial rites and incantations.* One of the brigands broke away and, screaming savagely ran wildly into the *maquis.*

Darius fired his gun, spewing bullets after him.

"No! Let him go," Vivaldi commanded. "You too, go," he told the third. "Spread the word, a Fornari Bonifacio spills no innocent blood. Convey to Chamois Barbone that this incident will not go unrewarded." He spat into the ground, slipped a knife from its sheath, and flung it, stabbing the ground. It quivered to a standstill. *The sign of war!*

"C-Chamois B-Barbone? But, *signore,* what has he to do

with this? Any of this?'' The Corsican lifted his eyes from the knife.

Vivaldi aimed his gun menacingly. Matteus, moving in, pushed aside the barrel. The Corsican cowered in fear.

"If not Chamois Barbone—who gave orders for the abductions?"

"You killed Moto, he is the one who possesses such knowledge."

Matteus lifted the death's-head. "The truth is not in you. The amulet does not lie."

The brigand gestured obscenely. "Kill me. I can offer no more than my life whether you believe me or not. I speak the truth. The orders came from Rome. We took orders from Moto."

"*Rome?*" Vivaldi tensed in the stance of a warrior. "You lie."

"Why would I lie? I have no reason to lie. Moto made the contract and you killed him."

"He worked for Rome?" The Moor pressed.

"And other places and people."

"I know your face, Corsican. If you lie to me, you shall be dished a death worse than what befell your hapless leader. Dare to raise a hand against the Bonifacio family and you'd better make peace with Satan for you will surely join him in the eternal fires and afterlife. No, go! And Corsica—pass the word. Speak wisely of what you witnessed here this night, if any courage remains."

The frightened brigand, a skilled marksman, a deadly blade man, unprepared to match wits with Satan, jumped into the truck, turned on the engine and, after three bad starts finally got the engine to sputter to life. He headed the machine into the thicket, lost in the night.

Darius, noting Daniel and Robert's shaken reaction, called to them. "Come, let's get into the lorry."

"Don't tell us what to do," Daniel countered.

"Do what your brother tells you," Vivaldi commanded brusquely.

"He's *not* my brother!" Daniel retorted snidely.

Darius's shock was total. Vivaldi struck his firstborn across the mouth. "Get into the lorry before I take a whip to you. You too, Robert. Darius! All of you."

They obeyed their father. Never had he displayed such anger with them. Darius felt sick. Confused by Daniel's hostility and his wild denial, he sat at the rear of the lorry, jostled about, as the machine rode over the rough terrain. Darius finally asked, "What do you mean I am *not* your brother, Daniel?"

Daniel clammed up.

Robert, the more affectionate of the two, the mediator with his mother's dark eyes, pacified Darius. "Pay Daniel no mind. He is jealous of the attention you get from Father."

"I know. I too am displeased. Only tonight I spoke to him about this very subject. He promised things would change between us." Darius's voice conveyed his displeasure.

"We've been promised that ever since you were born!" Daniel snapped. "Does it change? No. It's always Darius this, Darius that. Darius gets the best of everything!"

"Not the best, Daniel," Darius replied thoughtfully. "At times my dreams terrify me. I feel as if Father had molded me into some diabolical machine of destruction. Very early yesterday morning, I killed two men—"

The lads were shocked. "Why?" Robert asked.

"I'll tell you later. That's why you were nearly abducted, I think. Yes, that's why."

It wasn't. Vivaldi lost no time explaining after supper. The matters were unrelated, he assured his sons. He schooled them to exercise care and caution, never move about without their guns. "Never venture off the property without the guard dogs," Vivaldi spoke tersely. "And *never* without Matteus. Say nothing of this to your mother. I don't want her unnecessarily worried."

A half hour later Darius was in Matteus's quarters, his curiosity exceeding all bounds. Pointing to the death's-head amulet on the belt, he said simply, "Explain it, please."

Matteus unhooked it carefully from the belt, held it between thumb and forefinger of his right hand. "*Baraka*-magic powers. Be careful in handling, it is razor sharp, lethal. For centuries it has been a secret weapon of my people. Wise men, spinners of Islamic tales, claim it is a device of Moloch, keeper of hell, who takes charge of all tortures of the damned. Moloch, the most inventive of Satan's lower-world kingdom, received his high position because of his ingenious devices of death."

Darius studied the innocuous-looking death's-head. "Such a small weapon to create so torturous a death? Explain its properties, please. Before you do, explain why the brigands were permitted to go unpunished. Excluding the dead man, of course."

"Your father freed them to spread the word. The Bonifacio family is not without resources to protect their own."

"Ahhh. You rule enemies by instilling fear in them?"

"Not sham, but true fear." Matteus found himself unable to disguise his pride and respect for Darius. Vivaldi was right. Not the Spaniard or his two sons, only Darius would have the power.

"What makes the death's-head powerful enough to kill a man?"

Matteus removed the amulet carefully from Darius's hand. He placed it on the table, walked to a wall cabinet, removed a vial of liquid, and placed it on the table alongside the amulet. A skull and crossbones, crudely drawn on the vial, indicated its contents.

"Strychnine . . . the most horrible of deaths . . . after intolerable suffering. You saw how long it took."

"You dip the death's-head in the poison?"

The Moor shook his head. "A bottle this size could kill five hundred men. Observe, Darius. See here? a cylindrical shaft within the amulet. The poison is poured into the empty shaft. The poison is released—these outer ridges turn into sharp blades—when I press this lever." He demonstrated. Sharp blades protruded at the touch of a lever. "The blades cut the skin; simultaneously, the poison enters the blood stream."

Darius pondered the amulet. "Will I be expected to use such weapons when I grow into manhood?"

"If you do, know well in advance the consequences as well as the mechanics, including possible antidotes."

"Matteus, are you my ally?"

"It is a role to which I have sworn an oath and dedicated my life."

"Why?"

"In due time," Vivaldi spoke out, entering the Moor's spartan quarters.

"Yes, yes, I know. A time and place for everything."

"Because the learning process is not instantaneous; a process of daily repetition must be applied before man's most precious weapon, his brain, acts instinctively and intuitively. Come, we shall retire to the vendetta room."

Moments later each took his place in a throne chair. Vivaldi removed a letter from his shirt pocket, the letter from the Jesuit,

Franchetti, and read aloud. " 'Signore Bonifacio: I feel it my duty to describe the nature of Darius's mind, where his strongest inclinations lie. His uncanny ability to perceive the weakness of defenses in areas of combat results in offers of spectacular alternatives. His unique gift is a constant source of marvel to the Holy Fathers. Although, the clergy abhors violence, we are aware of the place military strength plays in our existence. In reviewing Darius's potential, we consider it ill advised to suppress these superior talents. We therefore recommend St. Cyr Military Academy to test his talents.' "

Darius's heart raced furiously, "Yes, Father. And your decision?"

"Not yet. Time enough for playing soldiers with uniforms and brass braid and pompous parading about *after* you learn more about man and human relationships."

"But I should have gone long ago. I told you. Daniel and Robert too! Why do you resist? You only delay the inevitable. I seem unable to convince you of the dire necessity. Time is of the essence, don't you see it?"

"Darius, bear in mind I make the decisions in the Bonifacio family. No military school until I say you are ready."

"The life of a monastic acolyte in Bastia stifles me."

"Your knowledge of men needs refining. Yesterday you killed two men and showed no remorse. Yet you confronted men of terror and held your own. Tonight you demonstrated the courage of ten men. Matteus and I are proud of you. Such self-assurance comes *not* from the Jesuits, but from what you've learned here, at Terra Bonifacio."

"*Men of terror?* What men of terror? Explain, please."

"Those Corsicans you confronted in the hills of Niolo tonight dedicate their lives to creating terror in the hearts of men. They are members of a secret society, as is Don Feruggio. Surely the Jesuits have taught you of such things? The S.J. Society, as they were named centuries ago, were considered men of terror in their long and varied histories . . . Now you shall learn of the relationship existing between Matteus and a certain family of Spanish nobles."

"Shall I call Daniel and Robert?" Darius's voice grew defiant.

"Darius. Do not provoke my displeasure. Neither Daniel nor Robert is prepared to absorb this discussion." Vivaldi nodded to the Moor. Instantly Matteus brought a bottle of wine and three glasses to the table between the throne chairs.

Vivaldi allowed his hands to rest on the arms of his chair. The golden ring of the Marten on his forefinger refracted light prisms from the overhead candles.

"In the past we've spoken of the Garduna Parchments." Vivaldi raised his wine cup in a toast. They all drank.

"I don't see how they affect my life."

"Centuries of family history in another country before we came to Corsica . . ." The gold ring glittered brightly.

Darius nodded, his eyes on the ring.

"Can you hear me, Darius?"

"Yes."

"You understand all we've discussed these many years?"

"Everything."

Vivaldi related the strange de la Varga odyssey, speaking well into the predawn hours. When the session was finished, Matteus picked up Darius and carried him to his bedroom and covered him with a blanket.

Later Spaniard and Moor spoke. "Those men earlier involved in the abduction attempt," began Vivaldi. "Do you believe the orders came from Rome?"

"Who in Rome would order the abduction of Bonifacio's son?"

"Who, indeed, if he learned of his wife's indiscretions?"

Matteus stared hard, contemplating the implication.

"Only through the contessa's closeness with Bonifacio's wife could such deviousness be achieved," Vivaldi added, when the Moor saw the connection. "Go to Don Feruggio. Ask him to make proper inquiries. We must know the origin of the contract. Nothing must happen to Darius, understand?"

"Did you listen sharply to Darius's concern over impending war?"

"Not now, Matteus. St. Cyr can wait. It *must* wait for another year."

The Moor left directly, unable to assuage his disquiet. Something was happening to Darius. He grew wary of the curious lights sparking in the lad's eyes.

Chapter Twenty-four

Sophia Bonifacio, needing desperately to sort out her thoughts and emotions, left the house at nightfall to go walking in the forbidden *maquis*. At fourteen, she evidenced the shadowy beauty of a madonna, a stunning product of her Spanish and Corsican bloodline. Her pale porcelain features were offset by violet, doe-shaped eyes, fringed with double rows of lashes. Her enigmatic smile held fascination, and all who passed her in Ajaccio were compelled to look upon her more than once. Sophia had no need to spend endless hours dressing her hair; she wore the mass of curls shoulder length. Sophia was physically mature beyond her years, the strain and wonder of adolescence confusing to her. At the first swelling of her breasts, she felt a rush of embarrassment. No matter how gently Dariana explained female biology, she begged for an *apodesmos* to flatten her breasts. She thought if she concealed the swelling, the sudden estrangement she felt from her father and brothers would abate and her life would return to normalcy. It didn't.

This year her life had drastically changed; she understood nothing. In the past hugs and kisses were profuse between brothers and sister, especially from Darius, whom she loved with boundless passion. His remoteness lately disturbed her and she felt utterly abandoned. Sophia loved her father and also feared him. She sensed something hidden in him which could explode and destroy if he were pushed far enough, but she never spoke of it, not even to her mother. Lately she seemed unable to please her father, nor her brothers Daniel or Robert. Their protective ways stifled her. They eyed her covetously; if a stranger glanced at her in that curious way only men knew about, her brothers would glare, act as if she had provoked or encouraged their glances.

Sophia still didn't know what went on in a man's mind when he held special thoughts about a woman. It didn't seem likely she'd ever know! Even Dariana seemed preoccupied with more than her usual household chores. Sophia felt like a stranger in her own home, a trespasser at times.

She moved quietly through the wooded glen. She imagined, in her uncertainty, there existed some intimate secret in her body that repelled her father, brothers, and especially Darius.

Every year as far back as she remembered, an exuberant Sophia waited with a wildly beating heart for June 15 to arrive, the date marking Darius's vacation. From June 15 to August 20 Sophia would come alive. The interim months were spent missing Darius, counting the days until his homecoming. Her inability to articulate what she felt for Darius and why she didn't entertain the same feelings for Daniel or Robert confused her.

Now it was worse. Everything this summer was different, strange; and unendurable. Darius had spent no time with her. He deliberately avoided her. She knew it and it nearly drove her mad. Tears welled in her eyes as she ambled along a spongy moss-carpeted earth.

The estrangement must be her fault! What had she done to reap such unjust rewards? All her life she had experienced the pleasure of all things sensual, the fragrance of the floral banked *maquis*, exquisite tastes of sauces and wines, the invigorating heat of the sun on her bare body while swimming in the lower pools. She'd felt the caress of sea breezes, fell prostrate to the exotic scents of herbs. And the touch and feel of her loved ones had fed her, nourished her, kept her alive. Now she felt dead, disconnected.

A coppery moon lay on the rippling sea. The night was filled with soft whistlings, the call of nocturnal animals. Something rustled in the underbrush. She tensed, listening. The mountain quivering in brilliant lunar lights was playing tricks on her. At ease now, she moved forward toward Virgin's Point.

The birthday cake! Darius's sixteenth birthday! She and Dariana had baked an elaborate cake iced with roses and cupids. No one seemed to care—not even Darius. It lay in the butter room growing stale. Sophia had not forgotten. Four nights ago she had knocked at Darius's door several times. Dariana had appeared. "Darius is sleeping," she whispered. "He had a narrow escape with the *moufflon*." Dariana had closed the door, telling her little else. Later that night Sophia had returned, but Darius was gone.

What did it matter? Tomorrow Darius was returning to school. God! She needed assurance that none of this strange sickness over her family was her doing. Not knowing was a heavy weight to bear for someone with as fragile an ego as Sophia's. What a strange summer! Never, as long as she lived, would she forget it.

Suddenly, she stopped. She peered about, all her senses honed at once, her hand gripping the knife at her waist. There . . . up ahead, the dark shadow etched against the lunar lights, standing on Virgin's Point!

Instantly her body was aglow. She recognized him.

Darius!

She approached soundlessly, her heart pounding, her delirious joy overwhelming. She wanted to embrace him, feel the comfort of his arms upon her.

"Why do you avoid me, Darius?" she whispered quietly, restraining her enthusiasm for fear he'd bolt.

Darius, startled, frowned, annoyed that he'd failed to sense her approach. Quickly his eyes darted about the night, alarmed. Satisfied no imminent dangers lurked, he looked into her eyes, noting the veiled radiance.

"It grows more intolerable each year," she continued. "Life without you is no life at all. Why are you estranged from me? I understand nothing of late."

Darius was unable to gaze at her. His emotions signaled cryptic, forbidden messages to his body. "The moments spent with you are my only reality. Do you believe me, Sophia?"

"Mine, too. Then why place such distance between us?"

"Soon I shall lose you to a suitor."

Sophia panicked. "No! It's not true! There is no one but you for me."

"Don't be a silly cuckoo bird." He forced a smile, unable to brood in her company; her spirit, her *joie de vivre* was infectious. "You're fourteen, soon to be swept off your feet."

"What has age to do with anything? It's you I love. Nothing will separate us—nothing! I shall never marry anyone, only you."

"Sophia! I am your brother. You cannot marry me."

"I know. *I know!*" She wilted. "What a terrible penance," she despaired. "Won't you explain the riddle of love to me. I am so confused."

How could Darius explain his own emotional befuddlement? What he felt for Sophia extended beyond the bounds of filial love. At school he had confessed his secret yearnings to Father Franchetti, his confessor. The Jesuit had feigned total helplessness, but spoke with a bemused countenance. "It's a natural thing to love one's sister; it's the purest, most elevating of earthly loves. But in time it passes, for it is love that must *not* be consummated, unlike love between husband and wife. The feeling will pass, my son. It will pass." Nothing had helped except deep immersion in his studies. Images of Sophia's charm and her sweet innocence embraced him throughout the school semester. It was true, this past summer he had avoided her. His feelings toward her frightened him. His religion had taught him these sensations and desires were sinful, hardly the balm to soothe an inflamed heart.

Now, in her presence, as she expressed her love, his manhood begged for union.

Sophia slid her arms around his neck, kissed his astonished, wanting lips. Darius stiffened. "We'd best return to the house," he said huskily with false bravado. Paying him no mind, she kissed him again. This time his unquenchable ardor was aroused. He returned the kisses as he'd dreamed of kissing her since they reached puberty. Hearts pounded furiously, amazement was scrawled across their faces as they breathlessly pulled apart, searching the other's eyes, wondering at the warm sensations flooding them. Neither had learned how to kiss and breathe, an art perfected only by time and experience. They gasped for air, kissed again, hearts racing. How marvelous was this rush of excitement. She abandoned herself to the fulfillment of desire, melting against him, startled by his uncontrollable hardness. Darius pulled away. "Sophia, we mustn't! It isn't proper."

"Who decides what is or is not proper?" she asked quietly.

"The church. The Holy Fathers," he stammered, taking deep breaths of air. "Whoever makes the laws by which men and women choose to live." Sophia challenged the rights of lawmakers. Raising both hands to his face, she cupped it firmly, forcing his eyes to lock with hers. "I love you, Darius, my brother, my heart, my life, lover in my dreams. At this moment my ache for you is such, my stomach hurts unbearably."

Darius moaned softly. He tenderly held her face, caressed it, committing it to memory. "I too ache for you. I dream of you, speak to you in my solitude. Whatever I do, wherever I go, I ask myself first, would Sophia enjoy such moments? But, beloved Sophia, we are growing up. We must set aside childish dreams and face reality."

He laid her head on his breast, the sweet scents of her body melting his resolve. Her husky voice was plaintive in the night. "I am frightened, Darius."

"If it's of any consolation, I too am frightened." His lips moved down her neck to her shoulders, his trembling hand reaching for the outline of her lush full breasts. Sophia's body shuddered violently until the exquisite feeling of surrender was upon her. In the rapturous moment Sophia pledged her heart and soul to Darius. She would do anything for him, *anything!*

Suddenly a foul, loathsome presence violated the scene. The moment would prove a turning point in Darius's life and to Sophia would forever remain a nightmare.

"Isn't this a touching scene?" sniggered the loathsome voice.

Startled, the couple pivoted, searched the darkness. Darius stiffened. He pulled Sophia protectively to him. *Lucifer be damned! He had brought no weapons!* Earlier, instinct had urged him to retreat, but emotion, the one luxury he could ill afford, had clouded his judgment. Sophia's eyes projected controlled terror. "We are surrounded," she whispered. "I sense three, perhaps a fourth."

It happened swiftly. Strong arms from behind pulled Darius off the rock, locking his arms behind him. Two shadowy figures approached the girl, circling her. Darius struggled against the two hands of steel pinioning him; he was unable to move. "What is it you want? My purse? Take it and be gone. Don't harm the girl. I warn you, let her go. Sophia—run!" he cried out in warning. A heavy clout at the side of his temple shot pain through every nerve in his body. Vaguely he saw a man advance toward Sophia. She backed away, unafraid.

"Take what you want from me," she muttered. "But don't harm him." She reached for her knife; it was wrested from her hand and fell with a thud to the ground.

Sophia, who knew every inch of the terrain, looked for an

avenue of escape; there was none. She sprinted frantically to the right, to the left, at all sides to avoid the assailant. She was caught, her long black hair twisted around coarse, crude hands. He dragged her toward him and with his free hand gripped her dress and pulled hard. The fabric resisted. He used his knife to slash at it until the fabric fell away. Tiny bubbles of blood dotted her skin where Masso's knife had pierced her skin. Sophia did not scream. Her fears for Darius multiplied. Masso, one of the assailants, bent over her, sucking the blood droplets with gusto, taking more privileges squeezing her breasts, swelling his passion.

At the sight of Sophia's nakedness Darius exploded in wild rage. Breaking the hold on him, he dove for Masso, landing on the bull moose's back, pummeling him fiercely with both fists. Instantly pounced upon by the other two savages, Darius was clouted, kicked in the ribs, forced back along the jagged boulder and lifted against it. They banged his head against the rock until he fell limp, blood oozing from his nose, lips, eyes, an open wound at the base of his skull. His lips formed the word, "S-Sophia," before he lost consciousness.

Sophia screamed at the ghastly sight, paying little mind to her own plight. She kicked, fought, struggled, and let loose a string of curses. She dislodged herself for one fleeting moment, rolled off the rock into the nearby embankment and came back in a crouch, brandishing another knife retrieved from her boot. She faced her assailants with the courage of a lioness. Unfortunately what was needed was the ferocity of a tiger and strength of a bull. She was sadly lacking in both.

The determined trio jeered with bemused tolerance; her courage seemed comical to them. The hirsute brute, Masso, advanced toward her. He gestured obscenely, his trousers falling to his ankles. Without warning Sophia's boot connected in a swift kick to his testicles. He howled, doubled over in pain, swearing vilely. He shouted to his cronies. "Get her! Get her good!" Forgetting the anticipated pleasure of deflowering a virgin, he continued to curse and damn her. Sophia, at once helpless, about to be ravaged by the two men, named Orso and Izzolo, was pinned to the ground. What remained of her clothing was ripped away. They taunted and teased her, touching her roughly in tender, private areas that brought shame to her. Her sense of propriety totally shattered, she forced her eyes shut so no images would imprint themselves in her brain. The brute, Izzolo, a short, rotund man with a fat belly, pounced on her unprepared, unwilling body, tearing open her flesh as he penetrated the unlubricated virginal chambers. Sophia was not certain which was worse, the periodic thrusts until he split her open or the stench of rotting teeth, foul breath, stale tobacco, and fetid wine. She felt sick, defiled. The first thrust was one of unbearable violence, the second excruciating; the third tore her apart, spilling blood. She clawed at him, leaving bloody tracks on his face. He growled, moaned with each savage thrust.

It was Orso's turn. He forced his swollen tumescence inside her in vicious assault. Sophia resisted. She clawed and scratched with the fury of a wildcat. The initial shock and degradation surged to the boiling point. Feeling disgustingly contaminated, she brought both fists crashing down on his skull, pummeled both his ears. Orso slapped her across the mouth, drawing blood. He backhanded her open hand, then delivered a hard blow to her head. Blood gushed from her nose.

Sophia lost consciousness.

Darius regained his.

Fiery pain shot through his head. Under thickly lidded eyes he saw his beloved Sophia struggling under the abominable assault. An overwhelming urge to kill shuddered through him. He took no time to analyze his feelings, gave no thought to offensive or defensive tactics. All he knew was he wanted to kill, brutalize, tear those beasts who brought suffering to Sophia limb from limb.

Darius crawled in the shadows, pulled back against the black boulder, garnering strength. He fell to a crouch, his blurred eyes trying desperately to assess the scene a few feet from him. *Easy now, take it slow, and now!*

He sprang, plowing into the backs of the rapists' knees, knocking them off balance. He pounced on the man named Orso, twisted his body, pulled the gun from his waist, and with one arm in a lock around his throat held the gun to his head. Darius pulled him back onto the flat rock. He ordered Izzolo to toss his gun over the cliff. "I can kill you both, easily," he hissed. Masso busy fornicating hardly saw what was happening.

Orso gave Darius's words no importance. He struggled free, twisted to one side, rolled over, jerked his leg wildly, trying to connect to Darius's groin. Darius pulled the trigger and blew Orso's head off. The decapitated head, shot geysers of crimson and fell at Izzolo's feet. A savage cry escaping his throat, Izzolo came at Darius, clawing the air, murder in his eyes. Gathering momentum, he made a flying leap at Darius, who sidestepped. Izzolo went sailing into space over the cliff. He fell, impaled against the jagged peaks at the edge of the sea.

Darius, on one knee, steadied himself. *Two down, one to go!* The sight of Masso taking his pleasure with Sophia infuriated him. Masso lifted himself off the girl, his eyes riveted to the wide-eyed stare of Orso's head. He cried out in a primitive roar, lifted bloodshot eyes, fixing them on Darius. Two hundred and fifty pounds of solid muscle came flying at Darius. "Bastard! I'll kill you with my bare hands!" he cried. Darius evaded the thrust, throwing Masso off balance, but he was no match for the brute. Darius played the fox.

The fox, favored by fortune, conquers the tiger, favored by strength!

Lessons learned from Matteus. He moved in and out of shadows, now visible, now hidden, tossing rocks in the opposite direction to bewilder Masso. He saw Sophia moving. Inches from her was her knife. Awake now, she cried.

"Darius! He has a gun!" Darius leaped out from behind a thicket into the moon's light, deftly catching the knife she tossed him. Aiming it expertly, he tossed it just as a bullet tore into his left shoulder. He couldn't last much longer; he was losing blood too rapidly. He leaped into the air, pounced on the hulk, knocking Masso to his knees. Darius straddled him. He beat his face to a bloody pulp. He followed the monotone command, Kill! Kill! Kill!

"Darius, stop! Please, Darius, stop! He's dead! Don't you hear me? He's dead!" Sophia pulled at him, forced herself heavily upon him, trying to pierce that inner world where Darius dwelled. Darius's failure to respond instantly frightened Sophia. She recoiled, huddling in a fetal position, staring incredulously at the scene. Exhaustion finally upon him, he ceased. He stared from his swollen, bloodied, throbbing hands to the mass of unrecognizable dead flesh on the Corsican's face. He saw Sophia's knife stuck into Masso's jugular.

Strange . . . he felt no elation, no contentment at the act.

Still dazed, he stared at Sophia, her near nudity barely registering until his focus sharpened. He was dazed, weak, but the sight of Sophia's lacerations, swollen eyes, bloodied nose and lips, caked blood on her breasts, tore at his heart. Her dark hair was matted with blood and sweat around her face and neck. He moved toward her, pulled her close, protectively. Together they trembled against a moonscape and crashing waves on shore.

Matteus, with Dobermans and lanterns, found them together a half hour later, still clinging together mutely, shivering in the wind. One look around the scene summed up the story. Removing the identification papers from the dead Corsicans, he shoved them into his pocket and heaved the remains over the cliff to the rocks below. He applied a tourniquet to Darius's bullet wound, covered Sophia with his jacket, and, leaving the Dobermans to stand guard, ran swiftly back to Terra Bonifacio for Vivaldi and the lorry.

An hour later Matteus had removed the bullet from Darius's shoulder, tended the lad's other injuries while a near-hysterical Dariana tended to her violated daughter. From Sophia they learned of three assailants, not two. The papers Matteus had retrieved from the bodies of the dead men identified them as Masso and Orso Pontevecchio, brothers of the mayor of Corte. "What business took them so far from home, at so late an hour?" Vivaldi agonized.

"Whatever it was ended in dirty business for Sophia and Darius." The Moor's remark did not go unheeded.

"With two deaths under mediation," Vivaldi said solemnly, "three more complicate matters beyond conciliation." Vivaldi's stormy eyes fixed on Darius as he tried to solve a situation that grew more complex by the moment. Darius sat upright on the bed, mute, eyes open, lost in another world. Having shot him with morphine, Matteus was now cauterizing the bullet wound with a hot iron. Darius didn't flinch.

"They violated Sophia," he muttered stonily. "I was helpless . . . helpless." He ranted, raved, with stepped-up momentum. "Helpless!"

"It's over now, Darius," Vivaldi said, trying to calm him.

In shock, he barely reacted when Vivaldi shook him. But when he slapped him to stop the chanting, neither Spaniard nor Moor was prepared for what followed. Darius, cringing under the blow, reacted instinctively. He sprang from the bed, lashed out against Vivaldi violently. Matteus leaped across the bed, restraining Darius. Vivaldi recoiled, stunned by the assault, that sent him reeling. Pulling himself together, he stared at Darius, observing the phenomenon taking place. Darius's eyes rolled upward before he fell forward in a heap.

"Curse the blackhearted soul of Moloch!" cried Matteus at the sight of the bloodied mass at the base of Darius's skull. He laid him gently across the bed. "He's not in his right mind, Vivaldi. It wasn't Darius who lashed out at you, but a demon inside him stirred to life by the travails of this blighted night." He turned. "You have been hard on him. He knows little love."

"I know. I know!" blurted Vivaldi. "How serious is the wound?" Circling about him, he examined the base of Darius's skull. He wrung out a towel in the bowl of water nearby, cleansed the wound solicitously, and frowned. "Matteus, at dawn the train from Ajaccio to Bastia passes through the junction. Darius must be on that train. Agreed? Good. Go at once, fetch the physician at Piana. I will go to my wife and daughter. Darius will sleep with the morphine."

At five A.M. Matteus and Vivaldi stood on the rickety platform at the Arrêt de Campodilora as the train carrying Darius disappeared from sight. Neither Spaniard nor Moor had the slightest inkling that many years would pass before they ever set eyes upon Darius again.

Ancient villages flew past the train window, drawing no interest from Darius. He sat rigid, his head bandaged, his arm in a sling, his eyes staring at some unfolding inner vision in his mind.

Berger fires dotted the Corsican landscape before sunup, sending smoke spirals skyward. Flocks of sheep grazed. The shabby little huts of Canaple, hewn from rocks centuries ago, seemed less shabby in the glare of first light. Darius saw none of these things en route to Bastia.

He couldn't pinpoint the exact moment of revelation. The monotonous rotations of the train's wheels working in tandem with the groaning, swaying cars, lulled him into a near-hypnotic state, reactivating the sights and sounds of the nightmarish horror of the past several days. The words of Don Feruggio exploded in his mind.

I am destined for a natural death, but you, young hammer, must look to your flanks for the rest of your life!

Prophetic words? For sixteen years, nothing untoward had occurred, but in the past six days—a tempest! *A tempest of alien and oppressive acts! He had killed five men!*

The magnitude of the hidden forces within his soul overwhelmed him. The desperate love he felt for Sophia, his inability to come to grips with incestuous thoughts, fueled his discontent. Her ravagement by the Corsican brutes forced him to reexamine his own brute savagery and lack of remorse toward his victims. Inconceivable to him was the appearance of an inhuman beast of indeterminate strength locked inside him, ready to spring. He understood little of what happened.

Apathetically he gazed down at the small box, a parting gift from Matteus. He opened it listlessly, staring at the contents without emotion. The death's-head amulet.

The death's-head amulet! Matteus knew! Matteus knew what lay buried inside him ready to spring out at any given moment!

By the time the train pulled into the depot at Belgodere, Darius knew where his future lay. He detrained. He had carefully constructed a foolproof blueprint for his disappearance. Now, to put the plan into action.

He hired a coach to Calvi. The Moor, if he tried, might track him to Belgodere, but never to Calvi. Coaches in Corsica ran on no regular schedules. Each driver, for the proper sum, would transport his fare to any island destination.

Darius's diligence, strength, and sense of purpose gave him new life. By late afternoon he finished the first leg of his journey. He boarded the ferry to the mainland, Marseilles. Before him stretched a limitless sea prepared to take him in whichever direction he pointed himself. He pondered how swiftly his absence would be noted in Bastia by the Jesuits. A week. Perhaps two at the most? Communication to Vivaldi by the Jesuits would initiate a search for him. A two-week start gave him the needed edge. Who would find him? He had covered his tracks expertly, every step of the way. Once he was declared dead, his family's life would be easier.

Earlier Darius had found in his small travel case his semester allowance plus a purse of spending money. A few francs spent in one of those Calvi waterfront hovels had bought him a travel visa and necessary papers to enter the port.

Before he turned his back on Corsica to focus on the next phase of his life, his eyes swept the glittering sea before him.

He felt the fatigue of his journey. He took the medication Metteus had given him. The pain wracking his body soon abated, numbed by the narcotic. He turned now, staring back at Corsica, contemplating with profound sadness the scenes of his youth. He was headed for the only place in the world where a man could get lost in a sea of mankind. *Who would know? Who would care?* St. Cyr would have molded Darius, shaped him into a warring French general. Instead he was relegated to uncivilized worlds where the surfacing of his brute force would create neither hardship nor shame for his family.

How would he endure the solitude, despair, loneliness waiting for him. The teachings of the Jesuit fathers were ingrained deeply in his conscience; he wondered what penance he'd pay for the five lives he had taken?

He was sixteen years old, felt fifty, and already he'd killed five men! What cruel hoax had destiny played upon him? What madness directed him toward a new tableland of horrors?

Night descended swiftly. The lights of Marseilles harbor lit up brilliantly, sending their beams many miles over the sea.

As Darius pondered his future and what lay in store for him elsewhere, throughout Europe, forces greater than any mankind had imagined were busily at work, preparing a marketplace in which to retail his extraordinary talents, a future he was too young to envision for himself, a world that would soon shrink in size, and one in which man would one day journey to the moon. It would be a world in which Darius would play a vital role, prepared long ago by the forces of destiny.

At Terra Bonifacio, Vivaldi had just affixed his signature to a letter to Father Franchetti.

"Your recommendation to enroll Darius at St. Cyr Military Academy has been taken under consideration. I am herewith giving you my permission to ensure this comes to pass. I fully agree with your observations. Yours in gratitude, Vivaldi Fornari Bonifacio."

Chapter Twenty-five

ROME, ITALY
October 15, 1935

It had begun! The waiting. The ultimate snub done to the man who practically placed Il Duce on the throne of Fascism!

Minister Zeller's usual calm was absent as he paced the outer office of Il Duce's *sanctum sanctorum,* feigning interest in the art works adorning the marbeled halls. The resounding onslaught of Wagnerian opera echoing through the halls burst his eardrums. Il Duce's favorite, *Götterdämmerung.* Why not *Verdi? Puccini?*

Not since Zeller began to construct his power empire, using as its nucleus those treasures amassed on his journeys from Zurich to Austria, Italy, and Spain had he felt the superstructure of his invested depredatory wealth shudder on its foundations. He fine-combed his memory determined to uncover *who* or *what* in the fascist chain of command had spurred the irreconcilable breech between Il Duce and himself.

Zeller's silent, unseen army of loyal eyes and ears had reported an aggregation of disturbing facts to him, over and above the usual vicious gossip that stood in the shadow of political luminaries constantly stalking them.

Glancing impatiently at his watch, Zeller strutted to the window overlooking the Palazzo Venezia. He seethed with rage. Never, *never,* had he been subjected to waiting to confer with Il Duce!

What caused the undercurrent of disquiet? The increasing turmoil festering in the fascist regime? Miscalculations and confusion in Il Duce's foreign policies had not abated. Unable to pinpoint the source of mixed signals—a task Zeller always conquered in the past—his frustration increased.

How in hell had he permitted Zurich to seduce him once again?

The Madrid Assignment had taught him no lessons, damn it! He had permitted the beguilement to be foisted upon him, hadn't he?

The Italian Assignment! Zeller reflected sullenly. . . .

Antonio Vasquez's disappearance from Spain in February 1921 had paved the way a month later for the emergence of Amadeo Zeller in Seville. Files of adulterated legal documents had supported his position as executor of the de la Varga estate. Gone were all traces of Vasquez. Dark glasses, worn constantly, shielded his telltale eyes. The hot sun, he lamented to those who questioned the dark lenses, created blind spots in his vision.

A visit to the cloister, where he'd learned Victoria Valdez had disappeared, had dismayed him. He'd made such marvelous plans! Once the proper transfers had been documented in the courts, expropriation of the de la Varga wealth commenced. A systematic sale of smaller property holdings followed, converting to cash those he found a waste of time. Once he grasped control of the wealth he embarked upon his personal search for the Seven Garduna Parchments.

Zeller knew exactly where to begin the search. Using Brother Xenofonte's essays, he journeyed to the underground dungeons of the ancient castle ruins and located the vault. A burnished wood-and-gold chest resting on a stone pedestal base was flung open. The contents were gone; Zeller mused over the predicament. Obviously this underground crypt had secreted the parchments for centuries. The question was: who had made off with the treasure? Francisco was dead. The Guardia Lieutenant Fuentes had sworn that his men had shot the Spaniard and his body floated to sea. Then, who? He had no idea. He pondered the traces of dried blood on the floor of the vault leading into what appeared to be a solid wall. Mystifying? Indeed . . . but he wasted no time pondering unsolvable riddles.

Two months later he arrived in Zurich enormously wealthy, with bargaining power and monetary clout. Presenting himself to the jurist, Kurt Von Kurt, he demanded an audience with the hierarchy.

Von Kurt, without expression, denied the request. Zeller, smiling craftily, had expected the refusal. His second demand, more assertive, contained enough ominous undertones to pique the jurist's interest.

"If the consortium desires to acquire the Seven Garduna Parchments, advise them, Von Kurt, that they shall be forced to deal with me." Before departing, he added, "I am sole executor of the de la Varga estate."

Von Kurt, daubing at the sweat on his hairless brow, glanced at the legal documents thrust under his nose, offered as corroborative evidence to Zeller's revelations. Masking his stupefaction, at the peripeteia confronting him, he promised to effect the desired encounter. He dismissed Zeller briskly, eager to substantiate the authenticity of his boastings.

Zeller wasted little time in the interim. He placed on deposit in the rival Guggenheim bank an enormous sum of money. Later that morning he negotiated the purchase of choice real estate overlooking the cobalt *Zurichsee*, midway between Rapperswil and Zurich, paying cash for the magnificent French chateau. A cash transaction of such magnitude sent shock waves through the banking community, precisely the reaction Zeller hoped to achieve. Before the ink dried on the title transfers and before the property deeds were filed, Zeller was contacted by courier at his hostelry. A meeting with the consortium hierarchy was scheduled for ten A.M. the following day.

Zeller arrived promptly at the *Suisse Banque Royale* on the Parade-Platz. He was ushered into a spartan office, graced only by a desk and two chairs. The consortium, conspicuous by their absence, had sent a *goddamned* buffer in their place! Zeller was furious.

Sigmund Weiderhof, a compelling man of forty-odd years, sat in a chair. He was a man of medium build, wore his straight black hair off his face, cut short, without sideburns. Weiderhof's discerning dark eyes behind pince-nez glasses carefully measured the man opposite him. "Congratulations are in order, *ja*, Zeller. Your good fortune in the Madrid Assignment is viewed as miraculous." In the same breath, he apologized for the hierarchy's absence. "At times their insensitivity at the feelings of others . . ." He waved his hand in a helpless gesture. "Suppose you convey to me the information meant for them?"

The snub was obvious. Zeller bridled indignantly, yet with measured precaution he asked, "Are you part of that hierarchy?"

"If I were, Herr Zeller, I would not ignore you, not after your success in Spain. Measured by any standard, it is impressive."

"Do you share equal confidence with the hierarchy as do the jurists who trained me?"

Weiderhof's unreadable eyes lifted to Zeller's in silence. He waited. The query came as expected.

"How much does the consortium pay you?"

"Enough."

"I'll double the sum. Come to work for me."

Weiderhof smiled a smile that could have meant anything. He glanced at the data on his desk, shuffled and stacked paper. "I never discuss personal business on my employers' time. Do you know the Odeon? The bistro across from the Bellevueplatz? We meet in thirty minutes, *ja*?"

The meeting was promptly convened at the bistro. "James Joyce penned parts of *Ulysses* here," Weiderhof explained. "Lenin himself resided close by once. I suggest the bratwurst and *rösti*, unless you prefer confections and chocolate, *Herr* Zeller."

Over a delicious luncheon, Weiderhof kept his silence. He was sipping cinnamon tea when Zeller's quiet voice swam across the table. "Have you considered my proposition?"

"It wasn't exactly a proposition. You merely stated you would double my salary. No mention was made of what I must do to earn such largesse."

"Exactly what you do for the consortium."

"And that is?"

"You tell me."

"Good try." Weiderhof laughed good-naturedly. "I may look it, but I promise you *Herr* Zeller, I am not considered a naive man. Tell me what is in your mind. I shall make the determination—if I am the right man for your needs. If not I can recommend—"

"Look, Weiderhof, we can yodel and dance the polka for a month. I have no time for charades. Did I ask you to identify the consortium? No. I know *who* they are. I need only know *what* they are! The purpose behind their anonymity. In addition I want to buy a bank."

"A bank?"

"The Suisse Banque Royale."

Weiderhof suppressed his amazement. "The *Suisse* is not for sale."

"Anything is for sale for the right price."

"Not the *Suisse*. Forget it."

Zeller brazenly pulled a small black book from his jacket pocket. He opened it, prepared to quote facts and figures, peering casually about the crowded room. Abruptly he changed his mind and placed the book before Weiderhof. "Glance at the entries, *Herr* Weiderhof, the figures. Assets, losses, liabilities, investments, manipulations of trust funds that are *not* trust funds at all but *coverups* to finance revolution in several nations. Shall I remind you of the mysterious disappearance of certain Russian nobility whose deposits were removed by the bank's agents to be split fifty-fifty with the informants? Informants who also disappeared as mysteriously as the unsuspecting Russians?"

"Fortunately, the Almighty endowed me with sight, *Herr* Zeller. I can read without assistance. Had I known you intended to make shocking revelations I might have suggested a more discreet rendezvous."

"How many of these entries can you substantiate? And don't bother to lie to me. I have in my possession confiscated classified ledgers labeled *Ramen Ruski*."

Weiderhof paled at the words. He returned the book to Zeller. "What will you pay for my testimony?"

"I told you. Double what the hierarchy pays you."

"I'll settle for half interest in the bank."

Zeller observed the Swiss finish his lunch, his eyes narrowing in distrust.

"*Herr* Weiderhof, understand me . . . to be taken lightly when I negotiate business is anathema to my nature. When Zeller is not appreciated, he becomes a difficult negotiator. Having traveled enormous distances, at great personal risk, to confer with the banking hierarchy, I have no intention now of remaining someone's lackey. My recent inheritance makes me ten times a millionaire!"

"*Herr* Zeller—" Weiderhof removed his glasses. "Do not place yourself in the unenviable position of perjuring yourself. So that you understand *me*, I suggest I know everything about you and how you came by your—*legacy*. The papers you saw on my desk earlier represent a complete dossier on you from day one, beginning with your illegitimate birth, your orphan days, your delinquency, printer's apprenticeship, up to and including your matriculation at Lausanne University where our agents recruited you—*after* your secret liaison with the Okrana.''

"*Our* agents?''

"Our agents.'' Weiderhof reset the pince-nez over his nose.

Zeller, tensing, made a swift reevaluation.

"Earlier you claimed you knew the identity of the banking hierarchy, that you wanted to buy the *Suisse Banque Royale*—''

Zeller stiffened imperceptibly.

"I assume you do not know the name Weiderhof. If you failed to uncover the name of Sigmund Weiderhof in those secret Russian plots, my job was exemplary. You still don't understand, do you, Zeller? I am Sigmund Weiderhof, owner of the bank you are anxious to purchase. For sentimental reasons I will not part with it. However, for a price you may buy forty-nine percent.'' He packed a pipe with rum tobacco as he spoke.

Zeller, having just committed the faux pas of the century, was unprepared for failure on the heel of his recent victories. Forced to reexamine his thinking as they ambled quietly along the *Bahnhofstrasse* from the *Aldstat*, heading toward the newer section of the city along the lake, he listened as Weiderhof pointedly suggested possible business expansion. He explained the benefits of Switzerland's neutrality during the last war and its growing financial stability despite global depression, how international organizations held business conferences in the various Swiss cities. He enumerated the advantages of their confidential banking systems, how they attracted foreign interests and the important future of Swiss banking.

"No gangsterism is necessary to ensure the future of Swiss banking profits. They are incalculable.''

They stood along the waterfront, observing the boats dotting the lake. Only then did Zeller ask the magical question. "How may I buy half the bank?'' And Weiderhof pulled no punches.

"Get close to this man, Benito Mussolini, in Italy. Become our liaison, steer him away from his Bolshevik leanings. We witnessed disaster in Russia—want no repetition of a Workers' World. This man in Italy has caught the fancy of wealthy Italian and European industrialists. He lacks one essential you command: organizational genius. A genius to which I bow deferentially. We shall provide this iconoclast in Milano with a campaign chest of unlimited funds. In return, you and this exuberant, iron-jawed politico will give birth to a new ideology—fascism. And our personal remuneration to you for your endeavor is forty-nine percent of the bank.''

The Italian Assignment, Zeller told himself in a nutshell! He paced the marble floor. His bargain with the golden Midas devils signed, he had met with Mussolini, prepared to back the former journalist to the end. As the political empire grew, modifications were made; favors asked by Zurich were promptly given. In the early 1930s they had exacted from Il Duce a promise that no Jewish problem would exist in Rome for the duration of his tenure as head of the Fascist party.

Just as Mussolini remained outside the Quadrumvirate, so did Zeller. He loathed the visibility forced on him in Rome. The anonymity his Zurich colleagues enjoyed wasn't his to comfort him. In his role as liaison minister of finance to Il Duce, Zeller channeled needed funds from Zurich to the party whenever contributions waned. Under this guise and on orders from the consortium, Zeller put to work a secret network of spies who reported all subversive activities, no matter how insignificant or irrelevant they appeared. In the early days the information was passed on to Il Duce. Recently, because of the deteriorating relationship between them, this news was withheld.

Zeller lit a cigarette, inhaled deeply, reflecting on the causes of alienation between himself and the Italian despot. He couldn't pinpoint the exact moment. For over a decade the relationship had flourished, all commitments had been honored. Yet?

Zeller had frequented Zurich following the initial meeting with Weiderhof. One day Weiderhof thrust a copy of Dr. Theodore Herzel's *The Jewish State* into Zeller's hands along with the writings of other Zionist scholars. At the time world opinion concerning the Jews didn't touch Zeller. To him, Zionism became an avenue of thought to explore, not one in which to participate. ''The Jewish Problem will soon become a *cause célèbre*, my good friend,'' Sigmund had told him.

So willing was Zeller to become part of the hierarchy—perhaps one day the entire ruling body—he agreed to all suggestions by his mentors. He became amenable to the marriage contract between himself and the Austrian contessa arranged by Weiderhof's cronies. If Marie Clotilde had ten heads and moved like a centipede, it wouldn't have mattered to him.

Weiderhof taught him all he cared to know about the Jewish

Problem. If Zionism was a stepping stone to higher plateaus, if he must embrace a new politic to reach his goal, so be it! The lessons to be learned from the Zurich banking hierarchy were vast in scope, beyond imagination. But the lessons learned in observing the duplicity of Il Duce were the essence for Zeller's future dealings—concession. How cleverly Il Duce had pacified the papacy by making enormous concessions. Weaning the powerful religious body to his side had strengthened the dictatorship. Il Duce, placing expediency above all else and prepared to ride roughshod over his anticlerical feelings, had made sweeping concessions to a religion he detested. In return the enormous influence exerted on his behalf had made his position impregnable. Mussolini's adaptability, his tactful offer of the olive branch to the Vatican, brought success to the fascist leader where others before him had failed. The never-to-be-forgotten object lessons learned under fascism would work in Zurich, at the *right* time.

Zeller glanced at his watch. Fifteen minutes! He'd never forget or forgive this humiliation, never! In a showdown, would Il Duce remember Zeller's value to him? Who *knew* the state of Il Duce's mercurial mind these days? Recently the fascist powerhead had defended his political *fait accompli*—better described as products of trial and error—refusing to critically examine increasing debts and diminishing profits from his determined efforts to expand the fascist empire.

Consider survival, Zeller. Calculate and reexamine your position within the infrastructure of fascist power. This is no time to question Il Duce's positions on anything—not in so turbulent a political climate!

Inside the gigantic marbled study designed to intimidate and humble any man from king to streetcleaner, Il Duce sauntered to the balcony window, lost in contemplation of Amadeo Zeller.

For too long the man had occupied his thoughts. Rumors concerning his minister's associations with men deemed enemies of fascism were roosting on Il Duce's doorstep. Disconcerted by world talk, the lack of confirmation or denial from Zeller, the fascist leader brooded. No question, Zeller was unique. His was the mind of a contriving novelist who designs plot upon plot with uncanny expertise. To possess the heart, mind, memory, personality, and motivation of numerous personalities and keep them separate and apart from others was indeed an unqualified display of genius.

Something about Zeller rankled him. The man considered himself a political genius. He was not a majority of one in this evaluation; others close to the dictatorship believed it. A measure of this was evidenced by the fact that his colleagues had trusted him for well over a decade. The exceptions, his decriers had kept him toe-dancing through perilous scenarios from which he never failed to extricate himself. So many confidants envied Zeller's status, his accomplishments and innate talents, but in recent days there'd been a groundswell of discontent concerning his liaison finance minister because of his harsh vocal Zionist persuasions. What was this damnable game he played? What was the true purpose of his chameleonlike personality changes and subtle innuendos dropped in the *right* watering holes at the *right* time? So! He had Il Duce in his hip pocket—did he? These were the dusty rumors coming home to roost. Worse, he, Il Duce, who'd sworn a decade ago that no Jewish Problems existed in Italy would be forced to reevaluate the situation in a new light.

Curse Zeller for his political charades! He must do what was right for Italy and the dictatorship—not for Zeller!

What stuck in his craw, and transcended any secret ploys, religious or political, were the contents of recently compiled dossiers on Zeller. precisely it was the lack of information in the period prior to his emergence in Italy in 1921 that lit fires of discontent. The caliber of man whose life lacked documentation spelled clear messages in Il Duce's mind. *Only a man with a terrifying past did not exist on paper. An assassin, perhaps?*

The corpulent file contained a formidable list of aliases Zeller had used in incredible involvements, unbelievable feats. Il Duce's immediate reaction was wild denial. Following a trip to Austria he had good reason to amend his initial reaction. Hitler, with whom he liaisoned had made a chance remark about Zeller that had provoked his curiosity.

"Rome's Minister of Finance. Is he the man who owns property at St. Bartolema in Bavaria? I stumbled across property deeds, on lands adjacent to mine at Berchtesgaden."

The ominous question wasn't merely a chance remark, but a studied statement of fact designed to provoke thought. Feigning indifference, Il Duce treated the inquiry as inconsequential. A question from Hitler provoked a deep-rooted curiosity. Later perusal of the property deed in question indicated an out-and-out property grant to Zeller by Brother Heinrich Schuller *without* monetary compensation. After further inquiry, the date of transfer was discovered to be one month *after* the monk was found dead in Admont, Austria. Further probing uncovered a great deal, but most enlightening was the report from the Austrian authorities naming one possible suspect: Professor Fabrizio Caragini! *One of the many aliases assumed by Zeller!*

By now, Il Duce knew Zeller well—too well! Imparting none of his findings to Zeller, he had locked the damaging files in his personal safe and remained remote to him. Inquiries about Zeller, he learned recently were emanating from Corsica. Corsica, eh? Well, it's best we get the show on the road.

Il Duce glanced impatiently at the gold and porcelain clock on his desk. He summoned an aide by pulling a cord near the window. The young officer entered from an anteroom, clicked his heels, saluting smartly. Il Duce made a small brushing movement with his hand, gesturing to admit Zeller. The man who showed no emotion was the man to be carefully scrutinized.

Zeller entered the lavish chambers. Protocol demanded he stand perfectly still until Il Duce acknowledged him.

Silence . . . protracted, infuriating silence. Zeller endured the interminable snub. He played the game out, waiting at attention until the imperious dignitary turned, nodded perfunctorily, and, jutting the famous jaw, gestured to the chair opposite his desk. No attempts were made at handshaking. The gesture was considered gauche by the dictator; he was convinced it made him vulnerable to an assassin's attack. A clever trick used by Sicilian Mafia before he had trimmed its sails.

"Minister Zeller?" Beneath the obligatory cordiality of the black-shirted leader's voice, storm clouds massed. He removed his gold braided tunic, hung it over a nearby chair, and, rubbing the small cyst on his shaven head, strutted pompously, hands on hips, lips unsmiling. His standing post assured him of dominance in conversation, a ploy he used frequently. "What is so pressing it couldn't wait another week?"

"Two weeks have passed, Excellency. Your constituents and financial bankers demand assurance from you."

"*Demand!* By what right?" Black fascist eyes burned through Zeller's glasses.

"Very well, they request—"

"*Assurance!*" The bleating voice arose in furor.

"They strenuously object to rumors of a possible alliance with Germany and demand reassurance from you—"

"Object! By what right do they object to *my* policies?"

"Your word promising no anti-Semitism would take root in Rome appears false in view of your recent vacillation."

"What gives *you* or any of them the impression Il Duce has broken his word?" The atmosphere turned oppressive.

"The intended alliance with Hitler. Hitler's name is synonymous with anti-Semitism. Anti-Semitism means the destruction of the Jews. Zurich will not permit it."

"So! I should permit your Zionist comrades to dictate fascist policy?"

"They demand positive assurance that you keep the promise made them nearly a decade ago. You permit speculation where none should exist. You reflect too many sides. You are at once revolutionary and conservative, Catholic and iconoclast, socialist and bourgeois, both a proponent of law and justice, yet its most vociferous opponent. You create cynicism and disquiet among these *special* constituents. In the past, despite all visible contradictions, they trusted you. They believed in your good intentions. They insisted that you employed such stratagems to delude the enemies of Italy. Now they ask, is the delusion theirs or yours?"

The pause was ominous, the tension, electric. "No more than your delusion when you persuaded me to assist Franco in Spain." Il Duce sucked in his breath and, pivoting on one foot, faced the man he distrusted more by the moment. "Be careful, Zeller. You may overstep your position. You are a man of colossal self-confidence." He heaved his thighs, wriggled them, shaking out the stiffness. "I have never brought you to task for matters best left to the past. None of us is perfect. But you! You bloody fool, have brought yourself to the attention of the *Führer*!"

Zeller peered past the dictator, his features paling slightly. "I don't understand. Why to Hitler?"

"*Damnation!* How should I know? You're the clever one! Rumors breed worse in the Quirinal than mosquitoes in the Pontine Marshes, Zeller. Your loyalty is at risk. Do I have reason to question your loyalty? And there is talk you are a *gabbamondo*. Are you a cheat, a swindler, an imposter?"

"That," replied Zeller without missing a beat, "is malicious gossip spread by enemies who envy our long-enjoyed relationship, Duce." The voice possessed infuriating calm.

"Loyal citizens in Italy who remain loyal have no worry from Il Duce."

"You recently demanded all Italian Jews must cut ties with old-world Jewry," Zeller pressed brazenly.

"The British Zionists are a threat to fascism!"

"Why do Italian Jews fear and oppose this whispered alliance with Hitler?"

"Ask them! They are *your* people—not mine!" Il Duce said snidely.

"Oh, I have asked *my* people. It is for them I speak." Zeller removed his dark lenses, his opaque eyes as determined as Il Duce's. "These same people who helped fill your war chests state that if you fail to avert the German alliance, you set the pace for the beginning of your downfall."

Il Duce, appalled at Zeller's audacity, flushed, turning a mottled purple. "You dare? You dare threaten Italy? To threaten Il Duce is to threaten Italy! *You dare?*"

"Benito, it is not I who issue ultimatums. I am liaison for the men of Zurich. My associates would dare threaten God Himself if needs be."

The iron jaw jutted, black eyes furious. Il Duce turned his back on Zeller and strutted to the window. "Italian Jews know me to be a friend to all Jews. Zionism is their enemy—Zionism! Tell that to your associates in Zurich!" He returned to his chair behind his desk. He did not sit down; he stood cautiously, poised like a spider at the edge of his web, waiting to pounce on his prey.

"I have withstood the crisis of revolution, attacked the early fascists because they were false prophets who used death, destruction, and villainy as tools, even as I was forced to use violence to suppress the opponents of fascism. Understand this, *Minister* Zeller, there is little I would not do to preserve my fascist dynasty. By now you should know my gift of infallibility."

The underlying threats couched in the dictator's words were unmistakable, "Politics, as you know, is a cold-blooded, cruel, heartless business," Zeller said with a superficial cleverness that failed to deceive the Italian leader.

Il Duce picked up a decanter of wine, poured two glasses. He handed one to Zeller, held the second before him. "Drink, Amadeo. Let us put aside this quarrel. We will survive these agitators. Too many years of personal success form an impregnable relationship between us." They clinked glasses. Zeller glowered inwardly.

You drink, Duce the magnificent. Your days are numbered.

They both sipped the wine, smiles fixed on their lips.

You drink, Zeller, master chameleon. You have shed your last disguise. Already you are a forgotten man.

They placed empty glasses on an ornate silver tray.

"Remember me to the contessa with much affection."

"The contessa sends the godfather of our son her love."

"Victor will make a fine militarist. I am enormously impressed by the progress reports from the academy."

"He wishes to be the image of you. As a small child he mimicked you and named himself Il Duce."

Mussolini did not smile. He nodded a curt dismissal, observed Zeller as he left, backing out as one did with royalty.

In the room adjoining his office, a sultry-eyed, delicately featured brunette was waiting for Il Duce in a filmy black silk négligée. Benito made the error of allowing the erotic image to weaken his resolve. The pressing business with Zeller could wait until after the sexual interlude. He needed, if only for a few moments, to forget politics, and war. He needed respite from the Vatican, the Youth Movement, and most of all Hitler, who was putting the squeeze play on Austria—something he promised all Austrians he would not permit. He felt drained. Three foiled assassinations on his life in one week. At times he longed for the good old days when the sounds of mazurkas and waltzes stirred his heart, stepped up his life forces, and made him come alive. However much he was fed by his virtuosity at propaganda and showmanship, he was growing tired of beguiling the masses, at home and abroad, into becoming his accomplices. He needed a rest—a sea cruise, a time to be alone.

He shifted focus to Amadeo Zeller. An instant replay to the earlier scene between them brought even more to light. Compelled by forces stronger than his sexual appetite, he pushed the woman aside, pulled up his breeches, stormed back into his office, and jerked at the phone on his desk, barking harshly to the voice at the other end. "Set the wheels in motion. Immediately!"

Too late! The Burgatti-Bertelli sedan had an hour's start by the time the *Squadristi* and Italian intelligence agents arrived at the Zeller palazzo with arrest warrants.

The contessa, descending the massive spiral staircase, recognized one of the arresting officers. "What is it, Major Fiumo?"

The major removed his beaked cap, apology in his hangdog eyes. "With your permission, Contessa, the minister has been placed under official arrest."

Her slender hands fluttered to her face. "What? Surely I didn't hear you correctly? But why?" Her hand gripped the gilded banister tremblingly.

"The charge, dear Contessa, is treason against the government of Il Duce."

Clotilde didn't bat an eyelash. "What of the minister's family? Are they also under arrest?"

Major Fiumo shook his head. "Personal regrets from Il Duce himself. He was unable to spare your feelings, but he wishes you to know you and your family are under his personal protection. You have no reason to be concerned."

No reason to be concerned. Clotilde bit back any response and observed the men in the performance of their duty. An hour later, after the house was searched and the officers had left, Marie Clotilde ordered dinner for herself and daughter Clarisse. The girl, the image of her father, snapped, "I daresay, Mother, Il Duce grows more confusing daily. Does he actually believe he can make charges of treason stick against his minister of finance? He must have discovered one of his whores cheating on him and decided to blame father. What a lot of rutting men, these fascists!"

"Clarisse! Really! Is this what you learn at *that* school?"

"You make me associate with silly, horrible women whose only thoughts are fornication and you *dare* ask so inane a question? Why can't I go to a school that would at least permit me to expand my mind? The girls at school are silly, empty-headed geese. Observing them, I loathe being a woman. I should dislike growing up like them. They all possess the morals of alley cats."

"Clarisse! I urge you to stop this at once!" Clotilde gazed at her daughter, fearing the worst. Everything she'd tried to prevent was rearing its ugly head. Scowling, she poured tea. Clarisse shoved back her chair and stormed out of the room.

The contessa sighed deeply, her mind floating back to the day Victor was born.

In Ajaccio, Dariana had received an intimate note attached to the gold-lettered announcement: *A son, Victor, was born to the Contessa and Amadeo Zeller on December 17, 1923.* Setting aside the announcement, she had read the note. "Victor resembles me in temperament. Physically, he is a composite of both his parents save for the shock of black hair and brooding gray eyes. Thank God they aren't colorless. Pray all is well with your children. Love, Clotilde."

Dariana had quickly responded, sending a gift, congratulations, and a brief sketch of her children's accomplishments in their first year of life. She pointedly elaborated on the exceptional promise of her son Darius.

In Rome, reading the notes, her heart racing at the loss she felt by not sharing Darius's first year of life, Marie Clotilde had overcompensated by recording every moment of Victor's life in a diary. She doted on him, attended to his every whim and caprice, and managed successfully to spoil him, incurring her husband's wrath. "He'll be no mama's boy!" the infuriated lord of the manor had declared, keeping his plans for a son well guarded.

A year later, Clarisse was born. Thereupon a steady correspondence flowed across the sea from Rome to Ajaccio. Each mother chronicled the lives of her children. She didn't disappoint the mother who had abandoned her son so that he might live. Clotilde, in turn, described the changes in her children.

Clarisse is fair of skin, blue eyed—not colorless, thank God—but arrestingly electric. She has cunning manipulative ways and a maddening precocity. I swear to you, Dariana, she promises to be Amadeo's incarnation! But *not* if I have anything to do with it.

Victor demonstrates a penchant for the military. My heart quells at the thought. Is it just possible? Will Victor be the link to Napoleon my relatives sought for so long? Yesterday my husband firmly announced to me, "Victor will enter Il Duce's Fascist Youth Organization. Following his Catholic and philosophical studies he will go to St. Cyr Military Academy in France to be trained as a fitting officer for duty in the Italian Army." If he thought to receive any argument from me, he was mistaken.

When Il Duce glowingly asserted his rights as godfather to my son, as if Victor were his flesh and blood, he promised that Victor would be in the elite Italian intelligence division as a trusted officer. Amadeo's eyes sparked. It was a lucky day for me when I confided in Il Duce, concerning the disposition of my trust. I am now among his most highly favored, and fall under his protection just as I intended when I designed the plot to outwit Amadeo. Of course, I made substantial donations to the fascist private charities, with the shrewd assistance of his personal *avvocato* Donato Donatelli. My dear, he converted the trust secretly, in ways Amadeo won't detect for years.

In another letter to Dariana she confided,

In Victor's absence from the palazzo, while he's away at school, I am kept busy with countless charities and social functions. I confide to you, my dear Dariana, that I grow more alarmed at Clarisse daily. She is too much like her father. The prophesy I imparted to you, fanciful at the time, is becoming reality. Observing her, I am convinced I must find a proper finishing school, somewhere in France, even Switzerland. I must steer her away from her father's influences. I daresay I have checked out schools as meticulously as a veteran horse breeder checks out pure-bred mares for his champion stud.

And Clotilde had labored prodigiously, finecombing those schools that stressed artistic accomplishments, eliminating those that offered radical studies and belief that a girl's education went deeper than the skills needed to find a proper husband. A school in Geneva, selected the moment tutors in Rome retired from their position at the palazzo, she prayed would solve her dilemma over Clarisse.

Clotilde's free time, with both children away at school, was spent reading and rereading Dariana's cherished letters, which spanned the period beginning shortly after Darius's birth to his sixteenth birthday. Over the years the letters had nourished the ache in Clotilde, enabling her to endure life with Zeller without disintegrating. Amazed at her own resilience, she marveled at the swiftness of time and how she had courageously braved the Zeller storms. Zeller had never protested or contested the story from Positano that made headlines in Rome. Moreover he had never harked back to the subject. Sensitive to his erratic moods,

Clotilde marked time. Somehow, some way, soon, Zeller would demand his pound of flesh and drain the blood from her.

Clotilde was right. The Positano affair had left Zeller dissatisfied. Oddly enough, on this day as he sped out of Rome into exile, Zeller's thoughts wrapped around the day he had returned from Libya to Rome. How could he miss the obvious changes in his wife? By radiating so brazen a hostility she had incurred his suspicions. Damn that conspiratorial aura she had projected and continued to flaunt at him for nearly sixteen years! Daring him to challenge that seraphic purity she exuded . . . She could fool anyone—but not Zeller!

Zeller—a cuckold? Never! He'd never permit it. That determination made, he waited until the time was ripe. How many times had he replayed the scenario?

Gazing out the rear window of his chauffeur-driven Burgatti-Bertelli sedan at the Tuscany countryside, his thoughts focused on the Zeller bloodhounds. Turned loose on his departure, they never returned to Rome to recount the details of their assignment. Zeller knew all about the Bertelli love nest high above Rome on one of the Seven Hills, and of the near miss on Bertelli's life. But the Positano shoot-out, never clearly explained, had provided him neither balm nor information.

Four trusted men dead! Inability to confirm or deny his wife's adulterous activities had left him up in the air. *Satan be damned!* The identity of Bertelli's paramour, a mystery until the auto tycoon identified her as a foreigner, had titillated all of Rome. A closer study of the mystery woman's photographs had evoked gasps of astonishment from Zeller. She bore an uncanny resemblance to Clotilde. He had searched the face carefully, studying it from every angle for hours, trying to assure himself she was not the contessa. The differences were slight: the wrong tilt of the nose, the slant of the eye, the imperious chin. Definitely, she was not Clotilde, *and,* Zeller *knew* he was being had. The presence of his men in Positano, the discovery of their dead bodies, had confirmed an indisputable fact: somehow Clotilde had blazed a hot trail to that southern love nest! His men were sharp, unequaled in their professional know-how. Mistaken identities were possible but hardly likely.

The loss of three trusted, personally trained assassins had struck him a severe blow. When the fourth met his death in a freak train accident, Zeller discerned the machinations of a masterfully executed plot. If he but whispered a word about love tryst, condemning fingers could easily point at him, spotlighting his personal guilt in the events that followed. He could accuse no one. Worse, the indignity of feigning total ignorance seared his insides.

Zeller, a man who knew when to chalk up his losses and move to greener pastures, focused covertly on Bertelli, ordering an indepth dossier on the auto tycoon. The dossier had expanded to a large portfolio presently secreted in a locked file in his chateau in Zurich.

Destroy Bertelli! Destroy Bertelli! The words, repeated as a daily litany, burned fires of vengeance in his soul. In the past, every avenue was closed to him since the industrialist was held in Il Duce's high esteem. Now he no longer felt these constraints. He would bide his time, await personal satisfaction, and when the time was right . . .

While he was caught in the cross-currents of raging jealousy and infuriating anger at his impotence in the Positano affair, Clotilde's announced pregnancy had both thwarted and secretly elated Zeller. The image of an expectant father was appealing to his political cronies. Among the fascists, the birth of each child added a measure or two to a man's stature. He pompously heralded the event far before its time. Later, when Clotilde returned from Corsica to sadly announce the infant was stillborn, he was forced to refute the then accepted fact.

"Try, try again, Amadeo," Il Duce had counseled his finance minister. "You cannot imagine how your stock soared among your colleagues at the earlier news." The statement both cut Zeller to the quick and proved informative. His popularity on the wane with Il Duce, he pondered the statement, turning it over and over. He got the message clearly.

So he reluctantly brought himself to Clotilde's bed chamber to conceive their son, Victor, born nine months to the day after his decision. Then, once again, when Clotilde's body was capable, he bedded with her to conceive Clarisse. Following the birth of Clarisse, Amadeo grew disgusted with the rash of emotional changes and ailments she experienced during her pregnancies. Disdaining her, he paid court to his numerous concubines.

Clotilde be damned! Let her raise the children! Let her become the darling of fascist society! Let her become Il Duce's most sought-after hostess! And she had—*in spades!* Her popularity with the "in" crowd ate away at Zeller. The mask he wore to hide his hatred had peeled away, disintegrated by the poisonous evil chewing at him. No chance for rapprochement between the contessa and himself. He could barely stand her now.

Yet, no matter how he scorned her or flouted his promiscuity before all Rome, Marie Clotilde's solid ties with Italy's glorified leader had served Zeller in good stead for more than a decade. The changing political climate had posed serious threats to him in the recent years. And Clotilde! Imagine, that bird-brained Clotilde, who once had difficulty speaking, was becoming too powerful, too clever, too public a commodity to be insulted or treated derisively by her own husband. Her image smiled back at him from every society column in every Rome newspaper.

You bloody, bloody fool! You've brought yourself to the attention of the Fuhrer!

The words spoken earlier that day by Il Duce swam before him. Zeller flinched, his brows knit in a scowl. What the devil did Benito mean by this statement? He mulled the words over. Who the hell knew the Machiavellian workings of Il Duce's mind? He knew the man used words to evoke emotional responses from his prey. Il Duce bore the unmistakable mark of a political virtuoso who wasted little time questioning the importance of any given task—he merely went ahead and did it, impulsively and without fear. The energy he burned in his sexual escapades could light the city of Rome for a millennium.

Whatever Il Duce meant by his reference to the *Führer* meant little to Zeller presently. He let his thoughts trail back to the contessa. The day he learned of lawyer Donatelli's cleverness in manipulating the de Bernadorf trust, he was sent into borderline shock. Why hadn't he suspected then, the end was in sight? Yes, he reflected it was this action that caused the sudden reversal of political circumstances, of playing the defense instead of offense. What really galled Zeller was the lack of precious time needed to sort out the intrigue behind his wife's cleverly designed conspiracy to put him in bad stead with the fascists— most especially, Il Duce.

Zeller, flicking his fingernails, lit a Turkish cigarette as the sedan continued northward, heading for Milan and the Swiss border. Monday-morning quarterbacking was not a fascinating occupation for Zeller, but now, forced to recap the events, he blamed it all on too busy a schedule, lack of time to sort out the rotten apples.

What an intriguing scenario! How was it, Il Duce had learned of the impending collapse of Austria's largest bank, the Credit Anwalt, and he, Zeller had not? Moments before that nation's abandonment of the Gold Standard, Italian diplomats, engaging in some banking sleight-of-hand, had managed to salvage the majority of Clotilde's trust by converting those assets into sound investments! Was it Il Duce's conspiracy with Donatelli? Or was it a tip from some powerful businessman? One man, an industrialist, *Miguel Bertelli*?

Zeller attempted to ferret out why his Zurich associates had signaled the impending Wall Street Crash in 1929 in time to avert disaster and failed to signal the impending Austrian banking crisis in 1931. The matter sat ill with him. His Zurich colleagues had insisted couriers had been dispatched to him and delivered the sensitive material directly to the minister's office. Zeller's employees—his most trusted confidants—had denied the allegation. Whereupon Zeller, poised between two formidable perils, the Zurich pythons and the Italian mongoose, temporized. Between the two opposing forces, the truth would one day be known.

Zeller wiped beads of sweat from his creased brow. A tic forming at the corner of his mouth twisted his thin lips into cruel white scar lines. He removed his dark glasses—he always wore them—seldom appeared without them. Wiping them clean, he reset them into place. He opened a gold pill case, removed a morphine tablet, placed it in his mouth, and washed it down with cognac from a silver flask. Morphine to quiet his duodenal ulcer.

Storm clouds on the Zeller domestic front were nothing compared to what was brewing in the fascist political arena, thought the new exile. His outward calm, abetted by the morphine tablet, concealed sparks of inspiration, forming a mosaic in his mind. Internally, he saw himself transformed into a prognosticator, capable of divining the future. The object of his scrutiny, Il Duce, infuriated him.

Il Duce! Il Duce! Why hadn't he anticipated the man's move?

The reality of an approaching Axis alliance and Il Duce's apparent willingness to accept Hitler's domination spilled enough acid on Zeller's intestines to burn a dozen holes in his stomach. Why hadn't he assessed his position with Mussolini sooner? Puffing thoughtfully on his cigarette, he rolled back his memory.

The antics and political ambitions of a man named Adolf Hitler, usurper of incredible power, posed a frightening shadow of might on the German horizon. This Goliath of spectacular persuasive powers had ridden herd over most of Germany, audaciously proposing the creation of a supernation. Every survival instinct in Zeller had sprung to life. Riding the crest of fascism, Zeller found little time for the lowly Hitler. To have assessed him when he first appeared on the political scene would have proved a fruitless exercise. Now, nearly two decades after the Great War, Germany no longer struck with a viscious breakdown was under the leadership of this nondescript little corporal sporting a small brush mustache.

Zeller opened a rear window of the sedan, inhaling the scents of Tuscan vineyards. Before nightfall they should reach Florence, he thought, closing the window.

Hitler . . . Adolf Hitler . . . He knew the entire game plan shortly after the burning of the Reichstag in February 1933. Zurich was backing it. The Reichstag burning flushed out the industrialists, who had secretly supported the *Führer*. One of them, the steel magnate Krupp, openly "Heil Hitlered" acquaintances on the street. Krupp had written his congratulation to Hitler. Krupp's reward? Appointment as czar of German industry, to sanctify the marriage between big business and National Socialism. When Sigmund Weiderhof was appointed president of the Reichsbank, Zeller knew the overall schematic. Oh, possibly not the fine print, but he knew what was in the offing. And when Weiderhof called him to Zurich, suggested he begin to talk alliances between Il Duce and Hitler, he became a spectator and coconspirator, without a block of stock to vote his own considerations in the matter.

The Reichstag fire marked death for German democracy. The Weimar Republic collapsed. And Zurich ensured the *Fuhrer*'s meteoric rise to fame. The Nazi party seized control of the tottering Von Hindenberg regime and with whirlwind strategy suspended civil liberties in Germany. Then Hitler moved. By God how he moved, purging communists, Social Democrats, and anything smacking of parliamentarianism. In rapid-fire order, Hitler swung out against the trade unions, intellectuals, and pacifists alike. The process of Nazification had begun. Before it ended, an entire nation, the world itself, would cow before Adolf Hitler. Zeller *knew* it.

And when Weiderhof suggested he should climb aboard the band wagon, Zeller pulled back, uncertain whether he should give his allegiance to the swastika-wielding behemoth, until he extricated himself from Il Duce's fascisti. "Would you object to becoming Hitler's finance minister?" Weiderhof pressed.

"Not while I am in bed with Mussolini," Zeller had retorted, ending the planned seduction. Periodically he received nudges from Weiderhof.

"Not only do bureaucrats and industrialists support Hitler, but intellectuals and literary figures find it possible to serve the *Führer*," he insisted. "They espouse the regeneration of Germany!"

Zeller sipped cognac from the silver flask. His secret files contained highly classified information, enough to plunge ten nations into war. He felt exalted to be part of the network that ruled the world, part of an elite that designed global scenarios and pulled the strings that made the world jump. He vividly recalled that day when the world, rotating smugly on its axis, had received a satanic goosing.

Black Thursday . . . October 1929. A host of avenging demons ripping through Wall Street had laid siege to world economy, toppling governments, devastating the lives of millions of speculators while paradoxically making millionaires out of those rare few in-the-knows. Zeller, one of those rare few, given word early in October, had sold his holdings. When the market plunged to rock bottom, he bought at give-away prices. The Great Crash, prelude to the Great Depression, had devastated many nations. Canny politicos produced a new messiah who promised his people a National Recovery Act. Americans, anxious to discard the old deck of cards, voted FDR and his New Deal into the White House.

In April of 1933 Zeller had traveled to Berlin to find the city in fear, filled with whisperings of illegal midnight arrests, of prisoners tortured in barracks cells. Mass meetings, parades, pageantry distracted the people. Uniformed Germans in large, swaggering boots thundered up and down Adolf Hitler Platz, and Herman Goering Strasse. Solid citizens rallied to Hitler's support. An outcry from liberals abroad infuriated Hitler.

The first of April he instituted a boycott against Jewish businesses. On the eve of the boycott the Italian ambassador had urged him, in the name of Mussolini, to soften his attitude toward the Jews. Hitler countered, "There are few Jews in Italy and Il Duce has no comprehension of the Jewish Problem."

Mussolini's animosity had given Zeller hope in the early days before soldering irons were put to alliances, because he knew the fascist leader was marking time to create a far more complicated scenario in what remained of the 1930s. He felt confident that

Hitler's comet would zoom and spend itself long before Il Duce's time on earth.

Zeller, part of the elite who watched warring generals warm up in bullpens, could point with certainty to the day war would commence. War, already born in the mind of Zurich's finance titans, was merely a tool in the game of international monopoly. Nations stood poised—not as ready as Germany—but poised enough to make preparations.

It was not for nothing the smoke signals of war were ignored by several nations. Zeller knew the scenario intimately. Each nation falling into desperate economical straits, needs the monetary boosts war provided. So industrialists, munitions makers, corporations who profited from war, wound up propaganda machines. It was all part of the war game.

That Hitler's solution to the Jewish Problem would one day spill over into Italy and most of Europe was a foregone conclusion, vividly imprinted in Zeller's mind. All that remained, now that he knew his position with Il Duce, was to burn his bridges behind him and heed the precautionary whisperings coming through to him in the direct pipeline to destiny.

The pictures in his mind progressed, adjusting themselves.

In the past he was careful not to disagree with Il Duce. He tried, against his nature, to remain serene in the company of the deluded Caesar who placed himself above Roman nobles. He had kept tight ties with the man for fear others would ingratiate themselves to the dictator. Now it was finished. He could systematically begin the downfall and destruction of the idol with feet of clay.

He could devote himself to the darker side of the libretto, the part in which Zeller excelled.

Chapter Twenty-six ·

Il Duce's sudden disaffection with Minister Zeller sent shock waves through the Quirinale and the Fascist party. When word spread that Il Duce himself had signed the arrest warrants, frantic efforts were initiated by highly placed fascisti to sweep their offices clean of any taint of the former minister. Surely the *Squadristi* and intelligence forces would retaliate against any man who had fraternized with Zeller in the past. No one, not the highest-ranking fascist or the lowliest clerk in government, held Il Duce cheaply because he'd erred in judgment. The fascist leader had made few mistakes in his career and knew the wisdom in cutting his losses at the appropriate time. He was a jealous, spiteful man who never forgot an embarrassment or an injustice done to him. Most wagered Zeller would be caught and chopped into tiger bait before nightfall on this momentous day.

They were wrong. The only man who *knew* the inner machinations of Il Duce's mind and manner of retaliation had already escaped his clutches and was presently headed for Milano and the Swiss border.

Zeller's exodus from Rome coincided with the birth of Claude St. Gallens, banker, financier, director of the *Suisse Banque Royale* of Zurich.

It was a stunning autumn afternoon as his chauffeur-driven sedan sped through the lush Lombardy countryside. Claude St. Gallens applied the finishing touches to his disguise, survival uppermost in his mind. His eyes covered with dark glasses, gray wig in place, a thick salt-and-pepper mustache affixed to his upper lip, he viewed his handiwork in the mirrored lid of his case. Good . . . very good. New identity papers, visas, passports, all stamped with authentic fascist seals. He applauded his foresight. No longer did he feel like a man in jeopardy. Fascism was behind him.

For a time he'd harbored suspicions but refused to believe in any possible alliance between Germany and Italy. Recently Il Duce had publicly denounced Hitler, charging the Nazi leader with the instigation of the Austrian revolt. Disgusted with the *Führer*, he had openly declared the Germans to be murderers. Further he charged Hitler with the murder of Dollfuss in 1934. In the ensuing storm, Il Duce proceeded to hurl vitriol against the great world powers. "Are you all blind not to recognize the German dangers? You fail to recognize the coalition racking up against me? Hitler will make war! Alone, I cannot stand up against his whirlwind force! Something must be done and quickly!" These were Mussolini's words! Empty words spoken to the world. It seemed then that nothing would mend the breaches between those two nations. Now the political beasts of the earth had become bed partners!

Empty words, Il Duce! Empty words for which you shall soon pay!

St. Gallens etched these words into his consciousness. His day would come. And when it did . . .

Claude St. Gallens, about to choreograph a *danse macabre*. began with a simple order: "Stop the automobile, Maggiore, I must relieve myself."

The chauffeur eased the car to the side of the road. He turned off the engine, opened the rear door, observing the minister. If Maggiore regarded Zeller as an eccentric, he kept his thoughts to himself. Zeller had often donned disguises to escape detection by a jealous mistress or two as he flitted from flower to flower in the garden of Rome's sweetest, most delectable blooms bent on climbing the slippery slopes of fascist society. This martinet knew the wisdom of chaining his tongue. Now, as he waited in the early dusk the urge to urinate came upon him too. He unbuttoned his fly, moved awkwardly across the narrow road, and watered the vegetation of the steep incline. Whistling a fascist tune, he failed to discern a pistol affixed with a silencer pointed at him.

Phhhfffttt! Phhhfffttt! Phhhfffttt!

Three quick bursts from the gun felled the older man. St. Gallens moved in quickly, crossed the road, pulled Maggiore into the bushes, and promptly undressed him. He retrieved his discarded fascist uniform from the car, dressed the dead man in it, and planted the Zeller ID on him. Peering cautiously in both directions, he darted to the sedan, started the engine, and wheeled it across the road to the outer edge of the ravine, and set the hand brake. Quickly he propped Maggiore behind the steering wheel, retrieved his satchel, and placed it on the ground. He gathered the discarded clothing, shoved them into the trunk box, and lit a match to them. Swiftly he moved around to the driver's side, released the hand brake, and, shoving hard, heaved the auto over the precipice.

St. Gallens jumped back, watched the powerful machine careen over the cliff, soaring into space, then hitting the ground, bouncing deeper into the endless chasm below. An explosion shook the earth, a burst of flames shot up skyward, consuming the vehicle. He smiled. The fire would make positive identification impossible.

Dressed in a sedate, navy-blue serge suit with a topcoat over his arm, he picked up his satchel and moved along the corniche, caught at once in the high-beamed headlights of a speeding roadster. A loud screeching of brakes coupled with the stench of burning rubber split the early twilight. The careening auto lurched to the left, then right, then spun out in a ninety-degree turn, ran up an embankment, burying the snout of the automobile in dirt and leafy foliage of the hillside. The loud, angry blasting of a horn and an enraged voice pierced the tranquillity of the night. A woman cursed, railing at him, her features indiscernible.

"*Stupido! Imbecile!* You scared the living devil out of me!"

St. Gallens approached the car cautiously. "Do you suppose you didn't frighten me coming around that bend at breakneck speed?" He mopped the sweat pouring from his forehead. "Two near fatal accidents in one night are more than I can handle," he muttered feebly, feigning near prostration, tapping the area of his heart.

The woman composed herself. "I regret your run of bad luck, *signore,* but I too am without composure after so close a call. What happened to you?"

"My car overturned back there. Nature beckoned, you see. And I, utterly without wits, failed to set my hand brake . . . the gears were in neutral . . . see, down there . . . the fire. At the bottom of the canyon . . . remains of my machine . . . consumed by fire." He sighed.

The woman calmed herself, listened politely, then made several attempts to start the stalled auto before the engine finally turned over. Shoving the gears into reverse, she gunned the motor, backed down, easing it off the incline and pulled forward to the side of the road. She set the hand brake, turned off the engine and got out from behind the wheel of her splendid Burgatti-Bertelli roadster.

She scurried across the road to the edge of the cliff, peering down in disbelief at the spiraling black smoke and angry flames.

"Give thanks for God's favor, *signore*. You could have been killed! May I offer you transportation to Milano? If the Germans do not detain me at the border, I shall travel to Switzerland." Her hesitation was marked. "Uh—are you a fascist?"

"No, *signora*. Swiss," he lied deftly.

"Ah, I can speak frankly then? Why Il Duce permitted the Germans free access to Italy is total insanity. They assume unimpeachable authority. They ask impertinent questions as if they already *own* Italy! Germans! Outrageous peasants!" She led the way across the road to her car, pausing briefly to assess the damage. Dismayed, she picked at the foliage and dirt stuck in the grill, dislodging portions, grimacing distastefully at the mess on her gloved hands. She was fastidious in her attempt not to smear her tailored suit with the messy clods.

In the play of lights she saw the accident victim in profile. "Poor soul, I frightened you to death," she exclaimed. The apparent stoop of his shoulders, the list to one side as he walked, evoked a more solicitous attitude from *Signora* Amadora Bertelli Donatelli. She apologized for frightening him earlier. "Come, you shall report the accident to the authorities in Milano," she said, turning her face skyward, feeling a cool drizzle on her face. "We'd best hurry."

Moments later, driving along the dangerous corniche, she broke the silence. "I know of a marvelous inn that serves food directly from the table of angels." She kissed her fingertips with a flourish. "There is a shortcut to the border where civilian border guards, not fascisti, or Nazis, will hassle us."

St. Gallens probed. "Are you *avoiding* border patrols, *signora*? Is it necessary to be devious in crossing the border these days?"

"Only because I am fleeing from my husband. What a horrible quarrel we had. Now I want him to suffer." She stopped abruptly, apologetically. "How rude you must think me to be." She introduced herself.

Claude St. Gallens froze. *Signora Donato Donatelli!* The wife of Il Duce's chief legal adviser! He stiffened. *How curious are the ingredients fate stirs into her cauldron of intrigue!* Turning imperceptibly in his seat, he attempted to discern her features in the soft glow of lights bounding off the dashboard. He could not. But he'd know her anywhere. "Permit me, *signora*. I am Claude St. Gallens at your service. I am grateful for your kindness." A year ago the Donatellis had attended a gala at the Zeller palazzo in Il Duce's honor. Much more added to his frustration. She was impossibly beautiful and bore a frightening resemblance to the woman he'd never forgotten, the unrequited love who had eluded countless investigators hired to track her down—Victoria Valdez! So many years! His thoughts trailed off. She was speaking.

"You *don't* recognize the name?" Her laughter filled the car. "Should I?"

"How refreshing. How positively refreshing! You fail to genuflect at the same Donatelli. Oh, Monsieur St. Gallens, you are a breath of fresh air." She banked the roadster on a sharp turn without breaking, driving her passenger into borderline apoplexy. "The name Donatelli suffocates me. I am sick to death of its pretentiousness. Shall I describe the agony of proving myself worthy and deserving of so glorious a name?"

As she spoke and he listened, St. Gallens did a quick evaluation of the liabilities posed if he remained in her company. On the one hand, the estranged wife of *avvocato* Donatelli was too quick to trust in strangers. If the military detained them, if stopped by border guards, would she impede his progress, limit his chances of concealing his true identity. He could not abide a jealous husband, needed no sticky involvements in domestic squabbles, not at this juncture. On the other hand . . . ingenuity, a primary requisite in maneuvering in and out of Milano, and her invaluable knowledge of *safe* border crossings, was a positive plus factor in her favor. *Everything hinges on circumspection! Do nothing untoward or alarming. Nothing to frighten her. Exercise patience!*

They drove in silence. The roadster's bright headlights sliced through the dark hazy drizzle, lighting the precarious road and the soft shoulders where a foot or two in either direction might spell doom.

"There, up ahead," she indicated. "The glow of yellow lights against the black sky is Milano. We're almost there. I am famished. How about you, St. Gallens?"

Her driving expertise on this dangerous mountain road took his breath away. His tightly clenched hand gripping the passenger strap didn't ease up until they reached the outskirts of Milano. Nor did he breathe easy until she geared down to a more acceptable speed. "The way you handle yourself behind the wheel would shame a Grand Prix driver, *signora*. You seem born to the skill."

Amadora laughed pleasantly. "Discerning of you, *monsieur*. If I were any less a driver, my family would disown me. I am a Bertelli. My family manufactures the automobile I am driving. What you see before you, St. Gallens, is one of the rare elite of women drivers, a partially emancipated woman."

In the darkness she saw neither his lips go slack nor the fiery sparking of his colorless eyes behind dark glasses. The color drained from his face. If Amadora Bertelli Donatelli had seen these changes, could she have averted the horrors of the remaining hours of her life?

The picturesque inn, once a farmhouse and part of a landed estate in the Lombardy countryside was sequestered from curious eyes by a bricked-in courtyard and high stone walls. The car turned into the courtyard.

The modest dining room sprawled through an open brick archway to a long, rambling alcove banked with potted palms and cut flowers in massive bouquets, where companions dined discreetly without fear of interlopers. Various eyes glanced up briefly at the mismatched couple as they passed, but took no real interest in their presence. They were seated near an open fire, secluded, yet not totally cut off from other diners. A service bar was concealed behind an ornate Oriental silkscreen. In the dimly lighted interior Amadora's burnished red hair and green eyes shone dazzlingly.

He stared at her, struck again by the incredible resemblance to . . . It was so long ago. . . . Would the dream of her never fade?

"Amadora Bertelli Donatelli. It is quite a mouthful to speak."

She didn't detect the rancor when he spoke the name Bertelli. "Too heavy a responsibility to live up to in one lifetime. Both names are traditions in Italy—not names." She sipped an amber sherry. "*Far bella figura*—keep up pretenses, the whole world looks upon you as a role model. The watch words of my existence—*far bella figura*." She clinked his glass in a mocking toast.

"You sound like a rebel," he said quietly.

"A familiar refrain, St. Gallen, one I've heard all my life. Perhaps I was born at the wrong time, in the wrong place, to the wrong parents. How I bridle at restrictions placed on us, on our minds. Yes, I am a rebel. Here we are not privileged to speak our thoughts. The shadow of Il Duce stands over us, peering into our hearts, minds and, souls. *Misericordia!* When we fornicate it is only to make babies for the dictatorship!"

He sipped his wine. "You think things are different elsewhere?"

"But of course! They must be." She smiled wanly. "You've heard the story, I'm sure. A few years ago, King Emmanuel selected twelve of the brightest men in the country to train for government office. He sent six to England and six to America to study the economic and political systems. The six who went to England were exceptionally smart. They hold important positions in Italy's government today."

"And the six sent to America? What of them?"

"They demonstrated far more intelligence. They remained there." She smiled engagingly. "I, St. Gallens, must be totally lacking in intelligence. I languish in my baronial mansion in Roma, think only what I am dictated to think, speak words I am fed to speak. *Signore*, at home I have a parrot who experiences more freedom than I. But enough of me. Are you retired? How do you occupy your time?"

"I am a banker. Sedate, a bit of a curmudgeon, but not as old as I appear," he said. She was the first woman to excite him in months. Could he resist the temptation? Red hair, the color of a fiery sunset . . . eyes the color of jade jewels. Why couldn't he forget Victoria? It was so long ago.

St. Gallens sipped his sherry, suddenly arrested by the thought that had earlier petrified him. "So. You are the sister of Miguel Bertelli? The continental playboy?"

She laughed. "Ah then, *monsieur*, we are not strangers?"

"Who in Italy has not heard of Burgatti-Bertelli and their automobiles? And, of course, your brother."

"Most *especially* my brother, is that what you're saying?"

"His exploits, or should I say, conquests, were chronicled in the newspapers with amazing regularity. Headlines, no less."

She inclined her head, weighing the thought. "Yes, conquests. Long ago, perhaps, but no more. He was once my idol. Then one day, *pouf,* he fell in love, real love, and destroyed the image. No more Casanova, no more Don Juan. Romeo himself faded into the sunset. True love is a mystery."

"He married the American automobile heiress, no?"

Amadora placed her empty wineglass on the table. A waiter appeared, refilling it. "You *do* know my brother!"

"Only through the tabloids, I assure you."

They dined on a sumptuous *lasagne* casserole in silence. The sounds of mandolins and accordions came from somewhere, but the musicians remained invisible.

Amadora swallowed her last morsel and picked up the conversation, unable to resist the foray into the recent past of her adoring brother, Miguel. "Not with the American heiress—not the one he married—but with the other woman, it was a true story book romance. She was the only one he truly loved. In defense of Miguel, he was not the Casanova the tabloids painted him. He is remarkably sensitive, very talented and creative, actually—a genius."

"Your brother?"

"Of course, my brother. Would I speak so candidly of a man I did not know intimately?"

"I thought perhaps you presented me a profile of your husband."

"My husband!" Green eyes flared to fire points. "That insensitive oaf? What can he know of love? It's always, Il Duce this or Il Duce that. No romance courses through Donato's veins, only lire, Swiss francs, negotiable securities, and fiscal profits."

"He sounds like a banker." St. Gallens shoved his plate aside, sipped his espresso, his face relaxing into lines of fatigue. How he loathed empty chatter.

"He is a lawyer. Money and politics are his idols. Certainly he is no romantic. Forgive me, I must seem tedious to you. I mean no disrespect to my husband or other men who rule their worlds. Such men should entertain concubines—not marry or, if married, have mistresses."

"You champion infidelities?" He perked up. "*Signora,* with such talk you construct exquisite riddles that cannot be solved."

"When two people are in love who can call it infidelity?"

"Uh—your church. The papacy . . . laws . . . government . . . society . . ."

"*Basta! Basta!* You force reality upon me. I tire of reality. For once I too would enjoy to live a dream."

"Like your brother's dream, eh?" *Careful now, or she'll bolt.*

"Why not? At least he *lived* a dream, enjoyed it, no matter how short-lived it was. Too soon, it came to an end—the affair, not his love. Does it not wring your heart?"

He shook his head in feigned wonder. "Unfortunately, *signora*, I am incapable of commiserating with you. Bankers deal in facts, sums, data, fiscal profits, not melodrama. You see, I too suffer your husband's ailments. My mistress is money. She is far more reliable than the intangible, undependable emotion of love."

"Would you marry a woman you do not love? Force children upon her to be raised in a loveless marriage while your heart pines for a woman whom you truly love?"

"Ah. That's what ails your marriage, is it?" *Couch your goading cleverly.*

"No, no, no, no, no! Not me! My brother's marriage. You aren't listening. Very well, I won't bore you. I shall desist"

"Please, proceed. Tell me everything. The bloom of a rose is on your cheeks when you speak of him. He must mean a great deal to you. Please, I shall be attentive." He signaled the waiter for more cognac.

"It is a sad story, mind you," she continued, a bit mawkish. "No happy ending. My brother fell in love with a fairy princess. Well, not exactly a princess, but nearly. A true contessa. Unfortunately the contessa is married to a man she loathes. She bore him two children. My brother married a woman he does not love and gave her two children. Is this a sensible arrangement, St. Gallens? Why is love the loser? I see it around me, *all around me*. Why do we suffer laws to keep us miserable? Love and happiness should be trusted to work things out. Laws make people miserable."

"Can you imagine how many children would flounder about homeless if your philosophy were adhered to? Already there are enough orphans to populate the nation." He glanced at her with a sudden, chillingly inscrutable smile. "Did your brother confide the details of his illicit bliss?" he asked negligbly.

"*Miguel?* But no! Are you crazy? He speaks to no one of his emptiness." She watched the waiter preparing flaming *zabaglione*. She leaned in confidentially. "The servants. You know servants!

They know everything!'' She spooned the dessert. ''*Molto delicioso*. Imagine. What audacity to suggest a love child was born to my brother's paramour. Such absurdity! *Miguel* would never part with a son, never! *Signore?* Is something wrong? Shall I summon help?''

Momentarily pale, he raised a protesting hand. ''No, *signora*. A touch of malaria . . . comes and goes . . . it passes in a minute.'' He removed a pill from a gold pill box, washed it down with wine. ''Continue, please. Did the husband learn of the love child?''

''Who knows. The cuckold was absent from his home too often. Some important man in government. A brute as I understand it. Believe me, St. Gallens, if the cock does not protect the hen house, the fox will make away with the chickens.'' She touched her forehead. ''But I did not say it was for certain that a love child exists. Only rumor, rumors from unreliable sources, servants.''

''Are we ready to leave, *signora*? Are we far from the border?''

Amadora stared at him, burst into laughter, a look of impishness on her face. ''St. Gallens, are you in some difficulty?'' She shoved a compact mirror at him. ''See, your mustache is crooked.''

Accepting the mirror, he sheepishly patted the truant accessory into place. ''I was in difficulty earlier, but no more. You rescued me, remember?''

Amadora remembered. Suddenly she was afraid. ''Who are you, *monsieur?*''

Don't frighten her! You need her as an ally until you cross the border.

''You are not the only one fleeing a loveless marriage. I too am escaping a domineering wife, a chain around my neck.''

Amadora relaxed, gave him a look of long suffering. ''Then perhaps you will remove the wig too, and let me take a better look at my escort, no?''

''The moment we cross the border.''

''You said you were not as old as you look. How old are you?''

''How old do I look?''

''Sixty.''

''That old?''

''An exaggeration. How old?''

''Younger by nearly thirty years.''

She stared at him, a peculiar excitement stirring in her. ''Who knows, St. Gallen, perhaps you are the fairy tale romance I thirst for," she said softly.

"Anything is possible."

An hour later they arrived at Lugano to find the border closed. Forced to return to Lake Como, they spent the night at the *Quattro Fiori Inn*.

It was nearing dawn when they abandoned further explorations and sexual advances. Spent and exhausted, Amadora drifted off into a twilight sleep. She failed to recognize Minister Zeller in the dark bedroom but found his sensual eagerness acceptable.

St. Gallens lay awake smoking a cigarette, examining his present situation. Amadora Donatelli presented complications he could ill afford. She knew too much. Earlier, before they booked lodgings at *Quattro Fiori*, they had slow danced to Italian love songs, the merging of dynamite to a lighted fuse. Then, here in this room, they had melted in sexual embrace. Now he was forced to make a decision. He could not permit her to live. He felt her hand on his body. He hardened, sprang forward to her delight. She moaned, rolled over toward him, wide awake. She reached for him, guided him into her feverish body. Her perfume, an aphrodisiac to him, stirred him intensely. The sight of her nude, uninhibited body, shaking, writhing on the bed, stimulated him beyond his ken.

Uncertain when the delusion began, he stared at her in the dim candleglow. She was Victoria . . . Victoria, his beloved. An insane quality shaped his lust; a madness unleashed a fierce animal reaction in him. He prodded her body deeper, deeper, driving her into a wild delirium. He called to her, "Victoria, Victoria, *mi alma, mi vita, mi amor!*" His illusion of Victoria became intertwined with images of Marie Clotilde; his mood alternated between loving and loathing.

Amadora, no match against his strength, tried desperately to release herself from his steely grip. She gasped, tried to suck in gulps of air. Quickly he covered her lips with his, siphoning off her air supply. Her arms flailed wildly, balled fists pounded against his shoulders and arms over and again. He would not release her. In a last-ditch effort to pierce his sexual euphoria, Amadora jackknifed her legs and thrust them out stiffly.

"Stop!" she screeched. "Beast! You are suffocating me!" She gulped greedily at the air, unable to settle the spasms racking her throat.

And the pain . . . sharp first, then icy cold, her stomach burning, then nauseous as if she'd been trampled upon by Caesar's warring legions. And her face, swollen, raw, her eyes puffy, nearly closed.

At once apologetic he leaped off the bed, darted to the sideboard, poured water from a porcelain pitcher into a bowl, and splashed it on his face. He opened a window, inhaled, and turned to her, his tone affectionate. "Please forgive me. I don't know what came over me."

"Is Victoria your spouse?" she asked in a thin, scratchy voice. She was not a forgiving woman. He nodded, then she understood.

Or thought she did. She glanced at him, in profile, lighting a cigarette from the gaslight. "You are—could be a marvelous lover, St. Gallens. But God Almighty! You get too caught up in fantasies. You are some libertine—skilled in the art of pleasuring, yes?" He did not answer. He poured the remaining wine, handed her a glass. "Because this is Italy," she said, her voice nearly restored. "If we were found together like this we could be prosecuted, charged with adultery," she said flippantly.

"In this artists' colony? I think not. Como is far more lenient than Rome in such matters." God, he loathed talk after sex. She began to annoy him. Senseless, emotional women, chatterboxes, the lot of them! He preferred men. What was his name? That man, the cleric in Austria? Schuller . . . yes, yes, Brother Schuller, a connoisseur in the art of sexual pleasures. *Why think of him now, after so many years?*

Amadora's mouth began to move again. She chattered, questioning him about his return to Italy. Would he see her again? Perhaps take up where they left off? Providing she could slip away from Donato? She hadn't recognized him as Zeller—but she would. Her kind usually ended up with what they went after and didn't rest until they scored.

He wasn't certain when the comparison to Marie Clotilde began. Marie Clotilde, his *loving, pure* wife who had adulterously conceived a child with the seed of another man's loins. The thought incensed him.

Something clicked in his brain, his focus changed into kaleidoscopic revolutions on three women in his brain: Victoria, Marie Clotilde, and in the dim background Amadora *Bertelli* Donatelli!

A sudden outpouring of loathing gathered momentum in his brain, a rash of violence spurted like a pus-infected boil. He turned Amadora over on her belly, sodomized her, and muffled her screams by burying her face into a pillow. He mistook her frenzied reaction for enjoyment. *The bitch, in heat, loved it!* Imagine, the whore couldn't get enough! He'd show her. He forced his swollen member into her mouth. Kneeling over her, he moved in vicious animal thrusts, shoving deeper into her oral cavity. Before his eyes, the woman's image changed. It was Marie Clotilde taking the mortifying indignities.

"Pure, cool, tolerant, well-loved, highly respected Contessa de Bernadorf de Zeller, the celebrated sanctimonious saint who moves through the cloisters of Rome like some goddess, donating money, *my money,* to charity!" He spat, picking up momentum. "All the while you and your lover made a cuckold of me! Of me, Amadeo Zeller! Bitch! Whore! Marie Clotilde! I was right all the time! It was you and Bertelli! I'll find that bastard child of yours and kill him! *Kill him!* You hear? I'll do it before your very eyes, I swear!"

Amadora heard him, knew at once the error of her loose tongue. Her eyes widened in stark fear. She attempted to break the rhythm of his frenzied thrusts, strained against him, scratched at his burning flesh, leaving slashed ribbons of bloodied fire on his face. The darkness was closing in on her. Her eyes struggled vainly to fix on a small point of light for orientation. Wild-eyed, suffocating, unable to escape his steely grasp, she made out those opaque eyes, colorless fiery beams, scorching her flesh. Images crossed her brain. His blasphemous words pierced her heart. She resisted in a mad leap, lurching to struggle free of him, her body electrified, forcing her to marshal whatever strength remained. She shoved, pounded him, jackknifed and landed on the cold floor.

Memory came in bits and pieces. She cowered, crawling backward as he came after her, inadvertently shoving herself into a corner.

"Bastard! You brutal perverted bastard!" she screeched in a cracked, distant voice. She doubled over in violent retching. It was a ghastly slimy vomit, blood mixed with semen and acid burning her guts and throat. Overcome by a rash of violent chills, compounding the agony of the bloody rips and tears in her body, she writhed on the floor in agonized spasms.

He picked her up, tossed her on the bed, still ranting and raving. "You and Bertelli will rue the day you forced deception upon me." The maniacal, rasping voice cut into her like acid. Then she remembered the eyes, the colorless eyes, but it was too late—too late for Amadora Donatelli.

In a moment of clarity, she saw herself standing at the edge of a precipice, thousands of feet above the clouds on pinnacles of frigid spires, hanging suspended in space.

She was floating on an enormous icy mass.

Loud animal grunts escaped his throat. Flushed with adrenaline, his ejaculation came strong, hard, long in duration. Gurgling, throaty death throes returned him to the moment.

Amadora Bertelli Donatelli was dead. He had slain Marie Clotilde and her lover in his execrative fantasy. And for a time he found relief. Focus came in moments. He stared at the woman on the bed, at her ghastly, distorted, bloodied lips, at the spill of blood commingled with semen dripping from its open corners. She lay motionless, the life force drained from her, her wide, glazed, uplifted eyes reflecting the horrible ignominy of death.

As his eyes adjusted to the light of reality he calmly lifted himself off the bed and, without a trace of emotion, showered, dressed, returned to the bedroom, and began to remove all traces of Amadora's existence. He rolled the dead body onto a bedsheet, tossed her clothing into the bundle, and, tying both ends into square knots, dragged the corpse to the balcony. He had to work swiftly. Peering about the dark, deserted courtyard, satisfied no one was in sight, he heaved the corpse over the iron balustrade. It fell with a loud dull thud into the thicket below. *Perfect*. He picked up his satchel, scrutinized the room. He moved to the door, glanced again at the large room.

Good . . . nothing remained to incriminate him. He locked the door behind him, hung a DO NOT DISTURB sign on the door, and proceeded along the deserted corridor, exiting through an open window, hoping to avoid the attendant on duty at the desk at the foot of the stairs.

He climbed down a trellis, stepped into a tangled mass of dewy foliage, and crouched down protectively in the shadows. *Easy, you're not in the clear yet.* He moved in the predawn shadows, then stopped abruptly as the bent-over figure of an aged watchman moved along the portico on rounds.

St. Gallens lay flat against the building, not daring to move or breathe. Then he froze, bathed in a fan of light from the headlights of a Mercedes sedan turning into the *Quattro Fiori* courtyard. The driver gunned his motor and swept past him, pulling up short, not far from where St. Gallens was trapped in a play of light and shadow.

A couple emerged from the auto. The driver called to the watchman. Was it permissible to leave the machine where it was? The guard assured him he'd park it after his rounds. The couple disappeared inside. The watchman lumbered out of sight.

St. Gallens moved swiftly. He removed the keys from the Mercedes, unlocked the trunk, and stuffed Amadora's body into it, with all her personal effects. He locked it, replaced the key, and, peering cautiously about, reached Amadora's roadster. He started the engine, wheeled it easily out the courtyard onto the country road leading to the main highway. He headed northeast of Lake Como toward the Swiss border. He presented his papers to the border patrol and crossed into Switzerland, where he was accorded every courtesy due an affluent banker from Zurich.

At Brunner he scuttled the flashy Bertelli roadster, pushed it off a high cliff into the lake below. He hitched a lorry ride to Zug on the Zuger Sea and there purchased a serviceable, conservative car. He abandoned it in Lucerne, boarded the train to Zurich.

In Zurich the St. Gallens disguise was scrapped. He became himself, Amadeo Zeller, locked behind the sanctuary walls of his remote French chateau overlooking *Zurichsee*.

Winter's ghostly trees melted into spring and through it all Zeller paced marbled and carpeted floors of the chateau, fighting the demons of his recent past. The images of Victoria Valdez—no longer pure—superimposed upon images of Amadora Donatelli struggling in the throes of death, haunted him. Marie Clotilde's infidelities ate corrosively at him. His lack of control frightened him. His hatred for his adulterous wife, whom he blamed for his falling out with Il Duce, spread through him.

Doctors plied him with sedatives, forced him on a diet to ease the pain of his ulcers. The anxiety refused to abate. Prolonged periods of sleeplessness, an increasing denial of reality and gradual substitution of fantasies and hallucinations were labeled as symptoms of *dementia praecox* by physicians. It was the first of many sessions with medical doctors called psychiatrists; at these sessions Zeller began to marvel at the wonders of the brain.

Suddenly a year had swiftly evaporated and Zeller, on the mend, was able to combat the cross-currents of a thousand complexities running herd in his mind. Calmer, controlled, he sorted, shuffled, rearranged them in order of importance and began a systematic approach to finding solutions for each one.

The contessa. She was an integral part of his plans. He'd deal with her at the proper time. Meanwhile, she was safe in Rome. Il Duce would *never* harm her, never! The love affair between Clotilde and Bertelli was nothing new to Zeller. And her accomplice—that—that *Corsican*, Dariana! Shortly before his exodus from the fascist regime he had engaged his spy network to probe deeper into the life of Dariana de Rocca Bonifacio and her husband to determine who, among their brood of children, might be the illegitimate issue of his adulterous wife and her lover. Unfortunately the plot to kidnap the sons, was bungled, and he was left none the wiser. Caught red-handed, one of the plotters died violently, another went mad, and the third had made no sense at all.

Zeller's decision to probe Bonifacio's past hinged on the contradiction that was Dariana de Rocca. Her emotional nature was too complex to contemplate. Zeller, a dealer in cold, hard facts, found it incredible that so sophisticated and worldly a woman, after being exposed to the power of Rome, would marry some crude Corsican peasant. The anomaly had jarred him these many years. Now, as he touched the rugged contour of his earlobe in recollection of the rape, he determined the Corsican hussy would pay! What tied the loose ends together, not perfectly, but in some semblance of order, concerned the transfers of finances from Clotilde's trust to Dariana Bonifacio and the shadowy manner in which *avvocato* Donatelli had *converted* that trust! He was still trying to ferret out the machinations involved.

Zeller, forced to concentrate on those Faustian banking titans dominating his life, set aside domestic upheavals, realizing a modicum of peace for a time. The hierarchy remained anonymous, aloof as ever. In closer proximity now with them, his bridges to Il Duce, irrevocably burned and impossible to reconstruct, he focused on the Zurich hierarchy, thirsting for their power, cohesion, know-how. His objective: to own them outright. But first on the agenda, the prerequisite to the accomplishment of this miracle, was the imperative of making himself indispensable to them.

Sigmund Weiderhof, you are first on my list!

A month after Zeller's arrival in Zurich, the November 26, 1937 issue of Il Duce's propaganda newspaper, *Il Popolo d'Italia* ran the following headlines:

WIFE OF DONATO DONATELLI IN
ACCIDENTAL DEATH

Signora Amadora Bertelli Donatelli dead in an automobile accident near Lake Como. The accident merely underscores what Il Duce had tried to impress upon Italian women. That they lack the mental discipline to drive machines of enormous power. Woman's place is in the home, to raise babies, care for her husband, and tend to womanly duties. Our deepest sympathies are extended to *avvocato* Donatelli and *famiglia*.

An in-depth investigation of his wife's demise proved the incident to be an entirely different matter. Il Duce received the report before his legal counselor did. In the privacy of his office at the Palazzo Venezia, he read:

Signora Donatelli's body was found in the trunk of a car registered to Brago Costanzo. The mutilated, sexually molested remains had been wrapped in a blanket from the *Quattro Fiori* Inn at Como. The authorities acting on a tip received at the border were searching for contraband. *Signore* Costanzo, long a suspect in the smuggling trade, claims no knowledge of the woman. He persists he is innocent. Admits to being at the inn with a woman companion. The woman substantiates his story. When questioned, the waiters in the restaurant reported that a woman answering to *Signora* Donatelli's description dined with an elderly man. It is further reported the *signora* placed two long-distance calls, one to the residence of her brother, the other to her own villa. *Signore* Miguel Bertelli confirmed his sister's call and plans to go to Zurich to spend time with unnamed friends. Most strange was the false mustache affixed to the *signora*'s upper lip, much like those worn by actors and stage performers. The Donatellis were patrons of the arts who enjoyed the company of performers. All artists who knew the Donatellis are under surveillance. Reports will follow.

Il Duce fulminated. He flipped the calendar on his desk back to the day in October when he signed the arrest order for Zeller. *Son of a bitch!* Zeller disappeared the same day the Donatelli woman disappeared from her villa, both obviously headed for the border!

He opened the file labeled HIGHLY CONFIDENTIAL. Inside the title page, the name *Amadeo Zeller* was typed. The last report, dated October 30, 1937, read: "The body and automobile of former Finance Minister Zeller were found demolished, burned beyond recognition in a steep ravine a few kilometers to the south of Milano. The road is treacherous, the curves and bends . . ."

"How many lives does the bastard have?" cursed the dictator aloud. "Wherever you are, Zeller, you had best beware of the fascist fist!" The horrendous plot unfolded, and Il Duce remembered what Hitler had said about the man who was his neighbor at Berchesgaden.

The next day Zeller was forgotten. Il Duce was setting the Roman stage with pomp and circumstance to greet Hitler with fife and drum. Rome was being dressed like a glittering Circus Maximus. Statues, fountains, and buildings along the old Roman triumphal way were adorned with searchlights. Night turned into day. The Colosseum, glowing in the brilliant wash of bright torches, came alive to pay tribute to the modern day gladiators. Cheering crowds lined the parade route and the African cavalry charged down the *stradas*. All the panoply and fanfare marked Il Duce's nod to Hitler's attempt to gobble up Czechoslovakia and set up the global arena for a European crisis. A fascist fist and a Nazi boot began gearing up for world domination.

IN ZURICH . . .

Reich Bank President Weiderhof explained patiently to a small influential group that he could not complete his task of economic recovery unless the *unlawful* activity against the Jews ended abruptly. Jewish importers were canceling large orders. Didn't they understand it was ridiculous to imagine any nation capable of succeeding economically without Jewish business? In private he met with another select group, among whom Amadeo Zeller sat listening in rapt silence. "We must take measures to protect our commercial interests. Is it understood?"

Secret conclaves, clandestine meetings between the most unlikely men took place in Zurich, Geneva, Lausanne, and Trieste. Wheels set into motion were directed toward Trieste, a city rife with partisans and espionage agents. International intrigue was hatched. Gold bullion was exchanged for new loyalties against the Axis nations. Messages were sent to the disaffected. Word returned from places deep within the hierarchy of the Third Reich and Wehrmacht.

In Zurich, Amadeo Zeller gloated.

There were friends among the enemies!

There was nothing money could not buy!

BOOK FOUR

I Have a Rendezvous With Death
At Some Disputed Barricade,
When Spring Comes Back With
Rustling Shade
And Apple Blossoms Fill the Air—
I Have a Rendezvous With Death . . .
—Alan Seeger (1888–1916)

Chapter Twenty-seven

*"VOUS ÊTES SOLDATS POUR MOURIR ET JE
VOUS ENVOIE LA OUT L'ON MUERETE!"*

ALGERIA, NORTH AFRICA
June, 1940

Sidi bel Abbes, the sink of the world, was a city of squalor, lechery, degradation, filthy wine shops and gaily tasseled braying camels: It was the end of the earth where stinking desert tribesmen plotted endless revolts. Sidi's chief stock in trade was the wholesaling of pubescent Arab girls who performed lewd sexual debaucheries designed to sate the perverse, salacious, degenerate sexual appetites of man; its second, the Foreign Legion.

As devastating as Sidi's diseased brothels and the constant menace of the *ghilbi*, fierce, hot desert winds, was the prattle of unhuman tradition pleading for extreme unction and burial rites. The Foreign Legion, a recalcitrant tradition, teeming with deficiencies, inconsistencies and, worse unable to catch up with the twentieth century was sabotaged by its worst enemy—the pomposity, pride and vanity of egomaniacal French officers. The beribboned, bombastic uniformed robots, St. Cyr graduates—by tradition—believed, *actually* believed in their own omnipotence. Existence for them was delusion, outmoded customs, belief in unhuman principles of soldiering and, a constant retailing of all past glories.

Camarone! Magenta! Le Livre d'OR! All were nobly recounted as if they were yesterday's battles, not those of a century before.

The French wore fatalism and superstition around their necks like valor badges. These were the genre of men to whom Darius turned upon leaving Corsica two years ago when he'd unwittingly traded one hell for another!

Capitaine Darius Bonifacio, warily searched the darkening sky, stepped briskly from the mule-driven *gharry*, paid the *gharry wallah*, cursing the giant plume of whirling dust rising off the hot desert floor in the near distance. A *ghilbi! Damnation!* Desert squalls could last from five minutes to five days with blazing gales up to ninety mph! Darius, measuring time against distance began to wind his way through the junk shops of a hot, dusty bazaar, along narrow, twisting streets. He must reach his destination before the *ghilbi* struck full force. He must!

The accursed screams of *dragomen*—camel drivers—accompanied the clangor of bells. Thousands of unique intonations ringing from every doorway produced a weird cacophony of sounds against the howling winds rumbling through corkscrewing alleys like an angry sea.

It was madness! A glissade of wild people spilled into the streets from open doorways, behind filthy ratty curtains, an avalanche of human lava shoving, pushing, desperate to reach their destinations before the *ghilbi* reached its zenith.

Darius passed open windows overhead with half naked women leaning over the streets, gaping at passersby, making obscene gestures in attempts at last-minute negotiations.

Suddenly, furious gusts of hot, oppressive winds, raising temperatures unbearably, tunneled white sand, fine as ground glass, through the narrow streets. Darius quickly pulled his desert goggles into place, shielding his eyes and, wrapping his neck scarf mummylike to protect his nose and mouth, moved on.

Men in billowing burnooses, boosted by the inflated winds, scattered crazily about like wild, disoriented birds. Some, lifted bodily off the ground, fell, rolling into the streets, stepped on by others running helter skelter to their destinations. Overhead, jalousies clattered, banged noisily against the buildings. Whirlwind glimpses of flimsy clothing, arms, legs, silver bracelets, gaudy attire, as people fled to the closest sanctuaries. A mad dog, foaming at the mouth, cavorted about like a savage devil, leaping wildly, whirling like a dervish. A skittish, stiff-legged mule, running free of its cruel master, went wild, kicking everything in sight.

Darius, tugging fiercely on his *kepi blanc*, its neck flap snapping loudly in the unrestrained winds, could go no farther. Sighting a tobacco kiosk up ahead, he made for the temporary shelter.

The next few moments, as bewildering as they were chaotic, Darius felt a stinging thrust, a sharp, biting impact as crowds jostled and shoved hard, plummeting him towards the kiosk. A shadow leaped over him, barely visible in the swirling density if sands and wind. It happened so fast, Darius failed to see the knife buried to its hilt in his upper left arm until pain sizzled through him. Stunned, he stared at it in disbelief.

Instinct had failed him! The blade, meant for his heart had ripped savagely into his arm. *Damnation!* He searched through thickening sand flurries, half blinded. Hot wind rushing past Darius's earlobe propelled him fiercely against the kiosk door.

Loud crashes, barking dogs, running feet, screams pierced the air. Darius, wiping his goggles saw a whirling frenzy of man and beast engaged in lethal gymnastics. The savage dog he'd seen earlier had sunk its rabid teeth around the Arab's leg. Darius's panicked assailant hopped, skipped, jumped about in mad frenzy, scuffling in the dust desperate in his attempt to shake off the deadly cur. Combating the approaching death throes, the assailant stumbled, fell, lurched and, scrambling to his feet, unable to dislodge himself from the frothing beast, reached for his gun and blew off the dog's head.

Another gun blast! An expert bullet emplacement killed the assailant. Darius squinted searching for the second gun. The hand holding the gun holstered it and in whirlwind force its owner, at once at Darius's side, propelled him inside the tabak shop, insisting in his rapid, regional French, "Pursuit is pointless, *mon capitaine.*" Legionnaire Lucien Pascal led Darius to an unoccupied corner of the grubby, overcrowded shop. "The wog is merely one of a horde of Hassan's nameless, faceless assassins."

"What perfect cover the *ghilbi* affords assassins, *oui*?" Darius clenched his teeth in pain. Blending swiftness of motion and a well-braced capacity for stress into an expert move, his right hand grabbed the hilt of the blade and yanked hard. *Voilà!* He extricated the knife, staring at the hilt.

Pascal, whipping off his neck scarf, moved in swiftly, bound his captain's arm, and, using a camel crop for a tourniquet, twisted it to stop the flow of blood. Darius studied the crest embedded in the hilt. A triangle between two circles, pierced by a double dagger, with a serpent wound through it, jaws open, displaying venomous fangs.

"*Muhammad Abou Ahkmed Hassan!* It has begun, sooner than expected," Darius muttered grimly. "I expected it, but not before the ink was dry on the accords!"

"What are you saying, *mon capitaine*? How can Hassan be certain when we ourselves know little?"

"I must leave, Pascal." Darius glanced warily through the dirty kiosk windows. The storm blackened the sky; visibility was nil.

"No, you cannot move until the winds abate."

Darius pulled his sand goggles down below his chin, removed his scarf, letting the sweat pour off him freely. He brought the tip of the dagger to his lips, tasted it carefully. "Kismet favors me, Pascal," he said dryly. "No poison on the blade." He wiped it clean on his trousers and slipped it into his tunic pocket.

"What need have they to dip it in poison when the filthy blade carries enough infection to do the trick. Come, I will take you to a friend. No, not through the streets. This way." He led him to a door at the kiosk's rear, draped by a filthy curtain.

Darius hesitated, scanning the faces of people seeking sanctuary from the storm. None posed a threat. He tarried a bit, purchased a pack of English Ovals from a squinty-eyed clerk as Pascal conversed with the man in Farsi. *Dinars* changed hands. Cautiously, certain no one observed their movements, Pascal stepped before him through the alcove, service pistol drawn, leading Darius down the dank stone steps to the cellar. They waded through a filthy, rat-infested sewer for several minutes, pausing before an alcove lit up with a burning torch in a wall niche.

Pascal knocked three times. A judas hole opened slightly. He spoke the magic, open sesame. The door swung open, the sentry waved them on. They scurried up a flight of stone steps to another door opening into a clean, antiseptic-smelling cubicle. "The back room of the barber shop across the street from the kiosk," Pascal informed Darius, "connected by underground tunnels dating back to the days of the famous Barbary pirates. Clever, *oui, mon capitaine*?"

Before Darius replied, a squat, barrel-chested Arab entered, his fawning smile freezing at the sight of the legionnaires. The intelligence insignia on their arms petrified the man. Recoiling at once, eyes bulging, his fear flowed in gibberish. Pascal's persuasive appeal, plus a few *dinars*, pacified the *specialist*. The barber, dentist, healer, doctor, blade and gunshot specialist regained composure. Recently, the penalties imposed upon him for performing what the Sidi police classified as illegal medical skills became so prohibitive the specialist had added two additional skills to his arsenal: bribery and extortion. Extortion from those requiring his skills, bribery to those protecting him.

Darius removed his tunic and lay back in the barber chair. He was given a glass of fig wine laced with *qat* to lull him into a drugged stupor, enough to anesthetize him for as long as it took to cleanse and dress the wound. On this day, no time could be wasted waiting for the command-post infirmary to open.

Darius slugged down the brew; icy numbness chilled him; the powerful narcotic turned him euphoric, dulling pain. Pascal's penetrating eyes fixed on the wog signaling retribution. "Should you fall victim to errors in judgment or lack perfection in tending my captain—" He cut off the menacing words and, using his forefinger drew an imaginary line across his neck.

The wog *specialist* understood. As he cleansed and dressed the wound, conflicting thoughts crash-landed in Darius's mind demanding careful scrutiny. The precarious state of politics creating the Legion's recent untenable position and the appalling events of the past three days demanded reevaluation.

France needed time! An entire world needed time to catch up to the nightmarish reality of that unrestrained madman running herd across Europe. A modern-day Alexander, wearing a small brush mustache and sporting a mechanical salute of a wind-up toy, had stretched Axis frontiers along the Russian border in the east to the Atlantic coastline of France in the west. Darius's predictions of impending global warfare tottered on the brink of reality. France had fallen on June 14, 1940, to the sounds of the German goosestep through Paris streets.

Darius's eyes lidded heavily as the Arab skillfully applied herbs and exotic balms to prevent infection. His attention fixed on the yellowed, fraying wall posters camouflaging cracked, scorpion-infested walls. The posters, like advertisements for a popular motion picture, depicted handsome legionnaires against a background of swaying date palms and yasmasked dancing girls. Across each poster, scrawled in bold French print, was the Legion's motto: A LEGIONNAIRE IS A SOLDIER IN ORDER TO DIE AND MUST BE EXPECTED TO BE USED FOR THAT PURPOSE!

Hah! What a farce! Bitterness flashed briefly in his eyes.

Mentally and spiritually he belonged to St. Cyr, wearing the prestigious French officers' uniform. Instead, he was relegated to wearing the insignia of a homeless recruit in a land where men, treated like scum, acted like scum. St. Cyr, for Darius became a rapidly diminishing dream.

Oh Christ! The bloody wog was efficient. He gestured to Legionnaire Pascal to pour more *qat* into Darius. Pascal complied. Darius's eyes lidded again. The wog prepared to stitch the jagged wound under Lucien's critical eye.

Euphoria expanded for Darius. He recollected his exodus from Corsica vividly as if it were only yesterday—not two years ago. A year in this part of the world was like a century, he thought, marveling at his own survival.

Enlistment at Fort Jean near Marseilles had bloomed into *règlemente* at Sidi bel Abbes. Survival for Darius meant existing in an alien tradition created to rid men on earth. Despite all odds he had survived foul, deplorable conditions, mind-bending, doglike treatment imposed on him by men not fit to wipe a camel's ass. He had asked himself a hundred times a day why, how he had endured? Was it due to some obscure, perverse instinct in him, a determination to brush against the parameters of death, testing for a future bout against unknown, unseen enemies in an uncertain future? *What?*

All the human flotsam discarded by other nations ended up in Sidi bel Abbes. Horrible distillates of humanity, united in this hellhole, trained to fight until each ended up a statistic, were entered into the Legion's log book of history with a vague allusion to bravery beyond the call of duty.

Merde! It was all bullshit!

Two years ago the men in Darius's company had sold their civilian gear, traded old identities for new names and lives. Convicted felons, afforded new leases on life, had flocked to Sidi in droves. No one questioned enlistment motives; a man's past was his and his alone.

At the outset Darius had grossly resented being lumped into this sea of murderers, arsonists, and fugitives. Worse, appalled by the French officer mentality that made it clear they considered all recruits unfit to be disciplined soldiers, that their existence served a singular purpose in the Legion, to be used as cannon fodder for the enemies of France, he wondered why he joined this arm of France's military, to be treated as a dog! To compound the degradation, German recruits, on enlistment, automatically assumed NCO status, whether or not they qualified! Their brutal, terrorizing tactics—highly respected by the French—were considered a solid basis for soldiering. *A solid basis for soldiering indeed!* Men became beasts in this despotic Tower of Babel. Recruits, speaking different tongues, were swiftly reduced to sign language for means of communication. Guttural vocal expressions, obscene hand gestures were employed to express their needs. Most remained mute with shock following *règlemente*.

Règlemente! became the antidote for Darius's painful memory of Sophia. For a time her image had sustained him, but *règlemente's* caustic reality had instantly dissolved her image like blips on a radar screen. Despite *règlemente*, Darius had survived.

He had survived! He was a legionnaire now; he must make the best of it.

Lucien Pascal, a stocky, well-muscled, morose Corsican with straight black hair shaved to bristlebrush length, possessed an unusual propensity for taking offense. An ardent patriot, he was "Bonapartishly" bound to loathe everything British and he looked upon the Arabs with equal distrust. Waterloo, St. Helena, and Darius Bonifacio were engraved upon his heart. The first two inhered in his genes; the latter was acquired since their encounter during *règlemente*. In argumentative moments he'd thump his chest like an ape and assert himself. *"C'est Lucien qui vous le dis!* Lucien has spoken!"

Now, he glanced at his watch, his anxiety accelerating. *Merde!* A half hour had passed. His captain should be regaining consciousness. He growled his concern in Farsi to the barber, who reappeared in the cubicle with two steamy cups of black Turkish coffee. The burnoose-garbed specialist nodded, indicating a few more moments.

Pascal sipped his coffee, his eyes fixed on Darius, considering how he had matured these past two years. Sagacious, toughened, more resilient than most men, he was exceedingly handsome. He looked ten years older than his eighteen years. Minute scars on his face, upper arms, and chest spoke of bodily harm done him in skirmishes with desert savages. Just a few lines furrowed his deeply tanned forehead, colored to golden chestnut by the Sahara sun; wandering white lines, minute interruptions, the leavings of violence adding intriguing dimensions to his enigmatic presence. The compelling intensity of viridian eyes, working every second, honest eyes that didn't look away when spoken to, all-seeing, all-knowing eyes instantly arresting those who met or passed him in the street.

Pascal, viewing this man in countless circumstances, some extremely dangerous, had yet to fault him in any way. He'd handled himself like a royal prince in each instance. Darius, he noted, exuded a unique form of magnetism that both attracted and repelled men harboring duplicitous thoughts. A man contemplating enmity with Captain Bonifacio reconsidered before taking an adversary position. To Pascal, invisible power hovered over Darius, a mystic presence setting him apart from other recruits. He had no peer among the officers. The French officers at Sidi, during the coffee and cognac hours, compared the young maverick to military figures of past eras. Darius remained an enigma to them.

Scuttlebutt naturally roosted on Darius's doorstep; it failed to bring the slightest trace of a smile to his lips. Not even comparisons to Napoleon, General Charles Gordon, and the famed Lawrence of Arabia caused him to react. This only heightened the intrigue surrounding him.

"Captain, it is finished. Are you awake?" Pascal shook him gently at the first sight of activity under his eyelids.

Darius opened his eyes; images came slowly into focus. He felt a burning sensation in his arm. He reached for it; the touch was painful. Pascal forced the hot coffee on him. Darius sipped it slowly, grimacing at the bitterness and staring at the expertly bound arm, silently questioning Pascal.

"Good as new, *mon capitaine.* You wish me to remain with you?"

Darius caught sight of his watch. It was 10:45 A.M. "No." He snapped out several orders. "Return to the office, Sergeant Pascal. Locate His Highness Ben-Kassir. It is imperative—life or death—understand? I must rendezvous with him at once. I shall return from Fatima's—if all goes well, by noon at the latest. I know, I know it's siesta. But damn it, today is crucial to the prince, to us, to France! *Comprenez-vous?* Instruct Delilah's Dream to prepare for anything on a moment's notice. I mean *anything!*" His voice dropped to a conspiratorial hush. "Word came from Compiegne this morning. Marshal Pétain signed the armistice. The Germans are now our allies!" He spoke incisively, the meaning unmistakable. "You will not leak a whisper of this, Sergeant, got it?"

Pascal's jaw fell open. "The Germans—our allies? *Merde!*"

He hooted devilishly, rolled his eyes. "Does Muhammad Abou Ahkmed Hassan know of this? What hell to pay when that religious zealot gets wind of such news!"

"Go! Carry on, Sergeant. And—Pascal, *merci beaucoup*."

Outside the winds abated. Darius exchanged glances with his sergeant, then, assured it was business as usual in the streets, they parted. Darius embarked on his mission, Pascal backtracked to the military complex.

There . . . up ahead. Darius entered the tangle of streets leading to the red-light district of Sidi bel Abbes.

Le village nègre . . . another world. Door-to-door cribs, bars, cafés, and brothels displayed the vice of Sidi in its most primitive form, crammed into a few blocks of narrow streets. Sanitary Patrol guards saluted the captain, their busy eyes searching for legionnaires remiss in signing the register on entering the district. Any legionnaire contacting *chaud pesse* was shown no mercy. Tossed into the brig, there he stayed until cured of the gonorrheal infection.

Outside the hawkers touted, "Enter ye all into the most remarkable brothel in the world!" Truer words were never spoken, Darius thought as the doors swung open to Fatima's Pleasure Dome.

Two colorfully dressed Punjabi doormen, Indian imports, gave the brothel added class. Darius strode past them through a circular foyer jutting five stories high to a stained-glass rotunda.

Darius negotiated his way through the world of scantily clad prostitutes, adorned with baubles, bangles, and glittering multicolored threads and beads woven through thickly oiled hair. It was always the same. Nothing ever changed here.

The jarring cultural shock of coming off the streets into Fatima's forced Darius to make continuous adjustments until his senses attuned themselves to the place. The smells of stale beer, opium and hashish assaulted his senses. He'd never get used to them.

With an outward display of complacency and good humor, he approached the bar beyond the spiraling steps leading to a cavernous room fanning out before him, separated from the noisy tap room by a partially drawn curtain. At once, catcalls, knowing winks, whistles, rousing cheers, and cheshire-cat grins came from men in his old regiment. He waved at them as he passed the twelve-year-old girls adorned with bizarre blue tattooing on their faces and legs and thick vermilion-painted cheeks and lips. Outstretched henna-dyed hands clawed and beckoned to him in sexually suggestive gestures. A mammoth silver-ornamented Nubian, a favorite of the legionnaires, solicited customers by making obscene gestures over intimate parts of her body.

Darius threaded his way past women painted thickly with garish cosmetics to cover their diseased bodies. Spanish, Maltese, Sicilian girls, stolen from their homes by white slavers who dumped their prize catches in Sidi, were sold to the highest bidders. There were girls with wide innocent eyes that could kill or flatter, eyes, learned in the ways of man, eyes batting thickly fringed lashes at whoever entered this commercial marketplace. A few coppers and a drink could buy any of them.

No wonder homosexuality was rife among legionnaires!

Darius, glancing in all directions, couldn't remember when Fatima's was so packed this early in the day. Had word from Compiegne been leaked? Had most followed the herd instinct and gathered here for protection and assurance?

Discordant, Oriental music bursting through the curtains of Le Café up ahead, drew him into the electrifying atmosphere like a magnet.

A clash of cymbals sent shivering echoes to the sky. The room darkened to a tumultuous applause. Men packed tightly at tables about the elevated stage riveted their attention to a minuscule beam of light at center stage, expanding to reveal Fatima's unique, highly heralded star, Lomay St. Germaine. She stood dramatically posed in flashes of illumination as the Arabic music and the erotic dance of the seven veils as only St. Germaine interpreted it began.

Under the splintered glow of a rotating Moorish grilled lamp, she moved sensuously, finger cymbals punctuating her erotic undulations and body gyrations. Necks craned. Heads jerked. Eyes strained to observe the spectacular, never-to-be-forgotten performance.

Lomay St. Germaine, a theatrical phenomenon, manipulated an audience the way a virtuoso fingered a Stradivarius, working them into rapturous journeys of enchantment and frenzied expectations. She was sheer artistry in motion. St. Germaine knew it, the audience expected it and applauded hysterically as she artfully worked each veil before discarding it. Screams of delight alternated with husky, encouraging howls and uncontainable applause, permeated the room, shaking its rafters. St. Germaine galvanized her audiences.

Darius smiled at their frenzied, high-pitched response. His

eyes fastened on the voluptuous beauty. Even he felt the
audience's building tension, their expectation as St. Germaine's
pulsating, undulating body swayed. She held the seventh veil
aloft, stretching the moment, controlling like a high priestess the
high-pitched hysteria and bacchanalian cries of the audience until
the room fell into a hushed awe. Slowly and precisely she
negotiated the shimmering gauze, permitting it to wind around
her naked body until it seemed to take on a life of its own.
Dimming colored lights, playing on her nudity, formed ambiguous shadows. Slowly, bit by bit, she simulated the slightest hint
of orgasm. The audience unleashed hoarse shouts and adulations,
shouting, coaxing her, "*encore, encore!*" At the moment they
seemed unable to endure the unbearable suspense, the lights
faded to black.

The thunderous, unrestrained applause, whistles, and affectionate obscenities refused to abate. The lights came up swiftly. St.
Germaine had departed. In her place, under a flattering spill of
colored lights, twelve of Fatima's most desirable passion flowers
began to sway their bodies rhythmically one way, their belly
undulations another, keeping time to the cacophony of Arabic
music. A bidding for their services commenced.

Darius smiled reflectively. Irresistibly naive on his arrival
at Sidi, shocked, scandalized at the naked display of feminine
mysteries, a brotherly protection had surfaced. How could he save
them from the lower depths of degradation? *How?* He couldn't.
Time provided necessary insight. Fatima's was an Edenic existence
for them compared to the unhuman conditions meted them at home.
No longer did the demimondaines, street whores and prostitutes
incur his pity or censure. Let them coo, beckon seductively with
their sing-song provocations "*Jes suis une putain de Legionnaires,
et j'ien sui Dieri, que j'em suis fiere!*" Darius had become
immune to them.

Favoring his injured shoulder, Darius stood at the bar sipping
cool German beer. If the shocking events of Compiegne were
known to these revelers . . . A familiar scent of musk rode
herd on his senses. A soft hand touched his arm; a husky voice
purred loud enough to be heard by those in close proximity
to them.

"*Bonjour, cher ami.*" The most stunning woman in Sidi bel
Abbes stood unbearably close to him, slithering her slender arms
about his neck. She kissed him passionately on the lips, simultaneously moving a black silk-stockinged leg sensuously up and

down Darius's leg in a gesture designed to set off electrodes of
sexuality in the most docile and recalcitrant of men. Onlookers
whistled, applauded, shouted exaggerated praises, each gesture
encouraging her into more overt expression. St. Germaine rained
kisses on Darius. Daringly she groped for his crotch, pulled him
provocatively up the winding staircase to the second landing and
her boudoir—off limits to nearly everyone. She slinked coquett-
ishly around the corner, disappearing behind closed doors.

Lomay St. Germaine. Her frail beauty, like that of a delicate
flower, lay over her face like gossamer. Satiny, bronze skin,
stretched taut over a firm, well-proportioned body; small waist,
large firm breasts, exquisitely rounded hips, long shapely legs,
and a patrician face molded with spectacular bone structure came
alive with violet eyes outlined with black kohl, framed by thick,
double-fringed lashes, luscious pouting lips, and a straight nose,
flaring nostrils, uptilted at the end. She moved with a unique
dégáge. Naturally curly black hair, worn waist length, dotted with shimmering gold papillon ornaments, fluttered animatedly.
A black jeweled garterbelt, long black silk stocking, and high-
heeled shoes were her trademark, covered by a diaphanous hip-
length jacket that barely concealed her body or the provocative
movements of her deliciously shadowed breasts. In Sidi, St.
Germaine was sui generis. She amused with witty remarks, sang
clever, titillating songs with a cool remoteness that spiraled
the imaginations of men. She was the quintessential fantasy of
all men.

Inside her cluttered, perfumed boudoir, festooned with ball
fringe and tassels, her comportment took on a variety of dimensions.
The tools of her adopted trade yielded to an acute professionalism.
Locking the doors behind them, she turned up the radio volume,
reached for a silk wrapper to cover her nudity, belting it securely
at her waist. Darius's appreciate gaze brought a decided blush
to her cheeks.

She wagged a finger at him, shook her head in silent, affectionate chastisement, and pulled him like a schoolboy caught cheating,
toward the lace and beruffled bed adorned with a massive array
of French dolls. She fumbled with a wall panel concealed behind
the brass spindle headboard until a wall section slid open.

"Voilà! Entrez s'il vous plaît, cher ami."

The alcove was crammed with a small desk, file cabinet, radio
receiver and transmitter, the walls covered with maps of North

Africa and the Sidi command post tagged with colored flags to mark key positions. Darius reached for Lomay, held her tightly in his arms, nuzzled her playfully, and whispered, "When will you make an honest man of me, *ma chère*? I burn with desire for you." He planted a kiss on her astonished but willing lips.

Her rich, husky laughter and Fifi D'Orsay voice admonished him. "One of these days, *Monsieur* Casanova, I shall call your bluff. Then we shall see the measure of your manhood."

"Ah, but you have already seen its measure. Ah, *ma chère*, what we sacrifice for La Belle France."

"*Qu'est-ce-que-c'est La Belle France?* What is this la belle France, business, eh? Always you make ovations when time is of the essence. One day," she said with pouting, teasing wet lips, "shall come a day of reckoning." Then in sudden transition, she got to business. "Enough of this whimsy. As usual grave dangers imperil all of us, *mon capitaine*." She switched on a ceiling fan, stirring a faint breeze. "*Mon Dieu!* The *ghilbi* is not to be believed!" She swept fine sand granules off the desk and chair and agitated the air with a bamboo fan.

Darius draped his tunic on the chair, sat down, mopping the torrents of sweat dripping off his brow and neck. "*Encore*, the glory of La Belle France, *ma chère* is always first and foremost."

Lomay, fanning herself, pulled the chain to the goose-neck lamp on the desk. She unlocked a desk drawer, retrieved a manila envelope, handed it to Darius, her free hand tracing his bandaged arm. Mild alarm in her voice.

"*Qu'est-ce-qu'il y a?* What is this? What happened, *mon cher*? *Mon Dieu!* So much blood!"

He shrugged. "One of Hassan's charmers." Under the spill of light he spread the contents before him on the desk, sorting photos and dossiers. Pausing briefly, Darius fished a pack of Fatima cigarettes from his tunic pocket, handed it to Lomay. He propped the three photos against the lamp base and placed the respective dossiers before each, critically eyeing each.

St. Germaine traced the belly dancer logo with a scalpel-sharp knife, lifted the cutout, extricated a microdot with a long-pronged tweezers, and, holding it against the light peered at it critically. She excused herself, departed the alcove and, inside the bedroom, pressed a second wall panel leading to an adjoining room, a makeshift photo developing lab aglow with infrared lamps. Her intrusion momentarily startled a gargantuan hulk named Karim, whose hand, hovering over a knife at his waist, relaxed in recognition. She handed him the microdot. He moved to the developing pans and went to work.

Karim, a bull-necked Mongol, a deadly man, was Lomay's fiercely devoted factotum and bodyguard. Avoided by others as if he were a leper, he served a dual role at Fatima's. He wore a garish, theatrical attire of golden lamé harem trousers, partially tarnished by tropical temperatures, girdled by a wide leather belt adorned with innocent-looking fetishes—quickly converted into lethal potions—and a bull whip. Behind the garish facade and menacing eyes worked the cleverly trained brain of an adroit espionage agent. His black almond eyes, set deeply into pockets of flesh over high Eurasian cheek bones, gave way to a flat, mushroom nose, unsmiling face, and a Samurai's muscled body. Nightly, as he moved through Fatima's rooms, protecting his charge, his pet parrot Coco perched on his shoulder, he was transformed into as spectacular a sight as the two colorfully garbed Punjabis at the entrance.

Twenty minutes later, Lomay left the photo lab and returned to the sweltering alcove where Darius cursed the elements. His brow was banded with a twisted kerchief to retard sweat from burning his eyes. Lomay fanned him with the bamboo to ease his discomfort. Her eyes trailing to the photos, she let loose a string of expletives.

"You recognize the unholy triumvrate, *mon cher*?" She spat.

"What a question!" He grimaced. Ernst Von Luden, Hans Hesse, Fritz Schmidt! "The faces are etched in acid in my brain. German NCO's recently transferred to Columb-Bechar. If it were my job to determine their fate, I'd put them in chains for life. Unfortunately they deserted their posts the first week in June."

"*D'accord, mon cher*. The truth is these are not merely German legionnaires, but high-ranking Nazis from the RHSA, foreign intelligence division of the Berlin *Reichssicherheitshauptampt*!"

"Your sources as usual, are impeccable, Lomay. Since we are both professionals who know the rules, I won't question them." He studied the second and third sheets of the dossiers, his features stony as he confirmed his worst suspicions. "What's in the microfilm?" Lomay picked up the Hesse photo.

"Hesse terrifies me. I get the distinct feeling he will demand retribution." Her body was gripped by fear.

"Worse than Von Luden?" Darius spat.

She grimaced in chilling recollection. "Von Luden? *Von Luden*. By comparison Von Luden is a cub." St. Germaine quickly changed the subject. "Darius, explain my confusion. Evidence transmitted these many months to Paris, proof of German espionage infiltration in the Legion's ranks, brings no results. Frances does nothing. Why?"

"To paraphrase Paracelsus, men who do not hear or take action are not to be invoked or shouted at for they may be in communion with spirits whose voice is not heard by humanity."

"Platitudes have no place here, in Sidi, now, as our nation prepares to give up the ghost. If a remedy fails us in North Africa, France will be forgotten, relegated to history."

"The film, Lomay," Darius pressed, "what did it contain?"

"*Bonjour, Capitaine*." Karim entered the alcove, placed the photo enlargements on the desk before Darius. Darius acknowledged the Samurai, his eyes affixed at once to the photos, astonishment flooding his face. Lomay moved in behind him, her eyes darting from the photos to Karim in growing alarm.

"*Merde!* Are these to be believed! Just what Prince Ben-Kassir *needs* in these crucial times!" Her whole body was trembling. "All morning I have tried to contact the palace. Have you been more fortunate?"

"Lomay, I am sorry. Nothing . . . I sent Legionnaires Pascal and Longinotti to track him down. We'll know soon enough."

She shook her head. "You're wrong. We won't. It's too late." She stood motionless, her face pale, her breathing erratic, but the fear was not for herself. It was for Youseff Ben-Kassir.

"You'd best get her a drink," Darius instructed Karim.

"No. No. I'm fine." Lomay steadied herself. "You realize what will happen—"

Darius shifted his focus to the enlarged photos. "Here Von Luden, Hesse, and Schmidt audaciously wear their German uniforms! You are correct, the lowest-ranking officer is Schmidt, *Oberstleutnant*."

"And with them, most appalling of all, Muhammad Abou Ahkmed Hassan!" Lomay snapped caustically. "You know what it means—this presence with the Germans?" she sputtered.

"I know." Darius's voice was calming, his eyes on the photos. The Arab chieftain in his *djellaba* and roped *kuffiah* gripped the knife sheathed at his waist. "For whatever it's worth, note the fury in his eyes."

"Faces can be fraudulent; therefore looks mean little to me. What counts are the stockpiled weapons crated ceiling high in this warehouse. This is a vicious collaboration."

Darius, with a magnifying lens peered critically at the crates; rifles and machine guns were scattered about the floor. The photo confirmed the reports he'd received these past weeks.

"If the rumors are true, and these photos support that truth, then Hassan, avowed enemy of France, plans to launch a holy war against France and its staunchest ally in the Tell—Prince Youseff Ben-Kassir!"

"I pray God it is not true, yet these photos prove beyond any shadow of doubt a military mobilization is already underway."

"Should a deadly altercation ensue at so ill-fated a time, when the Legion is unable to defend its fortification—" Darius couldn't air his innermost fears, not yet. He scanned the crate markings with a magnifying lens, cursing aloud. "*Merde!* Canadian, Spanish, and Belgian markings! Hassan's allies. These weapons were bound for Norway in the Narvik Operation. They're part of the hijacked shipments forwarded through German intervention to a Moroccan underground network of desert guerrillas working with Von Luden, Hesse, and Schmidt. Karim, where were those photos taken?"

"The warehouse of a spur track on the Oran waterfront in Morocco less than a week ago." Karim signaled Darius, with his eyes to Lomay.

"No need to spare me, Karim. I know the consequences. Youseff faces grave peril now that France has fallen. Bloodshed, massacre, destruction will follow. With Hassan is it *guerre a mort!* War to the end!"

The Italians say, "*guerra cominiciata, inferno scatenato*, when war begins, all hell loses." Lomay's spirits sank.

"This morning, Darius, in a railroad car in Compiegne—Hitler humiliated France. Marshal Pétain signed the armistice with Germany!"

Darius's shock was total. "You know? Already? You *know* the details? Intelligence headquarters is attempting to confirm the news burning the wires this morning and *you* already know the details?" He shook his head in stupefaction. "You never cease to amaze me."

"When I learned Hitler ordered the railroad car removed from the Paris museum, I knew what was intended."

Darius knew precisely where the unimpeachable information had originated. Tight-lipped concerning his source, he muttered dispassionately, "For too long France paraded like a preening peacock, doing *nothing* to avert disaster. Now it's done. A post mortem serves no purpose. We are allies now. Germany and France are allies."

"Germany and France—allies!" Lomay echoed the feeble words. "You'd best not wager a sou on that probability, *mon ami*. Forces within France resist this alliance and desire to form a new government, declaring this armistice null and void. Would you, Darius, fight for a free France or prefer to live under the heel of the German boot?"

"You ask so foolish a question of me?"

"Meanwhile Youseff is untenably positioned. As an avowed Axis enemy, to whom can he turn for protection?" Her concern for Prince Ben-Kassir left no doubt in Darius's mind where her loyalties lay. *"Cher ami*, can NAIS withhold the information out of Compiegne? Ben-Kassir desperately needs time. The moment confirmation arrives, Hassan and the Germans will kill him, usurp his power—"

Darius's face drained of color. His hand darted to his injured arm, recalling Hassan's assassin. He muttered, "If it isn't already too late. Surely the Germans received word, perhaps before us. But what of you, Lomay? This dangerous game you've played here in Sidi places you in dire jeopardy. If you are found out . . . Lomay—if we suddenly depart from Sidi, what becomes of you?"

"Karim will protect me. Will Colonel Furstenberg withhold the truth until we contact Youseff Ben-Kassir?"

Both she and Karim solemnly observed Darius collect the dossiers and photos and place them in a false lining of his *kepi-blanc*. Karim withdrew from the alcove, his features unreadable, but the undercurrent of listlessness and depression unmistakable.

Darius followed St. Germaine out of the alcove. He glanced at Lomay, noting her efficiency. "Why do you do this? Why risk your young, beautiful life in so perilous and thankless an endeavor? You live in a nightmare world of conflicting principles and confused emotions, in this god-forsaken world where Christ and Christianity are swear words. In this climate of uncertainty, where a promise is always contingent, truth is relative, courage unstable, and loyalty a question of weighing the balance of personal advantage. My God, Sidi is hell!''

''Why do *you, mon capitaine*?'' she retorted softly, her full lips trembling slightly.

Darius drew her close to him, embracing her with affection. Lomay pulled away slightly, placing her lacquered fingernail over his lips, silencing him. ''One day I shall explain the mysteries of Lomay St. Germaine.'' Glancing at the clock on her table, her hand gripped Darius's arm tightly. ''You cannot depart. It's not even noon. We must continue to play the game as usual,'' she urged as a knock on the door brought up their heads.

Hurriedly, she grabbed his *kepi* and tunic from his arms and tossed them on a chair. She placed his gun belt and holstered service revolver on the night stand next to the bed. She mussed his hair, raised the volume on the radio, and released a stream of bubbling laughter. Off came her silk wrapper and sheer bodice. In a few sure movements she slithered her fingers through her thick, lustrous hair, shaking the riotous mass into wild disorder. She smeared lip rouge onto Darius's lips and face, sprayed him with cologne despite his protestations at the strong, heavy musk. Darius, not idle during this artfully constructed scene, moved with agility, sweeping the dolls off the bed and pulling back the covers; he managed to lay back bare-chested, his trousers open and boots off. All was performed in less than sixty seconds. St. Germaine inhaled several breaths of air and, lying next to Darius on the bed, to depress the area next to him. Then she leaped from the down mattress, calling tartly, *''Entrez! Entrez! Sacré bleu!''* She bolted across the room, out of breath.

She unlocked the door, admitting a servant, Fayola, a dark-skinned Arab girl with inquisitive ebony eyes. Fayola glanced at Darius lying indolently on the bed, her eyes missing nothing. Quickly she lowered her eyes to the tray she carried, laden with champagne, glasses, and a basket of flowers. Darius thought her to be unfriendly, not hostile as her blank face indicated, but dominated by fear and superstition. Her movements were shaky. Had she not appeared so circumspect in placing the floral basket on the night stand, Darius might have disregarded the tocsins firing his brain.

''It took you long enough to get here!'' Lomay snapped in Farsi.

''But, madame, I came before! You did not answer my knock.''

"Indeed?" Lomay winked at Darius. "You hear, *mon cher*? We did not answer her. Was our ecstasy such we failed to hear the knock?" She snuggled next to Darius, a litany of solicitous murmurings and whisperings falling from her lips as Fayola poured champagne. "I try, *mon capitaine*, to keep Fayola off the streets, but she insists on emulating me. My life isn't always a bed of silks and exotic passion, I tell her. Men like you are the exception not the rule, and do not beat women in the custom of her people. *Sacré bleu!* I do believe Fayola desires you to pay some attention to—"

Darius, playing the game, one eye on Fayola, kissed Lomay with passion. His body hardening against hers surprised him as well as her. Lomay pulled back, eyes widening, searching his in penetrating silence. The moment passed. Under Fayola's piercing scrutiny, Lomay's manipulations could not stop, nor did his caresses. *How much more could either of them take?*

Darius pulled her atop his body, gently easing her *away* from the night table, the life-saving gesture obscured by the heat of passion. St. Germaine saw it! Danger was dramatized in his eyes. Hesitant only for a moment, she played the game, coloring it with caution. "You tell me you love me, *oui*? How do I believe you? You spend precious little time with me. Your mistress is the Legion!" she muttered petulantly. Surprised by his tenacious grip, she sputtered, "Who in Sidi can do for you what St. Germaine does, eh?"

Darius couched his warning in warm, whispered overtones, a seductive smile on his face. "Do not move, *ma chère*, unless you are expecting a Lucretia Borgia for luncheon." To Fayola, whose intent eyes were fixed like an adhesive on them, he ordered, "Go, leave us, woman. What we intend is not for innocent eyes." He kissed Lomay fervently, inching both bodies to the opposite side of the bed. Under lidded eyes he held a bead on the young Arab girl as she backed out of the room, her furtive, inquisitive eyes straining to see, her ears to hear, before exiting.

Darius unceremoniously dumped St. Germaine on the floor, admonishing her to remain immobile. In an agile move, he sprinted from the same side of the bed and padded swiftly to the door, bolted it, his finger to his lips gesturing Lomay to silence. Darius, knife in hand, stealthily approached the floral basket. St. Germaine, observing him in fascination, wondered as he pointed to the flowers. Then, quicker than the eye could see, he stabbed at the basket, time and again, lopping off the flowers, and in a final gesture swept the offensive things to the floor.

By this time St. Germaine, crouching behind him, exclaimed in a muffled voice, "*Naja Haje!* But how did you know?" She stared—amid the tattered blooms were the bloodied remains of a deadly black viper. "*Sacré bleu!*"

"Those pretty blooms, *ma chère*, are *Strophantus*, from which the natives distill deadly poison. The *Naja Haje* thrives on the plant and is curiously drawn to the scent of your perfume. Recently the government forbade growth of the plant due to its flagrant misuse. Too many mysterious homicides, *comprenez-vous?*" Her eyes darted to the door.

Although terror welled in her heart, Lomay, the consummate actress, groaned and moaned erotically, emitting ecstatic sighs. Then she rattled off some French love words and endearments that brought a blush to Darius's cheeks. Peals of syrupy laughter poured from her throat. She jumped on the bed, bouncing up and down, then springing catlike from the bed, she circumvented the overturned mess on the floor. She pressed the button under the night stand.

She stared at the overturned flowers and the the black asp, its arrow-shaped head lying disconnected from its body in bloody sections on the floor. If Darius hadn't been here . . .

In the corridor, Fayola's ear flattened against the louvered door. Karim, striking his bull whip menacingly against the walls, approached. Startled, panic-stricken at Karim's presence, she shrank against one wall. He growled at her in Farsi. "I shall brook no insubordination, wench! Back to the kitchen!"

If Fayola was terrified of Karim, that terror multiplied tenfold at the power of Muhammad Hassan and his tribe of desert zealots. Her loyalty to Hassan was absolute. Not an iota of this loyalty escaped St. Germaine. "It's far more sensible to feed Hassan's spies misinformation than dismiss them. Let their master mete out punishment when the information proves fraudulent," she had confided to Darius at his reporting of Fayola's duplicity.

Now she brooded. "It is insufferably hot. My head aches and I long for the consolation of cool sea breezes, rest, and quiet," she told Darius, hurrying him from her boudoir. "France is lost. You must reach the prince, you must! Now, go, *mon cher*. You've saved my life. Forever I am in your debt. Go with God."

Lomay St. Germaine, thought Darius as he departed, was the bravest woman he'd met.

St. Germaine bolted her door, swept aside the remains of Fayola's lethal plot, and, seated at her desk, wrote a communiqué in invisible ink to Monsieur Craneur Creneau, Postal Station C-1000, Compiegne, France.

Mon Ami:
  The news is shattering. Vast military strength arrives daily in the Libyan ports of Benghazi and Tobruk. Natives overwhelmed by massive deliveries of new guns and ammunition, far superior to the Sidi stockpiles. Internal uprisings are rife. Penetration of Italian fortifications reveal embryonic operational strategy that, if implemented, means *finis* for France. Strategy confirmed by trusted field agents and aerial reconnaissance photos. Germany too plans alliances with Libya. Massive offensive, OPERATION SPHINX awaits your approval for launching. Desperately need immediate counteroffensive preparation or France and the Legion are doomed. Undercurrents of unrest might require instant flight. Prince Kassir in dire jeopardy. Hassan and Germans mounting fierce offensive from Morocco. Death plots occur with alarming consistency. Advise return courier . . . Zahara.

Lomay sealed the coded communiqué, summoned Karim to dispatch it in the usual manner.

Only one man knew the truth about the desperate game Lomay played. Monsieur Craneur Creneau. This high-ranking French military officer, unknown to Darius or Colonel Henri Furstenberg, Chief of NAIS—North African Intelligence Service—was Lomay's espionage conduit to *Interalle*, France's espionage hierarchy.

Both Lomay and Creneau preferred anonymity. The name, Craneur Creneau, an invented one, translated "swaggering battlement," a perfect description of the French officer. Only Creneau knew Lomay's humble, yet infamous bloodline. To all others she remained a mystery.

Born under a black cloud of death, a plot to murder her before birth was foiled by either Satan or God. Born two months prematurely, she had escaped the German firing squad that executed her mother. Lomay, the illegitimate issue of the infamous Gertrude Marguerite Zelle in July 1918, was whisked out of prison, transported at once to North Africa by one of her mother's lovers—not her real father—and a wet nurse. The beleaguered lover had joined the Foreign Legion, determined to forget Gertrude's transgressions.

Her earliest memories were of soldiers, the blistering sun of the broiling desert, of M'Bata, her foster mother, who had nursed her and provided the only love she'd known. M'Bata gave Lomay life, love, and a reason to live. On her fourteenth birthday, Lomay's world exploded and crumbled to bits.

Tragedy descended, altering her life irrevocably. The French officer responsible for raising her was killed in a desert skirmish with warring desert tribesmen. M'Bata arrived in Lomay's room, her arms laden with manuscripts, letters, and zealously guarded diaries compiled by her dead lover. Her soft black eyes filled with inconsolable sadness, she placed them on the girl's bed, soothed the trembling child, counseling her to read the diaries. "Peruse them well, my child, contained in them is the key to your life." M'Bata retreated from Lomay's bedchamber and entered the room where her dead lover lay. She plunged a knife in her breast, fell atop him, her blood commingling with his.

Lomay learned of M'Bata's death the next day when the servants summoned her to the room. Shocked, she stared, trembling at the macabre scene of lovers united in death. The nightmares in the diaries had stunned her into insensibility.

Devastated, she found the inner strength to support her through the double burials and subsequent dark days filled with loneliness and indecision. Rummaging through the memoirs, the rash of faded, yellowed newspaper clippings, photographs, letters of a secret past of vast international complications drove her for a time to borderline insanity. She cursed her foster father aloud. "Why didn't you let me die! Why raise me to bear this burden of guilt?" Her refusal to yield to self-pity, coupled with her instinct for survival, forced her to peruse the legacy. What was it M'Bata had counseled before taking her life? *The key to your life is contained herein.*

With vigilance she pored over the diaries written in her stepfather's handwriting. Revealed was the story of the death of her real mother at the hands of her lover. It was he who had committed the final act of betrayal. The very man who had raised Lomay—another man's child as his own—the Legionnaire officer she had called *papa* all her life—had turned her mother, Gertrude Zelle, over to the Germans in a fit of jealous rage and suffered the guilt of the opprobrious act forever after.

Conceived out of wedlock! Delivered prematurely, deprived of her real mother and father—all of it would affect Lomay her entire life! But nothing, nothing shattered her as did the knowledge that her real mother was the infamous Mata Hari!

Lomay, in a rage, needed to destroy all memories of her ignominious parents. She took camel crop in hand and smashed all the African fetishes, the tribal masks adorning the walls, the personal articles of adornment in M'Bata's room and brought crashing to the floor her father's lavish Legion decorations, a fourteen-year chronicling of his meaningless life in exile in a desert firing oven where life was cheap but not as cheap as he felt.

Recrimination followed the destruction. Frantic efforts to restore order ensued. She perused the diaries again, fascinated by her mother's infamous existence.

Fighting a fierce compulsion to right the wrongs done to France by her mother's treachery, Lomay dispatched a polite letter of inquiry to a man whose name she found in the legionnaire's diary. She was going to do great things for France, she knew it, felt it in her bones. He couldn't refuse, he wouldn't! While awaiting his reply she rode her camel daily, against Legion regulations, beyond the limits of the post compound, returning daily for the next month, exhausted, forlorn, unfulfilled, and disappointed when no mail arrived.

She aimlessly fed her menagerie—a baby jackal found in the bush, a mangy cur with questionable bloodline, a parrot trained by a dead legionnaire to utter gross obscenities, and a green-eyed, black cat.

Well-meaning friends of M'Bata offered condolences and advice. If Lomay scorned speedy matrimony, they warned, she'd fall prey to the only fate meted out to a girl of fourteen whose maturity was ogled at constantly by salacious legionnaires. Her only recourse was prostitution, if she remained, or to enter some trade school to learn secretarial work. Lomay listened politely over tea, her contempt for their suggestions pyramiding to disgust and loathing. She marked time, refused all company, remaining alone in her modest house. The day she received an affirmative reply to her letter, Lomay disposed of her menagerie, closed down the house, and booked passage for Paris. Fate intervened, spreading darkening war clouds over the face of Europe. The added bonus fired her plan.

Four years later, Lomay emerged from espionage school outside Paris, a full-fledged spy, a skilled technician fluent in the application of basic cloak-and-dagger techniques. She was a natural!

The next two years Lomay worked in the Deuxième Bureau, in Vichy, an espionage control center, using the cover "Zahara." She continued to remain a mystery to all except the enigmatic, but powerful Monsieur Creneau who had sponsored her.

Which was perfectly fine with St. Germaine, who at age eighteen had unfolded into a ravishing flower of beauty. Her beauty worried her mentors. A recognizable beauty, unless expertly manipulated within the scope of special intelligence forces, could bring death. She was brought to the attention of the espionage hierarchy, *Interalle*. Six men and women specialists critically appraised her smoldering sensuality and elevated her from the rank and file of Special Services and mundane bureau activities. Like a rare, vintage wine she was cultivated, nurtured and properly aged to realize the highest profits. Musicians, inspired by a fierce loyalty to France, dragged reluctantly from retirement, taught her voice placement, singing, ballet, interpretive dancing.

Lomay was happy. Even the art of walking properly to bring instant attention to her superb body became an arduous but fulfilling endeavor, drawing her a step closer to her goal. She was proud of her achievements. Drama coaches dug deep inside her to uncover a wealth of talent buried behind a stony wall of shy reserve. Lomay came alive on the stage in a way she seemed unable to in real life.

Her mentors delighted in her achievements and began to chart an unparalleled course for Zahara, certain she would emerge as France's most valuable secret weapon. Their enthusiasm spread to Zahara, infecting her senses, dazzling her beyond belief. The next year, jam-packed daily with new, exciting adventures, fled past swiftly.

But Lomay St. Germaine still felt unfulfilled.

She had motored to Compiegne, seeking solace and advice from Monsieur Creneau. What she got was an outpouring of his wrath at the wave of vandalism sweeping through synagogues. He read her the newspaper account dated November 7, 1938, of a young Polish Jew who had killed the secretary of the Third

Reich at the Paris embassy to protest the Nazi treatment of his fellow Jews. What followed in Germany was called *Kristallnacht*, Crystal Night. Thirty-five were killed, thousands arrested, and fines totaling one billion marks were levied on German Jews. Creneau tossed down the paper in disgust. "Already, *ma chère* Lomay, I can hear refrains of "*Deutschland über Alles*" echoing through the streets of Paris. Next shall come the goosestepping German boots! But we must not let it happen! Do you understand me. Never!"

Lomay had never seen the *swaggering battlement* under fire. She never wanted a repeat performance. Following a glass of his favorite Bordeaux, he simmered down. "Now, Lomay, what is troubling you?"

She explained. "I feel like a failure. I am completely inept, unable to control myself. I regret shaming you after your kind, considerate assistance. It's best I give up now, before endangering any man's life. I am frustrated, locked in the tenacious grips of inhibition. They are enemies detroying me from within. Secret enemies preventing me from attaining perfection in my profession. The results I envision in mind are perfect, monsieur, but when put on the spot, forced to perform, I am lost! Frightened out of my wits! What a disappointment I am to you!" She felt terrible about bringing her problems to him when he had far more important matters to ponder. But Creneau listened, lit a Gauloise, puffed on it, taken by the remarkable changes in her. Her presence lit up the room.

"My dear child," Creneau began, trying to subdue the memories she stirred in him. "Dry those tears. What you're afraid of is merely deception in art form." He explained that espionage, like acting on stage, was donning a variety of disguises that shield you from detection. On stage the actor, masked by the character he plays, walks, talks, moves his body in ways to accommodate the role he portrays. An actor speaks another man's words, the singer utters another man's words, keeping time to music, and if he's good he expresses emotions to best convey the composer's emotional key. "You see, merely deception in art form," he repeated.

Deception in art form! If one word explained Lomay's life, *deception* had colored hers. Green lights flashed, alarms went off in her head. *She was free!* On intimate terms with deception since before her birth, she returned to Paris that day, prepared to employ it with the artful *dégagé* air of a butterfly.

Hadn't her drama coach defined her movements on stage as a butterfly in motion? *Voilà! Les papillons* would become Zahara's trademark. She would wear costumes and jewelry decorated with butterflies.

Lomay St. Germaine was ecstatic.

Interalle was dismayed. Zahara stubbornly pursued and realized the North African Assignment, temporarily shelving their infinitely more rewarding plans for her. Her fluency in wog dialects, compatability with torturous desert temperatures, and knowledge of the harsh realities of a legionnaire's life were powerful assets. *Interalle* capitulated when precious agents abandoned Sidi bel Abbes, afflicted with dysentery and gonorrea, and, unable to cope with erratic climates, ended up statistics.

Lomay St. Germaine, a.k.a. Zahara, the shy, retiring girl who had departed Sidi six years before, had flowered into an enchanting seductress wise in the ways of men. She had taken a tempting role any actress worth her salt would kill for.

One impediment had loomed unexpectedly. Thrown together in clandestine activities for France, she had fallen in love with Prince Ben-Kassir. *C'est la vie!* But, *c'est la vie très dangereuse!* And everyone could tell you, espionage and love did not mix! Couldn't they?

Lomay pressed the panel opening the alcove. She entered and fussed with the radio transmitter, headphones in place over her head. She spoke rapidly: Zahara calling Ajujui . . . Zahara calling . . . Come in Adjuijui . . . Imperative you respond . . . Do you read me? . . . Black lion of the desert in jeopardy. Imperative you make contact . . . Zahara.

Chapter Twenty-eight

It was twelve o'clock noon, the temperature was 115 degrees and still climbing. Darius, busy at his desk in the NAIS office sorted dossiers on the German Non Com officers.

The office, quartered in a two-story stucco building inside the Sidi military compound overlooking the parade square contained a profusion of radio and wireless apparatus, desks, wooden files, phones—all dominated by a temperamental ceiling fan. Today it was incapable of handling the heat overload. Maps of North Africa, Algeria itself and Sidi bel Abbes were flagged to indicate the location of all post commands in the High Atlas. Open grilled windows afforded no breeze except at night when temperatures dropped to freezing.

Darius picked up a phone, rang Prince Ben-Kassir's palace. He counted: one . . . two . . . three . . . six . . . eight rings. *Merde! Siesta!* The Wogs had learned it from the indolent French—no work from noon to 3 P.M. He slammed down the phone. For several moments he studied the spindle-stabbed messages, at once jarred by the shrill ring of the phone. It was Ibrahim, Prince Ben-Kassir's secretary, returning his earlier call.

"Is His Highness free to converse with me, Ibrahim?" He was not. His Highness had left early that morning to confer with several desert chieftains about pressing business.

"Perhaps, *Capitaine* Bonifacio, if you try *Saida* or *El Bayadh?*"

Darius thanked him and rang off, his eyes peering at some inner mental scene. An ominous feeling knotted his stomach as if he'd been kicked in the guts.

Getting back to the business at hand, he propped up the photos of the German NCOs at the Oman warehouse on his desk and placed before each the confidential dossiers compiled by NAIS on each. Something nagged at him. Youseff Ben-Kassir's image came alive in his mind too often to ignore it. He moved to the communications desk and began tapping out Morse code to *Saida*.

DELILAH'S DREAM TO BELLY DANCER . . . CONFIRM PRESENCE OF BLACK LION IN VICINITY REPLY IMPERATIVE . . . signed, SAMSON.

The reply came in moments:

BELLY DANCER TO DELILAH'S DREAM . . . NEGATIVE . . . BLACK LION ABSENT FROM VICINITY . . . TRY SNAKE CHARMER . . . CONFIRM RUMORS . . . STATE POSITION . . . DO WE ABANDON? . . . REPLY . . . signed, MOONSTRUCK.

Damned! News from Compiegne had spread like typhus. To promote fear now would be counterproductive. Darius tapped back a message:

RUMORS UNOFFICIAL . . . KEEP COOL . . . WILL ADVISE ON CONFIRTION, BELLY DANCER . . . OVER AND OUT . . . signed, SAMSON.

Darius switched at once to the El Bayadh coding and transmitted,

DELILAH'S DREAM TO SNAKE CHARMER . . . CONFIRM BLACK LION'S PRESENCE AT ONCE . . . IMMEDIATE REPLY URGENT . . . signed, SAMSON.

When the fourth consecutive attempt to reach the Legion outpost at El Bayadh failed, Darius noted and scored the time in his log—twelve-thirty P.M.—then scribbled, "Try again in half hour." Back at his desk he decoded one of the messages procured from St. Germaine earlier that day. It was from a Ben-Kassir agent and dated four days ago:

CONFIRM PRESENT STATUS . . . HASSAN ARMED TO TEETH BY GERMANS . . . PHOTOS CONFIRM LAUNCHING OF MASS OFFENSIVE. DO WE MOVE ON OPERATION SPHINX OR COME OFF THE DESERT TO RECONNOITER? . . . IMPERATIVE YOU REPLY. SIGNED AHUIHUI

Darius pondered the message. He had no ready answers—not now. He shot a glance at the temperature—120 degrees and *still* rising. He poured alcohol over his bare upper torso to cool down. Nothing helped. He resigned himself to the work at hand.

Precisely what the three German NCOs—Von Luden, Hesse, and Schmidt—meant to Darius personally and professionally remained part of the revolting nightmares of Sidi bel Abbes. Darius frowned at the onslaught of demons springing to life from his subconscious. Earlier at St. Germaine's, he'd contained them admirably, but now they rode herd behind painful memories of the recent past. Would he never be free of them?

He rose from his desk and moved beyond the wooden gate to the large grilled window overlooking the deserted Sidi parade square. It was totally devoid of life, save for an occasional snake or lizard scurrying into some hole for cover; the prostrating heat had sent every living creature into a three-hour hibernation. He stared at the blinding white sand. Vaguely the echoes of a bugler's call reverberated in his mind. A cruel tableau took shape in his mind. Images paraded across his cranium, a reenactment of indescribable, inhuman violence done to him and other recruits.

The internal scene refined itself, growing clearer, more perfect than the original. Voices rushed at him and came alive. The desolate courtyards filled with anguished, agonizing cries and tortured faces, the faces of the damned! Darius remembered vividly . . .

It was October, 1938.

High noon!

The sun beat down on the debilitated recruits marching the last legs of a torturous five-hour, full-pack drill in the bleached Sidi square. Dragging themselves about with superhuman effort, each recruit saturated with sweat and covered with sand hardened to cardboard consistency was driven by a rewarding thought—it was nearly over.

Règlement c'est finis! Merci Dieu!

Eight solid weeks of sadistic orientation conceptualized by the fiendish German NCOs was about to end. The unholy triumvirate—

Hans Hesse, Fritz Schmidt, and the ugliest of beer-bellied Germans, Ernst Von Luden—had finished their dirty business. The recruits had won.

It was finished, wasn't it? In moments it would be ended, wouldn't it?

A bugler sounded *finis*. A sergeant, somewhere off in a distant tunnel, dismissed his men. The grueling pack drill had ended for the tormented men. *But had it*?

The disoriented, dazed recruits had straggled off the parade square zombielike, blindly groping the space before them. Devastated by the debilitating effort, their depleted bodies unable to receive muddled brain messages, most had to be pointed in the proper direction; others, led back to barracks, collapsed and could not be carried. An incoherent babbling of voices arose in feeble protest. Their thoughts—if any remained—disconnected. The entire platoon, Darius included, had lapsed into a mental state of insensibility known to legionnaires as *cafard*.

Cafard! The point at which blind spots explode your cranium and irrevocable holes are burned in your memory! It is the utter hopelessness and despair of the mindless. When *cafard* descends, cruel tricks played by the senses leave you a step inside the pale of madness.

This was their reward for *règlemente!* This was the state of mind to which Darius and the new recruits fell heir to that day. Barely aware of time, direction, and distance, they fell prostrate in various stages of collapse, only a few making it to their bunks. Their throats were parched, their eyes swollen, scratched by sand granules; most were unable to speak or signal their suffering. Darius like the others had barely shed his backpack before oblivion swallowed him up.

Words, tunneling at them from a vast distance, barely penetrated their consciousnesses. Behind Darius's swollen closed eyelids, sound waves bounced about in unbearable cacophony. Nothing worked. Not his senses, not his motor functions, *nothing!*

"Squaaaaadron leaders, Attennnnnntion! . . . Failure to remove, unload and fieldstrip your weapons has just earned you three weeks at hard labor in the penal battalion at *Abu Hammid*."

If anyone heard the command, understood the orders, no one stirred, no one moved.

Words. *Dreams? Illusions?* Flickering apparitions piercing blistered walls to their brains? No one, including Darius, knew for certain. *What did it mean*? Pulled to their feet, stripped of their packs, weapons and uniforms, forced to don prisoners' garb the dazed recruits were herded back onto the broiling sands unsure of what was transpiring. Manacled at wrists and ankles, heavy linked chains bound them to mule-driven lorries.

The nightmares commenced at once. And for what? *For what?* Five hours of dehumanizing torture inflicted for a minor infraction of the rules! Incredible! Unbelievable!

But did it end here? No. Honey, sadistically applied to their wounds as they moved dirgelike through the crematorium desert converted them into ghoulish banquets for dive-bombing mosquitoes, vicious red ants, and waiting at a respectful distance in a timeless patience, hideous vultures circled overhead. Nearby deadly scorpions, sensing feasts above the sands manufactured venom in assembly line swiftness.

The pathetic train of men moved leadenly toward their destination. Darius's clogged, clotted eyes, incapable of focus in the excruciating pain errupting over each sun-scorched eyeball, followed the pull of chains. Blistering hot steel manacles burned into each wrist left open, bleeding sores—perfect refuge for blood-sucking bugs and insidious ants that delighted crawling into their ears, noses, lips and even bored holes under the men's skins to lay their eggs.

What insanity is this? Memory, for Darius spurted alive and collapsed leaving fragmented blips, unspoken gibberish on the transmitting screen of his mind. No longer the naive, sixteen-year-old Corsican, Darius sat at the periphery of madness, unable to circumvent the diabolical events surrounding him. Behind his numbed faculties lay a coiling anger at the inhuman treatment. A spear of ice pierced his heart. A thousand satans could not have conceived such brutal torture.

He was actually contemplating the deaths of the German Non Coms.

If ever men deserved to die . . .

By five P.M. total insanity beckoned from the desert. Their sun-scorched brains had turned the regiment into blithering idiots. Yet, they moved forward for God knows how long determined not to give in to these German pigs.

Von *Luden!* That devil took perverse delight in beating the mules' rumps with a thick cane, forcing them into a fast trot. Prisoners who were unable to keep pace with the mules were dragged along the sands until they lost consciousness. Through it all, the sight of Von Luden's belly shaking with laughter, pierced

Darius's thickly curtained mind. It was a sight he'd never forget. Compassion, a marked deficiency in the German legionnaires, Darius found them oppressive, ruthless and without souls. Reflected in their beastly features was a fixed haughtiness, an insufferable superiority and fierce dedication in finding ways and means to break the backs and spirits of the recruits. Actually it was difficult to comprehend their sadistic bent when Germans got the best in the Legion. Why then the resentment? *Why?*

By sundown, the prisoners, more dead than alive, straggled into the barren courtyard at Abu Hammid, a Legion outpost in the High Atlas. Herded into an enormous two-story stable within the complex, the men fell prostrate, babbling incoherently. Darius's hatred gave way to apathy. How differently the recruits had planned to celebrate the death of *règlemente*.

Night descended mercifully.

Kabul a twelve-year-old Arab with street savvy had accompanied the prisoners from Sidi. He was permitted freedom in the compound and now moved about wary-eyed in a somewhat officious manner. Under the piercing scrutiny of the Germans he jeered at the prisoners, poked fun at their infirmities and cursed in Farsi, insulting them with colorful expletives.

None of the suffering recruits took umbrage at him for without Kabul they'd be dead. He secretly plied them with morphine, quinine and salt tablets filched from the dispensary under the very noses of the NCOs.

Thanks to Kabul, a walking apothecary, the prisoners slept that first night devoid of pain.

The punitive routine at Abu Hammid was consistently brutal. Awakened before dawn by a vicious clubbing done to the soles of their feet, doled sparse water rations and ill-fitting sandals, each man was then stripped to his waist, issued a quarry hammer and pick, then marched to the construction site where he was ordered to smash towering rock piles into tiny pieces. Leather-strap harnesses were fastened to their backs enabling them to tote bags of rocks from the work site to an area where mules transported them to another location.

Hourly the mules received water rations—the recruits got no such considerations. The fact that animals were treated with more consideration didn't escape the men, not for a moment.

Time, for Darius, stopped. And why not? He belonged to the living dead. And with the others was afflicted with hallucinations, devilish images and mirages attacking one and all in this *danse macabre* flawlessly orchestrated by the German NCOs.

Silence . . . the quintessential rule of the penal camp hovered over the men in an unsung death threnody. Should they violate the rule, the Germans devised worse punishments. Beatings with hard canes, plus an additional thirty days for insubordination. Fed salt tablets, refused water? What did it matter? They did not talk—not for fear of punishment but because they lacked the strength to even swat a fly.

The purpose of discipline is to instill fear so pervasive that power can be marshalled and held without opposition.

Words . . . Words . . . only words. Droned at them during *règlemente* preserved neither their sanity nor the will to live.

Darius was losing touch with reality in these critical hours. He desperately needed a miracle to keep him going. God Almighty!

A miracle was provided. *Moufflon!* Yes, *Moufflon*.

It happened on the afternoon of the third day. He remembered that day atop the snowy peaks of Mount Cinto. A mental image of that day flashed on him as he swung his rock pick crushing stones. The image wouldn't fade; it returned and clung tenaciously to him until a curious sensation shook him. Darius shivered noticeably. For a moment he thought, *malaria!* I've got fever! But no—it wasn't that! An inexplicable, intangible alchemy of sorts was taking place in his mind. An enigmatic force cooled his body, actually reduced his body temperature. By concentrating on the snow, he could actually cool his body. Amazing! What a powerful tool—the mind!

By the morning of the fourth day nothing of earth-shattering importance had occurred to change things for the hapless recruits. The motley collection of ex-pickpockets, second-story men, muggers, bank robbers, political terrorists, murderers—now turned legionnaires—accepted the brutalizing stoically. Hunched over pick and shovel, pitiful, grotesque in appearance, as unrecognizable to his companions as they were to him Darius labored, *pour passer le temps*.

Until . . .

It happened without preamble.

Duncan "Limey" Whitehall, a weasel-faced, small-fry con man from Liverpool, swung his pickax languidly, shifty eyes under a predatory brow fixed on the object of his loathing—Hans Hesse. Who could tell what went on in Limey's confused mind at the sight of the imperiously strutting German moving about the rock pile with two guards holding a large umbrella over his head while he swilled water from a canteen, purposely spilling precious drops onto the sand? Desperately thirsty, the prisoners, forced to endure the appalling waste, sent daggers of hatred in the direction of the beast.

The movement was swift. Darius barely saw the outline against the broiling sun as Limey's pick, raised in midair, was about to come smashing down on Hesse's head. Caught from behind by Darius's pick, Limey was restrained. Turning to face Darius, he fell to a crouch, seething, ready to tear his obstructor apart. A whirlwind of action arose. Dutch "Irish" O'Reilly, a broad-shouldered, barrel-chested brute with a thick Irish brogue, leaped into the melee, his chains clanging, and crashed into his companions. He screamed, *"Snake! Snake! Snake!"* and pointed to an imaginary serpent at a point between some rocks.

The guards shot aimlessly, the bullets spitting sand into the prisoners' eyes. O'Reilly signaled Darius and Limey to silence. This was a first for Darius! The first time any recruit had shown consideration for his companions. He resumed his work, glancing periodically at the red-haired Irishman peppered with a crazy quilt of freckles from head to toe.

Dutch "Irish" O'Reilly. His body was a mess. Homesteading bugs had penetrated every open orifice in his body. Their poisonous bites had infected and swelled his penis and testicles to treble their normal size. He wore a shabby breech clout, rags hanging from a slow slung rope at his hips providing little protection for the hairy balls hanging like so much red meat between hairier beet-red legs. Pausing briefly to bind his bleeding hands Dutch caught sight of Hesse staring at his crotch. His black pygmy eyes under shaggy red brows grew smaller. "Eat yer bloomin' friggin' 'eart out, ya friggin' Kraut bastard!" he muttered *sotto voce*.

Hesse moved in closer, straining to hear, his eyes never leaving the area of Dutch's crotch. Dutch's expression turned into an idiot's grin; the poor man resembled a boiled lobster. As Hesse moved away, his attention focused on the others, Limey made an obscene gesture. "Kiss me arse, ye ring-tailed faggot!" In that moment, every man stood still. If the German heard the remark, he seemed oblivious to it, and moved on.

Pasquale Longinotti, a twenty-year-old Italian army deserter, swiped at a family of burrowing insects on his body; flinging them furiously from his body, he hammered away at them with maniacal glee. He cursed in Italian, assailing all the devils in hell and saints in heaven, blaming them for his infirmities. Once, Longinotti had laughed with gay infectious laughter and told an endless parade of humorous stories. But during *règlement* and especially since the events of the past few days, he had locked himself in a never-never land.

Another recruit, Jean-Louis Delon remained impervious to the German presence. The twenty-six-year-old Frenchman, the eldest of the recruits looked an emaciated fifty. He took time this day to meticulously rewrap his bloodied hands with a filthy rag. As usual he kept his distance from the others, and stoically accepted the brutality dished him. He held his own counsel, bottled up his feelings and made no effort to communicate his inner thoughts to the others.

Darius, glancing at Delon felt a shudder course through him. He'd learned many lessons in the Legion, namely that a subdued nature meant one of two things, gentle breeding or the reflection of the inner world of a dangerous psychopath. Which of the two fitted Delon? In any event you steered clear of such men or were caught up unsuspectingly in their insane delusions. Raising his pickax over his head he commenced his destruction to the larger rock, one eye peeled on the enigmatic Hesse.

Hans Hesse, labeled by the legionnaires as a fornicator of animals, strode among the prisoners with pantherish strides, observing the men with icy remoteness. No one knew Hesse's true story, but it made for interesting conjecture among the recruits.

Lucien Pascal, a brooding Corsican, stood five feet six inches tall. His dark square-knotted cropped hair was covered flimsily by a kerchief to protect his head from the brash sun. Shaggy brows formed an unbroken line over a wide capacious nose and flaring nostrils. Black agate eyes defied any man to invade his privacy. Pascal ignored the Germans. His was the only pick and hammer working in a steady, unbroken rhythm. Behind a mask of indifference lurked a marked curiosity about Darius's activities. If, however, the liability existed in this curiosity it was unknown to Darius. Pascal walked in Darius's shadow from the moment he arrived in Sidi, a few weeks after Darius.

Clarity wafted in and out of Darius's brain. When thoughts crystallized, the inescapability of their common predicament weighed heavily on his mind, then as quickly faded and nothing mattered, not even the moment. When you lose the capacity to think . . . What was it called—mental dysfunction? Before Darius could nourish this isolated thought, a flurry of activity drew his attention.

One head, then another and another, all the way down the rock pile, jerked up as Hesse disappeared inside the tent a short distance from them. The men tensed, aware that Von Luden's appearance was imminent.

There he came, exiting the tent, arrogant, cocksure, belching, frequent *petard* orchestrated in between. He strutted behind two armed guards, their guns at the ready, his hands on his hips in that swaggering pose popularized by Il Duce. A stunning handlebar mustache, brushed, curled, waxed daily into a masterpiece of perfection, was the only visible growth of hair on his body. His head shone like a round yellow melon.

Von Luden, a contemptible boozer who dallied in drugs, was shunned by Sidi's whores. Those among the Legion's traveling bordello avoided him, sniggered behind his back, repeating his disgusting sexual debaucheries to anyone perverse enough to listen. The only way a woman could excite Von Luden was by defecating on his face. His specialty was sodomizing young Arab boys. "Hell," Delon had confided to Darius. "The entire command post looks upon Von Luden as the personification of a pus oozing syphilitic."

"Why do the French select such men to train new recruits?" Darius, the neophyte who still dreamed of St. Cyr, had asked. Now, as he peered at the disquieting man from under puffy lids, he wondered what, if anything, he had to learn in all this. By God, French thinking escaped him!

Von Luden remained briefly among the prisoners. He was escorted back to his tent to be fanned, fed and fornicated by a fresh retinue of Arab boys.

Darius failed to see the lighter side of this grisly scenario. Assaulted by physical and mental fatigue, he was unable, once he formed a thought, to hang on to it. Earlier he sensed a spark of courage flaring in the men. Limey Whitehall had actually lunged at Hesse! Here, where prisoners outnumbered the guards three to one, was it possible to spark a flame of revolt? What held them back? They were treated worse than the wogs treated their wretched, starving mules and *gharry* horses; how much more could they endure before they fought back? Darius tried to find some semblance of order in this nightmare. The men didn't lack courage. If they wanted to fight back, they could. Then what was it? Darius had seen it before. A sense of futility whipped the men into obedience. They had nothing to return to, for each had left his country, fleeing from the law for one reason or another. They weren't ready to trade one hell for another—not yet.

At midday Kabul distributed rations, a half pound of stale bread and a pint of water. Darius noticed the lad tarried longer than usual. In a quick, deft movement he hid an extra pint of water behind a boulder and casually dropped a pack of Fatima cigarettes at Darius's feet. The young Corsican glanced curiously at Kabul from under swollen lids, saw the stamp of cruelty and pained grimaces etched into the lad's features. As he had asked a hundred times in the past, Darius repeated the same question this day "Why do you stay, Kabul? Go! Flee this German Moloch."

"Why I stay, Bonny-suh?" Kabul's black eyes oozed indescribable sadness. "My house provides no better, Bonny-suh." He winked broadly. "Besides I steal all I can," he said slyly, and with the deftness of a thief dropped a vial of morphine and quinine tablets into Darius's hands. One of the men hooted; Kabul, alerted, collected himself.

Hesse was returning. In a voice that generally inspired amusement Kabul sternly repudiated an imaginary opponent. "No more rations, infidel dog! Me, boss-man!" He thumped his chest. "You, camel dung!" The lad limped cockily off toward the tent. Hesse plodded up a slight rise on the rocks, his cold, martial eyes overseeing the prisoners.

Darius slipped a morphine tablet between his bleeding, cracked lips, passing the rest to the others. As impotent in the circumvention of their fate as he was his own, he gazed lethargically at his companions, continually awed by their Sisyphean labors, his own included, when boiling dangerously under a hair-thin layer of each man's mind was a bitterness, a battered self-esteem that signaled mutiny and rebellion. Not since he'd left Corsica had the savage urge to kill surfaced in him as it had these past four days. Matteus's death's-head amulet, suspended on a leather strip around his neck, served as a constant reminder of how simple an act death could be. It burned his chest and fired his courage, silently crying out for vengeance, yet he had resisted. Questioned incessantly about the amulet by the other recruits, Darius had remained mute.

He resisted the overwhelming desire to terminate Von Luden's tenure with life and the Legion. He failed to understand his reluctance for no man deserved death more than Von Luden. In those moments when the disorder of his mind abated, he asked himself a thousand times what lesson he must learn from all this. He didn't know yet and never dreamed he would one day give thanks for the lessons taught him at Sidi bel Abbes. *Never!*

Sundown. Abu Hammid. The apathetic prisoners lay prostrate on their prayer rugs in the enormous stable, converted only recently into prisoners barracks. Lighted torches blazed from wrought-iron brackets along the broken stone walls, creating eerie plays of light and shadow extending to the Moorish dome.

How curiously the men accommodated themselves to this hovel. A Y-shaped stick like a miniature crutch, hooked under one arm, elevated one side of their bodies; each man's propped-up shoulder served as a pillow for the man next to him. "Bloody uncomfortable, but bloomin' safe from blood-lusting scorpions bent on nesting in yer ears and hair," insisted Limey Whitehall. "A trick I picked up from the bloody wogs in Equatorial South Africa."

Darius gazed up listlessly as Kabul entered the barracks. He watched the young business entrepreneur peddling skins of wine and hashish. He tossed Darius a pack of Fatima cigarettes. Darius flung them back. "I didn't pay for the last pack. Besides it isn't my brand."

"Oh, yes, Bonny-suh, you pay." Kabul tossed the pack back to him. He tapped his forehead. "You do not remember. You *cafard,* maybe. Always you say, 'Kabul, I like Fatima smokes.' Yes, Bonny-suh, maybe you *cafard*?" He shook his head balefully and negotiated his way among the others, periodically peering back at Darius.

Kabul adored the young Corsican recruit. On his arrival in Sidi he had singled Darius out, clung to him, choosing him as a friend, his eyes full of hero worship. The cunning, street-wise wheeler dealer in contrabrand continuously provoked Darius's curiosity. He was a fount of knowledge, an incessant talker whose endless barrage of questions baffled Darius. He considered the lad too bright to be working the streets.

Kabul's mendacity annoyed Darius, so caught up in the rigors of *règlement.* To devote time to the customs and moralities of a race of people about whom he understood little seemed a fruitless task.

When was it? . . .

Two weeks ago, Kabul, sadistically buggered by Von Luden, had run to Darius's barracks, bleeding, injured, and a bit *cafard* from the drugs forced into him. At the dispensary, medical treatment was refused because Kabül was a wog. Darius, outraged, had beaten up the medic, confiscated medication, and warned the bleating slob of the merits against reporting the incident.

Now, Darius, dazed by the day's events, sat on the prayer rug, disquieted by Kabul's erratic antics, unable to unscramble the puzzle the lad posed. Leaning against the hitching post at the center of the stench-filled shelter, convinced something was terribly wrong, missing, distorted or out of kilter in this comedic tragedy unfolding before his eyes he was unable to tear his eyes from the lad.

Kabul's actions bordered on the ludicrous. He clapped his hands, stomped his feet, finger cymbals tinkling like bells, keeping time to imaginary music, performing a damnably bad and outrageous imitation of a belly dancer. To compound the absurdity he chanted a wog verse in atrocious pidgeon English taught him by Limey Whitehall.

"Me handsome wog boy . . . look a' me . . . look a' me . . . under belly of dancing Fatima abound many treasures . . . See—me swing to east, me swing to west, but place Fatima swing the best is under belly . . . under belly."

Now all this was fine for entertainment, but his suggestive looks in Darius's direction, coupled with the crazy play of his eyes, brought a ripple of amusement from the prisoners. Darius blinked blandly at the performer. The morphine tablets had dulled the pain, sharpened his thinking. He was able to hold a thought a bit longer than earlier. A good sign?

Tamir Mandel, a twenty-year-old Polish Jew, had escaped the storming of the Warsaw Ghetto and lived to tell of the horrors he endured before the Germans stormed Poland. Slight of build, blue-eyed, with nerves of steel, the Polish exile was not a talkative man. Oppression does something to a man; it warps his insides, twists his mind, body, and spirit into a kind of fanaticism. Observing Kabul, vacant-eyed, certain the lad was demented or possessed, by Beelzebub, Tamir irresistibly joined in the dementia. He pulled out a wooden flute secreted in his boot and played a tempo in rhythm to Kabul's gyrations.

Darius, unable to concentrate, made little sense of Kabul's animation. The wailing flute mysteriously stoked a deep melan-

choly in him. *Think. Think! What is happening to Kabul? Dope—
was that it? Had he smoked his own hashish? What?* Darius
peered at the others, at their vacant-eyed stares. Did they sense
something amiss? Was it a blur in his own brain or had he—but
wait . . . Darius perceived, in this ridiculous act, something
specific, something that escaped the others. Kabul's flashing
dark eyes darted to the pack of Fatima cigarettes on Darius's
rugs. Kabul was indicating . . . what, for God's sake? Couched
in the lad's crazy behavior, Darius sensed he was attempting to
communicate something.

*Disregard nothing! Everything has a purpose, even that which
is hidden from the naked eye.* A lesson taught him by Matteus.

Darius painstakingly sorted facts. What was this business with
the Fatima cigarettes? They were *not* his favorite. Kabul insisted
they were. He hadn't paid for the pack; Kabul insisted he had
paid. Why had Kabul overwhelmed him with Fatima cigarettes?
Why? Was he afflicted with *cafard*? Kabul intimated it. Darius
turned in Kabul's direction. The boy was gone.

Darius stared apathetically at the others; each, involved in his
own private hell, drank freely from goat skins containing a
potent concoction called Thessalus wine.

Thessalus wine! A cheap, light, deceptively innocuous wine;
when laced with Pernod, the concoction, aptly named "earthquake" by the legionnaires, became devastating. Few hardened
drinkers could withstand its effects; the less hardy suffered a
twenty-four hour continuing of inter-cranial explosions.

Dutch O'Reilly, hit swiftly by the doctored Thessalus lay on
his prayer rug ticking his coppery spiked beard with the vacant-
eyed diligence of a mad baboon. The sideshow effects of the
psychedelic afforded the observers an unusual show. He began to
sing out of tune in a dirge tempo. *"VOUS ÊTES SOLDATS
POUR MOURIR . . . POUR MOURIR . . . POUR MOURIR
. . ."* Limey Whitehall joined in, totally out of the sync, *"ET JE
VOUS ENVOIE LA OUT L'ON MUERETE . . ."* He dragged his
words turning them over in his mind. Delon, then Longinotti
chimed in. Dutch, deciding his Irish-accented French was not
appreciated, switched to English. "You are soldiers born to die
. . . born to die . . . born to die . . ." He convulsed into
maudlin tears.

Tamir Mandel, unable to keep time with his flute, tapped it
against his hand, certain they were all going mad, and retreated
to his ration of Thessalus and the dark corners of his mind.

Darius, his swollen-lidded eyes blazing, shouted, "No! No, I tell you. We became legionnaires to live—not to die!" He began at once to invert the words, singing louder above the others. *"We are legionnaires to live—to live—to live!"* If the prisoners heard, they remained impervious to his rallying spirit. Dejected, he sank into deeper apathy.

"You expect miracles in this hell?" Tamir asked in French. "Only Jehovah can make miracles." He launched into incomprehensible esoteric mumbo-jumbo in Yiddish. giving praise to *Yaweh*.

Delon set aside his ration of "earthquake" and smoked dope that turned his eyes magenta. He never described the inner visions brought on by the drug. His facial contortions ran the gamut from ecstasy to agonizing torture. Darius on occasion had witnessed Delon transform from a human into a elipatoidal beast. Why the Frenchman inflicted such torture upon himself was as inexplicable as was his presence in Sidi.

Nearby Lucien Pascal, the only sober man besides Darius, engaged in calisthenics. His perseverance was remarkable, thought Darius. It was as if somewhere beyond the vast Sahara lay a world in the future only he perceived beckoning to him. Daily he prepared for that eventuality, immune to the trials and tortures of the moment.

What am I doing here? Darius had asked himself a hundred times a day since his arrival. He felt a breed apart from these men, yet here at Sidi, at Abu Hammid, they were all equal.

Four stray temple cats with shrunken skulls and luminous eyes were buggering one another unmercifully. Darius fixed briefly on them, then focused on his bleeding, swollen hands wrapped in soiled rags. Nothing in this daytime nightmare made sense. The black mood of the prisoners spread like a malignancy in the heavy, oppressive atmosphere. A few began to masturbate, uttering obscenities. Darius looked away, sickened. Then, as quickly, he listened.

Silence . . . pervasive, unnatural silence, was underscored by the occasional scratchings of the buggering cats, the heavy breathing of the men playing with themselves. Darius, sensing something amiss sat up, peered about the compound, head cocked obliquely.

Lucien Pascal, similarly disturbed by unknown, unseen forces, abandoned his exercises. He too strained to hear. The buggering cats had ceased their thrashing about and, congregating in a body, listened, disturbed by unseen forces. Then, skulking about the stable, micturating at random, they suddenly arched their backs and fled.

A hair-raising scream split the air. Darius and Pascal's eyes locked. The others barely flinched or indicated concern. More screams, agonizing shrieks, blood-curdling cries permeated the stables. The sounds of torture inflicted upon some wretched soul grew louder, came closer. The screams rose to a harrowing pitch.

Loud crashes . . . the sounds of running feet growing louder. Darius bolted to his feet. They were not the cries of jackals or desert hyenas—they were human! Pascal angled his head toward the stable entrance. Frantic, hurried footsteps approached.

There! Suddenly coming at them . . . a ghastly sight!

A human torch! A screaming, terrorized, human torch, zigzagging in a frenzied purposeless direction, came at them, startling the other prisoners. Darius, first to break through the frozen wall of panic and horror that immobilized the men, swiftly grabbed his rug, raced toward the burning mass, lunged at it, knocked it down into the dirt, and, beating ferociously at the hot, angry flames, managed to wrap the body with the rug, all sense of reason and survival forgotten in his attempt to save a life.

Faces, from the shadows, stared in mute paralysis. Fear provided the men a prudent circumspection, rage increased their madness. Some sobered at once, a few still reeled under the impact of *earthquake*. Now this atrocity dumped at their doorstep brought reality into focus. Closer they came, approaching cautiously, drawn to the smoking, writhing carpet roll. The odor of burned human flesh was nauseous, overpowering. Black smoke billowed from the burning mass. The men coughed, sputtered, fanned the nauseous fumes. Nothing sufficed.

Two brutish legionnaire guards followed by a third man rushed into barracks, guns at ready, prodding the prisoners with bayonets keeping them at bay. Ignoring them, Darius unfurled the charred contents, his eyes riveted to the smoking mass. Slowly as he discerned what the grisly scene held for him, he shook his head in wild denial. "Kabul! *Mother of God, it's Kabul!*"

The men, sickened at the sight averted their eyes, then with considerable reluctance trailed back to the ghoulish sight. The lad, burned beyond recognition, whimpered, his body racked with pain and shock. Weakly he supplicated to Allah.

Darius, shocked and appalled beyond all sensibility, stared in horror, uncertain what to do for Kabul. He was alive and conscious—a miracle in itself—yet his body was burned to the bone. His body, a trail of massive blisters on his legs, some open, some like balloons failed to conceal the brutal sodomy done to him. Set afire for reasons known only to the depraved perpetrator of the ungodly acts, Kabul had fled to the only possible refuge at the outpost, the only place he felt safe—to Darius. And Darius, enraged at the sight of his little friend felt the urge to kill those responsible.

The next few chaotic moments erupted into savagery when one of the guards chose the wrong time and the wrong person to prod with his rifle—Darius! Leaping at him, with feral skill, Darius wrested the gun free, the strength of Samson unleashed in him. Swinging in blind fury, he knocked one guard senseless with the rifle stock, then, wielding it like a lacrosse stick bludgeoned the second; he swung at the third, smashing his head with the butt. Felled by his savage blows, guns spilling from their hands, the guards remained where they landed, astonishment and pain whirling them insensible.

Jolted by the galvanic energy of Darius's action, Pascal sprang to his feet, followed by a dazed Limey Whitehall, Longinotti at his heels. Each grabbed a rifle. Tamir Mandel flung his wine botta into a wide arc across the stable, and picking up a bailing fork, followed the leader.

Darius led them stealthily out the barracks entrance into the lengthening shadows of darkness, skirting ramshackle buildings, tracking cautiously across the compound toward Von Luden's quarters. Their objective: to get past the manned towers at either side of the main gate within the walls of Abu Hammid without detection. There was little time to think. Action was called for, cool, level-headed action. They approached the gate. Darius raised his hand in signal halting the others. *No guards in the towers!* Before he could contemplate this, the shrill sounds of a bugler's alert drew them back in the shadows of the wall; they flattened against it, their stormy eyes peering furtively about the area, confused as hell.

A second bugle alert!

"What in friggin' hell is coming off?" Limey Whitehall nudged Longinotti. Blinking to sharpen their focus they sobered at once. Pascal, as bewildered at the others sprang from the shadows, listening. About to question Darius, he was silenced by Darius's gesture. He waved his companions against the wall, listening. *Motors? In the distance? Was it possible? A supply convoy this late? Unlikely.*

He darted up the stone steps, swung to the catwalk leading to the ramparts. Darius peered beyond the fortification wall at the black moonless canopy of starry sky. There! Twelve bright lights moving unsteadily in the darkness—headlights of six desert utilities.

At once four battery-powered spotlights mounted on the post command's towers came alive. With the six desert utilities came a dozen man-mounted camels thundering toward the fort.

French officers and Arab chieftains with crack riflemen, less than five minutes away.

Darius, making split second decisions scurried off the catwalk, waved his men back to barracks. "Damn Satan's hide! Something is happening. A small army approaches. Von Luden will keep. Hide the rifles. Limey, go to the dispensary, steal all the medication you can lay your hand on. If the orderly puts up a fight, *kill him*. Pascal, you, Tamir and Longinotti tend to the guards we left in barracks. I must tend to Kabul."

The men responded swiftly. It didn't occur to them until *after* they returned to barracks, *after* they stuffed and gagged the guards, bound their hands and feet, and tossed them into the dry well at the edge of the stable wall how easily they had followed Darius's orders, as if it were the natural order of things.

Darius approached the galley crouched low between the ramshackle buildings, keeping to the shadows; once inside, caught the cook off guard, sacked him, filched a keg of fat from the stores. He tossed a keg of ice into a leather harness, and toted the goods back to barracks.

When he reached Kabul, he removed the charred clothing fragments stuck to the lad's tortured body. He forced morphine tablets between the burned, bleeding, swollen lips. Scooping fat from the keg, he spread it tenderly over the blistered, charred, bloodied remains.

Delon, wafting in and out of his drugged stupor, observed Darius critically. Limey returned, a cheshire-cat grin on his pockmarked face. He flourished a cache of morphine and opium vials. Delon, springing to life, glanced impatiently at the narcotics, admonishing Limey, "Can't use poppy juice without a needle." Limey grinned. With nimble dexterity he flourished a hypodermic syringe from his pocket. Delon, demonstrating surprising expertise, moved in and took over the process of caring for

Kabul. He listened for a pulse. Delon, an enigma to the other recruits, adopted a brusque manner.

"The odds in his favor diminish rapidly, Corsican. He needs hospitalization."

"Keep him alive!" Darius snapped. "If not for Kabul, who among us would be alive?"

Kabul's body was placed on linen stolen from the quartermaster's stores, and packed in ice. "He'll feel less pain," said Delon, preparing another morphine injection. "Pain is the killer, if infection doesn't spread its putrefaction first." He injected Kabul in the neck area and scooping a handful of fat, rubbed it onto his own sun-scorched skin, then passed ice over the burns. Observing him, the other prisoners did likewise.

By now Kabul's wretchedness had heightened the men's sobriety.

The crass braying of camels and the whinnying of lathered horses brought up their heads. The men exchanged concerned glances. Darius, captured by a voice, a barely audible whisper, knelt over Kabul.

"Bonny-suh—" Darius leaned in closer, placed his ear to the lad's lips. "B-beneath b-belly . . . d-dancing . . . F-fatima . . ." Kabul's strength siphoned off. A drugged stupor fell like a scrim over his eyes.

"Kabul—what the devil are you trying to tell me?"

The sounds of loud brash voices and squeaking leather boots were heard. Darius saw a flurry of activity at the stable entrance. He quickly covered Kabul with Delon's prayer rug.

French officers from Sidi entered the confines, paying obvious homage to a grandly robed Arab chieftain and his entourage of crack riflemen. The scent of French perfume mingled with the raw scent of the herd, created disquiet among the prisoners.

Colonel Henri Furstenberg, the Legion's chief intelligence officer, sauntered about languidly, his usual peacock strut absent. A spry man in his midfifties, his addiction to hashish and cognac were evidenced by the sagging folds under his red-veined eyes and his flabby jowls. This cold, stony-faced officer, a dreaded man to tangle with, was more awesome out of his lair.

Why was he here? For what did they search? Questions nagged at Darius. When he asked himself why he should care one way or another, he fell into a brooding silence.

At a nod from the intelligence chief, a squadron of legionnaires, bayonets at ready, fanned out like a swarm of locusts, scurrying in all directions for cover. Their prodding bayonets jabbed and stabbed, violating every dark corner of the two-storied stable. A few climbed to the lofts, plunging knives into bales of hay. They yanked bridle paraphernalia, and harnesses off the walls in storage areas, and tossed them aside like so much garbage.

Ferocious-looking Arabs, guns ready, stood in a semi-circle around the veiled Arab chieftain observing the legionnaires.

Suddenly the action shifted to the stable entrance. An embarrassed gravel voiced corporal in total disarray, half in, half out of uniform, stumbled in. He saluted the French officer, barked harsh commands, forcing the indolent prisoners shakily to their feet. Standing red-faced and apologetic to one side of the colonel, he glared at the pack of dehumanized prisoners, angry-eyed, silently promising swift retribution for their insubordination.

Ignoring this bleating bull, Colonel Furstenberg addressed the splendidly garbed Arab chieftain deferentially. "Highness, what led you to believe your brother was at Abu Hammid? Certainly the royal brother of Prince Ben-Kassir would not fraternize with such degenerate scum."

Couched in Furstenberg's words was a silent warning to all prisoners. An unwritten tenet had been drummed into the recruits' heads throughout regimentation: *legionnaires stick together against the wogs!*

The royal Prince Ben-Kassir, a legendary figure among the legionnaires, moved about the confines, his face veiled, in deathly silence, his electric onyx eyes sweeping the bleak, rat-infested stable, revolted, but wisely keeping his thoughts to himself. He nodded to four of his men. Instantly they descended on the confines like giant birds of prey, their robes billowing as their suspicious, dagger eyes, aloof to the infirm prisoners searched every nook and cranny, missing nothing. When they finished searching the outer perimeters of the barracks, they walked dislocated circles in and around the huddled prisoners at the center of the stable, scrutinizing the vacant stares fixed on them for some telltale sign of guilt.

"See for yourself, Highness. None among these dispossessed is your brother." Colonel Furstenberg strutted about, striking a camel crop harshly against his spit-polished boots.

The prince, moving among the prisoners as if he searched for buried treasure, stopped before Darius, studying the Corsican's face with the prolonged scrutiny of a lapidary before cutting a gem. Slowly, with dramatic panache he undraped the lower half of his face, revealing a handsome, clean-shaven, distinguished-looking visage with a black mustache and an arch expression. His right hand fingered a jeweled dagger at his waist, his eyes never wavering from Darius's eyes. Before he could speak, a muffled voice drew his attention.

"*Allah Akbar*! M-most m-merciful—"

The prince's turbaned head angled sharply. His arms, outstretched like a symphony conductor, commanded silence. Behind him the colonel's features jerked. The others tensed, exchanged troubled glances.

"From whence came that voice?" Prince Ben-Kassir asked in French. repeating the query in German. Behind him, gun bolts clicked. The Arab riflemen held the guns menacingly.

"Colonel Furstenberg, I demand to know," Youseff Ben-Kassir's compelling eyes scanning the prisoner's face fell upon Darius and held with a riveting magnetism that shook Darius.

Darius perceived instantly that a tragic error had been made, one of extraordinary magnitude. A price would be exacted: Von Luden's life, he hoped. The prince moved closer to Darius. By now, everyone's focus shifted from the prince to Darius, from Darius to the prince.

Youseff Ben-Kassir studied Darius's emaciated features, his dark eyes lingering on the death's-head amulet around his neck, the pack of Fatima cigarettes in his belt—and knew him at once. The Corsican's was the face of a true prince, harsh, powerful, yet just. *Kabul was right: he can be trusted.* Darius, instinctively sensing that the prince was a friend, stepped to one side, leaned down and lifted the prayer rug, exposing the hideousness that was Kabul. A gasp arose from the Arabs. The prince reluctantly averted his eyes. When he saw the ghastly remains, he glanced sharply at Darius again.

"Merciful Allah! Pray who might this be?"

"An infidel dog!" boomed Von Luden's Germanic voice, filling the barracks like black thunder. He was followed by Hesse and Schmidt, their faces the color of *pâté*.

"Indeed? An *infidel dog* who speaks my language without accent? Who supplicates to Allah in princely fashion. I think not!" He clapped his hands twice. Four of the robed Arabs converged at Kabul's side, kneeling before him, inspecting the pitiful body while chanting Moslem prayers. A scorched, golden lion's-head chain, removed from Kabul's ankle, was handed to the prince.

Ben-Kassir's veiled loathing shifted to Von Luden, then he

examined the chain quietly, his jaws rigid; he fell on one knee, head bowed before his young brother, chanting Islamic prayers. Behind him the chief of intelligence glared hotly at the Germans. Von Luden's bald head glistened with sweat; his dilated eyes bulged grotesquely as the truth struck him. Hesse and Schmidt stood rigidly at his side without expression.

No one could have been as shocked as Darius and the other prisoners at the turn of events. *Kabul—a prince? The brother of Prince Ben-Kassir?* Shaken to the core, each of the prisoner-recruits retreated slightly. As certain as they were of the moon's phases, they *knew* a day of reckoning was at hand.

"Kabul, my brother, speak to me," the prince cooed in Farsi. His lean, slender, jeweled hands hovered in a holding pattern over the lad, not daring to touch him. He agonized over Kabul's fate.

"You have much to account for, Von Luden," the Colonel snapped.

"But, *mein Oberst*, he was a street beggar. I tell you it is a mistake. *Gott in Himmel!* Tell him, Hesse! Schmidt!"

"His papers identified him as a Berber," Hesse said lamely. Schmidt parroted Hesse.

"I shall get to the bottom of this infamy, Highness . . . Order a litter at once." He barked orders to his men.

"No! No infidel dog touches the brother of Ben-Kassir and lives to speak of it."

Delon sprang forward. "Highness, I am—was a physician. Kabul must be hospitalized at once. We sedated him with morphine injections to reduce the pain. Packed him in ice to reduce his temperature. Yet, without proper instruments to gauge the—"

Youseff Ben-Kassir's eyes trailed from Delon to the areas of his brother's mutilated body revealing the extent of the debaucheries done him. Crusted blood hung in black charred clumps between his legs and genitals. The prince's expression was ghastly; his deadly eyes held on Von Luden in loathing.

Darius would remember this moment forever. It enabled him to know—when it became vital that he know—*who* and *what* the Germans really were. Moreover, he *knew* that Prince Ben-Kassir also *knew* who bore responsibility in this god-awful deed.

In the deepening vinous haze Darius listened to the fraudulent expressions of remorse, entreaties for understanding bandied about in this unusual circumstance. Von Luden pleaded to ineffectual stupidity, but his expressions of appeasement failed to dent the prince's tough exterior. Ben-Kassir neither obliged the French by pretending to understand, nor allowed himself to collapse emotionally before him. He maintained a deadly silence, and continued in this posture until he and his entourage, with Kabul on a litter departed Abu Hammid. Darius knew, by this silence that Prince Ben-Kassir had constructed a design of future retribution, payment to be exacted from those responsible for the atrocity.

An hour later, Darius, unable to mask his turbulent feelings shook his head in confused astonishment. "Kabul—the brother of Prince Ben-Kassir? A prince himself? Incredible!"

"So this is the powerful black lion of the desert?" Longinotti marveled with a bite of rancor. "The wealthiest man in the Tell permits his princely brother to be a receptacle for German sperm?" He spat disgustedly in the dust.

Tamir Mandel, silent throughout the unexpected tragedy and what ensued shook his head in awed disbelief. "I've heard tell of Arab rites and rituals . . . *Feh* on them!"

Limey was a bit circumspect; he scratched his beard thoughtfully. "The wog chieftain is sure to summon up a bloomin' bloody war quick enough. We'd best be lookin' to our own arses. I been through one of 'em bleedin' holy wars," he shuddered. Give me a thousand set-tos with the bloody coppers at 'ome any day. If it 'appens, it's curtains for us bloody blokes. We ain't got a prayer in the world against 'em."

"We dinna hear it at Sidi," said Dutch. "But at Fatima's the men's tongues get loosed and they been atelling us this duffer Hitler is making a name for hisself. Ain't gonna be no livin' with 'em bloody Krauts now. We should 'ave killed 'em bloody faggots sooner. Nothing personal, Tamir. I jus' hopes ta Christ His Royal wog Highness plucks the bloomin' tail feathers off them Kraut NCO arses!"

"You tell them," Tamir said, bluntly retrieving and draining his wine *botta*.

Dutch was right, Darius thought. There'd be no living with the Germans if Hitler's conquests continued. He felt a sense of outrage at the French. Why in God's name did the French permit the Germans such autonomy here in Sidi bel Abbes? *Why?*

The next morning Abu Hammid was turned inside out. Unprecedented events took place. Sentences were terminated. Lorries transported the exonerated prisoners back to Sidi. Hospitalized at once, treated for fatigue, exposure, and a variety of infirmities, they were bathed, fed, and given red-carpet treatment. Choice foods, vintage wines, cigars, newly requisitioned clothing—all this was lavished upon them, and each emerged as legionnaire, private first class. Stunned, and a bit leery, they examined their good fortune with trepidation. They all agreed. Their silence in the Kabul tragedy had bought them, for a time, a pasha's existence.

For Darius an unprecedented event was about to change the course of his life.

Colonel Henri Furstenberg possessed the perceptions of a master criminal, the eyes of a stalking tiger, and the nose of an anteater when it came to ferreting out Intelligence data. His was an abiding dislike for Legionnaire recruits. However much he concealed his feelings behind veiled tolerance, he projected the exasperation of an intellect exposed to minds feebly lacking in brains. His constant immersion among men far beneath his social strata had caused this prim, proper Frenchmen to long ago set aside the gentlemanly class conscious code of St. Cyr. At first, however, in his naiveté he had intended to use the Foreign Legion as a podium from which to preach the glories of France and expand the tradition of gallantry and self-sacrifice to cattle car recruits. Tragedy stalked him at once. Within a year of his arrival, his wife, unable to adjust to the desert rigors and spartan existence of a legionnaire, had killed herself and their three sons. A six-month period of besottedness followed. Henri drank himself into a daily stupor, until one astonishing day he sobered up, reestablished himself as captain of his soul and master of his fate and demanded the most dangerous assignments. He dedicated heart and soul to the Legion, clung stubbornly to the barren lands as if Sidi bel Abbes and the High Atlas were gold dust treasures which he defended with fierce tenacity and a hand-picked battalion of daredevils. This veteran of the Moroccan Campaign and World War I was involved in the surrender of Abd el-Krim in 1933.

Something terrible had happened at the battle of *Djebel Baddou*. No one knew for certain, or if they did know no one talked about the massacre, but Colonel Furstenberg had returned hardened, embittered, battle-scarred and with a violent loathing for the wogs.

Today, Furstenberg paced his sterile office sipping cognac,

waiting for Private Bonifacio. On his oaken desk, a warped relic recently given a face-lift by a plate-glass top, lay an open dossier on Darius Bonifacio. The intelligence chief was not in a good mood. Decisions made over his head and against his better judgment failed to sit well with him. Yet it remained for him to execute the orders. He glanced impatiently at the wall clock, the time barely visible through the thick coat of white dust; he looked at his pocket watch. It was two P.M.

He damned well knew his opening speech would zero in on the merits of punctuality. The fleeting thought was dismissed at once by a knock on the door; his aide entered to announce Legionnaire Bonifacio. He nodded to the aide, turned his back on him, and gazed out the window at the courtyard below. Darius entered behind the aide and stood braced at attention, saluting, eyes straight ahead. It wasn't his first visit to this office to see this dreaded man; it wouldn't be his last.

The colonel languidly placed a cigarette into a carved ivory holder. He lit it, inhaled deeply, muttering at long last as he condescended to turn to him, "At ease, Private." He studied Darius critically through smoke spirals and returned to his desk. Seated, he gestured to a chair. "Praise is a rare commodity here at Sidi, Bonifacio. Where it concerns you there's an apparent glut on the market. I've read the reports on your training." He picked up the report. "Your grades in weaponry: exceptional. You're a crack shot, *oui*? Discipline: above and beyond reproach. Leadership capabilities: remarkable. Military strategy and tactical warfare: unequaled among your peers. Which doesn't say much for you, since your platoon is a group of dolts." He flipped the file cover shut, tossed it on the desk. "Reports indicate you've earned the trust, confidence, and respect of your companions. Now in this sewer of humanity, where lives are meaningless and a man's character isn't worth *merde*, that says something." His red-veined eyes probed Darius's, his tone aloof, slightly hostile. "Now tell me, just who the devil are you?"

"I don't understand, sir." Darius faltered, taken aback.

"You—don't—understand." He drew the words out one at a time, scoffingly. "Don't play games with me, Bonifacio. It wastes precious time. Military strategy is not a subject taught at Jesuit school!"

"Ah. I see. You've compiled a file on me, is that it? Well, sir, that may well be, but I was formidably taught the history of Napoleon's military strategy by the holy fathers you disdain. I daresay they can expound on battle skills in a more proficient manner than most officers here at Sidi.''

"You know, then, the brains behind Napoleon was Lazare Carnot.''

"I know, if recorded history is dependable, that proper military science is a subordinate branch of the science of statecraft.''

"Good. I'm happy to hear you don't put all your eggs in one basket, Bonifacio.''

"No sir, I don't, unless I intend to make an omelette.''

"Why did Napoleon lose to the Russians?''

"You ask a direct question when no one answer can suffice. Ask me why the sun shines each day and expect a succinct answer; I can better reply to that than the question posed concerning Russia. If I were pushed to the wall and forced to reply, I would suggest it was due to the czar's decision to engage only in an inconclusive rearguard action to begin with. If the Russians had put every resource into attempting a decisive battle against the onslaught of Napoleon's army, Bonaparte would have inflicted a decisive military defeat on them. Instead Bonaparte was permitted to occupy Moscow. Blowing up the French-occupied city signaled virtual defeat and Napoleon was forced to exploit his fatal logistical error by retreating. You see, sir—''

"Never mind! *Never mind!* We all know the result! Now tell me about Corsica—why you left.''

"The Legion stresses the privacy of a man's past,'' Darius replied testily.

"Bonifacio, these are hectic, complicated times. With war imminent, every man's past here at Sidi becomes *my* business.''

Darius's lips pursed stubbornly.

"Very well, we do it *your* way.'' The colonel unbuttoned the top three buttons of his tunic, rose from behind his chair, and paced about the room. "You did *not* change your name at enlistment. Therefore I assume you were not in disfavor with the law in Corsica. On that assumption, my aides made further inquiries. A certain Jesuit father named Franchetti stated that you have a rare penchant for the military. You come from a respected, affluent family. Why, with your talents, were you not sent to St. Cyr?''

"Why do you persist in penetrating a past I choose to forget?''

"Any officer who discovers a potential Napoleon in his command—''

"That's preposterous!"

"It's not *my* observation. Prince Ben-Kassir has taken an interest in your career."

"Why? What am I to him?"

"We shall discuss that in a moment. Your sudden departure from Corsica intrigues me. Why, instead of returning to school, did you choose Sidi bel Abbes? The Jesuit father wrote to me, describing what held fascination for you."

"Father Franchetti is a fanciful dreamer."

Furstenberg turned from the window with the eyes of an intent serpent. "Falsifying your age is grounds for discharge in the Legion." He returned to his desk, poured two brandies.

"Thank you, I do not drink." Darius declined the outstretched drink. To drink with this man would imply a weakness in his own character. He wanted no such illusion to enter the colonel's mind.

"Are you married? Did some woman complicate your life at home?"

"No to both questions."

"Look, Bonifacio. This is no inquisition. I must ask these questions prior to offering you a lieutenant's commission in the Intelligence Corps."

"A commission? Intelligence?" He was stunned.

"*Oui*. Espionage. Intelligence gathering."

"Front-line action is more in line with my talents."

Furstenberg was exasperated. "Your talents? *Mon Dieu!* Such talents are not meant for conversion to cannon fodder!" Darius's hostility drew reproving looks from the French officer. "Listen, Corsican, life in the Legion is unlike the pampering a cadet receives at St. Cyr, but it does produce supermen. The men in your company, measured by the same yardstick as you, demonstrated few or no special aptitudes."

"What do you expect after the beastly treatment meted us by the Germans?"

"You received no special benefits!" Furstenberg fired back. Listen, I am offering you opportunities commensurate with your abilities. Only a select breed of man is provided such opportunity. In thirty years, to my knowledge, it's happened twice. If you remain in the infantry, your highest expectations are an NCO rating." Disconcerted by Darius's inscrutable gaze, the colonel sat forward, his tiger eyes narrowing. *"Sacré bleu!* This is not to be believed! Here I am convincing you to join my intelligence forces, when usually I deter men from the corps. Few men qualify as intelligence material. Damn it, any jackass can follow front-line orders and get himself shot up!''

''Who recommended me for this special promotion?''

''France's staunchest ally, Prince Ben-Kassir. Understand, Bonifacio, once your decision is made, defection is unacceptable. France will be your mistress for life. Entrusted with highly classified matters, you cannot take the position casually. *Cave quid dicis quando, et cui.* Beware what you say, when and to whom at all times. You must learn never to make yourself vulnerable to the enemy.''

''Is Kabul alive?''

''Barely. Plucky little bastard. He gathered more information on spy infiltration in Sidi than any ten of our men.''

Furstenberg stared at the smoke spirals at the end of his cigarette, ''Imagine what he learned while those beasts buggered him? A Frenchman wouldn't subject himself to such debauchery unless he enjoyed it. But these wogs! Imagine praying zealously to Mecca, daily, without let up, only to debauch and whore with libidinous license.''

''That makes them no different than most religious zealots, doesn't it, sir?'' The tone of Darius's voice brought the colonel's head up sharply.

''It wasn't condemnation, Legionnaire, merely an observation.''

''That night at Abu Hammid,'' Darius began resolutely. ''You *knew* Kabul was there, yet you acted as if he wasn't. Why the attempt at deception if Prince Ben-Kassir is our staunchest ally?''

''*Cave quid dicis quando, et cui.* Beware—''

''Yes, yes, I heard. Beware of what I say, when and to whom. In other words the scene was staged for the benefit of the Germans, Von Luden and Hesse?''

''Bull's-eye!''

''But what happened to Kabul! That terrible accident—''

''Wasn't planned. Not that tragedy!''

''Why would Prince Ben-Kassir permit his brother to be so debased?''

''Don't try fathoming the wog's logic. It is incomprehensible.''

''But how did he know of Kabul's accident?''

''It was *no* accident.''

''*The prince knew in advance?*''

''Only what his brother told him. Von Luden was becoming suspicious of Kabul, and Kabul's message to Youseff to bail him out was a signal of impending danger, you see? What you did for Kabul . . . the emergency care . . . well, the prince is forever in your debt. I shudder to think when the wretched lad examines his reflection in the mirror . . .'' He poured another cognac. ''Amazing, Legionnaire, you don't drink. You will . . . you will. Oblivion, here at Sidi, is a blessing.''

''Oblivion is a luxury I can ill afford, sir. *Especially* in Sidi.''

Furstenberg ignored the innuendo. ''The prince wishes to orient you to the mechanics of his spy network.''

Darius's brows arched questioningly.

''Understand, Bonifacio, he is as loyal to France, as was his father against Abd el-Krim and and Ouskounti at Djebel Baddou in the High Atlas.'' He slugged the cognac down in a gulp. Tough, cynical, and trained to keep his own counsel, the chief gave Darius a brief rundown. ''Youseff Ben-Kassir's mother was French . . . Kabul's mother was a wog . . . Bloody Arabs have a number of concubines, you see. I don't pretend to keep track of them. The prince's father saved my life. I am beholden to him. Here, this is for you.'' He tossed an envelope to Darius. ''An invitation . . . engraved. You're to be at the palace for dinner on Friday evening.''

Darius picked it up, opened it, glanced at it cursorily, and slipped it into his tunic pocket.

The next few days were exciting, every moment packed with activity. Darius returned to his barracks at night mentally exhausted yet exhilarated at the challenges hurled at him. Prior to his meeting with the prince Darius sat at his desk in the early shank of an evening, and began to compile a journal. Pen in hand, he pondered a moment, then articulated his thoughts.

LEAVES FROM DARIUS'S NOTEBOOK
DECEMBER 1938

Bright and early three days ago I swore an oath of fidelity to France in a simple, unpretentious ceremony, received a lieutenant's commission, and moved into new quarters in the Intelligence Division. I was measured for a new uniform. Since then I've plunged headlong into a thorough training program, which demands my absolute skill in wireless and radio transmittal and receiving, cryptology, and reading aerial reconnaissance photography.

Military intelligence briefings are opening new corridors of thought and awareness. I am intrigued by the compilation of intelligence, the highly confidential and classified report on troop movements, the Legion's strategy in attack and counterattack. Desert warring tactics and strategy are related to the environment; the use of nature itself is essential to triumph. Yet I despair at the antiquated methods of battle, worse, the impoverishment of weapons. Everything at Sidi is vintage World War I.

INTERNAL AFFAIRS ... previously alien to me; now I must know intimately each legionnaire placed in key positions. The meticulous reports are as reliable as the officer collecting the data. Unfortunately the data compiled can not be identified! I see volumes of holes in such procedure, the possibility of misunderstanding and confusion. Nothing to me is as good a gauge of man than personal contact under battle fire. The theory, however, I am told, is debatable.

ESPIONAGE ... The procedural reports, clever ruses and guises employed by the Legion's best spies, hold fascination for me. Something a man cannot be taught in a matter of months, perhaps years. Shaping in my mind are several approaches to existing problems demanding immediate solutions. The ever-constant arrival of recruits from Germany bothers no one but me. Am I paranoid?

I look forward to my visit with Prince Ben-Kassir on Friday night. Before I keep that appointment, I have pressing work to attend to. I still am unable to accept the strange circumstances surrounding Kabul's death.

Friday night . . . the Moorish palace, camouflaged by high walls and a natural barrier of date palms, fell short of Darius's expectations until he rang the bell cord and two armed guards admitted him to an inner courtyard of indescribable beauty: man-made waterfalls, exotic tropical blooms, stunning aviaries filled with birds of multicolored plumage, transported Darius to a world of Persian delights, of Aladdin and the stories of his childhood. Inside the palace he was confronted by the *Arabian Nights* setting he had half expected to see in Sidi bel Abbes. Darius was awed by the profusion of marble. mosaic tiles, stained glass, rotundas, tesselated latticework and walls; perfumed pools fed by crystal waterfalls. In the larger salons the decor was superb:

low, silken sofas, ottomans, brocaded pillows tossed about lazily, and the entire setting drenched in palatable incense to explode the senses.

He was overcome by the stunning odalisques in diaphanous jellicks, wearing gold-threaded breast cups, hinting at firm, virginal breasts. Adorned by tiny bells at the wrists and ankles they moved about with a soft syncopated tinkling that pleased the ears. Greeted by two bright-eyed, modest servants, their dazzling smiles faintly veiled behind sheer *yashmaks,* he was led to a smaller salon dramatically lit with Moorish lanterns. He sat down on an ottoman, his eyes trailing the opal and emerald play of lights, the geodesic patterns of half-moons and circles fanning obliquely from the revolving glass balls affixed to the lanterns. The giggly girls salaamed, fussed over him, removed his boots and socks, laved his feet with scented oils, and fit him with open sandals of leather that felt like baby skin. Truly, he felt like a nine-tailed pasha of rare distinction.

A clash of cymbals sent several white doves in nearby cages into a flutter. A strutting peacock, fanning its plumage, screeched a mating call to a hen. A golden pheasant spurted into the air. And at the center of this incredible scenario came Prince Ben-Kassir dressed in a simple golden lamé robe girdled by the jeweled knife sheath Darius had seen at Abu Hammid.

The dignified prince greeted Darius as he might a long-lost brother, his disarming continental manners, as infectious as his accolades were dignified and regal. "My indebtedness to you for saving Kabul's life cannot be measured, Lieutenant."

Darius, stunned by the opulence, spoke in near apology. He waved his hand about. "Kabul had me convinced—"

"That his house was more squalid than those at Sidi or Abu Hammid?" The prince smiled wanly, a vast shadow in his eyes. "Who could reason with Kabul? Please, please sit down." He handed Darius a crystal glass of pomegranate ice. "My brother demanded autonomy, the right to assist me in my work and take on his share of the Ben-Kassir responsibilities. It was his way or none. Six times he ran away from home. Six times I brought him back. My fatigue at clashing sabers with him became chronic. Admittedly I did a great deal of soul searching before agreeing to any participation in this ghastly affair. I did so with the honest belief he'd tire of the role. Did he? Indeed not." He sighed, sipped the iced drink, and sank into a nearby sofa,

"Although I used his talents economically, Kabul proved a valuable asset."

"But at *what* price, Highness? What price?" He was unprepared for the reply.

"The cause is great, Bonny-suh. One man is expendable."

"Darius, Highness. Call me Darius."

"And you shall call me Youseff." He clapped his hands twice.

Beginning with the pomegranate ice, laced with a subtle Rosé d'Anjou, spooned from golden cups, the banquet was manna for the gods. Wild pheasant dripping in fragrant wine and mushroom sauce, wild rice, baby artichokes marinated in lemon sauce, topped off by chocolate torte and Turkish coffee.

Youseff, a superb host, became expansive. The conversation, superficial at best, touched light on global topics and heavily on France, its *raison d'être* in the changing world. This Sorbonne- and Oxford-educated Algerian prince who graduated from St. Cyr with honors smiled reservedly. "Forgive me if I boast a little ethnicity. Frenchmen consider themselves esthetes and intellectuals, interested only in the higher things in life. Foreigners think of France as a land of brilliant intellectuality—which it is—a land where art thrives—which it is—a land of immorality—which it is not—a land of political refuge—which it is—but never as a land of the bourgeoisie. Yet this above all is what France is."

Darius listened attentively, wondering what course the conversation would take. He studied his host at closer proximity than he had had time or the mental capacity to do at Abu Hammid. Breeding and refinement oozed from every pore. His English was superb, his French excellent, his German surprisingly unaccented, his Spanish textbook Castilian. He was a master of Farsi and a half-dozen North African dialects. Darius wondered what he was doing in this man's company? What was this interest Youseff demonstrated in him?

By nine P.M. Youseff demonstrated no inclination to end the evening. Darius, sensing the prince to want something else, finessed the approach. They sipped brandy in the study, a real man's room: walls adorned with animal skins, mounted tiger heads, elephant-tusk trophies from African safaris. Formidable gun collections under glass occupied a major portion of one wall. A softly lit stained-glass rotunda, three stories tall, towered over one end of the room, accessible only by a spiral staircase. First editions, costly paintings, and marbled statuary were tucked into various niches along the wall.

Youseff stood to one side of an enormous painting. "My father, Prince Ali Ibrahim Ben-Kassir," he said quietly.

"How proud you must be of him. His bravery is legend."

"Without question. See here, Darius." He indicated the countless portraits—international dignitaries, chiefs of state, kings, queens, ambassadors—adorning the remaining wall. "My father was a friend to France, because France proved a sincere friend to Algeria. The friendship was costly. Enemies sprang up at all sides. Religious fanatics, zealots bent on keeping our people in bondage made Holy War on us. You see, the zealots use fear and superstition to herd people into primitive existence. Their fear of progress is incomprehensible. They prefer to smoke hashish, sip *qat* and pass through life in total ignorance. War is nothing new to my nation. Beginning with the Arab invasion in the seventh century . . . No! I won't bore you with past history. Present history is frightening enough. Troubles for the House of Ben-Kassir began with my father's enemy, Abd el-Krim. The suppression of the Krim regime in 1933, his subsequent exile led the way for the rise of a new enemy, Muhammad Abou Ahkmed Hassan, a myopic fanatic who equates mankind's existence with bloody savagery and whose appetite is whetted by a modicum of power he wields. Hassan, my sworn enemy leads a fierce band of desert tribesmen. who are swelling in numbers. The inevitability of our encounter on a battlefield has already been written, only the date is uncertain."

Darius muttered lamely, "*Muhammad, Abou Ahkmed Hassan!*" The very name chilled him. He flashed on the psychopath. "I have met your enemy, Youseff. I do not envy you. A frightening savage, that man . . ."

"Indeed? I presume the encounter was distasteful to him. He loathes the Legion, and all legionnaires." He swirled the brandy snifter, inhaled its bouquet barely glancing at his guest.

"Strangest thing," Darius mused. "Nearly two months into *règlement*, Legionnaire Pascal and I were on bivouac with a platoon of recruits in the upper desert of the High Atlas caught in the midst of a squall."

Darius launched into the story . . . of the harrowing experience

"Aware that the squall was bound to evolve into a *ghilbi*, we sought overnight refuge in a cave amid a scattering of high boulders. I awakened before dawn. A flaming pink sliver of light wedged its way between desert and sky at the horizon's edge. No sooner had I rubbed the sleep balls from my eyes when the droning sounds of swarms of locusts drew me over the craggy tors, to a sharp precipice. Below me was a spectacular sight. The scene was so elaborate I felt I had wandered into a dream. It was a wild landscape, Youseff, with black boulders strewn about like sinister shadows. At the middle of a triangular courtyard, at the edge of Ksar-el Boukhar, a mass of brightly dressed natives lay prostrate on prayer rugs, supplicating Allah. In the deceptive panoply of unbearable lights, unlike any I've seen save those preceding the desert sun in daily birth, I stood transfixed. By now my friend Pascal, awakened by the primitive sounds, joined me on the upper ridges, sharing my stupefaction at the surreal sight. Something nagged at Pascal. His cat eyes and animal sense constantly at work, he suggested we leave at once. He peered about in astute surveillance of the area, but detected nothing threatening near or far; still he took a moment or two to offer a Catholic prayer to God.''

Darius sipped his brandy, observing Youseff's rapt interest.

''There is simply no way to explain what happened in the next several moments. I shall try to put it in perspective. Sensing something awry, I turned to see Pascal gripped by momentary paralysis. Words stuck in his throat could not be prodded from him. Terror-stricken eyes tried to signal me. At that moment I felt a dark shadow looming over me. Swirling around abruptly, I saw a bearded, black-eyed monster standing over me, saber uplifted in both hands, ready to inflict an epithetic *coup de grace* upon me. Suddenly, something bizarre occurred. Precisely at that moment, the sun spoked over the horizon, washing us in blinding light. And Youseff, incredibly, the Arab stopped as if the very hand of God held him back! The saber froze in midair. He cried aloud. '*Allah Akbar! La Ilyaha, Illya Allah!* Allah is merciful! Allah is beneficial. Allah, the God of all Gods, has decreed a miracle!' He proceeded to credit Allah with every known miracle! Slowly his arm lowered and, eyeing me like a savage beast cheated of prey, he resheathed his saber.

'' 'Consider yourself fortunate, infidel dog,' he told me. 'Our paths crossed at the rising of the sun. Truly a sign from the Great One you are favored by Allah and shall not be killed.' I was confounded by the disparity between his earlier ferocity and sudden servility. Behind him in the near distance, appearing seemingly from nowhere, a formidable camel train approached, escorted by armed riflemen on horseback. The picture, veiled by tricky dawn lights, was clear to me; his words were not. 'Go,' he told us. 'Mount a camel and be gone. But be forewarned, infidel. Do not seek that which is not meant for your eyes.'

"Twenty-six heavily laden camels lay below us. I presumed we had stumbled on a smuggler, perhaps a gunrunner. Worse, an enemy of France. I confess, survival took precedence. What chance had two men, alone, but to escape and report our findings to our CO? We salamed to him, pressed our hands before our eyes. I spoke deferentially. 'Since Allah the merciful arranged our encounter at so auspicious a moment, my brother, these eyes shall remain blind, the ears deaf, the lips mute. I shall not permit an infidel's curiosity to shorten my life.'

" 'Well spoken, infidel,' he retorted. 'I am Muhammad Abou Ahkmed Hassan. The uniform you wear is anathema to me. That by which you are called is not. Identify yourself.'

"I complied. Thereupon he spat several unmentionable curses, leaving no doubt in our minds what he thought of the Legion.

" 'Bah! French infidel dogs! Today you were favored by Allah. The next time we meet, the Hand of Fatima, whose five fingers evoke the Law of the Koran, shall guide me according to my inner beliefs—not Allah's law.'

"Hassan lingered. His eyes were riveted to the amulet I wear about my neck, sufficiently startled as if he viewed an apparition. He raised both hands over his head, the sleeves of his robe winglike. Against the extravagant morning lights he glowed like some wild Brazilian bird and cried aloud in supplication, 'Allah the most wise has outdone himself this day. Your humble servant departs!' With these words Hassan strode off the boulders, joined at once by a phalanx of camel-mounted riflemen, some of the fiercest I've seen. Each muttered incoherent monologues, independent of the others. Neither Pascal nor I understood. Those who did peered up at us as if we were something incomprehensible to them and rode off in clouds of dust. A tethered camel awaited us at the foot of the boulders. I began the descent but Pascal urgently beckoned me to the ridge, pointing below.

"Howling, savage cries arose, followed by rapid bursts of machine-gun fire. Grenades exploded craters in the earth, sent bodies flying into the air. Savages on camels, lusting for blood, charged the courtyard of Ksar-el Boukhar, stampeding, crushing underfoot all those not felled by guns. Wild bearded men with flashing murderous eyes and ragged burnooses flying in the wind leaped forward in charge after charge, screaming, brandishing new rifles. What powerful guns, Youseff! We in the Legion had not seen the likes of them. Soon the sands were littered with the dead and the near dead.''

Darius, on his feet for half of his story, paced the polished wooden floor of the study, his frustration evident. ''The supplicating Moslems, impotent against those desert butchers, fell in massacre, rivers of blood flowing from their broken bodies. The air was rife with the stench of cordite, and death hung in a pall over that open graveyard muffling the agonized shrieks, groans, and death howls. It was charge . . . assault . . . retreat over and over again. Hassan's warning echoed in my ears.

'' 'Do not seek that which is not meant for your eyes!'

''Our first indoctrination to tribal laws of the desert both sickened and appalled us. Feeling as useless as eunuchs in a harem, we scurried off the rocks, mounted the waiting camel, and beat it the hell back to Sidi, never to forget the nightmare of Ksar-el Boukhar!''

''And?'' Youseff poured more brandy and coffee. ''The story doesn't end there, *does it*, Darius?''

''No, and you *know* it doesn't. Correct, Highness?''

''Correct, but indulge me.''

''By the time we reached Sidi, word of the massacre had spread throughout the entire garrison. The Camel Brigade, five hundred men and camels in all, was already lined up in battle formation, prepared to depart. What panoply. What color!

''Buglers sounded battle cry! The brigade, eager to catch up with that desert hyena, Hassan, fell into battle formation behind their commanders with drawn swords

''Before the raucous camel brayings and thundering of hooves faded into echoes over the desert floor, beyond Sidi, Pascal and I were arrested, thrown into the brig for failing to file reports of our overnight outing! The punitive measures bewildered us. The next morning, flanked by guards, Pascal and I walked that dreaded corridor to Colonel Furstenberg's office. That man, brass and leather to the core, kept us braced for ten minutes before he condescended to recognize us. The message in his eyes read: *guilty before interrogation!* Sometime between our arrival in his office and our departure, someone entered the office and stood behind us. Still braced, we did not move. A loud whooshing sound came from behind us. Something hurled over our heads, landed in the colonel's hands. Just as quickly he flung the object to me. It was a rifle. Not an ordinary rifle, a *Lee Enfield*! By then the interrogation picked up momentum. Furstenberg badgered us. Where did we get the rifle? How many did we have? Were we hiding more? What exactly were *we* doing at Ksar-el Boukhar? I had never seen the rifle! But the colonel was not amenable to truth—not that day. He stormed at us, called us liars. The gun was found in a saddle holster under the camel riggings of the beast we had ridden back to Sidi!

"I handed the rifle to a glowering Pascal, failed to appreciate the one-sided inquisition. Neither of us had taken time to inspect the riggings, Youseff. But the colonel added insult to injury.

" 'How strange, *oui*? Two *Corsicans*, lost in a storm return from bivouac, with one of hundreds of rifles used to kill Ben-Kassir's people?'

"Furstenberg's sobering condemnation his injudicious remarks reinforced our determination to obscure the Hassan encounter. If a knife were thrust at Pascal's throat, his lips would remain sealed.

"Furstenberg thundered about the office, cursing at us. 'The fastest-operating bolt rifle in the world! The consequences of such arms flowing into Hassan's hands are incalculable!' He tore the rifle from Pascal's hands, tossed it to the mystery man behind us, insisting we both repeat our stories again. We complied, adhering to the contents of our written reports, eliminating of course our tête-à-tête with Hassan. I think you know the rest, Youseff.

"Three days later, less than half the Camel Brigade whipped shamefully into retreat returned to Sidi, sorely discouraged. Those who lived blamed their defeat on the antiquated weapons France provided the Legion. The superior weapons brandished by their enemy were the talk of the Legion post. *Dammit,* Highness, in addition to the impressive Canadian Enfields, they managed to scavenge a few Belgian and Spanish carbines!"

"Why did you conceal the truth from the colonel?" Youseff queried.

"What point would be served in the recitation of actual events? Would he have believed the truth? That death, defaulted by a rising sun and the superstition of a savage had spared our lives. Hah! Can you imagine the colonel believing such a tale?"

"No."

"Precisely. In candor, neither would I. I too might have

shared the colonel's doubts if I'd heard this wild, yet honest tale."

"Your report contained several inconsistencies. Your story to the colonel was *less* credible. But because the savage mind, its superstitions and the origin of the death's-head are known to me, I believe you."

Darius pivoted on one foot, caught Youseff's knowing glance. "Ahhhh. It *was* you that day in the office? *You* are the mystery man."

Youseff lifted the snifter to his nose. "What gave me away?" he asked suppressing a smile.

"You wear a distinctive cologne. I smelled it first in the colonel's office, then again at Abu Hammid. Tonight the same scent permeates your villa, over and above floral and spice fragrances." On another tack Darius apologized. "Pascal and I, two men against a horde, were impotent to help your people against Hassan. It was out-and-out massacre, Youseff, a bloody awful sight. So much bloodletting . . . unnecessary killing . . ."

"Rest assured, Hassan is aware that your promise of silence was held sacrosanct. The incident may work in our favor, Darius. Now tell me how you come by that amulet? Kabul told me about it; it enabled me to know you at once that night at Abu Hammid."

Darius peered down at the death's-head, pulled it away from his body, and studied it intently, a shadow passing over his eyes. "A gift from an old, dear friend. Why was Hassan taken by it?"

"You don't know? You *really* don't know?" Youseff poured more brandy. "It is a relic, a symbol of power dating back to the high priests of the Almohad Empire, the largest Muslim empire ever founded in North Africa. The Almohad Dynasty, comprised of the highest of the highest Moorish warlords, conquered Spain, Portugal, Sardinia, Corsica, and other Mediterranean islands. Those veiled men of Almohad blood, Allah's chosen, were endowed with near-supernatural powers, meant to be handed down to each generation."

As he listened Darius regarded Matteus and Vivaldi and the esoteric teachings of his childhood. Locked drawers in his mind sprang open. Trigger words popped out: *Seven Garduna Parchments . . . A power greater than any known to man . . . Unione Corse Brotherhood . . . Family Cohesion . . . Vengeance! Vendetta!* Something shaped vaguely in his mind. . . .

"Darius? What is it? Something disturbs you. Darius!"

"Uh—no." He snapped from the reverie. "My mind wandered."

''You turned pale as ash. May I offer you more brandy?''

''No, *Shoukran*, Highness. You've been most generous. I must depart.''

''Darius, Kabul spoke to you of the dancing Fatima, *oui*?''

Cave quid dicis quando, et cui. Beware what you say . . .

''The night of his accident, he gave you two boxes—''

''Odd you should ask. I had a feeling you might want them.''

Youseff's eyes lighted expectantly. Darius removed them from his tunic pocket. The sight of their mutilated condition brought reproval from Youseff, ''These are inappropriate. I am sure you know why.''

''I do. Contact was made.''

''*Contact!*'' Youseff exclaimed in shock. ''*With whom?* You dared make contact without exploring the implications? This is a highly imprudent act, Darius. I hope my belief in you was not misplaced.'' Youseff in a captious mood held his censure.

Darius advanced the name quietly. ''St. Germaine.''

''*St. Germaine?*''

''Communication with Kabul was impossible.'' He began at the beginning. ''That night Kabul's antics were wild; the lyrics he sang mystified me. Unfortunately my mind was unreceptive, until *after* our return to Sidi, *after* I rested and received treatment. During my convalescence I nourished memories of Kabul. How those crazy antics played and replayed in my mind. One day it fell into place. There is only one Fatima's in Sidi bel Abbes—''

''Fatima!''

''I approached Lomay St. Germaine—''

''*You gave the boxes to her?*''

''No. Only the film extracted from—to use Kabul's words—*under the belly of the dancing Fatima* was turned over to her. St. Germaine, a sly vixen, treated me as if I were *cafard*.''

''You took a terrible chance. Karim is a—uh, a *specialist*.''

''Yes. I was convinced the moment I laid eyes on him.''

''You gave her the film, *not* the boxes?''

Again the boxes. Darius tossed them to Youseff. He observed the prince gracefully slide a stiletto from a concealed wrist sheath. Delicately he slit open one end, peeled off the printed cover paper, and extracted a thin parchment. He performed the same expertise on the next box, retrieved the second parchment, and, beckoning Darius to his desk, turned on the desk lamp, flooding the top with a pale, blue-white glow. Placing the parchments side by side, he slid one up, the other down, until the markings matched. He decoded the Arabic writing, relief on his face. "You were lifted from the ranks, Darius, transferred to intelligence upon my recommendation," he began.

"*Oui*, Highness, *merci bien*. Destiny needed prodding."

"Judgments made to take you into our confidence limit what I can reveal to you. My status here carries heavy burdens. The lives of a vast network of well-trained, trusted, respected men and women depend upon my discretion. . . . The Germans," he asked quietly, "Von Luden, Hesse, and Schmidt—where are they presently?"

Darius's commission was a week old. He had hoped it would extend far longer. Youseff was asking for classified information.

Silence . . . resolute, underscored by a dismayed sigh, the opening of another brandy bottle, the sounds of liquid pouring from bottle to decanter . . .

"Darius, don't make this difficult. To which outpost were they transferred? It is imperative that I know."

"You pose questions only the colonel can answer." Darius, a guest in the palace, felt like *merde*.

Youseff read from one of the coded messages: "The Germans, Von Luden, Hesse, and Schmidt, are Nazi espionage agents attached to Bureau VI, the Foreign Intelligence Division of the elite *Reichssicherheitshauptamt*. These agents penetrated the Foreign Legion at Sidi bel Abbes, organized a secret command of five hundred German patriots. Frequent liaisons with Abou Ahkmed Hassan indicated they are prepared to move the moment word arrives from a private bunker at the Wolfsschanze." Youseff placed the communiqués on his desk. "These men are examples of the mass hypnosis done on Germany by the *Führer*. Von Luden's treatment of Kabul increases his worth to me. I will be avenged, Darius!" His eyes flared like black suns.

"That, Highness, is *why* you must obtain the information from Colonel Furstenberg. My orders were explicit in this regard."

The prince understood. He didn't like it, but he understood. What's more, his opinion of Darius soared. He had selected the *right* man! He was certain of it.

The next six months sped by swiftly. Darius and the prince liaisoned three times a week, more often if possible, to reorganize the Ben-Kassir spy network and counter the damage done by German spies who had infiltrated the ranks at Sidi bel Abbes and in North Africa.

Operation Sphinx was conceived, a plan to ferret out all the subversives in the Legion. To Darius, it became increasingly evident that Adolf Hitler nurtured and prepared long-range war plans while an entire world slept. Thousands of Jews, Bolsheviks, and other anti-Nazis escaping repression in Germany continued to seek asylum in Sidi bel Abbes, piquing Darius's curiosity no end. Why, after vituperative remarks about the Foreign Legion made by the German press, did German recruitments swing upward rather than decline? A ruthless screening of the ranks began in a clandestine manner.

A select group of twelve legionnaires, supporters in an underground endeavor, met in a sequestered room in Fatima's cellar. Six of the men had endured *règlement* with Darius and shared the Abu Hammid nightmare: Limey Whitehall, Lucien Pascal, Dutch O'Reilly, Pasquale Longinotti, Tamir Mandel, and Jean-Louis Delon. Darius came to trust these men with his life. Together the intrepid dozen, known as "Delilah's Dream," underwent rigorous training under Darius's personal tutelage and soon evolved into a superbly synchronized body whose precision teamwork was the envy of every French officer in Sidi. Their task was to infiltrate dangerous corridors and steal valuable classified information from the enemy—with a *kill-or-be-killed* credo. Strict rules were enforced, oaths of silence and allegiance sworn to, and once the physical endurance tests melted into past history, Darius taught them the art of separating fact from fiction and the vital need for incisive, on-the-spot judgments.

From its inception Delilah's Dream offered the NAIS something unique in the Legion's long and glorious past. Amid life-or-death situations, plagued at every turn by uncertainties, Darius broke through their xenophobic barriers to impress them with the imperative unity. He was shaping and molding their minds as Vivaldi had shaped and molded his mind. "Each man an integral part of the whole must fuse together perfectly," he told them, unconsciously spouting tenets of the Garduna Parchments. "Should any man fall to his death, the man closest to him must be prepared to take over for his fallen comrade and do the job of two men."

By November 1939 *Operation Sphinx* was born.

An idea came alive in the North Africa desert amid the utmost secrecy. The discreet, ingeniously devised spy went to work.

The purge began. *Operation Sphinx* snorted fire.

Spies, weeded out from the ranks and relieved of duty, were

reassigned to desert outposts. Contact with the outside world was virtually impossible. The unsuspecting German spies were fed misinformation and led to believe the expansion of French forces in North Africa was under way. Believing in the Legion's confidence in them, none of the Germans protested reassignments to grueling road construction sites at Columb Bechar deep in the heartland of the broiling Sahara until they awakened to an undisputable fact. Escape was well nigh impossible.

· In March 1940, Darius was promoted to captain. His proof that a saturation of Nazi spies in North Africa was connected to Arab insurrectionists was growing more apparent daily.

One month later Hitler's secret alliance with Libya surfaced. The possibility of German control in North Africa and the Middle East devastated the French. It was becoming a reality . . .

Most answers arrived on June 8. The German army had crossed the Aisne and Somme rivers. Two days later Il Duce, not to be outdone by his German counterpart, raised a powerful fascist fist in the air and prematurely declared war on France and Great Britain. Fascist forces invaded southern France.

Darius, moving away from the window overlooking the Sidi parade square, locked his memories back into his mental vault. He ambled back to his desk, dejected. Paris had been declared an open city, and on June 14 Hitler entered it in triumph.

The following day the Nazis captured Verdun.

And this morning—*this unforgettable morning*—the disgrace of the armistice reached Sidi bel Abbes!

Operation Sphinx had just rolled over, gasping in its final death throes. *Would it survive? Would it?*

Darius could make no assessments, not today!

Chapter Twenty-nine

A telephone's brash ring pierced his concentration. Darius glanced up at the wall clock. *Merci Dieu!* It was two P.M. Siesta was nearly over. He stacked the Von Luden, Hesse, and Schmidt dossiers and photos, locked them in a file drawer, ignoring the damnable ringing phone. Finally rankled by the steady buurrrrp . . . burrrp . . . burrrpp, he yanked at it, then listened to the unleashed torrent, a frown creasing his brow.

"Central command headquarters here, Captain," shouted the urgent voice. "All hell's breaking out. We're receiving bloody confusing messages. Will you decode and declassify for us, Captain Bonifacio?"

Darius listening intently, began to jot down the gibberish, a growing consternation etched into his features. "What it says, Lieutenant, is: *German legionnaires are opting for expatriation.*" He flared with annoyance. "Now, what's so bloody difficult with this? It's plain and simple. Why did you need me?"

"C'est bon . . . c'est bon, mon capitaine. We decoded precisely but it makes no bloody sense. None at all!"

"Ah! *Je comprends* . . ." Darius, suddenly enlightened, studied the message. "I'll get back to you." He hung up. He understood all right; the message, sinister in content, could prove disastrous. He pondered the implications. The phone rang again.

543

Before he snarled his discontent into the mouthpiece, Colonel Furstenberg growled at him, long distance, from Algeria. "*Before* we verified news of the armistice, Captain, *before* we confirmed with our ministry, orders arrived from Compiegne. The world is coming apart. Hitler *demands* the immediate transfer of Von Luden, Hans Hesse, and Fritz Schmidt from Sidi to Paris! And mind you, Captain, they are only the top of the barrel!"

"You are *verifying* the reports from Compiegne, sir." Darius was crestfallen.

"Captain, I traveled from Tangiers to Bizerte and back to Algeria. I'm in no mood for levity. The news is the same. Military intelligence fell apart somewhere along the way. Trust us to learn *after* the event! We are being sabotaged, Captain. Sabotaged! I'll find the goddamned leak. Meanwhile you round up the Germans!"

"Colonel, just how do I go about performing miracles? A Merlin I am not. The Germans escaped from Columb Bechar ten days ago. Surely you received my communiqués?"

"Disaster! It's total disaster!" Furstenberg shouted in a mood uncharacteristic of him. "Let me make one thing perfectly clear. I don't know *how* you'll do it. But—*do—it!* Another thing. Herr Hitler also demands the return of all Jews, anti-Nazis, antifascists, Bolsheviks, and communists who sought refuge with the Legion these past two years."

"Colonel! You don't expect me to obey those orders! We have a moral responsibility to those men!"

"A moral responsibility! Don't give me moral responsibility! In less than twenty-four hours there may be no Foreign Legion— and you give me moral responsibility!" His scoffing voice dripped vitriol.

"Perhaps I'd better make myself clear," Darius began. "Before I followed such a command, I'd resign my commission."

"Captain! Perhaps *you* don't understand! The ministry in Algeria is in chaos! Can you imagine what's happening in Paris? Compiegne? All of France? Now don't question my orders. We must demonstrate efficiency, understand. There's no time to choose up sides at this moment. That's already been done for us in something called German one upsmanship."

"Chaos. You said chaos, sir. In this turmoil orders can become scrambled, *oui, mon colonel*?"

"Bonifacio! What in the satanic black demon of hell are you thinking? This is an inappropriate time to play games."

"Only that orders received in this madly paced bedlam can easily be misinterpreted. Wires cut or dismantled, *oui*? Who would know? I refuse to part with Tamir or Longinotti or any man on that list!"

"It's not enough that the Legion is disintegrating. Now I am faced with mutiny? Insubordination. I'll have nothing to do with your disreputable proposal. I didn't reach you. We haven't talked."

Darius hung up the phone, grimly determined not to break up Delilah's Dream. There was no way in hell he'd send Tamir Mandel or any of his men back to Germany. *Especially* not Tamir!

The blue-eyed, bewhiskered Polish Jew, was a quiet man, a voracious reader. Unlike most legionaries of his sexual persuasion, he neither flaunted his homosexuality nor wore it like a badge of valor. His knowledge of languages had posed an enigma to Darius when he arrived in Sidi. He'd witnessed Tamir's orderly remoteness convulse into wild disorder when provoked. Tamir's withering stare and acerbic tongue, governed by a hair trigger temper, were capable of cutting people in two; and he saw murder in the man's eyes on occasion. Through Pascal's encouragement, Tamir had begged to join Delilah's Dream. Darius's disinclination to include him in the rigors and risky clandestine involvements stemmed from the feeling that Tamir's skeletal countenance, masking killer instincts and the volatile temper and burning racist fanaticism was an anti-social personality aching to be prodded. One day Darius had sent for him and laid his cards on the table. "Let me make our function perfectly clear, Tamir. The fact that the men of Delilah's Dream must function in symbiosis, each dependent on the other for survival in life or death situations, alters the qualifications of the men to very specific requisites. Your temper and racist mentality, however much I understand them, have no place with Delilah's Dream. They interfere with sound judgment and split-second decision making. Besides," Darius added with a smile. "I trust no man who consults God before he consults me."

"I agree with you. I understand perfectly, and I promise I shall change. I too recognize my liabilities. And their destructive forces."

And so it began. Somehow Tamir got hold of the works of the noted psychologist Émile Coué on autosuggestion and hypnosis, determined to alter his thinking and outmoded way of life. Changes gradually appeared in him with such forceful impact that Darius called him back on a trial basis, and on the condition that he instruct the other men in the work of Dr. Coué. In time it worked magic, strengthening the ties between each of Delilah's men.

Give up Tamir to the Germans? Never! He'd sooner part with his right arm. New names and identities would be provided for Tamir and the others.

Damn! The French mentality continued to elude Darius.

French officers, trained to spot incongruities in the behavior of their men yet blind to the handwriting on the wall, had failed to take action. Darius had developed a feral instinct for truth, a nose for sniffing out facts. Hans Hesse was no ordinary NCO nor was Fritz Schmidt, who made himself important to men like Hesse and Von Luden and feasted off them like a parasite off a host. And *Von Luden!* Ah yes, Von Luden, that repulsive misfit. Observe his repugnant countenance closely when he took orders from the French and you knew by his subtle flinching where his loyalties lay.

Forget it! It's nearly over! Mistakes were made, costly mistakes!

But how would the French absolve themselves of the guilt of allowing the Germans to commit atrocities under their very noses? Could they wash away memories of German brutality among the ranks?

For the next ten minutes Darius's repeated attempts to reach El Bayadh, requesting immediate response from the Legion outpost, brought no result. Nothing! It was vital that he contact Youseff to authenticate the aerial recon photos St. Germaine had turned over to him that morning and show him evidence of Hassan's cache of weaponry.

Allez-y . . . Allez-y. Dépêchez-vous!

Darius was livid. Siesta or no siesta, Legion outposts were under strict orders to keep communication command operational twenty-four hours a day.

By two-fifteen P.M. his discontent was aggravated by the silence. A two-hour silence! *Merde.* Something was terribly wrong.

Back at his desk, he doused himself in alcohol to cool off. He slipped into his shirt, snapped the cartouche gun and holster into place, grabbed his *kepi* and briefcase, and bolted out the door.

He collided with Dutch and Tamir. Instantly the two were bombarded with orders. Moving under the force of their captain's commands, they manned the communications consoles before Darius had finished.

"And Dutch, get El Bayadh on the horn one way or another. I've gotten no answer for the past two hours. Find the bottleneck. *Pressor so dépêcher!* You Tamir—round up Delilah's Dream! Instruct the fearless dozen to gather all the arms they can carry. We're going for a sortie to El Bayadh. Departure time—ten minutes. Clock it. Do you follow?" Darius bolted out the door, and down the steps.

Dutch, seated at the wireless, earphones in place, dexterously tapped Morse coded messages to the Legion outpost. His free hand played with radio frequencies on the short-wave transmitter. He barked into the microphone, "Snake Charmer . . . Calling Snake Charmer . . . This is Delilah's Dream . . . Come in Snake Charmer . . . Come in, do you read? You friggin' bums, answer me! Come in for Christ sakes!"

Tamir, on the phone, attempted to wade through the busy trunks to the main post command. A string of Yiddish curses escaped his lips. "*Ich vil da toifil izu schneidan dina batzen!*"

"Ya better move your friggin' buns, Tamir! Go round up the others, ya hear? Time's frittering away," Dutch shouted, pointing to the wall clock between his own frustrating machinations.

Tamir needed no nudgings. He leaped over the wooden office gate and out the door, an unexpected whoop of jubilation echoing after him.

Action at last!

Fifteen minutes later three dusty Benz utilities sped over the broken desert floor south to El Bayadh in 124-degree temperature. The jeeplike vehicles, mounted with machineguns on swiveling tripods, were manned by twelve grim-faced, begoggled, very special legionnaires. Tense, alert, the sweat pouring profusely from their bodies, binoculars to their eyes, they scanned every deceptive inch of the broiling sands.

An hour out of Sidi, the white stucco towers of El Bayadh loomed in the distance, jutting high over the Legion outpost wall. French and Algerian flags, mounted on a standard over the Legion's colors, fluttered in the mild breeze of the Saharan Atlas. The fort, a speck on the horizon, formed a deceptive composite. Actually five miles away, it appeared to be less than a mile in distance.

Darius slowly turned the focus wheels on his binoculars, adjusting them as the distance changed, to see what seemed to be legionnaires manning the crenellations between the merlons on the battlement. Closer . . . closer, as the utilities jostled their occupants, Darius shouted aloud, signaling his driver to stop. The other utilities skidded to an abrupt stop and, kicking up cartwheels of dust, eased abreast of the lead vehicle.

What Darius had perceived to be legionnaires a mile back had turned out to be hulking creatures with eight-foot wing spreads.

"Jesus Christ!" Longinotti began cursing in Italian. *Madoditi avvoltoio. Goddamned vultures!* The others, spotting the vultures now whirling arcs over El Bayadh echoed his sentiments in their native tongues.

It was a dreaded sign. Winged predators had already sniffed out a banquet of death! Metallic sounds cracked noisily as the men clicked magazines out of their guns, inspected them, and shoved them back into place, their stony features grim, eyes deadly.

Dutch O'Reilly cranked his battery-operated radio in frenzied attempts to contact the fort. Longinotti's hawklike features and ferret eyes signaled danger. The Italian was a bloodhound. Most of the men, unfettered by higher education, had retained and refined their animal instincts and could detect the proximity of death as a physical odor.

"Can't get a friggin' answer, Cap!" Dutch lamented.

Delon tossed off a mock salute toward the fort. *"Morituri te salutamus!* We who are about to die salute you!"

"I dinna think that ta be amusin'," Dutch snapped, repeatedly cranking the phone apparatus.

Darius signaled the others forward. The vehicles lurched, zigzagging crazily over the sand, the means of diverting rifle fire should volleys unload on them.

Ten minutes later as the jeeps geared down at the outpost gates, Darius, scanned the towers, gravely concerned.

No guards! No one manning the gates! He waved the men ahead, pacing them two car lengths apart. Darius, in the lead jeep, eyes everywhere at once, stiffened with tension. They proceeded tentatively past the kiosks, through deserted, bottle-necked streets greeted only by specters. No one need tell them the fort was abandoned, the question was why?

"Look, *capitaine*!" Dutch pointed to the ganglia of wires dangling against a building wall. "The bloomin' bastards cut the friggin' wires."

The awesome silence of a phantom-filled desert hung ominously over El Bayadh. The scene turned sinister. Rotting garbage formed hillocks in the narrow alleyways. Familiar sounds, the usual shouting and confusion were absent. No greedy, grasping beggarly hands reached out to the legionnaires pleading for *dinars*. No dope sellers or illegal wine vendors skulked about. No infirm natives cried, "Alms for the love of Allah!" They saw no prostrated natives on prayer rugs facing Mecca. Where once a hot, dusty bazaar with its usual rotting fruits and stale breads had snaked along the paths there was nothing. And where once had strolled filthy, diseased prostitutes, beckoning with smiles masked by shabby lithums, offering sure-fire annuities of clap or gonorrhea, there was no one.

Only silence . . . interminable, foreboding silence, underscored by the straining and screeching of skidding tires as jeeps turned sharp corners leading to the core of the Algerian fortification which resembled a sprawling village.

Sweat rolled off their bodies, fear nibbled at their calm. The men in Darius's jeep exchanged silent glances, their eyes communicating angst at the unknown forces arrayed against them. They approached the stark white stone and cement Moorish construction with its monumental foundations, long flat roof with crenellations and fortified gates. The central tower, pierced by tiny, off-angle empty windows oversaw a vast sea of hidden death, until . . . *Delilah's Dream* entered the courtyard.

Suddenly Pascal, driving the lead utility slammed hard on the brakes. The jeep lurched spasmodically. The engine stalled. Screeching tires! Crashing iron! Heated curses pierced the deathly silence as each jeep rear-ended the machine in front of it.

The legionnaires stared, appalled at the ghostly El Bayadh.

These men had seen everything, but nothing on the scale of this wholesale slaughter. Broken, dead bodies were piled into towering dunes and strewn in wild disarray as if a giant bulldozer had razed everything in sight and dumped it all onto one burial ground.

Slowly, the men, guns at ready, spilled from their vehicles and moved zombielike through the violent and motionless tableau.

Death, no stranger to Delilah's Dream had vomited forth horrifying spectacles in the past but nothing like this. Covering their noses with their mufflers, Darius and the others walked dislocated circles about the dead. *If only the stench would abate*.

Flies, as thick as clustered drones around a hive feasted voraciously on the bloodied carnage. Sand, cartwheeling through the courtyard stuck to human entrails giving them the appearance of so much breaded meat. Decapitated heads encased in soiled turbans lay alongside the mutilated bodies, swelling in the sun. Gargoyle lips covered with pink foam, swollen tongues jutting from mouths, lopped-off ears, noses, fingers, picked clean of jewelry were scattered everywhere. The raw stench of human flesh broiling in the desert heat anathematized the senses. But, it was the sight of children impaled on lances that caused a collective dry heave among the men.

A tribal uprising between desert enemies? Not this atrocity.

As Darius studied the carnage, it was the obvious touch of professionalism, one that extended savagery beyond the pale of decency, that prodded him. Something wasn't jibing properly. The *modus operandi* of whoever had committed the atrocity, ghastly in its execution, would have you believe this was tribal warfare. It wasn't. It lacked one essential element.

Testicle sacs and penises on the male bodies were intact!

This was no Berber atrocity—this was white men's doing! Darius's eyes moved from one body to another, and another. His face, under a desert tan, turned gray, expressionless; his eyes, green dead stones, were devoid of luster.

Suddenly in the distance the sound of an approaching horde was heard. Darius and the others rushed to the high-walled gates to see the sun flashing on hundreds of dilated eyes; it bounced off rifle barrels like glints of mirrored steel. A tumultuous roar arose; savage screams and howling yells jolted the legionnaires to life. Wailing bullets bit chunks of concrete off the walls in wild ricochet.

"The gates!" Darius shouted. "Shut the gates!"

The men scattered. Four wheeled the gates shut, barricading them with enormous quebracho beams. Six legionnaires scurried up the stone walls to the ramparts, fixing their rifles between crenellations and firing volleys at the charging horsemen who descended on them with flying burnooses, roped *kuffiahs* and some of the fastest automatic weapons the defenders had ever encountered!

Darius scaled the narrow steps inside the tower three at a time. He cursed aloud! Three machineguns against a horde? They'd never make it, *never!* He raced back down the steps, out one door and through another, kicking in the arsenal door. Stopping short, he cursed again. *Merde! Damnation! Not enough ammunition for a twenty-one gun salute!* He ran outside. The men were unloading the extra cache of weapons they'd transported from

Sidi. Darius loped past them, scaled the steps to the ramparts to assess the assaulting forces. He studied their inconstant outline against the blazing sun. He counted forty in all: some came on horseback, a few on camels charged and fired at the fortification. From the east came a dozen horsemen dragging brush over the sand kicking up thick aprons of invisibility. Forty riders moving constantly could give the impression of a battalion of hundreds!

Darius's instincts at work, saw more than the design of destruction, far more here than met the eye. Forty horsemen converging on El Bayadh from nowhere? Uh-uh, he didn't buy it. Chances were perhaps hundreds were en route to rendezvous with these fierce fighting Arabs. But why? *Why?* It was inconceivable to him that a captured Legion outpost, summarily deserted would sustain two assaults in one day. Not without vital reason.

Vital reason. *What in damnation had brought these devils back en masse? What had they missed the first time?* A dozen unanswered questions in Darius's mind plagued him. He speculated on their chances of survival, measuring the odds. Without radio or wireless, outnumbered, outgunned, under bombardment by weapons superior to theirs they were as doomed as their predecessors. He prayed for a miracle.

And a miracle occurred.

Prince Ben-Kassir! Lucien Pascal found him more dead than alive. Waving his hairy arms, like a human semaphore he called, "Captain! Captain! Over here!" Pascal bent over the inert robed figure in the dust.

Darius found no recognizable traces until after he washed the grime and blood from the face with water from his canteen. The blood drained from Darius's face. It *was* Youseff! "How in the name of sweet, sweet Jesus did you recognize the prince?"

"Six bullets in him, *mon capitaine*. I didn't count the knife wounds." *Mon Dieu!* His neck had been slashed!

"Go! Find Delon. Bring him quickly." Ducking bullets, Darius glanced about for shelter. Youseff's lips moved. He strained to speak. "Don't move, Youseff! For the love of God, don't talk! Your injuries are serious."

Ben-Kassir's eyes flared wildly; the milky film over his eyeballs cleared. His lips formed words. Darius, held captive by the effort, leaned over him, placed his ear closer to the prince's lips and listened. *Please Youseff—live. Live!*

"Are you certain?" he asked, as hope sprang eternal.

Youseff blinked. Pascal and Delon scurried back toward them. Darius shouted to Delon, "Save him, you hear? Delon, save the prince's life! Understand?"

Delon scanned Youseff professionally, then glanced at Darius as if he'd lost all senses. Shrugging, he helped them carry the body into a nearby shelter. Darius shouted, "Pascal, come with me to the tower! Tamir, you too!" He shouted as the others approached with bad news—they were running low on ammunition. They loped after Darius, calling to Dutch and Limey Whitehall, waving them off the catwalks, bidding them to follow.

Darius, without a second to lose, moved with the speed of a meteor, sprinting, vaulting, skirting dead bodies. He stopped before the solid oak and iron-padlocked door, shot off the lock with his service pistol, shattering it. He kicked in the door and stood transfixed at the amazing sight. The men rushing behind him whooped aloud, shouting joyously.

An arsenal! A goddamned arsenal! Was this to be believed? Reason enough for the second assault!

Rifles, grenades, flame throwers, machineguns, automatic rifles! "Collect all the arms you can carry!" Darius shouted. "Get back to the wall and send the others back!"

Within moments Delilah's Dream prepared for the enemy's onslaught. Machineguns, swiftly positioned in the towers overlooking the main gate, began the overture. Automatic rifles opened fire at the charging horsemen, lifting the advance riders from their saddles as horses buckled their knees under fire and spilled blood onto the sands. A few horses, spooked, reared, eyes flaring. Some exploded under a hurled grenade and came down stiff-legged, entrails ripped open. A second charge came on the heels of the first. Darius's men opened fire and blew the enemy out of the Sahara. At the main gate, six robed men, breaking through the barricade, were blown to bits by well-placed grenades.

A minimum of rifle fire, several machinegun bursts, a handful of expertly aimed grenades and luck combined to rout an unknown enemy. Sober-faced legionnaires, shoving their *kepis* to the back of their sweaty heads, stared at the men in flight, marveling at the powerful weapons and whooping for joy. On the cracked floor of the desert, near the main gates, a baker's dozen of men lay dead.

"Open the gates!" Darius shouted.

They leaped off the catwalks and ramparts to examine the

faces of their dead enemies. Hunkering down on their haunches, waddling from one dead man to the next, Darius heard his men's astonished gasps, their audible curses.

"No fucking ordinary Arabs, these!" Dutch O'Reilly interjected.

"Friggin' Krauts!" Limey Whitehall spat viciously. "Whaddya suppose they were trying ta pull off, Cap?" He scratched his beard ferociously.

"What else?" Darius muttered. "The arsenal! They returned to retrieve the weapons and stumbled onto a surprise—us! Believe me, they'll return. We've no time to spend on conjecture. *Allez . . . Allez! Déménager!* Delon—your first priority is to keep His Highness alive!" To the others, he commanded, "Next we strip the arsenal. Load all you can into the utilities! Then we get the hell back to Sidi. *D'accord?*"

Delon and O'Reilly loaded Prince Ben-Kassir into a utility, Darius beckoned to Pascal and Tamir to follow him to the arsenal, quickly explaining the intended strategy. "Our timing must be perfect, our actions swift. Don't look back, *comprenez-vous? Alors,* we've no time to spare. When it begins, get your asses back to the main gate on the double. No bungling; ready?"

Pascal and Tamir, nodding, geared themselves for the life-or-death relay. Darius signaled. The intricate, lethal ballet commenced. Loping precariously from opposite directions, heading for the gate, they bit pins from grenades, hurled them behind them. The target: the arsenal. Explosions rocked the earth. Detonation followed detonation. Buildings on all sides of them collapsed, raining dust, debris, and sand down on them. Shrapnel, stones, wood, plaster, and glass descended. The main tower crumbled like broken tiers of a wedding cake. The trio blindly charged on through the congestion, zigzagging, ducking, lurching, sidling past obstructions, sprinting breathlessly to the gates where drivers gunned the engines. In a mad leap they boarded the moving utilities, speeding the hell out of El Bayadh. The utilities, gunned to the floorboards, skimmed over the parched cracked floor of the desert as sunset began its death chant for the day.

The life of a brave prince hung in the balance. Oh, Christ!

Tamir Mandel brooded. Well muscled now, his skin tanned a tobacco brown by the sun, his fiery personality had been tempered in the past year. He was becoming a professional who thought he understood tactics and strategy better than his companions. Momentarily he glowered inwardly, unable to comprehend the importance of saving one man's life if rescue meant certain death to each man should the Arabs ambush them. Then Longinotti explained that the prince was not merely any man, but a very *special* man who meant a great deal to France. Still Tamir shrugged, unconvinced. By now he knew the unlikelihood of selecting a field of battle tailored to their specific needs and talents, for in the Legion battles can erupt anywhere, on any terrain, at any time, and you must prepare for the worst. But to deliberately risk the lives of twelve specially trained legionnaires to save one man, royal Arab or not, didn't jibe in his mind. All his life he'd been taught that one man's life was expendable if the cause meant life for the majority. Would he ever understand the Corsican captain's mentality?

Approaching El Bayadh along a southeasterly spur track, a Nazi supply train snaked through blistering sands like a thirsting behemoth anxious to reach the Legion outpost before sundown. German swastikas, emblazoned on the doors of the dust-laden Daimler touring cars and Wehrmacht trucks were barely discernible in the blinding light. Nazi flags on front fender standards barely fluttered in the dead heat of the desert. Engines roared and stalled. Gears shifted raucously as the cars, trapped in sand, sought escape. Wheels spun crazily, spurting bursts of sand granules, and congested the paths of the worming supply train.

From up ahead, cutting back over the desert floor came the constant *baroooom . . . barooom . . .* of gunned motorcycles, running interference for the snaking train. They had lumbered past labyrinths of desolate hills, bare and as round as baby buttocks, grown claustrophobic while traversing narrow winding roads between high skeletal walls of ebony stone sculpted by the inexorable winds of the High Atlas and had finally descended into latitudinal valleys, made chaotic with boulders, jagged pillars and volcanic rocks.

Now, thought *Sturmbannführer* Hans Hesse, seated in the lead car behind the escorts, we penetrate a portion of this limitless desert, then on to victory. A well-deserved victory! He removed the dead cigarette from his gold holder, tossed it into the sands, a satisfied expression on his Aryan face. It wasn't over yet, but the tide was turning. The indignities suffered at Sidi bel Abbes had ended. This *coup*—the capture of El Bayadh—would mark the beginning of Nazi domination in North Africa. Hesse foresaw one solitary obstacle—*Muhammad Abou Ahkmed Hassan!* And the desert chieftain was poison.

The way Hesse saw it, the success of a chancy but clever plan necessitated intimate cooperation from a dubious, unstable ally, Hassan. But to be forced into an untenable situation, solely dependent upon the mercurial temperament of such a man sat uneasily on Hesse's mind.

It was not for nothing that Hassan promised his manpower and warring desert expertise to the Germans; Hassan's rewards for turning El Bayadh over to the Nazis was the head of his mortal enemy, Prince Youseff Ben-Kassir. It was a pact devised by Lucifer himself, but Hesse felt no qualms about the exchange.

Earlier this day, before Intelligence reports had verified Ben-Kassir's presence at the Legion outpost with his tribal chieftains, Hesse's advance squadrons, disguised as Arab tribesmen had integrated with Hassan's butchers and struck at El Bayadh with the intention of decimating the inhabitants and to stash an enormous train of new weapons in the arsenal, awaiting Major Hesse's arrival. When verification of Ben-Kassir's presence at the fort arrived at the Hassan encampment the marauding butchers had returned to search for the prince's body. Instead, they encountered bold resistance from Delilah's Dream. Their forces scattered, and badly depleted in the fray they had returned to their chief emptyhanded.

Unfortunately for Major Hesse, he'd received no briefing on the second assault. Delirious with his clever strategy, he patted his tunic into place, flicking at the residue of cigarette ashes, planning more strategy. El Bayadh, at the center of the High Atlas was the perfect spot from which to launch a German offensive at Foreign Legion Post Commands. Now to prepare for the North African Campaign.

When Berlin got word of this day's victories . . .

This military coup would catapult him that much closer to his goal: Bureau III, the SD—*Sicherheitdienst*—Security Service inside the Reich. To be noticed and commended by the *Führer* himself would certainly mark the culmination of his career.

Hesse, like Schmidt and Von Luden a member of Hitler's German Youth Movement, was indoctrinated at an early age and had betrayed his family. Trained in the army, he joined the Waffen SS and was later recommended for the RSHA.

Hesse's shattered personality and egomania was concealed behind an imperturbable countenance. A man in whom blind ambition had coupled with hatred for a vast army of incompetent subordinates, the *Sturmbannführer* never forgot a slight. Not content to even a score, he demanded total annihilation of an offender if it took a lifetime to avenge the wrongdoing. Violently passionate in matters of venereal decadance he'd spent his lifetime experimenting with the darkest mysteries this side of hell.

Hesse, a man with arrested emotions, who seemed totally fearless, gobbled men like Hassan for breakfast and shat them from his bowels before sundown.

Now, sighting clouds of dust up ahead, Hesse raised binoculars to his eyes. The advance guard was speeding back along the road toward the train. He swept the sky with the glasses, studying the huge birds of prey whirling on the distance, icy blue eyes narrowing to slits behind his goggles.

A young officer on a motorcycle slid to a dusty stop alongside of the touring car. He saluted. "Heil Hitler! The situation is grim, *Kommandant*! El Bayadh is a smoking cemetery for hundreds of dead men!"

"Send in the advance infantry. I want a report the moment I arrive." Hesse smiled inwardly. So far so good.

Ten minutes later, in stony-faced silence, Hesse stepped out of the Daimler inside the ruined fort. Wading through the sea of dead men, he maintained an inscrutable, condemning silence. His aide, *Oberstleutnant* Fritz Schmidt, followed Hesse like a stalking hunter waiting for the beast to snort fire. It exploded sooner than he'd expected.

"Order a detail to dig trenches beyond the gates. Dump the bodies and burn them," Hesse said, covering his nose. "It should have been done before my arrival!"

"*Jawohl, Sturmbannführer!* At once." Schmidt hesitated. "May I suggest we search for the corpse of Ben-Kassir before Hassan and his entourage arrive? He was promised the head of his enemy, and what that disgusting man wants, he gets."

"That *disgusting man* is *our* ally!" Hesse snapped, daubing delicately at his sweaty brow. "Light the torches," he ordered. "I had best assess the damage personally."

El Bayadh was a shambles, the stench of broiled human flesh unendurable, luring desert jackals, hyennas and wild dogs to a feast.

Hesse located and staked out for himself one building untouched by fire and explosives. He ordered a detachment of engineers to repair communications centers and prepare decent quarters for himself. Within the hour a retinue of personal aides and drones accomplished the impossible. Carpets, desks, file cabinets, and maps in place, now the room formed a semblance of order.

An hour later Fritz Schmidt appeared to report what he dreaded to report. "Prince Ben-Kassir's body is not among the dead!"

"Impossible! The dead do not get up and walk away!"

"This one did."

Hesse's eyes turned deadly. "Explain how? The radio was silenced, *ja*?" Schmidt stood deathly still, unable to conjecture. Wheels turned in Hesse's mind. Suddenly revelation punctured his consciousness. "Those men! *Delilah's Dream!* Those clever men trained by the Corsican!" He spat venomously. "But how? How could they travel the distance from Sidi on camels more swiftly than we made it from Oujda in motor vehicles? *How?*"

"Perhaps they came by other means, *after* our men demolished El Bayadh. Perhaps they caught our men off guard . . . forcing them to flee . . ."

Hesse tossed his aide a look of long suffering. "How else, *Dummkopf*? Pray Abou Ahkmed Hassan's appetite for heads can be forestalled."

Schmidt, ignoring the stinging rebuke, was struck with sudden inspiration. "Perhaps Hassan's appetite need not be forestalled, sir."

"What exactly do you suggest, *Leutnant*?"

"Most bodies are mutilated beyond recognition. If we substitute one body for another—"

Hesse's lips, twisting into a leer, froze. Muffled, yet clearly enough for Schmidt to hear, came the word, "Genius! At times your thinking astounds me, but this is sheer genius, Schmidt!"

Schmidt was tempted, but the moment wasn't ripe to push for promotion.

A staff sergeant rushed into the room. "Heil Hitler, Major! The arsenal . . ." He hesitated, looking from Schmidt to Hesse.

"Yes, yes, the arsenal—"

"Is kaput! Blown up! Nothing remains but ashes, *Sturmbannführer*."

Hesse cursed aloud; his blue eyes turned cobalt in fury. He pounded the desktop in a rage. "Send the communications officer to me at once, *Dummkopf*! Everyone is a *Dummkopf*! Why must I be saddled with the sons of jackasses?" Guzzling schnapps, he fumed at Schmidt. "Take a message, Schmidt!"

Schmidt deflated at once; his battered self-esteem dropped to an all-time low. He picked up a pad and began to write.

* * *

The sun, a flaming orange disc, had sunk below the horizon, leaving in its wake a billowing twilight of purple fire that hovered over the campfires at the encampment of Muhammad Abou Ahkmed Hassan. Here and there along the dusty path leading from the entrance through the scattering of tents to the main tent of Hassan, boulders, the color of polished lead, were strewn like shattered mirrors, reflecting the purple flaming ribbons of sky. The omnipresent wind in the High Atlas rolled and swept over the deathly immobility of rock, desert, and precipitous cliffs like a tremendous shadow of doom.

Robed, bearded men and camp followers sat before braziers, eating *kumis,* drinking *qat,* and smoking hashish in utter indolence. A few glanced up with provincial curiosity as three swift riders galloped swiftly to the center of camp, pulling up abruptly before the tent of their chieftain. Swinging from their tasseled saddles, they paused to wet their lips, swill wine from goatskins, and then salaamed and made their presence known.

The hesitant trio, bearers of bad tidings, found Hassan seated cross-legged before a brazier vigorously eating *cous-cous* from a bowl with dirty fingers. Nearby on a gold stand in this pretentious, carpeted tent was the Holy Koran, bound in lugubrious leather binding and tooled in the finest gold. The couriers bowed obsequiously, reluctant to impart the bad news. Their reluctance stemmed from the dread of two possible perils: death, if the news displeased their chief and it certainly would, and death, if they were forced to return to El Bayadh. Still they salaamed, paid homage to Hassan. At least one brave man, their spokesman, displaying tremendous deference, spoke tentatively.

"Blessings and peace be upon thee, Lord Hassan." He began to impart the news.

Hassan paused in the act of chewing loudly, his face turning a mottled purple. He spat the food from his mouth as if it were contaminated. "What?" he roared in outrage. "Substitute another body for that of my sworn enemy?" He bellowed like a bull in a voice that threatened to bring down the whole of the Sahara encampment. "Perhaps I failed to hear my emissary well?"

His black-dagger eyes stabbed at the hearts of the panic-stricken couriers. He flung his bowl across the tent, wiped his bearded lips with the back of his hand. His animallike teeth showed yellow and savage. The sounds deep in his throat, unlike any human, snarled at them.

"So! This is the way it must be? Our enemy the sheikh of Kassir eludes even the German infidels! Truly he leads a charmed life! Verily he is protected by Allah, blessings be upon him. Verily by Allah Himself!" Rising from his lotus position before the brazier, he summoned up the extent of his rage. His ugly face darkened malevolently as he raised his arms to the heavens. Fiery gold and orange lights from the brazier threw shadowy lights onto his features gave him a supernatural appearance. He chanted in a mixture of Persian and Farsi.

"So that all Islam shall witness our power, we shall arise and slay the infidel dogs who trespass on our lands. Our Lord Muhammad, blessing be upon the merciful one, has commanded me to rid our lands of all infidels, to invoke the laws of Islam, to wage war so that all Islam will bow and tremble before me. The infidels have thirsted for supremacy in our lands. They arm us, men they hate. Into our hands are placed supernatural weapons. Is it to help us? Oh, no. The infidels *pretend* to be our friends. The Germans make promises they do not keep. We shall not cower before them. They shall not conquer us. No conciliatory talks shall sully the people of Muhammad Abou Ahkmed Hassan. We shall be the conquerors! Arise, my brothers, spread the word. The Great One has commanded. *Destroy! Destroy! Destroy El Bayadh and the traitors with their own tools of destruction!*" His cry arose like a vast fury, shaking the poles of his tent. Outside, the sounds sent skulking camp dogs loping and cavorting crazily onto the desert.

On the arduous ride back to Sidi bel Abbes, Darius, growing anxious over Youseff's weakening condition, ordered the driver to floor the accelerator. Unaware that Hesse had occupied El Bayadh, he glanced impatiently at his watch. Youseff needed immediate medical attention. His thoughts drifted back to a recent conversation with Colonel Furstenberg and Youseff. When was it? Three, four days ago?

"France will fall in a matter of hours, days, less than a week," Darius had prognosticated, studying a map of German advances in the Rhine at the NAIS chief's office. "With his Western Front covered, Hitler will either bombard North Africa or cross the Channel into England. Which takes priority?"

"Does it matter?" Furstenberg had replied acidly. "We shall be at peace with Germany. No question, France is defeated."

"France and Germany shall enjoy peace." Youseff indicated his displeasure. "But Hassan and I shall be at war. Perhaps the bloodiest war to be written in the pages of history. Germany's alliance with France spells the annihilation of my people. Hassan will throw everything he has against me. I am not Hitler's ally. Nor shall I permit Hitler to feed Hassan's military strength."

A silence prevailed as all three men digested Youseff's words.

"I sense a distortion in all this," Darius said. "Hitler shows no inclination to wage a two-front war. He tackles his enemies one at a time, picking them individually and with psychological planning. Thus far his inclination and success lies in waging short wars, economical in manpower with minimum destruction to the German economy. Poland was scarcely a contest. There his campaign was short, sharp, and brutal. His Stukas operated as precision artillery, pounded defense positions and fortifications. The French army was ripped in two on the Meuse, and the British, escaping from Dunkirk, are living proof of the type of warfare Hitler engages in. Now France has fallen, due to her operational stupidity. Neither she nor the British offered bold offenses. They tried to defend and were crushed in the attempt."

"What is it you're trying to say, Darius?" Youseff had queried.

"We must plan *offenses*! Offenses, Highness, not defenses. I am one Frenchman who fails to delight in the thought of living under German domination. Von Luden, Hesse, Schmidt, and the other German Non-com Officer at Sidi cured me of any such delusions. How many more Frenchmen share my feelings?"

How many more Frenchmen share my feelings!

Ben-Kassir came alive. "All who oppose Pétain's armistice proposals."

"How many would you estimate, Highness?"

"The figure is too awesome to contemplate." He embraced Darius vigorously and left the colonel's office bent on summoning powerful forces.

Now, agonized Darius, what was the good of all their comings and goings? Death hovered close to Youseff, frantically seducing the great prince to its eternal bosom.

Sidi bel Abbes was in chaos! Everywhere people milled about the bottlenecked streets, making them impassable to the desert utilities. Pascal floored the jeep, cutting corners, blowing his horn impatiently, cursing at the stragglers as he sped to the infirmary.

"Delon," commanded Darius. "Guard the prince with your life until I return." He shouted to the others, "Learn all you can of this commotion. Meet me back at headquarters!"

Darius leaped from the jeep and ran to his office. Two messages awaited him. He tore open the one marked URGENT—TOP PRIORITY. He read:

> TWO HUNDRED GERMAN LEGIONNAIRES DESERTED FORT JONNART TO
> UNITE WITH NAZI TANK DIVISION IN LIBYAN DESERT. DESTINATION:
> TRIPOLITANIA. YOU ARE TO LEAVE AT ONCE WITH YOUR SPECIAL SQUAD
> WITH THE 13TH DEMI-BRIGADE UNDER SEALED ORDERS. JOIN BRITISH
> TASK FORCE IN ALGERIA FOR RELOCATION. H. FURSTENBERG.

The second envelope was marked SEALED ORDERS—OPEN IN MIDFLIGHT. He placed it in a canvas courier belt strapped to his body under his shirt. Moving swiftly about the office, he opened files marked HIGHLY CLASSIFIED, sorted through them, and, selecting only those coded in purple, placed them in his briefcase. The others he pulled and dumped into a metal trash bin, setting fire to the contents.

Sweep it clean . . . destroy remaining records . . . leave nothing for the enemy! He completed the ritual in less than seven minutes, smashed the radio transmitter, dismantled the wireless, and poured more files into the fire until he finished.

It was done! Finished.

Dutch O'Reilly dashed into the office and stopped short, eyes peering at the destruction. A bulldog ferocity settled onto his features. Pascal, followed by Tamir, rushed into the office. "It is urgent?" Pascal asked, staring in dumb amazement.

Darius, nodding, thrust the briefcase at Pascal. "Guard it with your life. Delilah's Dream will depart Sidi with the 13th Demi. Get cracking! On the double! And Pascal, we take Prince Ben-Kassir with us!"

All three men, about to protest at the dangers involved in transporting the prince, were instantly arrested by the look in Darius's eyes. His voice weighed heavy. "If we leave him behind, he'll be killed. Hassan or the Germans—take your pick."

They left to round up the others. Darius suddenly remembered.
St. Germaine!

He bolted after the others, down the steps, into the jeep, and, gunning the engine, swung the utility around and back over the narrow congested streets to *le Village Négre*.

More madness in the streets! Pandemonium was the order of the day! He abandoned the jeep before a kiosk, muttered, "*Mon Dieu!* Was it only this morning?" He rubbed his arm, remembering Hassan's specialist.

Crowds thickened. The streets were mobbed. Something crazy was happening, but he couldn't take time to find out what. The implications, flashing in mind, quickened his gait. Legionnaires were shouting! Darius, catching bits and pieces, put it together. The 13th Demi-brigade was massing at the edge of Sidi, preparing to troop-train it to Algeria. The NAIS was preparing to join Colonel Furstenberg in the capital city. Nothing made sense. A skeletal staff of legionnaires would remain behind. A skeletal staff would remain behind to man the fortification? *For what?* To be massacred by Hassan's men? Very little made sense.

St. Germaine's precarious position loomed vividly in his mind. He had to rescue her, take her with them. He must!

Café Fatima—the pleasure dome! He rushed past the Punjabi, then stopped short. Incredible! No one seemed aware of what was happening outside the doors. There were no distortions? None at all. It was business at usual inside, which to Darius was not usual at all. He searched through the smoke-filled rooms for St. Germaine. She was nowhere to be found. *And Karim!* Where was Karim? Darius moved forward, languidly climbed the stairs, passing couples negotiating prices. Inwardly alarmed at the rising disquiet knotting his stomach, he sidled along the deserted corridor, service pistol in hand, a growing irritation at the lack of attendants who usually patrolled each floor. His eyes darted to the spill of light from under the louvered door to Lomay's boudoir. Sweat poured off him.

Darius sprang soundlessly to one side of the door, listening. In a sudden, knee-jerk action, he kicked in the door, fell to a crouch, gun at ready. Slowly, as his eyes panned the room, he straightened up.

The room was a shambles!

Madmen, turned loose to vandalize and destroy, had reached their objective. Jalousies, torn off their hinges, lay in broken slats on the floor. Feminine garments lay strewn about, shredded to ribbons. Bed and bedspreads slashed, the mattress stabbed randomly; goose down fluttered about in cloudy clusters. The French doll collection lay strewn about, beheaded, dismembered, their porcelain heads, arms, and legs crushed as if by heavy boots. Lomay's perfume bottles lay in broken shards on the floor; their scents combined with acrid hashish turning Darius's stomach.

Darius, gripped by angst, felt light-headed, faint. He gulped air to subdue the nausea. Heading for the secret alcove behind the bed, he touched the control.

Another shock! The room had been stripped bare. All communicating devices—gone! Only that morning . . .

Lomay! Lomay, where are you?

Closing the wall panel, he opted for the photo lab. He dreaded opening it, yet he must. It slid open on contact. Darius recoiled at the ghastly sight. *Karim!* Mother of Christ, Karim! What had they done to him?

Stripped naked, garroted by strips of unfurled negative film, his face lay in a pan of photo developing fluid. Darius couldn't tell—had he been choked by the negative or drowned in the fluid? Did it matter? He was dead, brutally sodomized, bloodied from the hips down, his flesh ripped open by lashes from the bull whip he carried.

The protector was dead! Where was the protected?

Darius closed his eyes at the appalling sight. He sensed his error at once. A steel-muscled arm snaked around his neck from behind and yanked hard. He was being choked, harder . . . harder . . . cutting off his air supply. Someone was trying to kill him. He could not move. He could employ no diversion to distract his obstructor. A wild growl, a victorious grunt from an invisible face, preambled Darius's impending death and echoed vaguely in his bursting head. In a fierce attempt to break the hold, Darius twisted, squirmed, heaved, convulsed, tensed, and relaxed. The concentric circle of thought was fading. Immobilized by a hard punch to his kidney, Darius still managed to jackknife forward, doubling over, the movement dislodging his right hand. He groped for the amulet inside his tunic, tore it off, and, slicing the death's-head over and behind his own head, managed to slash at his assailant's face. Momentarily the grip on him slackened. Darius moved swiftly, breaking the hold on him. He gasped for air. He backed away, holding the amulet menacingly at arm's length. His voice cracked hoarsely. "T-the w-woman! W-where is s-she?"

Hassan's butcher fell against the wall, groping behind him, searching for something to provide backward leverage. He sank to his knees, terrified eyes bulging, fixed in dread on the amulet. Darius kept stabbing the air with the awesome amulet, praying, *Don't fail me now!*

"Gone! She fled, master." The Arab's agate eyes rolling in their incandescent whites shone grotesquely. The assassin was shaking. Somehow he managed to unsheathe a hidden dagger from his arm. He lunged at Darius, slashed fiercely, catching him in the arm. In that instant, Hassan's murderous devil froze in midair. Blood spurted geyserlike from his lips. The savage clutched his throat, gagging, choking, his tongue chewed to shreds as the strychnine took effect. Briefly his expression flashed fear, terror, and awe before he collapsed at Darius's feet. Darius, observing the man in the final throes of death, momentarily caught his breath. Good, the pain was easing up. But wait . . . Clearly this man hadn't ventured to Fatima's alone! Somewhere others sought St. Germaine. Pray God they didn't find her!

He pocketed the amulet, bound his arm with a silk scarf he swept from the floor. *Twice in one day? Did the gods seek to destroy him?* Darius peeled a red garter from a wall peg, slipped it around his arm, securing the scarf. The movement agitated a picture frame. His eyes riveted to it; he moved it gingerly to one side with one finger, then with more impetus. A panel slid open, revealing a cubicle filled with a stack of letters. Darius peered about the room, out the corridor, then quickly retrieved the letters written to Lomay by a Monsieur C. Creneau, postmarked Compiegne, France. Hesitant for a moment, he shoved them into his tunic. He mussed his hair, set his sand goggles into position, and mosied out the door, creeping along the corridor and down the stairs, feigning inebriation. He swaggered to the entrance, saluting those who saluted him. He was one step out the door when suddenly from behind a commotion broke out; bacchanalian cries crashed through the whorehouse, the loud slamming of doors, the sounds of running footsteps. Turning Darius saw four burnoosed Arabs enter from the rear and scale the steps like hooded winged creatures.

He bolted past the Punjabi, crashed through the doors, running wildly in the darkening night haze. He elbowed his way past street whores and hawkers, stopped abruptly at the entrance to the red-light district, searching for the jeep. *Merde! Gone! Stolen! Well, move! Don't just stand here with egg on your face!*

Darius ran toward the mobbed gates of the city. A quarter hour later he caught up to the tail end of the evacuating 13th

Demi-brigade. Lorries, bumper to bumper, turtled along the roads. Coming at him at a fast clip, the weaving headlights of a jeep lighted his way. It was Lucien Pascal.

"Climb aboard, *Capitaine*. I've searched everywhere for you."

Darius complied. In this moment, he wondered why was it that everywhere he went trouble brewed. Pascal was always at his side like some protective force. *Or is it my imagination?* The thoughts ended as Pascal swerved and the jeep careened precariously, then sped back along the sandy road to position itself in the troop train, behind Dutch O'Reilly, who transported a heavily sedated and thickly bandaged Prince Ben-Kassir.

Darius swung over the side of his jeep, ran forward, leaping aboard the first jeep. "How is he?" he asked Delon.

"The best I could do," replied the former physician dubiously.

"I'll be in the rear utility, Delon. If you need me." Darius stepped off the moving utility and trailed back to swing aboard Pascal's jeep.

"Who cut you this time?" asked the observant Pascal, glowering blackly at the bloodied rivulets streaming down Darius's arm.

"It's nothing," Darius insisted, feeling the bulk of Lomay's letters in his tunic. *Where the bloody devil was St. Germaine?*

Operation Sphinx had given up the ghost. This time it was official.

What did the future hold for him? His men?

A cold wind crept over the desert. By midnight the desert stars suspended from the black bowl of night sparkled like chips of ice. Hyenas no longer prowled and snakes sought warmth in the burrows and holes of the High Atlas. From Hassan's camp came the bloodthirsty legions of crack riflemen on fleet-footed Arabians, two hundred strong, galloping swiftly to the outer perimeters of El Bayadh. There was little pomp and ceremony, no flags fluttering in the breeze, no standards bearing colors, only murderous-eyed men with a singular purpose: the destruction of El Bayadh and the German infidels.

Major Hans Hesse's planned duplicity was about to be aborted. For Hesse's failure to keep a promise made in a vainglorious moment, Hassan, with the guidance of the prophet Muhammad, intended to settle the score by feeding the unworthy carcasses of his German enemies to the desert jackals.

Hassan had never encountered German soldiers in military

combat. His direct communication pipeline to the prophet Muhammad and his God Allah had not revealed the dedication or formidable warring skills of the Wehrmacht soldiers. Hassan's had grossly underestimated them. He had compared them to the usual legionnaire recruits at Sidi, who, lacking dedication and honed skills, were repeatedly defeated and humilated by antiquated, highly inferior weapons.

So, Hassan's horsemen surged forward at a swift gallop, moving like sweating, clattering, flame-belching beasts to grind an enemy force into broken flesh and running blood under their pounding feet.

El Bayadh, such as it was after two mortal assaults, was operating under the direct orders of Major Hans Hesse. Had Hesse not learned his lessons well at Sidi, had he not developed insight into the wog mentality and their barbaric warfare, he might not have anticipated Hassan's disfavor and prepared to tactically defend his perimeters against possible onslaught.

Hassan's first charge never paused, nor did it reach for tactics. For two hours, his men charged and hurled grenades, fired automatic rifles with everything they had, but the Germans prevailed.

From his position on a rise of porphyritic boulders overlooking El Bayadh, Hassan discerned the skeletal remains of the fortification, sagging dejectedly in the day's defeat. Torches lit a path outside the walls, where dead bodies had been hurled into freshly dug ditches. Hassan was not aware that these soldiers who returned volley for volley were not defeated men but fresh battalions prepared to fight to the finish with sophisticated weapons. He signaled his horde back to reconnoiter and prepare for more assaults. They came off the craggy boulders yelling savage war cries across the desert floor. Still the Germans prevailed.

Major Hesse stood on the ramparts of the ruined fort, under heavy fire, observing the fine Wehrmacht soldiering resisting Hassan's terrific charges time and again. The belly-deep booms of 88s and rapid machinegun fire split the night with repeated white fire.

Finally, in Hassan's last-ditch effort to bring down the walls of El Bayadh, his forces regrouped; they were exhausted, running short of ammunition, and utterly devastated by German warring strength. Now they thundered over the sand, resisting the heavy fusillades, and charged murderously, hurling grenades, one after another devastating the outpost walls, crumbling them to bits. The assaulting horde swiftly retreated, scattering in the night.

Howling screams of pain on the heels of German curses crashed through Hesse's throat. A grenade, landing inches from where he stood, exploded before he could take cover. Crouched against a stucco wall, screaming in pain as dust and crumbling concrete congested the air, he stared in frozen horror. On the ground lay his bloodied left hand, its fingers, powered by live nerve endings, moving grotesquely.

Hesse regained consciousness aboard a plane flying out of Morocco to Paris. He was told he had decimated Hassan's forces, that the body count outside the fortification had numbered one hundred and twenty. It offered Hesse no balm. Groggy from a heavy morphine injection, he stared in revulsion at the bandaged stump, sick at the sight of the imperfection. *They'll pay for it! By God they'll pay! Hassan, the Legion, and especially you, Captain Bonifacio, will pay!*

The giant transport groaned forward toward a private airstrip runway easing into takeoff position. The fuselage shuddered under the acceleration of its motors and a swift boost of power as it rolled forward lifting into the air. Inside, the huddled legionnaires were shaken by the turbulence; their faces blanched perceptively.

Struck by the incongruity, Darius burst into spontaneous laughter. Their unspoken fear was not to be believed. These warriors and survivors of unholy massacres and diabolic Berber atrocities sat petrified in their seats, knuckles on clenched fists white from tension. Men oriented to blazing guns and crude desert warfare were scared witless of this, their maiden aircraft voyage. This, too, was his first plane trip. How casually he accepted it.

In a sense this flight was the culmination of a painfully frustrating learning process. Once Darius believed he'd joined the Foreign Legion as the result of a logical reasoning process born in a spur of the moment decision on the day he left Corsica. He knew better now. Destiny was leading him to an unknown and uncertain future and he could do nothing to circumvent it. The moment he arrived in Sidi, he knew he'd entered a world of violence, one he'd secretly envisioned for as long as he remembered. It had given him little peace, yet afforded him clear comprehension of an inner compulsion he'd struggled against in his formative years. All his life, it seemed, had been preparation for Sidi bel Abbes and what lay ahead.

Règlement had provided him with priceless objectivity, the ability to detach himself from a situation and examine it without emotional impediments. Mysterious perceptions, surfacing periodically, had forced images upon him of a man he had never met yet knew more intimately than any on earth—Amadeo Zeller.

Who was Amadeo Zeller? Why was he driven to destroy the man?

Darius loathed the disturbing black feelings and memories of this man. He didn't know that by consciously dwelling upon such thoughts, he was drawing closer, like a magnet to a force field, to the thing he anathametized.

Frequently he got the distinct feeling that some despotic contest was about to commence, swollen to larger, more grotesque proportions.

Darius knew something was lacking, something he desperately needed in his life. *What?* He did not know, couldn't describe it, and felt the worse for it.

Sophia's image lingered unbearably in his mind. Darius closed his eyes, dwelled on her face, luxuriating in the images of his beloved.

Oh God! He should have written to Sophia. At least to Dariana! But how could he *after* the deaths of the Corsicans? How?

It was time to open the sealed orders. Darius removed the courier pouch strapped to his body, broke open the NAIS seal and read:

13TH DEMI IN NORWAY UNDER HEAVY AERIAL BOMBARDMENT BY LUFTWAFFE IN FULL RETREAT. PROCEED TO FINAL RENDEZVOUS . . . UNITE WITH BRITISH LION AND FRENCH COMMANDERS. DESTINATION ADVISED ON LANDING . . . ADIEU, *BON CHANCE* . . . H. FURSTENBERG

Chapter Thirty

WAR JOURNAL ENTRIES BY
CAPTAIN DARIUS BONIFACIO
STROKE ON TRENT
June 30, 1940

It was too late! France has fallen, the army collapsed, and the government has bowed in final surrender to Adolf Hitler!

The 13th Demi-brigade of the Foreign Legion stood at attention on the parade field at Trentham Park Camp near the Wales border. Exhausted, rag-tag valiant survivors of Hitler's lethal Panzers, Messerschmidts, and Junkers in the Narvik Operation, dogtailed it back to England by whatever means they could to join us and commiserate with the rest of us from Sidi bel Abbes. The fatigue of defeat solidifies our fear.

Today, the world stood for us, all of us. A never-to-be-forgotten moment in history was in the making. We had gathered here to listen to the only man in the world we believed we could trust. All eyes were on him, our savior, our only hope.

He stood in fierce profile against the gray dawn, tall, powerfully built, uniformed, gold braid and bright buttons glistening in the early lights. The visor of his white forage cap was pulled low over piercing blue eyes.

Brigadier General Charles de Gaulle, instant stimulant

569

to a dispirited battalion of anxious men, made the issue perfectly clear:

"There are now two nations called France; one a vassal of the Nazis, the other free. Which do you prefer to serve?"

The 13th Demi-brigade split. Half the men elected to serve de Gaulle, the others chose Pétain and Vichy France. Decisions followed swiftly. General Marie-Pierre Koenig, from the Norway operation, chose to serve de Gaulle. Colonel Furstenberg and his NAIS forces did likewise. I moved in swiftly behind the colonel with Delilah's Dream. Our orders are to remain in England, receive special commando training by British MI6 before moving on to NATO (North African Theater of Operations). Nothing shall ever be the same for us. In the division, Sidi bel Abbes became Vichy France. The free French will have no home base of operations until France is free of the shadow of the German boot. The world, about to come apart at the seams, will never be the same for any of us.

A brisk knocking on the door interrupted Darius's stream of thought. Startled, he shot a look at his watch; he was late. He crossed the spartan barracks room, opened the door. The messenger confirmed his thoughts. "Beggin' your pahdon, suh, you are requested to depart posthaste to the officer's rec room."

"Thank you, Lieutenant. I was just leaving." Darius closed the door. Back at the desk he capped his fountain pen, closed his notebook, shoved both items into his attaché case, locked it, and placed it in a gray metallic locker, padlocking it. He poured water into a porcelain bowl, washed his face and hands, and, glancing at his image in a mirror over the commode, brushed his hair. He slipped into his dress tunic, a perfect fit miraculously provided him by the quartermaster and, squaring his *kepi* on his head, left the room, closing the door behind him.

Darius saw her from across the crowded recreation room at Briarsbruck, one of those secret training camps that sprang up all over England. Unable to distinguish her rank or company insignia by the uniform she wore, he thought, What did it matter? At stake was the thundering of his heart. He felt an extraordinary breathlessness, a pounding at his temples. He glanced away, then back again, to assure himself she wasn't an apparition.

She wasn't. A casual tumble of hair, the color of fire, spilled from under her visored hat, and twisted into a neat coppery coil at the nape of her neck. A few wispy strands fell fetchingly about the unbuffed face bearing the slightly drugged postcoital drowsiness of a motion picture vamp. She was the most beautiful ghostly creature to ever stand braced over a champagne glass. Pensive viridian eyes, a classical Garboesque beauty without a hint of Garbo's sexual ambiguity; there was, thought Darius, a certain languor in her lips, a suggestion of fatigue—or was it melancholy?—that pulled her features delicately down into a pout. Unable to see the rest of her, Darius imagined her to be as perfect below the shoulders as she was above. Now she was smiling. No—actually laughing, flashing even, white teeth. She wore a bag suspended from a leather strap. It looked as innocuous as a handbag, but it wasn't; it was a compact gas mask. The mask brought home the reality of war. Here, amid a sea of laughing faces, Darius saw remarkable courage in the British, a denial of the circumstance of death facing them.

The orchestra played medleys of romantic French, American, and British music. Slow-dancing couples moving dreamily packed the floor. A generous bar and buffet was manned by bright-eyed, cheery-voiced Red Cross and women's volunteer groups. And all were so bloody optimistic they seemed out of synch with a nation under siege.

"It's the timbre of England, Darius. The subject on everyone's lips is Hitler, his indomitable Panzers and the brilliant tactical Luftwaffe strategy," said Prince Ben-Kassir. "Blitzkrieg and the dreaded Messerschmitts lie across the Channel, but the British will always find time for revelry." He attempted to explain the British mentality. "They are a stouthearted lot."

"Warriors admiring warriors," Darius said, smiling, his eyes searching the crowd for the uniformed woman who had stopped his breathing. The prince, following Darius's line of vision, smiled.

"Excellent taste, dear Darius. I'd say she's got that *fin-de-siècle* disillusionment built into her bone structure, *oui*? Her shoulder slopes into that somewhat fatalistic shrug, yet, let's see—her eyes are direct, challenging, and her lower lip is terribly unsatisfied. Other than that I'd label her exquisite."

Darius wasn't sure why he was startled by the assessment. Perhaps it was too accurate? He turned, astonished.

"I regret the bad timing, *mon capitaine;* unfortunately that passionate jungle kitten must await another time." Youseff's slightly drawn and battered features relaxed into a wan smile. His arm was in a cast supported by a black silk scarf suspended from his neck. He leaned heavily on a handsome lion's-head cane to disguise a noticeable limp. Visual reminders of El Bayadh would dissolve in time, but the internal scars of the massacre of his people and his own near death fired an insatiable lust for vengeance. But that was in the future; at present he was the picture of impeccable British tailoring in his black silk suit, unadorned by anything save a gold pin in his lapel bearing the Ben-Kassir coat of arms. He glanced urgently at his watch. "Come, Darius, we must be off. Time to learn *her* identity later."

Darius, reluctantly compliant, moved with Youseff past the uniformed dancing couples, alive with laughter and seduction. Casting backward glances at the bewitching she-devil aspiring his heart, he craned his neck, kept her in his sights, and trudged along the perimeters of the crowd to the corridor until he lost sight of her.

They stepped through blackout curtains into the ebony folds of night, then boarded the waiting vintage Rolls limousine.

As it lumbered off the compound grounds, heading north, Darius peered out at the stark silhouetted buildings against the moonlight. The compound, unnamed for security reasons, consisted of a ganglia of interconnected buildings housing hundreds of soldiers preparing for war. An unusual camaraderie existed among men, who had come from diverse backgrounds to join in the effort against a common enemy—the Nazis. Both British RAF and Canadian RAF were housed in nearby quarters. A recent tour of the complex had shocked Darius. Radar tracking screens, radio direction finders, critical communications centers were manned by women! Women occupied every position on the post command that relieved men for active duty. "Incredibly, they prove damned efficient and draw astonishing raves from the War Admiralty," Youseff explained.

Youseff's voice hadn't returned in full strength after the surgery to his damaged vocal cords. He hardly spoke above a whisper. "While Hitler plots Britain's annihilation, stouthearted Britishers have reshuffled the Parliament. A new prime minister has replaced the old, Darius. Tonight he will be tested at St. Andrew Hall."

St. Andrew Hall at Marboro. The estate loomed into view, shadowy, vague in the darkness, yet enormous, sprawling, as elegant as a Roman palace. Armed guards carrying battery-operated red torches, official blackout issues in one hand and snarling killer dogs straining against choke chains in the other, lurched forward. Pulled by the canines, deferential British agents checked their credentials and the guards backed off as Darius and Prince Ben-Kassir entered the manor.

An aide led them through a brilliantly lit foyer over harlequin-tiled flooring, along walls covered with numerous dramatically lighted Renaissance oil paintings. They moved past a wide circular staircase through a large mahogany door, carved with lion's-head panels, into a large library and trophy room, carpeted in crimson. The room was filled with priceless antiques, burnished woods, leathers and imperial furbishings. Youseff, limping across the room with unmistakable familiarity, pulled back the drapes on one wall revealing a framed, wide panel of smoked glass. Darius was bewildered. It seemed to serve no functional purpose until Youseff pressed a panel of switches. Instantly the glass was transformed into a window, permitting visibility into a larger salon, actually a conference room, where several stodgy middle-aged men sat around a gleaming oaken table sipping brandy from snifters. Layers of blue-white smoke wafted over them.

"Unfortunately, the minutes of the meeting in that chamber are classified, highly confidential to all but a privileged few," the prince said in that raspy whisper. "Tonight you'll see history in the making." He indicated a nearby table laden with refreshments. "You will honor me by making yourself at home," he said, excusing himself before leaving the room.

Darius reveled in the elaborate scene. Startled somewhat as he recognized the famous men whose names would live in history, he moved closer to the window, scanning the austere faces at the conference table against a background of baronial elegance. Framed strategically on one wall, above the stoic British lion's crest and coat of arms, portraits of the royal family, peering down their majestic noses unmistakably orchestrated the tempo of events as prestigious world-famous statesmen mapped out international diplomacy and warring strategies.

Darius saw Youseff enter the grand room through a door at the far end of the salon. At once the others stood up, bowed deferentially to the prince as he passed. Youseff, leaning on his cane, nodded to them in acknowledgment. He shook hands with a rotund, heavily jowled man smoking the longest black cigar Darius had ever seen and moved on to embrace the uniformed

Brigadier General Charles de Gaulle. He positioned himself at the Frenchman's right.

In Darius's salon, two U.S.A. military officers entered and nodded to him, moved to the display window, at once absorbed in the conference-room activity. Moving slightly to his right, Darius glanced peripherally at the insignia patches on their arms, unable to make them out. The lieutenant spoke to the captain.

"You can tell Kilroy hasn't been here yet."

Both Americans laughed at some private joke. The captain spoke in confidential tones. "The bulldog at the head of the table, giving the stogie hell, is the new prime minister, Churchill. The French uniform is de Gaulle, for whatever that's worth in this inning of the ball game. The black business suit is a North Africa VIP. A sheikh, a prince, or one of those bloody desert chiefs who bats a thousand with these birds. The wog owns St. Andrew Hall, loaned it to the British for the duration. How about them apples?"

The American's hot assessing eyes swept Darius, as if seeing him for the first time. "I'm Captain Brad Lincoln," he said, flashing an ingratiating American smile.

Darius disdained the outthrust hand. Handshakes to Corsicans implied bodily threats and ulterior motives.

Lincoln in mock umbrage, drew back his hand as if he'd touched fire. "Uh—this is Lieutenant Jim Greer."

Greer did not extend his hand. "Interested bystander? Are you French? English? I don't recognize the insignia on your sleeve."

"The uniform is British, the insignia is 13th Demi-brigade, North African Intelligence Service, Foreign Legion, Sidi bel Abbes."

"French Foreign Legion? I didn't think they really existed. Where ya stationed? The Firs? Hampton Hall?" The Americans exchanged secret, playful glances.

"No," said Darius, sensing their mockery. He was not over-joyed at his first encounter with the American military. He coolly scrutinized the solidly built Lincoln, his short crew cut hair and his spanking-new uniform, mirror-polished boots, and shiny buttons. Lieutenant Greer, a ruddy-skinned, craggy-faced man with a thick neck, broad shoulders, and pugnacious Irish-American jawline, was a fascinating study. His jaws were in constant motion. It was Darius's first exposure to the American phenomenon, gum chewing. *Five chews, and a snap-pop without a miss.* Incredible!

Behind their bland, innocent expressions lay deadly personalities. Darius sensed it at once. He had no idea they were American OSS agents. He studied the gold griffin insignia over a red arrow on a blue patch—unmarked U.S. army personnel. Something connected.

"Ah, you are Cloak and Dagger?" His attention trailed back to the conference room.

"Uh—not exactly," Lincoln replied cagily. "I'm at Bletchly Park with John York. You know—Ultra. The lieutenant is with Cloak and Dagger in the Signals Development Branch. Our work is classified. You know, super-secret. Magic and Ultra—that's us."

"Ah, très bien. Parlez-vous français? Je regrette. Je ne comprends pas la langue des États-Unis," Darius muttered.

"Whoa, whoa there. Just a doggone minute, Captain. You're going too fast for me." Brad held up a protesting hand. Greer intervened.

"He wants to know if we *parlez* in his lingo. He claims he doesn't understand the language of the Americans." To Darius, he said, "It is the same—English. You were speaking English, earlier?"

"English, *oui*. But not American idiom. But I shall try. If your work is, uh, super-secret is it not best we do not discuss it, Captain?" Darius's brusque posture and cool words irked the Americans. *Good. Perhaps they would all enjoy a few moments' silence.*

Darius's interest centered on a young, well-dressed woman entering the adjoining conference room. She wore a tailored two-piece brown suit; her blond hair, pulled back severely from a remarkably beautiful and poignantly familiar face, formed a thick coil at her neck. Her vaguely mannish shoulders and tough-cookie eyes telegraphed a brisk, brassy beauty free of nuisance emotions like affection, appetite, and desire.

Instantly the men at the table rose to their feet, affording her defference and every courtesy. As she moved to the empty seat at de Gaulle's left, Darius gasped aloud in recognition.

It was too late! Too late to conceal his reaction from the Americans. Captain Lincoln slickly maneuvered Darius on the spot. "You are acquainted with the young woman, Captain?"

"No," he lied. "For a moment, she seemed familiar, but no, she is a stranger to me." He loathed questions, especially from strangers.

Lincoln didn't buy the lame answer. "You don't, eh? That's

odd. NAIS, you said. And you don't recognize your own Mata Hari?'' Both Lincoln and Greer tensed. "I find it peculiar, don't you, Lieutenant?'' They thrust mental jibes at Darius, unaware they were attempting to corner a fox. She's a French espionage agent, Captain. The best goddamned spy in NAIS. So how come *you* don't know her? Suppose you show me your credentials, Captain Boneface—''

"*Bonifacio*.'' Darius corrected the steely eyed American, glancing scathingly at both. In his most impeccable English he asked, reservedly "What reason have I to prove myself to you? Perhaps it is more fitting I should request *your* credentials?''

"No sweat.'' Lincoln brandished his ID. "Now, *yours,* Captain, uh, *Bonifacio*—you did say Bonifacio? Fair's fair. I just passed the ball to you.''

The moment for Darius was irresistible. He held himself in check, studied the outthrust ID with Dali Llama inscrutability. "What means these initials, OSS?''

"Same as yours, only we don't spell it out for the enemy. Office of Strategic Services is more palatable than Office of Espionage or spies and all that rot. Wouldn't you say, old chap?''

The old chap wouldn't say. Revolted by the patronizing tone, confounded by the brassy Americans he inserted a verbal blade. "Did I miss something en route to England? Is the U.S.A. at war? Or does your government no longer believe in *laissez-faire*?''

"America, for your edification, believes in being prepared. We're a young and curious nation, see? If we go skinny-dipping with strangers, we gotta know who's gonna be looking up our arses. And if we, unfortunately, get into water over our heads we gotta make sure all the life-saving equipment works, see?''

Darius shook his head in bewilderment. "If I understood one solitary word you spoke—''

"Setting aside American idiom, why do you pretend not to know Zahara?''

"You are a stranger to me, Captain, not even an ally. Explain to me, *s'il vous plaît,* why I should discuss such sensitive matters openly, here, with you and your companion?''

Lincoln gestured negligibly. "Of course. I stand corrected. Rather dolty of me.'' He turned from Darius and, peering through the window, muttered to Greer. "Were you briefed on Zahara? It's a well-kept secret that . . .''

Darius's dislike of the outspoken, hard-nosed, outrageous and certainly uncircumspect Brad Lincoln escalated by leaps and bound. So undisciplined an officer whose inquisitorial nature lacked the usual discretion could present dangers unless . . . Could it be a ploy of sorts? Yet, to speak openly of Zahara, disclosing her position with NAIS, presented a thorny problem. *I could be a German spy for all they knew.*

In the conference room Prince Ben-Kassir rose to his feet. St. Germaine moved swiftly to his side. Reflecting a bohemian androgyny she grasped her portmanteau and, poised regally, walked with Youseff out of chambers. Darius noted the interest the Americans displayed at the couple, the exchange of silent, knowing glances.

"Well, what have we here, ole buddy?" Lincoln muttered. Brad's sudden volte face disconcerted Greer. Why had he lost control before this French legionnaire?

There was a knock at the door. A British military aide entered, saluted the room's occupants, and addressed Darius. "Captain Bonifacio, His Highness is prepared to leave." Lincoln's brow shot up in annoyance.

The aide was unceremoniously shoved aside as St. Germaine swept grandly into the room, her perfume scenting the air before her. "Darius! *Mon cher ami.*" She flung herself into his arms, uttering a profusion of French endearments and trying as she did—in rapid French mixed with Farsi—to bridge the gap between her exodus from Sidi and her arrival in London. Darius, stunned at the changes, could not be done with staring at her.

St. Germaine, suddenly aware of the Americans, subdued her exuberance. Sensing the Americans' censure, Darius introduced them, taking special care not to address her by name. "This is Captain Lincoln and Lieutenant Greer, *ma chère.* Both Americans."

St. Germaine's face lit up in cordial recognition. "Ah, *très bien. Vous êtes Cain and Abel, oui?* You are Cain and Abel, yes? We are to rendezvous in a few days, *mes amis?*"

Darius glanced from one to the other, thunderstruck. Youseff stepped inside impatient at the delay. He nodded to the Americans, listened a moment in silence.

"That's right, ma'am. It is a pleasure. We consider it the capstone of our career to be working with the incomparable Zahara."

"And I with Cain and Abel. Your reputations precede you."

Darius, disquieted by these superficial accolades, retreated slightly from the circle. And Youseff sensing his oblique disenchantment, eased into the room. "It is well you met today, soon there shall be a joint venture, Darius. Recall your theory concerning Hitler's reluctance to wage war on two fronts?" Darius nodded. "*Alors*, according to the blokes at Bletchly Park who broke the *Ultra Code*, it is only a matter of time before the Germans open a second front. The prime minister has an accurate picture of German strategy; they are now preparing operation Barbarossa, a Russian offense."

"I don't think Captain Bonifacio trusts us," Greer said.

"Captain Bonifacio has sufficient reason not to trust anyone," the prince retorted defensively, his eyes growing distant.

"Well, cheerio, blokes," St. Germaine muttered to the Americans in a fair facsimile of Cockney. She slipped one hand through Darius's arm and guided Youseff to the door. They moved out the room, chattering like bluejays. Darius paused, called to the Americans,

"*S'il vous plaît, Capitaine*. Who is this *Kilroy* you spoke of?"

The American officers conveyed their amusement. "Top American super-secret, Captain."

It was their first encounter; it would *not* be their last.

Darius had no way of knowing how inextricably bound together would be their lives. That his past would one day become a part of their future was inconceivable to him. That their future and the future of mankind would one day rest in the palm of Darius's hand was so remote he could lend it no shred of credibility. What he knew at this moment, and was forced to focus on, was the reason for his dislike of the Americans.

Chapter Thirty-one

Valentina Carter Valdez Varga. An American volunteer to the British war effort held a unique position as the personal driver of General Marie-Pierre Koenig of the "Free French" army. Darius's initial encounter with Valentina, arranged by Prince Ben-Kassir, instantly galvanic, struck them both with the impact of an exploding meteor in midsky. Her beauty, far more compelling at close proximity, overwhelmed Darius. The sound of her husky voice, the touch of her slender white hand sent his heart pounding.

He somberly regarded her and the impact she had on him, the first time they slow-danced on the crowded floor of Briarsbruck officer's rec room to the dreamy refrains . . .

Kiss me once and kiss me twice and kiss me once again . . .

Darius knew he wanted to kiss Valentina more than drawing his next breath. He held her closer, inhaling her sweet fragrance, trying to still his wildly beating heart. Her lassitude, he discovered was more a sensuous affair. The tristful fatigue he detected in her at first sight carried a needy, expressful force which she demonstrated subtly.

It was crazy! Their first meeting and what followed . . .

During the first four weeks, his involvement in intensive commando training permitted him no leaves of absence. After that he was free four nights a week. While British and Free

French warring moguls plotted strategy for the North African Campaign, Lieutenant Varga arranged her schedule to be with Darius each of those four nights. Other women—nurses, ambulance drivers, clericals—at Briarsbruck used every feline trick to lure him from Valentina. Darius paid them no attention. For him, only Valentina existed. Their love swelled to uncontrollable passion. His sexual exigency, her willing desire, fired daily by their secret thoughts sought expression—and it had to be soon.

Their first kiss—it was as if they'd been eternal lovers. From the first they complemented one another in a thousand ways. She *knew* when his silence meant nothing but blissful contentment and when it meant preoccupation with something unrelated to her. And Darius's heart melted by her soft affection and warm outpouring of love. Valentina was filling the void he'd felt all his life and couldn't identify until she entered his life.

Then it came—his first weekend leave.

In a veil of rhapsodic joy they motored out of London to Dover and leased a cottage on the legendary "white cliffs" overlooking a vast sea. The magnificent, soul-inspiring scenery evoked in Darius the urge to rave over Corsica's natural splendors. He described *Les Calanches,* the phantasmagorical gorges, and mysterious floral-filled *maquis*—aware suddenly he was homesick.

But he was also in love! So ecstatically in love he could think of nothing and no one save Valentina Varga. The couple saw the seashore and other panorama on their arrival and departure. In between they clung to each other in rapturous embrace, loath to part.

To Darius, Valentina was stunningly provocative, utterly feminine with firm, high breasts, full, delicately hued as the finest porcelain, but much softer. It was incredible what love they felt. If this was love—God on high had given them a taste of paradise.

They spent the first night moving up and down and around each other until their bodies found the proper fit, contorting, moving in concert to a mysterious symphony playing in their minds. Neither took time to think. They wanted only to feel, create memories, leave imprints of themselves upon the other for eternity. Their kisses were deep, soulful, demanding, She beseeched his body with trembling exploratory hands. Her rosy-hued nipples stood hard and erect under his touch; her body quivered like violin strings at the slightest provocation. And each time he made love to her, prolonged her orgasm, coaxing her to the heights of ecstasy, she trembled and her flesh stood on edge. Darius worried that he might be too large for her fragile body. She laughed, insisting she was far more durable than her appearance suggested. She wanted Darius and made no effort to disguise her desire. She had known from the first time she looked at him that he would be perfect for her. To think, she'd traveled halfway around the world to find him.

All Darius could think of was the intensity of his need and desire for her. Their first mating had been so fierce, so explosive and sensuous, he hadn't realized until much later she wasn't a virgin.

Somehow it didn't matter. So much for tradition.

What a woman! She was to Darius an irresistible thunderstorm of golden, silvery lights, moist as a blood rose on a dewy morning. She orchestrated personal colors that made sensational noises until he realized it was his tumultuous blood thrumming through his head that left him breathless and wanting. His whole world was revolving around him like a magic carpet upon which he couldn't get a foothold. He was possessed by Valentina Varga and was certain she felt as he did. Silence enfolded her like a gypsy moth. He'd watch her lying sensuously on the bed, her hands guiding his, currents passed through her like shuddering ripples in a stream of brook trout, his body had never felt as alive, afire with urgency.

And then . . .

Odd how magic turns against itself, how reality wipes out an eternity of magic. And you wonder, did it exist at all? For how long? At some point their passion became catharsis a purging of their souls, but Darius got the distinct impression it barely touched Valentina's mind. Strange . . . how strangely this woman warded off tenderness. She gave freely of her body, her lips, her love, but withheld her immutable mind. She reminded him of a hermit who compels you into the wilderness to keep him company but refuses to impart the wonders of the wild. Moments after coupling, Valentina resumed a cold, statuesque beauty, an imperturbability that erected barriers between them, and these barriers disturbed Darius as much as he failed to understand them. Valentina it seemed saw out the corner of her mind's eye all day long; it was nerve-wracking and a bit frustrating to him. Yet just as quickly, something throbbed from her, absolutely galvanizing him, rippling into his blood, and he couldn't do without her.

Very well, she wasn't a virgin, but it no longer mattered. What mattered were her words—*words*! It began between moments of their lovemaking, while they were seated cozily before a fire, munching something unique to Darius called a sandwich. Slices of cheese, roast beef, a dash of mustard piled between two slices of bread—a tasty, convenient treat.

Valentina asked, "How much longer will you be in England?"

"I don't know. Please, let's not think of separation. Our time together means a great deal to me. Truly you are enchanted." He said lovingly, "You've spun witchcraft on me."

"Nonsense, we Americans don't believe in esoteric whimsy."

Darius flinched slightly as if he'd been reprimanded for baring his soul. He refused to retreat. "How practical are Americans in matters of the heart?"

"Sensible. Quite sensible, I believe." Valentina found herself saying things she'd had no intention of saying, as if an alien voice within her deliberately incited her to push Darius from her despite her desire for him. She failed to understand what was happening; she knew only she was being flippant and crass. "What is it you want? A mistress? An arrangement of sorts while you're here? Four times a week for as long as you remain in England?"

Darius was offended. She saw it immediately. "Do you realize how much like a retailed affair you are making our love?" He stared at her. The glow of the fire had turned her skin and hair to golden copper. Her hair fell around her shoulders like iridescent threads of golden fire. He whispered huskily, "Valentina, have I done anything to offend you? Said anything that deserves this reaction?"

She shook her head. "It's just that you are offering me the whole world when all I want is a thin slice. Can you understand?"

"No. I offer you three, perhaps four weeks of my life—that's all I have to offer—and you call it the world?"

"I'll be yours as long as you want me. The question is how do you want me? On call? On a moment's notice? To be available only when you are available?" A sudden vagueness dulled her eyes.

"Valentina! What's wrong? Why do you talk like a cheap—"

"*Whore!* Go ahead, say it. You think it because I'm not a virgin, so speak it! *My love is a whore.* It's easy."

"*Mon Dieu, chérie!* I said nothing." His confusion was total.

"It's in your eyes. I sensed it the moment you penetrated me without difficulty. You condemned me without trial or jury."

"Do most Americans think as you?"

"Don't most men?"

"I do not consult with men. I am neither a compiler of data nor an interrogator of sexual matters. Oh, *merde*! Tell me how we arrived at such a point from where we began?"

"I'm not promiscuous, Darius. But tell me, will you be *fucking* anyone other than me while we are together here?"

The word *fuck* amused him. Years later he'd remember that Americans had introduced the word to Europe, in World War II along with nylons, chocolate bars and Coca Cola. *Fuck* covered a thousand situations and emotions no other word could. Europe would be grateful for it one day. At the moment, Darius asked her to explain. She did. He replied. "I can't imagine wanting anyone after you."

"That's easy to say in the afterglow of an affair."

"Could you be mine? All mine, Valentina?" He could make no commitments, not now.

"I have not been with a man as I have been with you. Can it be any better with another?"

Momentarily outraged, Darius stared at her, wondering, was she being facetious, playing games with him? Before he could decide, she compounded the anger mounting in him.

"Very well, Darius. I shall be your mistress if you promise not to be sentimental. You Corsicans are a tender-hearted lot with your women. You kiss one and think you're in love. I thought only Americans suffered those delusions."

Awash on an icy floe he said coolly, "I suggest we motor back to London."

Valentina moved across the floor to him, snuggled her head against his heart. "Don't be cross. I don't know how to be with men." She traced the shape of his stern lips with her fingertip, stroked his face, cupped it between both hands, kissed him lingeringly. He melted. "I never knew my father. He died before I was born. My mother met him in Spain during revolution. Bound together by a marriage contract . . ." She told him the love story of Victoria Valdez and Francisco de la Varga. "I don't know all the details only that it left Mother sad, embittered and sparked with fires of retaliation."

Darius shot her a probing look. Something indefinable stirred in the deep recesses of his brain. As quickly his libidinous nature took over.

"She never remarried. She still makes daily entries into her diary, after all these years. What I'm trying to say is I don't want to emulate my mother, live in the past with only memories to comfort me. Can you understand?"

Darius barely heard her words. The urgency of her need for love took over. Holding Darius for dear life, she slid her legs over his thighs, up and around, gripping his hips to take all of him. Valentina lay back working the muscles of her vagina, squeezing his penis inside her gently until he was left gasping at the exquisite sensations. It was an escalation of pleasure point to pleasure point until they reached the pinnacle where retreat became impossible without release.

Engulfed in a lethargic aftermath of orgasm, Valentina blinked, her eyes inscrutable. Pursued all her life by a vague sense of menace, she lit a cigarette and wondered what was this thing inside this black-widow spider behavior? What compelled her to annihilate the love she needed desperately?

I know precisely what I say and do when I say and do those things that alienate, but why am I unable to abort the words or understand the forces compelling me toward those ends?

Now, more than ever in her life, she needed the love of this strange Corsican, but she had alienated him. Nothing she could say or do would ever erase the spoken word! She shivered.

A gusting wind fell on southeast England, and Valentina, feeling chilled to the bones, felt the need of air. She dressed in slacks, a sweater, and scarf, and leaving Darius sleeping slipped out the door. She walked over the rocky cliffs, gazing at the billowing gray slate clouds hanging heavily against the Straits of Dover. She stood still for a time, gazing across the Channel, mesmerized by nothing she could define, but suddenly on this July 10, she felt an unendurable chill. For no reason, save she couldn't bear being apart from Darius, even for a moment, she returned to the cottage, still gripped in an icy paralysis. Darius was still asleep. Quietly, she boiled water, steeped a pot of tea. The chill lingered even after two cups of the strong brew, laced with a jigger of brandy. She felt incapable of dispelling the frost in her bones and in her spirit.

Valentina lit the prepared kindling for a fire and sat in a cozy chair wrapped in a down comforter content to feast her eyes on Darius. Her eyes traced every fine line and scar on his body, his full lips and stern jawline, committing him to memory like an inspired artist who might never again set eyes on his subject.

She fought to maintain her usual cool indifference. Never in her life had she felt so secure, yet thoroughly frightened. The love she felt was both demon and angel, pushing, pulling. She didn't want to be a disappointment to Darius so he could easily dismiss her from his life. What could she do to hold him, when the demon pushed him away?

Time, the bitterest of enemies for lovers had run out. The witching hour was over. It was time to don the masks again and rejoin the mad charades of a world gone crazy. They dressed in silence, both in British army uniforms, their arm patches indicating their branch of the Free French service and, taking a lingering last look around the quiet cottage where they had coupled in love, prepared to depart.

Valentina felt it first. Darius shouted, "*Mon Dieu!* See—the cupboard is shaking! What is it? What's happening?"

A distant roar of thunder unlike anything they'd ever heard brought a wondrous angst to their eyes. Swiftly, they ran outside.

"In the sky!" Val shouted, shading her eyes. "In the direction of Calais!"

A guard escort of six Hurricane fighters tagged a moving convoy steaming westward from the Thames estuary. "Look, Darius! Coming from France! Oh, God! It's begun in earnest!"

Darius spotted the concentration of enemy planes. He'd heard from the men in the 13th Demi how the Luftwaffe had pulverized them in Norway, but observing the magnificent Messerschmitts and Junkers in action was an awesome sight. Seeing an actual dogfight set him aquiver with anticipation. The sky blackened with aircraft.

Seventy, or was it eighty German planes against six Hurricanes? It spelled suicide for the RAF fighters! But wait . . . it wasn't six! Swarms of Hurricanes and Spitfires from surrounding Squadron HDQS shot into the sky. They came, piercing silver-lined clouds, scrambling to the rendezvous over the Straits of Dover.

The battle lasted thirty minutes. Darius didn't learn the statistics until he returned to Briarsbruck. One ship from the convoy was sunk; the enemy lost four fighters, the British three. But that day, as he watched he sensed a peculiar strategy born in German minds. The more aircraft Germany could entice into the skies, the sooner the RAF would be crippled. The Luftwaffe outnumbered the RAF by an enormously wide margin.

He and Valentina drove back to London in protracted silence.

"They came down on us from behind the clouds like ruddy thunderbolts," she said at last. "I shall never forget the sight of those Spitfires bursting into flames in midair. You bloody well don't stand a chance in aerial combat, do you?"

"Only when skills are matched," he replied solemnly. "Bear in mind, Val, the Germans' killer capabilities were sharpened in areas of real combat, not in exercises or war games. Those German pilots we saw were part of the Condor Legion, which contributed to Franco's victory in Spain. Each is trained to make the best use of sun, clouds, and sky as well as an enemy's weakness." As he spoke Darius was storing his observations for future use. *What a formidable lot, the Luftwaffe!*

"Darius, did you ever get the feeling that God is a clock, ticking away minutes, hours, days, months, years, a lifetime. We are lucky only if we manage to see His face without the dial, without hearing the ticking sounds."

Darius took his eyes off the wheel for a second, stared at her profile, then flashed on the narrow, dangerous road again. He made no comment. Valentina Varga was the strangest young woman he'd ever met. She laughed with a discerned tenderness. He had witnessed and tasted the burning passion lying beneath the cool porcelain exterior. Absent from her character was the insufferable superiority of the intellectual and the very wealthy. How many sides to this wench had he seen? How many lay shielded by impenetrable walls? Still, he returned to London this day feeling he didn't know her at all. Her complexities, like his own, drove deep without end.

Darius wasn't certain what it was—this thing between them. The fact was he cared deeply and made no attempt to conceal it. It was in his eyes, gestures, words. Everything about Valentina, despite the alienation she advanced aroused a poignant tenderness in him. Before they parted that day, Darius cautioned, "You know what to do if the Germans invade us, here, *chérie*. Promise you'll be circumspect in all you do."

Valentina alighted from the auto before the barracks compound, saluted him, reciting by rote, "*What do I do if the Germans have landed?* I remember this is the moment to act like a soldier. I do not panic. I stay put. I say to myself, 'Our chaps will deal with them.' I do not say, 'I must get out of here.' Fighting men must have clear roads. I do not take to the road, not on bicycle, not on foot, nor in a car. Whether at work or at home, I stay bloody well put!'' Before Darius heaved a relieved sigh to indicate his satisfaction, she laughed at him. ''Good grief! Have you bloody well forgotten that I am one of *our chaps*, along with you?''

He hadn't forgotten, but he flushed crimson, and gunned the motor, fishtailing the utility out of sight. He didn't know her at all!

Some weeks later on August 28, Valentina, panic stricken, rushed out of London in a speeding utility en route to a secret air field. Confusion and bedlam greeted her. She broke through the thick lines of uniformed Tommies weighted by full gear and through the supply trains being loaded into the belly of large army transports, searching in every direction for Darius. Finally, in an area dimly washed by a minimum of blackout lights she spotted Darius's plane, its passengers boarding. Darius, lingering behind, searching the murky, vaporous fog banks, finally caught sight of her. Breaking away from the others, he ran to her and, gathering her into his arms, swung her about, raining kisses on her face. Brushing a few truant tears from her cheeks, he asked softly, ''Will you ever remember me?''

''You ask that *after* Dover?''

''Valentina, Valentina, will I ever understand you?'' He wanted desperately to bare his soul, describe the extent of his feelings. Forced into the likelihood of suffering the humiliation of rejection after the Dover fiasco, he said firmly, ''Don't mistake intimacy for love.''

Aware of the instant rebuke in his eyes, as if she'd been slapped hard into a stunning awakening, Valentina backed off, saluted him smartly. He returned the salute as if they were strangers. What were they at this point in time, was but what the world had made of them—actors on a stage. And the curtains had just rung down on the first act. Only God and global affairs could predict a second or third act . . . if any.

Darius boarded the transport. Valentina, barely visible in the enveloping darkness, watched the enormous transport taxi into position, then move along the runway, lifting off, airborne. Some way, somehow, I'll make a future together, she told herself, ignoring a blinding veil of tears.

''The enemy of my father, Abd el-Krim, has just declared himself a Vichy loyalist, Darius.'' Youseff, dressed in his smart

Free-French brigadier-general uniform, sipped black coffee from a thermos.

Darius, buckled into his seat in the transport's fuselage, glanced sharply at Youseff, mentally calculating the grave problems this simple statement caused for him. The prince sighed despairingly.

"Yes, yes, I know what you are thinking. It is undeniably stupid to sit here and pretend the risks are minimal."

"Not exactly. God knows I was there too. I am aware of your limited powers since the armistice, Youseff. What has Abd el-Krim to offer Hassan?"

"Hassan? Ah, if it were only Hassan, the situation would pose far less perils. You recall I told you Krim was exiled to Madagascar in 1933? Well, *mon ami*, through Vichy intervention, German and Italian espionage agents arrived at and departed from the Krim palace, plotting ways to twist that desert serpent's complex interests to their advantage. Krim's sons are both in St. Cyr learning to be Vichy French officers, and the enemy of Free France, *my* enemy, resides on the Riviera in grand opulence, closer to me now, plotting with the hyena, Hassan, my annihilation and my people. If I sound bitter, I am. My memories are all blotted with blood, and a terrible sense of loss."

"Don't go back, Youseff. Come with us. Create new memories, a life."

Youseff's eyes lit up for a brief second. Just as quickly the flame dimmed. "Hassan and Krim must pay for what they did. It's that simple. Enough of my woes. What burdens you so heavily?"

What burdens me so heavily? A life, not of my choosing, explodes and falls down around my shoulders, drawing me like quicksand into a grave uncertainty and I advise Youseff to create new memories, another life?

Darius patted the back of Youseff's hand affectionately. "What can I do to help? You have only to request my services from Colonel Furstenberg—or have matters changed in the last twenty-four hours? He is still my superior officer, I take it?"

"Henri's a good man. Don't censure him for what occurred following the Ksar el Boukhar massacre. His compassion, understanding, and loyalties are not skin deep. Not all Germans are Nazis like Von Luden and the others. It's time you know what motivates that iceberg personality."

Darius had no choice. Youseff's narration commenced without preamble.

"It happened at *Djebel Baddou*, a natural fortress in the High Atlas. A desert chieftain, Ouskounti, prepared to defy, with two thousand warriors, a modern-day army of twenty-five hundred men. French intelligence officers regarded the fortress as impregnable; neither ground shelling nor aerial bombing could reach the rebels inside the honeycombed caves. They were right. Yet, the French persisted in the futile effort, perplexing the devil out of Henri. He was only a captain then; his word carried little weight. . . . Two columns of soldiers, led by Henri, proceeded, with daring, to climb six-thousand-foot peaks in a foolish attempt to overcome the enemy. The officers fell at once, picked off by sharp-shooting snipers. Furious at the situation, Henri, with daring bravado, indifferent to death and danger, demonstrated a bravery that became legend at Sidi and in North Africa. He ran forward in a crouch position, hurling grenades at the Berbers, only to be pounced upon by marauders lying in ambush behind stone parapets. He was shot, mutilated, left to die."

"Mutilated?" Darius held his thermos in midair. "In what way?" he asked naively.

Youseff gestured animatedly. Darius flushed crimson at the revelation. "His manhood was taken from him, an event that no doubt hastened his wife's suicide. My father found Henri, transported him back to the post command for surgery. In the interim, French and Spanish forces annihilated Ouskounti and his forces by outwaiting them, until their need for food and water drove them from the cave sanctuaries, forcing their surrender."

Darius shook his head balefully. "And still the *fucking* war continues! Did they learn nothing from their errors?"

"As a matter fact, yes, Henri reviewed the Foreign Legion's battle tactics during his convalescence. *Djebel Baddou*, historically logged as an exercise in futility, taught him, at the price of his manhood, a bitter lesson and a profound respect for essential intelligence gathering. Henri made NAIS what it is today." Youseff snorted, and a tinge of irony crept into his words. "In light of its present shaky condition, it hardly seems worth the effort, eh, mon bon ami?"

Darius mulled over the revelation in silence. Below, Cairo airport was in their sights. He peered out the hatch window, unprepared for Youseff's next remark.

"Allah willing, Darius, at war's end Lomay shall become my princess."

Darius expressed his delight reservedly. "She is an exceptional woman, Youseff. May Allah grant you both the secret desires of your hearts. But in earnest, she is treading dangerous waters."

Youseff was exasperated. "My attempt to dissuade her from taking so active a part in the Resistance failed sorely. Her determination as admirable but foolhardy. Darius, if you would speak to her—"

Darius laughingly wagged his finger at him, citing his own failure to dissuade Valentina from the career she chose to pursue. "Headstrong women are a contentious lot."

Nearly an hour later Darius stood in the balmy Cairo night bidding Youseff *adieu*. The prince boarded a chauffeur-driven limousine provided by the Egyptian and British High Command. Youseff, in exile since Vichy France occupied Algeria, headed for his secret villa near Alexandria, assuring Darius they'd catch up in the war soon enough. Each saluted the other snappily in parting.

Darius had purposely declined discussing Lomay St. Germaine with Youseff. The day following their encounter at the secret mansion Darius visited St. Germaine in her suite at the Dorchester to deliver the packet of letters she'd left behind at Fatima's. If he hadn't noted her ashen features, he might have thought he'd been euchered into delivering the parcel. St. Germaine recovered admirably over tea and in a voice swollen with the backwash of shock, hesitantly posed the question she could barely whisper. "Did you read the contents, Darius?"

"I'd be a blatant liar if I denied doing so. You were no place to be found. I hoped the contents might clue me to your whereabouts. In addition, *chérie*, if I must serve as courier, it was only fitting that I insure that I was carrying no state secrets."

"State secrets? *Mon Dieu*! You transported explosives!" St. Germaine's hand had darted to her heaving breast, her eyes lowering demurely. Then, half whispering, half afraid to form the words, she finally asked, "Do you—is it your intent to discuss the contents with anyone? I mean, anyone special?"

"If you wish me to forget the contents, it is done."

She had flung her arms around his neck, a torrent of tears spilling down her cheeks, as if her life was instantly out of jeopardy. "It would serve no purpose if the world learned the truth, Darius. It might bring harm to a very great man, destroy his credibility at a time a very desperate nation needs him.''

Darius had understood and sagaciously agreed with her assessment. What purpose would be served if the world were to learn that the mysterious Monsieur Creneau was Lomay's real father?

Chapter Thirty-two

DARIUS'S WAR JOURNAL ENTRIES
PORT TAUFIQ, EGYPT
November 10, 1940

If Sidi is called the sink of the world, the Limey's irreverent, yet quite correct description of this place, is "the arsehole of the Suez." The air is black with flies, the area polluted with every foul stench imaginable and the scum-studded harbor lies sweltering in a breathless heat like a surface of simmering water. Despite this, the port reeks with a curious, unbearable excitement. You'd think the soldiers landing here and those on permanent duty were going on lifelong leaves, not to their deaths in the heat of battle. They are actually filled with unmistakable euphoria. The Italian entry into the war has effectively closed down the Mediterrean to all merchant shipping on the Suez run, and convoys to the Middle East are forced to make the long haul around the South African Cape. The port is crammed with all types of installations—quays, cranes, lighters. However hoplessly inadequate, it is still the repository for enormous numbers of troops, thousands of guns, tanks and other warring vehicles, always in constant motion. Across the bay the burnt out hulks of several converted troopers bore witness to the successful Italian bombing attacks on the port. When I first spotted the armed merchant cruiser requisitioned by the British Admiralty to convey the SAS

592

commandos to me, I found it incredible that they had made it! The twenty year old hulk, barely able to do 17 knots, reconverted to a trooper and ˙˙cated to the RAF carried a small permanent staff of ojjicers and NCOs responsible for the embarkation, billeting and discipline of all troops and special detachments aboard ship to whatever service they belonged. This British mentality is crazy! The buildup of the British Desert Army under Churchill's incessant drive, coupled with the long delays imposed by the bloody slow sea journey around the Cape have created hectic delays. Will we ever catch up with the German timetable? Two dozen key men, trained impeccably for commando warfare, are special men who should have flown to Cairo with me! When I caught sight of the Georgic steaming into port I was elated. When I saw my men up close after several hours delay, finally cleared by the Billeting Officers, and heard a long list of grouses, concerning foul quarters, limited fresh water, slow ration fatigues, poor ventilation, the intense heat, and biting cold—my dismay communicated itself to them and I commiserated. Why the bloody blue devil train these men to razor-edge physical and mental prowess, then subject them to a month's debilitation? Once we were together, their complaints ceased. Immediately I conveyed the men by lorry over the scorching sands to Cairo and a few days' respite before shipping off to our destination. I listened to their varied experiences, en route to the Suez. The most harrowing were their near encounters with U-boats operating in wolf packs near Gibraltar.

CAIRO, EGYPT
November 15, 1940

We lunched on the open terrace of Shepherd's Hotel. Delon, Mandel, Pascal, and O'Reilly grow impatient. After four days of rest, their energies back, the incipient vestige of relaxation rapidly vanishing in the expectation of orders, they began an amusing guessing game, selecting, among the proliferation of espionage agents, those preparing to out-cloak-and-dagger the competition. Our timetable leaves us little time to enjoy the tourist traps. My desire to see the *crumbled ear on the Great Sphinx reputedly shattered by Napoleon's cannon, must wait. The sight of so many strange troops staggers us. British global warring forces! My, what a colorful tour de force.*

Regally garbed Indian Sappers, Australians, New Zealanders with handsome slouch hats, South Africans serving His Majesty's government are everywhere! Soldiers from wherever His Majesty's royal arse had sat are descending on Cairo in force to be dispersed to the fighting zones. During lunch, there came from across the desert the wailing artillery fire and the booming of great guns as the British army sent up practice rounds. We paused in conversation, listening. The men frowned as the reality of war moved in closer to us.

Delilah's Dream has been fully integrated into the British Eighth Army. We wear British uniforms—khaki shorts and ghutrahs on our heads. We are now called the SAS commandos (Special Air Service). Originally the SAS were composed of paratroopers—hence the name—now we are a ground-based force. We are specialists trained to wreak havoc on enemy fortifications slither about at night, performing a wide variety of tricks. If pursued, we fade into the desert, unable to be tracked or destroyed. The risks are incredibly high. As their commander I am exceedingly proud of my men and their accomplishments. I hold high expectations for them. In the past the desert has been midwife, wetnurse, and mistress to them. At Sidi bel Abbes we weathered the fiery side of hell. Soon, very soon we shall be put to the test.

Captain Darius Bonifacio supervised the loading of his men onto a train and sat at the rear of the car, on an endless spur track en route to Syria. Delon had told him he'd seen Lieutenant Valentina Varga before they left. Now Darius regarded her. Smitten by her, amused, thrilled and bedazzled by her sensuous body and vulnerability, he was also confounded by her peculiar dilettante behavior at Dover. He had deliberately refrained from seeing her; then when orders arrived announcing his departure from England, he was irresistibly led to call her base headquarters. Darius pondered. Had he detected a change in Valentina? Her parting words still echoed in his mind. "Without you, Darius, I feel as empty as a walnut with its insides gone." How could anyone feel that empty? His mind had constantly wandered back to her and those idyllic, yet strange days spent at Dover. If only they understood each other, they could share rapturous love. The differences in their culture—she American, he Corsican—seemed monumental, unbridgeable. Something about her, a vulnerability he was unable to resist screamed at him, demanding love, then as quickly another side of her personality shut him out. He didn't understand. And lacking understanding of so complex a personality, he poured every energy into his work.

December 10–30, 1940

How is it possible to describe what is in the hearts and minds of the homeless Free-French recruits integrated into the British Eighth Army? For the past four months before our arrival, continuous war was waged against the Italians at Kassala, the forts of Montecullo, Umberto, and Massawa. We, all of us, are war machines pointed at an unknown enemy in a land where nature combats us with far more efficient and deadly elements. Malaria runs rampant, yellow fever, and constant undiagnosed afflictions plague the soldiers. Beyond Deir Ali, near Damascus, the Free French met their brothers of the Vichy army, fighting with the Nazi forces. Deeply rooted feelings sprang to life and commotion ensued. "Are you Vichy or Free French?" came the cries before they fired the coup de grace. " 'The Marseillaise' is our song too!" came the anguished cries. From across the sands came the cacophony of music, refrains of the "Horst Wessel Lied," the official Nazi song. Instantly the Free-French band struck up a heated rendition of "The Marseillaise." For a time it seemed as if the war existed between two musical forces; whoever outshouted or outplayed the other was determined the victor. Ah, if only war were that simple! Frenchmen on both sides refused to fight. It was bedlam. Finally it was the British Aussie regiment with their slouch hats, pushing through the Gardens of Damascus, who skillfully halted the melee of heated emotions by forcing the Vichy into surrender.

What the enemy is thinking at this moment is anyone's guess. We leave Syria at the end of the month. The infantry to whom we are attached are ignorant of our destination.

The advantage of being in Special Services and intelligence is you get to know in advance your approximate, targeted destination. "Between point of departure to point of rendezvous, you can vomit all you will," I instructed my men. "But you'd better be prepared for anything on arrival."

One week ago we rendezvoused with several SAS officers going on leave. Strange bedfellows these. They are the toughest lot of ruddy men I've ever seen. Strange, what I see reflected in their eyes is what I saw in the eyes of Hassan's assassins—death! We shall be together for approximately a year—if we survive—to see if the stuff we're made of isn't cream torte. We held our own at Briarsbruck, but will we cut it in the actual warring arena, against the most formidable army ever to mobilize in the twentieth century?

SOMEWHERE IN NORTH AFRICA
January 31, 1941

Morale among the homeless French soldiers is at an all-time low. Recently Winston Churchill declared "I have not become the first minister to the Crown to preside over the liquidation of an empire!" A week later British air squadrons in an all-out attack destroyed half the Italian fleet in Taranto Harbor, in southern Italy. What inspiration Winston Churchill provides! Pray the Free French can be inspired.

On a recent trip to Paris, I met with Lomay St. Germaine. She gathers unto herself an overwhelming force of silent combateurs *called the* Resistance. *An insidious force of dedicated men and women determined to wage internal war against the Germans until they are driven out of Paris, out of France forever. Act of Sabotage as done to factories and railroads. Underground radios and mobile communications centers spring up in Paris sewers, and preaching to the people is the* Voice of Freedom—Zahara *herself. As the Voice of Freedom, she issues encouraging bulletins, boosts the morale of the oppressed, and spreads hope for liberation. The Resistance aims to erode the German power structure. I worry over St. Germaine. The danger is intense; her position grows more precarious daily. An old enemy has surfaced, she confided, heralding the news over Nazi Radio, in hourly doses threatening to find Zahara and hang her bloody Voice of Freedom neck from the Arc de Triomphe!*

Sturmbannführer *Hans Hesse of the RSHA swears he'll crucify her. He has yet to learn Zahara, the thorn in his side, is St. Germaine!*

War grows less palatable by the moment.

TRIPOLI, LIBYA
March 12, 1941

The Moorish city of swaying palms, gentle sea breezes, golden-domed mosques, wide piazzas, and Barbary pirate fame spills over with international news correspondents, photographers, and British intelligence agents desperate to learn the identity of General X, *Hitler's mystery commander sent here to goose up the North African Campaign. Today we learned the truth!*

General Erwin Rommel! *Commander of the 7th Panzer Division—the Ghost Division—fresh from those audacious victories in the battlefields of France. His presence stunned the press and undercover agents when he passed in parade with Italian Commander Italo Garibaldi. The news sent shudders of disquiet among French and British officers.*

General Erwin Rommel and his elite Afrika Korps. *The news was instantly dispatched to British HDQS at Cairo. I shudder to think how the brass will take this. They dislike every phase of the upcoming operation, a feeling that is not shared by the rank and file, who for some reason adore Rommel.*

Lucien Pascal, Jean-Louis Delon, and Tamir Mandel were with me today. We observed the parade disguised as Arabs, wearing burnooses and kuffiahs roped around our heads. Periodically the men filmed points of interest with our minicameras, managing to focus on the 5,000 Afrika Korps troops standing at parade rest in spanking dress uniforms, jodhpurs, mirror-polished knee boots, and Safari helmets. At the appointed time, they massed and rumbled along the main piazza in an endless column of 25-ton

Panzer III and Panzer IV tanks painted a desert-sand color for camouflage. Perfect, I might add! They strutted their stuff, two and three abreast. What a sight! Tank commanders in uniforms of the same color, death's-head badges adorning lapels and collars, stood at attention inside their turrets, saluting their commander in chief in passing. The spectacular show of strength, designed to intimidate, achieved its purpose. The British commanders, receiving first reports of this indomitable power, I learned later, took immediate inventories of their own garrisons.

An hour into the parade, something nagged curiously at me. Some of the tank commanders looked familiar to me. Did I know them? From where? I tried to match faces with events in my recent past. Nothing came alive in my brain. It was time to separate from the others. We planned to rendezvous at the international bazaar in one hour. I snaked through the throngs of excited parade watchers, skirted around the corners of the piazza following the parade route, trying my damnedest to place the tank commanders' faces. Actually I began doubling back along the avenue behind the parade square before the clever scheme came together in my mind. To my amazement and utter amusement, the parading tanks moved four blocks to the north and made a sharp right turn, prepared to reenter the parade square and once again pass in review! Incredible ingenuity! The tank commanders looked familiar because I had already seen them twice in the same parade! Rommel had run his Panzers around the block several times, stretching the regiment into the appearance of a full armored tank corps!

General Rommel, the Desert Fox, had arrived with a brass band, colorful pageantry, and a bag of tricks! I would have given a year's salary to peek into that bag of tricks. My subsequent reports to Colonel Furstenberg, contained serious discrepancies when compared with those submitted by British agents. British MI6 had reported 500 tanks. My count was 120 tanks. Contained in my report to my CO was the explanation.

We now know Hitler lost the Battle of Britain. His superior Luftwaffe air power was unable to break the British Lion's back. Hitler's strategy boggles the mind. If he had persisted another few days, Britain's surrender would have been imminent. The British High Command in Cairo took time to laud the victory with three PIP PIPS and a CHEERIO. Oddly enough they ended the celebration vaguely down-spirited. They danced around the issue, I am told, but frankly, they remain disquieted. The calm-before-the-storm sort of thing. Our orders came through. We're off for a two-month sortie in the desert where I fear we'll be bombarded by 88 guns and artillery fire dusting the shorts off us.

GAZALA, LIBYA
May–December 1941

Gazala . . . On most maps, if you look close, the province of Cyrenaica from Tobruk to Benghazi along coastal, littoral waters resembles the enormous hump of a Dromedary camel. If you include Bardia to the east, a camel's head takes shape. Gazala, approximately sixty miles west of Tobruk along the rugged Mediterranean coast, sits on the rise of the camel's hump; Benghazi occupies the camel's rump.

Cyrenaica is the field of action. Behind a sandy plain of beach, a high desert plateau, strewn craggily with enormous boulders juts five hundred feet skyward. A precipitous escarpment, barely passable, leads to a plateau on the palisade. The access is perilous. Rough terrain plays havoc on tank treads, truck wheels, and axles. But this is the site of war where men will face enemies to the bitter end, both beset by an even fiercer enemy—the desert. Beyond this enormous natural obstruction, the Libyan and Great Western Sahara stretches five hundred miles to infinity, with hell in between. An unbearable sense of isolation grips you when you first catch sight of it, a wide expanse so vast it resembles an uncharted sea.

Cyrenaica, the battle arena, and its chief Ports of Benghazi and Tobruk, is coveted for its strategic location; next to Egypt, it provides the gateway to Cairo and the Suez. Work has already begun on something vaguely referred to as the Gazala Line.

Here the desert sets the pace, makes direction, and forces man to plan strategies around it. No one conquers it. The natives, eyeing us warily, wonder why under all of God's earth the battles must be fought against such horrendous odds. Man must adapt as do primitive nomads. Desert warfare, like sea warfare, has no front; its governing principle is mobility. Men are hunted as a destroyer hunts another destroyer on the high seas; you do your best to annihilate the enemy; the rest is dependent upon the desert.

A bit about the SAS commandos . . . Admittedly we are a reconnaissance group buried deeply behind enemy lines. The Sahara, both our bitterest enemy and our refuge, permits us to wage war against the Italian and German armies, a unique war, one for which no military manual has been devised. We are unique to North Africa and move about with the skill of Bedouins. We've grown thick scrubby beards; the sun has blackened our skins and we begin to look more indigenous to the area. We travel in desert utilities equipped with powerful machineguns, caches of weapons, ammunition, and, of course, a deadly assortment of devious tricks. Every enemy military installation and fortification is known to us. We work skillfully together, executing our business with perfect synchronization. Our sorties into the desert last for two and three months at a hitch. It is incredible how we abuse our bodies, exist on half a pint of water daily and iron rations barely enough for an infant. We are adept at navigating this trackless wilderness. We, the silent forces, move under cover of night in lightning raids on enemy depots, airfields, and redoubts. We blow up valued equipment, killing key personnel and leaving massive destruction in our wake, then fade into the desert. We traverse this endless sea of desolation to perform the impossible. We exist in the impossible, leave it periodically only to be ordered back to perform more of the impossible. We take on many disguises, often wearing the uniform of the enemy. We speak their language with proficiency and ease. We enter verboten areas, plant bombs, explode enemy aircraft, destroy fuel dumps, often speeding out of the bloody aftermath a hair's breadth from total annihilation. Our time bombs explode Luftwaffe planes in midair, blow off the turrets from Panzer tanks, turning their iron inside out. We cause enemy weapons to jam, misfire, and explode in the hands and faces of men who fire them.

Oh Christ!

We are lethal men. What a rewarding testimonial! We are fierce. Tough. Hard as nails! We are vigorous primeval brutes with skins tempered like steel.

We are lost men! God help us! Conditioned to the present we rarely speak of a future. What will become of us if we survive this ghastly hell on earth? Will any of us be fit for normal lives. We don't dwell on such thoughts for fear it will impair our dedication in this cause. I no longer recognize myself, nor any of my men. We do our best to exist only in the moment.

March 1941

Musaka Mubende, an SAS recruit came in off the desert with his squadron. The others collapsed but Mubende insisted on transfer to our outfit, determined to enjoy no interim rest. There is something special about Mubende. A tall, well-muscled Nigerian with a warrior's heart, he comes from a long line of Nigerians called Black Phoenicians. Musaka holds himself superbly with natural, unaffected poise and unmistakable regal bearing. The impact of his personality is indescribable. At all times, even under the brutal cruelty of our desert sorties, the man radiates a positive energy; it differs from what passes among most men as virtue as a masterpiece differs from a bad reproduction. His skin is a deep bronze; more unusual are his black sapphire eyes that at times resemble burning golden suns. He radiates an aura of goodness; he is simple, direct, positive, and constant.

Mubende, by all standards, is perfect homosexual bait among the legionnaires. Yet none dares approach him, not for fear of physical harm, but due to a powerful, intangible force he exudes, one more formidable than physical strength. Some among the SAS believe him to be sainted. It was in the way he walked among animals of the compound, at once subduing the fiercest among the jackals, hyenas, dogs, even the snakes. I cannot explain this enigmatic soul, only say he is special.

In the course of briefing, after studying his dossier, I asked why he had volunteered for commando duty. His response didn't vary from his initial reply. "To learn the power of the white man—the power of the gun."

His dossier revealed Musaka Mubende to be the son of a dethroned Nigerian king whose tribe had been driven into the bush. In his lifetime he'd seen enough undersized, potbellied, spindleshanked, diseased, broken, and degenerate remains of a defeated tribe to sicken him for life. What remained of his people was consumed with tertian fevers and tuberculosis. Refusing to hunt for even small game in which the country abounded, they were breeding themselves out in sheer apathy and wretchedness. Mubende's dream was to one day gather his people unto him and restore them to a pride and heritage that was once theirs.

June, 1941

Word has arrived. Hitler has embarked on a mission called Operation Barbarossa, aimed at annihilating Russia. He's launched a Blitzkrieg with a force of over three million troops into Russia? Shades of Napoleon! What is the Führer thinking of? Russians cannot be knocked out in a single blow! Not unless Hitler has some secret weapon of which the world knows nothing!

December, 1941

So many global events at once! The Japanese bombed Pearl Harbor. Days later the Führer did what he insisted he'd never do—declare war on America. Ah, well, so we learn Hitler is human after all. Three mistakes in a row; first abandoning the Battle of Britain, second occupying Russia, third war against the USA. What is the next? I wonder did anyone consider madness in Hitler's bloodline. How far can Axis tentacles reach before lifelines weaken? It will happen soon. We know it, feel it. North Africa will be a testing ground that decides many issues.

January 31, 1942

We are back in Gazala. In our absence General Rommel launched a full-scale offensive, entered Benghazi, helped himself to large stores including fifteen hundred trucks. Within two weeks, he pushed the British back to Gazala. British losses: 40 tanks, 40 field guns, 2,000 men.

Global events taking place thousands of miles away from us exert powerful influences in this war. Politicians in Zurich, London, and in the USA have diverted vital material and men from North Africa to the Far East following Japan's all out war in the South Pacific.

On our recent sorties into the desert, the SAS hit installations at Maaten el Garra, Msus, Mechill, Charruba, Breda Fomm, Antelot, Mersa Brega, Sidi Oman, Suillieman, and Azuz. We crisscross the camel's hump to destroy . . . destroy . . . destroy. Destroy! What good is it? New fortifications and German redoubts spring up all around us.

War is abomination! War is depravity! War is the quintessential evil! We are drained, totally debilitated. We are afflicted with the desert disease—mirages! Unless we get respite from the grim rigors of commando warfare . . .

Voilà! O'Reilly just gave me the news. Two weeks sojourn at the seashore for us!

February 20, 1942

I am setting forth a message received from Cairo British Command. Ten, twenty, even fifty years from now no one will believe it. It reads:

ATTENTION: FREE-FRENCH COMMANDERS AND THE NAIS, INCLUDING OFFICERS OF BRITISH INTELLIGENCE. . . OUR FRIEND ROMMEL IS BECOMING SOME SORT OF BOGEY MAN, A HERO OF SORTS TO OUR TROOPS! I MEAN TO STATE HEREIN AND UNEQUIVOCALLY, ROMMEL IS BY NO MEANS A SUPERMAN, ALTHOUGH HE IS ENERGETIC AND ABLE. EVEN IF HE WERE A SUPERMAN, IT WOULD BE HIGHLY UNDESIRABLE IF OUR MEN SHOULD CREDIT HIM WITH SUPERNATURAL POWERS. YOU SHOULD, THEREFORE, DISPEL BY WHATEVER MEANS AT YOUR DISPOSAL, THE IDEA THAT ROMMEL REPRESENTS ANYTHING MORE THAN AN ORDINARY GEN-

ERAL. PLEASE ENSURE THIS ORDER IS PUT INTO IMMEDIATE EFFECT AND IMPRESS UPON ALL COMMANDERS THAT FROM PURELY A PSYCHOLOGICAL POINT OF VIEW, THIS IS A MATTER OF THE UTMOST IMPORTANCE AND MUST TAKE PRIORITY OVER ALL ELSE. HIS TRICKS AND TURNS HAVE MADE THE TOMMIES CHUCKLE, WHICH IS SCARCELY THE PROPER RESPONSE TO THE ENEMY IN THE TIME OF WAR. SIGNED, AUCHINLAUS.

Colonel Furstenberg postured about as I did, in amused bewilderment.

Chapter Thirty-three

Darius stretched out lazily on the bleached sands of a secluded cove between Tobruk and Benghazi occupied with the screeching of seagulls bobbing up and down, snatching fish from the sea in endless repetition.

The sun, that detestable, unrelenting, prostrating force in the desert had metamorphosed into a comforting, invigorating ally here along Mediterranean shores. Trickling from him, bit by bit, bringing him peace and new perspective was that definitive numbness born of constant living in close proximity to death. Draining from him was the sinister intent of violence and duty.

Those endless months of assault and kill had dissolved—*Merci Dieu!*

Now, as gentle breezes cooled him, a soft azure sky and bewitching tide lulled him into Daedelian euphoria. He felt winged, able to transcend the lower rungs of hell to higher planes of thought.

Inevitably his thoughts included Valentina Varga, but the inescapable present—and General Rommel, shoved her into the dark recesses of his mind. The inescapable present . . .

Fifty miles away, along the western shores of Cyrenaica, a modern-day warlord planned the conquest of Egypt and the Suez by applying Blitzkrieg tactics to desert warfare! Darius's reports to the British High Command, substantiated by incredibly accurate photographs of German redoubts, made no impact on the king's elite officers in Cairo. *Ineffectual desk-bound soldiers— the lot of them!* Why risk the lives of commando specialists in daring intelligence gathering if the information wasn't put to use? British tactics! Darius raged internally. War generals who placed pomp, ceremony and decorum before strategy and skilled tactics were no opponents for a Rommel! Hell, the British had not bothered to *know* their enemy! Rommel a dedicated soldier whose only interest was warfare was a formidable, galloping exponent of the open-ended defense. Did the British prepare themselves against Rommel's tactics? No! A year ago, when Darius had first sighted General Rommel in Tripoli, a sense of *déjà vu* engulfed him; he'd felt a kinship of sorts, as if they'd known each other in a previous lifetime. The experience shattered linear reality for him, and Darius found it damned hard to view Rommel as the enemy when his respect for the warrior was fierce. It wasn't finished, and Darius, having observed first hand the German's exceptional warring tactics felt a foreboding, an inner trepidation.

Pray God the British and French *knew* their own blueprints. If it was patience they demonstrated, that was one thing, but entirely another if they floundered about without definitive strategy. Darius shuddered at the ominous possibility.

Stop it! Stop this negative thinking! Yours is but to do or die, not think or question why!

Damnation! The war scenario in Libya had been thrust into outer limbo for some mysterious reason he seemed unable to grasp. No one was talking. Not a hint of the warring scenario was hinted.

So, take time out to rest in between acts, Darius.

He removed his war journal from his rucksack, opened to a page on which he had sketched a map of Cyrenaica, and studied it. From Gazala he drew a line extending to the area to the south known as Bir Hakeim—Chief's Well—some sixty kilometers to the south of Gazala. Sipping cold beer from a canteen, he picked up his pen and began to write.

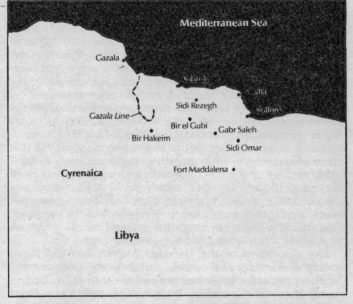

THE BATTLE OF BIR HAKEIM AND THE GAZALA LINE

May 10, 1942.

THE Gazala Line . . . a sixty-mile-long chain of defenses built by the British Eighth Army from Gazala to Bir Hakeim runs a jagged course southeast for forty miles, then elbows northeast for twenty more. Scattered at wide irregular intervals along the line to the east are a series of strongholds called boxes, each manned by soldiers. Each of these boxes, girded on their perimeters with rolling cartwheels of barbed wire, slit trenches, and pillboxes, is stocked with stores to withstand a week-long siege. Between these boxes British tanks roam freely, prepared to intercept enemy tanks advancing across their sectors and to race up and down the line to the aid of any box likely to fall under attack.

The Free French, under the command of General Marie-Pierre Koenig, are based at Bir Hakeim, a caravan crossing at the southernmost tip of the Gazala Line. The general, spit and polish to the core, is thoroughly St. Cyr. He is a clean-shaven man with attentive, stabbing eyes, a dedicated professional who commands enormous respect from the men. Under his aegis, nearly 3,500 troops have entrenched the perimeters of the box. Gun pits, command posts, and utility trucks are fully entrenched, in the sand. God forbid a Khamsen or ghilbi descend on the fortification to bury it forever amid the sands of time.

The perimeters of the six-sided French box measured nearly ten miles. The general immediately extended the frontiers to twelve miles and ordered the men to dig in and firmly entrench themselves. What Koenig orders gets done!

The thoughtful British bought an entire stock of Palestinian wine for the legionnaires. It arrived in steel containers, sizzling in the sun, not fit to use as vinegar.

Five hundred thousand antitank mines, planted along the Gazala Line from stem to stern are intended to defend Tobruk, strike at General Rommel's Afrika Korps, and decimate them. Is this a toss-up between equal forces? Or plain suicide on the part of the French?

Good question. One worth pondering. But, not now.

May 15, 1942

The soldiers grow indolent from lack of action. Rommel makes no move against the British! Last November he laid siege to Tobruk; now as he waits he lacks equipment replacements. Constant British bombardments pressured him into retreat, forty miles west of Gazala. Operation Crusader rendered the British sensationally victorious. Actually Rommel suffered his first defeat. The statistics: 33,000 Axis soldiers taken prisoners, 300 tanks destroyed. The British, in the SAS absence, lost Cyrenaica and regained it two months later.

Now Rommel waits . . . The British wait . . . The French wait and we wait. Only God in his mysterious heaven knows why the bloody devil we wait.

The Indian Sappers cut off their beards, losing a bit of dignity and colorful panache. But what use is dignity and panache if your life ends? Swiftly they engaged in gas-mask drilling. Rumors spread: the Germans intended using poison gas.

Speaking of rumors . . . Valentina Varga is here. I haven't seen her, but since General Koenig is here, it was only natural she'd be here. The possibility of her presence here both alarms and offends me. What the bloody blue blazes is she doing in a land not fit for hardened man or beast? What? Yet the thought excites me.

May 17, 1942

On the move again. We received aerial recon photos of German installations from the RAF. Each night, using Bir Hakeim as our base, I take twenty men out on patrol to launch surprise attacks on the enemy and rescout the area. Several photos indicated heavy concentrations of Panzer III and IVs in the vicinity of Ben Gania southwest of Bir Hakeim. We made our move last night. Our orders: destroy the German redoubt!

Two hours out of Bir Hakeim, we confirmed the RAF photos. Three nights previous to this, this spot was an ocean of vast desolation; now armored tanks, lined abreast and twelve deep, stretched to infinity. The men, unable to *contain their astonishment at the spectacular array, communicated their frustration. How the bloody blazes could such massive armor get through our lines without our detection? This formidable display confirmed our worst fears. Rommel was gathering a staggering force to hurl against the British and Free-French forces!*

Curiously enthralled by the display of might these seductive iron ladies, armed to the teeth with powerful guns, presented my mind flirted flagrantly with the gross inconsistencies. I scanned the entire fortification through binoculars. Radical distortions piqued my curiosity. How was it possible?

Valuable equipment guarded only by barbed-wire fencing. Two guards. Only two? No machinegun towers ... no managed gun posts ... ostensibly no armed squadrons to protect this mass of valuable warring assets? Nothing made sense. I sniffed the air, hoping to detect something alien in the winds. We, all of us, listened for a sound, unusual movement, anything to help ferret out the truth. Could it be a trap? Soldiers lying in ambush behind the rocks, inside the tanks, in the black shadows of night, just waiting for the SAS to break cover?

Instinct directed caution. The fiasco at Tripoli has never left our minds. Pascal, O'Reilly, Mandel and I crept forward, covered by the other men, their guns ready, itching to be used. We slid off the rocks and crabbed forward, faintly shadowed by four battery-operated floods stationed at the four corners of the armored depot. We inched forward over sand dunes and open brush, approaching from the rear. A half hour later we slipped under the wire. Crouching low, we loped in closer to the rear row of tanks and parted. Dutch was taking photos with an infrared lens. I moved in with my own special camera and took additional shots, stopping at once. I crept in closer, my hands running over the smooth armor. I stood up, moved on to the next and the next, shaking my head in exasperation. I saw Pascal doubled over in mirth, hands clasped over his mouth to suppress all sounds. Tamir's classic expression, one of confusion, bewilderment, and disbelief as he discerned the deception, is one I shall never forget. Dutch O'Reilly, deeply involved in his task, hadn't caught on, yet. He looked around for us and beckoned us toward him. Just then he patted the armor and got the same reaction we got. The puzzled astonishment on his face as it registered broke us up. "Captain!" *he growled softly.* "Didya see what I jus' saw? They'll never believe us! They'll think us drunk or cafard!"

And when I ordered them back without issuing demolition instructions, their puzzlement grew. Let the Germans wonder why we didn't set up explosives and lay the entire depot to waste. I didn't take time to explain. We sped back to Bir Hakeim. I dismissed the men, wrote up my report while the lab boys processed the film.

Captain Furstenberg summoned me to his quarters on the double. He demanded an explanation, one he could understand. Canvas and cardboard tanks? What the devil was I thinking of? How could he inform British intelligence that his super commandos out on recon stumbled on a redoubt of cardboard tanks? "Why the bloody hell didn't you blow them up and let us take credit for something?" *Pacing the floor, snorting like a charging bull he fulminated and cursed vociferously.*

I explained. I thought it best not to let Rommel know we're on to him. If he believed his display of strength, however fraudulent, had us cowed, he might experience the false sense of security I preferred he enjoy for a while. The colonel stared at me with unreadable eyes, my words conjuring unwanted images in his mind.

"Begin at the beginning," *he instructed me. I complied describing the length and breadth of the depot and indicated to the cardboard tanks in the photos.* "Cleverly adapted canvas and cardboard exteriors mounted on Volkswagen and Fiat chasis." *A rare smile appeared on the colonel's lips, unspoken praise of a unique human war machine— Rommel, himself.*

May 19, 1942

Still no action for the infantry! *Soldiers drill religiously, grow adept at the hit and run tactics of Jock columns. Serviced by traveling bordellos, and Thessalus wine, pleasure and serenity lull both the officers and rank and file. Each night they tune into Radio Belgrade to hear the sad, soul-stirring lament about the broken hearted girl, still waiting under the lamplight by the barracks gate, and not a dry eye can be found among them.* Lili Marlene, *the dream of every soldier listening to the tremulous voiced rendition, is rapidly becoming the official lament of every desert warrior, British, French, German and Italian alike.*

Worse than waiting for the Germans to make their move is the immense, trackless, devastating desert. Its agonies to the uninitiated are excruciating. Fluctuating temperatures soar without warning; broiling by day, plummeting to freezing at night. Sand clogs rifle breeches, inflames the eyes, fills nostrils, permeates every crack in vehicles and tents. It buries food and equipment, reduces visibility to a foot or two. And mirages! The men are afflicted by them like a raging pestilence.

God! Could hell be any worse?

Never, never *did the legionnaires dream they'd give thanks for the gruelling* règlement *endured at Sidi! Legionnaires, as it turned out were less prone to prostration than the British Tommies. What a toughened lot we are! What was it Colonel Furstenberg told me?* Sidi bel Abbes produces supermen? *I am a believer now. The British applaud the French stamina and look upon the SAS as something extraterrestrial.*

Brigadier-General Ben-Kassir is here. We met in Gazala. He's had a bit of bad luck with Hassan in the west and joined our forces to the end, whatever our fate. The Vichy government holds Algeria. Youseff is optimistic. He expects American intervention shortly. I suppose we all expect miracles. We pray for them!

If dragoman *curses cannot move stubborn camels and obstinate jackasses, surely our curses will not evaporate Rommel and his forces. He controls the west. The sixty-mile line of defenses stands between him and his return to Tobruk. Why does he wait? He has both ground and air power! Christ! Waiting makes us desperate men. I dare not put into writing what I think of the British High Command at this point and run the risk of sounding treasonous.*

Early on the morning of May 20, Darius, sand goggles shielding his eyes, skimmed over the sand in a utility, transporting Brigadier-General Ben-Kassir from Gazala to Bir Hakeim. Youseff was scanning a sheaf of reports. Darius pointed out several English boxes—the Knightsbridge, Londonderry, Chelsea, and many other encampments where naked soldiers scrubbed their uniforms with sand to remove the sweat, grime and dirt. A few used gasoline, but never water. Water, a scarce, jealously guarded commodity, was *verboten* save for drinking and cooking. The soldiers waved and saluted to the officers. Farther along the Gazala Line to the south, clusters of scantily clothed men, patiently cleaning sand-clogged rifle breeches, shouted greetings.

Darius pointed to a demolished mass, a giant open crater in the sand. A pitted sea surrounding the large one. "See, Youseff . . . a recent hot wind rising off the Sahara, generating a massive jolt of electricity, blew up an ammo dump—right here."

Youseff stared in hard, stony silence, weighing the massive destruction.

Closer to the French box, pith-helmeted soldiers, their heads swathed in mosquito netting, like hive keepers to ward off carnivorous insects and flies, dug out sand-buried provisions. Glancing up at the passing vehicle, they saluted apathetically and returned zombielike to their tasks.

"Is it as bad as the reports indicate, Darius?" Youseff stared at the pathetically disoriented men and their mechanical movements.

"Worse."

"Rommel needs Bir Hakeim to get to Tobruk."

"True, but the British Eighth needs it more. We won't give it up."

"Why does Rommel wait? The reports say it's been three months."

"Rommel's a master of the unexpected, and genius at psychological warfare knows the British mentality, as schizophrenic as it is."

"The British stiff-upper-lip attitude is a devil to reckon with," Youseff said, grasping the jeep's safety bar as they rode rough-shod over the craggy terrain. "Their bloomin' mumbo-jumbo and the ploys invented by London politicians drive us all bracketing to madness. It's a controlled situation, Darius. Without the faintest idea of what goes on here, they move squadrons of soldiers into positions on political chessboards to provide themselves with political comfort."

"*Political comfort!*" Darius slammed hard on the brakes, fishtailing the jeep precariously. "Political comfort?" He raged. He turned off the engine, pulled himself up on the back of his seat, perched behind the roll bar, scanning the area through binoculars. "Is that what I've been doing this past year? Have I put my life and that of countless brave men at risk just to provide the blasted politicians with political comfort? *Jesus!*" Darius's suppressed fury erupted. "Politicians are anacondas! Here, look for yourself. We're at midpoint on the Gazala Line. The French box is a goddamn sitting duck! The entire damnable line is a series of sitting ducks. With twenty men—my men—and plenty of grenades, we could blow every friggin' box from Bir Hakeim to Tobruk. Now, tell me, General, if *I* perceive the inadequate defenses here—wouldn't Rommel? . . . Shall I tell you how intimately that intrepid Desert Fox knows the essentials of desert warfare? The need for speed and surprise dominates every tactic he employs in the warring arena. His grasp of both speed and surprise, plus his ingenious, split-second timing, violates text-book principles and throws the British into mass confusion. The man gets around an open flank into enemy defenses like nothing I've seen. The desert is perfect for tank warfare and he deploys those iron behemoths with the skill of a man born to the desert. Where does that leaves us, eh? Thus far his deceptive show of strength, undetected or *ignored* by the British prevents us from advancing, giving Rommel the quick strike advantage." Darius stopped talking. Thoughts forming in his mind stirred a dubious hesitancy in him. He began slowly, speaking each word clearly, so as not to be misunderstood. "General, tell me, if I detect Rommel's *modus operandi*, why can't the British High Command?" . . . Darius paused dramatically. "Oh, no . . . don't tell me. It's too painfully clear. We're being set up for some dirty business! Tell me, Youseff! I need truth from someone I can trust."

Youseff scanned the line defenses in tight-lipped silence. Darius was dismayed. "Oh Christ! Christ, I *knew* it! The look in your eyes . . . you *know* the truth." His voice dropped an octave. "It's suicide, *oui*? *Je ne le comprends pas!* Not the French or the British! If the men in the ranks got the faintest whiff of the contents of my reports, they'd desert! And I wouldn't blame them. Rommel and his Panzers lie in readiness with mobilized columns. How long before they descend on us?"

"Less time than it takes Messerschmitts to wipe Bir Hakeim off the map," Youseff said quietly.

"Precisely." Their eyes met, held in knowing dread. "I don't need to remind you the Gazala Line is in the gravest of danger."

"You don't need to remind me."

"Suppose the BHC in Cairo intends to use Bir Hakeim for some political deviousness? Surely, Youseff, a bit of euchring is taking place. . . . I ask myself, what can be accomplished if thousands of lives are sacrificed? It sure as hell had better be worthwhile, *oui*? Oh sure, I can conjure up tricks to match Rommel's and prolong our stay. But, assuredly, once the Junkers begin aerial bombardment it is *finis* for Bir Hakeim. Even if Spitfires and Hurricanes roll over and dogfight them to kingdom come, it only prolongs the suffering. More Junkers and Stukas will divebomb us off the map. I fail to see the treasure at the end of this human rainbow bloodied by the death of Frenchmen. Do you see it, Youseff? if you do, please explain it to me."

"What your SAS men do is not written up in military manuals or logged in war diaries as victories. But what you've done had to be done, and because of your efforts the British were able to chalk up plenty of victories in this skirmish."

"Christ! I'm not talking yesterday! I'm talking today! Now! This moment! The Gazala Line is our weakest defense. Oh, hell, Youseff, we're not here arguing philosophies. It's war and you kill, else you'll be killed."

Youseff cut him off with a sharp glance. "No need to refresh me on the rules of war, Darius. I understand perfectly. The British go by the book—"

"By—the—book! How do I get through to them? They underestimate Rommel! Christ, it's in all my reports. Rommel, the miracle maker in France, with his Ghost Division makes miracles here, daily. Still they underestimate him. The man's a genius! A logical, insubordinate genius who constantly disobeys the German High Command and makes his own rules because, goddammit, he's learned more about desert warfare in less than a year than the fatuous British who colonized this accursed land have learned in centuries!"

"Be fair, Darius. The BHC is dictated to by Prime Minister Churchill."

"And Churchill is motivated by the need for popularity in the House of Commons. I know! I know. It's a sickness!" Darius groaned.

"In addition, he must please the queen."

"Politicians! Bah! Give me malaria, sunstroke, dysentery, the penal battalion, but don't give me *fucking* brain-fried politicians who make decisions thousands of miles from the battle site!

Right now, at this moment, the British High Command sits in fan-cooled dining rooms in Cairo, sipping Pimms Cup, planning desert strategy! Is that a kick in the balls?'' Darius watched the gentle breeze whirlpooling sand drifts. ''All this official warring fantasia is laughable. Listen, two field commanders were sacked recently. Another needs sacking badly, but the general says, 'It's bloody rotten for a soldier's morale to lose confidence in his CO.' Well! I say bloody rotten for any soldier to lose his life needlessly. *Damn it*, Youseff! The British aren't imaginative! They can't beat Rommel at his game by adhering to protocol! We need a commander who can outwit the Desert Fox. *The German Fox, favored by fortune conquers the British Lion, favored by strength!* Shall this be the sobriquet that marks the downfall of the Free French in North Africa? Rommel's making it come to pass. By God! He's done it. Rommel came in support of the Italians and stole the whole show! Ordered by the German High Command to take defensive action—so say *our* intelligence reports—the general arrives in North Africa and does precisely the opposite. Listen, Youseff, Rommel arrived in Tripoli in secrecy. The first thing he did was to board his Storch Aircraft to engage in personal aerial· reconnaissance of the Libyan desert. He took photos, studied the battle arena, probed the desert and its secrets long before an unsuspecting people hailed his arrival. He detected opportunities and, like the military genius he is, struck for victory. The bloody British don't *know* desert warfare! They should be adept at it. What but the desert lends itself to tank warfare? Rommel has enough savvy to take one look at the Gazala Line and wipe out each command post in a twinkling. Explain British thinking to me. I am baffled by their insensitivity to warring tactics.''

''The British are France's allies. The real France . . . Free France.'' Youseff played with the rotation wheel on his binoculars, assessing the drastic changes in Darius these past many months.

''Is that supposed to excuse them for gross errors? Are we not permitted, as allies, to point out their errors in judgment? Youseff, for God's sake! You don't beat a Rommel by going by the book!''

''Face it, Darius, who has the daring and guts of a Rommel?''

Darius slid into his seat, positioned behind the wheel. He started up the jeep. Youseff settled in his seat alongside him. Darius sped along the Line, the spinning utility wheels kicking up gusts of sand, en route to the post command HDQS at Bir

Hakeim. "I had hoped you might use your influence to tell it like it is, Youseff. I am certain Colonel Furstenberg is aware of the precariousness of our position. But he remains mute. See, it's the damnable silence before the storm that keeps me jittery. I *know* what's in store for us and feel impotent, unable to circumvent catastrophe."

"I shall try, *mon bien ami*. But I promise you no miracles. The British, a lugubriously elite fraternity don't take kindly to advice from anyone outside the group."

A half hour later they entered General Koenig's spartan quarters at the post command. Darius, sniffing the air, whipped off his sand goggles, spun about, blinked hard. *It couldn't be! It simply was not possible. It was a mirage!*

He was wrong. Valentina Varga was no mirage. She stood before him in the flesh, a breath of spring in the drab quarters. For all it mattered to her, he could be ten thousand miles away. She moved past him, ignoring him, and, taking General Koenig's briefcase, turned around to smile at Youseff. She nodded perfunctorily to Darius, saluted, and stood to one side, waiting for the general. Koenig moved from behind his desk, shook hands with the prince and Darius, and, apologetic, left with Lieutenant Varga. "I shall return momentarily," he told them, leaving Captain Bonifacio stunned and waffling outright.

Darius's heart ached. As swiftly his mood blackened. "What the bloody hell is she doing here in the midst of this insanity? Who hatched this brainstorm?"

"Why are you so angry, Captain?" Colonel Furstenberg entered, saluted Youseff, and shook hands warmly.

"Angry? Who's angry? Not I, Colonel. Bir Hakeim is a friggin' hellhole. The men are animals. It's no place for a frivolous woman seeking thrills to write home about!"

"Odd. Lieutenant Varga never impressed me as a frivolous woman." The colonel checked his amusement. "Highness, do you take her for a thrill-seeking woman?" Before Youseff replied, Darius made his excuses and bolted out the door.

He stood in the partial shade of a tent awning, rising anger the capper to an unproductive day. He lit a cigarette with shaking hands, furious at himself for losing control. Somewhere along the bloody trail of war he recalled thinking how would he ever fit into the old pattern of life? He couldn't. Now, as emotions charged through him, coloring his thoughts, the sight of Valentina shook him to the core. The unresolved dark part of his nature must be dealt with soon, *very* soon, he told himself.

That girl, that American girl with a name like a prolonged musical phrase, had managed to make him forget the war, the SAS, and his duties for as long as it took to smoke half a cigarette! Without speaking, she had managed to lecture him on the eternal tragedy of love in war! *Damnable, bloody girl!*

Inside, Youseff, alarmed at Darius's outburst, peered through the grilled window, of the adobe studying his friend intently. "Henri, would I only be scraping the surface if I diagnosed his malady as a case of arrested love? What's wrong with Darius, do you know?"

"What's wrong with Darius?" The colonel sighed despairingly. "You know, Highness, we, none of us, came to the North African Campaign seeking fairy tales. It's not out of the bloody *Arabian Nights*. A year in the SAS does things to the mind. Is it a bit immodest to say that without our Corsican captain there'd be no SAS? Your belief in him has been Free France's godsend. But he shoulders the entire load. He needs time to rest, recuperate, and I don't mean for a week or two. He needs a solid month—more perhaps—and we cannot spare three hours!"

"He sees things *too* clearly. What will become of him? You realize he considers our ancillary role with the British contemptible, below our dignity." Youseff lit a cigarette, inhaling deeply.

"That's a thorny one. You see, I concur with him. Since the British are subsidizing us, we have little say in this war, Highness. Oh, they confer with us to salve our ego, yet despite the fact that the general hocked half of France's ass—*payable after the war*—there's no question we occupy a subordinate role."

"Henri, let me speak confidentially and tell you how Darius perceives our situation here at Bir Hakeim, *oui*? And we shall think on it."

May 25

The war shambled forward, overburdened with inept, unimaginative commanders. Bir Hakeim Post Command HDQS contained only the barest essentials. One thing it boasted of with fierce pride was an excellent war room.

Today, the war room's atmosphere was heady with the presence of British and Free-French intelligence officers and the

French commander, General Koenig. Koenig, one of the better commanders was a man who wore fatalism around his neck like a cross. Always found at the center of the thickest frays, forever admonishing his men to keep their helmets on during heavy bombing and strafing, today, as he played host to British and French intelligence officers, he moved quietly, studying a bas relief table model of the scaled-to-size Gazala Line. He peered scrupulously at tank positions, artillery, and field concentrations, mined areas identified by colored flags, somewhat astonished at the numbers of enemy troops and full battalions arrayed against them.

Brigadier-General Ben-Kassir, Colonel Furstenberg, and two British officers moved alongside him, eyeing the scale model critically, listening as they did to Captain Bonifacio's comprehensive observations, summations and denouement of an audacious remedy to an already intolerable situation.

Major General Kenneth Brack, a slim, raccoon-faced man with a long nose and waxed mustache, pursed his lips in thought. Brigadier-General Martin St. John was short, wiry, with broad shoulders and light brown hair. He moved swaggeringly about the table, smoking a cigar. Both men belonged to that tight clique of brother officers above the rank of colonel who resented and feared outsiders.

Both British M16 officers represented the wide disparity between men at the front and those at Cairo HDQS. British staff officers never referred to the soldiers in the warring zones as humans but as the regiment, the platoon, or the squadrons. They refused to connect faces and names to the dirty, lice-infested, sun-scorched, fever-plagued bastards who were forced to fight wars conjured up in the minds of the esoteric brotherhood of British officers.

Brack opened dialogue on Darius's report. "I say, Captain, your intelligence gathering contains an excellence beyond my expectations. I quite agree that one must fight fire with fire. Tobruk is now a fishbone in Rommel's throat. Our Aussie, Polish, and British forces holding this seaport fortress pose considerable threats to Rommel's supply lines. *Ultra* signals from Rome and Berlin indicate that Rommel is obsessed with reducing Tobruk and retaking it."

"Rommel," said Darius firmly, pointing to the table model with a long wooden pointer, "will strike in less than twenty-four hours!"

"I say, *rahthah!*" muttered Martin St. John.

"He doesn't quite fancy leaving Tobruk to the Italians," Darius continued. "His orders are to press on to Egypt. But I know General Rommel, gentlemen, I know him well. He will not give up a choice dessert like the Gazala Line." He tapped the area of the Knightsbridge box. "He will strike here! Meanwhile he intends to hurl the entire Italian Ariete Division, supported by full armor to the south, and approach from the rear of Bir Hakeim, drill up the center, ensnare Gazala, and pick off each box along the line to the north."

Youseff's lower jaw slackened. He blinked in amazement. Darius had predicted this strategy a week before.

"Rommel is perpetually running out of fuel," said Brack. "He began sending *Ultra* signals to Kesselring in Rome, complaining bitterly about the lack of supplies, demanding new equipment, and criticizing the Italians for failing to land supplies at Benghazi instead of Tripoli, some five hundred miles farther from his advance troops."

"Precisely." Darius returned them to his scenario. "The Italian division, accordingly, will attack the French box at this point." He indicated the elbow-joint turn off the main Gazala Line. "Once *that* defense is crushed, the Italians will move in behind Rommel, pick off stragglers, gobble up British armor, knock out the line from the rear! Then, gentlemen, it's on to Tobruk and victory for Rommel!"

"I say old chap, rahthuh!" St. John muttered respectfully.

"Rommel's overconfidence—if we play it right—might win us a sorrily needed victory," Darius continued. "He leaves Bir Hakeim to the Italians. That should tell you what he thinks of our chances." Darius waited-for the statement to sink in, then laid his plans at the feet of the military and intelligence brass.

"I say, rahthuh!" St. John's apparently limited vocabulary covered everything from admiration to frustration. The officer shifted his focus from Darius to the table model, eyes lighting, then dimming, as the ingenuity of Darius's proposal sank in. "You're certain it will work?"

Major General Brack's face turned ferruginous. "It's the most abominable plan I've ever heard!" Then his hard features relaxed; an inescapable grin tugged at his lips under the waxed mustache. His eyes cautious, fixed on Darius, sized him up. "I know nothing of this conversation, is it understood? I wasn't here today to listen to this perfectly abhorrent, yet utterly delightful, discussion. Have I made myself clear? I'll have no part in these negotiations.''

"Nor shall I," St. John echoed Brack's condemnation, his short-toothed smile appearing hesitantly, eyes sparking. "Jolly clever of you, Captain! Ah, you Corsicans! Like Napoleon, what an uncanny, utterly ingenious lot! I say, bloody marvelous . . .''

Both St. John and Brack saluted stiffly and departed hurriedly, their remarks and laughter muffled as they boarded their vehicles.

In the war room, General Koenig listened to the gunning of motors as the British officers sped off. "If I had an ounce of sense I'd subscribe to Brack's and St. John's neutrality. French valor will not be lost to the world. We must stay the hand and outfox this German Fox who chases his hunters back and forth across North Africa as often as they have chased him. The British have lost face and have yet to redeem themselves. So, it's up to the French to stand up and be counted—Well, Captain Bonifacio, shall we make it a spectacular show? *Ecoutez,* I too know nothing of this tactic you speak of, unless it is successful. Then, of course I shall admit to authoring this bit of *jeu de guerre théâtre.* General de Gaulle will be so pleased if we measure to Rommel's innovative genius. *Jeter de la pudre aux yeux, mon capitaine!* Throw dust in their eyes, deliberately mislead them! What a coup!''

"First, sir, I shall need six cases of Thessalus wine laced with Pernod . . .'' Darius said solemnly, winking at Youseff on the sly.

ITALIAN ARIETE DIVISION HDQS
LIBYAN DESERT, LATE AFTERNOON

A French lorry laden with the Thessalus wine careened wildly at the perimeters of the Italian redoubt. Stopped at gunpoint by the Italians, the schnockered driver was arrested, tossed into the brig, his truck and goods confiscated. The thirsty Italian tank commanders scheduled for the Bir Hakeim offensive in the morning partook heartily of the spiked Thessalus wine, imbibing well into the wee hours. Dawn arose and with it came the devastating after effects of the brutal concoction. Agonized groans permeated the tents as the stupefied soldiers prepared for battle. Each member of the elite Ariete held his tormented head between both hands hoping to subdue the pounding anvil inside. Never mind that their dilated eyes impaired their vision; never mind that their overheated blood-seared veins and arteries or that the pain blazing trails inside their craniums caused their flesh to run hot and cold. No one dared to report to sickbay—not after the abrasive browbeating flung at them the day before by that insufferable German C.O. General Ernst Von Luden!

Santo Dio! What were they to do?

BIR HAKEIM

Shortly after dawn a column of sixty tanks driven by the hungover Italians of the Ariete division glided over glowing pink sands. Concentration paramount in this mission, the tank commanders permitted no insidious thoughts of possible defeat to invade what little space remained inside their aching heads. Defeat? Were they crazy to think it? *Dio Maledetto!* The word itself was forbidden.

Overly confident in their mission, no advance guards ventured forth to run interference for them. They plowed forth in battle formation toward their objective unaware of the meticulously laid snare awaiting them.

Darius and the SAS were ready for them. Using sensitive radio and tracking devices, Darius intercepted the Italians' radio frequency and, speaking unaccented Italian, he beamed directly into the tank commanders' headphones. He spoke in a gentle monotone, guiding them unwittingly toward the densely mined fields. Mirrors, strategically placed in the sand, magnified the sun's blinding glare creating havoc among the Ariete, throwing the battlefield into mass confusion.

The British Eighth Army brass, concealed in cover positions overlooking the field of action fell witness to the craziest antics ever staged in a war theater. As the prestigious Italian Ariete metamorphosed into *commedia dell'arte* players, the scene became burlesque at its most hilarious to everyone but the players.

The Ariete lead tank, heaving laboriously over rough terrain, lurched without warning to a sudden stop. The tank immediately at its rear whacked its iron head onto the first, its tracks piggybacking the lead vehicle. Repeated attempts made by the drivers to dislodge themselves from the pile-up failed. Chaos ensued as approaching tanks blindly rear-ended those ahead of them and in turn were rear-ended by those behind. Many were struck broadside. Loud crashing sounds echoed over the desert sands.

The British and Free-French officers, in good humor vented a gnawing year-long frustration. It was slapstick; the result was rousing laughter. Binoculars in place, the officers swung them every which way trying to catch every improvisational act in the comedic vignette. At the sound of clicking camera shutters voices overrode the prevailing disorder. "There! Look over there! See this! What a bloody rout! Delightful enough to write home about!" Hearty laughter lit up their faces, echoed across the sands.

In the warring arena there was bedlam. Tank commanders gunned their motors, strained, struggled, heaved their irons forward in short, spasmodic jerks. Those managing to disencumber themselves from the melee ended up nose-down in open craters. Hatches flipped open, helmeted heads appeared, one after another. Bewildered drivers and gunnery soldiers pulled their sand goggles to their chins and whipped off their helmets. Desperate, pain-filled eyes squinting at the unbearable sunlight were instantly shielded by hands, helmets, anything to deflect the glare. Italian curses and audible groans bounced off the hot iron of the tanks. *"Dio Maledetto! E un bel pasticcio! Ma che c'e? Managgia! C'e teste terremoti!"*

That voice again . . . coming through on their headphones!

"Soldati bravi, fa un bell' effetto. Attenzione! Sfaccendare."

"Soldiers of the elite Ariete, this is your commander speaking. Do not despair. Follow my instruction and I shall guide you safely through the blinding maze. *Allora, allestirsi. Squadrone, avanti!"*

The Italians, unwittingly following Darius's instructions disappeared into the tanks and secured hatches. The less thinking the Ariete engaged in this day, the better for Italy, for history.

Following to the letter the course charted for them by the smooth-talking unidentified Italian piped in through their headgear, the Ariete squadron pulled forward, steamrolling unsuspectingly into the mined areas. Before the cunning radio deception was detected, thirty tanks blew up. Six tanks groped blindly through the mines unscathed, plunging headlong into the French box, crushing the Legion post command. Scrubby-bearded legionnaires in shorts, sandals, and mosquito netting about their heads leaped onto the tanks, tossed grenades into the open visors, jumped off and picked off any of the crew left alive and able to force open the overhead hatches. Several tanks picked off by French 75mm guns were later salvaged and picked clean of weapons. Squads of Free-French soldiers sprinted like jack rabbits, zigzagging through volatile mines, to blow up what remained of the crippled tanks. The soldiers looted supply trucks at the rear, returned to the French box heroes, toting hams, cheeses, tins of jam, wine, chocolate, and barrels of precious water.

It was sheer genius, it was! Whoever thought up this act . . .

Five hours later . . . *retaliation*! It was ghastly. German Commander Ernst Von Luden, buoyed by fresh squadrons of the 90th German Armored and Italian motorized Trieste divisions, encircled the French defense, trapping two detachments under heavy fire; none in this sector survived.

The SAS commander leaped from their cover positions in an abandoned well near Bir Hakeim, and, scurrying forward, hurling grenades, destroyed eight tanks, four trucks, and knocked out a powerful 88. Returning to the well, under cover, Darius was informed the post command at Bir Hakeim was under heavy bombardment by both German and Italian forces.

"Get Command headquarters on the phone, Dutch," Darius shouted, measuring the effect of the enemy bombardment through field binoculars. Broken lines of barbed-wire fences, a jumble of coiled steel brambles at the outer perimeters, left enormous gaps and weakened the defenses.

"Captain! There's no answer at headquarters!" O'Reilly shouted.

The sweat-soaked commandos hunched over the well's rim barely heard Dutch. Focused on Darius's line of vision, they lowered their sand goggles and peered into the distance.

"What the bloody hell?" Darius crept over the sand-bagged rim of the well and crabbed his way forward to a slight rise.

Tamir Mandel cursed aloud. "That ain't no damn mirage! We'll be drowned in a sea of blood."

"We've been in worse straits," said Pascal, leaping over the rim, landing in a cloud of dust next to Darius. "*Mon Dieu! Capitaine!* What a spectacular sight! What a show of strength!"

God Almighty! It's over, thought Darius. We're done for! Pascal pulled a reluctant Darius back into the abandoned well. Darius quickly grabbed the periscopic sights, turned them to the incredible array of strength approaching.

General Rommel himself, leading ten thousand vehicles around the British flank south of Bir Hakeim approached, closer . . . closer . . . closer. . . . The commandos prayed aloud in their native tongues. Binoculars fixed like adhesives to their eyes, each witnessed history in the making, their optimism slowly draining away.

Rommel and his Afrika Korps were close enough for Darius to smell the hot iron of the sand-colored Wehrmacht trucks and heated diesel oil permeating the desert air. He sighted the dust-covered palm-leaf markings and bold swastikas emblazoned on the tanks. *Damn it!* A warring prowess, an unmistakable aura of victory hovered over the Germans. Darius, holding binoculars on General Rommel, actually saw a penumbra of light around the intrepid Desert Fox. How did they do it! Every soldier was nattily dressed like a soldier should dress, seemingly impervious to the prostrating effects of the desert.

General Rommel, master of the unpredictable followed through with an unpredictable move. He directed his massive army right past the SAS commandos, headed toward the French box. Instead of knocking it out—and he could have with a huff and a puff—he circled Bir Hakeim, fanned his troops out to the northeast, headed for the British boxes.

Later Darius learned that the British 3rd Indian Motor Brigade had served to whet Rommel's appetite. For salad, entree, and dessert he had gobbled up with gusto three additional British armored and motor brigades.

The momentary victory of the Thessalus wine ploy fell flat. Darius with the sting of momentary defeat smarting, sorely frowned in consternation. If the fortifications to the north of Bir Hakeim fell . . .

Oh Christ!

"*Sacré bleu!*" Lucien Pascal, the first to sight it, gasped in dismay.

Darius spun around, his eyes on Pascal's line of vision. "Not again!" he sputtered at the enormous black cloud appearing on the horizon.

"A *khamsen!*" Limey Whitehall cursed.

"A *ghilbi!*" Delon muttered, wiping the sweat from his brow.

Every legionnaire along the Gazala Line knew that the hot hurricane winds rising off the Sahara floor were their mortal enemy. Temperatures could soar thirty-five degrees higher, winds rage ninety miles per hour. The *ghilbi* stopped battlefield movements, halted tanks, grounded planes, pinned down troops to a standstill. The commandos prepared for the worst. Neck cowls wrapped around their heads, skin-tight sand goggles lifted over their eyes, in moments they metamorphosed into bug-eyed mummies.

Darius, peering apprehensively at the billowing sands on the darkening horizon, measured distance against time. Could the SAS make it back to Bir Hakeim? To remain in the abandoned well was suicide. He cursed aloud. He tugged down on his goggles, peeled his sand mask apart, and placed binoculars to his eyes. He signaled toward the storm. His men, sprinting over the sandbags, ready to flee to headquarters, glanced in the direction to which Darius pointed.

Holy Christ! It was neither *khamsen* nor *ghilbi*!

Tracking forward at a fast clip from the north, kicking bowls of sand from the desert, came brand-new U.S.A. twenty-eight-ton Grant tanks equipped with 75mm guns. Off came the masks and goggles!

American tanks? Help from the U.S.A.? The men whooped for joy.

Was it possible the tide was turning in their favor?

That night Darius broke protocol. He permitted the SAS to imbibe a few bottles of wine.

DAWN THE NEXT DAY

All hell broke loose! General Von Luden, leading the embarrassed Italian Ariete brutally assaulted the French box. Two infantry divisions, supported by air power descended upon Bir Hakeim, shells bursting, shattering buildings, supply depots, razing portions of the post command.

Observing the devastation from their cover positions, the SAS huddled solemnly behind the rim of the abandoned well in grim silence. Then, Longinotti, spitting a mouthful of sand raining on them pointed to the sky. "*Capitaine*—see up there!" Darius whirled about staring.

Junkers! Bloody Junkers! Here it came, the dreaded aerial strength he had expected to support the enemy ground forces.

Christ! It was unbelievable! The SAS stared impotently at the awesome sight. Diving Stukas flung stick bombs into the French box. Deafening sounds rumbled over the desert floor. Entire sections of the garrison propelled into the air exploded and fell to the ground in pieces. The French ground forces fought with all they had, a pitiful sum of weapons and ammunition against the

Stukas and 88s. Yet, they brazenly picked off assault troops with bullets and shells. Astonishingly Von Luden's troops fell to retreat, letting the aerial assault demolish a greater part of the French perimeters. It was a bloody damn rout, the French casualties ran high.

Impenetrable curtains of black smoke hovered over the southern perimeters of the Gazala Line. Machinegun spurts sounded like popping champagne corks. The pervasive stench of demolition bombs commingled with charred flesh permeated the desert heat, grew intolerable.

The flare-lit sky revealed a concentration of troops and lorries herded together in a narrow corridor and Darius saw the legionnaires redouble their assaults on the encircling lines. Hand-to-hand combat ensued, slaughter with bayonet, grenades. A lieutenant in a Bren carrier overran a couple of machinegun nests and, charging headlong at an anti-tank gun, was killed. The men of his company, incensed, broke through the first, second, and third enemy lines while lorries carrying the wounded and salvaged material lurched and skidding precariously over the sand toward the post command.

Tamir Mandel from his cover position shouted, "*Capitaine*, look to the east!" Darius whipped around, stunned at the sight. Less than five hundred yards from their position German gunners began wheeling deadly 88s into position.

The Free-French soldiers shouted, "*Demerde-vous!*" as other sections of the garrison blew into the air. The battle raged on unmercifully.

"Bloody damn rout!" Darius shouted snapping orders to his men.

And into the fray . . .

As the SAS loaded incendiary and fragmentation bombs, Darius heard, "*Captain!* Captain Bonifacio!"

Darius, sporting a month's growth of beard, his skin charred from the blistering hot sun and winds, fixed haunted eyes on the moving target approaching them. He whipped off his sand goggles, blinked hard. Sunlight, bouncing off the men's bayonets distorted the image.

Valentina Varga! Here, in the bowels of hell! Damnable woman! She came at them gunning the motor of her utility, kicking up flumes of sand. Christ! If the Germans spotted her? . . . How could they escape the cloud bursts of sand blazing her trail? *Damn, it was Valentina!* For a moment he thought his eyes played tricks. Panic gripped him. He refused to permit the backwash of shock to paralyze him. Quickly he turned in the direction of the German 88s, measuring time against distance. *Don't let the Huns spot her!*

Valentina slammed hard on the brakes, skidding rakishly, exploding more sand geysers. Jumping free of the vehicle, she ran toward the well, shouting, "Captain! . . . Captain Bonifacio! Can't you hear me?" Her smile evaporated at the glowering expression on his face. She saluted him, instantly reverting to protocol. "Lieutenant Varga, here. General Koenig's orders, sir. As your driver I am to transport—"

"My driver? *My driver!* Goddammit, I don't need a bloody driver! Get your derriere the hell back to the general before the nasty Nazis turn you to vulture bait. That's an order, Lieutenant!"

Abashed at his abrasiveness, Valentina quickly recuperated her poise. "General Koenig's orders are to return you to the post command on the double! What I do with my hind quarters is my business. As a member of the armed forces I resent your attitude. You don't like the orders? Fine! Take them up with General Koenig! *Damn you anyway!*"

Darius came toward her. Despite her obvious exhaustion and without an ounce of cosmetics, she was more stunning than he remembered her. Or was his desire so great . . . They stared at one another, oblivious to the war at all sides of them.

"Where do we go from here?" she whispered softly. "Two whole years without word from you, Darius! Two whole years!"

"I'll tell you where you go from here," he began softly, seductively. "Go the hell back to where you came from! You hear? Move it, Varga! Get cracking. Goddammit, I said go!"

"I stay!" She hurled the words at him like a grenade.

He descended on her in growling menace, under the mocking eyes and amused grins of his haggard and emaciated men, and swept her up in his arms. She struggled fiercely as he toted her back to the jeep and dumped her into the driver's seat. "I hadn't expected to see you again against so dramatic a background, *chérie.*" Leaning in closer to her, he shoved a wispy tendril of copper hair from her face. "I'll settle with you later. Now, *move* before you get us all killed!"

Too late! A mortar exploded nearby, rocking the jeep. The SAS shouted warnings as they dived for cover. Darius cursed blackly under the barrage of bursting shells. He lifted Valentina from the utility and tossed her to the ground, then fell protectively over her as the German 88s opened fire on their position. The last thing Darius needed was a woman's presence in hell!

Any soldier worth his salt kept himself attuned to the sounds of shells. He could discern by approaching sounds if they'd land close enough to be lethal; by the curved arc of a falling bomb, he determined if they'd fall close or far away. He *knew* thirty yards from an exploding missile was safe—any closer, forget it. Darius had learned to sniff the proximity of danger and knew it existed only at the time and *moment* of danger, not before, not after. Only the tough, smart, seasoned soldiers survived hell. The rest became carrion. Dreams and ambitions did not exist beyond the moment of battle, and because they did not, a soldier learned to be cold, brutal, and tough or he was destroyed.

But how could he put all these lessons to use when his senses were beguiled by this woman? How, for the love of God?

Darius was raging mad. Mad at the war, at Valentina, at the lame-brained general who had sent her into a raging battle! What were field telephones for? He denied the tightness in his throat as memory stirred feelings he had buried deep inside him. Her nearness, the smell of her, activated all the old yearnings.

Ten minutes . . . an eternity later, the bombardment ceased. Darius scrambled to his feet, then fell to a crouch. Peering into the distance, he moved stealthily forward, cautioning Valentina to stay put. He thanked his men for not returning the gunfire. "If you had, we'd all be statistics by now." He glanced back at Valentina.

Goddamned! What a woman! She wasn't in the least bit shaken. Covered with dust from head to toe, coughing, spitting out the sand, she got to her feet, slapped the sand from her uniform, shook out her hair, tugged down on her short-sleeved tunic, and reset her visored hat into place. Then she strode back to the jeep.

"Varga! Don't move! The Italians have us in their sights, *dammit*. You must wait until dusk!"

"Fuck you, Captain!" she spat at him contemptuously. "If you haven't learned by now the inaccuracy of the 88s and the odds against their landing *precisely* on target, or the improbability of bull's-eye aerial strafing by now, you never will!" She sank into a pothole to her knees. "What the bloody damned hell are you angry at? I don't know you anymore!" She scrambled out of the hole remarkably well poised and swung into the jeep.

She started the motor, gunned the engine, spun out the wheels crazily in the sand.

The SAS grinned broadly at Darius's ferocious scowl. He turned to them menacingly. "Not one word, hear? Not a fucking word from any of you!"

Two hours later Pascal, Tamir, and Longinotti returned from reconnaissance with stunning news. Tamir gushed aloud, "Rommel's immobilized!"

"Immobilized, Tamir? Rommel's immobilized?" exclaimed Delon.

"What?" Darius shouted. "Rommel's immobilized? How? Where? When? In God's name, spill it!" His spirits soared.

"The new USA Grant tanks went after Rommel, trapped him along the Gazala Line. Two Panzer divisions lost! One third of their tanks gone! The Germans are backed up into a moon-shaped retreat, surrounded on all sides by British boxes and mines!" Pascal reported concisely in rapid French.

"Rommel's immobilized!" Darius repeated incredulously. The unthinkable had happened. "O'Reilly, get on the phone to headquarters, relay the news to Bir Hakeim!"

A half hour later Darius paced the earthen floor of General Koenig's office, addressing himself to French commander, Ben-Kassir, and Furstenberg. "I tell you, now! Now is the time to strike! Mass Rommel's armor! Crush him! Take him by surprise!" Darius insisted. "General, don't you understand? Rommel is vulnerable, for God's sake! We must move now. If we don't strike before he's had a chance to regroup . . ."

Delon rushed into the office with two communiqués, one from Cairo, the other from the Knightsbridge box where Rommel's position grew increasingly untenable. Colonel Furstenberg read the first message with considerable annoyance. "Italian engineers have just cut open a supply line to Rommel." He tossed the second message onto the general's desk. At least the British High Command in Cairo agrees with you, Captain Bonifacio. They've ordered the field commanders in Gazala to take instant action."

"And?" General Koenig pressed eagerly.

"General Ritchie is—uh—not ready. He's taken the matter to committee."

"To comm—" Darius stopped, as appalled as the others. He searched Colonel Furstenberg's eyes, critically, then with sagging shoulders he fired a verbal *coup de grace*. "Is it time to destroy the files?"

"The dust of defeat hasn't settled upon us yet, Captain."

"Give it time, give it time," Darius said, deflated.

The others flinched; they didn't dispute him. "Beyond Bir Hakeim, to the west," said Ben-Kassir quietly, "is *El Kalahara* a German redoubt that keeps Rommel supplied. If Captain Bonifacio and his commandos can destroy it—"

Furstenberg interrupted, "There's no time to set up strategy for the mission." He shot Darius a tentative glance. "Well, captain? Is there?"

Darius deliberated two full minutes, silent as he studied El Kalahara fortification charts. "We know the area better than the tail end of a camel's ass, sir. With luck and a choir of angels on our side. . ."

"*Très bien!* It's settled. I shall accompany you," Youseff said tersely.

"No, Highness. I cannot permit it." Darius was firm.

"The captain is right. An odd man at the center of such risky business would impede, if not destroy their objectives." Furstenberg's voice oozed authority.

Darius signaled a silent thanks. Youseff glowered.

EL KALAHARA
9:45 P.M.

A full moon rising off the desert floor flushed the area with light, bringing the caravan crossing a short distance from the massive German fortification into clearer view. A scattering of date palms, several large boulders spilled around an oasis provided meager but adequate cover, Darius continued to plot strategy en route to their destination.

The whites of their eyes showed incandescent against root-stained faces. Disguised as Bedouins, the commandos approached El Kalahara navigating bad-tempered dromedaries. Darius and twelve of his men dismounted, tethered the camels at the oasis, and scurried forward toward the formidable German redoubt. A dozen French soldiers trailing in machinegun mounted utilities pulled into cover positions in the shadow of the date palms. They alighted the jeeps, covered them with camouflage tarps, and took their positions, guns at ready. They observed the advance commandos through binoculars until they disappeared from sight.

Wide, luminous arcs swept the black sky. Generator-powered kliegs from the fortification fanned the nearby area. And the music! Brassy percussion instruments booming Wagnerian music through loudspeakers echoed for miles in the night.

For Darius, internal tocsins shouted above the din. *It was all wrong!* The moon! Spotlights! Music! All wrong for the mission he planned this night.

Distance and sound, deceptive in the desert at night, the German redoubt, a mile away seemed less distant than two city blocks. The music seemed a hundred yards away. The seasoned commandos arrived at the redoubt's southern wall, crabbed forward on their bellies up the slight rise of a sand dune, avoiding the sweep of spotlights mounted on high towers.

Darius signaled the explosives and wire men ahead while those preparing fuses worked to prepare a systematic series of explosions. The first wave of commandos crept stealthily forward, timing their movements against the sweep of converging spotlights, moving only in the twenty-second intervals of darkness.

A signal to Longinotti, Whitehall, and Tamir brought them out of the shadows and onto the main path toward the large gate. The trio squabbled loudly among themselves in Farsi. One moment they begged shelter from the German guards, the next the guards were garroted and dealt a taste of instant eternity. After pulling the dead men out of the light, the trio removed their robes and donned German jackets and helmets. In moments they stood guard at the gates.

Darius frowned. Fifteen minutes and no explosives! No wire men! That blasted music! *Tristan und Isolde!* Preempting Wagner periodically came morale boosting speeches by the *Führer* venerating *Deutschland.* "Psychological ploys work wonders," Darius whispered to Delon lying alongside him. "Hitler will never know the excellent cover he provided us this night," hissed Delon noting the time. "Fifteen minutes were up four minutes ago, captain."

"We wait," Darius snapped. He focused his binoculars on the towers; the relaxed guards were talking, drinking in repose. The fuse man had finished; he waited for the others.

Two minutes passed . . . four . . . six . . . eight . . .
Jesus Christ! Hurry, goddamn it! Hurry!

"There! By the wire fencing!" Delon indicated. "Let's go!"

A hooting signal was heard. *A warning! Something was wrong!*

"We wait!" Darius commanded. Two men crept under the wire. Two more followed a hundred yards behind them.

Suddenly hell broke loose. A fusillade of gunfire came at them from within the compound. Spotlights swiveled about, focusing on the south wall. Guns from the towers opened fire. Bursts of white lightning electrifed the night. Screeching sirens mercifully obliterated the *Führer's* voice.

"The lights! Shoot out the friggin' lights!" Limey shouted to Pascal. They each aimed at separate corners and shot. *Bull's-eye!*

Commandos at the eastern perimeters fired, drawing attention from the southern wall. Additional spotlights swung about and came to life. German machineguns spewed flame-streaked bullets at invisible targets, shrieking ricochets.

The men were out. Darius signaled the fuse man, who detonated the box. Nothing! Frustrated, he tried again. *What the hell!* Nothing! Duds! Goddammit, duds! Darius shouted, *"Move it! Goddammit! Move!"*

Darius signaled his men. They beat a hasty retreat back to El *Kalahara. What had happened? Dammit, what went wrong?* The damnable explosives: *that's what went wrong! Merde!* Rapid fire bullet fire exploded at their heels, on all sides of them, snapping the air above them, every which way.

At the redoubt, loud angry shouts pierced the night. It was bedlam! Everywhere was disorganized chaos. German soldiers sprang to the utilities, started the engines, gunned the motors, lurching forward into the courtyard as gunners manned the mounted machineguns. More soldiers in partial stages of undress sprinted alongside, boarding the vehicles wheeling toward the locked entrance gates. "Shoot off the locks, *Dummkopfs!*" shouted the officers. A few spurts from the burp guns exploded obstruction. The Benz utilities shot out into the night in hot pursuit; three squadrons followed, armed to the teeth.

At El Kalahara . . . commandos holding the well viewed the action through binoculars. The first team was returning, sprinting through the night. Instantly the riderless dromedaries were driven off into the desert toward Bir Hakeim, kicking up a smokescreen of sand.

A diversionary tactic! It worked. The Germans sped past the sequestered men at El Kalahara in pursuit of the braying camels. Clouds of dust, raised by galloping camels and speeding Germans, curtained the night. The Nazis opened fire on the invisible moving targets, giving the commandos a moment's respite.

At El Kalahara, Darius, fulminating at the failure of the explosives, perceived their untenable position at once. The commandos were boxed in by the German fortification to the north, and the three squadrons bound to return in hot pursuit the moment they spotted the deception. As he saw it, he had two choices: prepare an ambush, battle the returning Germans and risk being blown to kingdom come by the 88s at the redoubt or . . .

A barrage of gunfire dusted their perimeters. German 88s dictated Darius's second choice. Flares bursting overhead lit up El Kalahara like fireworks on Chinese New Year. *Damnation! Walkie-talkies!* Better than field-radio apparatus! The next surprise for the SAS came on the heels of the first.

Tracer bullets! Accursed tracer bullets!

Darius snapped orders to his men. These stone-cold professionals usually plowed right in, did the job expertly, and got out. Tonight, confronted with aborted plans—the frizzled explosives— they were forced to wing it. Now, as the Germans sped back over the desert toward El Kalahara, they listened to Darius's alternate plan, eyes glittering in expectation, committing his instructions to memory.

The Germans, aware of the fraud perpetrated upon them, pulled up at the oasis, spilled from their utilities, and took cover, shooting wildly into the night.

Silence. No gunfire was returned.

Brigadeführer Ernst Von Luden shouted, "Cease fire!" Signaling his men to silence, he crept forward with a squad of men, waving his hand toward a cluster of date palms. "They are out there!" he shouted. "Go! Find them!" The sweat rolled off his glistening face.

Darius swiftly assessed the odds against victory. Outnumbered five to one, facing the power of a military redoubt with enough sophisticated weaponry to grind them to dust, what chances had they? He carefully winnowed out from his men the members of Delilah's Dream. They had one chance for survival: *hand-to-hand combat! Every dirty trick in the book!*

With the Germans in their sights, the commandos waited.

Von Luden and his men approached. Darius signaled. With Delilah's Dream in the lead, the SAS crept forward like stalking cougars, each step drawing them closer to their objective.

The German soldiers, ignorant of commando warfare, were caught off guard. They dropped like flies under the soundless, lightning assaults.

Guns proved impotent against well-placed blows to pressure points. Here, an unsuspecting soldier, struck with a chop to the jugular was felled, killed on the spot. There, another, garroted from behind by unseen hands, sank to his knees, dead before he hit the ground. Bodies were dragged out of sight, hidden behind date palms and boulders. Wehrmacht soldiers, rated the finest in the world, fell to the unique artistry of men who hadn't seen a grenade launcher or known about tracer bullets until recently.

Darius picked off a German coming at him. Another assailant never knew what struck him, a quick move forced the German to his knees, his arm twisted behind his back, his air supply cut off. The body sagged, fell to the sands, dead.

Another, then another German came flying at Darius. Was there no end to the Nazis? He chopped the cricoid cartilage in one man's neck with a sharp, precise blow and, pivoting in a wild arc, lunged for a second. His upraised fist froze in midair. Darius gasped in loud dismay as shafts of moonlight, stabbing through the date palms, lighted the face clearly. "Youseff! I could have killed you! What the devil are you doing here! I told you to remain behind!"

Boom! Baroom! Baroom!

Darius scrambled up a rise of boulders, binoculars to his eyes. *Merde!* The Germans at the redoubt had got their bearings from the tracers. Now they unloaded the 88s at them. The Germans caught at El Kalahara sprinted for cover, retreating behind boulders, and opened fire on the SAS. Quickly the commandos leaped from cover positions, scooped up stray, abandoned carbines, and shot after them, wasting most.

Valentina was right! The 88s were not always accurate! In that moment's reflection, Darius was struck by a bullet in his arm. Fire sizzled through him. He picked the soldier off with his service revolver, then felled another with two heart implacements. A third was struck, groaned aloud, and sank to his knees, his automatic rifle firing wildly as he fought the throes of death. Darius's forehead, ripped open by stray bullet fire, spurted blood. The hot, sticky crimson fluid streamed into his eyes. Spinning from the impact, he fell back against a boulder, searing pain in one eye and came face-to-face with a man from his past, a man he loathed. Ernst Von Luden! Recognition contorted the German's face.

"*Schweinhund!* Corsican dog!'' the former Legion NCO spat venomously, blood oozing from an open wound in his left arm. He dived at Darius, teeth bared, hatred in his eyes. A knife sank into Darius's shoulder. Darius shot wildly. Through his bloodied eyes, he caught sight of Von Luden, crouching before him, sneeringly beckoning to him. With a bold arrogance and swagger, he made the grand gesture. He tossed aside his gun to even the odds. Now he lunged at Darius, a wild guttural cry crashing through his throat. Darius evaded him, grabbed his enemy's injured arm, twisted it, flipping him on his back. Stunned, enraged by the unexpected blow, Van Luden sprang shakily to his feet; he stalked again like a frightened tiger moving in for the kill. He yanked off his helmet, his head glistened like a billiard ball.

Before Darius could strike, a whirlwind force came from behind pouncing on Von Luden. A wild, inhuman howling brought up Darius's head. A voice shouted, "*Schweinhund!*''

A long, sharp blade, shimmering like silver fire in the moonlight came down slashing, cutting, stabbing Von Luden. It was Youseff Ben-Kassir! Reflected in his royal maniacal eyes was the man who had brutalized his brother, Kabul, the brute who had sodomized and torched the young prince! Darius, attempting to intervene, was flung back against the boulders striking his head. He took a moment to clear it. Pascal restricted his movements, pinioned him, shouting, "No, Captain! His Highness is entitled to his brand of justice!''

Darius, reeling dizzily under a mounting nausea capitulated. He was rapidly losing blood. He sank into Pascal's arms. Lucien forced brandy through his lips. He called, "Delon! Tamir! *Dépêcher!* Hurry! I need help with the captain!''

Jean-Louis moved in hurriedly, his neck cowl pressed against Darius's forehead to retard the blood flow. Tamir moved where he was most needed, assessing the damage, and with the wire men, manned the German utilities. He shouted, "We shall finish the job left undone earlier!'' Donning the Germans' helmets and jackets, they sped off toward the redoubt under a storm of live fire.

*   *   *

The skirmish had ended, mission accomplished. Three German squadrons wiped out and . . . It had taken Tamir, Whitehall, Longinotti, and O'Reilly six and a half minutes to blow up the German fortification, including precious supplies and weapons.

Victory! Yet back at El Kalahara no joyous shouts spilled from the commandos' frozen lips. Grim of face, their emotions in limbo, they moved in frigid silence, witnessing the grisliest sight they'd ever witnessed: the vengeance of Prince Ben-Kassir.

Ernst Von Luden's dismembered, bloodied remains lay strewn about rocks. Youseff, at the hub of activity, was chanting Islamic prayers. The barbarous ritual immobilized the commandos. Yes, they had killed before, yet, as they huddled about in a mute circle, they were unable to comprehend the savagery. None seemed able to break through the terrifying frieze of butchery save one man, Musaka Mubende, a newcomer to the SAS commandos. His dark sapphire eyes stared at the ritual in mute understanding.

"Stop, Highness!" Darius's anguished voice cut through his men's stupor. Four men moved in, barely able to restrain the prince. Twice he broke their hold on him. Hands upraised to the heavens, he cried in supplication, "You are avenged, Kabul, my brother! Praise Allah!"

Darius reentered the world of violence as if he'd never be done with it. Collecting himself, he moved about, shakily instructing Pascal, Tamir, and O'Reilly precisely how to dispose of Von Luden's remains. Listening to their commander, their eyes sparked at the ingenious ploy.

Scrambling into the Germans utilities, the flaming sky behind them, explosions still shaking the earth, the commando task force sped back over the cracked floor of the desert to Bir Hakeim.

Mission accomplished!

Retaliation came, worse than expected. Those two days the British generals had delayed in overtaking Rommel at the Knightsbridge box gave the Desert Fox time to regroup. Italian supplies got through to him, enabling him to smash a bigger hole in the Gazala Line, destroying one hundred British tanks, taking 3,000 prisoners. By eliminating the 150th Infantry Brigade, Rommel knocked out the British box.

General Erwin Rommel turned toward the south, his sights on the French box, prepared to retaliate for the severe losses of critical supplies and weapons sustained at El Kalahara.

GAZALA LINE
June 1–9, 1942

For nine days and ten nights a succession of nightmares fell upon the Free French like a plague. Each morning the gray dawn shone obliquely through the iron-barred windows of the scrubby, dilapidated barracks. Each day—no better, no worse than the last—began at sunrise as monotonous light striations converged in colorless bands. Trembling light molecules, exploding an infinity of hell in the minds of vacant eyed soldiers, barely able to focus on anything clearly, unable to discern the features of his closest friend. To these men, the beginning of one day, the end of another, meant very little. What did it matter? Days and nights, strung together in unending nightmares, committed each soldier to his own private hell. The dead and the near dead lay where they fell; no medics, no stretcher bearers sprang to their aid.

Severe cutbacks in rations, especially water, turned them into animals. When the RAF mercifully dropped canteens of water from the sky, the men metamorphosed into human pack rats, scrambling in all directions, devouring what they could, secreting portions, denying the injured and near dead, prepared to turn their guns on any man who tried to filch their stash. And to cap their humiliation, propaganda leaflets rained down on them from Luftwaffe planes. Under normal circumstances this would have triggered volatile French tempers into fierce combative energy. Now the men barely flicked an eyelid at the printed paper.

> EUROPE BELONGS TO HITLER! DON'T FIGHT! SURRENDER AND SURVIVE! IN THE GERMAN ENCAMPMENTS THERE IS PLENTY OF FOOD, BEER, WATER, AND WINE FOR ALL!

For nine days of living hell, they were bombarded day and night by a hair-raising malediction called "carpet bombing." Stukas appeared on the horizon each dawn, soared high, rolled over on their sides, flew in low, and strafed everything in their sights; the entire Gazala Line glowed under white-lightning bursts. The constant hammering of the Stukas, the sickening consistency of spiraling bombs erupting from Junkers drove the French soldiers closer to madness. Outmatched, outnumbered, outgunned, the valiant French continued to exchange volley for volley, like mechanical soldiers and bloody well held off the German 88s better than their British allies. French and continental music was played to elevate the sinking spirits of the deteriorating French troops. Intermittently Hitler's voice, intruding on another frequency, commended them for putting up a stout show. He suggested surrender, pointing out the utter futility of their plight.

The French soldiers no longer jeered at Hitler's canned voice. Most became supine, infected with a sort of mind paralysis. A protective arrogance no longer concealed the shame of defeat. The morale at the French box had sunk to an all-time low.

THE NINTH DAY

Junker 87s came without warning, piercing dawn-lit clouds. They rolled over and came in strafing. Sleek silver Messerschmitts, in bomb formation, outlined against eastern skies shook the French to the core. As falling bombs whined sickeningly to earth exploding, Darius, driving a jeep to the supply depot, spotted the Luftwaffe planes. He leaped from the utility, into a nearby trench miraculously escaping the first assault. Forced to wait until the air cleared, he coughed out the sand granules. He craned his neck over the rim of the ditch for a look-see.

Oh Christ! . . . Valentina Varga! In the direct line of fire!

Emerging from a supply shelter, carrying supplies to the open bonnet of General Koenig's car, she seemed impervious to the steel thunderbirds raining down lethal pellets. Darius panicked. Was she crazy? He swung his focus to the skies. Another Stuka rolled over. Jesus! He shouted to her! "Take cover! Take cover!"

Valentina looked up, trying to locate the source of the voice, then she gazed at the sky, thunderstruck, yet unwilling or unable to move. Darius loped across the strafed path of dust bursting like miniature volcanoes and caught her in a flying tackle. He felled her, shoved her into a nearby pothole, and covered her with his body.

Overhead, enemy planes in low altitude strikes spit hot bursts of gunfire, spewing shrapnel, laying siege to everything in their sights. Under a raining downpour of debris, Darius peered over the pothole. General Koenig's auto had been blown to bits.

Valentina struggled against him, trying to surface. *"Stay down!"* he shouted. "Down, goddammit! The main building clusters have taken direct hits! The prefabs along the western line . . . razed to the ground. Fires are spreading. . . ." Black smoke spirals and hot red flames darkened the sky. Darius tried to assess the immediate damage. He couldn't.

Oh God, the bodies! The naked and the dead lay like so many rag dolls, scarlet ribbons of blood spewing from holes on their flesh. For many the wretched existence of the past two years was over, thought Darius. For others, who wished they could join their comrades, the worst was yet to come.

The planes had circled around and prepared for another barrage. Moments remained . . . only moments to leap to a more secure position. Go! Darius pulled Valentina out of the pothole, shoved her forward between the medics' tents and a lean-to containing engineering supplies. Nearby, soldiers, manning machineguns mustered last-ditch efforts. Their firing, ineffective at best, barely came within range of the strafing Stukas. A loud cry arose from the French soldiers like a wailing of locusts.

Merci Dieu! Hurricane Intercepters! Dotting the sky like huge birds, the Intercepters came from the British boxes to the north. RAF Spitfires soared valiantly into overhead skies scattering the Luftwaffe planes. Instantly the arena of aerial warfare shifted to the air space south of the French box. The sky was littered with planes as enemies engaged in bitter dogfights.

The French soldiers held binoculars to their eyes to observe the miracle on the horizon. Ground danger for the southern sector was temporarily clear, loudspeakers cracked the stillness left in the bombing aftermath with the music of "Lili Marlene."

Darius did not release Valentina, not yet. "I owe you an apology," he said softly. She struggled to free herself. "Not yet, not until the ground fire ceases. You look terrible," he told her with affection.

"You're no Tyrone Power at the moment."

He studied her features critically. As emaciated as the men, she had shared the same iron rations and water allotment as they had. She had dug in her own vehicle, slept in a slit trench alongside it, done more than was required of her these past nine days. Her courage was the talk of the French box. He whispered softly, "Why, when I see you, do I want to fall in love with you?"

"Don't," she implored. "Love is more frightening than war."

"If we survive, Valentina, perhaps we can be together, even on your terms."

She glanced at him, frowned, and grew flippant. "If I didn't desperately need a bath and my hair wasn't packed with Sahara grit, I'd kiss you for saving my life."

"You Americans are too fastidious for your own good." He kissed her lightly, released her, and began to rise to his feet. "I must go."

"Darius—what are our chances, really?" she asked on a solemn note. "General Koenig tells me nothing. He doesn't have to. I know we face a multitude of dangers. We've suffered inordinate losses. Is it worth it? The sacrifice of so many men— and for what? To save face for France?" She stared vacant-eyed at the dead piled high around her. "Just tell me, do we stand a chance of survival?"

Darius averted his eyes. "We'll know in twenty-four hours."

"If we don't survive, will you be among a band of angels or a legion of devils?" She knew of his SAS forays.

"That depends on the *high* court."

"Fine. We'll meet in court, then. How shall I recognize you? By the smile you no longer use or the frosty-eyed terror in your eyes?"

She walked out of the makeshift shelter. Darius pulled her to him, forcing her eyes into his. "I'd know you anywhere, no matter how you looked." He moved away from her. "It's back to business, *ma chère*."

Her heart quivered. She watched him plow through the rubble. Once he left her line of vision, she glanced at the remains of General Koenig's auto, shuddering. Had she purposely ignored the deadly ballet of strafing Stukas? Was she growing careless? Unobservant? Was it a death wish? Valentina, a stranger to fear, now confronted it squarely and shook inwardly. She felt fear as never before. Now she wondered, could she again feel love? *Real* love? The love she'd felt with Darius two years ago and thrown foolishly aside? What in hell was wrong with her? She didn't know.

Introspection lay dully on her mind.

God! She'd questioned her sanity in leaving Chicago a thousand times. Now she had the answer: his name was Darius Bonifacio. In two years she'd discovered the intensity of her love for him. His departure from England had left her feeling empty; she had told him so. She felt that a part of her was missing, that she'd never feel whole again. She had lost weight, grown pale, listless, and apathetic. On their arrival in North Africa, General Koenig had read the riot act to her. "Shape up or ship out!" And when he saw her reaction to Darius at HDQS, the general had pulled her aside. "Lieutenant Varga, I want no human disasters to disrupt my command. Demonstrate any idiotic femininity and I shall cashier you at once! Do I make myself perfectly understood?" Sobered by his remark, Valentina had snapped to, and continued, robotlike, in her work.

Now, as she moved back through the debris and smoke, wading through the moaning, bloodied bodies, she shuddered. Then she moved on, numbed, pausing at the sound of loud gunfire. She turned to the activity at the main gate of French HDQS. A cluster of French officers observed Rommel's squadron of white-flag-bearing soldiers fleeing under a barrage of bullets.

Rommel's sixth request, asking for French surrender had been denied; would there be another?

An hour later on this decisive ninth day of devastation, Lucien Pascal waved his arm to Darius from inside the well in the field HDQS. "*Sacré bleu!* We are finished!" He pointed to a plume of dust along the eastern sky. Darius scaled the rock pile, pulled his sand goggles to his chin, and set binoculars to his blackened eyes, focusing on an incredible sight in near-hypnotic fascination.

The entire crack German 90th Division, led by Rommel himself, was headed toward Bir Hakeim, supported by an entire armored division and coordinated air power. Darius signaled his communications man. "O'Reilly, relay the news to the post command—British Eighth headquarters in Gazala!" The answer was radioed back at once. O'Reilly, under the dirt and grime, blanched. "The SAS will remain in position . . . fire at will . . . keep the post command at Bir Hakeim and Gazala apprised of all enemy moves!"

Darius inhaled deeply. *How in the name of fucking Christ could the SAS conjure up miracles against so indomitable a force?* German iron monoliths of destruction approached the Gazala Line. Pascal's instant prognosis loomed as irrevocable truth! *They were finished!*

In the face of such opposition, the audacious French opened fire on the advance assault troops! A barrage of 75mm airburst shells toppled a few Panzers. The SAS opened fire with all they had. The fighting continued without letup. Incredible! Over three thousand Free-French troops were hedged in on a burial mound of pebbly ground by German and Italian armored infantry divisions, strafed by Junkers and bombed by Messerschmitts but still fighting valiantly. Eyes, deep in their sockets, ringed white with emaciation, the French expressed the impotent rage of wild animals forced to cower and tremble under the whip.

"Wars, unfortunately, are not won with rage!" General Koenig assessed their bravery to Colonel Furstenberg and the group of British officers observing the deadly devastation. The British officers, in radio contact with Gazala, issued the dreaded orders. *"Retreat!"*

Over the deafening sounds of deadly 88s and wailing dive bombers coming in to lay waste to the ·French box, buglers sounded full retreat.

Full retreat!

The dreaded moment lay upon them like a plague. The long wait had ended; it was over. Of the 3,700 troops entrenched at the French box, General Koenig led some 2,500 into retreat in the darkness.

The Germans were not finished. They threw squadrons of tanks against the retreating French bracketing them by salvos of shells the moment they stepped foot outside the perimeters of the box. The desert exploded all around them. Tanks and desert utilities bounced over rocky, bone jarring ground. Soldiers on foot zigzagged across the sands, hitching rides where they could. German flares formed an umbrella of illumination over the French enabling them to picked off half the fleeing trucks and Bren carriers.

On and on ran the retreating, debilitated soldiers harried by desert squalls, vomiting from fatigue and fear. Darius and the SAS made several runs over retreating lines, picking up stragglers, driving them forward to the lorries and utilities. The retreat was mass hysteria.

By early dawn Darius made his last trip to the rear lines, loaded every straggler, dumped the heavy guns to make room for humans. A pre-dawn sun set the battlefield into appalling relief. Every rise was littered with burned-out tanks, some still smoking, the charred skeletal remains of bodies spilling out of turrets and hatches were partially covered by shifting sands. A hot wind coming off the desert would bury them forever, thought Darius. He and the others stared solemnly at the horrible aftermath of the battle. Vultures circled overhead, swooping down on the prey, tearing flesh from the corpses. Tamir Mandel picked off a few with his rifle. Longinotti cursed, tossed a grenade where a wall of voracious vultures congregated on a pile of rocks. A few wild-eyed soldiers, on the verge of madness, dashed forward and picked off the jackals and hyenas with their service revolvers.

By midmorning, as the last of defeated soldiers straggled into British Eighth Army lines near the Egyptian border, Darius noticed British engineers and turbaned Sikh sappers, of the 4th Indian Division engaged in the complex, nerve-shattering task of scouring the grounds, delicately probing with bayonets for buried explosives. Anything from heavy saucepan-shaped teller mines, whose blasts could blow a tank inside out, to the small S mines, which, when set off by a footstep, sprang to shoulder height and shot forth hundreds of tiny steel fragments. The turbaned Sikhs displayed cool, uncanny expertise on these vast sandy fields where hidden death lurked unseen.

CAIRO, EGYPT
WAR JOURNAL ENTRY

Bir Hakeim; an unheralded battle in the war has ended. Only the post-mortem remains. A last-ditch effort to save the French box by thirty-five thousand American troops had failed. The Americans were green, inexperienced, unused to daily barrage of enemy fire so stoically endured by the British and French forces for the past two years. The worst thing about being a novice in the war was not knowing what to look for, listen to, or smell. No training behind the lines could teach you what it was like to move out to where the enemy waited to kill you. Handling your fears was another thing altogether. Give the voices another six months . . .

Chapter Thirty-four

CAIRO, EGYPT
November, 1943

"She zigzagged across the black desert like some crazy . . . In and out of potholes, over crater rims onto the sands. Well, I ordered Lieutenant Varga to stay clear of shell craters and she shouted back at me, 'Fine, General, I'll do just that if you tell me how to stay clear of the *fucking* holes doing fifty in the darkness without headlights!' "

The others laughed as they listened to General Koenig's description of his retreat from Bir Hakeim.

"She had a point there, General," said Colonel Furstenberg, the first smile Darius could remember playing across his lips.

Valentina Varga stood at the edge of the parade square at British HDQS talking with several RAF officers. Ben-Kassir sidled up to Darius and, following the Corsican's line of vision, smiled.

"That flame needs quenching soon, Darius. My house is your house. *Comprenez-vous?*

"*Qu'est-ce que c'est? Que voulez-vous?*"

The prince laughed. "You understood me the first time."

"*Merci*, Highness."

"*Pas de quoi.*"

*   *   *

Two hours *after* the parade, *after* the citations, *after* tribute was paid to the Free-French forces by the British High Command, *after* General Koenig received the DSO, and *after* Valentina Varga was decorated with the *Croix de Guerre* by General Charles de Gaulle, new orders were issued to Darius. He received his new commission as major from the recently elevated-in-rank General Henri Furstenberg. Before he did, General Koenig addressed the Free-French forces.

"You men of the Legion will prepare at once to leave for El Alamein. Our task is to seize control of El Himmeimat. I want you to show the same bravery and courage you did at Bir Hakeim."

General Koenig dismissed his men and left the large room.

"Uh, not you, Major Bonifacio," General Furstenberg called to him. He closed the door behind the others, in the quarters provided for them in the British fortifications in Cairo. He turned to Darius. "Your assignment is far more critical. Our commander in chief personally requests you take command of a new offensive, Operation White Coral. Corsica, Major, is under enemy occupation. The Italians landed November 12. Your orders are to depart for Corsica, following briefing with your SAS, send the Axis soldiers into retreat, and prepare for the liberation of France."

Darius stared at Furstenberg, speechless.

Ten days! Ten *whole* days and nights to be together *after* a two-year deprivation? Their time together promised to be idyllic. Youseff had provided them the use of his Mediterranean villa near Alexandria to live, love, luxuriate, swim in perfumed pools, make love on the beach under star-studded skies; to listen indolently to waves crashing on the shore under an invigorating sun, against a background of weird sounding Egyptian music played by instruments with no names.

Valentina had so much to tell Darius. Nothing beyond the villa, not even the glorious lore of ancient Egypt could lure the star-crossed lovers. Servants cared for their every need, fed them marvelous foods and vintage wines neither could enjoy. It was too much! Too soon! After a two year sojourn of iron rations, their sensitive stomachs rebelled. The first three days were spent in great discomfort; after that, the lovers blended intimately.

The changes in Darius, evident by the almost savage intensity of his lovemaking, both overwhelmed and frightened Valentina. He demanded more, gave less, and his moods, more mercurial than she recalled had intensified. Lurking beneath his charm, she sensed violent rages and a melancholia waiting to surface at the slightest provocation. The quenchless fires within him needed constant fanning and feeding. The intensity of her own love for him, was reciprocated more powerfully than at Dover. At times, she tried desperately to understand and be tolerant of the moods falling upon him, but felt immobilized like the victim of the spitting death's-head spider that enveloped its prey in a mucilaginous secretion until after the ritual mating was done. She was unable to resist him.

The first night erased the two year separation at once; it seemed they'd never been apart. Darius spoke very little and when Valentina felt inclined to talk, he'd move in closer, kiss her to silence. "Let's just feel, Val. Let our feelings come alive. Stretch, air them, give them new life. We've both lived through the dark side of hell, repressing our feelings for too long. We, the lucky ones, lived through hell while thousands of luckless bastards died horribly. I don't know why we were spared, but I don't want to relive those memories, not while so much lies ahead of us." She agreed.

Valentina tried several times to express the depth of her love for Darius. She wanted him to know she no longer entertained those foolish ideas she had promoted in Dover. Each time she was held back, inexplicably, by something profound and threatening. Something distant in him, an aloof, cautious reserve restrained her. Although she gave herself wholeheartedly to him she sensed he kept a part of himself in cautious reserve—untouchable. Her love for him was so desperate she asked herself why she felt miserable, unfulfilled. Would she forever be haunted by those stupid words spoken at Dover? *"You offer me the whole world when all I want is a small slice!"* What a fool! Now, she wanted the whole world, Darius at its center.

On Wednesday, Youseff flew into Alexandria from Cairo, insisted on taking them on a short sightseeing jaunt up the Nile. Valentina accepted the idea with elation. Curiously Darius seemed relieved. He carted along his camera and film.

They flew south from Cairo enchanted with Youseff's narration.

"It is impossible to glimpse the Nile and not have visions of eternity," he began pointing out a narrow strip of green vegetation shadowed by palm groves that ended abruptly in a broad, slow-moving, mud-brown river. "More than ten thousand years ago man settled along the life-giving Nile. The land prospered and in the fourth millennium before Christ burst into splendor under the first of the Pharaohs . . ." It was a marvelous journey and Valentina's expectations were high.

At Giza they saw the Great Sphinx. It was stunning. Darius photographed it from every angle. West of Saqqara they flew over the Step Pyramid. Countless other pyramids, surrounded by a high wall, rose from a plateau of billowing sand and stretched endlessly to the west. Further south another came into view. "The Bent Pyramid," Youseff told them. And Valentina, united with a sense of timelessness rhapsodized, "Just think, Cleopatra and Anthony sailed a barge up this same river."

The men exchanged amused glances. *Just like a woman!*

The Sikorsky soared over upper Egypt, past Hermopolis to the Valley of Kings. "The Colossi of Memnon." Youseff pointed to the gigantic monoliths standing before Deir el Bahri. "There, the Temple of Hathor." In moments the helicopter soared over the Temple of Amenhotep III. The spectacular statues and temples were awesome. By the time they reached the First Cataract of the Nile Valentina had fainted dead away in Darius's arms.

Darius, alarmed, stroked her damp forehead, broke an ammonia capsule under her nose, and implored Youseff to fly back to Alexandria.

But Youseff had other plans. His reason for suggesting this excursion in the first place was to assuage his inner fears for their well being. He landed at Cairo airport. A dusty black Mercedes awaited them, and drove them to a building in downtown Cairo not far from the Shepherd's Hotel.

Dr. Mustafa Sharaffian, once a resident at Johns Hopkins, completed his examination of both Valentina and Darius, He spoke with a clipped British accent. "Nervous exhaustion compounded by a flagrant disregard for proper diet and bodily care. You should have attended to this condition long ago. You are both suffering from malnutrition, anemia, combat fatigue." He gave them injections of Vitamin B, loaded them with medications, and prescribed four to five meals daily and plenty of rest for the next two months.

*   *   *

"Two months!" Darius chuckled. "Your doctor must think we're on a grand party, Youseff," he said as they finished lunch on the terrace of Shepherd's Hotel. "You are not the most subtle of people, Highness," he added, raising a condemning eyebrow. "I appreciate the concern."

"*Valentina! Valentina Varga!*" They all turned in the direction of the voice. The terrace was filled to capacity with British officers, civilians, and a rash of patched-up soldiers on the mend. They peered through the unrecognizable throng, searching. Valentina shrugged indifferently.

"Valentina! *Damn, it is you*, Val! What a sight for sore eyes." Coming gushingly forward was a U.S. Air Force pilot. "It is you, isn't it? My God, woman, you look terrible. Are you all right?" He approached with two American officers and an Egyptian wearing the British uniform of a first lieutenant. The exuberant young officer glanced at her companions, but he zeroed in on her.

Valentina broke into an ineffable grin of delight. "Hart? Hartford Lansing! What a surprise!"

He picked her up in his strong arms, swung her around in a circle, kissed her lingeringly as the others looked on.

Darius's face flooded with anger, his eyes turned frigid, hostile. Youseff's restraining hand on his arm and the look in the prince's eyes arrested him. "An American custom, Darius, take no offense."

Vaguely he heard Valentina's voice. "May I present Major Darius Bonifacio . . . His Highness Prince Ben-Kassir. Gentlemen, Captain Hartford Lansing, a friend of mine from home."

The men shook hands. Lansing turned back to Valentina, ignoring the others and the momentary awkward silence.

"I can't believe my eyes," he rhapsodized. "You're the talk of Chicago. The *Croix de Guerre* no less. Congratulations, honey. Being here in the thick of things before Uncle Sam took a shine to war . . . Same old daredevil, eh, kiddo?"

" 'Fraid so, Hart." She glanced at his companions pointedly.

"Forgive my manners. May I present Captain Brad Lincoln—" He stopped. Prince Ben-Kassir was already shaking hands with the OSS captain. "Well, that's Captain Lincoln. This is Lieutenant Jim Greer, another apple-pie man, and this is Lieutenant Mustafa Qir, a British soldier attached to Egyptian intelligence. They are showing me the sights."

Valentina, quick to notice the displeasure in Darius as he recognized the American OSS officers he'd met in London, nodded curtly. "If you'll excuse us, we were just leaving."

"Oh, no you don't! You can't escape me so soon. We've got a lot of catching up to do." He was handsome, well built, with a golden tan and blue eyes that turned all the female heads he passed.

Darius loathed him at once.

"Sorry, Hart," she begged off. "The war, you know. Commitments . . ."

Two hours later they were back in Alexandria at Youseff's villa.

Silence . . . protracted, impenetrable, like a wall between them . . . *Jealousy* . . . from Darius? *Inconceivable!* Still, Valentina entertained a budding delight deep in her soul. Jealousy? Was it a sign he cared for her far more than he wanted to?

They sat on the terrace overlooking the sea. Valentina was perspiring profusely. Darius moved in closer, studied her pale features. "You look feverish. Come, let me take you inside. The sun can enervate you swiftly."

Before she replied, she collapsed in his arms. Moments later Darius laid her on a large bed, on a raised dais overlooking a sparkling, scented pool. She awakened briefly, smiled, and fell asleep. Darius covered her with a thin sheet of silk, unloosed the mosquito netting, and left the room, closing the door behind him.

In the library he found Youseff's enormous record collection. He too had fallen for the sad lament of "Lili Marlene" and played the recording endlessly while he pored through the library. At last he fell asleep, consumed by exhaustion.

Valentina awakened early in the evening. She summoned a servant, ordered a fresh glass of orange juice and sipped it slowly, taking each of the pills Dr. Sharaffian had prescribed. When she asked, the servants told her the major was asleep in the library. Should they prepare dinner as usual? They should, she said, lying back against the silk pillows, staring at the iridescent play of lights reflected from the crystal pool nearby. She'd seen hell firsthand and, like the battle-hardened infantry, had developed a protective apathy in the face of violence and death. With the *dégagé* air of an actress filming dangerous action scenes before a process-screen background, Valentina had moved through the bloody battles of war without consciously relating to the events. That haunted, empty-eyed look called shock, combat fatigue and a hundred other misnomers was in fact the outward repression of acute numbness. Today she'd been hit hard. Was it, she wondered, an excuse to cover her real feelings? She was in love with Darius as she had never dreamed of loving any man, and didn't know what to do about it. She didn't want to lose him, knew less how to hold on to him. He was slipping away from her; and the war, no ally was determined to make them strangers again. What could she do? You don't lasso a man like Darius and say, "Hey there, I'm in love with you, and because I want you, no one else gets you. You're mine forever, see?"

Uh-uh, not to Darius. *Think, girl, think.*

She tried to get up, felt woozy, and sank against the pillows, confused, angry. Never ill a day in her life, why here and now when she wanted to feel strong, vigorous, and alive? She fought sleep. She didn't intend to waste a precious moment of time by sleeping away the few days remaining of her leave.

At nine P.M. Darius entered the bedroom, carried her onto the terrace, and placed her on a comfortable chaise lounge. A tray of food lay on a nearby table. He began to feed her, solicitously.

"How Youseff manages during war to make miracles . . ." Darius smiled. "Tonight, just for you, a surprise. American films, with sound. A pastime until we both regain our strength."

"I love you for including yourself on the infirmed list, Darius." She watched him roll down a screen from a recessed wooden ledge on one wall inside the library. "What's the star attraction?"

"*Jesse James,* starring uh—Tyrone Power," he said with the emphasis on the name.

Valentina laughed, recalling that day at the French box during the Stuka raid when she had alluded to the fact that he was no Tyrone Power. Unknown to Valentina, Darius had asked of his companions the identity of the mysterious Tyrone Power? Delon had clued him in. "A famous American cinema actor who married Anabella, a Frenchwoman."

At the end of the film, Darius turned to Valentina somberly. "No one is as handsome as Tyrone Power." She laughed heartily.

Assuredly they enjoyed the films, but it was Laurence Olivier's performance in *Wuthering Heights* that both intrigued and disturbed Darius. It brought into definitive focus the vast differences between his world and Valentina's. He recollected what Youseff had told him at Bir Hakeim. Marveling at Valentina's heroic comportment, her courage, stamina, and discipline, the prince had candidly expressed his amazement. "A wealthy heiress who could and should be sitting out the war in luxurious comfort? What the devil is she doing here?"

Darius wouldn't let the remark pass. He questioned Youseff, who suggested, "Study her security clearance, if you don't believe me, *mon ami*." And Darius did precisely that. It was true! According to the report she was as rich as Croesus. Why in hell was she risking her life in a war? His mind was cluttered with possible answers. *Eccentric! Certifiably insane! Possessed with a death wish!* Or all three? Whatever she was, whatever Darius was, he knew one thing for certain—they were ill-fated lovers who came from separate worlds. At war's end she'd return to her world and he to his. Darius knew it was only natural that she would cling to America. It never occurred to him that he might be equally as wealthy as Valentina; the thought of wealth did not occur to him at all.

They spent the next two days strolling lazily along the beach, enjoying the moment, both commenting on the unfathomable mysteries in life. "Less than sixty miles to the west, along the shore, one of the most decisive battles of the war is taking place at El Alamein between Rommel's forces and that British, Bible-reading, teetotaling son of a bishop, General Bernard Montgomery." Darius told Val about Montgomery. "Beneath that cantankerous and flamboyant facade is a dedicated professional soldier with a keen sense of how to handle front-line infantry soldiers. What I wouldn't give to watch those two in action."

"War fascinates you enough to *know* so much about the commanders?"

"If you know the leaders of both sides, you can almost predict their moves," he said quietly.

They walked in silence for a time. Valentina yielded to introspection, then began to speak freely of her childhood, of growing up fatherless. She spoke of the man she'd only known through her mother's eyes, a man who was guilty, even if by death, of abandoning her. Speaking freely in catharsis, Val realized this love-hate relationship with a man she'd never known had influenced every moment of her life. She learned she had posed conditional love to the men in her life so that no man could ever abandon her. When she thought of the wasted years . . .

Darius, mystified by the complexities of Valentina's life, couldn't imagine Sophia being inundated with so many problems. Corsican and American lives contrasted sharply. Would he ever understand her?

Two days remained of their leave. Youseff, in Cairo, fighting to extend their leaves for another week, got nowhere fast. War waited for no one. Didn't he know the enemy was waiting in the wings?

Friday got off to a bad start. Darius screened the film *Beau Geste*. He fulminated at once. "What rubbish—this portrayal of the Legion! You Americans do not depict real life in films! Are you all shallow, superficial, lacking in strong basic values? How, in God's name does man cope with the real world if he measures reality against the lies depicted in those films? People do not live the fairy tales shown in the screen!"

"Darling, why are you so angry?" Valentina asked.

Darius said nothing. He turned on the record player. "Lili Marlene" filled the solarium. He dived into the indoor pool. Valentina slipped in after him. They swam vigorously, frolicking like children for a time. Darius lifted her from the pool, carried her to the chaise lounge; he held her close, their bodies, wet, cool, and languid, turned hot, steamy, fervent in locked embrace.

Valentina was euphoric, unaware she was storing memories to get her through the coming months of hell. In the background . . . always "Lili Marlene" and the war.

Darius stroked her face; it was filling out, the hollows less pronounced. Her hair, the color of dancing fire, billowed about her head like eternal flames. He entwined strands between his fingers, held captive by the play of sunlight on it. Eyes bore into eyes, reaching their souls. Darius uttered a soft moan and gathered her into his arms. He held her close and proceeded to tell her what he had wanted to tell her, what was welled up inside him.

"You were right that day in Dover, *mon amour*. Your words did offend me that day; now I admit to their wisdom. Commitments between us are impossible when our future is obscured by war."

"Darius." She stroked his face gently. He drew her hand to his lips, kissed her fingertips. "I was wrong—"

"Shhh, *chérie*. Do not let words spoil our last few hours."

"But I must tell you. I've thought about many things—"

His lips fell over hers, silencing her. "It is enough to know we love," he said, pausing between kisses, "and feel deeply for each other." His body fit into hers, cutting off thoughts. She trembled against him like a blood filly on a rein. God! she loved him madly. Why didn't he understand? Why did he refuse to acknowledge her love? She moved under his touch, trembling, but she had to ask.

"Do you no longer want me as you wanted me two years ago?"

His soul trembled, but he pulled back, pausing in their love-making with superhuman effort. He reached over her, poured two glasses of champagne, handed her one, withdrew gently from her body. It was as good a time as any to tell her what had eaten at him like a cancer for days.

"We come from two separate worlds, *chérie*. I will never fit into yours. God knows mine would not entice you. I am not familiar with the comforts to which you were born."

"I've had *such* luxuries these past few years?" she retorted acidly her heart sinking.

"Here, at Youseff's villa, I've watched how you fit into such surroundings. I don't belong to this world, Valentina. Oh, perhaps for a week or two, but a lifetime of such luxury would dull my spirit."

"If I had wanted the life to which I was born, I'd have stayed at home in Chicago, done all the dutiful things expected of American girls. I found love in you, Darius, the love I need—*your* love. I thought you loved me."

"You are talking foolishly," he snapped curtly. "Soon we become travelers embarked on separate journeys into the unknown. My path journeys me back to the darker side of hell. Go home, Valentina. Please, so I don't worry about you. I dare not speculate what lies ahead, perhaps disaster for all mankind."

She paled slightly. "If I returned home, would you come to me at war's end? Would you?" She turned his face, forced him to look deeply into her smoky turquoise eyes.

"You demand promises from me I am powerless to make."

"A simple yes would do it if you mean it."

"Now, at this moment, yes. Between now and then too much can happen. How do I make promises when the future is uncertain?"

"Then I'll come to you. Where will you be at war's end?"

"My God, Val! Don't you understand? How do I answer you?" He saw the futility of his words. How could he fence with Eros? He flashed on her world, one of light, not of darkness, death, and vendetta. "I preferred you as you were in Dover," he snapped.

She fell under the hammer blows to her heart, stunned by his words. Reflecting on the wisdom of not letting any man get close enough to her to hurt her, how quickly she tucked her bruised, vulnerable libido behind invisible barricades and sipped her wine, each swallow nearly choking her. Couldn't he see she was no longer the glib, spoiled, mixed-up brat of Dover? *Oh, God, how do you make the blind see, the deaf hear?* Darius was speaking. Did it matter?

"I am Corsican. With the heritage comes a responsibility to my family, a tradition no outsider can understand. At war's end, if I survive, I shall return to Corsica, pick up the pieces of my life, spend the rest of my life there. To you, Corsica would be merely an experience. It is *my* existence, Val. My way of life." He searched her face. "Don't look at me like that—like a widow with the ghost of a dead man etched on your pale face." He turned from her, stared into the crystal pool. Words, promises, childhood memories rushed at him: sweet, loving Dariana; an austere, reprimanding Vivaldi; Matteus, the bold, defiant Moor; his resolute, unloving brothers, and—he felt a tug over his heart—his beloved Sophia.

Darius dived into the pool and vigorously swam several lengths until he was spent.

Valentina watched him, saw the darkness in his eyes turn to something malignant. What caused these sinister shifts in mood? He seemed a stranger to her. If she lived a lifetime, would she ever know him? He'd never permit her to glimpse what was sealed inside him. What was this attraction between them? Was she growing up? What? Could she differentiate between mature and immature love? If only she could tame Darius? *Can you tame Bengal tigers on the rampage? Silly girl!*

Darius rose from the pool like a golden sun god; it was an image she'd cherish all her life. He came toward her, picked her up. Her arms slid around his neck; her face lay flushed against his cool, wet body. Her heart ached, but she was a sucker for punishment. "After the war—if we meet again—will you at least reconsider our love? Seriously?" she asked above a whisper.

He nodded, entered the bedroom with her. It was enough,

all she could hope for. *Hope!* Without it she couldn't go on living.

I'll be seeing you in all the old familiar places. . . .

The record played on and on.

That this heart of mine embraces all night long . . .

Their lovemaking grew more passionate, more ecstatic than ever.

Kiss me once and kiss me twice . . . *and kiss me once again.* . . .

"It's Been a Long, Long Time" would become Valentina's song, just as Darius and thousands of others had laid claim to "Lili Marlene."

Valentina's orders arrived before Darius's. She packed, donned an attitude of bravado, for Darius's benefit. Moments before her driver picked her up, Darius held her lingeringly, her song playing in the background. "You belong to someone like that Yankee flyer of yours, Val. That man, that Lansing chap we met in Cairo. He is of your world, your way of life."

Stunned by the remark, she blurted, "I hardly know Hart Lansing. His sister and I went to the same school. How do I explain? Americans encountering fellow Americans abroad are extremely cordial—*bon ami, comprenez-vous?* I suppose you view it as a social deficiency afflicting Americans? What do I know?" In her attempt to explain Lansing's ardent, affectionate display she began to talk too fast, repeat herself. She stopped abruptly, quit while she was ahead and gestured helplessly.

Her last glimpse of Darius as he stood on the terrace in the courtyard under swaying palms was his smile, that dreadful, friendly smile, an obituary to their love, the most ghastly of all things that register on a human's face. Valentina cried all the way to the Cairo airport, annoyed with herself. If she rattled off all the platitudes appropriate to the occasion none would help mend the rend in her heart. Find something in Darius to loathe, to appease your sorely bruised heart, she told herself, and felt worse because she couldn't. Didn't he *know* all there was to life was here with her? Hadn't they both seen the utter ridiculous farce they had played in that unreal world where men savagely killed themselves off instead of taking time to talk, listen, feel and express a brotherly love?

Both she and Darius had agreed that only in love would man one day find peace. Caught in a web of manmade atrocities, how dare they speak of anything but the moment? Darius was right. He had clearly defined the guidelines. The future was remote, the past, grotesque, and the present? Oh God, the present was all they had left. Why must they share it with the insanity of war?

Prince Ben-Kassir spoke most of the afternoon, filling him in on the U.S. involvement in the war. Darius listened intently, and finally asked, "What will I be in Corsica—cloak and dagger or *Mozarabe?* All this talk of clandestine activities is puzzling me."

"You will wear both hats and at all times be circumspect. To complicate a most complex scenario, since I've already back-grounded the involvements of Cain and Abel, the OSS agents with whom OWC is planned, let me emphatically stress these men are *specialists.* They report directly to General 'Wild Bill' Donovan."

Darius sipped his iced tea recalling the incredible feats bandied about by this more incredible man who was at all places at all times involved daringly with British SIS and the War Ministry.

"A recitation of all global involvements occurring in tandem to your involvement at Bir Hakeim and Gazala, is impossible. More impossible is the task of convincing you that Donovan alone orchestrates a dozen clandestine acts at all times at once. He's created a formidable network of spies within the ranks of nations strung across Europe. Now imagine, Darius, that in each nation he traversed to secure his goals there stood opposing forces, equally as intelligent, equally as determined to win and equally determined that God shone only for them. Put such opposing factions in one arena and you have chaos. Put these same opposing factions on a small island—Corsica, and you'll witness a throbbing eruption of humanity, a circle of hell undreamed of even by Dante in his *Inferno.* If you think the NAIS or even my modest network of spies are impressive, you've seen nothing in comparison to the Allied operation in store for you."

"*Merci bien,*" Darius said wryly.

"General Furstenberg will brief you on his arrival here."

Chapter Thirty-five

"We, Darius, are obsolete. We, the Legion, camels, traveling bordellos, belong to a bygone era. The recent fiasco at Bir Hakeim proved our obsolescence. Your reports were accurate, all right. You foresaw defeat. You didn't understand the difficulties in teaching old war horses new tricks. I tell you we waged antiquated war, lived on past glories and fond memories for too long. It is ended. God willing, we shall be united in France." General Furstenberg's words, spoken over dinner prior to Darius's briefing on Operation White Coral, was a eulogy to a dying tradition.

"General Rommel summed it up the day he recaptured Tobruk. He stood before the British prisoners, commending their endurance and plucky fighting, and said, 'The British fought like lions; unfortunately, you were led by jackasses.' "

Smiles tugged at the corners of Youseff and Darius's lips.

"Your briefing for Operation White Coral—OWC—commences in the morning. These years spent in intimate hell with your men have bound you to them, almost symbiotically, Major. Now let me stress a few caveats, *oui*? How easy it can be for you to overlook telling quirks, *n'est-ce pas*?"

"I am not certain I follow you," Darius said deferentially.

"Be generous in your assessment of your comrades. But at all times maintain objectivity. Remember, first and foremost they are subordinates. American and British intelligence forces together with the French Resistance have received fine-combed dossiers on all the men involved in OWC. There might be a few rotten apples among them. Take proper precautions.''

Darius shot him a sharp, piercing glance.

"It is imperative that an officer know his men better than they know themselves.''

"I thought I did.''

"Once you approve them, Major, they are *your* responsibility. You must try to maintain the icy imperturbability you find distasteful in me. You saw it at Sidi—''

"Yes, sir, and I thoroughly disapproved.''

"You—disapproved! You saw their clays laid bare at Bir Hakeim. How stellarly did the legionnaires perform in contrast to their British counterparts? And *you* disapprove?''

"Sidi bel Abbes was a lifetime ago. You're trying to say the end justifies the means.'' It was not a question, but a condemnation.

Furstenberg bowed smugly, as if he'd scored at bridge. "At Bir Hakeim, despite your personal objections to strategy and delayed tactics, you bore up well. Now, I beseech you to bear with France and her allies with equanimity—*sangfroid,* if you will.''

Darius felt it coming. *"Contingencies!"*

General Furstenberg shrugged helplessly. Youseff stared at the brandy snifter he twirled in his hand. "Technically Corsica is *your* baby. Unfortunately decisions—all of them—are subject to the approval of British M16, the American OSS, and Resistance leaders. And *yours* of course.''

Darius was outraged. "I protest! You would place me in a position of insubordination? Perhaps mutiny? Other jeopardy? I cannot agree—in all conscience—to conditional limitations I know in advance I shall violate.'' Darius, on his feet, paced the large solarium, paused at the edge of the terrace, staring hard at the gibbous moon reflected on the silvery sea. He spun around, livid. "General! Did we learn *nothing* from the mistakes the British made against Rommel? General Ritchie's ambivalence cost us Bir Hakeim! Delays cost us Tobruk! Delays spell the difference between life and death, success or defeat in Corsica!''

"I know! *I know!*'' Furstenberg bleated with a disorganized gesture. "Work around it, Major. You *must work* around it. Orders from the Allied top brass are clear! France alone is incapable of bringing the task to fruition; she needs Allied help. Decisions, made in London, for the time being are irrevocable!"

Darius set his drink down. He opened his tunic, dunked a serviette into a bucket of ice water, wrung it out and applied it to his face, neck and head. He puffed air out his mouth vigorously in total exasperation. "You propose an untenable situation in which my personal and professional posture are at the outset indefensible. You shackle me with invisible chains, General. This posture may do irreparable damage to the cohesive bond existing between my men and me. To see me falter, when in the past I took action? . . . I am not certain I wish to risk the deterioration of their respect for me, to say nothing of their shattered morale."

"As an old war horse I deplore the situation. I find it reprehensible but I ask that you accept the task, conditions and all."

"Why?"

"Because it will please General de Gaulle. You were his personal choice for the mission."

Darius blinked, half disbelieving. He caught Youseff's nod. "It's true, Darius, Henri speaks the truth. I was there. You came highly recommended."

"The alternative is replacing you with another officer who knows nothing of Corsica or its people. An OSS officer; Captain Lincoln," Furstenberg added. "Yes, that's his name. He and Lieutenant Greer."

"Exactly *who* recommended me?"

"An old, dear, and trusted friend—Zahara."

"*Zahara!*" Darius expostulated. "And if the Axis forces decimate me, float my body across the Bay of Marseilles as another statistic of war to be buried next to the tomb of the Unknown Soldier in the shadow of the Arc de Triomphe, all you old war horses will sip your brandies with pained expressions, and pontificate, 'We sent the best damned man to Corsica. We tied his hands, but he was the bloomin' best!' "

Furstenberg twisted the foil from his cigar into curious shapes. "That's it in a nutshell," he said quietly. "However, Major, we have no disagreement. You will *not* end up a statistic. You will outlive us all. You are the most logical man I've met, the most perceptive. You see before a problem is posed. You, lad, are going to Corsica, with your Corsican's bag of tricks to perform miracles for Free France. You are not a reckless man. You are not insubordinate. Nor will you mutiny. You will do your ingenious best to meet your schedules, while I many miles away in London, intend to do my damnedest to see you are not thwarted on major issues. Do you understand me? As a matter of fact I pray you'll do a Rommel on us."

Darius studied the general testily. There was more; he sensed it.

He was right. "It falls incumbent upon me to inform you, beforehand, you will remain an unsung hero, Major. On the day you present Corsica to General de Gaulle and the Allies you will continue to remain an unsung hero for your personal protection. Oh, the rewards are incalculable. Perhaps a position in the new government, an ambassadorship, a representative of your nation with a salary commensurate—uh, more than commensurate—with your talents. But *not* the glory, Major. The glory of your deeds must forever remain unpublicized. Can you live with anonymity? Obscurity, if you will. Every great man must nurture his ego at one time or another. Can you deny yourself the glory, the public acclaim?" Both Youseff and Henri's eyes bored into him.

"I don't know. I am not certain what a hero is, sung or unsung."

"Shall I tell you?" Youseff claimed the honor. "You, Darius, are the unsung hero of Bir Hakeim."

Laughter exploded from Darius's lips. "I don't agree."

"You knew in advance, through technical sightings, careful calculations, dangerous reconnaissance, the outcome of Bir Hakeim. Yet you tackled your duties resolutely, injected hope and optimism in your men, and by employing several tricks managed to keep us alive. The deadly alternatives, had you employed them, could have caused mass desertion."

Darius, impervious to the flatter, harked back to a question nagging at him. "Explain, please, why we sacrificed so many lives, lived in conditions unfit for dogs, holding the Gazala Line when its indefensible position was defined six months in advance. It was insanity!"

"Insanity? Perhaps. No one can call Bir Hakeim a victory for France. We did halt the Afrika Korps . . . dissolved General Rommel's instant hopes of conquering Egypt and the Suez. More important, by holding out as long as we did, we allowed the politicians to put France back into the war. In that time, Hitler's priorities changed. Russia, we pray will become his Waterloo."

Politicians. Oh, how Darius was learning about politicians.

Youseff walked to the phonograph, turned a switch, and returned to Darius, handing him a slender package. "A gift from Lieutenant Varga," he said as her music flooded the room.

Kiss me once and kiss me twice and kiss me once again. . . .

"She instructed me how to give it you, Darius, music and all."

"A solid-gold watch!" Darius was flabbergasted. A sweep second hand and in one corner a compass. A button, when depressed, played "Lili Marlene." He turned it over, read the inscription: *"Win the war, mon amour."* A Chicago telephone number was inscribed under the date. Darius removed his old watch, clasped the new into place admiringly.

Observing the sentimental event, General Furstenberg interjected, "An additional imperative, Major. Our agent, Zahara, must never, I repeat, *never* be referred to as Lomay St. Germaine. Too many Germans from Sidi will recognize the name. Can your men be trusted to hold inviolate that order? Her life is in your hands."

"You infer we will be working together in Corsica?"

"Directly or indirectly, I can't be sure, but certainly in some covert manner. Ah, yes, the SAS will remain in North Africa for a time, save those you carefully winnowed for OWC, including those of Delilah's Dream. Those men are dead and buried as far as the enemy is concerned. Henceforth you will be known as the *Mozarabe.*"

"*Mozarabe?*" Darius pondered a moment. "Christians fighting in an Arab world? A bit late, isn't it? We just left the Arabs."

"It's a catchy phrase. It was the general's choice—de Gaulle, that is. Well then, Major. God be with you. And I must say I don't envy God."

Darius and Youseff embraced fraternally. "Take care of Zahara for me, Darius. Hopefully I shall join you soon. First I must mend a few fences in my nation." Darius nodded mutely.

As he prepared for the immediate future, his thoughts and senses wrapped amorously around Valentina Varga. Darius felt such love for the American that his soul had felt ripped in two when he had forcibly restrained himself during their recent lovemaking. Now, as he negotiated the near future for himself and the *Mozarabe* in Corsica, he wondered how he'd fare dismissing Valentina from mind. He couldn't. What was the sense in trying?

He touched the button on his watch releasing the tinkling sounds of "Lili Marlene" and saw Valentina before him, felt her presence inside him, and he clung to the image tenaciously.

Somehow Darius knew it hadn't ended between them; that it never would; that he'd love her eternally.

And, he knew that somehow, someway they would meet in Corsica.

GLOBAL 2000:
BOOK III

THE STING OF THE SCORPION

The fiery passions and intrigue of EYE OF THE EAGLE and THE JACKAL HELIX continue in THE STING OF THE SCORPION.

The final pages of THE JACKAL HELIX separated the star-crossed lovers, Valentina Varga and Major Darius Bonifacio, and Darius was given a top-secret briefing on Operation White Coral by General Furstenberg.

Before plunging into Operation White Coral, to be staged in Corsica, the story moves to a spymaster's nest in Zurich, Switzerland. There, Major Victor Bonifacio of the Italian Intelligence Division meets in secret conclave with his father, the super-villainous Amadeo Zeller, and finds himself unwittingly at the center of political intrigue on a scale he'd never imagined. Amadeo infiltrates the Allied espionage establishment, centering on the OSS (Office of Secret Services, USA) whose later rebirth as the CIA makes it the most formidable intelligence, counter-intelligence, and sabotage agency in the world. Victor, at the center of plots and counterplots, is besieged by both treasonous impulses and guilt feelings. As he encounters his father's evil plots, involving dissemination of false information to both Allied and Axis powers, misinformation tactics and revolutionary devices capable of destroying nations, he is outraged and feels compromised. The evil Amadeo Zeller is a quintessential power-broker who uses both sides, and Victor, a devout Fascist and protégé of Il Duce, enters into a barrage of verbal fisticuffs with his father and departs Zurich believing his father to be a madman.

Victor, later nearly felled by assassin's bullets, is saved and recuperates, determined to eventually expose his father's treasonous plots.

The times grow more precarious as Il Duce injudiciously flexes his muscles against Hitler, annexes Corsica and places Victor in command of the invasion. Victor's use of Terra Bonifacio in Corsica creates chaos and upheavel in the Bonifacio household. Sophia's mysterious disappearance after Major Victor Zeller's arrival at the estate in search of Darius, begins an awful peril to his family. Should the enemy learn the true relationship of his family to the monstrous Amadeo, they will be in grave danger. Other webs in the plot involve Major Hans Hesse, who, recuperated from the El Bayadh massacre, is back on duty in Paris, more ambitious than ever. A clever British spy intrigues with him to sell Allied operational plans while the capture of Zahara, the Resistance's thorn in his side, also occupies his attention. Soon he is reassigned to Corsica, where he clashes with Victor Zeller.

As World War II shambles on, everyone's personal lives become increasingly entangled in incredible cloak and dagger scenarios. Darius and the Mozarabe become the unsung heros of Operation White Coral, and more intrigue follows, orchestrated by political ghouls, as the Zeller machine's post-war global machinations force Darius from his recuperation after the final battle in Corsica.

In 1984, after a forty-year interim in which Darius forms an impregnable world organization to counter the global strife still being concocted by Zeller's zealots, the heroic Darius moves on to a formidable position of strength.

As the ace in an hole, the Moufflon task force, a secret group originating in World War II, prepares a survival location in the face of impending nuclear holocaust.

As his final heroic act, unless Darius can make the secret of the Scorpion's Sting part of mankind's consciousness, all humanity will be at the mercy of the relentless ambitions of the silent oligarchy that seeks to control the world.